CLOSE ENCOUNTER

"Exactly what are you implying?" she demanded, quivering all over with fury, her eyes narrowed feline slits as she sprang to her feet.

"Just what I said, honey! Maybe you were just playing hard t' get? Maybe you *wanted* that oily son of a bitch t' catch up with you?"

"Why, you foul-mouthed cad! How dare you insinuate that I encouraged his filthy attentions!" she cried. Swinging about, she drew back her hand, intending to slap his face with all her strength and wipe the mockery from it.

But in that moment, the carriage rounded a street corner. The turn unbalanced Angel. She was lurched off her feet, flung across the vehicle's interior, and thrown heavily across Nick's lap.

He grunted and his arms went around her. He fully intended to restore the conniving little witch to her seat, but somehow, it didn't work out that way. Somehow, his arms went around her and stayed there. And somehow, his dark head dipped as he arched her across his lap, and he drew her close, closer, closest, knowing he was a fool, but doing it anyway; knowing he'd hate himself later, but unable to help himself in that moment, he wanted her so badly. . . .

PENELOPE NERI

Cherish The Night

ZEBRA BOOKS
KENSINGTON PUBLISHING CORP.

ZEBRA BOOKS

are published by

Kensington Publishing Corp.
475 Park Avenue South
New York, NY 10016

First printing: February, 1992

Printed in the United States of America

Love 'n marriage are only for gamblers,
Who'll wager their hearts on a whim.
At the turn of a card,
They'll give up the free life—
They'll hang up their saddles,
Hitch up with a housewife—
Lassoed by some gal's shapely limb!

O, Love is for lonesome young cowboys,
Who melt with a female's false smiles.
But it ain't 'til she's got you
Corralled with a ring—
'Til you've wedded and bedded
That purty young thing!—
You discover her four-flusher's wiles.

Smart is the bachelor fellow
Who won't bet against Lady Luck's whim!
All the days of his life
He'll hoard money and heart—
Should his stake reach the rafters
From neither he'll part!—
Love makes no gamblin' fool outta him!

Prologue

It was 2 A.M. and drizzling steadily as the hackney cab rolled to a halt before the vestibule of Bligh's, the most popular supper club and gaming house to be found in Soho, London.

A bulldog-faced doorman who managed to look like a convict, despite his smart green livery, lumbered head down to the curb, hastening to assist the new arrivals from their vehicle to the pavement.

"Cor, blimey! If it in't Colonel Cody!" the doorman exclaimed, grinning broadly as a bearded gentleman in a showy white suit and matching Stetson hat alighted. "I saw yer Wild West Show last Saturd'y, sir. Bleedin' wunnerful it was, too, gov'na! It's a pleasure t' have yer here at Bligh's t'ght, sir. Step right this way!"

Beaming, the American—Colonel "Buffalo Bill" Cody, former buffalo hunter, former Pony Express Rider, former Indian fighter, and now showman *extraordinaire*—followed the effusive cockney doorman to the door of the London club.

At the entrance, he paused. "Well? C'mon, boys n' gals! Hurry it up!" he urged his companions over his shoulder. "Darned if I don't feel lucky t'night!"

"You've said that every night this week, sir," Frank Butler reminded him with a grin as he handed his pretty, elegantly dressed wife, Phoebe, down from the coach. Tucking her elbow through his arm, he noticed that she seemed quiet and a trifle nervous. He chucked her beneath the chin and gave her a reassuring smile. Phoebe—better known to the American and British public by her professional name of Little Annie Oakely, the sharp-shooting "Maid of the western plains"—considered gambling and frequenting supper clubs a most unladylike pastime. She'd had to be cajoled to come with them tonight.

The third man, who sprang down from the carriage after them, observed, "The way I see it, Frank, the colonel figures his luck'll *have* to change sooner or later. If he says he feels lucky every night, sooner or later, he'll be right!"

The four were laughing as they swept inside the club.

Directly ahead lay a cloakroom. Off to the left, a dining room opened up, intimate little booths with pink-shaded Tiffany lamps casting rosy light over tables with snowy cloths. A curving flight of stairs with a highly polished bannister led up to the gaming rooms above, but even from below, the new arrivals could hear the whir and click of the roulette wheels and the singsong calls of the croupiers. Above this, on the rarely mentioned third floor of Bligh's, were several rooms where bored young ladies lounged in various stages of undress, awaiting their next customer of the evening.

"Damned if I ain't hungry enough t' eat a bear!" Cody exclaimed, handing his white Stetson to the gaping cloakroom attendant. The Butlers did likewise with their capes. "Shall we go in, Phoebe, honey?" he suggested, taking Phoebe Butler's arm. "Durango? Butler? You boys ready for some chow? I hear the grilled oysters are mighty fine here."

While Butler and his wife murmured in the affirmative, Nick Durango, the Wild West Show's "King of the Cowboys" shook his dark head. "You go on in and start without me." He grinned. "I've a mind to try my luck first."

Cody nodded. "Suit yourself, son. Come along, Phoebe. Tell that husband of yours we're ready to go in."

As a fawning waiter shepherded Colonel Cody and the Butlers to their table, Nick took the stairs to the second floor, instead. He nodded politely to the young women wearing elegant pastel evening gowns and long white gloves who passed him on their way down. The women blushed and looked quickly away, but seconds after they'd passed him, he heard their nervous titters and knew if he looked back, they'd be staring after him, wearing their silly, vapid smiles and exclaiming about his foreign attire. Wherever he went, it was the same.

The second floor of Bligh's was divided into three large, elegantly appointed rooms where various games of chance were in progress—roulette, faro, ving-et-un, and so on. Looking around, Nick found himself a quiet corner out of the crush of noisy high society snobs where he could sit quietly, enjoy a drink, and observe the goings-on for a spell, before trying his hand at the tables.

The crowd jostling around the blackjack table was typical of most of the supper-cum-gambling clubs they'd visited since the Wild West Show's arrival in Britain a few weeks ago. Bored young heirs and heiresses, they considered themselves the cream of society. They were out on the town looking for some excitement to give an edge to their indolent lives—and frittering away the family fortune in the process.

Nick doubted that they, living their pampered, cocooned lives, even knew of the existence of the poor, the hungry, the homeless in the teeming London slums beyond these walls, let alone cared. The men appeared a spineless, affected lot, concerned only with the acquisition of thoroughbred horses, pedigreed hunting dogs, and, perhaps, suitable wives, in that order, if the snatches of conversation he caught were anything to go by. The young women appeared equally unlikely to have a single intelligent thought between them; these lovely, exquisitely gowned butterflies no doubt passed their days husband-hunting and adding to their collections of jewels and gowns.

The quartet that had caught his eye was typical. The two young men were both gussied up in perfect evening attire, though the elbows of the fair-haired fellow's coat appeared somewhat shiny and worn. They and a young, dark-haired debutante wearing green silk were clustered around a blond beauty in lavender, who was seated at the blackjack table.

Idly, Nick watched as the dealer dealt her two cards. She

9

peeked at them and sighed. Her shoulders drooped, but then she nodded to the dealer, giving him the go-ahead to deal her another card. Seconds later, she folded with an expression of quiet desperation on her pale face.

Nick was intrigued. The upper-crust set usually handled their losses with laughter and a dismissing wave of the hand. Not so Blondie. Leaning back, he watched over the rim of his glass as the girl lost time and time again. But, just when she seemed determined to give up and leave the table, lo and behold, she'd win a hand! Her despondent expression would lift, the dealer would beam and congratulate her, her trio of friends would exclaim with delight—and she'd be suckered into trying her luck again. Too good to be true? Nick thought so.

Frowning, he called for another Scotch and turned his attention to the deft hands of the blackjack dealer. Smooth, white, and perfectly manicured, they were a professional gambler's paws, if ever he'd seen a pair. His frown deepened to a scowl. Several hands followed before he was sure of what he'd suspected. Once he was, he uncoiled to standing and wove his way between the crowd, heading for the blackjack table. The least he could do was whisper a few words of warning in the girl's ear. The poor kid seemed to be taking losing harder than most.

He was still some feet away when the blond girl sprang to her feet with a muffled cry. Thrusting past her companions, he saw tears fill her eyes as she stumbled toward him, blindly seeking an exit. As she did so, she collided with Nick, slamming into him full-tilt.

"Whoa, there, little lady!" he exclaimed, grasping her upper arms to steady her.

She looked petrified as she gaped up into his face, though what she saw in his features or expression to terrify her so, he had no idea. Whatever its cause, the fright in her eyes soon dwindled, corraled by an iron will he couldn't help but admire. Drawing herself up to her full height of perhaps five-feet-five inches, she looked down her nose at him and demanded frostily, "Unhand me this instant, sir!"

With an apologetic shrug, he did so, taking a step back. But before he could offer his warning, she made as if to sweep past him. Reaching out, he gripped her elbow.

"Yes?" she asked as she swung around to face him, her gray eyes smoking with annoyance now. "What is it?"

"Ma'am," he drawled softly, turning her aside, reluctant to let her companions—who'd followed her—eavesdrop on what he was saying. "Ma'am, I'd like to offer a few words of warning about your losing streak back there . . ." he began.

"About my losing streak . . . ?" she cut in, but then her voice trailed away. He felt her arm grow rigid under his light hold and a tremor passed through her slender body. As she lifted her wide, smoky eyes to his, he saw that the fear was back. Her lush lower lip quivered as she whispered hoarsely, "Why won't you people leave me alone? M-Mister Bligh and I have already discussed the matter of my . . . losses, both t-to his satisfaction and my own!"

"Ma'am, I don't know who you think I am, but I have nothing to do with this establishment."

"You don't?" she came back immediately, suspicion in every line of her lovely face.

"No, ma'am. I just wanted to warn you about that dealer . . ."

"Lewis?" Her brows rose. "What about him?"

"He's crooked, ma'am—he deals from the bottom of the deck."

"The bottom of the . . . But that's preposterous!"

"No, I'm afraid it's closer to fact, ma'am," he insisted.

Hectic color flamed in her cheeks. Her smoky eyes flashed at him. "Then I suppose I should thank you for warning me, shouldn't I?"

His jaw hardened. "I wasn't looking for thanks, ma'am. Just trying to help out."

"I see. Then if there's nothing more, good evening, sir!"

With that, the beautiful little bitch kicked her full skirts aside and was gone from him with a furious rustling of petticoats, leaving only the fragrance of her perfume in her wake.

As the trio caught up with her, he heard the dark-haired woman exclaim, "Angel, darling, who on earth was that man you were speaking to?"

11

"Couldn't you tell, Diana?" the tall, fair-haired man supplied with a bored yawn before "Angel" could answer. "A brash American, by the looks of him. London's teeming with 'em, lately. Good God, didn't you notice his attire? Positively outlandish! But then, none of these colonial bumpkins have the foggiest idea what's appropriate and what isn't." He sighed.

"An American! No wonder he looks so deliciously . . . dangerous!" Diana exclaimed in delight, looking back over her shoulder. "For all his eccentric attire, he's terribly handsome, isn't he? What in the world did he say to you, Angel, darling?"

The girl with the honey blond hair turned away as she answered, the others crowding forward to listen. Nick didn't catch her response—or give a damn that he hadn't. Instead, he took her seat at the blackjack table.

"Good evening, sir."

"And to you. Deal me in, pardner," he told the dealer cordially.

The man smiled and nodded. He shuffled the cards with a practiced zipping sound, allowed Nick to cut them, then his small white hands flashed as he dealt.

Like a rattler striking, Nick's hand snaked out. His steely fingers closed around the small-boned dealer's wrist like a vise. He squeezed hard, grinding bone against bone until the deck fluttered from the man's slackened fingers. He yelped.

Nick smiled in a thin-lipped, tigerish manner. "Now, listen up, Lewis, you cheatin' son of a bitch," he gritted softly. "I've been watchin' you, and I'll be damned if I like the way you deal! If it's all the same to you, pardner, I'll take my cards from the *top* of the deck, *comprende?*"

The dealer's sullen nod confirmed he had indeed understood—and without need of translation, either.

Chapter One

"Oh, do stop it, poppet! Bemoaning one's gambling losses is both vulgar and common. It's simply not done in polite circles, don't you know?"

Angel grimaced, casting Reggie a hurt look. It was all very well for him to take that supercilious tone. It was common knowledge that he didn't have a penny to his name, despite his title, yet he still managed to act as if he hadn't a care in the world! She, on the other hand, was in debt to the tune of three thousand pounds. Neither her conscience nor her upbringing would allow her to shrug off such an enormous debt so airily!

She sighed, blinking back tears. Her father, Sidney Higgins was the dearest man who ever lived. He trusted her completely—and she couldn't bear the thought of him finding out that she'd deceived him. If he ever got wind of her sorties to the gambling clubs of London in the wee hours of the night while Brixton Towers slept, how could she ever look him in the eye again?

"But what am I to do, Reggie?" she wailed. "Tell me that? Won't you lend me a few pounds, so I can try to win it back? One last fling, to make or break me . . . ?" Her thick dark lashes were spiked with tears now. More swam in her lovely smoke gray eyes. "I simply have to pay off that horrid Bill Bligh!"

"I wish I could help you, old girl, really I do. But we both know I don't have a bloody farthing to my name," Reggie admitted, inspecting his immaculate fingernails. "Actually, I was rather hoping you could see your way to

lending *me* a few pounds again—just to pay my tailor?"
He scowled. "The cheeky blighter had the temerity to force
his way into my club the other evening and demand
payment for those last two suits. Dashed impatient beggar,
that Neville! But then, what can one expect from a
tradesperson?"

He thought for a few moments, drumming his fingers
on the green baize tabletop before continuing, "You
know, there's a beastly fellow in the East End who'll lend
money when a chap's down on his luck—astronomical
interest, of course, but no questions asked. I could give you
his address, if you like?"

"Me, go to a moneylender? Oh, I couldn't . . ." She bit
her lip, looking more like a frightened little girl than a
young woman of eighteen, despite her elegantly upswept
blond hair and a lavender silk gown with a daring
décolletage.

"Now, be sensible, poppet. After all, what choice do you
have, really?" He withdrew an embossed calling card from
his pocket, flipped it over and scribbled an address on the
back with a tiny gold pencil.

Angel watched him hopefully. In the light that spilled
from the gas jets, shaded by fringed pink shades, he looked
dashing, debonair, every young girl's dream. *Her* dream.
Someday, she told herself, *someday, I'll become Angelica,
Lady Smythe-Moreton, Reggie's wife, and I'll have the
title to go with Da's millions! Then these past wretched
weeks will be nothing but a bad dream, and the society
snobs who've looked down their noses at me and Da for so
very long can go to the devil!*

"There you go. And Angel, darling, don't mention my
name to Bloomstein, there's a love. He's under the
impression I still owe him a guinea or two, that old
Shylock!" Pushing a stray lock of pale blond hair off his
brow in his languid, upper-crust fashion, he yawned
ostentatiously as he withdrew a gold pocket watch from
his waistcoat. Flipping open the patterned lid, he peered
at the watch face. "Oh, good Lord, it's already half past
two! Angel, I really must be running along. I have to
remind William to lay out my tweeds. Did I mention I
have a shoot planned with the Fieldings down in Suffolk

14

tomorrow? See you when I get back, poppet. Oh, and good luck, old girl!" Planting a perfunctory kiss somewhere above the area of her ear, he left hurriedly.

As Angel wove her way between the knots of elegantly dressed gamblers, intending to follow him out and have her own carriage sent around, she saw the reason for Reggie's hasty exit. Bill Bligh was lumbering between the tables, heading toward her! Her heart gave an anxious little flutter. There was but one way out—the door Bligh'd entered! There'd be no avoiding the club's proprietor.

"Why, Mr. Bligh! What a pleasure to see you again— and looking so very—um—robust, too!" she trilled, extending her hand to him and wondering nervously if he'd bite it rather than kiss it. He certainly looked capable of doing so. Standing over six feet tall, Bill Bligh had coarse black hair, coarse features that had been blurred by countless bouts of fisticuffs, and a coarse bluish shadow over his cheeks and jaw. His fleshy bottom lip jutted pugnaciously, as if he were always ready for a fight. As, no doubt, he was.

"We'll 'ave none o' your sweet talk tonight, Miss 'Iggins. You know what I want, without beatin' around the bush. The three thousand quid you owe me, plus interest! So. 'Ave you got it yet?" he demanded bluntly.

Her hand drifted back to her side unshaken. Her palms were damp. "No, Mr. Bligh. I'm afraid not. Not yet. But I'll get it, very soon, I—I promise!" she added in a whisper.

"Soon, my arse!" Bligh cursed vulgarly. "Soon was a month past, when I first tried t' collect from you! Let me tell you, Miss Angel 'Iggins, my patience is growin' very thin. Very thin, indeed! I've a mind t' ride out t' the Towers an' 'ave a word with your dad, I 'ave . . . !"

She paled. "You mustn't do that! Really, Mr. Bligh, you mustn't! Da—well, he'd—he'd never forgive me!"

Bligh appeared to consider her words for a moment or two, then gave what passed for a smile, but was more a carnivorous baring of teeth. "All right, then. I'll wait. After all, I'm a reasonable bloke. Everyone sez so! I'll give you another fortnight t' come up with what's owin'. But if you're not here, cash in hand, the Friday arfter next, I'll

15

have some o' my boys rearrange the bones in your pretty little neck, afore you can say 'Gawd Save the Queen'! Got it, *luv?*" he jeered, his deep-set shifty little eyes cruel as they pierced her ashen face.

"G-G-Got it!" she echoed, nodding repeatedly.

"Right. Two weeks it is. 'Til then . . ."

With that, he lumbered away.

Bligh was counting the evening's "take" from a green metal cash box when a shadow fell across his accounting register. Without looking up, he removed the cigar from his mouth to snarl, "Back so soon? Whadda you want, Cousin?"

His unexpected guest chuckled and perched uninvited upon the desktop. "Surly as ever, eh, Billy-boy? You could at least ask how I am, offer me a drink or a cigar, perhaps? We are partners, in a manner of speaking, after all."

"Stow it, Cousin—and stow the bloody accent, too. After a night of bein' polite t' those bleedin' toffee-noses, I'm in no mood t' hear any more o' that fancy jabberin', thank you very much."

"All right. I'll speak plainly. It's been a month. Has our little pigeon come through with the money yet?"

"Not yet. An' I don't know as 'ow she ever will. I reckon you've misjudged this 'mark.' Angel 'Iggins strikes me as the sort wot'll break down an' spill 'er guts to 'er old man, rather than pay up and shut up! I spoke to 'er t' night, I did—put the fear o' Gawd inter her. Told 'er I'd set me boys on 'er if she didn't pay up soon. She had a desperate look when she left 'ere, if ever I've seen one!"

His cousin smirked. "How long did you give her?"

"A fortnight."

"Two weeks. Hmm. Good enough! And if it doesn't work, no matter. Like I told you, we can always switch to our other plan, instead." He grinned. "Dearest Daddy Higgins is a millionaire several times over. He'll pay anything we ask to get the chit back. Though of course, he won't be getting her back alive, if it should come down to that, will he? No. We couldn't possibly take the chance of letting her live, once she'd seen us . . ."

16

Bill Bligh shook his head, staring at him half in admiration and half in contempt. "You're a cold bastard, you are."

"Now, look who's talking—bloody Jack Frost 'imself!" the other observed, smiling mirthlessly. "If you're having second thoughts, Billy-boy—perhaps getting cold feet?— we could dissolve our little partnership right here and now . . . ?"

Bill Bligh frowned. Much as he disliked his cousin, he couldn't deny his talents as a confidence-trickster were second to none. He'd proven bloody useful in the past, effortlessly carrying off role after role. And not one of their stupid "pigeons" had seen through his acts until it was too late for 'em, neither! Nah, he didn't like him, and he trusted him even less—but he was handy t' have around, he was. And this Higgins caper just might prove the juiciest one yet. . . .

"Nah, I'll stick it out, mate. Pour yourself a drink then, scarper. Pansy'll be here soon. I want you gorn by then."

"Ah, yes, your divinely beautiful Miss Loveness! She— um—she wouldn't be bringing a pretty young lady friend with her tonight, by any remote chance?"

"Drink up—and don't press your bleedin' luck, Cousin," Bligh snarled.

Angel was still shaking from that awful lout's threats as her carriage pulled away from Bligh's.

How in the world was she to recover the three-thousand pounds, plus interest, that she'd lost at the tables? The problem was no longer merely worrisome. It had taken on life-and-death importance to her now! Gulping, she stroked her neck. Oh Lord! She could almost feel Bligh's fingers tightening around it . . . squeezing . . . choking the life from her!

Only two weeks, to raise what it had once taken her father ten years to earn at the cotton mill. It was the same old story all over again, Angel thought with bitterness. There were times when she cursed Harry, Lord Brixton, the eccentric old millionaire who'd brought them to this pass with his gratitude. Now they lived in a sort of social limbo, accepted neither by the working class to which she and her da had been born, nor by the circles of the wealthy and titled members of London society that inheriting the Brixton fortunes had thrust them into. Great wealth was no automatic guarantee of entrée into society. For that, you needed bloodlines, breeding, a name, or a title, and she and Da had neither. . . .

It had all begun eight years ago, in '79. She'd been a little girl of ten at the time, and although they'd both missed Elsie, her ma, who'd succumbed to rheumatic fever when Angel was only eight years old, she and Da had been happy, after their simple fashion.

They'd lived in the best slate-roofed cottage of a row of such small cottages in the village of Brixton, Lancashire, a hamlet that had sprung up the century before in the shadow of one of Lord Brixton's four cotton mills. Da had been a foreman over at the mill—and a bloody good one, too—the day Lord Brixton had come to inspect his concern. Brixton's manager had appointed Sidney Higgins, Angie's father, to show the owner around the mill.

They'd completed the tour and the two men were standing outside in the mill yard, watching the smoke rising from the mill's lofty chimney stacks, when a runaway mason's horse pulling a laden cart had come clattering down the village high street. Without checking its gait, it had rounded the mill yard wall, bearing down on Lord Brixton at full speed!

"Look out!" her da had yelled.

According to her father's modest description later, he'd merely shoved Lord Brixton aside, out of the path of the galloping animal. But onlookers who'd witnessed the near-fatal accident were more generous in their praises. They said Sid'd turned, seen the danger, and leaped across the yard like a veritable lion, performing a champion flying tackle that swept Lord Harry from the path of death in the nick of time.

Muddied but otherwise unharmed, Lord Brixton had scrambled to his feet, dusted himself off, and thanked Sid profusely. The millowner had stood Sid his dinner of hot

18

pot and ale at the nearest pub, the Brixton Arms, then walked him home, frock-coated and cravated peer-of-the-realm strolling arm-in-arm with a humble mill foreman in his moleskin breeches, shirt sleeves, and flat cap, just as if the two were not only equals, but old friends.

Lord Brixton'd stayed for an hour or two in Sid's humble cottage, enjoying the steaming cup of tea Sid's wide-eyed little daughter, Annie, had shyly offered him, along with a bit of bread n' scrape that he'd eaten with all the enjoyment of caviar on toast. Later that evening, his Lorship'd made his farewells, leaving father and daughter with five gold sovereigns in appreciation for Sid's bravery. Harry'd vowed never to forget that he owed Sid his life.

Both father and daughter had thought they'd heard the last of the matter with Lord Harry's departure, but far from it. The following Christmas, a Brixton servant had delivered a huge turkey, a plum pudding, expensive oranges, nuts and sweets, and a bottle of Scottish whisky, to their humble cottage. With these had come a porcelain doll, elegantly clothed in the height of fashion, and a dress of scarlet velvet with white lace trimming for little Annie to wear. Its grandeur had left her speechless.

To his credit, her da'd tried to return the gifts, but Brixton's servant had insisted. Eventually, they'd had no choice but to accept.

There'd been a similar visit the following Christmas, then six months later, as a result of his hard work and on his own merits, her clever da had been raised up to the position of mill supervisor. The extra five pounds a year he was to receive in wages had seemed a king's ransom, and the future had seemed rosy almost beyond belief for the Higginses. Dressed in his Sunday best, Sid'd carried a bunch of gladioli, Annie, a posy of daisies, and hand in hand they'd walked to Elsie Higgins's grave in the churchyard of St. Augustine's Church. The two of them had stood there by the grassy mound, heads bowed, and told Sid's wife all that had happened, wishing with all their hearts that she were still alive and there with them to share their good fortune.

When Harry—Lord Brixton—died in his bed of advanced dropsy less than two years later, the village of Brixton had draped the mill windows with black crepe, and mourned the loss of a master who'd been fairer than most, while wondering with some apprehension who would inherit his concerns and what sort of master he'd prove. Sid and his daughter had done likewise, believing Harry's passing had closed an exciting and prosperous chapter in their otherwise humdrum lives.

But, less than a week later, the Higginses learned from the black-coated solicitors who descended like crows upon Sid's cottage in the village that Brixton's generosity and gratitude had not ended with his death, as they'd thought. The eccentric, childless lord had changed his will soon after that fateful day, bequeathing all he possessed—with the exception of his title—to "his dear friend and savior," one Master Sidney Arthur Higgins of Brixton, Lancashire, who was "as good and brave a man as any who'd ever walked the earth."

The fortune had been considerable—mind-boggling to ordinary working-class people such as Sidney and his little girl, who'd considered the five sovereigns a fortune in itself! In truth, they could barely begin to absorb the full extent of his lordship's true wealth. He'd owned four flourishing cotton mills in the north of England, worth well over a million pounds combined, along with a cotton warehouse in Cairo, Egypt; a vast country estate in the mild southeast of England called Brixton Acres, with a thriving, working dairy and sheep farm; a town house mansion and grounds on the outskirts of London called Brixton Towers; a charming villa named Villa Allegra in northern Italy; a sugar plantation in the West Indies; a tea plantation in Ceylon; vast grazing lands in the western wilds of North America; a diamond mine in South Africa; timber lands in Canada; and so on. Furthermore, his several bank accounts had held a fortune in pounds sterling exceeding the sum of all his holdings put together. The extent of his wealth had been staggering!

Once Sidney had recovered from the shock of his good fortune and been persuaded that he must accept the inheritance as his due, he'd proven remarkably astute for one raised in poverty. Knowing he needed trustworthy advisors to assist him in administering his inheritance, he'd immediately enlisted Lord Brixton's solicitors' aid in retaining the best financial advisors his newfound wealth could buy him. A condition of their hire had been that they instruct him in everything he needed to know in order to be able to eventually administer his own estates in return for a generous bonus. Meanwhile, he'd added in his broad Lancashire accent, gray eyes twinkling at his daughter, "Our little Annie must go off t' school, mustn't she?"

"Eeh, Da, I musn't!" she'd protested. Leave her da, whom she'd taken care of like a grown woman since her mam had died? Her forgetful da, who went without supper rather than go to the bother o' cookin' it up himself, if she weren't there t' do for him? Nay, by gum, she'd never do that! "Give over wi' ye, Da! Me leave you an' go t' school! Not bloomin' likely!"

"It's all settled, our Annie. You're goin' to school, like it or nay. You'll learn 'ow t' be a lady there, an' that's that. I'll hear nowt more about it, my lass."

Having money had changed Sidney Higgins to some degree. He was more confident of his abilities, more ambitious to prove himself, but it had certainly not dazzled him. He'd seen the good having money could do, if properly managed, the gates it could open, the worlds it could explore, and he had vowed his little Annie would one day rule as queen of them all. And a queen, he'd said solemnly the day he'd lifted her up into the pony trap which would carry her to the train station on the first leg of her journey to boarding school, must know how t' read and do sums.

Wearing his shirt with the sleeves rolled up, and his braces and cap, just like any other mill worker, her da had stood by the hollyhocks that grew up about their front gate and waved goodbye.

The next two hard years she'd spent away from Brixton and the home she loved, but the memory of the pride that had shone in his eyes that day had made her vow she would never let him down.

The prestigious Ellen Clarke Boarding School for

Young Ladies had been a living nightmare for twelve-year-old Annie, whose schooling had been sketchy at best, and whose polish was nonexistent. The pupils, all daughters of Britain's titled aristocracy, had considered the Higgins girl common and vulgar and had made no bones about expressing their ridicule.

"Annie! Such a common name! Papa has a Labrador bitch he takes pheasant shooting named Annie."

"Mama's maid is named Annie, too, I believe. Or is it Alice? It's so tedious to remember! Servants do all tend to look alike, don't they, Diana?"

"Where on earth did you get those dreadful clothes from, girl? The rag-and-bone man?" they'd asked.

Seeing the hurt and confusion in the little girl's face, the sheen of tears lurking in her eyes, they'd nudged each other and tittered behind their smooth pale pink hands. Knowing their gibes had struck home, for days, then weeks, they'd mocked her name, her broad northern accent, her clothes, everything about her.

"The new girl said 'Nowt'! How quaint! Did you hear, Diana? 'By gum,' it can speak!" they'd taunted.

Poor little Annie had cried herself to sleep each night in her bed in the hostile, darkened dorm, praying that God would strike her dead during the night—or at least whisk her away to her beloved Brixton and Da, there to stay forever.

But alas, He'd done neither.

Weeks had become months, and both God and her father had left her to the teasing and spiteful whispering, the cruel torture that young girls know how to inflict so very well on those they perceive as different from themselves.

And, little by little, Annie had realized that in order to be accepted, to make them stop taunting her and defuse their scorn, she must either grow a far thicker skin—or change and become like them. And so—since she knew she could never completely ignore them or grow immune to their spite—she'd decided to change.

She'd start with her name, changing it to one she'd admired in a book: *Angelica*. It was close enough to Annie to remember easily, but far grander sounding. She also vowed to study hard at her lessons in reading, writing, arithmetic, botany, French, Latin, music, and art, and someday, one day, she'd put the high-nosed lot of 'em t' shame, by gum!

Once she had formed the resolution, she stuck to it religiously, for in tenacity and raw intelligence, she was her father's daughter to the core.

While the other girls went on chaperoned strolls along the banks of the Thames, Angelica studied. While they sketched under fragrant lilac trees and vied for the honor of being invited to take Sunday high tea at Miss Clarke, the headmistress's home, she conjugated French and Latin verbs with ink-stained fingers, or practiced deportment, gliding down the halls with a pile of books on her head whenever she thought herself unobserved. In an effort to improve her speech, she worked on her elocution, carrying on elegant conversations with imaginary callers whenever she was alone.

"It's frightfully good of you to call again so soon, my dear Lady Wadsworth," she'd simper. "Do say you'll stay and take tea with Papa and myself?"

Over the next year, her teachers were amazed by Angelica's rapid progress. Her broad Northern vowels, so reminiscent of Lancashire, had softened, shortened. One could scarcely tell that her well-modulated speech had ever been different from that of the other girls. And, although never attaining the top of her form, a heady status she'd craved, by the end of the second year she'd settled into a comfortable and respectable position in the top third, and was considered enough of a threat academically to make the others girl look nervously to their laurels.

The months flew past. The seasons changed and changed again. She'd not seen her beloved da for over two years, he'd been so involved in learning the intricacies of his own complex new lifestyle. And, though she'd written often to tell him about school and her new life, his letters had been few and far between, and those disappointingly short.

So it was that when Sidney Higgins was finally able to visit Miss Clarke's establishment with the herd of other parents there for the school's annual Parents' Visiting

Day, he was thunderstruck by the changes in his daughter. At fourteen, she was a lovely young lass—a lady, by God!—and she showed every promise of becoming a beauty in the near future, like her mam'd been.

"Eee, by gum, Annie, love, ye look a proper treat, you do!" Sidney Higgins had exclaimed.

In her elegant, white afternoon gown with its fitted bodice and narrow layered skirts, the hems trimmed with tiny silk rosebuds, she'd known she looked her best as she basked in his praises.

Diana Forsythe, the most daring of all the girls, leader of her own "fast" little clique and the last word in what was fashionable, had been flattered by Angel's hesitant request for advice about what to wear for Parents' Visiting Day. On discovering that the Higgins' girl had simply loads of money, but no wardrobe to speak of, nor any doting mama to advise her on such matters, a bored Diana'd agreed to take Annie under her wing, sending for her own seamstress to sew the unfortunate child a completely new ensemble, from underdrawers to tea gowns, ball gowns, night chemises, bicycling knickers, bathing costumes, gloves, and more. The results had been stunning, and the Northern girl's gratitude surprisingly rewarding. Angel suspected that Diana had considered the matter an amusing little interlude in what had been an otherwise tedious school term, but had decided it was worth swallowing her pride in return for Diana's expertise in regard to such matters.

"Thank you, Papa," Angel murmured decorously, in answer to her father's compliment. "Shall we take a stroll in the gardens before luncheon is served?"

"All reet, then, Annie, love. Lead the way," her bemused but grinning father had urged, fascinated by his new, genteel Annie. By gum, his little lass looked proper quality, she did! "Or—should I?"

"You should, Papa." Smiling, she'd offered him her hand, and Sid, after a moment's hesitation, took it and slipped it through his elbow.

"Like this, is it, love?" he asked uncertainly.

"Just like that, Papa," she approved softly, turning radiant gray eyes up to his. Oh, it was so wonderful to see

24

him after so long, she could hardly stand it! "And if you could remember to call me Angelica, or even Angel while you're here . . . ?"

"I'll try, lass. Aye, your old da'll give it a try—but I won't promise nowt. You've always been my little Annie, and I reckon as 'ow ye always will be!"

Behind the box hedge, hidden from the mocking eyes of the other girls, she dropped all decorum, flung her arms around his neck and kissed and hugged him in her old, boisterous fashion. "Oh, Da, Da, I've missed you s' bad! Ee, it's been reet lonely here wi' out ye!"

"I know, our Annie. I've missed you summat awful, too! Aye, love, I 'ave," he'd agreed huskily, hugging her back every bit as hard, and sniffing to hide his tears.

And now, here she was, four years later, desperate to conceal her excesses! She swallowed, feeling sick to her stomach. *Oh, Angel, how could you have been so foolish?* She'd frittered away a year's allowance at the gaming tables in less than a month, and for what? To impress Reggie and Diana and the rest of her so-called friends. But they didn't care about her, not really. All they cared about was keeping up appearances and their endless rounds of parties, not common Annie Higgins or her common, *nouveau riche* father. They wouldn't bail her out now, she knew, even if they could!

Perhaps she could pawn her few remaining pieces of jewelry? She sighed. No. That wouldn't do. Mabel, her maid, had told her that pawnshops paid one only ten percent of an item's true worth. Even if she pawned her diamond ear bobs and the Indian sapphire necklace Da had given her on her last birthday, she'd still be short. Then what . . . ? *What?* There must be *something* she could do?

Beyond the carriage windows sprawled the dark warren of streets that were Victoria's London, lit by gaslight under a veiling of fine spring rain this April morning. Puddles reflected the eerie yellow light tenfold. The smell of the distant wharves and of soot, of onions, hot meat pies, and strong brown ale carried faintly on the soggy

night air. Even at this ungodly predawn hour, a few unfortunates were strolling about in search of "trade," their
huge hats and their shabby black boas long-since wilted by
the damp weather. A caped bobby clopping by on
horseback sent them scurrying back into a nearby alley
with muffled giggles.

But, her vision blurred with tears, Angelica saw nothing,
heard nothing. Like a mouse running around and around
on a treadmill, her thoughts were centered on one thing
alone—the money.

When the idea came, it did so quite out of the blue, as if a
guttering candle had suddenly flared up in her mind,
illuminating the shadows of despair, dispelling both fear
and doom. Yes! It was perfect—and it would work, she just
knew it would! But—there was no way she could carry off
her plan alone. She needed a partner, someone with cool
courage and backbone, someone she could trust not to get
cold feet, or—someone whose loyalty she could buy with
cold, hard cash.

The memory of a bronzed, hard face swam into view; a
rugged, devilishly handsome face dominated by a pair of
ruthless silvery-blue eyes that would have damned the
devil himself to hell . . .

The American.

"Simmons!" she cried excitedly, rapping on the
carriage wall with her knuckles to alert her driver.

"Yes, Miss 'Iggins?"

"I've changed my mind about going home. Turn the
carriage around! Take me back to Bligh's."

"At this hour, miss?" Simmons sounded dubious.

"At once, Simmons. The faster the better!"

Chapter Two

She spotted her "quarry" leaving Bligh's, just as Simmons reined in the horses before the gambling hall's entrance.

A cheroot jutted from between his teeth, the tip a glowing crimson sequin against the dreary night and the sooty brick walls of the buildings that lined the narrow street on either side. He wore neither cape nor greatcoat, making no concession to the bone-deep chill and damp of the night but that his broad shoulders were hunched, his hands tucked into the pockets of his peculiar fringed suede jacket. Wearing a strange hat with a brim that curled up on either side, he was striding along with the long-limbed, easy grace she'd observed in the gambling hall. He was, in all likelihood, headed for the Haymarket, where music halls abounded and painted streetwalkers were everywhere, lingering in shadowed doorways and murky alleys, though a man like the American would have little need to buy women. He would draw them like a magnet. . . .

Hands trembling with apprehension, Angel raised the partition to speak to Simmons. "That man—the American—follow him!"

"What's that, miss?"

"I said, follow him, Simmons—and hurry up, do, before we lose him at the corner!"

The coach pulled away from the curb. At their driver's urging, the horses picked up their gait, moving at a spanking trot down the rain-washed, gaslit street. When they drew abreast of the American, Angel signaled Simmons to stop with a sharp rap of her knuckles on the coach walls.

"Shall I call him over, miss—?" Simmons offered, his tone doubtful, but his mistress had flung open the coach door before the wheels had even stopped turning.

"I say, sir, you over there!" she sang out.

The American kept on walking without so much as turning around.

"Excuse me, sir!" she tried again. "Could I—could I have a word with you?"

He halted and swung around, his expression unfathomable in the amber puddle spilled by the nearby gas lamp. Drawing the cheroot from his mouth, he tossed the butt to the ground, where it sizzled and extinguished itself on the rain-wet pavement.

"Are you talkin' to me, ma'am?" he asked, his tone puzzled as his silver blue eyes assessed her. Framed as she was in the open doorway of the handsome vehicle before him, the lamplight bathing her in gold, she was breathtaking. Her honey-colored hair, piled in lustrous ringlets, cascaded down about her shoulders like satin ribbons. Her thick-lashed eyes were seductively dark against the cream and rose of her complexion. Delicately moistening her lips, she met his searching gaze, then quickly looked away, showing none of the disdain with which she'd rebuffed his well-intended warnings a while ago. A slender, graceful hand fluttered to her throat, betraying her uneasiness as she murmured, "Yes, I am."

Oh, Lord, the American seemed even taller, broader here on the wicked streets of Soho than he'd seemed in the brightly lit, noisy gaming club! And compared to the Englishmen she'd met, he was impossibly handsome, impossibly tan, larger than life. Indeed, standing there with his weight thrown on one hip, looking her straight in the eye, he exuded an aura of male arrogance and a casual self-confidence that was palpable. He also seemed extremely dangerous, in retrospect: so much so that her momentary burst of courage almost deserted her!

What on earth had encouraged her to act on such a foolish impulse and accost such a man? What did she know of him, after all? She could be taking her very life in her hands!

But then, remembering her plan and the unhappy consequences of failure, she realized she had very little to lose. She managed to whisper huskily, "I'd very much like a few words with you. That is, if—if you'd be kind enough to oblige me, Mr. . . . ?"

"Durango. Nick Durango."

"Mr. Durango. Yes, well, I thought—that is, I was *hoping* you might be willing to join me in my carriage for a brief—er—discussion? It won't take but a few moments of your time."

"No, ma'am, I don't—"

"Oh, please, don't say no—at least, not until you've heard me out—? You see, I have a proposition—a business proposal, rather!—that I thought you might find . . . interesting . . . ?"

His guarded expression said he'd recognized her from Bligh's and was far from eager to renew that brief and unpleasant acquaintance. Setting his jaw, he shook his head. "Nonetheless, I don't think I care to—"

"Oh, but please, at least let me say my piece! What harm can it do? I know I was dreadfully rude to you earlier, but—but I was upset about something. I snapped at you and I'm really and truly very sorry. Please hear me out, Mr. Durango. It won't take long, I promise it won't."

The dewy sheen in her lovely eyes now swayed him. Unless he was way off the mark—and he didn't think he was—she was close to tears. And, as hard as he'd become over the years, he was still a sucker for a pretty damsel in distress. With a curt nod, he took the two long strides toward the coach and mounted the single step.

The coach rocked as he swung himself inside, pulling the door shut after him. Angel shrank back against the farthest side of the ox-blood leather seat while Durango chose the one facing her.

"Drive on, Simmons!" she called shakily through the partition, thoroughly unnerved by the nearness of the man. Somehow, in these confined, dark quarters, his presence was unsettling; it was as if he radiated energy in some peculiar way. Her heart was racing and her breathing shallow.

"Where to, miss?" Simmons asked.

"Anywhere—around the block will do nicely, Jim. Just—just drive, and keep on driving until I tell you to stop!"

"Right you are, miss," came Simmons' sour response, and the vehicle started forward.

"All right. Spit it out," Durango urged softly, his tone brusque. "I'll hear you out—but I don't have all night, ma'am."

She bristled at his ill-manners, but said nothing. After all, what had she expected? That brashness and nonconformity were among the very qualities that made him the perfect choice for what she intended to do! Any self-respecting Englishman would have turned her proposal down flat, told her her plan was disgraceful, devoid of any redeeming aspects. She was encouraged that the American would not reject it out of hand. . . .

"Very well, I won't beat about the bush," she began, clasping her hands together so tightly in her lap, the nails dug painfully into her palms. She drew a deep breath. "As a result of my own . . . foolishness, shall we say? . . . I find myself in something of a quandary, Mr. Durango. A financial quandary."

"And?"

Ignoring him, she continued, "Over the past two months or so, I've accumulated a—a rather considerable debt with Mr. Bill Bligh—the owner of Bligh's gambling hall. Mr. Bligh is now demanding payment—somewhat forcefully demanding it, too, I might add. He has made certain . . . threats . . . of a rather violent nature toward me, but threat or no threat, I simply can't make good on my markers because I'm completely—"

"Strapped?"

"Quite!"

"Well, I'm sorry t' hear it, but I don't see how this concerns me. Is it a loan you want, ma'am?"

"Oh, certainly not! I wouldn't dream of asking you for a loan."

"You want my advice, then? What about asking your family for the money? You do have one?"

30

"I have my father, yes. And he happens to be a very wealthy man. He is also very fond of me. Unfortunately, he is also violently opposed to gambling! Mr. Durango, I simply cannot ask him for the funds to cover my losses. I would sooner face my creditors! Consequently, I—I was desperate to find a means to repay Mr. Bligh, until I hit upon a simply marvelous plan tonight. It's a very simple plan—but one I'm unable to carry off alone."

"Ah. And that's where I come in?"

"I'd hoped so, yes!"

"I see. And exactly what is this plan of yours?"

She wetted her lips again and despite himself, he found his eyes drawn to the moist pink pout of her delectable lower lip, wondering what it would be like to kiss her there, and maybe lower, where the fluid elegance of her pale throat flowed into the high curves of her breasts, glimpsed beneath the folds of her gaping evening cape of luxuriant fur.

"Well, it's actually quite a simple plan, really. I thought I'd—that I'd have myself—you know, *kidnapped*," she mumbled, feeling heat flame in her cheeks.

His dark brows rose. "Kidnap yourself?" He whistled softly and shook his head. "Hell, that's some plan you've got there, lady! And I suppose you're confident your father'll meekly hand over the money t' get his little gal back safe and sound, no questions asked? Money that you'd then use to pay off your gambling debts?"

"That's it, exactly," she acknowledged, relieved that he'd understood so quickly.

"Ah huh. And unless I miss the mark, I'm t' play the part of the big, bad ole kidnapper, I take it?"

When he described her plan in that contemptuous tone, it sounded utterly despicable, rather than the flash of divine inspiration she'd seen it as earlier. She averted her eyes, her cheeks afire with shame now beneath his insolent gaze. Oh, Lord! Could he see her mortified expression in the shadows? She hoped not. Now that she'd set the wheels in motion, she had to see it through—this was her last chance, her last hope! She couldn't let anything deter her. Setting her jaw, she gritted, "Something like that, yes, though I wouldn't have described it quite so—

harshly—myself."

"Prettyin' it up with nice words doesn't change it any, honey," he growled. "But—might I ask why you settled on me as your accomplice? After all, it's not as if we know each other, is it? Or as if we've even been formally introduced, come to that?"

"Well, I thought of you mainly because you're an American, aren't you?" she began, the words spilling out in her rush to explain herself. "You—you struck me earlier as someone who would have the—the necessary nerve, shall we say, to see my plan through to the end? And besides, everyone knows that Americans have far less scruples than the British do—I mean, insofar as making money is concerned. Naturally, I wouldn't expect you to help me without a payment of some kind," she added hastily, for his impatient expression had turned ugly.

"Oh, naturally," he echoed sarcastically. "But, surely there's someone else you could ask?"

"Not in the circles in which I move, no. My father and I are—let's simply say we have very few friends. I don't know if you're aware of it, but in British society, it's practically considered a sin for anyone to make a penny from any sort of commerce or trade. The only respectable means to become wealthy is by inheriting wealth from your family—and my father came by his fortune quite by chance."

"Well, kidnappin' is hardly respectable, honey. It's not even legal, damn it!"

"That's why I know nobody will lift a finger to help me, not even Diana, and she loves to try anything new and dangerous . . ." She was gabbling on about irrelevant matters, she knew, things that had no bearing on her immediate problems, but in her nervousness, she couldn't seem to shut up! Besides, she didn't dare confess to this Durango that she'd *really* chosen him because he seemed tough enough to do the job, and see it done right . . . !

"So let me get this straight. You approached me—a stranger—with this little plan of yours because you thought an 'unscrupulous American' would jump at the chance to get mixed up in your sneaky little scheme and make a few dollars?" There was a cold edge to his tone now, one that was chilling.

"Yes! No! Oh, please, Mr. Durango, I really don't mean to insult you, not for a minute. It's just—it's just that I need help so very desperately, and I have no one else to turn to. Perhaps it is a sneaky little scheme, but I would never even consider doing this to my father if I didn't have to, and I'll make jolly well certain I never have to do it again. Surely you understand, it's not as if I *want* to do this?"

"Oh, I understand you all right, honey. You're desperate enough to break the law to keep from getting found out—and selfish enough not to give a damn who gets hurt in the process! But tell me, what's in it for me?"

"You?"

"Yeah, me." He leaned forward, planting a heavy hand on her knee. "See, Blondie, you mentioned payment, but the way I see it, you're doing this because you don't have a nickel to your name in the first place, 'less good ole Daddy gives it to you. If that's true, how were you plannin' on payin' me off?"

The silence in the wake of his question yawned between them like a gaping pit. The lids drooped over his eyes like curtains, leaving only a silvery glitter in the shadows, but she knew he was watching her like a hawk, and the knowledge unnerved her. Her knee seemed afire beneath the weight of his fingers. She itched to pluck his hand away—but didn't dare. Oh, Lord, what had he asked her! She couldn't even think clearly enough to answer him!

"Well? I'm waitin'. What did you plan t' buy me off with? The family jewels? Your furs?" He paused, catching a flicker of something in her expression, then added softly, "Yourself?"

Aghast, she wasn't certain at first that she'd heard him correctly, but he continued in the same taunting drawl, "Was that the deal, sugar? My help, in return for your . . . favors?"

"Certainly not!" she flared, flinging his hand off her knee. "You're utterly contemptible to suggest such a thing!"

"And by my reckoning, ma'am, you're 'utterly contemptible' to be putting this little con over your pa, just to save your hide!"

"All right. If that's the way you feel, get out of my carriage! I don't have to listen to your insults a moment longer!"

"Nor I yours, honey. But it was *you* who invited *me* in here, remember? Not the other way around."

"You're a cad—a perfect bounder! I must have been mad to ask you for help!"

He laughed mirthlessly as he sprang to his feet, looming over her. "Well, what else would you expect, from an American, hmm?" Hand on the coach door, he mockingly tipped his hat to her. "I'll be on my way now, Blondie, but a word of advice before I leave. Go to your father. Tell him everything. If he loves you, like you said, he'll forgive you anything . . ."

"If I wanted your advice, blast you, I'd have asked for it!" she flared, knowing in her heart that every word he said was true, and squirming with guilt because it was. "Now, just—just get out of here!"

"Good evenin' to you, ma'am. I'd like to say it was a pleasure meetin' you—'cept it wasn't . . ."

With that, he flung open the door and stood poised in the doorway, ready to spring down to the cobbles when the carriage slowed its pace.

His imminent departure brought Angel to her senses like a slap in the face.

"Wait! Oh, please don't go! You're quite right, I don't have any money, and I'm sorry for the awful things I said. But—but if you'll stay, if you'll agree to help me, I'll—I'll pay you from the ransom money, I swear it. I'll pay anything you ask. Just . . . just name your price!"

"Thanks—but no thanks," Durango gritted after an endless pause, then he sprang down from the carriage, slamming the door behind him and leaving her alone in the gloom.

Craning her head through the rolled-down window moments later, Angel saw him standing beneath a gas lamp, his collar turned up. His head was bent, his hands cupped to light another cheroot. As she watched, the match caught and his face was illuminated in its sulphur flare for a few seconds, darkly handsome, hateful. He glanced up, saw her watching him and saluted mockingly as her coach rolled on through the darkened Soho streets.

"Damn you, Durango!" she hissed as she flopped back onto the leather seat. The few words they'd exchanged had left her weak, exhausted; left her already frayed nerves in shreds. Oh, she'd been a fool to ask a stranger—and an American stranger, at that!—for help. Durango was dangerous, wild, and unpredictable—anyone could tell that a mile away. The horrid brute was proof positive that he and his countrymen deserved their dubious reputations! Well, no matter. She'd have to look elsewhere for help, that was all; she would have to find another accomplice to whom the successful outcome of her plan would be as vital as it was to her. Someone she could handle. Someone who needed money just as desperately as she did. . . .

A relieved smile curved her lips as the perfect person came to mind. Of course—*Reggie!* Why on earth hadn't she considered dear Reggie from the first? He was the obvious choice. And if she hurried, she just might catch him before he retired for the night.

"Simmons!"

"Yes, miss?"

"Turn the carriage about, at once. Take me to Lord Smythe-Moreton's town house!"

"Again? At this hour, miss? It'll be dawn in a little while!"

"Don't argue with me, Simmons. Lay on!"

"Very well, miss."

Chapter Three

"Oh, really, Mabel! It's not as if I were asking you to sacrifice your life, for heaven's sake. I just want you to tell a teeny little lie for me," Angel indicated with her fingers just how tiny, but her maid was not convinced.

"It in't tiny and it in't little, and I in't havin' nuffink t' do wiv hoodwinkin' the master, so there!" Mabel refused with a sniff, glaring at her young mistress, who sat before her dressing table, unpinning her hair, the following night.

"But Mabel, you simply must say yes. Reggie and Simmons have already agreed to do their part. All I need now is for you to agree to do yours, and this entire charade will appear genuine."

"I won't do it."

As if she hadn't heard Mabel's refusal, Angel set aside her hairbrush and counted off the steps of her plan on her fingers. "From the milliner's, Simmons will drive me to Reggie's town house tomorrow morning. Then, after a suitable delay, he'll bring you back here. You'll run directly into the house, sobbing that your beloved mistress has been kidnapped. Just make absolutely sure that you give Da the ransom note, and your part's done with. Finished! It's as simple as that."

"Sobbing, my arse. Simple or not, I want no bloomin' part of it." Mabel crossed her arms over her bosom.

Wearing a tiny lace night cap perched on her Medusa's mop of hennaed curls, and a voluminous flannel nightgown that could have doubled as a campaign tent, her maid-companion reminded Angel suddenly of a squirrel dressed in human attire. A squirrel that, at this very moment, she would dearly have loved to shoot with a very large blunderbuss.

"Oh, you're absolutely impossible!" she accused instead, whirling around, stomping across her bedroom, and flinging back the bedcovers.

"And you're a spoiled brat what's 'eadin fer a bad end, you are!" Mabel flung back. "Sneakin' out at all hours o' the nights wiv them randy toffs, up to Gawd-knows-what mischief, or wiv 'oo. Gamblin' an' dicin' your dad's money away . . . Next we hear, you'll have a bun in the oven, I shouldn't wonder—!"

"Oh, get out, you horrid woman! Go back to suckling your gin bottle!" Angel flared, feeling guilty about Mabel's reference to her gambling.

"Don't mind if I do, Miss Hoity-Toity 'Iggins."

Mabel left, slamming the door in her wake.

Standing before the cheval looking glass, wearing only her lace-trimmed bodice and long ruffled underdrawers, Angel undressed. As she did so, she considered how very hard it was to be the mistress of a household with servants of Mabel Blunt's ilk.

That frightful woman! Mabel was rude, disrespectful, and lazy. She obeyed only those orders she felt inclined to obey and was inordinately fond of the gin bottle. She sighed heavily. Still, what choice had her poor da been given, but to engage such—such riff-raff as Mabel to run his London household? No self-respecting servant worth their salt would seek employ at Brixton Towers, for servants—after their own fashion—were every bit as snobbish as those they worked for. And Sidney Higgins—although the Towers' new master and a millionaire many times over—was most definitely not possessed of the old master's blue blood, or anyone else's come to that.

She had tried—however clumsily!—to explain this subtle distinction to that odious American, to demonstrate to him that it simply wasn't accepted in society for one's wealth to be earned, however rich one might become from trade or whatever. Old money—inherited money—was the only acceptable form of wealth—provided it was inherited through one's own bloodlines. And her poor da couldn't even make that claim, his millions having been the bequest of an ailing, eccentric stranger.

For a fleeting second, an image of the American's handsome, sun-bronzed face, hard with anger, popped into her head. She shuddered. What madness had possessed her to approach such a man—and a foreigner, at that—with her foolish proposition? And what must he have thought of her, waylaying him on the streets in the wee hours of the morning as she'd done, then brazenly inviting him into her coach like a common trollop! She'd made an utter fool of herself, then made a bad situation worse by insulting him terribly in the bargain. She really hadn't meant to insinuate that his countrymen had no scruples to speak of. In her nervousness, her carefully thought-out speech had simply come out wrong. She would have tried to explain, but he'd been so very angry, the air had crackled as if a storm were about to break. And the contempt in his sensual, silvery eyes had been palpable! Even now, it still made her shudder to remember it. On reflection, she shouldn't have been surprised when he asked if she meant to pay him off with her favors. She'd deserved his insults. Thank God she'd never have to see the man again!

A timid knock sounded at her door. "Who is it?" she asked.

"It's me. Mabel."

"I didn't ring for you, Blunt. Go away."

"Open this bleedin' door, Miss Uppity, 'else I won't be responsible for me actions!" Mabel hissed through the keyhole.

With an irritable click of her teeth, Angel complied, flinging the door open wide.

Mabel flounced into her bedroom and slammed the door shut behind her. She sashayed across the carpet and plunked herself down upon her young mistress's bed as if she, rather than Angel, owned the place.

"I'll take two arfternoons orf from here on, 'stead o' just the one I've bin 'aving. A week's 'oliday in August, when the weather's 'ottest, and a little bottle o' somethink 'medicinal' when I'm feelin' poorly," she declared firmly.

38

"Are these your terms for helping me?" Angel asked in an icy tone. The gall of the woman!

"They are. Take 'em or leave 'em."

"I'll leave them, thank you."

"How's about the gin and no 'oliday, then?" Mabel wheedled, considerably deflated now. She'd expected Angel to hang her head and agree.

Angel shook her head. "No." If nothing else, Diana had taught her that servants needed a firm hand.

Mabel's tight little mouth drooped in a sulky pout. "Oh, all bleedin' right, then! You win. I'll do it fer the extra arfternoon off, you horrible little chit—but I in't happy about it. Mark my words, you'll come to a right bad end with your pinchpenny ways. I can smell it a mile orf! I don't know 'ow a loverly bloke like Sid could've fathered a selfish, toffee-nosed brat like you, I reelly don't!"

"It's *Mr.* Higgins to you, Mabel," Angel reminded the young woman. Becoming the mistress of Brixton Towers was a fond hope of Mabel's—and Sidney Higgins's most dreaded nightmare. Accordingly, Angel never missed the chance to disabuse her of any such notions. "Now, shall we go over the plans again? Or do you think you can remember it all?"

"Go over the part about me sobbin' me eyes out 'cos you've been snatched and 'orribly mutilated," Mabel suggested with obvious relish. "Who knows? If I pray 'ard enough, it might come true . . ."

"You've hardly touched your grilled kidneys, our Angel. And come t' think on it, ye look a bit flushed this morning. Not comin' down with summat, are ye?" her father asked the following morning, regarding her fondly across the breakfast table.

Swallowing her nervousness, she summoned a smile.

"Of course not, Papa. I feel marvelous! I'm just in somewhat of a rush this morning, that's all. I have an appointment at the milliner's at ten to select my Ascot hat, and afterwards, my old school chum, Diana Forsythe, is expecting me for a light luncheon at the Square. Her wedding's in two months, you recall, Papa? Dini's relying on me to advise her about the—er—with the—er—"

"Flowers?"

"Yes, that's it. The wedding bouquets and floral arrangements." For a moment, her mind had gone quite blank.

"I'm not surprised. You was always real handy wi' them hollyhocks and daffs we 'ad back in Brixton! 'Our Annie's got a proper green thumb,' I always used t' say." His gray eyes, so like his daughter's, twinkled.

"Oh, Da. You never did! And besides, the hollyhocks grew wild! It was Mam had the green thumb. She planted them, remember?"

"Aye, lass. I remember as if it was yesterday."

Angel smiled. He was still so very handsome, her da, with his neatly trimmed moustache and side-whiskers and those fine, intelligent gray eyes that met one with such appealing directness and warmth. The new tailor she'd found for him had proven a marvel, knowing just how to dress Da to make the most of his slight build. He was truly becoming quite dapper and distinguished in appearance, was Da, wearing those dashing tweed suits and vests he'd come to favor, and with his dark brown hair now a silvery pepper-and-salt at the temples! Only in his late forties, he was still far from old as yet. What a pity he'd never found someone to equal her mother in his affections. . . .

She peered at the tiny gold fob watch pinned to the smart gray-and-pink striped fitted jacket. "Oh, heavens! It's past nine. I really should be running along."

She took another hasty sip of breakfast tea from a fragile china cup, then pushed back her chair before the footman could assist her. Hurrying around the table, she kissed her father's cheek, hugging him a little longer and a little tighter than she usually did. "I should be home by midafternoon, at very latest. Cook knows what to prepare for supper. You don't have a thing to worry about."

"Nay, lass, not with you t' look after things for me, I don't. I don't know what I'd have done wi' out you, my pet, after your mam passed away." He frowned and came to take her in his arms. "But . . . what about you? Are you happy, love? Eeh, I do fret about ye, sometimes. Being rich does 'ave its own share o' problems, don't it?"

"I'm very happy, Da, honestly I am," she reassured him, and it was no lie. If not for that nasty business with Bligh, she'd be delirious—over the moon with happiness! *Tomorrow*, she promised herself. *By this time tomorrow, it'll all be over, and I'll never, ever have to lie to him again.*

"But you've no 'usband yet, lass! You need a good man—a stout-hearted, God-fearin' lad with a bit o' old-fashioned pride who'll love ye for yer sweet, bonnie self and want t' support ye—not come courtin' ye for your father's 'brass'!" He shook his head ruefully. "But I'll be blowed if I can figure a way to tell the wheat from the chaff—or the fortune 'unters like that bloody Smythe-Moreton from the good 'uns what'll do right by ye."

"Don't worry. When I meet him, I'll know, Da."

He sighed. "Aye, lass, happen ye will. Eeh, I hope so."

"I really should be going . . ."

"Aye, if ye must, ye must. Ta-ra, then, my Angel. See ye later, love."

"Ta-ra, Da," she murmured.

With a nod, she was gone in a flurry of pink silk and floating scarves, turning away too quickly for him to see the telltale moisture in her eyes.

"I swear, Mabel Blunt, that if you do anything— *anything at all!*—to ruin this for me, I'll—I'll—"

"Have me guts fer garters?" Mabel supplied gloomily.

"At least!" Angel agreed, for want of a more bloodthirsty threat of her own.

"Oww, stop carping on, do! Where's your faith in human nature? Your trust? I've said I'll do it, an' I will. Now, give over, both o' yer. It's time t' do the dirty deed, so I'm off home, t' see it done right!"

Reggie shook his head as Mabel—with that dramatic farewell—toddled to the door, then through it, under the frankly aghast eyes of his valet, William.

"Good Lord, Angel! That awful baggage reeked of spirits," Reggie exclaimed with a shudder after she'd left. "I do believe she was a little *tipsy*—and it's barely tea time! Are you certain she's capable of carrying this off without your pater suspecting anything?"

Angel grimaced as she sat down on the sheepskin rug before the fireplace. Although it was April, Reggie's old brick town house was as drafty as a mausoleum, and a fire was burning merrily in the grate.

"Quite certain," she said confidently in answer to Reggie's question. "Once Mabel's promised something, she's a bastion of reliability, believe it or not. Now, pass me the toasting fork and the crumpets. I'm positively starving!"

"Beastly nerves given you an appetite, have they, poppet?" Reggie asked softly, ruffling the wispy dark gold curls that trailed like delicate golden vines about Angel's delectable nape.

"I rather think they have, yes," she admitted, spearing one of the crumpets on the three-pronged brass toasting fork. She angled it over the glowing orange coals of the fire. "Oh, Reggie, I feel so awful about deceiving Papa! Why did you have to set the ransom at five thousand pounds? You know very well I only need three!"

"So that you'd have two thousand pounds in reserve, remember? Just in case you should ever be tempted to such folly again?"

"I know that but—!"

"And don't forget, you did promise to lend me fifty guineas to pay my tailor."

"How could I forget, Reggie, darling?" She scowled, her delightful snub nose wrinkling. "You keep reminding me over and over! Sometimes, I wonder if it isn't just my father's money you love, rather than me."

"What nonsense, my darling," Reggie denied breezily, without meeting her eyes. He handed Angel a cup and saucer from the silver tray William had set before the fire on a low folding table, then took one for himself. Raising the dainty cup, he proposed a toast. "To us, old girl, and to the success of our endeavors!"

"Hear! Hear!" Angel agreed fervently, touching her cup to his.

The two middle-aged men, both wearing well-cut tweeds, came to a halt before the entrance of Brixton

Towers and looked about them.

The two-story mansion and its grounds were situated on the outskirts of London. Built from mellow Cornish stone, the Towers rose from a formal English garden, complete with a box hedge maze and lily pond. Geometrically shaped flowerbeds created a stunning splash of color with seasonal daffodils, tulips, and hyacinths vying with crocuses, narcissus, and more.

The house boasted a small tower at either end, much like a miniature castle, having the main entrance at the middle. Several broad white steps led up to an imposing double-doored entryway, which an overhanging semi-circular glass dome protected in inclement weather. Two gray stone elephants, their trunks raised, flanked the doors, *howdahs* overflowing with trailing ivy plants. The high stone walls that enclosed the gardens and the curlicued wrought-iron gates showed evidence of having been freshly painted.

"It's remarkable what you've done, Sidney, old chap. Quite remarkable! I can't get over the renovations you've made since I was last here—not to mention the repairs you've already completed! The stables are returned to their former magnificence, and the greenhouses and the orangery—! Why, the Towers looks as imposing as when I was a young lad, before Pater carted us all off to India to live. Father and Lord Brixton were awfully close, you know. Practically brothers. Did I mention that before?"

"Aye, Teddy, lad. You've done so a time or two," Sidney admitted with a wry grin, clapping Edward Hardcastle, Esquire across the back to show that there were no hard feelings. Though he spoke like a toffee-nosed gent—as if he had a plum in his mouth—Sidney liked Ted and had come to consider him a good friend.

They'd met three years ago when Teddy—also a widower who'd never remarried, though himself childless—had retired early from a career with the East India company due to recurring bouts of malaria, which India's climate had exacerbated.

Accordingly, upon his mother's death Hardcastle had returned to England to live, and in due course had come to the Towers to pay his respects to his father's old school chum, Harry, Lord Brixton.

He'd been shattered to learn from Sid that Harry had passed on some years before, and that the Towers had a new heir. Being of a kindly nature, Sid had insisted Teddy stay and poured him a stiff brandy to compose himself.

That first visit had led to others, for though worlds apart in education and breeding, the two men had enjoyed each other's companionship from the very first. Together they went to the horse races at Epsom Downs and Newmarket, followed endless cricket matches at Lords, and—from time to time, unknown to Sid's little Annie—enjoyed the fond companionship of a pair of very attractive widows in the West End of London, who were decidedly generous with their favors! After a lifetime spent abroad, Teddy declared, he felt uncomfortable among London society. Sid, more comfortable among working class folk, felt the same. The two fish-out-of-water had soon become fast friends. . . .

"Come on inside wi' ye, Ted, my lad. Let's you and me have a drop o' summat over a game o' billiards."

"Right-o. Loser pays for these!" Grinning, Teddy whipped out three cardboard rectangles.

"Tickets?" Sid appeared suspicious. "And what might those be for? If it's the bloody opera again, I'd as soon pass it up, Ted, thanks all the same. All that 'orrible screechin' an' wailin' in that I-talian talk—! Eeh, it's murder on the ears, it is! I swear, I don't know how you can stand it, lad! Nay, give me the musical halls any old time! A bit o' singing, a bit o' dancing, a lot o' laughs. A naughty lass or two, flaunting her stuff. Eeh, a lad knows what he's getting with them music halls, he does," Sid declared, leading the way to the billiard room down a long hallway carpeted with a Turkish runner. "But that opera—!" He was shaking his head in disgust as they went inside the large room that smelled faintly of cigar smoke and fine brandy.

"'Pon my word, Sid, it's not the opera. I *know* you'll enjoy this show!" Teddy promised with a knowing chuckle. "I'll give you a hint. These tickets are harder to get in the city right now than gold!"

Sid frowned. "The circus?"

Teddy shook his head. "Does the name 'Buffalo Bill'

44

ring a bell?''

"What's this? You've tickets t' the Wild West Show?''

"Better than that—three *front row* tickets, to be exact!
One each for you and your lovely Angel, and one for me.
They're for Friday evening. I thought we'd all go
together—make a real occasion of it. Have a spot of supper
first at Wellington's, perhaps, and then on to the show.
What do you say, old chap?''

Teddy didn't need to hear his answer. Sidney's eyes
shone! He'd read about Colonel William F. Cody's Wild
West Show in all the London newspapers. Eeh, who in
Britain hadn't? Ever since her Most Gracious Majesty,
Queen Victoria, bless her, and His Royal Highness, the
Prince of Wales, bless 'im, had expressed their delight in
the entertainment by viewing it an unheard of *three* times,
Sidney'd been itching to see it for himself! In fact—though
he'd never admit it to Teddy—he'd tried to get tickets
himself, but had no success.

By gum, the thought of seeing that American show was
an exciting one. Two whole days t' wait—how would he
stand it! Sid felt exactly like a little lad in short trousers
promised a visit to the circus!

It was said there were five hundred members in the
troupe, including real American cowboys, real American
Red Indians, real Indian chiefs—Sitting Bull and Red
Cloud—and the stars, Nick Durango, the Cowboy King,
and the famous sharpshooter, Little Annie Oakley, along
with five hundred horses. The troupe reenacted stage-
coach and wagon-train attacks with screaming savages
firing flaming arrows; deadly shootouts between rival
gunslingers, rough-riding, roping, horse races, shooting
contests, and Colonel "Buffalo Bill" Cody himself, astride
his prancing white horse—! Eeh, by gum, it promised to
be a champion show! He couldn't wait to tell Angel that
they were going. . . .

"Does that ridiculous grin of yours mean you find the
idea somewhat entertaining, old chap?'' Teddy asked,
removing his coat and selecting chalk and a cue from the
rack against the wall.

"Aye,'' Sid agreed, pouring them both a glass of whisky
from a crystal decanter on the side table and trying to

smother his broad smile without success. "I reckon it does. I must admit, I've—*whoa!*"

At that moment the door to the billiard room flung inward with a resounding thud. It slammed against the wall, dislodging the scoring board and sending it crashing to the ground. Chalks and cues followed with a clatter and a puff of white powder.

Mabel Blunt, her cheeks hectic, her hair and hat awry, her wine-colored feather boa wound untidily around her throat, all but toppled into the room.

"Good God!" Teddy Hardcastle exclaimed, astounded by the woman's deranged, wild-eyed appearance.

"I'll give 'er 'Good God,'" Sidney snapped, furious. "You've been at the gin again, 'aven't you, our Mabel? You're nowt but a young sot, lass, that's what you are!"

"I in't touched a single drop t'day, I swear it, sir!" Mabel denied indignantly. "But—oh, sir, never mind me. It's Miss Angel! She's gorn, sir! Vanished orf the face o' the earth! Disappeared without a trace! Them 'eartless villains have taken my poor mistress!"

"What!" Sid exploded.

"Owww, the dirty rotten scoundrels! The dastardly blackguards! What ever are we to do without her, sir? She were so bleedin' good to me, she were. So bleedin' gentle an' patient. Always s'bleedin' sweet and generous. And now she's gorn—and we'll never see 'er again! Owww, owww, woe is me! Woe . . . woe . . . woe . . . !"

"Summat's happened t' my Annie? Damn it, spit it out, lass!" Sid thundered. Grasping Mabel by the upper arms, he shook her like a wiry fox terrier shaking an untidy rat, his gray eyes feverish. In fact, he shook her so violently Mabel's burgundy feather boa unwound. Her shabby black hat slipped from her head and hung from her frowsy red hair by a single, lethal pin.

"That's wot I said, innit, sir? Miss Angel's been kidnapped, she has. Vanished orf the face o' the—"

"Yes, yes, but how? When? And by whom? Speak up, my good woman!" Teddy Hardcastle demanded, trying to bring some sense to the moment. Sid appeared to be in shock, now that he'd digested the import of the woman's news. He reeled away, completely felled by that Blunt

46

creature's terrible announcement. He appeared incapable of thought, let alone taking charge!

"It musta happened when she was leavin' the milliner's, sirs!" Mabel cried, sniffing and wiping her nose on her knuckles. "Miss Angel told Simmons to return for her at eleven. Jim waited an' waited, he did, but Miss Angel didn't come out. So finally, Simmons went inside t' ask after her. That Miss Prudence said she'd left ages ago! And then, when Simmons got back t' the carriage, he—he—he f-f-found this n-n-n-note what some dastardly criminal had left on the seat! The poor lad can't read, can he, sir, so he didn't know what t' make of it, but I did. Here. Take a gander at this, sir!"

Noisily blowing her nose, Mabel thrust a grubby, much-wrinkled sheet of what appeared to be butcher's paper into Sidney Higgins's face. Hands shaking, he unfolded it and smoothed it out. In crude smudged capitals it read:

To Mister Sidney Higgins
Brixton Towers, London
   Bring five thowsand pownds to the holer oak on Crofts Comon at dorn Thersdy if you want ter see your dawter agin Cum alone

Sined
The Kid Napers.

"Atrocious spelling," Teddy observed with a shudder, having read the note over Sid's shoulder. "But I think their meaning's plain enough, nonetheless."

"Aye," Sid said heavily, looking as if someone had just rammed him in the belly with a billy club and knocked all the wind out of him. His normally vigorous, ruddy complexion had turned gray. "It's plain, all right—plain as bloody daylight! Them sods've got my little Annie! And if I won't pay what those swine're askin', they mean t' kill 'er!"

Chapter Four

"Well? What do you think of my disguise?" Reggie asked, sounding a trifle petulant. "You didn't say, you know."

"You look perfectly sinister! I don't think I'd have recognized you on the street," Angel admitted, hugging a ragged blanket more tightly about her shoulders.

Reggie's blond good looks were hidden by a bushy black false moustache and wire-rimmed spectacles that had been his late father's. His fair hair had vanished beneath a barrow boy's soft suede cap, while a brown leather waistcoat worn over a patched cotton shirt and breeches of threadbare brown corduroy stuffed into shabby boots completed his disguise.

"Really?" Reggie said, sounding pleased.

He'd affected a rolling sailor's gait for his pose as her kidnapper, and walked with his thumbs hooked into his belt and his head poked forward. To be honest, she thought he looked like an ungainly question mark—but she'd never tell him that. "Really," she insisted. "Brrr! It's freezing out here!"

"You're just nervous, that's all," he tried to reassure her, despite sounding edgy himself.

Nevertheless, Angel was shivering as they walked across the dew-sodden turf of the common toward the hollow oak, their feet lost within the mist that curled about their legs like drifting smoke. The pink-and-gray striped silk ensemble she'd chosen to wear had been a foolish choice, she realized now, yet at the time, she'd quite forgotten how

48

cold an English spring morning could prove.

By tacit consent, they both halted before the hollow oak and looked about them.

Crofts Common was a popular courting spot on fine evenings in spring, summer, and autumn, when sweethearts in various stages of intimacy littered the coarse grass and heathered hollows, but at this ungodly hour it was deserted except for a scrawny stray dog. A few gorse bushes, some straggly broom, a tangle of blackberry briars, and perhaps a half-dozen wind-warped trees were the only vegetation. The murky half-light of predawn and the misty wisps floating above the ground gave everything a distorted, witchy feeling.

Angel clenched her fists, pressing them to her middle beneath the blanket. She had a cold knot in the pit of her stomach that had grown steadily worse as last night inched its snail-like path toward day. Guilt, no doubt, coupled with a hefty serving of remorse, had kept her awake most of the night. She hadn't been able to sleep for imagining her poor father reading the crude ransom letter Reggie had composed. And knowing how frantic he'd be to learn she'd been abducted, she'd been unable to eat a bite since the crumpets she'd gobbled down the afternoon before.

They'd left Reggie's carriage and walked the remaining half-mile to the common. But neither brisk exercise nor mounting excitement had succeeded in warming Angel. Her hands still felt like ice! Her knees still trembled!

Was this really happening? she wondered for the umpteenth time, or was it all a ghastly dream? Had she really stooped so low that she would defraud her own beloved father to conceal her debts? She had. And yes, she would, indeed—that she was here proved it! She shivered again, feeling as if she were living a scene from *Macbeth*. She would not have been surprised if the hags had materialized from behind the blasted oak to cast their gibbering spells, or had Lady Macbeth herself put in an appearance, wringing bloodied hands that Arabian perfumes could not sweeten. . . .

"Now, then, we need to find a spot for you to hide, poppet," Reggie observed, thoughtfully tugging on his chin. "Somewhere close enough for you to be able to see when your papa deposits the ransom in this hollow oak, but distant enough to draw him away from it once he spots you."

"Those briars over there?" she suggested.

"Splendid! Come along, old girl—and do step on it! The sun'll be coming up any minute. We must have you hidden before our little charade begins."

She nodded glumly as she trudged along beside him. Casting a side glance at her chalky face, Reggie clicked his teeth in disapproval.

"Angel, my love, whatever else happens, do promise you won't be sick? If there's one thing I simply can't stomach, it's someone being sick all over the place."

She bristled and assured him icily, "I am not and never have been of a nervous disposition." She looked about her. "These briars will serve very nicely, I believe. I suppose this is where we part company?"

"I'm afraid so, old girl. Now, remember. We rendezvous after church on Sunday next, to divide the 'spoils.'" He winked. "Any last minute questions?"

She shook her head. "None whatsoever. The plan's perfectly straightforward. A simpleton could carry it off."

"Good-oh. Then you should have no difficulties, what?" He dipped his head to kiss her brow in farewell, noting that her skin felt clammy—far cooler than the morning air warranted. Reggie frowned. He hoped to God she wouldn't go into a blue funk and ruin everything for him, for truth was, he needed the ransom money even more desperately than she did! His tailor was but one of a long list of creditors headed by the same thug who had Angel between a rock and a hard place. And Reggie had no illusions about Bligh. If he didn't come up with a miracle—and soon!—he was headed for a watery grave in the Thames. Goosebumps prickled down his arms, as if someone had walked over his grave. Too late, he'd realized that it wasn't at all prudent to welsh on men like Bligh, who had the most unsavory connections and were behind most of the crooked dealings in London's underworld! This plan of Angel's simply had to succeed!

"Well, here goes. Good luck, poppet! All going well,

we'll be toasting our success come Sunday morning!"

She nodded, suddenly too apprehensive to speak. Despite what she'd haughtily told Reggie, she did feel as if she might be sick, after all.

"Go on, old girl. Into the briars with you, then I'm off."

Obediently, she ducked between the briars, weaving her way between twisting bramble branches until she was hidden from the eyes of any chance passersby, but could still see the hollow oak. Shaking all over, she turned for Reggie's approval, but saw that he'd already vanished into the mist. There was no going back now. . . .

Pulling aside a briar that blocked her view, she settled down to watch the all-important oak. And, as she did so, the sun rose at last in a burst of gold, flooding the sooty rooftops and smoke-flagged chimney pots of London in glorious amber light. As if on cue, a thrush began to warble sweetly somewhere nearby. Night had fled. It was dawn!

Sidney Higgins reined in the chestnut hunter and looked about him.

To all appearances, the common was deserted except for a stray dog nosing for rabbits in the bushes. Dew sparkled like frost over the turf. A thrush was singing its little heart out.

"Dawn Thursday," the kidnapper's note had said, and dawn Thursday it was. "Crofts Common," it had read, and Crofts Common was exactly where he was. Now, where was the hollow oak?

He kneed the hunter toward it. The magnificent horse plodded slowly across the grass, its hooves thudding. Reining in at the tree, Sidney reached inside the inner pocket of his tweed riding jacket. He withdrew a bulky package tied with string and as he did so, his fingertips brushed the cold grip of his revolver. His gray eyes hardened, became the color of steel. His mouth narrowed to a harsh, ruthless slit that few who knew him had ever seen. Kidnap his daughter, would they? Try t' extort money from a Higgins, would they? Well, happen those louts'd would learn they'd bitten off more than they could chew. If they'd touched so much as a single hair on his

Annie's head, they'd not live long enough to regret it, he swore under his breath! He'd hound them t' the ends o' the earth—!

Dismounting, Sidney glanced over first one shoulder, then the other. He thrust the parcel deep into its knotty recess, then looked about him again. As he did so, the stray dog he'd noticed earlier barked furiously at something in the bushes. He turned his head to look. A blur of movement caught his eye as someone scrambled out from a thicket of briars, the mongrel worrying at his heels. A tramp who'd passed the night there, Sidney wondered, frowning—or one of the kidnappers?

"*Da!*"

He heard Angel's shout and both dog and tramp were forgotten as he spun on his heels.

"Over here, Da! It's me, Angel!"

Sidney needed no second urging. He was off and running toward her, booted feet eating up the turf to reach his daughter, who was weaving her way out of a briar patch. Her hair was a tangled mare's nest, her face scratched by thorns, but thank God, she appeared unhurt, otherwise.

"Annie, my little love . . . !" he cried, enfolding her in a hearty bear hug that threatened to snap her ribs. "Eeh, lass, are ye all reet? Did those bastards hurt ye?"

"No, Da, I'm not hurt—really I'm not. I'm just a—just a little—frightened still—that's all. They—they left me here, ages ago. Swore if I moved so much as an inch from these briars, they'd know it, and I should be sorry!"

"Happen they did, lass, but it's all over now," he told her grimly, clasping her to his chest and stroking her tangled hair. "There, there, my pet. Your old da's here, and he'll have ye safe home in two shakes of a lamb's tail."

Still with his arm about her, Sidney began leading her toward his horse, which was cropping the grass, reins dangling. "After a drop o' brandy, ye'll be right as—by God! There he goes!" he roared suddenly.

Sidney drew the revolver from within his coat and took aim. Before Angel could recover her wits, he'd fired in the direction of the hollow oak.

The bullet ricochetted off the gnarled trunk with a

52

metallic "ping," almost wounding the odd-looking kidnapper who—the ransom tucked beneath his arm—had clearly been attempting to make good his escape, despite the mongrel worrying at his breeches. As the bullet zipped past his cheek, the rogue let out an ungodly shriek before kicking up his heels and haring across the common, the mutt bounding after him.

As if the shot had been a signal, police whistles sounded from every direction. Angel's head snapped about in confusion as uniformed bobbies converged on the hollow tree, springing up from hidden hollows and dropping down from the trees fringing the common! Shouting excitedly, they swarmed after the fleeing kidnapper like a flight of bluebottles buzzing after a luckless nag.

"Da—?" she whispered, horrified. "You called the bobbies!"

"Aye, lass! Ain't they a grand sight?" Sid crowed, hugging her boisterously. "Our stout lads in blue'll arrest that ruffian right smartly, you mark my words. Justice will prevail!"

"Arrest him—!" Angel echoed, an awful vision of poor Reggie falling beneath the bobbies' wicked truncheons filling her mind. "Oh, Da, do you—do you really think so?"

"I *know* so, our Angel!" Sidney said firmly and with obvious glee. "By breakfast time, he'll be behind bars, awaiting Her Majesty's pleasure. Eeeh, lass, we planned it just champion, we did!"

"We?"

"Aye—me an' Ted and that Inspector Jamieson from Scotland Yard. Our plan worked a proper treat! I've but one regret for this mornin's work—!"

"Yes?" Angel asked, not certain she wanted to know. *Oh, run, Reggie, run!* she prayed silently, crossing her fingers as she awaited her father's answer.

"That I won't be there t' see the kidnapper's face when he opens 'is bloody 'ransom'!" Sidney chortled, beaming at Angel as he lifted her up onto his hunter's back. "It weren't brass he made off with, see? It were Bible *tracts,* our Annie, five thousand of 'em, each wi' the same verse." Sidney's eyes twinkled. "*'Thou shalt not steal'*—!"

53

As the import of her father's words slammed home, Bill Bligh's evil threat sniggered in Angel's ear:

"I'll 'ave some o' my lads rearrange the bones in your pretty little neck . . . Got it, luv?"

She felt the blood drain from her face. Her head reeled so badly, she swayed in the saddle. And, though Angel prided herself on never swooning or getting sick, she came perilously close to doing not one, but both, in that moment. . . .

"Angel?"

"Yes, Papa?"

"We didn't wake ye, did we, pet?" Sidney asked as he and Teddy Hardcastle tiptoed into the room to stand beside her bed.

"No, Papa. Come on in, too, Uncle Teddy, it's quite all right. I'm still far too upset to sleep." In all honesty, "upset" didn't begin to describe the way she was feeling! It was Friday. She had only one week left to come up with the money she owed Bill Bligh—and her last, desperate plan lay in smoking ruins all about her! "Did they—?"

"Catch 'im?"

Her heart in her mouth, she sat up and nodded.

Sidney sighed heavily. He sank down onto the edge of Angel's bed and, drawing her slim hand between his, shook his head. "Nay, lass. They gave it a champion try, but the bobbies lost 'im. 'Boobies' they should call 'em, I say, not 'bobbies'! The rogue ducked inside a pub, ran up the stairs, and climbed out onto the roof. While our brave lads in blue were busy searching below, the ruffian escaped across the rooftops. The police called off the hunt this afternoon—gave up an' went 'ome, the sorry clods! Eeh, I'm reet sorry, lass."

Her relief was so great, she closed her eyes and sank back upon the heaped feather pillows, murmuring, "He got away! Oh, my Lord! He escaped!"

"Aye, lass, I knew ye'd be upset t' hear it. So am I! I want that lout safely behind bars, but—there's no help for it. He got away and that's that. We have t' go on from there, and make sure this never happens again."

She nodded demurely to hide her relief. Thank God, Reggie had actually outrun the bobbies—and escaped across the rooftops, no less! Who would have thought him capable of such agility, or such daring either, come to that?

"Me and Teddy here, we've talked it over, right, Ted?" Sid continued.

"We have indeed, Sidney."

"And we've turned it round this way and that, but the fact remains. Your old da is rollin' in money, and you're my only daughter, dearer to me than anything in the world. Angel, it's just askin' for trouble!"

"I don't understand," she cried, her gray eyes round. "What is it you're trying to say?"

"That this could happen again, love! And the next time—!" He shook his head gravely. "Eeh, the next time, we might not be s' lucky."

"What your father is trying to say, Angel, is that, having escaped so easily, the kidnappers might well be encouraged to try their luck again, or persuade other ne'er-do-wells to similar efforts! Your father fears for your life with those rogues at large, my dear."

"Try again?" Angel echoed. "Oh, surely not, Uncle Teddy! I'm certain being hounded by the bobbies—forced to—to run for his—for their!—very lives has more than rid them of such notions!"

"Perhaps. But I can't take that chance, love. The beggars have t' be caught and put behind bars! If the authorities can do nowt more, me, Ted and the Inspector will continue the investigation ourselves 'til we find 'em. But—we must get you safely out of harm's way, meanwhile."

"I'm to go into hiding?" she asked, brows raised. "Is that what you're saying?"

"Aye, lass, sort of. Ye'd be safest out o' the country, 'til we 'ave them rogues apprehended, we reckon."

"Leave England? I'm to go abroad, you mean?" She was quite breathless at the thought.

"Aye, lass. Me an' Ted, we've talked it over, and we thought a Grand Tour might be just the ticket right now . . . ?"

"A Grand Tour? Oh, Da!" she exclaimed breathlessly,

her gray eyes glowing. "I'd love it, truly I would! When are we to leave?"

"Now then, 'old your 'orses, lass. I'll be stayin' here, like I said. Tryin' t' find them ruffians."

Her face dropped. Crestfallen, she murmured, "Oh. I'm to travel Europe alone?" The prospect of having no one to share such a wonderful adventure with quite dimmed her excitement.

"Nay, lass, o' course not! You'll take your Mabel along with you. She's been just champion since this kidnappin' business, I must admit. And I'll be hirin' a brace o' strapping lads, besides. A pair o' likely young fellows who'll look out fer your safety in them forrun parts. You'll not be alone, love, never fear."

"I see. And when shall I be leaving, Papa?"

"The sooner the better, we thought. Mr. Hamilton has already been put to work, planning your itinerary. There's a ferry for Calais, France leavin' Dover Harbor Monday at noon. If I've found some lads t' go with ye by then, you'll be on it, lass."

"So soon!" she frowned. "I'd best have Mabel begin packing our trunks immediately, then!" Monday, her father'd said. In just two days, she would be leaving England—and doing so just in the nick of time to avoid her deadline for paying off Bill Bligh. It was almost perfect—the answer to her prayers! By the time Bligh realized she'd flown the coop, it would be too late for him to do anything about it! And perhaps she'd have a solution by the time she returned, she thought, a sparkle of anticipation in her eyes now. . . .

"It's settled, then," he said with obvious relief. "You'll go."

"Errhum. Talking of going, old chap, we should be running along ourselves . . . ?" Teddy reminded Sid with a discreet cough.

"Ah, yes, the Wild West Show!" Angel remembered, smiling at the pair of them fondly. Da'd told her all about it the evening before, hoping to divert her thoughts from her "ordeal," she knew. Bless them! They were like two silly little schoolboys, beside themselves with excitement at the prospect of their outing. Wild West Show, indeed!

56

Her cheeks felt suddenly hot as she remembered the hateful American she'd met, the shameful way he'd looked at her and planted his disgusting hand upon her knee. What Da and Uncle Ted found so fascinating about a troupe of outlandish foreigners wearing ridiculous costumes as they galloped about, firing guns at each other, was a mystery to her!

"Aye, that's the one," Sidney admitted gruffly, trying hard to conceal his eagerness, but not quite succeeding. "You're sure you won't change your mind and come with us, love? Ted's got three tickets . . . ?"

"Quite sure. Don't worry about me. You run along—and have fun, both of you!"

"All right, then, love. Simmons has his orders, so ye've no call t' fret. I've armed he and the other lads with shotguns, so the Towers is near as safe as bloody Buckingham Palace tonight, I shouldn't wonder!"

"Oh, safer, Sid," Teddy insisted with a chuckle, bending to drop a farewell kiss on Angel's brow. As he did so, he popped a small round tin of her favorite foil-wrapped lemon bonbons into her hand. "Rest and recover your strength, my dear girl, and do try to forget your terrible ordeal."

"I will, Uncle Teddy. Thank you."

After a kiss from her father, the two men made an eager exit. She could hear them laughing and carrying on all the way downstairs, noisy as schoolboys.

Alone again, Angel lay back amidst her pillows and considered what her father had said. She was to make a Grand Tour, as the young men and women of wealthy families often did, either before their marriage, upon attaining their majority, or as their honeymoon trip. The prospect of seeing Paris, Rome, Madrid—perhaps even Egypt!—thrilled her, yet best of all was the knowledge that, in such distant lands, the evil Bill Bligh would be only a nasty dream!

Sidney Higgins and Teddy Hardcastle took their seats but moments before the Wild West Show began with a blaring bugle-blast.

Into the enormous saw-dusted arena galloped a magnificent white horse with flowing mane and tail, ridden by a distinguished-looking bearded man wearing fringed buckskins.

"Eeh, look, our Ted! That's 'im! That's Buffalo Bill 'imself!" Sid murmured to Ted in a hoarse aside.

With a showman's flourish, Buffalo Bill swept off his hat, stood in his stirrups and welcomed the audience, promising them the exotic entertainment for which his show had justly become world famous.

"Tonight, my friends, you will see daring roughriders risk death to demonstrate their skills—both in and out of the saddle! You will see defenseless wagon trains and stagecoaches attacked by hostile redskins. Marvel at the roping and riding of our Cowboy King, Nick Durango, and witness feats of marksmanship from our Little Annie Oakley that will leave you truly speechless!

"So, sit back, my Lords, Ladies, and Gentlemen. Prepare for an evening that you'll remember the rest of your lives! I give you the One, I give you the Only, the Authentically American, "Buffalo Bill" Cody's Wild West Shoooow—!"

With that enthralling announcement, which had every one of them perched on the very edge of their seats, Buffalo Bill spurred his horse into a gallop. He rode once around the dirt arena, then reined in sharply. The magnificent creamy stallion reared back on its hindquarters, its front hooves striking air in a breathtaking fashion that drew thunderous applause from the audience. Smiling broadly, Buffalo Bill gave a wild, blood-curdling whoop, drew his six-gun from its holster and fired into the air.

With this signal, a cavalcade of costumed riders poured into the arena, waving to the crowd as they trotted past, bearing flags that furled in the breeze. There were the two Indians chiefs, resplendent in feathered warbonnets, riding their curious spotted ponies, followed by bare-chested Indian braves, their faces painted with garish colors. They cantered past, brandishing feathered lances or wicked tomahawks. In their wake came a train of swaying covered wagons and stagecoaches—and behind them, the stars of the show: Little Annie Oakley and the "King of the Cowboys," the Deadly, the Dangerous, Nick

Durango, dressed head to toe in black and silver!

A roar went up as the pretty young markswoman and the rough-riding, hard-shootin' Cowboy King rode into the arena, both waving their Stetsons and blowing kisses to the crowd.

"Eeh, by gum, this here's champion, in't it?" Sid murmured without taking his eyes from the arena.

"Yes, Sid, truly 'champion'!" Ted agreed with a grin.

Chapter Five

"Got the luck o' old Nick hisself, you do!" Mabel declared, stashing pairs of Angel's satin underdrawers in a large sea trunk, along with the rest of her frothy unmentionables.

More clothing was strewn in heaps across the powder-blue candlewicked counterpane and stacked on the white wicker vanity chair. There were serge walking skirts with shirt-blouses to match, morning dresses of muslin or Calcutta, plaid and striped afternoon dresses, evening dresses of silk and satin trimmed with pearls or beads, sensible tweed suits, flannel night chemises, a dozen pairs of kid gloves, bicycling knickers and saucy berets, navy blue bathing dresses with striped matelot bibs and sailor collars, and hats, dozens of hats—Angel's secret passion!—several stacked in each box, one inside the other, from straw boaters to felt hats with feathers, dramatic toques, large-brimmed Gainsboroughs, and beaded pillboxes, to name but a few.

At that moment, Angel's bedroom resembled nothing so closely as a popular seamstress's salon, while Angel herself was primping before the mirror, admiring the figure she cut dressed for church that Sunday morning in a tailored cream suit. The narrow-sleeved jacket buttoned down the front and had cunning points like a waistcoat at the bottom edges. The matching cream skirt boasted elegant swags across the hips but fell in a fashionably narrow line beneath their fullness. A sable wrap was slung casually around her shoulders, while on the knot of curls

Mabel had swept up onto her brow, she wore a smart cream fedora, tilted rakishly forward. The hat's mannish effect was softened by a pouf of cream net that was almost but not quite a veil, pinned with a pearl and topaz butterfly. With her dark blonde coloring and gray eyes, the effect was elegant but modest, she decided, tilting her head to one side in order to admire the effect the hat created.

"You should have caught 'ell for wot you tried t' do to poor old Sid, you little bugger, and wot happens?" Mabel scolded. "Sid—bless him, the soft-hearted love!—gives you a pat on the bum and sends you orf t' the Continent with his blessing! I tell yer, there ain't no justice in this world!"

"It's Mr. Higgins to you, Mabel, not Sid," Angel reminded the woman tartly by rote. "And as for luck—! Well, I'm not sure that we had much, if it's any consolation to you. Poor Reggie was almost shot—and very nearly apprehended by the Law!"

Mabel snorted. "That one! Never fear, he knows 'ow to take care of 'imself, he does. He could fall in a puddle of pig muck, an' come up smellin' like a bleedin' rose. It's Reggie-Bloody-Smythe-Moreton first, last, and center, and don't let his 'Angel, my poppet' nor his bloody 'my dear girl' fool you, neither." Mabel's hard expression softened. In a gentler tone she warned Angel, "He don't love you, ducks. It's your Dad's loot he's after, not you, anyone can tell that. I wouldn't trust that toffee-nosed leech no further than I could see 'im on a foggy night, I wouldn't!"

"Blunt, you're speaking ill of the man I intend to marry. Pray keep your opinions and your advice to yourself."

"Marry, my arse! Mark my words, if you disobey your dad and run orf and marry that titled twit, you deserve everythink you got comin' to you, you spoiled little brat. But somehow, I don't think you're quite that daft, are you, ducks—'else you'd have gorn an' done it long ago . . . ?"

Angel scowled. "I think we've spent more than enough time discussing my personal matters, Mabel. Hand me my gloves, then finish packing this trunk and make a start on the other."

"Very good, Your Royal Bleedin' Highness." Mabel curtsied deeply.

Angel ignored the other young woman's sauciness. In all honesty, she'd grown immune to it over the past three years. "I'm off to church now, but I'll look in on you directly to see how the packing is coming along."

"Right you are, ducks. Who knows, per'aps our 'bodyguards' will arrive while you're gone?" Mabel jiggled her eyebrows, shot her a crafty wink and clicked her teeth. "I'm fairly itchin' t' give them lads the old Blunt 'once-over'!"

She grinned in such a salacious way that despite herself, Angel couldn't help but smile as she descended the curving staircase. Really, the woman was impossible—but mercifully far from dull! Mabel, by her own admission, "loved the lads," and was looking forward to meeting the two strapping young men Sidney Higgins had hired to protect their persons while abroad. To be completely honest, Angel was somewhat curious about them herself! Her da and Uncle Teddy had been acting very suspiciously since yesterday morning, when Teddy had called for her da in his carriage.

The two of them had left before eight, cutting short the leisurely Saturday morning breakfast that Angel and her father had come to enjoy. The pair of them had gone off together about their mysterious business, then upon his return, her da had smugly announced that he'd hired "just the very lads" to see to her safety while she was traveling. But to her annoyance, with her curiosity thoroughly whetted, he'd clammed up and refused to say another word, promising only that she would meet them soon enough, since they were coming to Brixton Towers on Sunday for luncheon! Nor had she been able to pry a word out of Uncle Teddy, whom she usually had wrapped around her little finger, despite her most determined coaxing. He'd presented her with a bouquet of spring flowers, asked fondly how she was feeling and what she most looked forward to seeing whilst traveling on the Continent—and adroitly avoided answering her!

*　　　*　　　*

Reggie was loitering in the churchyard of St. John's Church of England following the morning service, leaning indolently against one of the ancient yew trees that grew there. His posture, she remarked, was the only indolent thing about him. He had a wildness to his eyes that she had never seen before. There was, too, an almost tangible air of desperation to the look he cast her way.

After paying her compliments to the vicar for a delightfully uplifting sermon, Angel escaped her father and wove her way between the milling congregation to Reggie's side for what she anticipated would be a somewhat upsetting meeting, far from the triumphant rendezvous they'd planned. She was not disappointed. Reggie was livid at the switch her father had made, exchanging Bible tracts for the ransom money, and still more furious when she told him she would be traveling to the Continent.

"When shall I see you again?" he demanded, looking haggard.

"I really can't say. I expect to be gone for quite some time—eight weeks, at the very least, quite possibly longer."

"Perhaps I could join you in Paris? Angel, we could be married before we returned to England? What do you say?"

"Elope, you mean?"

"Why not?"

"Reggie, this is so sudden! I really don't know what to say . . ."

"Say yes, my darling! Oh, don't you see, Angel? Our marriage would solve both of our financial problems."

"I'll think about it very seriously. You have my word. Reggie, I really must go now . . ."

Her father was scowling as she hurried back to his side. "Was that that fortune hunter, Smythe-Moreton, you were talkin' with, our Annie?" he asked, his disapproval marked in both tone and expression.

"It was," she admitted. "I had to tell him about my Grand Tour!"

"Aye, happen you did," he agreed, surprisingly amicable about it. "We'll get on home now, then, shall we, lass?

Our Mrs. Prickard'll have a bit o' summat tasty waitin' for us, I shouldn't wonder. And I'll wager you girls have a spot o' packin' yet t' do, what with all the frills an' flounces you lasses lug about wi' you!"

"You're quite right, Papa. I do have loads to do." She smiled and side-eyed him mischievously. "And besides, I don't want to miss the arrival of those 'stout lads' you've been expecting anymore than you do . . ."

Knowing Angel'd seen through his flimsy excuse and guessed the real reason he was anxious to get home, Sidney grinned and followed his lovely daughter to their carriage. Sharp, she was, his Annie. Sharp as bloody knives. Just like her old da!

By one in the afternoon, Teddy Hardcastle and his friend, Police Inspector Hamish Jamieson of Scotland Yard—the fourth of their luncheon guests at Brixton Towers that day—had arrived, but the two eagerly-awaited young men had still not put in an appearance.

Despite Sidney's glum face and frequent jaunts to the front door to see if they were at that very moment arriving, Angel was at length forced to declare that they would delay the meal no longer. She instructed Mrs. Prickard to go ahead with serving, and on Uncle Teddy's arm, she led the small party into the dining room, saw them all seated, and the meal served.

As the maids and footmen were spreading snowy napkins over the guests' laps, passing them the silver serving platters, filling water and wine glasses and so on, Mr. Prickard, who served as Sidney's butler, valet, and general factotum, entered the dining room bearing a folded note on a tray. Standing at his master's elbow, he attracted Sidney's notice with a discreet cough.

"Aye? What's up, Albert, lad?"

"This correspondence arrived for you just a few moments ago, sir. A small boy delivered it."

"Did ye give the lad a threepenny piece for his trouble?"

"Indeed, I did, sir."

"Good lad! Go on an' 'ave yer own dinner now, 'fore yer missus gets riled-up."

"I shall indeed, sir. Thank you very much, sir," Albert said with a grin. Sidney Higgins might not be exactly the kind of master he'd been used to serving in the past, but that Albert liked him was obvious.

"Well, my friends, it seems our lads 'ave been detained," Sidney declared after unfolding the note and reading it. "But this note says they'll be around just as soon as they can. And, since I'm fair starved, and I've no doubt you are, too, let's eat!"

After a light but tasty repast of celery soup, poached red salmon—brought fresh by train from Scottish burns—boiled baby potatoes with mint, and assorted side dishes, the gentlemen loosened their waistcoats and, at Angel's urging, leaned back comfortably to enjoy their cigars at the dining table, instead of repairing to the billiard room as was the custom.

"The salmon was remarkable, quite remarkable. And this here's a verra fine smoke, Mr. Higgins," Inspector Jamieson observed in his Scottish burr, drawing appreciatively on his cigar.

"Cuban cigars, Inspector. A gift from my lass here last Christmas," Sidney told him, leaning back in his chair and critically observing the way the rolled leaves burned. Curls of fragrant tobacco smoke drifted upward to the crystal chandelier. "Finest tobacco in Havana—per'aps in the world."

"Aye, indeed they are. You're to be envied such a thoughtful daughter, Higgins," Jamieson complimented Angel, nodding in her direction.

The perfect hostess, she inclined her head to acknowledge the comment, giving Jamieson a brilliant if false smile to hide her true feelings of discomfort.

The inspector was a tall, wiry Scot with a fluff of receding ginger hair fringing his balding head. His fierce sandy moustache put Angel in mind of a wire-haired terrier. His eyes were disquieting, too. Fringed with lashes so pale they were almost colorless, they were of a piercing, penetrating blue that met hers without blinking or looking away. In fact, they seemed able to strip away lies and falsehoods and see deep into the hidden truths of one's soul! She swallowed. Whether it was her own guilt that

65

made her dislike him, or her fear that he would ferret out the truth of her "kidnapping," she did not know. But there was something about the police official that had made her edgy from the moment her da had introduced him and told her Jamieson was taking a leave of absence from Scotland Yard to continue the investigation into her kidnapping.

"I love my papa very dearly, Inspector Jamieson," she murmured in answer to his observation. "There is nothing I would not do to make him happy. A spot more coffee for you, sir?"

Jamieson nodded, a faint smile playing about his lips as he watched her, admiring the elegant picture she made. Her honey gold hair was wound around her head in a coronet of braids and she wore a smart gray-blue-and-white plaid gown with white collar and cuffs. She was pouring from the elegant Wedgewood coffeepot while she conversed as if butter wouldn't melt in her mouth, appearing born to the role of grand lady, rather than dragged up to it by her bootstraps. "Please!" he accepted.

Angel nodded to Sally, who stepped forward to pass the man's coffee cup to him. As she did so, a flurry of chilly wet wind swept into the room, stirring the lace draperies to a wild dance. "My word!" Angel exclaimed. "Gentlemen, it would seem we're in for some unseasonably windy weather this afternoon! Sally, run and close the French doors, dear. I do believe it's going to rain."

"Then let's hope it won't last long," Jamieson murmured. "In fact, I shall pray that the weather holds until after you've made your Channel crossing safely, Miss Higgins."

"Thank you, Inspector."

"And, if you're quite recovered from your terrible ordeal, I was hoping ye'd be up to answering a wee question or two before ye leave?"

She turned from his piercing gaze, drawing a lace-edged handkerchief from a tiny pocket in her afternoon gown and dabbing at her eyes with a muffled sniff. "It was an awful experience . . . simply dreadful . . . but of course, I'll be happy to do whatever I can to apprehend those dreadful men. Ask away, sir."

The inspector pursed his lips. "I've been wondering, Miss Higgins. Could ye give me a description of your kidnappers? For a start, how many of them were there? Two? Three? More?"

"I believe there were only two men. Or at least, only two that I saw personally."

"Then you did see them?" Jamieson pressed eagerly, leaning forward like an anxious red hound all aquiver on the scent of game.

"Ye-es," Angel fibbed uncertainly, her palms suddenly damp in a most unladylike fashion. Lie was piling up upon lie. Oh, where would it all end? How many more lies would she have to tell before it was over and done with? Wetting her lips, she continued, "I caught an odd . . . glimpse . . . here and there. You know, when the blindfold chanced to slip?"

"I see. And would you describe these men for me, to the best of your ability?"

"Of course!" She carefully set down her coffee cup and frowned as if giving the matter her utmost concentration. "Now, let me think. One of them struck me as rather tall, I believe. Not *very* tall, but certainly not short, either. Like Papa, say?"

"Then he was of middling height?"

"Middling, yes! That's exactly the image I was trying to convey, how clever you are! Yes, his hair was somewhere between blond and brown. Perhaps a tad more brown than blond—? Yes, very definitely brownish."

"Then one was of middling height and of average coloring?" Jamieson repeated with an edge of impatience. "Miss Higgins, that's not much to go upon. Was there nothing unusual about him that would serve to identify the ruffian?"

"Well, he wore spectacles," she volunteered.

"Aye, Miss Higgins, we have those in our possession."

"You do?" She knew her voice sounded a trifle shrill, but was frantically trying to recall if Reggie's late father's spectacles had had any identifying marks upon them. Oh, damn it all, she couldn't remember! She continued hurriedly, "Also, he had a moustache. Black. Very bushy and fierce. Quite . . . villainous, in fact."

"A theatrical moustache, Miss Higgins. One held in place by spirit gum. We also recovered a suede barrow boy's cap and a leather vest on the rooftop from which he made good his escape."

"A false moustache? Why, who'd have thought it!" she exclaimed. "Then I suppose his peculiar walk might also have been an act . . . ?"

"He had a limp?"

"Oh, most markedly so, Inspector! When he walked, he sort of hitched along, dragging one leg." She gave a delicate shudder. "A truly monstrous fellow! It was all most upsetting."

"I'm sure it was. And the other one?"

"You mean, the one with the patch over his eye?"

"If the other fellow wore an eyepatch, aye?"

"Oh, he was quite different!" Angel lied smoothly. "A great rough bear of a man, hugely fat, with wild black hair and a bushy black beard to his chest. He had a very pronounced accent. Russian, perhaps? Or was it Indian? His one baleful black eye held a hint of insanity, I thought at the time—though the other was covered by the eyepatch, of course."

"Och, o' course," Jamieson agreed, eyeing her doubtfully. "Now. Do you have any idea where these two men held you for the night, miss?"

"My eyes were blindfolded, Inspector. And I was both bound and gagged for much of my abduction."

"Aye. But they couldna cover your ears, lassie! Were there no sounds to give ye a clue as to your whereabouts? Like the ring of a blacksmith's hammer, for example? Or a smell, perhaps, t' indicate ye were near a fishmarket or a flower stall, say?"

Angel frowned, then brightened. "I do remember thinking at one point that I must be in a—in an abandoned warehouse. You know, down by the docks? I fancied I could hear water lapping nearby, and the air smelled somewhat unpleasant. It had that nasty, yeasty odor of grain one associates with the wharves?"

"I know just the odor you're talking about. The docks, eh? Well, thank you, Miss Higgins! I'm sure what ye've told me will prove verra helpful in apprehending your kidnappers."

So saying, Jaimeson withdrew a small lined notebook and a lead pencil from a coat pocket, licked the point, and proceeded to jot down all she'd said while Angel, inwardly trembling with fear of discovery, strove to compose herself and sip genteelly from her tiny demitasse cup, swallowing coffee she was too nervous to taste.

Jamieson left soon after, but the strain of his questioning told. She felt limp with exhaustion! Three nights without sleep, scant food, and the arrival of Inspector Jamieson with the penetrating eyes had taken their toll. She begged to be excused, leaving her da and Uncle Teddy bemoaning the dark skies and the sudden rain pelting against the window panes that ruled out a brisk canter to show off the paces of her father's new chestnut hunter.

"Are ye all reet, lass?" Sidney asked her, chucking her beneath the chin as she made to leave them to their own company. "Ye do look awful peaked t' me?"

"I'm just tired, Papa," she said with a brave little smile. "And, since we must make an early start tomorrow, I do believe a tiny nap would be in order now. Please wake me should the young men you hired arrive, would you?"

"Aye, lass, I will," Sidney promised, privately deciding quite otherwise. "'Ave a good nap, love, and sweet dreams—!"

"Thank you, Da." She gave him a quick peck on the cheek, did the same to Uncle Teddy, and escaped to her bedroom.

Mabel was nowhere in sight, but the two locked trunks and a brace of bulging carpetbags indicated she'd finished packing. All was in readiness, right down to the burgundy velvet traveling ensemble she was to wear for the journey, steamed and brushed to perfection.

A thrill of anticipation ran through her as she picked up the pert feathered hat that matched her travel attire and twirled it about on her finger. By this time tomorrow, all going well, she'd be in distant France, and her worries— along with that ferrety Inspector Jamieson and his questions, Reggie's moaning, and that horrid Bill Bligh and his menacing threats—far behind her!

To her surprise, she fell asleep the very instant her head touched the pillow, deaf to the violent spring storm that blew up soon after, battering Brixton Towers, shredding golden yellow daffodils and pink tulip petals and hurling a slate or two from the rooftops. Nor did she awaken when Mabel tiptoed in to pull a coverlet over her, or so much as stir when Mrs. Prickard rang the dinner gong at seven that evening.

Through the drumming of heavy rain, through the moan of the howling wind, through the loud, angry clatters of thunder and the bright white flashes of lightning that lit up the rooms as if by gaslight, Angel slept like a baby.

Chapter Six

Her bedroom was dark when she awoke. The fire in the grate was now only a heap of white ashes, giving off little light by which to see. Feeling drugged from such a long, deep sleep, Angel struggled to sit up, swinging her legs over the side of the bed with a groan, and realizing in the same moment that she was still fully dressed in the plaid gown she'd worn to luncheon, though someone had thrown a blanket over her while she slept. What on earth was the time?

Rising and throwing off the blanket as she went, she peered at the tiny clock set upon the marble mantlepiece. Two thirty in the morning? Good Lord, she'd slept for over twelve hours! She must have been more exhausted than she imagined. . . .

An urgent call of nature made itself felt then, but Angel ignored the flowered porcelain chamber pot set beneath the bed for that purpose and instead went from her room, out onto the long landing. Sidney Higgins had installed a flushing water closet at the end of the upstairs hall when he was having repairs and renovations made at Brixton Towers soon after Christmas. It was the very last word in modern conveniences, and far, far preferable to the undignified use of the chamber pot, in Angel's opinion, despite the necessity of having to leave one's bedroom for the drafty hall in order to use the convenience. Swinging her heavy mane of hair over her shoulders—for it had lost its pins while she'd been sleeping—she headed toward it.

She'd not gone far when an alien sound from somewhere drew her attention. Frowning, she went to the casement window that overlooked the front of the grounds, lifted the latch, and swung it open a few inches.

The night air that rushed inside was chill and sharp against her cheek, tangy with the scent of rain. She'd been right about the weather. It had rained heavily whilst she slept, although it was no longer raining. Instead, a pale spring moon smiled down upon the manicured lawns and flower beds, bathing them in ethereal bluish light. Beyond, the boxwood maze was a nest of deep shadows embracing still deeper shadows. Suddenly, she gasped, for within the shadows she fancied someone was moving about—a human form that separated itself from the stark geometrical lines of the boxwood!

As the form moved, she heard once again the metallic chink-a-chinking sound that had first drawn her attention. Looking frantically to the pale drive and the looming wrought-iron gates beyond, she could see no sign of Simmons or the grooms who were supposed to be patrolling, nor the dogs, come to that. Dash it all, where were they? There was an intruder lurking on the grounds of Brixton Towers—!

Her heart skipped a beat, righted itself, and hammered on. *Bill Bligh. It had to be him—or one of his boys. Perhaps both!*

Fear sent chills rolling in waves down her spine. Tiptoeing—though why, she really didn't know, since they couldn't possibly have heard her from outside—she retraced her footsteps to Mabel's room, next to her own. Trying the knob, she found it locked and groaned in frustration.

"Mabel?" she hissed at the crack where door met jamb. "Mabel, wake up! And do hurry!"

To her credit, the other young woman was not long in waking. Angel heard a colorful stream of curses, then Mabel opened the door. She was wearing a mobcap over her red ringlets, which were done up in curling rags for the night, and a voluminous night chemise.

"Wot the bloody hell do you want, waking a body up at this hour?"

"There's someone outside—! In the maze, I think!"

"Then happen whoever it is'll get 'isself lorst 'til morning, so's I can get some kip!" Mabel grumbled. "Good night!"

With that, she turned from the door, clearly intending to go back to her bed and do just that.

"But you can't sleep—not now!" Angel squeaked, diving into the room and grabbing the folds of Mabel's nightgown to drag her back out into the hallway. "I can't tell Da there's an intruder because—because I-I think—oh, Mabel, I'm certain it's Bill Bligh—or his cronies! Oh, Mabel, you must do something? They've come to murder me!"

"Bloody good idea, I say. Maybe I'll help 'em, you keep up this here nonsense! I'll strangle you wiv me own bare hands—!"

"Oh, you don't mean that, I know you don't. Please just—oh, please just come and look, won't you? Maybe—yes!—maybe I was imagining things?"

"Aw, all right then, you pest. Let me get a candle, and we'll have a look-see."

Moments later found the two women tiptoeing down the landing to the open window and peering through it. The grounds of Brixton Towers were still rain-washed and dripping, still bathed in moonlight that reflected off each tiny droplet like liquid silver. But to Angel's disappointment, the furtive movement she'd glimpsed by the entrance to the boxwood maze was gone, the silence empty of metallic chinkings. Nor did the tall, immaculately clipped hedges appear to hold any secrets.

"Oh. Whoever it was must have gone, thank God!" Angel whispered, her relief evident.

"Wrong, ducks," Mabel argued hoarsely, to Angel's surprise. Her head was cocked as she listened intently. "They in't gone, they're *in the 'ouse!* I can 'ear the buggers movin' around downstairs! Listen up . . ."

To her horror, Angel realized that Mabel was right. When she cocked her head to listen, she could hear muffled laughter and knocking sounds—as if someone unfamiliar with the darkened hallways and rooms of the Towers had banged themselves against the furniture or walls. Someone—maybe more than *one* someone!—was definitely in the house.

"What shall we do!" Angel moaned.

"Do? What we need is a gun," Mabel muttered. "That'd scare the blighters off right smartly, an' no mistake!"

"But the guns are all in Da's gun room—downstairs!" Angel murmured.

"Get the poker from your room for now, then. We'll go downstairs, sneak down the 'all t' the gun room and help ourselves. Once we 'ave, Gawd help 'em—!" Mabel said with relish.

With a nod, Angel scampered away to fetch the fire implement, weighing it in her hand as she returned to Mabel. The poker's handle was nine inches long, barrel-shaped, and made of heavy brass, an instrument that could play havoc with the delicate bones of a human skull, crushing it like an eggshell—if she could but bring herself to use it as a weapon.

"Here it is!" she whispered.

"Go on down, then, you twit!" Mabel hissed. "If anyone pops out, brain 'em! I'll be right behind you."

"Uh uh. You go first."

"For wot your dad's paying me, ducks? Not on your bloomin' life! After you, Miss 'Iggins . . ."

With a shrug, Angel brandished the poker before her, drew a deep breath and started down the long staircase leading to the foyer of Brixton Towers. Her mouth was dry. Her palms were moist on the polished bannister, her knees knocking together long before she reached the ground floor.

"See anyfing?" Mabel hissed from behind her.

She was about to say no, when someone turned up the gas jets, flooding the hallway with sudden light that all but blinded her for a few seconds.

When she could see again, she gaped, unable to believe her eyes.

The insolent American stood in the open doorway, looking for all the world like an avenging angel! Pale moonlight streamed down from the skylight above him, reflecting off hair blacker than the devil's hooves as he swept off his hat. The hard, handsome face beneath was equally striking—a study in spare contours and hard

74

planes, as darkly bronzed as any Gypsy's. Yet it was his hooded ice blue eyes that insolently met hers beneath moody black brows that chilled her to the bone. Merciful heaven! They tossed out a reckless challenge that struck sparks against her soul like a hammer against an anvil! *"Remember me, honey?"* they seemed to say.

Her mind reeled. Her hand moved to her temple, stroking the sudden throbbing there as she swayed dizzily. Oh, dear God! Why would the American have come to Brixton Towers, unless he meant to tell her father what she'd asked him to do—!

As she stood there, paralyzed by the certainty that discovery was imminent, a half-naked savage with long black hair leaped out from behind the gleaming suit of armor at the foot of the stairs! Thrusting his hideously painted face in hers, he brandished a wicked tomahawk over her head and uttered a bloodcurdling howl: "Yi! Yi! Yiiiihoooo!"

It was too much.

The hallway spun like a top as her eyes rolled up and the brass poker slid from her slack fingers. With a pitiful cry, she collapsed in an inelegant heap upon the floor.

"Señorita!" the horrified "savage" exclaimed.

"Oww, don't mind 'er," Mabel cooed calmly, batting her lashes as she stepped over Angel's prostrate form. She teetered past the "savage," crossing the black-and-white checkered foyer to stand before the towering cowboy.

"I'm Mabel Blunt, luv,—Miss 'Iggins's—um—personal companion and confeedunt. Oh, an' that's *Miss* Blunt, not missus, by the way . . . Welcome t' the Towers, ducks!"

"I'm pleased t' meet you, ma'am," the stranger echoed in a loverly twangy American voice that made Mabel's heart do flip-flops.

The maid giggled. "Oooww, you're a handsome devil, you are—and wot a big lad, too!" She looked him up and down, poked him in the ribs and winked cheekily. "Lor, I bet you can do marvels wiv them big guns, can't yer, ducks . . . ?"

Chapter Seven

Scooping Angel up off the floor as if she weighed no more than thistledown, Nick Durango carried her down a long Turkish runner into the fancy parlor Sid Higgins indicated.

She stirred as she came around, her gray eyes fluttering open first in bewilderment, then shock, to find herself in his arms.

Looking down at her, Nick smiled thinly. If this didn't beat all! The "beloved daughter" Sid Higgins had hired him to ride shotgun on was none other than Blondie, the highfalutin, snooty filly from the blackjack table who'd tried to buy his services as a kidnapper the other night—then treated him as if he was something the cat had spat up! Seeing him standing in the doorway must have given her quite a turn. And the sight of his partner, Juarez, wearing his "Panther Who Stalks" buckskins and war paint couldn't have helped any, either!

Still, she'd recover soon enough, he didn't doubt. If only half of what he'd found out about Miz Angel Higgins in the past twenty-four hours was true, she was a social-climbing hussy with a fondness for men, liquor, and gambling who had ice water in her veins and a cash register where her heart was 'sposed to be. To all accounts, she was tough enough to chew nails—and then some!

"I'm Nick Durango, Miz Higgins. One of the men your pa hired t' look out for your safety," he drawled, thinking he was more likely to be the one in need of protection.

Angel, fully awake now, went rigid in his arms. "Surely

76

you don't think I believe you? My father would no sooner hire someone like you than—than—than join the Foreign Legion! Now, put me down—at once!—or so help me, I'll scream!"

Nick's jaw tightened. The pallor of his eyes darkened ominously. Who in the hell did she think she was, handing out orders, coolly implying he'd lied? He'd be damned if he'd let Miz Angel Higgins ride rough-shod over him, the way she apparently did her pa! Since he'd given Higgins his handshake on the deal, he was honor-bound to see this Grand Tour fiasco through to the bitter end—but damn it, he'd wear the pants on this here trail drive, or know the reason why!

"Quit squawkin'," he growled, his poker face betraying nothing of his true feelings. "I'll put you down when I'm damn' good and ready."

Angel's stomach gave a sickening lurch of dread. Surely this Ringo or Dingo or whatever-his-damned-name-was couldn't really have been hired by her father, could he? But if not, what could he be doing here? Unless . . . he'd ferreted out her identity and come to Brixton Towers to tell her father that she planned to stage her own kidnapping, hoping to extort money from her da in return for the information . . . ?

"Take your hands off me right now!" she snapped in a tone icy enough to chill a Santa Fe summer. "I'm quite capable of walking unaided, thank you very much!"

"Fine. Have it your way." With a shrug, Nick obliged. Spreading his arms, he let Angel drop the three feet from them onto the horsehair sofa like a sack of beans. She bounced, just a pinch, he noted with pleasure. Her pretty white teeth snapped together with an audible click, and two red spots of fury flared in her pale cheeks. Her sassy gray eyes sparked like a spitting cougar's as she glowered up at him.

"Thank you," she gritted in a tone that consigned him to hell.

"Aw, shucks, little lady, it was my pleasure to be of service," he shot back, inclining his head and grinning nastily.

As his knowing, silvery blue eyes met her hostile, guilty

77

gray ones, the air about them crackled with tension. The silent exchange was about as close to a declaration of war as two people could come without uttering a word.

"As I was going t' say when ye fainted, lass, these are the lads I've hired t' escort you and our Mabel on the Continent," her father began, and any faint hope she'd harbored that Durango was lying dwindled miserably. "Mr. Durango, Señor Juarez, I'd like ye t' meet my daughter, Angel."

The two Americans murmured appropriately.

"Eeeh, love, ye look proper peaked as yet. Shall I 'ave the doctor sent round for?" Sidney asked, breaking the crackling currents as he anxiously knelt at his daughter's side. He drew her limp hand between his and chafed it.

Before Nick's startled eyes, "Iron-Drawers" Higgins melted. Her gray eyes lost their hostile spark and grew soft and tender with filial love. Her thinned lips softened, blossomed with a fond smile that utterly transformed her face. The angry tension in her slender shoulders evaporated as she became the very picture of a loving daughter.

Watching her performance, Nick felt a grudging admiraton stir and was hard-put to stifle the urge to applaud. Damn, but this little hellcat was *good!* On the stage, her act would have brought tears to the eyes of hardened, tobacco-chewing bullwhackers—maybe even brought the house down! Being a shrewd *hombre* himself, he made a mental note to remember her acting talents. After all, Blondie seemed about as eager to be rid of him as a calf with a panther on its back. And, since he was committed to seeing this through, like it or not, there was every chance she'd use those talents against him in the next few weeks!

"Really, there's no reason for you to worry, Da," she purred silkily. "I just fainted. It must have been the shock of seeing your two—your two American gentlemen standing there. I thought we had intruders, you see, so Mabel and I had come down to investigate. Then the gaslight went on—and the front door flew open, and—! Well, there *they* were!" Her nostrils flared.

Side-eyeing Nick, she gave a delicate, genteel shudder that would have brought encores for Sarah Bernhardt.

How in the hell did she manage to make her nostrils quiver like that he wondered, fascinated. Damned if he could do it, he discovered, trying.

"Señorita Higgins, I must offer you my humblest apologies," his fool cousin, Juarez, stepped forward to say, to Nick's disgust.

Juarez hovered like a goddamned buzzard over the sofa where Miz Iron Drawers lay in elegant languor, a queen with her humble subjects—Higgins and now his cousin, Juarez—worshipping at her feet. "Believe me, I did not mean to frighten you. Me and my *amigo* Nick, here, we thought you were expecting us. We—I!—wanted to amuse and entertain you, not frighten you. Aiee, *Señorita linda*, beautiful *Madonna*, say you'll forgive poor Juarez, *sí?*"

"Entertain—? Oh, *now* I understand!" she exclaimed.

It was then, Nick knew, that the girl realized her father's two "stout lads" were performers he'd hired away from Colonel "Buffalo Bill" Cody's Wild West Show. And, though she smiled and murmured consolingly that of course, Juarez must consider himself forgiven and the incident quite forgotten, her telltale gray eyes said otherwise as she glanced up at her father. Had he gone quite mad, her incredulous, disdainful expression demanded? Taken leave of his senses? Did he truly consider this American clod clothed head to toe in black and silver, and this other long-haired, painted savage—both from a common theatrical troupe, no less!—suitable escorts for her person . . . ?

But her indignation was effectively defused as a beaming Sidney rose to his feet, clearly prepared to accept her protests that she was quite recovered at face value. Sure enough, he clapped the pair companionably across the shoulders, for all the world as if they were old friends.

"Ye see, my lass? They're champion—the pair of 'em! Ye'll be in reet good hands with these lads, an' no mistake. I'll 'ave no bunglin' British bobbies t' see t' my little Annie's safety from here on. Only the best that 'brass' can buy fer my lass—and these two are the very best." He turned back to the two men. "Now. How's about summat t' eat, lads? Did you 'ave your dinners?" he asked.

They told him they had.

"And your 'orses 'ave been stabled proper?"

They'd already been sent down to Dover aboard a livestock train, they assured him.

"That's champion! Proper champion!" Sid declared. "Then you're all set! We have just enough time fer a drop o' summat t' wet our whistles before findin' our beds. Follow me, my lads!"

With this, Sidney started to lead them off to his study, obviously enchanted with his exotic guests.

"Da? Could I join you and these—er—gentlemen?" Angel plaintively asked, struggling to sit up on the sofa. She smiled bravely. "I think a spot of brandy might do wonders for my nerves . . . ?"

Sidney halted, looking at her as if he'd forgotten her very existence. He frowned doubtfully. "Join us? Nay, lass, not t' night. It's late and ye've had a rough time of it these past two days—and ye've still t' make an early start in the morning. Besides, I doubt ye'd enjoy listening t' us lads rabbittin' on—or that the talk'll be fit fer a young lady's ears, either, come t' that, eh, boys? Our Nick's promised t' tell me all about the Wild West an' the Redskins, haven't ye, lad? Our Mabel, I'd thank you t' see Miss Angel settled, if ye would, lass? I'll 'ave Mrs. Prickard send up a posset o' warmed milk t' calm her nerves."

"Right you are, Sidney, love," Mabel twittered. She received Sidney's nod of approval, a broad wink and a, "There's a good lass!" for her trouble as Sid left the room. Mabel basked in the master's praises, patently ignoring the livid look Angel shot her way.

A backwards glance over his shoulder as they left the drawing room brought an evil smile to Nick's face, for in that instant, he glimpsed a facet to Angel Higgins's character that her acting ability was unable to mask. Her expression was no longer sweetly kittenish, nor even graciously condescending, as when she'd accepted Juarez's apology. No, sir! Now, her lovely features had curdled like sour milk. The spoiled little Daddy's girl was fairly seething with jealousy at being casually dismissed, without so much as a second thought by her doting father!

"Your father's right, Miz Higgins," Nick murmured. "Y'all get a good night's sleep, and we'll see you—bright and bushy-tailed—in the morning! And if I might say so, ma'am, I'm *really* looking forward t' spending the next two looong months in your company."

"Over my dead body!" she spat, stabbing him with a venomous look that was filled with loathing. "I'll slit my wrists before I go anywhere with you!"

"Beggin' your pardon, ma'am? I didn't catch what you said?" Nick queried innocently, his raven brows quirking up like inky commas as he cocked his dark head to one side.

He'd heard her perfectly well, damn him! "I simply said 'good night,' Mr. Durango!" she snapped in a far louder voice, quelling Mabel's raucous titter with a glacial stare. "You may go now."

Those ebony brows rose. "Thank you kindly, ma'am," he drawled insolently. His pale blue eyes icy, he swept her a deep, mocking bow, melodramatically clutching his black Stetson to his chest. And, with that sarcastic leave-taking, he vanished after Sid and Juarez.

"Blunt? Stop it immediately! What the devil are you chortling about?" Angel demanded, glowering at Mabel once they were alone. "Do you find that—that impossible scalawag's impudence amusing?"

"Not half, I don't! He's proper cheeky, that Durango, in't he?" Mabel declared in admiration and delight, smiling from ear to ear. Her blue eyes sparkled with excitement as she twirled a hennaed curl about her finger. "'You may go,' indeed! Cor blimey, you acted like you were the bleedin' Queen of England, an' he was the skivvy wot emptied yer bleedin' pisspot! But he gave you tit-fer-tat with that bow, didn't he, Miss High-and-Mighty—set you down good an' proper, sarcastic as all get-up." She pursed her lips. "Yer know, I think I'm goin' t' like Nick Durango and that Warez bloke. Just imagine, you and me, off in them forrun parts wiv two likely lads, for weeks on end! Ooo, it'll be bleedin' heaven on earth, it will!" She sighed in blissful anticipation.

"Hrrumph. I'm glad you're so happy about it. Personally, I can't imagine what Da could have been thinking of, to engage such a pair," Angel complained sourly as if she hadn't heard a word Mabel had said. "First thing in the morning, I intend to see them both dismissed and replacements found! Then that Durango'll be laughing on the other side of his face!"

"We'll see," Mabel declared, jumping to her feet. "Now. I'll be off t' fetch you that warmed milk your dad ordered. How would you like it, Milady Sourpuss? In a cup—or shall I pour it in a saucer?"

Before Angel could retort with a sharp reprimand, Mabel had fled to the kitchens.

She might as well retire, Angel decided irritably, standing. As her father had pointed out, she had an early train to catch in just a few hours—and a suitable new escort to hire before she did so.

After they arrived at the train station the following morning, her da sent Simmons, the groom, in search of a porter to take care of her and Mabel's baggage. In moments, Jim returned with the information that there were no porters available to handle the mountain of luggage, due to the early hour.

"It's nowt t' fret about, our Jim!" her father declared. "We've strong arms and strong backs ourselves, right, lads? Between the five of us, we'll 'ave this little lot stowed away reet smartly."

Uncle Teddy and Da wrestled one heavy sea trunk down from the back of the carriage and lugged it off toward the train, while Durango and Juarez grappled the second. Jim Simmons picked up the two bulging carpetbags while Mabel, taking her cue from the others, gamely elected to carry four of Angel's hatboxes and hasten after the men. That left another four hatboxes stacked on the pavement outside the station, awaiting loading. Four boxes of her precious hats left untended!

Angel opted to stand there and wait for the men's return.

Shivering in the predawn chill, she hugged her sable wrap around her and stamped her feet to keep warm while she guarded her precious hatboxes from theft. Her toe-tapping increased as she waited impatiently for one of the men to come back for them. What on earth could be taking them so long?

Just then, out of the corner of her eye, she observed that brute, Durango, halt by the ticket window. He signaled the Red Indian to set down his end of the sea trunk and he strode back toward her. Was it possible the hateful clod had *some* redeeming qualities, after all?

Her hopes were shortlived, however, for Durango tipped back his hat and regarded first the hatboxes, and then herself.

"Seems t' me those boxes have your brand on 'em, ma'am," he observed in his infuriating, colonial drawl, his weight braced upon one booted foot and his thumbs hooked into his belt.

Startled that he would dare to address her directly, rather than waiting to be spoken to, as was proper, she blinked. "I beg your pardon?" she asked coolly.

He frowned and in a thundering voice repeated, "I said, this here looks like your share t' tote on out to the locomotive, Miz Higgins. Even got your initials on it, right here, ma'am. A period H period, it says."

Her finely arched brows rose. "I'm well aware of that, you don't have to shout so! And? What of it? You're surely not suggesting *I* should carry these boxes myself?"

Instead of responding to her demand, he cocked his ebony head to one side to inspect her arms, first right, then left, before suddenly flipping up her burgundy velvet skirts to expose her legs, baring them as far as her knees and the beribboned and ruffled hems of her pantalets.

She shrieked, desperately trying to replace her skirts modestly about her ankles. "How *dare* you!" she spat.

Unruffled, Durango's ice blue eyes narrowed, the contempt back in their silvery depths as he drawled, "Aw, I reckon you'd be mighty surprised at what we 'unscrupulous' Americans dare t' do, ma'am! But—that's beside the point. From what I can see, it don't appear that you're crippled anyplace. Are you?" he demanded insolently, a challenge in his eyes and his tone. "Maybe I missed something . . ."

He reached for her again, but she hurriedly backed off. Crimson color filled her cheeks as she turned her rigid back on him. "You did not! For your information, I'm sound in both wind and limb!"

"I'm relieved t' hear it, ma'am," he drawled. "And, that being the case, I reckon you could shift your tail t' carry a few boxes out to the train yourself—'else leave 'em where they stand. Either ways, you'd best get movin'. Train's gettin' ready to roll, by the looks of it—with or without you! Let's go, Juarez."

With that, Durango returned to his partner. The two men hefted the trunk once again and carried it to the train.

After she was certain he had gone, Angel turned around, her cheeks still flaming. "Shift her tail," indeed. What gall! But to her dismay, the ill-mannered brute'd been telling the truth. Great clouds of steam were shooting up above the ticket office into the dark gray sky as the engineer took on coal and water in readiness to pull out of the station. Furthermore, there was no sign that anyone intended to return for her remaining hatboxes—or, for that matter, herself!

Uttering curses under her breath that would have done credit to Mabel on a bad day, Angel leaned down and picked up the hatboxes. She foolishly loaded one precariously on top of the other, so that her view was blocked as she teetered on high heels across the cobbles. Complaining loudly, she stumbled blind through the station offices and out onto the platform, where the others were milling about, laughing and talking amongst themselves as if they hadn't even noticed she was missing from their chummy little group.

"Eeh, there ye are, our Angel! I was wonderin' where ye'd disappeared to, lass," her father greeted her. He took two of the hatboxes from her arms to reveal her scowling face, while Uncle Teddy quickly relieved her of the others.

Over Teddy's shoulder, she caught Durango's amused blue eyes and flushed angrily at the mocking smile he shot her way. How dare that—that *cowboy* expect her to carry her own luggage like a—like a common servant. She'd really put her foot down and insist that her father replace him, as she'd intended . . .

"Papa? Might I have a word with you . . . in private?" she asked sweetly, turning the full power of her charm on her father. Durango was watching them, shamelessly eavesdropping on every word she said, she knew.

Sidney hugged her fondly. "Eeh, ye don't 'ave t' ask for an appointment, lovie. Besides, your old da's been meaning t' have a few final words wi' ye, afore ye go. Come along over here wi' me, lass."

They sat side by side on a railway bench, her da's arm around her. "Well, it won't be long now an' you'll be off! I'm goin' t' miss you summat fierce this summer, but it's for your own good, love, an' I know ye'll have a champion time of it, so I'll get by. Don't worry your pretty head about me," he urged, squeezing her hand. "Ye just go an' have yourself a bit o' fun. God knows, you've earned it."

"I know I'll have a grand time, Da," she agreed slowly. "But . . . that wasn't what I wanted to speak to you about. You see, I really don't think that man, Durango, is in any way—"

"By gum, I clean forgot t' give ye the letters o' credit from me bank!" he cut in.

"No, you didn't. They're right here, tucked safely in my reticule. But that isn't what I—"

"Good! Keep 'em safe, love," Sid continued, "And should ye need more 'brass,' ye can take 'em to any bank on the Continent, and they'll see ye taken care of. Just use my name."

"Thank you, Papa. I'm sure I'll be perfectly fine," she assured him impatiently. "But, about Durango. Da, I don't think he's at all the proper person to—"

Wheeeeeeeeeeee-whoooo!

Her complaints were drowned out by the deafening whistle of the steam engine and by the station master's loud bellows of, "All *abooooard!*"

They were so close to the engine, Angel was forced to cover her ears with both hands to muffle the piercing sound. And, by the time it had ceased and she could both hear and make herself heard again, it was too late to complain about Durango!

Her da took her elbow and hurried her to the open compartment door, through which the others, with the exception of Uncle Teddy, had already clambered.

Teddy turned her to face him. "Well, I suppose it's Goodbye for now, my dear girl. Do have a safe journey and a simply grand time! Oh, these are for you. A little

85

something to nibble on the journey." He pecked her cheek in farewell, thrusting yet another tin of her favorite lemon bonbons into her hands.

"Thank you, Uncle Teddy. You really shouldn't have. Be good—and do take care of Da for me 'til I get back, won't you?"

"Rest assured that I shall indeed, dear girl. Bon voyage, Angelica!"

Stepping back, Teddy gave Sid room to say his own farewells.

"Up ye go, then, love," Sid urged. "But first, give your old da one last kiss, before ye get in."

Realizing it was too late now for changes, too late to do anything except accept her lot and make the most of the weeks that lay ahead, Angel flung her arms around his neck and hugged and kissed him fiercely. "Ta-ra, Da. Oh, I'll miss you so much. I do wish you were coming, too!"

"Aye, lass, so do I. But, it can't be helped. Per'aps next time, eh? Take care o' yourself, love—and God Bless."

With that, he handed her up the steps into the train's corridor, slamming the door firmly behind her. At once, she'd let down the window by its leather strap and craned her head out. "Now, you're the master of the house, remember. Don't let Mrs. Prickard order you around," she reminded him.

"Nay, I won't."

"And keep an eye on Sally. The silly girl's far too sweet on Simmons for her own good!"

"Aye, I will."

"Bye!"

"Ta-ra, love! Ta-ra!"

With a jolt, the steam engine snorted and threw itself forward, like a cart horse taking up the slack of the traces. The wheels squealed, sparked, and finally turned. Steam billowed from the engine's chimney stack as the engineer waved to show that he was all set. The signal man in his lofty box pulled the lever to work the cable that switched the signal arm from red to green further down the track. The stationmaster flourished his flag, blew his whistle—and they were off!

She waved until the station and Da were lost to view,

then staggered from the corridor into the private compartment, blinded by her tears, biting her lower lip as she envisioned touring the elegant city of Paris with the two outlandish Americans plus her outrageous Mabel in tow! The mental picture she conjured straightway worsened her slight migraine. Massaging the pounding in her temples, she wondered what on earth she was to do? What! The Hotel St. Pierre was, by all accounts, an exclusive establishment that catered to the upper classes. Why, she'd be an utter laughingstock, signing the register with her motley crew of servants in tow! Servants? Ha! The very suggestion that she had servants was laughable! Mabel was a law unto herself—and by his dreadful behavior at the train station earlier, that awful Durango had already made it very clear that on no account should she ever consider him a lackey, despite the no doubt exorbitant sum her father was paying him.

She closed her eyes and leaned back against the leather banquette, the throbbing in her head increasing as the train rattled on toward Dover.

Not five minutes out of London, and already she was wondering if throwing herself on Bill Bligh's mercy might not have been preferable to Nick Durango, after all. . . .

Nick watched Angel through slitted ice blue eyes, his black Stetson angled low on his brow. She probably figured he'd fallen asleep, but he'd been watching her beneath his hat brim ever since the milk train had rattled out of sooty London on its slow journey southwest down to Dover.

The Higgins girl was pretty enough, he had to allow that, he decided grudgingly. Truth was, most men would consider her beautiful, if they liked their women golden-haired, with a fresh peaches-and-cream country-girl complexion and wide gray eyes. Or if their taste in females ran to slender *muchachas* with only a few curves to keep a man warm in his bedroll on a cold desert night. She wasn't his type, though—not anymore. Since Savannah, he thought with a tightening of his gut and the tic of a nerve at his temple, he'd confined his womanizing to lush, dark-haired beauties with warm, flashing brown eyes and ample figures—in fact, about as far from the cool deceptive blond charms of the Angels and the Savannahs of this world as he could get. Once bitten, twice shy, that was the saying—and Nick had no intention of gettin' bit a second time around.

Although Angel looked for all the world as if warm butter wouldn't melt in her mouth, he knew otherwise. Beneath that innocent blond loveliness lurked a gambler, a liar, and a cheat. She was pure maverick, to the core—though you'd never guess it by looking at her!

Sid Higgins's generous offer of employment last Saturday morning had made Nick suspicious as hell. What, he'd wondered, could be wrong with Higgins's daughter? Why would a decent *hombre* like Sid offer two complete strangers a small fortune to escort the girl about Europe, rather than find two beefy English bullyboys to do the job?

Then Higgins had told him about the kidnapping, and the pieces of the puzzle had dropped into place. Remembering how the girl he'd nicknamed Blondie had tried to enlist his help to stage her own kidnapping, he'd put two and two together and come up with four—though he hadn't been absolutely sure Higgins's daughter and Blondie were the same girl until he'd seen her standing at the foot of the stairs last night.

By then, he'd done some nosing around on his own, and found out the girl had a bad reputation, and that she belonged to a wild crowd who lived life fast and loose. Gossip said she was courtin' a fancy title to enhance her father's millions, and would go to any lengths to coerce the titled yet penniless Reggie, Lord Smythe-Moreton into marriage, but that Reggie—knowing the girl for a rank social climber—swore only bankruptcy would force him into wedlock with a common millworker's daughter. . . .

Nick scowled. Poor old Sid Higgins! He trusted his perfect Angel. He had no idea his precious little daughter had been sneaking out of Brixton Towers to visit the gambling halls until the wee hours almost every night. Nor did he have a clue that she'd gotten herself into hot water with an unpaid gambling marker, or that a shady *bandido* named Bill Bligh had been threatening to rough her up if she didn't pay it off real soon . . . hence the phony kidnapping she and her greenhorn companion Reggie must have staged!

Yessiree, Angel was a deceitful little cat, a good-time gal without scruples who didn't hesitate to use those who loved her for her own ends, no matter who might get hurt by it. Sid Higgins, on the other hand, was the kind of father any man—or woman—should have felt damned fortunate to have, himself included, he thought bitterly, recalling the drifter, Gil Durango, who'd proven himself worse than no father at all.

Nick'd decided he didn't like Angel Higgins, but he'd been touched by Sid's obvious love and concern for his daughter, and had agreed to take on the job of riding shotgun for her for that reason alone.

Since he was a fair man, and what he'd heard about Angel was only hearsay, he'd tried to keep an open mind until he'd met the girl—but doing so had only deepened his dislike. The snooty, highfallutin, high-steppin' way she had about her made him itch to haul her across his lap and paddle her backside, just to see if she'd come down off of her high horse and be a real person, once the starch'd been paddled out of her drawers.

Still, whatever happened, it was too late to back out now. He'd wanted out of the Wild West Show and had jumped at Higgins's proposal, all money aside. Oh, he'd been good at his part, popular with the crowds who'd flocked to see them perform, too, but he'd quickly wearied of putting on a fool act each night. "King of the Cowboys"—hell! He was no born showman, like Juarez, who thrived on praise and applause. At heart, he longed to go back to his real life and his sprawling cattle ranch outside of Santa Fe, New Mexico. There, at Rancho Diablo, his rope and his gun were the tools of his trade, not just pretty toys to thrill and draw gasps of amazement from a gawking audience. Truth was, he thrived on real action, on adventure, excitement! They were his lifeblood, since the softer side of his nature had been eroded by a pretty woman's betrayal and his spineless father's weakness.

He sighed. So, why was he babysitting a rich man's

spoiled little girl—who promised to be Trouble with a capital "T"!—and riding the rails through the blooming apple orchards of Kent, instead of riding herd on his range in the foothills of the beautiful Sangre de Cristo? Damn, he must have been *loco* to agree to this fiasco, but . . . he'd promised Sid, and Nick Durango always kept his word, he told himself as he drifted off to the rhythm of the rails. . . .

Chapter Eight

Golden afternoon sunlight bathed the white cliffs of Dover, bleaching the wings of the screaming seagulls that wheeled and dipped over the churning waters of the murky English Channel. Some twenty-odd miles away, glimpsed through a salty haze, lay the low hump of land that was France.

Outside a small fish restaurant that perched on the steep cobbled street below the ruins of Dover Castle, Angel stamped her foot and glowered at Durango.

"What do you mean, we've missed the ferry? We simply can't have!" she argued hotly. Peeking at the fob watch pinned to her burgundy jacket, she held the timepiece up to the insufferable American to demonstrate the truth of her claim. "There, you see? It's only just noon, and the Calais Ferry doesn't depart until one o'clock. Simple arithmetic tells me we still have an entire hour to wait," she added scathingly, implying that simple arithmetic was no doubt beyond the American's capabilities.

With admirable restraint, Nick choked back the urge to feed her blamed watch down her lily white throat. He countered in an easy drawl, "You reckon so, do you, ma'am? Well, simple *eyesight* tells me that your watch has stopped. According to the clock up there, it's almost two." He shook his handsome dark head, his disgust plain. "I warned you you didn't have time t' eat before I went to make arrangements for the horses, but, no, you wouldn't listen!"

She unpinned the watch and held it to her ear, straining

for the tick that would prove Durango wrong. Alas, she heard not a tick nor a tock! And her covert glance at the church clock showed two, as he'd implied. "Oh, drat it all!" she grumbled, tugging off her sable wrap, which had become stifling in the spring sunshine. "Now I suppose we'll have to find lodgings for the night, and wait for the Tuesday ferry. Botheration! Our entire itinerary will be upset!"

"There's another boat leavin' for France in a few minutes. I was talkin' to her captain down by the quay while you were at the chuck wagon. But . . . forget I mentioned it. I don't reckon you'd be any too cosy on a fishin' boat, a re-fined British lady like yourself!"

How he did it, she could not fathom, but the dreadful, arrogant brute somehow managed to make the quite acceptable term "refined British lady" sound like the coarsest of insults—and a challenge—at one and the same time.

"Why not, pray? Is the vessel unseaworthy?"

"Don't reckon so. Her cap'n don't seem like a lazy fellow. And it didn't strike me he had a hankering t' commit suicide this perticular day! Look, she's down there. The trim little white tub riding at anchor to the left. Y' see her?"

Nick pointed, and Angel, Mabel, and Juarez dutifully shaded their eyes and squinted in that direction.

"The *Pelican*?" Angel translated the French name scrolled on the bows of the vessel he'd indicated.

"That's her."

"But she's charming!" Angel exclaimed, admiring the immaculate white vessel with its smart red trim that bobbed like a cork at her moorings alongside the quay. A quaint sailor in a knitted jersey, wearing baggy oilskins stuffed into rubber galoshes, was puffing a pipe on her foredeck, gazing out to sea. No doubt one of the *Pelican*'s trusty crew. "Do you think her captain would be willing to take on paying passengers?"

"Willing? Huh! Captain Raoul seemed about as perky as a newborn calf when I put the notion to him," Nick admitted wryly, scuffing the toe of a stilt-heeled boot against the cobbles.

"Then what are we waiting for, my good man?" Angel demanded gaily, quite forgetting her dislike of Durango in her relief and gratitude that he'd found them alternative passage to Calais despite her foolishness. "Let's hoist anchor and away!" Her gray eyes sparkled as she flung the sable wrap over her shoulder so boisterously, a corner prodded poor Mabel in the face.

"Eh, you! Wotch yerself! You almost blinded me, you twit!" Mabel complained, clapping a hand over her eye and blinking rapidly.

Angel had the grace to look repentant. "Oh, Mabel, I'm so sorry."

"So you bleedin' well should be . . ."

"You're sure you don't want to wait an' take the ferry tomorrow, ma'am?" Nick asked doubtfully. "The *Pelican*'s real small. And the Channel looks pretty darned wild t' me!"

"*Sí!*" Juarez agreed with a doleful frown. "Look, señorita! The water, she bucks like a bronco—!"

"Oh, really, you landlubbers!" Angel scolded airily, bestowing an amused, indulgent smile upon them all. "I've sailed on many a ship—boat—vessel in my time, and crossing the Channel will prove no more exciting than rowing across a millpond, I promise you. Everyone, follow me!"

With the air of an intrepid explorer leading her party of native bearers into the jungles of Darkest Africa, Angel struck out at a brisk pace, positively marching down the steep cobbled street toward the quay below.

"And when 'ave you ever been on a ship, that's what I'd like to know?" Mabel queried, dabbing at her streaming red eye as she tottered after her. "Far as I know, you've only been on the water once in yer whole life—when we went down the Thames on that pleasure barge Smythe-Moreton rented. T' see Kew Gardens and the tropical 'ot houses and all the loverly lilacs in bloom, remember? It were summer, two years ago—and you were sick as a bloomin' pig in the picnic hamper comin' 'ome."

"For your information, Blunt, I've sailed many times. It might surprise you to learn that my life did not commence the day you added your somewhat explosive person to my

93

household. I've had a great many experiences of which you, my good woman, know nothing about." With that sharp setdown, Angel continued on.

"Well, excuuuuse me," Mabel retorted, sticking her tongue out at Angel's retreating back. "I never knowed you were bloody Horatio Nelson, did I? Lead on t' the *Victory*, Your Admiralness."

"One moment. Your poor eye, Señorita Blunt. It sheds so many tears. Here, let me help you," Juarez offered gallantly.

Nick, shaking his head and grinning to see Juarez flirting with the *muchachas* yet again, passed the pair up and ambled down the steep street after Angel while Mabel hung back.

Although Nick'd discarded the black-and-white chaps he'd worn last night, and now wore a fringed buckskin jacket similar to Juarez's over his black shirt, red bandanna, and vest, he was still drawing eyes, Angel noted. The thought of the outlandish American being seen in her company appalled her, and so she quickened her pace to the point where she was almost running down the hill to the quay, leaving Nick far behind.

Meanwhile, Mabel watched as Juarez pulled an enormous snowy handkerchief, immaculately folded, from within his buckskins. His dark eyes gazing soulfully into hers, he took her chin between his brown fingers and tilted her face up to his. Then, with exquisite care and the gentlest touch, he patted the moisture from her eye and dampened cheek, murmuring, *"Aiee, pobrecita . . ."* as he did so.

"Are you reelly a Red Indian, then?" Mabel asked as he did so, made breathless by his closeness and his touch. Cor, this Warez bloke wasn't half a looker, she realized, suddenly conscious of the male beauty of his sculpted, high-cheekboned face. Ow, maybe he wasn't 'andsome in the same exciting, dangerous way the other American bloke was—him with those brooding dark brows and no-nonsense eyes that gave a girl the shivers just t' look in 'em. And maybe it *was* Durango you noticed right off the bat when the two were together, but this Warez bloke was really quite nice. Very nice, indeed.

"No, Señorita Mabel. I am not Indian, but Spanish, from the beautiful town of Santa Fe, which is in a place called New Mexico. When I heard that Señor Cody was hiring Indians for his Wild West Show, I decided to let my hair grow long and join his troupe. My full name is Antonio José Domingo de Montoya y Juarez."

"Blimey! Wot a mouthful!"

"*Sí.*" He smiled. "That is why my *amigos*—my friends—call me only 'Juarez.' There! It is done. Your little eye—so blue, so beautiful!—it has stopped crying now. But you must keep this, in case it starts again." He tucked the kerchief into her hand.

Mabel bit her lip, feeling uncharacteristically shy. All the lads she'd known, and not one of them had ever shown her such concern. "Ta ever so, love. It—it was ever so nice o' you t' help me out."

"*De nada.* It was my happiness to serve you, Señorita Mabella. Come. Shall we follow the others?"

Mabel smiled shyly up at him and nodded before slipping her hand through the arm he offered, suddenly aware of the stares the passersby were giving them—especially the girls, the cheeky, jealous buggers. She glared at them, then drew herself up proudly and flung the dangling end of her ragged boa over her shoulder. "Oh, let's, ducks!" she agreed happily.

It was soon apparent to them all that Angel had made a grave error of judgement in opting to cross the treacherous British Channel in the tiny *Pelican*.

The diminutive fishing boat rode each towering swell and dropped into each deep trough that followed with the wonderful buoyancy of a cork. But her small size made every lurch, every roll, every plunging dip and death-defying shudder far more pronounced than a bigger vessel would have. Up, up, up and away they went, soaring on the crest of a swell! Down, down, down, they plunged. And then, just when one was thanking one's lucky stars that it was over and one's innards had returned to their proper position in one's anatomy, it started all over again!

Perched on an overturned bucket on the briny deck,

clutching a thick length of cable for purchase and looking as utterly ridiculous as the rest of them in the floppy yellow sou'wester hats and fisherman's oilskin slickers the captain had provided to protect them from the wash and the salt spray, Angel was bitterly regretting the tasty luncheon of battered and fried Dover sole that she'd enjoyed in the restaurant while the ferry sailed without them. Her mouth watering, she'd ignored the Americans and Mabel's warnings to eat lightly—or not at all, as they'd chosen—in view of the imminent sea crossing. Instead, she'd made a perfect pig of herself at luncheon. Now she was sorry.

"Make it stop!" she wailed, feeling her stomach squeeze in rebellion as the *Pelican* rose to ride out another swell. "Oh, I beg you, I implore you, Captain Raoul, pleeease make it stop!"

"Nevair fear, we are already 'alfway to Calais, mam'-selle," the captain promised cheerfully, handling the wheel with the casual ease of an expert seaman. The stub of a Gauloise cigarette jutted from the side of his mouth, jiggling up and down as he spoke. "Soon you will be there, *no?* I can imagine the lovely mam'selle dining at some exquisite little boulevard restaurant in Paree, savoring *escargots,* sopping up the wine sauce with a little morsel of fresh bread . . . hmmm! *Les escargots sont magnifiques!* Fresh butter . . . a few herbs . . . a little garlic . . . heaven!" He kissed his bunched fingers, and rolled his eyes.

Escargots. Had he really said "snails"? With a sauce of—of butter? And garlic—? She gulped. Just the thought of it was too, too revolting, combined with the fishy stench that rose through the hatch alongside her. Her nostrils flared. Her lovely face turned a sickly greenish hue. Her belly squeezed, heaved. She gagged. Her hand flew up to cover her mouth, and in the same instant she was up and on her feet, positively flying across the slippery decks for the rail.

She threw her upper body over it with such violence, she almost toppled headfirst into the churning gray green waters of the Channel. Indeed, only Nick's prompt grab for her skirts kept her from falling overboard as she made a sacrifice of her luncheon to the ecstatic, screaming gulls wheeling about the boat.

"Oh! Oh, my! Oh my my my my my!" she babbled when he hauled her back upright. Standing on the lurching deck, tears streamed down her blotchy face. "I think—yes! I really believe that I—oh, aaaggghhh!"

With a strangled moan, she turned violently about-face and once again hung over the railing, making disgusting retching-gargling sounds that no true lady would ever have dreamed of uttering, however indisposed, but quite unable to help herself. When she again swayed upright in a most drunken fashion, she felt as hollow as a drum, and her face was the color of old bones.

Nick, his hands still clamped on her hips, eyed her warily. "All done?" he asked, keeping a safe distance.

Biting her tremulous lower lip, she managed to whisper a shamefaced, "Yes. I believe so."

"Then here. Suck on one o' these. It'll take the . . . er . . . trail dust out of your mouth."

He drew from a pocket in his oilskin the box of lemon bonbons Uncle Teddy had given her, which she'd thought she'd left on the train. Gratefully taking one, she placed it on her tongue. As it dissolved, the bonbon's fizzy sherbet filling did wonders to rid her mouth of the foul acid taste. "Thank you," she gritted, hating having to thank *him* but feeling duty-bound to do so, under the circumstances. "Er, would you care for one—?"

"Nope, thanks all the same, ma'am. See, I ride boats the same way I ride a wild bronc—with an empty gut." His expression was accusing.

"How very sensible of you," she agreed contritely, flinching at his graphic choice of words. Pushing back long strands of dark gold hair that had escaped both hairpins and skipper's hat and now flapped wildly about her face in the blustery wind and salt spray, she was suddenly very conscious of looking less than her best.

What a devilishly good-looking rogue Durango was, however brash and arrogant his manners might be, and however unpleasant the circumstances. While she looked windblown and dishevelled, his silvery blue eyes were sparkling, damn him, and the wind had whipped ruddy color into his blue-shadowed cheeks. His healthy tan complexion made a startling contrast to the attractive glimpse of white as he grinned . . . Realizing she was staring at him in the same uncouth way he favored, she blushed and quickly looked away, promising through pursed lips, "I shall remember your advice and do the same, next time, Mr. Durango." She shuddered as she eyed the heaving green swells beyond the fragile rails. "But for now, would you be so—so kind as to escort me back to the—er—to my bucket?"

"I'd be happy to, ma'am," he managed to splutter, for it was all he could do to keep from laughing, she looked so darned comical in that enormous sou'wester hat and outsized yellow slicker. Yessiree, damned if she didn't look like she'd been ridden hard and put up wet!

She blushed furiously. The odious brute was laughing at her! Well, the last thing she needed was his help or his arm. "Never mind! I can manage for myself," she snapped, tossing her head.

Before he could protest, she started off toward the wheelhouse, her arms outstretched on either side of her like a tightrope walker, to counterbalance the movement of the decks beneath her feet. Two steps to the left, then the *Pelican* would heave and she'd be carried two steps to the right. Hell, the way the fool woman was teetering across the slimy decks, she was jest asking to get dunked in the channel—and he wasn't about to dive in after her!

"Wait up, Miz Higgins," he drawled, reaching her side. "Let me carry you."

"No! There's no need for your assistance, thank you. I believe I've found my—er—my sea legs at long last. Your help is no longer necessary."

"Sea legs, hell, lady! One slip, and you'll go sliding overboard under the railing, into that pea soup—and right now, that's the last thing I need! Swallow your damned pride an' let me carry you." So saying, he reached for her, swept her up into his strong, capable arms before she could squirm free.

"I'm quite capable of walking, Mr. Durango," she said, though in a very small voice, resisting the compelling urge to cling to his neck and strong, capable body like a drowning woman clutching for a life ring or spar. "Your concern is quite unwarranted, really it is."

He laughed scornfully. "Concern, hell! Lady, if it was up to me, I'd let you drown—! But I promised your pa I'd look out for you, and Nick Durango keeps his word. Now, quit squawking, 'fore I change my mind and toss you in the drink myself!"

With those chastening words, he carried her back to the others and deposited her on her upturned bucket without ceremony.

"She is very beautiful, eh, *amigo?*" Juarez murmured knowingly out of the side of his mouth when Nick joined him behind the tiny wheelhouse for a smoke. It was less windy there.

"Beautiful, hell. She ain't my type."

"No? I'd say she's exactly your type, *hombre.*"

Nick scowled. "Then you'd be wrong, *amigo,*" he growled, casting his cousin a foul look. "Damned woman's been nothin' but a burr under my saddle since the word 'go'! Now, this here trip is strictly business, Cousin. We agreed to escort these two little fillies— nothing more. Try t' keep that in mind, huh?"

Juarez grinned. "Oh, I shall, Nick. But . . . can you?"

Nick's answer was drowned out by the scream of the gulls as the mud flats of Calais hove into focus through the salt spray.

France! They were there.

Chapter Nine

Paris—the City of Lights! Never had a name seemed so apt! Angel was so excited, the rented *fiacre* could scarcely contain her as they were driven to their hotel on Rue Cologne, through rainwashed streets flanked with brightly lit cafés or elegant hotels.

A smoky train had whisked them the one hundred and thirty-odd miles from Calais to Paris, along with provincial passengers reeking of garlic and wine, some carrying wicker baskets stuffed with live pigeons and chickens or strings of onions; others with fresh fish wrapped in newsprint. The cramped train journey had seemed endless to Angel, but now they were on the last leg of their journey, thank God!

Once a porter had been found upon their arrival at Gare du Nord—North Station—to unload her belongings, Nick had summoned her and Mabel a hansom cab—called a *fiacre* here. He'd told Angel that he and Juarez would follow immediately after they'd located their horses.

"Did you say horses?" she'd echoed, eyebrows arched.

"Yes, ma'am. My black, and Juarez's paint."

"Really? I wasn't aware that you'd brought your own mounts with you."

"Shoot, we never travel anywhere without 'em, ma'am," Nick had come back seriously. "Good cow hosses and trick ponies like ours are real hard t' come by."

It transpired that Nick had sent their horses down to Dover on a livestock train the evening before they left London. A livestock steamer had transported them across

100

the channel. From there, they'd been sent ahead to Paris by rail. According to Nick, the poor beasts were now awaiting their masters' rescue in a cramped boxcar stable somewhere in the station. Once they'd located them, he and Juarez would ride to the Hotel St. Pierre in the wake of the ladies' *fiacre*.

His affection for the beasts was apparent in both his tone and his eyes, revealing a softer side to his character she'd not anticipated. Angel had muffled a snort. Clearly he was far fonder of horses than he was of people in general—and herself in particular! His expression said as much. . . .

"Rue Cologne," Angel had told the cabbie in her best schoolroom French, mentally thanking Mademoiselle Tait for her repeated drillings in pronounciation. "Hotel St. Pierre, *s'il vous plait.*"

Moments later, they were off, driving through the gaslit, chestnut-lined boulevards of Paris.

A drizzling rain was falling over the Ile de la Cité, yet despite the lateness of the hour and the weather, late-night café-goers and opera and ballet aficionados were everywhere, either humbly dressed and strolling down the avenues arm in arm, or sumptuously attired in silks and satins glimpsed only through the windows of private coaches as they were whisked by.

"Smell the air, Mabel! It smells quite different from London here. It smells . . . French!" Angel cried, her fatigue forgotten as she angled her pretty head out of the hansom window. "Hmm, *c'est—c'est marveilleuse!* I can smell café au lait—and fresh bread—and flowers, too! Try it, Mabel."

Mabel shot Angel a jaundiced look and smothered a yawn before sniffing the air for herself. "Wet cabbage," she pronounced. "Old socks. Garlic. Cat piddle."

"Oh, pooh!" Angel dismissed her comments, disgusted with her. "I don't believe you have an ounce of romance in your soul, Mabel. Here we are in Paris—wonderful, historic, *romantic* Paris, and you can't find anything nice to say about it?"

"Me eyes are burnin', me bloody head's throbbin', I've got an upset stomach from being tossed about in that leaky

101

old barge we sailed 'cross the Channel in, and me feet 'urt. Happen I'll feel a mite more enthoosiastick about yer bleedin' Paris tomorrer, after a good night's kip. Fer now, give over, do!"

Angel bit back a cutting response, knowing from experience that scoldings were wasted on Mabel, especially when she was grumpy and tired. Instead, she continued to crane her neck out of the window, watching the inky River Seine that flowed slowly beyond the stone embankments lining the boulevards, or else slipped darkly beneath the arched gray-stone bridges that spanned her starlit, rain-dimpled waters.

Beyond, darker still than the night sky, rose the majestic silhouettes of ancient churches with soaring steeples that looked like fingers pointing heavenwards. Despite Mabel's request for silence, Angel began humming "Frère Jacques," feeling almost giddy with anticipation. Her battle with *mal de mer* that afternoon, and that arrogant Durango's timely if scornful assistance, now seemed as distant as the moon. If only the man himself were equally distant, she'd be looking forward to her Grand Tour without a single reservation—!

A few moments later, their *fiacre* jounced to a halt before an imposing building of gray stone that stood some three stories high, fashionably situated on Rue Cologne, less than one block from the Tour d' Argent. The cab rocked as the cabbie clambered down to open the door.

"Hotel St. Pierre, mademoiselle," he informed Angel with a Gallic flourish, before handing her down. "If you would care to go inside, out of the rain, I will 'ave your luggage brought up to your rooms immediately."

"Thank you, Jacques. Please do. Come, Mabel! Follow me."

So saying, Angel tipped him, drawing her cloak more closely around her shoulder. Her back straight, her head held imperiously high, she started up the immaculate steps leading to the etched-glass and brass-trimmed portals of Hotel St. Pierre. London society might snicker behind its back at her working-class origins, but she was determined her deportment and manners would give no one cause to do so here on the Continent.

A sleepy-eyed doorman appeared from somewhere to welcome them and escort them to the registration desk.

The enormous foyer was ablaze with the light of crystal chandeliers and far from deserted, despite the late hour, guests coming and going on either side. The ladies wore glittering Charles Worth gowns and jewels flashed from their throats and fingers. They were caped in flowing silk or velvet, or else swathed in costly furs as they swept through the foyer on the arms of their escorts, men who were equally elegant in their top hats, tails, and swirling opera cloaks, worn with white silk scarves draped over their shoulders.

Numerous green velvet chaises, tiny mahogany tables strewn with periodicals and newspapers, and elegant potted palm trees gave the St. Pierre's vestibule an air of quiet distinction. One could almost smell the money—the aristocratic old blue blood of France and Europe—in the air, Angel thought, sniffing appreciatively as she looked about her. It was her favorite perfume!

Angel rang the bell on the front desk. Within seconds, a tall beanpole of a man with a pencil-thin, stiffly waxed moustache and beaky nose came flying from a side door, hastily pulling on a coat. Breadcrumbs clung to his moustache.

"Good evening, mademoiselle. Welcome to Hotel St. Pierre! My name is M'sieu Paul Martine, and I am the hotel manager. How may I be of assistance to you?"

"Good evening, M'sieu Martine. I believe my father's business manager, Mr. Hamilton, telegraphed ahead to make my reservations? Mademoiselle Angelica Higgins, and party of three?"

With a dubious eye, Martine opened a leather-bound register and scanned the inked entries, turning pages rapidly. "'Iggins . . . 'Iggins . . . *Mais, non!* I regret we 'ave no such reservation, mam'selle. Perhaps you are in error? Another hotel, perchance . . . ?"

"It was this hotel, M'sieu Martine. The Hotel St. Pierre, Rue Cologne, Paris. Please be so kind as to look again!"

He did so, with the same results.

"But you simply must have our reservations! Mr. Hamilton is most efficient and reliable. He would never

103

have forgotten. Perhaps . . . perhaps a mistake has been made on the hotel's part?'' she suggested.

It was entirely the wrong thing to say. She realized it immediately. The bored congeniality on Martine's face vanished, becoming instead an expression of frosty hostility. He looked down his nose at her. "On the contrary, mademoiselle, I beg to suggest that perhaps the mistake was on the part of *your* M'sieu 'Amilton!" he said huffily. "The Hotel St. Pierre does not make mistakes, I assure you!"

It would be useless squabbling with the man, Angel sensed, gesturing at Mabel—who'd been tapping her foot with mounting impatience during the exchange—to exercise a little self-control.

"Nor, sir, are my papa's employees. But who made the error is unimportant at this late hour, is it not?" she coaxed in a gentler tone. "I have been traveling since before dawn this morning, and am quite exhausted, as is my maid. If you would be so kind as to find us alternative rooms immediately, I would so appreciate it . . . ?" She smiled sweetly, hoping to cover her *faux pax* of moments before. But both her smile and her drooping, travel-worn loveliness were wasted on Martine.

"I regret we have no rooms available for you, Mademoiselle 'Iggins," he informed her with ill-concealed pleasure. "Tonight, Luigi Mavorotti, the celebrated Italian tenor, opened in Verdi's *Aida* at the Grand Opera. Anyone who *is* anyone was, of course, in attendance." His tone and expression implied that she was obviously not included in this select group. "Accordingly, *mademoiselle*, all the finest hotels in Paris are filled to capacity. Why, the St. Pierre's rooms have been booked for many weeks! Perhaps you might be fortunate in finding a small *pension* for the night elsewhere, but at the St. Pierre—!" He shook his head with an air of finality. "Alas, *non.*"

Crestfallen, Angel turned away, biting her lip. In her fatigue, she was perilously close to tears. She was about to retrace her footsteps outside when the lobby's double doors flew apart. Nick and Juarez sauntered into the lobby, their boot heels and Nick's jingling spurs creating a minor stir. Her heart sank as she saw that they were wearing full western regalia, complete with Stetson, flapping chaps, Indian war-paint—and tomahawk!

"Oh, dear Lord, no!" Angel groaned. "Just look at them! Mabel, help me to get them back outside before they make us an even bigger laughingstock than we are already! Mabel? Mabel, please?" she implored, horrified to see that Mabel had perked up with Juarez's appearance and was now actually grinning as she waved at him.

"Lawd, no, ducks. Let the lads be! Happen that handsome Warez will scalp that bleedin' fairy, Monsewer Martine, when he hears they've no rooms fer us! Either ways, he can't do much worse than you did, can he, love?"

Ignoring Mabel's pointed criticism, Angel all but flew across the parquet floor to head off Nick's swaggering advance on the front desk. Plucking at Nick's elbow, she tried to turn him back toward the door he'd just entered.

"Mr. Durango, there's been a dreadful mix-up. They have no reservations for us here. We must leave at once and look elsewhere for accommodation," she informed him breathlessly, pricklingly aware of the amused and frankly curious stares they were receiving from returning hotel guests, and of Nick's darkly handsome, mocking face beneath the brim of his black Stetson. The loathsome man appeared just as amused as the passersby. Did nothing ever perturb him? "Please, do come back outside. We can decide there what must be done. In—in private."

"No rooms! Hell and damnation! 'S that right, Martine, you ole son of a gun?" Nick demanded in a thunderous voice quite loud enough to carry to the third floor. "You aimin' t' throw us cowpokes out on the streets, pardner?"

Martine's head snapped up. His hazel eyes ignited. Dropping the register, he beamed and threw up his hands in delight.

"Why, M'sieu Nick! And M'sieu Juarez, too! Welcome back—and what a pleasant surprise! We did not expect you again until August, *non?*"

Welcome back? Again? Angel watched with amazement as Paul Martine scuttled around the front desk to greet Durango personally, waving aside the grinning, suddenly perky doorman. The hotel manager pumped Nick's hand, then shook Juarez's in turn.

"Say, you ready for a shootout, stranger?" Nick challenged suddenly, backing away several feet. His fingers flexed. His cupped hands hovered over the brace of pearl-handled Colts that rode low in the holsters at his thighs.

"I sure am, Du-ran-go!" Martine twittered in a fair imitation of an American accent. He placed a fist on each hip, index and middle fingers extended like imitation guns.

"One! Two! Three! *Draw!*" a grinning Juarez counted.

On three, Nick's guns cleared leather with such speed, they were only a pearl and silver blur. He spun the Colts showily around his index fingers and had fired two deafening shots in rapid succession over his head before Martine's finger "guns" had reached waist level!

There was a splintering sound as two of the glass teardrops hanging from the fabulous chandeliers shattered, glass showering to the marble floor.

"Sorry, pardner, but you're dead!" Nick apologized to Martine with a rueful grin.

"Quite so, *mon ami!*" Grinning himself and appearing far from angered, Martine shrugged expressively. *"Mon dieu*, you are so—how you say? Fast as ze lightning when it is greased? Although I 'ave practice for many, many hours since you left, I am still no match for ze 'King of the Cowboys,' alas!"

"Aw, shoots, someday you'll beat me, friend," Nick reassured him, clapping him across the back. "Some fine day! Meanwhile, me and my Injun sidekick, old Juarez here, need a place t' spread our bedrolls. I hear you're all filled up? 'S that right?"

"Alas, yes . . ." Martine pursed his lips. "But for you, M'sieu Nick, I will make room, somewhere."

"I'm sure glad t' hear it, *hombre!* And say, while you're huntin' one up, why not make it a passel of rooms—a suite, maybe? Heck, two suites'd be just dandy! One for me and my pardner—and one for the little fillies here."

"Mademoiselle Higgins is with you?" Martine sniffed.

"Higgins, hell!" Nick grinned. "The little lady's bashful, I reckon. Don't want folks t' know who she *really* is." Leaning over, he added in a lower voice, "Guess you

106

didn't recognize Miz Annie Oakley in her city duds, eh, Martine, you old coyote?" He winked and nudged the manager, adding, "You know how it is, eh, Martine? The two of us jest had t' get away for a spell, so . . . we gave her husband the slip. Too-joors lamooor!"

Martine whirled to face Angel, his hands clasped to his chest in amazement. "Mademoiselle Annie Oakley—? *Oh, pardonnez-moi,* mademoiselle! How foolish of me. As M'sieu Nick said, I did not recognize you! A thousand apologies, my dear lady!"

Angel's features resolved into a mask of indignation. *Annie Oakley, indeed!* Her mouth dropped open as she prepared to deliver a scathing rebuttal, but before she could deny Durango's claims, Nick had taken Martine's elbow and drawn him aside. At some length, the two conversed in low murmurs behind a potted palm, ignoring her.

When they'd finished their conversation, Martine looked Angel up and down with a new light in his eyes and a knowing smirk that she itched to wipe from his lips with the flat of her hand. *"Alors!* I will 'ave you two lovebirds shown to your rooms immediately, *chère* Mademoiselle Annie," he promised silkily. "And may I be the first to wish you and M'sieu Nick a delightful . . . 'oliday?"

With that, he made her a half-bow before floating away, snapping his fingers to summon a bellboy for their luggage as he went. The cabbie and the doorman were lugging it into the lobby at that very moment.

Angel watched Martine's retreat before marching up to Nick. "All right, Mr. Durango. This has gone quite far enough. Out with it! What exactly did you tell that obnoxious fellow?" she demanded, glaring at him. "Besides the outrageous lie that I was Annie Oakley, I mean?"

Nick shrugged and rolled his eyes, feigning innocence. "Why, just what you tried t' tell him, ma'am. That we need two suites. Heck, he didn't have a lick o' trouble understanding me . . ." He paused thoughtfully before turning back to her and adding, "Y'know, ma'am, I reckon your Frenchy talk ain't near as good as you think it is . . ."

"I spoke to the man in *English,* you American clod!" she snapped. Durango looked too innocent by far to her eyes. He was up to something—she could smell it a mile off. But what? And what had he told Martine?

Yet again, he shrugged. "Then I guess Martine didn't understand your parlaying."

"He understood me quite well, Durango. And furthermore, I would appreciate it if you'd—!"

"Ma'am?" Nick cut in, clearly impatient. His ice blue eyes were snapping. "It's late. Do you want the blamed rooms or not?"

"I—of course I want them!" she sputtered, color filling her cheeks.

"Then corral that temper o' yours and hold your danged horses while I see about gettin' us some!" he growled.

"But . . . but . . ."

"You 'heard 'im, ducks. For once, stifle!" Mabel hissed.

An hour later found her standing before the dressing table of an elegant suite with delightful cream and rose-colored furnishings.

She unpinned and brushed out her long honey-gold hair, then washed her face and hands. Her flannel nightgown was spread across the bed in readiness as she contorted her body like a circus performer to untie the laces of her stays.

Drat it! The stupid laces had resolved themselves into tight little knots that defied her fingers. And turning her back to the mirror and risking neck dislocation to look over her shoulder served no purpose but to increase her irritation.

Would nothing go as it was intended, including her preparations to retire? She scowled at her reflection. Any other wealthy young woman would have her maid fawning over her right now, just waiting to whisk away her rumpled garments for pressing, or to brush out her hair. All she had was that idle Mabel Blunt, the lazy, saucy baggage, already sound asleep in the second bedroom adjoining the suite's sitting room.

Well, enough was enough! Mabel might be suffering from a throbbing head and exhaustion, but so was she, dash it all. However, there'd be no sleep for her with these torturous stays digging their nineteen-inch whalebones into her twenty-four inch waist. Mabel would just have to stir herself to untie the blasted knots. . . .

Resolute, Angel stalked across her bedroom and into the suite's parlor, which was scattered with long, low brocade chaises and tables bearing silver bowls of spring flowers. Before the door leading to the suite's second bedroom, she halted, turned the door knob, and pushed at the door once, twice. Nothing but a narrow crack opened inward. Muttering, she pushed again, but the door, although clearly unlocked, was stuck. The damp weather had caused the wood to swell, she decided.

"Mabel!" she hissed into the crack. "The door's stuck and I need your help with my stays! Pull the knob from your side!"

There was no answer.

"Mabel? Mabel, I'm warning you . . . If you don't answer me this very instant, I shall forbid you afternoons off!" she threatened, thinking: *If anything else goes wrong today, I shall go insane . . .*

But despite her threats, there was still no answer.

"Very well," she gritted, teeth clenched. "You have tried my patience to the maximum now, Blunt. I have no choice but to employ extreme measures. If you are behind the door, listening and laughing in your underhanded fashion, I strongly caution you to step aside to avoid injury—!"

So saying, she threw her entire weight against the door. To her shock, it flew inward! She careened over the threshold and into the dimly lit bedroom adjoining, the impetus of her thrust carrying her clear across the Turkish carpet to tangle with the lace curtains that billowed from the opened French doors leading to the balcony. Behind her, the door slammed shut with a loud boom that made Angel, already jumpy, whirl around.

In that same moment, she saw Mabel erupt from the bed with surprising agility for someone just aroused from slumber. The maid flung back the covers, reaching for something on the nightstand that gleamed dully in the murky light of a chimney lamp. She moved in a spare, fluid fashion, that left Angel open-mouthed in dismay, then spun to face her with the agility of a cat. An ominous, metallic "click" sounded.

"Reach for the sky, you thievin' rattlesnake!" growled a deep male voice. "You move s' much as a hair on yore blamed head, I'll blast a hole in you, so help me God!"

Why, it wasn't Mabel at all, she realized, fighting the wild desire to giggle hysterically. It was Durango—!

Chapter Ten

"This is not Colonel Cody's Wild West Show, Mr. Durango," Angel snapped with icy hauteur when she'd recovered her wits. "Pray, put up your revolver, then I believe an explanation of your presence in this room would be in order."

"*My* presence?" Nick snorted in disgust. "Damn it, woman, what about yours?" He was shaking his head as he moved to turn up the lamp.

"Don't!" she squealed, guessing his intention the moment before it became action, but she was too late.

Lamplight flooded the room, revealing her bare arms, her bare shoulders, her bosom framed by the lacy straps of her bodice, the tightly laced whalebone stays cinching her waist, and the horsehair bustle pad behind. Dear Lord! In an age when married men rarely—if ever—saw their own wives nude, her state of *déshabillé* was mortifying, to say the least! Dare she hope that Durango would turn away, avert his gaze as any gentleman would? Ha! A faint hope, indeed!

When Durango turned back to face her, the dark slashes of his brows rose in delight on seeing her state of undress. His light blue eyes sparkled wickedly.

"Well, my, oh, my!" the hateful cad drawled. "What would your pa say t' these here goings-on, Miz Higgins?" He clicked his teeth. "Tsk! Tsk! And all this time, I figured you were a lady!"

"Well, you're quite wrong!" she sputtered, decorously crossing her hands over the exposed curves of her bosom.

His jaw dropped. "You mean, you ain't a lady?"

"I mean, sir, that despite appearances, I did not come here for any—any scandalous dalliance with you!" she protested hotly. "Now. Where is my Miss Blunt? What have you done with her, you rogue?"

"Mabel?"

"Of course I mean Mabel! Where is she? In your—your bed?" The thought made her quite faint.

"Hell, no!" He scowled. "Red's in the suite down the hall, I reckon. Leastways, that's where I left her."

"In the suite down the . . . ? But, why? Why is *my* maid not in *this* room to answer my calls?"

"Because I set it up this way," Durango admitted with bald-faced nerve. "I fixed it so I'd be real nice and handy t' come to your rescue, in case those mean old 'kidnappers' decided t' lay hands on your lily-white body again, Miz Higgins." Both his tone and his expression challenged her.

"But . . . that's utterly ridiculous!" she blurted out without thinking.

"Ridiculous to think those rascals might try again? Your pa didn't seem t' think so. Or . . . ridiculous because there were no kidnappers? And no real kidnapping?"

"Of course there were!" she protested, flushing.

"Ones that you hired, after I turned you down that night, right?"

"No! I—I abandoned that idea, I swear it. What—what you said that night made me ashamed—made me realize just how foolish it was."

He eyed her in frank disbelief. "And you expect me to believe that just two days later, you really were kidnapped?"

"Yes! Because that's exactly what happened!" The enormous lie made her cheeks burn as if she had a fever. Oh, dear Lord, was she really having this conversation, standing here wearing only her undergarments—or was all of it, including that brute Durango, but part of a terrible nightmare from which she'd soon awaken? Ah, if only it were . . .

Durango snorted. "I'd have t' be loco t' believe you,

honey! But either way, your pa's back home and he's frettin' over you. And, since Mr. Higgins hired me t' ride shotgun on you *night and day*, hell, that's just what I'm aimin' t' do. Now, you run on back to your room and get a good night's sleep. And should anything come up, you just sing out, an' I'll come a'runnin'!"

He strode toward the connecting door she'd exploded through so inelegantly moments before, and turned the brass knob to open it. But once again, the door was firmly stuck. And this time, not even Nick's considerable strength could force it to open again.

"Door's stuck," he declared unnecessarily, his eyes roving over her bright pink face, then dropping to inspect the rest of her person in that insolent way he had.

"I'm quite aware of that!" she snapped, acutely embarrassed by her unclothed state and his leisurely perusal. Oh, how her flesh crawled! His eyes felt like hot coals as they traveled over her. "But what, pray, am I supposed to do now?"

"Weeell, you could sashay on out into the hall, maybe get back into your room through the hall door—*if* you left it unlocked, that is. Did you? Leave it unlocked, I mean?"

"Of course not," she confessed in a small voice. "I'd have to be stupid to do such a thing. Anyone could have walked in!"

"Guess that idea's out, then." He frowned. "I reckon you could go on down the hall and try to wake up Red?" he suggested. "Maybe bunk with her for t' night?"

"By 'Red' I presume you mean Mabel?" He nodded. "Ha! A fine chance that'd be, Mr. Durango! Mabel sleeps like the dead. But—you're right. That is a possibility. Except . . ." her voice trailed lamely away.

"Except you can't go out in the hall dressed like that?"

"Exactly," she agreed, relieved that he'd grasped her dilemma without the necessity of embarrassing explanations. "Perhaps you'd be kind enough to lend me one of your dressing gowns or a smoking jacket 'til morning . . . ?" she asked hopefully.

He laughed, appearing vastly amused. "Honey, me and Juarez took off from the Wild West Show without so much

113

as a howdy-do or a by-your-leave from Bill Cody. And folks planning on breaking their contracts with a shrewd fellow like Cody don't have time t' round up their duds! What I've got on my back right now and what you see slung over that chair in the corner are all the clothes I've got t' my name, 'til I can rustle up a change of duds from someplace," he lied, enjoying her dilemma. "But—hell, you're welcome to 'em!"

He made as if to unbuckle his belt and donate the black Levi-Strauss trousers that fitted so snugly across his flanks to her cause, but belatedly, she realized that those trousers were the *only* garment he was wearing. . . .

Her gray eyes glazed over as she stared at him, mesmerized, for she'd never seen a man unclothed—or even barechested—before. The soft lamplight played over his bronzed shoulders and corded arms like water. It gleamed on his broad chest, furred with a mat of curly dark hair that disappeared below a wide black leather belt. The belt, she noted, fascinated, fastened with a silver buckle in the shape of a longhorned bull. Below it were lean, hard hips and a row of buttons, across which the heavy fabric strained. She swallowed, and beneath that heavy cloth—!

Swaying, she gulped and looked quickly away, thinking how very scandalous it was that she was in a bedroom, alone with a young, barechested and no doubt disgustingly virile man, while only scantily clad herself! She caught her lower lip between her teeth in consternation. Durango appeared a man of few principles, from what little she knew of him. He might—oh Lord! He might attempt to take advantage of the situation and force his attentions on her, to ravish her, steal her innocence without thought or care for the consequences of his raging animal lust! The possibility made her cheeks burn and her heart flutter unbearably. Her mouth, she realized, was dry as cotton at the thought, while her palms were strangely damp. . . .

The blurred action of his nimble fingers as he freed the button fastenings of his trousers snapped her back to the moment at hand. "Please, no!" she cried with a shudder.

114

"That—that will not be necessary!"

"You sure about that?"

"Beyond all doubt, sir!"

"Suit yourself, ma'am," Nick acquiesed with a shrug. "But . . . I reckon that leaves you with only one other choice, doesn't it?"

"And that is?"

"To stay here for the night."

"Stay here? In this room? With you? Oh, never! Most certainly not! That's quite out of the question! My—my honor and my reputation would be compromised beyond redemption come morning!"

He scowled, his handsome, sun-browned face now brooding and impatient. "So would mine, ma'am—but you don't hear me bawling about it, do you? Make up your mind, what's it to be? You plannin' on standin' here, jawin' all night. On runnin' up and down the hall in your underdrawers—or on spreading your bedroll in here, next to mine?"

She flinched at his indelicate reference to her undergarments before murmuring bleakly, "I suppose I really have no choice but to—er—to spread my bedroll here."

With a nod and a grunt, Nick turned to his bed, scooped up the rumpled rose satin quilt that had graced it and dumped the coverlet at her feet. He did likewise with one of the two feather pillows. "There you go, ma'am. Now, good night!"

So saying, he reached over, turned down the lamp until only a small circle of light remained, then flopped down onto his bed.

Angel stood there, quivering all over with tamped-down rage. That—that bounder! She wanted very badly to ask him if he was accustomed to treating ladies in such a cavalier manner back in his odious Wild West? If it had not, for even a fleeting instant, occurred to him to allow *her* to sleep in the softer bed and take the hard floor for himself? But . . . his brooding scowl and impatient tone, his obvious bad temper, and her own fatigue—coupled with the necessity of asking yet another favor of the hateful man—made her bite her tongue.

115

"Mr. Durango?" she said timidly on the silence. "If I might trouble you again for just a teeny moment—?"

"Geronimo, woman! What's up now?" he growled.

"It's my—er—laces." Her face was flaming now. She could feel it! "Without Mabel's help, I can't untie them, you see. I would be forever grateful if you'd assist me?"

"In untying your shoelaces?"

"No, Mr. Durango. I was referring to the—er—the laces to my—er—stays." She turned her back to him expectantly, thinking as she did so that she would never, as long as she lived, be able to look him in the face again after tonight. She was torn between the shame of needing desperately for him to unfasten her, and by her woman's intuition, which dictated that he be kept at a safe distance!

To her relief, she heard the bedsprings twang as he left the bed. Seconds later, she felt his warm fingertips graze the bare skin of her back as he fumbled for the fastenings. His touch made gooseflesh crawl down her arms. Could he feel it? Could he tell that his nearness made her tremble uncontrollably?

"Damn if you aren't all trussed up like a Christmas turkey!" he muttered after trying in vain for several minutes to untie the small, tight knots. "Only one way I know of t' get you out o' this tonight. Want me t' try it?"

"Yes! Anything!" she whispered fervently. "Just . . . just get it off!"

She felt the current of air against her skin as he moved away from her, then her nostrils filled with the pleasant, masculine aromas of tobacco and shaving soap as he returned to stand behind her. His dark head dipped, so close she could feel the tickle of his inky curls against her spine, and the warm current of his breathing upon her back as he exhaled.

"Hmm. You sure smell pretty . . ." he murmured.

"Durango—!"

"And your skin feels s' blamed soft and silky, it's like butter . . ."

"Durango, I'm warning you—!"

"Aw, all right," he growled. "Man pays you a compliment, ain't no need t' get riled up, is there? Suck in

116

a deep breath and hold it, Miz Angel. I'll have you outta here in two shakes of a coyote's tail!"

Thank Heaven for small mercies, he was true to his word! She felt a metallic chill against her back, then with one quick motion, Nick slashed the infernal laces, knots and all, using a hunting knife with quite the largest, wickedest blade she'd ever seen.

Weak with relief, she turned to thank him, hurriedly gathering her loosened strays and underbodice modestly about her to conceal her bosom. Resisting the unladylike urge to scratch uncontrollably where the whalebone stays had bit into her tender flesh, she gritted, "Thank you, sir."

"My pleasure, ma'am," he acknowledged with a wicked grin that made his teeth flash wolfishly in the gloom.

She noted that he made no effort to move away as she turned about, nor to pretend he hadn't glimpsed the snowy jiggle of her pretty breasts as the offending stays fell away from her middle. Rather, the rogue stood a hair's breadth away from her and repeated softly, "My pleasure!" with such a wicked lustre to his ice-and-fire eyes, she almost swooned. What was more, his husky tone made her heart flutter so, she could barely think straight, confound the horrid man!

She scowled so hard, she went cross-eyed as she ground out, "Mr. Durango, before we retire for the night, I believe it's only fair that I warn you. Any attempts to—how can I put it delicately?—make amorous advances on your part, will be firmly repelled."

Amorous advances? Why, that prissy little bitch! Nick thought, furious that she'd suggest he'd take advantage of her! Who in hell did she think she was, anyway? Aphrodite? The Venus de Milo? Righteous indignation filled him, for truth was, his thoughts had been wandering along just those very lines. That she'd seen through him so easily flayed his guilty conscience!

"Angel, this might come as somethin' of a shock to you, being a lady an' all," he drawled, exaggerating his American twang, "but we cowboys ain't all droolin' at the mouth over stuck-up, rich city gals like you. Fact is, Miz Iron Drawers, I—how can I put it delicately?—wouldn't

117

take a roll in the hay with you were you stark naked and the last blamed woman on earth, besides! Now, good night—or what's left of it!''

And with that withering set-down, he lay down again and said not another word.

Muffling a resigned sigh that was almost a sob, Angel gathered up the quilt and spread it over the Turkish carpet, placing the pillow neatly at one end. Selecting the half she would sleep upon, she lay down and pulled the other half over her, as if she were the filling in an omelette, before trying to sleep.

But, try as she might, despite her exhaustion, sleep eluded her for what seemed like hours. It was hardly any wonder. She was too acutely aware of that hateful man just a few feet away from her. Too sensitive by far to the deep rise and fall of his breathing. Too aware of the pleasant scent of him that lingered in the room. And too vulnerable by far to the memory of his warm breath upon her skin, and the fleeting touch of his fingers . . .

Used to rising early in his native America to ride herd on several thousand head of unruly beeves, Nick awoke in the darkest hour just before dawn.

For a full minute he lay there, absorbing his unfamiliar surroundings, detecting the first twitters of the birds awaking in their roosts under the eaves, the first glimmer of daylight framed by the French windows.

A gentle snore to his right alerted him that he was no longer alone in his bed. Turning his head, he grinned and thought, *Well, I'll be damned!*

Despite her highfalutin insistence that *he* keep *his* distance, at some time during the night, Miz Angel Higgins had gathered up her quilt and crawled into bed alongside him!

Her honey-colored hair streamed across the sheets like old Spanish gold. And, in repose, without hauteur to mar her lovely features, she was just as pretty as a picture. Her high cheekbones were tinted a becoming rose. Her lashes were sable fans resting above them. Her pink mouth was charming, the upper lip prettily curved, the lower lip pouty as any sultry *señorita's*, the corners curving upwards ever so slightly as if she were about to smile. A pale, lovely throat flowed down to meet a high, full bosom and ivory shoulders. The teasing glimpse of a tiny pink nipple was just visible above the rose-colored quilt she'd wound around her like a satin cocoon. Sweet Christ! The illicit glimpse made his mouth water. . . .

Yes sir, asleep, he had to admit she was kind of fetching—fetching enough t' make any red-blooded man curious and a mite distracted—and he was about as red-blooded as they came! But . . . he knew the minute she awoke and began looking down her nose at him, as if he were a rattler or a buffalo chip, his curiosity would fade, and fast, taking with it the illusions.

Yessirree, the rare woman who attracted Nick Durango these days had to have more than looks alone to hold him for longer than a night or two. He liked sweetness, gentleness, and a sense of humor in a woman; intelligence, compassion, and kindness for others—coupled with an earthy enjoyment of what went on between the sheets. But, since Savannah's betrayal, honesty rated above all other qualities he sought from a woman.

Miz Iron Drawers, from what he'd learned of her so far, had about as much humor in her as an undertaker. And as for an earthy appreciation of the sensual side of life—hell! She acted like the sight of a naked man, or his lusty lovin' would send her screaming into the night—or make her swoon, at the very least! Moreover, he knew for a fact she was about as dishonest as they came. She and her pal, Reggie, had staged her phony kidnapping, or his name wasn't Nick Durango. She'd been lying through her teeth—and wasting her breath!—trying to convince him otherwise. . . .

He thought about Sid Higgins and the touching concern he'd shown for his daughter's safety and shook his head, thinking, *You poor, gullible son of a bitch, Higgins! She's got you strapped over a barrel, so blamed hoodwinked you can't see through the clever little act she puts on for your benefit!*

But he could. Hell, yes. He knew all about her little deceptions back in London, and didn't trust her a blamed inch.

Still . . . he gazed longingly at that pert little nipple. It was puckered now, made tight and pebbly from brushing up against the bedclothes. But—although his manhood responded predictably—he shook his head. *Down, boy! This little filly ain't for you!* he told himself firmly. No, sir. He wasn't about to mix business with pleasure, not this time around—however tempted.

Chapter Eleven

After that first dreadful morning when she awoke to find herself half-naked in Nick Durango's bed, balanced along the very edge of the mattress as if contemplating suicide, her luck changed for the better. To her surprise—and relief—Durango made no mention of the incident, and she began to thoroughly enjoy her holiday and the beautiful city of Paris despite him.

Her days took on a pleasant routine. In the mornings, following a light Continental breakfast of croissants, café au lait, and fresh fruit, served on the St. Pierre's stone-flagged terrace overlooking the Seine, she'd fallen into the habit of renting a mount and going riding in the Bois de Bologne, as did many well-to-do Parisiennes.

The Bois was a beautiful park. Deeply forested in many places, it boasted several cafés, restaurants, arbors, walkways, ponds, fountains, and even a race course. Angel enjoyed riding on those lovely Parisienne mornings beneath trees that dappled her face with sunlight and shadow, a powerful horse responding to her slightest touch.

By the pond, she'd rein in her mount and watch little boys skimming their tiny sailboats across the glassy water with sticks, or nod at the uniformed nursemaids with their adorable charges in fine permabulators, out to take the air. Most mornings, she'd also exchange a few comments about the weather with other female riders—in French, *naturellement*—or look coy at the outrageous compliments paid her by the gentlemen. Although impeccably tailored and quite correct in appearance, she'd discovered these French fellows were charming rogues, as bold as all get-up—yet terribly romantic for all that!

Unfortunately, she had a shadow during these rides—that dratted Durango—who saw to it that her little flirtations could not lead to thrilling assignations. Oh, not on your life! The American had taken her father's instructions too literally for words! But to his credit, he kept his black stallion—named, appropriately enough, Diablo, she'd discovered—at a discreet distance behind her, so at least she could pretend she was alone.

Durango.

During those morning rides, she often found herself wondering what went on behind those brooding black brows and silvery blue eyes, what he really thought of her? Did he find her remotely attractive? Pretty? Handsome? Or a plain-Jane? And did she intrigue him, irritate him, amuse, or bore him? She sighed. Irritate, no question about it. The thin-lipped, scathing looks he shot her, the impatient way he always spoke to her, said as much. She frowned. She couldn't fathom why, but he always seemed angry with her, despite her attempts to treat him cordially after that first night. And, although it shouldn't have mattered, she wanted him to treat her with the same teasing approval he showed Mabel and include her in his and Juarez's chummy group.

As day followed day, she began to look for glimmers of approval in Durango's cool, calculating blue gaze, like a puppy watching its master's hand, craving a pat, a few words of praise, some warmth of expression, tone, or manner. Her mood became ridiculously buoyant when she imagined she'd received either one, in however small a measure. She would laugh far too loudly, chatter too much. On the opposite side of the coin, she became ridiculously flat and depressed when, despite her efforts, there was no favorable response from Nick—or, shudder the thought, a scowl of disapproval. She didn't understand why she should be acting so strangely, but nor could she seem to stop. . . .

Following her morning rides, Angel would return to the hotel to wash and change. Then, suitably attired, she and

122

Mabel would stroll along the tree-lined boulevards of the Right Bank with other British and European *touristes*. Sometimes they shopped at the exclusive emporiums on Rue de Rivoli, Rue Saint Honoré, or Rue de la Paix, where Angel purchased several bottles of expensive perfume, a fringed shawl from Cashmere, a waist-long necklace of pretty pink glass beads, an ivory-ribbed fan with Chinese birds painted on the silk webbing—and still more flamboyant hats!

On other days, they went sightseeing, exploring the narrow cobbled streets of "La Mouffe," the open market where an enormous variety of items could be haggled for beneath the brown canvas awnings of the tiny shops that lined the busy, colorful street. They watched streetcorner musicians busking, craned over bridges to watch small barges loaded with coal or lumber plying the Seine, and promised themselves they'd ride one of the charming *bateaux mouches*, or "fly boats," before they left the City of Lights, for no other reason than that it promised to be fun!

At tea time, they stopped to drink bitter espresso coffee and devour French pastries at one of many sidewalk cafés. They'd gorge themselves royally on foot-long chocolate eclairs, seated beneath one of the gaily striped umbrellas that mushroomed along the famous Champs Élysées in full view of Napoleon's magnificent Arc de Triomphe, feeling sinful, gluttonous—and enjoying every creamy, chocolatey morsel!

Late afternoons were given over to more cultural pursuits. After tea, she and Mabel wandered the hushed galleries of the gloomy Louvre, once a palace but now home to many of the world's most famous works of art, and there puzzled over some of the more indecipherable masterpieces. They visited the magnificent cathedral of Notre Dame and the tomb of Napoloen, and marveled at the little Emperor's enormous conceit in having himself interred in no less than six caskets, placed one inside the other.

On one occasion, they paused to watch the construction of a massive steel tower being erected in the Champ de Mars gardens. The monumental work was taking shape under the critical eye of its designer, the brilliant engineer M'sieu Alexandre Eiffel, and was scheduled to be completed for the Exposition in '89, two years hence.

They crossed charming little stone bridges and strolled the quays of the Seine's Left Bank and the Latin Quarter. There they saw hungry-eyed street artists bent over their pallets and easels wearing paint-stained smock and berets, and heard intellectuals and students passionately expounding their philosophies in dark, smoky little cafés from which the lively strains of accordion music drifted. Book stalls called *boîtes* lined the quays, too, inviting them to leaf through their dusty wares, before returning to their hotels to bathe, rest, and change for supper.

And, after dark, the two young women discovered, Paris truly came alive!

Elegant restaurants and theaters blazed with gaslight and candles, grew vibrant with laughter and song every night, while the dance halls Nick and Juarez frequented after escorting her and a reluctant Mabel to the foyers of the Grand Opera or a performance of the ballet rocked to the wicked cancan, danced by red-lipped, sloe-eyed demimondaines who shamelessly kicked their legs above their heads, brazenly showing their petticoats, garters, and drawers! She knew all about this because Juarez had described it all to Mabel who, fond of the lurid and bawdy, commoner things in life, had immediately told Angel that she meant to see it for herself!

If London had often been compared to a frowsy bawd in character, Paris was a merry widow kicking up her heels; alive, naughty, often scandalous, but infinitely endearing!

By the end of the second week, Angel was head over heels in love with Paris—and even more obsessed with the horrid American.

As she clattered into the stableyard of the St. Pierre the following Thursday morning, Nick kneed his stallion alongside her rented mare and swung down from the saddle.

Before the hotel groom could help her down from the saddle, Durango reached up to do so, much to her surprise.

Placing a hand on each of his shoulders, she let him grasp her waist and slithered easily to the ground before him.

"Thank you," she murmured shakily, blushing scarlet to the roots of her hair. Standing there in the loose circle of his arms, their bodies almost touching, she was painfully aware of his closeness, terribly aware of him as a man.

A tiny smile quirked his slim-lipped mouth. He tipped his hat. "Don't mention it, ma'am."

She stared up into his face a little longer than was strictly acceptable, before blinking to break the spell and murmuring, "Well! I suppose I should be running along . . ." She turned to go.

"Miz Higgins?"

She whirled to face him as if jerked by a string. "Ye-es?"

"A friend of mine has asked me to dine at his home this evening."

"Oh. And you'd like my permission to accept?"

A scowl knitted his tan forehead. Ask her permission? Hell'd freeze over first! "No, ma'am," he managed to grind out levely. "I—er—just wanted to let you know my plans."

"Then feel free to go, by all means, Mr. Durango. I shall be perfectly all right in my suite with Mabel. We'll probably just enjoy a quiet supper somewhere, and retire early for once. I know Mabel has some mending to do." She made as if to go on into the hotel.

"Ma'am, Red won't be here. She and Juarez have made other plans."

"They have? I wasn't aware of it?" She halted, her jaw tightening in annoyance. There it was again—that chumminess that excluded her! Hurt became annoyance, then anger. That dreadful Mabel had said nothing about spending the evening with Juarez, let alone asked her for the night off, but she had no intention of letting Durango see that she was hurt or upset about it. "Then I suppose I shall be dining alone, shan't I? No matter. I'm sure there are restaurants in a modern city like this that will serve an unescorted lady."

"I reckon there are, but . . . I can't leave you alone."

"Don't be ridiculous! I'm not a child, sir."

"I know that, Miz Higgins. But, I promised your pa, and my word's my word," he insisted stubbornly.

"So you have said, many times. But in this instance, you'll just have to break it, won't you? You have no choice, if you wish to dine with your friend."

"I have a choice. You could go with me."

"Me?" Her brows shot up. She could hardly believe her ears. "You're asking me to accompany you?"

"I reckon I am, yes."

"Why, that's—it would be most improper . . ."

"It would be supper, ma'am," he pointed out with an edge of impatience in his tone now. "Supper, maybe some dancing. And that's *all* it'd be."

The idea of spending the evening with him was an enormously intriguing one. She frowned, disgusted with herself, for she was torn between wanting desperately to accept Durango's invitation, and the impropriety of dining with someone in her father's employ.

"There'd be a bunch of swanky titled folks there," he added in the manner of someone dangling a juicy bone before a starving mongrel—the mongrel in this case being herself, and the juicy bone, the promise of titled guests! "Antonio—my business associate—is a prince. An Italian prince," he added to emphasize the point.

"I'm sure he's a very worthy fellow, Mr. Durango," she murmured patronizingly. "However . . ." She caught the flicker of irritation cross Nick's features and wished with all her heart that she'd thought before she'd spoken so condescendingly.

"Ma'am, make up your mind. Either you'd like t' go with me this evening, or you'd prefer t' stay in your suite, in which case, I'll find someone t' stand guard on your door 'til I get back."

"Stand guard—! Ha! You don't leave me much choice, do you, Durango?" she flared, slapping her riding crop against the corduroy skirt of her habit as if she'd dearly love to slash his insolent face with it.

"No, ma'am," he acknowledged, with just a ghost of a smile. He couldn't help himself. Damn, but she was something to look at this morning in that sassy black top hat with a filmy white scarf trailing behind it, loose gold ringlets spilling down about her shoulders, and the high, angry color riding in her cheeks!

"Oh, very well, then," she said finally, with apparent reluctance. After all, what harm could it do, really? "I accept your invitation—on one condition."

"And that is . . . ?"

"I must insist you dress for the occasion in correct evening attire."

He made her a mocking bow, shrivelling her with the contempt in his ice-blue eyes. "Proper evenin' duds, you say? Now, why didn't I think of that, hmmm? Dang me, I was jest fixin' t' wear my cowboy gear!" The heavy sarcasm in his tone made her flinch, but before she could withdraw her acceptance, he nodded curtly and added, "It's a deal, Your Majesty!" then led Diablo into the stables before she could say another word.

The hotel manager, M'sieu Martine, beckoned to Angel as she strode angrily across the lobby, slapping her riding crop against her palm. He informed her that the post had brought two letters for her. Waving the envelopes before her nose, he'd added coyly that the senders had tactfully used her "false" name of Higgins when addressing them.

"Perhaps one is from your 'usband, *non*, mam'selle?" he suggested silkily, and winked.

Glowering, Angel snatched the letters from Martine's hand and avidly scanned the envelopes. Both bore English stamps and London postmarks. One envelope was even monogrammed in the corner!

"The staff of the St. Pierre would be honored to have a little demonstration of your sharp-shooting, Mademoiselle Oakley . . . ?" Martine hinted in his low, obsequious murmur.

"Alas, m'sieu, I'm afraid I can't oblige you. You see, my—er—six-guns were left behind, in England. With my husband and my horse," she added sweetly, as an afterthought. "So sorry!"

With that, she hastened upstairs to her room.

Once inside, she unpinned her hat and sent it flying into a corner, before flinging herself comfortably across the bed on her stomach to read her letters. Considering the fun she'd been having, she was surprisingly eager for news of home.

The first letter, as she'd expected from the handwriting, was from her dear da, she saw with a twinge of homesickness. He asked if she was well, bless him, and enjoying herself, reassured her that he was fine, but confided that he'd come no closer to apprehending her kidnappers. (Thank God for that!) He went on to inform her that, despite her warnings, Sally, the maid, had run off to Gretna Green with Jim Simmons, the head groom, but that he was interviewing replacements for their posts. Uncle Teddy had been called away to settle some problem with his estate in Wales. The cook, Mrs. Prickard, had had yet another of her "funny" turns and scared them all, but was completely recovered now. It ended with her da's fondest love and his instructions to take care of herself.

The second letter was from Reggie. As she tore open the monogrammed envelope, the image of his long-nosed aristocratic face and that adorable blond cowlick flopping across her brow filled her mind. Reggie's refined image was a welcome contrast to the unsettling image of Durango's brooding, dark good looks, which for some obscure reason plagued her thoughts of late.

Obscure? Hmm. Perhaps not. When she thought about her disturbing obsession for the brute coolly and objectively, she'd decided her preoccupation was akin to one's reaction to a gnat bite. The bite swelled. It reddened. It got beneath one's skin and irritated dreadfully. It wasn't pleasant to look at, nor to have. It served no worthwhile purpose whatsoever. And yet, for as long as the blasted thing lasted, it itched like the very devil—and the itch simply couldn't be ignored; it had to be scratched! Exactly like Durango, irritating fellow—though she would definitely never stoop to scratching *that* particular itch . . . Pursing her lips, she shook her head and forced her attention back to Reggie's letter.

My Dearest Poppet, it read:
Although you've been away for only a few days at this writing, I already find myself desolate without you. Bligh's is a bore and my luck at the gaming tables has been no better since you left. Neville

continues to pester me, and the Season is insufferably dull. Accordingly, I've decided to visit the Paris of my youth and be at your side, dear heart. Give the slip to your "gaolers" if you can, and come to the sailboat pond in the Bois de Boulogne on Friday next at ten o'clock. There, sweetest Angel, we shall rendezvous and discuss certain Matters of Import to us both. Until then, Au revoir, my darling! I remain your obedient, affectionate servant, etc.

It was signed simply, "Reggie."

She sighed, knowing by "Matters of Import," Reggie was referring to the subject of their marriage. But—Friday next? She checked the date on the top of the letter. Why, Friday next was tomorrow! How simply marvelous, she thought, delighted at the prospect of sharing Paris with Reggie, to whom the city was as familiar as London. She frowned. He'd said to come alone to the Bois, but—how on earth was she to escape Durango's surveillance?

Her eyes fell upon the hat she'd discarded so carelessly before flinging herself across the bed, and a naughty grin curved her lips as an idea popped into her head.

Perfect! Utterly perfect! Durango's comment that she was the last woman on earth he would ever wish to—er—"roll in the hay" with had rankled over the past weeks. Although she certainly had no desire to roll in the hay—or in any anything else, for that matter—with that crude scalawag, her female vanity had been pricked by his words. Hoodwinking Durango and sneaking off to meet Reggie would even the score! And, if she hurried, she had just enough time to outline her scheme to Mabel, before bathing and dressing for tonight's dinner. A villa—and an Italian prince, Durango'd claimed, one with "swanky titled guests." She snorted. Prince, indeed! She doubted this Antonio's claims to royalty, Italian or otherwise, if he was any friend of Durango's—unless the man was a "royal" bore!

Thank God she had her rendezvous with Reggie to look forward to, she thought with a shudder. With that prospect, surely she'd manage to get through what promised to be a disastrous evening, somehow . . . ?

She smiled.

Her smile lasted until much later that day when, gorgeously gowned in a ruby-colored creation with hugely puffed sleeves and a daring décolletage, her slender hips accented fore and aft by cunning swags of ruby satin like a well-dressed window over a narrow underskirt, she sailed down the marble staircase to the foyer.

As she descended the stairs, she scanned the crowded lobby for Durango, without success. Instead, her attention was caught by the impeccably tailored figure of a tall, dark-haired gentleman who, in the company of several other men dressed in evening attire, was obviously awaiting his supper companion by one of the potted palms.

The man—either Spanish or Italian, she judged from the glimpses she caught of his tanned profile—was clearly of the aristocracy of Europe. His erect, arrogant bearing, that fine, noble head beneath ebony hair, his elegant gestures, suggested a duke, at the very least. And, although his back was to her, the excellent cut of his dark gray frock coat bespoke taste, good breeding, and wealth.

She sighed as she paused for effect at the foot of the stairs, one elegantly gloved hand dangling languidly over the acorn newel post. Oh, that awful Durango! What would *he* be wearing when—and if—he deigned to make his appearance? Fringed buckskins? His showy black-and-silver Wild West Show costume? She shuddered. He could take lessons in dress from that handsomely turned-out fellow by the palm and still contrive to look uncivilized and dangerous, she thought.

The small oval train of her gown rustling behind her, she crossed the marble foyer to perch on one of the velvet chaises and wait for him.

"Mademoiselle!" exclaimed a voice. "You are simply ravishing this evening!"

"*Merci beaucoup*, M'sieu Martine," she thanked the manager with a graceful angling of her head, knowing he was right. Her hair was a mass of honey-gold ringlets that a flushed and excited Mabel had piled high on the crown

130

of her head, before leaving for the evening with Juarez. Her hair's rich coloring was set off by a cunning little ruby spray of leaves that caught the light of the chandeliers. She had never looked better, she knew, and the knowledge added a radiant luster to her appearance. What a pity! The effect would be quite wasted on that—that man! "Have you seen Mr. Durango this evening, Martine?"

"Mais oui, mademoiselle! There he is, by the palm tree, *non?"*

To her shock, she realized that the concierge was pointing to the impeccably attired man she'd admired from the stairs. Oh, but it couldn't be . . . ? Surely not . . . ? But it was! The man was neither count nor prince, neither Italian aristocracy, nor Spanish, but . . . Nick, the cowboy, Nick of the red bandanna, the hairy chaps and the jingling spurs, Nick, the incredibly handsome perfectly attired . . . gentleman!

While she was still open-mouthed with amazement, he turned, spotted her, and strode toward her. An amused half-smile curved his sensual mouth and his ice blue eyes danced with amusement as he noted her astonishment. *That's one in the eye for you, honey!* he thought, going to meet her as if he had all the time in the world.

Her heart skipped a beat as he drew closer, for his dark hair and tan good looks were striking against the snowy wings of his high-collared shirt. So striking that simply *looking* at him did peculiar things to her breathing. Of a sudden, her stays seemed far too tight, as if they were robbing her of breath—until she remembered that she wore none.

"Good evenin', ma'am!" he greeted her with a bow. "I see you're all gussied up and rarin' to go. Shall we?" Smiling mockingly, he offered her his arm.

"Why, yes, thank you, Mr. Durango," she agreed faintly as she took it, ogling him. My goodness, she was quite unable to take her eyes off him, he was so very striking. A god—an Adonis! she thought, feeling faint and wishing she'd thought to bring her fan. Her small hand, now tucked within his far larger one, trembled madly, though he seemed not to notice.

"Really, my dear, it's high time you called me 'Nick,'

don't you think?" he suggested with a wink for Martine's benefit, his playful expression suggesting she was carrying their little "charade" too far, since they were lovers.

"I suppose it is, yes," she agreed in a small voice, looking up into his ice-and-fire eyes. As she did so, something strange and powerful and somehow frightening stirred in the very pit of her belly. "Umm, Nick."

He nodded, an amused smile still playing about his sensual lips. "Good. Well, let's hit the trail, shall we? I have a *fiacre* waiting outside."

And with that, he led her away.

Supper at the Tour d'Argent went splendidly, much to her surprise. The table for two he'd reserved was in the very best location, offering a view of the gaslit boulevard three floors below. The atmosphere was elegant, the other guests obviously upper class, the waiters fawning and correct. Her handsome escort was also incredibly adroit at ordering for them both, acting as if he dined each night in such opulent surroundings. It was amazing. The rustic clod she'd dreaded having for an escort had been replaced by a man who was urbane, witty, charming—and devilishly handsome, to boot!

Angel was in her element! Removed from the censurious eyes of London's unforgiving ton, thrust into a setting where no one knew of her humble origins as a lowly cotton-mill foreman's daughter, she felt the equal of anyone in the room. Accordingly, she blossomed before Nick's eyes, like a tightly furled red rosebud uncurling its petals under the warmth of the sun—the sun, in this instance, being the unspoken acceptance of the nobby patrons all around them, some of whom she nodded to genteely as if she knew them intimately, damned little snob, Nick noted, shaking his head in amused disgust.

"More champagne?" he asked, leaning back in his chair and studying her from beneath dark brows. Her cheeks were flushed, her eyes bright—a result, he knew, of the several sparkling glasses of bubbly she'd already downed. He dropped his gaze to the curve of her breasts. They rose and fell rapidly above the deep neckline of her gown, and

Nick felt a stirring in his groin, despite himself. The rosy flush that bloomed in her cheeks had spread to pinken her bosom. The subtle blush of color warmed the creamy expanse of her flesh in a way that made his throat dry with the longing to touch, to taste. With perfect clarity, he recalled the delicate pink nipple he'd glimpsed upon waking to find her in his bed three weeks ago. . . .

"Oh, please!" she cooed in answer to his offer of more champagne.

"What?"

"The champagne! Just one last, teeny little glassful, please!"

Nick nodded absently and gestured to the *sommelier* to refill her glass.

She raised it, peering through the curved bowl and the bubbly wine at him. The rounded shape of the glass flattened out his features, she observed, smothering a giggle. It stretched them far to left and right like an elastic band!

"Hardly recognized you back at the St. Pierre, Mr. Durango!" she pronounced, and hiccupped noisily. "Oops!" Carefully setting down her glass, she waggled an accusing finger at him and added loudly, "By gum, you look right handsome with yer clothes on, lad!"

Several heads turned their way with her loud and shocking declaration. Aristocratic hands raised monocles to curious eyes that stared in their direction.

"You think so, huh?" he asked casually, fighting the urge to laugh out loud.

"Oh, aye!" she gushed, unsteadily resting her chin upon her cupped hand. Her elbow slipped off the edge of the table as she gazed at him with too-bright eyes and a silly smile. "Mind you, this isn't the first time I've thought so. N-no-hic!-no! I thought you were handsome the night I spent in your bed, remember? 'Now that's a champion pair o'shoulders, Annie, girl,' I told myself. You really should—hic!—should scratch that—that itch. Oh, yes—hic! Hic!"

"Itch?" Nick asked amiably. "What itch?"

"From the gnat bite, silly man. That's what—hic—happens when you roll around in the hay. You get—hic—

gnat bites! Heeey, wait! What are you doing? Take your hands off me, you lout! Where are you taking me—?" she protested, for Nick suddenly stood and gripped her by the elbow.

With a steely hand, he all but lifted her from her chair and half marched, half carried her through the elegant restaurant, smiling apologetically to the gaping patrons.

"Wait! We didn't have any dessert!" she wailed, hanging onto a doorjamb with both hands for grim life.

"You're drunk, you little idiot. We'll stop for Italian ices later," he growled into her ear, unplucking her fingers and boosting her tail through the door with his weighty knee. "Meantime, I reckon we need to get you sobered up! Some black coffee'll do the trick."

Yet despite pouring an entire pot of coffee into Angel at a tiny café on Rue Chanson, she was still far from sober when they arrived at Antonio di Sorriso's villa on the outskirts of Paris!

Chapter Twelve

"Ah, but she is exquisite, your little English miss. A pink-and-white rosebud, carefully nurtured, tenderly watered and fed, now but awaiting the lucky fellow who will make her bloom! Ah! That golden hair, that figure! That—that *signorina bellissima!* She is perfection! A flower!" The prince kissed his fingertips.

"Now, hold your horses right there, 'Tonio!" Nick sourly warned his rapt business acquaintance, drawing on the slim cheroot between his teeth as he watched Angel from the verandah. The ballroom behind the open French doors was crowded. Exquisitely gowned and suited couples were waltzing to the lilting music of a five-piece string orchestra at one end of the room, yet despite the crowd, Nick never took his eyes off her.

"Damned if you don't sound like you're hankerin' t' be the gardener!" he accused Antonio. Anger—and perhaps the tiniest hint of jealousy—fired his eyes with glittering sparks and made them pale to silver and grow dangerously brilliant against his swarthy complexion. His hands tightened into hard fists against his thighs, for Angel—her shoulders almost bare, her ruby satin skirts swirling beneath the sparkling crystal chandeliers—was dancing giddily with some old coot whose name he hadn't caught, and doing so despite his orders to the contrary, the hot-headed, obstinate little mule. Even tipsy, she was the orneriest, most contrary woman he'd ever met.

"Ah, my friend, what real man would not wish to cultivate such a blossom! Surely even you must won-

135

der . . . ? And then again, perhaps I am wrong!" the prince amended hastily as Nick shot him a murderous glare. Antonio shrugged his robust shoulders expressively, rolled liquid ebony eyes skyward to the sprinkling of brilliant stars in the night sky and sighed. "I am but a man, and Italian, no? It is a curse, this virility of mine, but I cannot help it, my friend. It—it is in our blood, you see? A fire in the loins, always raging out of control! I have a compulsion to conquer each beautiful woman I see! To—how you say? Add another notch to my gun? And the little English signorina, she is a virgin, surely—? So rare a prize, nowadays, virginity, eh? I confess, Nicko, I have a craving to possess her innocence, her loveliness! To see her change from little girl to glorious woman before my eyes!" 'Tonio's pudgy, oily face glowed.

"Lay a hand on her, pardner, and I'll see *you* changed—from bull t' steer!" Nick growled, tossing his cheroot stub over the verandah steps and into the shrubbery below.

Flambeaux of ornate wrought iron were scattered amongst the darkened gardens, burning bright as Olympian torches. Their dancing flames caught the diamond sparkle of the water in the stone fountains that burbled in secluded little arbors and alongside stone pathways; they flickered over erotic statuary, hidden now by shadow and the darker masses of shrubs and foliage. Nick glimpsed the pale blur of a woman's bared shoulders against the night, caught a trill of seductive laughter on the breeze as an amorous couple sought the garden's seclusion for a tryst, and his scowl deepened.

"Her pa hired me to watch over her. T' bring her back to him the same way she left him—and that's jest what I intend to do, you savvy, 'Tonio?"

"I understand, *sí*. But alas, I can promise only to do my best to withstand the temptation, nothing more! Now, if you will excuse me, Signore Durango, there are other guests I must welcome to my home . . ." With that, the prince—clearly miffed—shrugged apologetically and left Nick alone.

As the waltz ended, Nick elbowed his way between the glittering guests to Angel's side. Grasping her hand, he whisked her out of the clutches of the doddery old fool she'd been dancing with, who was all but drooling down her décolletage.

"Mr. Durango, please! My arm! There's no need to be so—so masterful!" Angel exclaimed, flushed and beautiful as she pouted and fluttered her lashes at him. "Silly man! You had only to ask, sir, and I would have promised the next dance to you! There is no need for force . . ." She dug in her heels and pulled in the opposite direction.

And, to Nick's dismay, at that moment the orchestra began to play again. He was trapped on the pink marble dance floor, committed to dancing with her or making a scene by dragging her from it! Resigned to his fate, he took her in his arms and started dancing, his expression that of a doomed man about to be led to Madame La Guillotine.

One, two, three. One, two, three. *Savannah—and Santa Fé!* He hadn't danced at one of these nobby goings-on since the Governor's ball there, what was it—? Two years ago? Aw, hell, he thought, turning Angel smoothly in time to the music, he reckoned it couldn't be much different t' riding. Once you learned how, you never forgot. . . .

And he hadn't. Angel was slender and supple in his arms. Although tipsy, she moved as gracefully as a willow sapling swaying in the breeze, though the champagne lent her a seductive boldness that made her press herself far closer to him than the dance warranted. Turning her, Nick was acutely aware of her hips brushing against his, of the rustling sound her skirts made against his trousers. The scent of her filled his nostrils with the fragrance of warm, flower-sweet womanhood and he found his gaze irrevocably drawn to the moist rose of her lips, the pearly sheen of her bared shoulders. Christ! It was hard to look away! Could he blame Antonio for wanting her? he considered angrily as he spun her with far more enthusiasm than the waltz demanded. Damn if he wasn't starting to want her himself—to imagine all kinds of interestin' possibilities between the two of them. Ideas he might be real inclined to act on—if he were less than a man of his word. And in that moment, he wished he were someone—anyone!—else. Wished to God he'd made Sidney Higgins no rash promises . . . or that he was a four-flushing sidewinder without scruples!

"You dance divinely, Mr. Durango!" Angel purred, plastered up against him as if they were pasted together at the hip. She pouted her lips coquettishly. "In fact, we're rather good together! So, why must you always look so— so very cross with me, Nicky, darling? Hmm?" She drew her hand from within his and reached up to stroke his ink-black hair, her bare arm pressed against his rough cheek.

Her gray eyes peeked up at him seductively from beneath a fringe of surprisingly thick, dark lashes that he longed suddenly to feel fluttering against his skin, perhaps as she kissed him . . . everywhere? Heat flooded through his gut as her fingers wandered through his hair, grazing his scalp, pressing lightly against the back of his neck. Geronimo! It was like being stroked by summer lightning!

"Oh, Nick," she whispered, her eyes darkening to smoke. "Why can't we be nicer to each other?"

His mouth dry, he swallowed. "Because right now, honey, you're still pickled," he rasped in her ear, gritting his teeth to maintain his control as he unplucked her hand. "An' because you don't know what in the hell you're saying or you wouldn't be saying it!"

"Oh, but I do, truly!" she protested, wide-eyed with innocence. "I'm as sober as a judge! Listen!" Clearing her throat, she recited in a voice loud enough to carry above the music—and maybe as far as the city of Paris proper: "Peter Piper pecked a puck of peckled pippers."

The orchestra stopped playing. The dancers stopped dancing. Silence reigned, yet in the interim, Angel continued to shout:

". . . A pock of packled poppers Peter Pecker pucked. There! I can say a tongue-twister, so that proves it. I can't be pickled, can I?" she declared breezily, tottering a little as Nick released her waist. *Ah, Mabel,* she thought, burping but smiling sweetly over her shoulder at the shocked dowager with billowy breasts and a dark moustache behind her as she covered her mouth. Dear, gin-swilling

Mabel would be so proud of her, holding her liquor the way she'd done tonight! There was really nothing to it but keeping a cool head and knowing when enough was enough. "You know, I'm not nearly as drink as some thunkle peep, really I'm not," she insisted to no one in particular.

"Time we got some more chow into you, Miz Higgins," Nick said grimly, aware of the onlookers recoiling in shock all around them, of women furiously fanning themselves. "That damned coffee sure didn't help any!"

Despite the raised eyebrows all about them, he dragged her from the dance floor and out into the cavernous dining room.

Buffet tables had been set up there, groaning under silver platters of smoked salmon, thinly sliced tongue and ham, an array of spicy Italian sausages and cheeses, artichokes, deviled eggs, stuffed tomatoes, olives, mushrooms, sardines, and so on.

Settling Angel on a chair against the wall and sternly cautioning her to remain there, he turned his back on her for only a few minutes while he served her a generous plate.

When he glanced over his shoulder, she was gone.

"Beautiful Angel! Let me worship you!"

Angel opened her eyes. She saw the Italian prince, Antonio di What's-His-Name, kneeling on the flagstoned gazebo floor beside the wicker chaise upon which she reclined. His pudgy fingers were reaching out as if he meant to embrace her, while his expression was that of a man who'd found heaven on earth!

Why in the world is that chubby little man looking at me like that? she wondered, smothering a yawn. She blinked at him sleepily as she struggled to sit up, waiting for his shiny moonlit face to assume a more proper expression. To her dismay, it did not. His hot black eyes continued to devour her. His fleshy lips were still puckered. His olive brow and upper lip were still oily with sweat.

She must be seeing things, she decided. Her eyes smarted and felt gritty—surely that was why? She rubbed them on her knuckles, trying to recall how she'd come to be out here, in the gazebo, so far from the house. She vaguely remembered Nick insisting she should eat something but nothing beyond that, other than feeling a little woozy and sleepy. In fact, terribly sleepy! Had she wandered out into the gardens alone? Or had she swooned, and the prince carried her out here for some air?

"Sweet little virgin, don't scream, I beg you! You are quite safe here, in my little bower of love. And please, don't be angry that I carried you away, *amore!* Antonio must have you, you see, or he will go mad—!" the prince whispered ardently, answering her question.

Before she had time to digest this information, he was lying half-across her on the chaise, his plump, sweaty hands plucking at her plunging neckline, trying to reach inside her gown to fondle her breasts! The gall! The utter gall of the man! Outraged, she screamed and tried to squirm from beneath him, but the bounder had her securely pinned with one fleshy thigh angled across her hips.

"Enough, *signore!*" she panted, thrusting against his chest. "Desist, or I shall be forced to violence."

"Violence!" His face shone. "Ah, *mi amore, mi belissima!* I knew from the first that you were a woman of strong passions!" Antonio exclaimed. "Antonio will be naughty—very naughty—and then you will punish him, yes? *Yes!*"

Flinging his arms around her, he rained sloppy wet kisses over her face, her throat, her heaving bosom, where the neckline of her gown had slipped.

Enough was enough! Angel brought up her knee and slammed it into his groin, elated when Prince Antonio recoiled so violently, he fell backwards onto the gazebo floor. He lay there, plump belly uppermost, arms and legs squirming like an overturned tortoise as he moaned horribly. Then, clutching his tender parts, he scrambled to his feet and danced a cunning little jig about the gazebo, first upon one foot, then upon the other.

Angel stood. She smoothed down her skirts, tucked a wisp of stray hair back into her coiffure and drew a deep, calming breath as she'd been taught at Miss Ellen's. "I believe my actions have served to express my feelings toward you quite adequately, signore. Good night," she said icily.

Lifting her skirts from the dusty flagstones, she stalked haughtily past him down the steps of the gazebo. She continued on without looking back, marching quickly past a towering chestnut tree whose foliage cast the pathways in dense shadow, then circling a mossy fountain where a trio of stone cherubs replenished the waters in unique fashion. Naked little boy cherubs, they appeared, she observed with a delicate shudder, to be doing what Mabel would term "piddling" in the fountain's basin.

"Come back here! No woman refuses Prince Antonio and walks away!" the prince bellowed behind her, shaking his fist.

She turned in the direction of Antonio's voice, prepared for further argument, just as he began a mad dash toward her. Heavens above! The lunatic intended to fling her to the grass and force his attentions on her!

But—whatever his plan—Antonio was destined never to fulfill it.

When he was a little over six feet from where she stood, she heard a strange whizzing sound. Something long and dark snaked through the air before her. A noose dropped down around Antonio's waist and tightened, pinning his arms securely to his sides. He gave a yelp of dismay, but before he could squirm free he was jerked roughly off his feet, into the air. For all his stout build, he rose swiftly skyward as if levitated by some playful poltergeist! Furthermore, he remained airborne, suspended from the overhanging bough of the towering chestnut tree. As he twirled on his string like a puppet, his stubby legs windmilling, furious Italian words that could only be curses rolled off his lips, turning the air quite blue.

Now, how in the world...? a fascinated Angel wondered, frowning and looking about her. Yet even as the question popped into her head, Nick appeared beside her. His hand snaked out, cruel fingers clamping around her wrist so tightly, she yelped in protest.

"Ouch!"

"Ouch hell! Move!" he hissed. His crackling silver-blue eyes dared her to argue.

"But . . . move where?"

"We're. Leaving. Now. The carriage. Walk!" he ground out, clearly unable to formulate complete sentences in his fury.

"Very well. But first, how did you—?"

"Antonio? Lariat. Rope trick. Quit jawin' an' git!" he snarled, chivvying her down the pathway toward the villa's carriage house.

Reluctant to anger him further, she "quit jawin" and "got."

Nick lounged on one side of the covered carriage, his shoulders slumped, his arms hugging his chest, and his long legs stuck out, while Angel perched primly on the seat opposite, her hands clasped in her lap like a nervous schoolgirl. Random gaslight spilled through the carriage windows as the horse clip-clopped back toward the city of Paris. It revealed that he was scowling horribly, and his livid expression irritated Angel. If anyone should be angry, it was her, not him.

"It wasn't my fault!" she protested, not for the first time.

"You drank too damned much."

"I'm not used to drinking! And besides, you kept offering it to me. If I am drunk, that's why!" she fibbed. "Because of you!"

"Little liar! You seriously tryin' to tell me you didn't drink at Bligh's? Come on, lady, I'm not the fool you take me for! I'd bet hard money you've been tippling since you were weaned from your mama's titty!"

Her cheeks flamed at his calculated crudity, born, she guessed, of his anger. And, in her upset that he would use such language in her presence, she didn't even notice that he'd mentioned Bligh's. "Well, perhaps I *did* overdo the champagne a tiny bit," she allowed grudgingly. "But I did

142

not go into the gardens with Antonio willingly."

"No?" he mocked. "Then what did he do t' get you there? Carry you off over his shoulder like a sack o' corn feed?"

"Yes! I suspect he did exactly that!"

"Aw, for Chrissakes!" he growled, disgusted with her innocent act.

"Believe what you wish, sir. That *is* what happened. He even admitted as much," she said defiantly, tossing her head.

"Sure, honey, sure. And he took you to that shack with no encouragement from you, right?" he jeered.

She blinked at his tone, sensing something more than anger in it. "Why, Mr. Durango! If I didn't know better, I'd swear you were jealous!" she accused suddenly.

Something flickered in his steely pale blue eyes. "Jealous, hell! Don't flatter yourself, missie. I'm just doin' my job. Nothing more. And you can thank your lucky stars I am. If I hadn't happened along when I did, you'd have been a—goner!" For want of a cruder word.

"Ruined, you mean? Dishonored? Ha! Don't flatter yourself, sir! It was a well-placed knee in the bounder's middle that saved me, not you, Mr. Johnny-come-too-lately!" she ground out.

"You reckon so, huh, you mule headed little fool? Why d' you think 'Tonio was loping down the path after you? To ask you t' tea? T' beg the last dance?" He shook his head and snorted in disgust. "No, darlin'—he was fixin' to get into your drawers!"

"My—*oh!*" His coarseness left her speechless. Faint.

"You heard me right. And come t' think on it," he drawled hatefully, "why in hell didn't you make tracks for the house once you'd broken loose, 'stead of hangin' around waitin' for him?"

"Exactly what are you implying?" she demanded, quivering all over with fury, her eyes narrowed feline slits as she sprang to her feet.

"Just what I said, honey! Maybe you were just playing hard t' get? Maybe you *wanted* that oily son of a bitch t' catch up with you?"

"Why, you foul-mouthed cad! How dare you insinuate that I encouraged his filthy attentions!" she cried. Swinging about, she drew back her hand, intending to slap his face with all her strength and wipe the mockery from it.

But in that moment, the carriage rounded a street corner. The turn unbalanced Angel. She was lurched off her feet, flung across the vehicle's interior, and thrown heavily across Nick's lap.

He grunted and his arms went around her. He fully intended to restore the conniving little witch to her seat, but somehow, it didn't work out that way. Somehow, his arms went around her and stayed there. And somehow, his dark head dipped as he arched her across his lap. His right hand splayed across the back of her head, weaving through her softly piled ringlets as he drew her close, closer, closest, knowing he was a fool, but doing it anyway; knowing he'd hate himself later, but unable to help himself in that moment, he wanted her so badly.

The flowery, powdery fragrance of her hair and skin filled his nostrils; the warm sweet curves of her body pressed against his—and he was lost! Deceitful little bitch she might well be, he thought, but she made a fever rage through him! Spoiled little liar she'd proven herself, time and again—but she made rivers of fire pound through his veins.

Twice he whispered her name like an anguished prayer, his voice low and urgent on the shadows. There was a lightning instant as the *fiacre* rumbled beneath a gaslight when their eyes met, silvery-blue to startled smoky-gray, then his hard mouth came down and covered hers, crushing her soft lips like rose petals beneath it.

His mouth was demanding, hungry, as he tasted her sweetness for the very first time. She whimpered as his tongue-tip traced her lips, parting them, thrusting between them as he kissed her lingeringly, igniting bonfires deep in her body. Their tongues met, played sensuously together, twisting, tasting, before he thrust deeper and still deeper inside her mouth, a pirate plundering its honeyed velvet.

His kisses surpassed her wildest dreams! They were so unlike Reggie's chaste, disappointing kisses; they were so dangerous—and far, far too exciting for safety! Knowing she should fight her body's treacherous responses, she uttered husky pleas for release—pleas she never intended or wanted him to answer! She squirmed, trying desperately to escape his hold—but perversely, she gloried in her helplessness when she could not, when he would not, free her. Against Nick's lean, hard strength, she was weak and oh, so vulnerable! He was too strong, too powerful by far. What else could she do, but succumb to his seduction? To struggle against such a man would be futile . . .

And so, absolved, she closed her eyes and arched her body to his, surrendering to the wicked sensations of his mouth, yielding all to the fiery torch of his lips as the coach rumbled on.

As they kissed, he caressed her straining curves, cupping each satin-clothed breast. He rubbed the tiny peaks that rose beneath the slippery fabric until they grew firm as nuggets of gold between his fingers. Then—with a suddenness that left her breathless—he pulled down the bodice of her ruby gown and bared her breasts for his hungry mouth.

He took each swollen nipple between his lips in turn, laving the sensitive flesh with his tongue, suckling her gently, then harder, until she gasped and moaned in bittersweet torment and knotted her fingers in his ink-dark hair. Dear God, oh, dear Lord! His bold caresses had awakened longings and sensations she'd not known she possessed before; stirred a sensual, pulsing warmth, fueled a dormant hunger, in the hidden, secret core of her being that only he could ease.

His mouth left her breasts. His hands moved caressingly over her rounded hips, swept down the length of her legs to the hem of her gown. Grasping the slippery fabric, he thrust up the layers of satin and silk that denied him the smooth softness of her bare skin. With a groan against her mouth, he cupped the firm globes of her bottom and drew her up, across his thighs, until her hips were pressed to the hard ridge of his arousal, cursing the wedge of clothing

145

that kept them apart. She wanted him! Wanted him as badly as he wanted her! The answering pressure of her soft curves as she molded herself to him drove him wild; wild with the need to have her, take her, to bury himself deep in her sweetness and warmth. . . .

Feeling the thrust of his hardness against her, she inhaled sharply. Her heart was thundering! Her breath came hard and fast as Nick twisted her beneath him, draping her across the black leather seat. Crouching over her, a dark panther poised over its kill, he showered her throat with kisses; trailed burning lips over the bared curves of her bosom. Then, reaching beneath her voluminous skirts, he thrust them up, thrust aside her layers of petticoats to stroke her stockinged limbs, to feel that silken flesh encased in more silk.

She swallowed, holding her breath as his hand rose higher and higher. The thunder of her pulse grew louder, faster in her ears, as his calloused hand parted her thighs. When she resisted, he took her hand in his and placed her palm over the straining buttons of his breeches.

"Sweetness, feel what you do to me," he demanded huskily. "I can make you feel the same—Let me show you, pretty darlin' . . . Let me . . ."

He caressed the sensitive skin of her inner thighs again, doing so with little feathery, circular caresses of his fingertips that were so very gentle, they made her shiver anew. With barely a pause, he slipped his hand down to her knee, inside her lacy garter, and smoothly loosened the ribbon to remove it, then rolled down her stocking to fondle her slender legs. She clung to him, drowning in need, making little gasping sounds deep in her throat as he slid his hand inside the leg of her pantalets and cupped the fleecy vee of her maiden hair. His boldness brought her up off the leather seat with a shocked gasp. "Oh! Please—you mustn't! Not there!"

But Nick only soothed her with still more kisses, raining them over her cheeks, nuzzling her throat and lips until she moaned and lay back, feeling delirious with the sensations bursting through her. He slipped his hand between her thighs, his finger gently plundering the silky

146

fleece to find the tiny, hidden bud of her passion. With a knowing touch, he stroked her there, caressed and parted the velvet petals of her sex, and brought her hidden blossom to dewy flower. Shameless now, wanton in her first passion, she pleaded with him to end her torment.

"Please oh please, Nick—!" she whimpered throatily, pride and anger vanquished in her passion. "Please, do *something!* I don't know how—oh! Help me!"

"Soon, sweet thing," he whispered. "Soon!"

He dipped his head, replacing his hands with lips and tongue. Shocked, she cried out in protest, but he caught her wrists and gently pinned them to her sides with a gruffly whispered "Don't! Let me . . ."

In one moment, she felt his breath rising hot and moist against her inner thighs, and then in the next, oh Lord, he was tasting the secret essence of her being, bringing her to a glorious, frenzied release in a way she had never imagined. A tiny shriek escaped her as his tongue stroked and teased her. Another second—another exquisitely pleasurable caress there—and she would surely die of pleasure! What he was doing made her burn with shame . . . ache with sweet agony . . . go insane with mindless desire!

"Yes, sweet thing!" he groaned huskily, holding her hips fast as she writhed beneath him. "That's how! Let go, little darlin . . . Let it all go—and fly!"

She sobbed and grew tense and still, for the towering wave of pleasure had suddenly crested and carried her over the edge to release. Surge after surge of the sweetest sensation was pulsing and pouring through her body, ending her agony, lifting her to rapturous heights of searing pleasure and breathless fulfilment, before letting her drift slowly, slowly back down to reality and quiet content.

For a few moments, she lay stunned, breathing shallowly. She was too drained to move, too sated and emptied to do anything but listen to the wild thunder of her heartbeat as it gradually returned to normal.

"Good?" Nick murmured as if from the end of a long, velvety tunnel. He smiled down at her in the shadows.

"Mmmm," she murmured drowsily and nodded, only dimly aware that he was freeing the buttons of his breeches. A still detached, questioning part of her mind wondered what on earth he was doing. . . .

"*Hotel St. Pierre*, m'sieu!" the cabbie suddenly sang out, rapping sharply on the *fiacre's* roof with his whip handle.

With a jolt of shock, Nick realized the *fiacre* had halted. That they'd reached Rue Cologne and the hotel. He swore under his breath. "Once more down the boulevard, Henri!" he growled. "Don't stop 'til I give the word, *hombre*." The timbre of his voice was husky, ragged with lust for the disheveled beauty sprawled beneath him.

"Very well, m'sieu."

But the cabbie's voice had acted like a deluge of cold water on Angel. It served to bring her back to the present—and her senses—in the nick of time. Shame flooded through her as she recalled her abandon of moments before . . . the wicked things she'd said . . . begged him to do . . . the shocking liberties she'd allowed him to take! Dear Lord, what had she been thinking? Had she gone mad, that she'd lain here so shamelessly and let Durango take his pleasure of her? Belatedly she understood what he intended to do next, and knew she couldn't—wouldn't—mustn't—go through with it. If she left now—at once!—if he let her leave—she might yet be able to chalk this horrid interlude up to experience, and keep her innocence intact.

"Stop!" she protested, pushing down her skirts as she struggled to sit up. She thrust Nick's hands away. "Please, I must go. This has already gone way too far. Cabbie, wait—!"

"Don't, Angel. Don't go—not now." Nick's voice was low yet insistent.

"I must. Really! This—this is utter madness. I should—you should—it should never have happened. None of it. Ever!"

"You wanted it—and you want me, just as I want you. Tell me, where's the madness in that? We've both been around some. We know the score, hmm?"

"I—I can't. We mustn't. An—an affair is quite out of the

question. Besides, you and I—we're worlds apart, don't you see that? It wouldn't work. It's wrong. And besides, I'm promised—to—to someone else!"

"Smythe-Moreton?" Nick hissed his contempt. "I've heard a bellyful about that greenhorn. But does he make you feel the way I do? Does he make you burn, Angel? Does he get you so blamed excited, you beg him to—"

"No!" she cut in, furious and, if the truth were known, mortified by her earlier behavior. "Of course I don't act like this with Reggie!" she denied. "It's the champagne—I drank far too much, or I would never have—! Oh, please, let me go inside? It's late and I'm feeling quite unwell all of a—!"

"Why don't you act this way with Reggie? Don't you love him, Angel? Don't you desire him? Isn't desire a natural part of love? Of marriage?"

"Yes. No. Oh, I don't know anymore!" she wailed.

"He doesn't make you feel the way I do, does he? He doesn't excite you the way I do, because you don't love him, do you? It's his title that's got you dazzled! Come on, admit it, Angel," he urged huskily, nuzzling her ear. "I've seen you side-eyin' me, honey. I know, because I've been doing the same damned thing! You hate yourself for it, but it's me you want . . ."

"That's a lie! He—Reggie would never treat me in this disgusting fashion, because he worships me. He—he would never dream of being anything less than a—less than a perfect—"

"—gentleman?" Durango jeered.

"Yes, damn you, you insensitive clod, a gentleman. And he behaves that way because unlike you, he respects me."

"The hell he does! Reggie respects your pa's loot! Your fortune's what he worships, honey, not you. Come on! Open your eyes!"

"That's a filthy lie. Reggie's decent. Honorable. He's—he's always proper and correct. He's everything you could never hope to be!"

"Reggie's an ass! A bloodsucking sidewinder who preys on fool women like you!"

"Oh? And what, pray, are you?" she demanded, furious

149

that he'd malign Reggie. "What makes you better than him? You're nothing but a lusting animal—a common showman! An eccentric nobody! A rough, dirty cowboy!"

"And what does that make you, Angelica?" he asked softly, his ice-and-fire eyes blazing in the shadows. "A lady?"

"Yes!"

He snorted his contempt. "No way, honey. It takes a lot more than what you have right now to make a woman a lady. A lot more than money, and a hell of a lot more than a fine school and fancy clothes. Maybe more than you'll *ever* have, sweetheart—unless you take a good hard look at yourself and how you treat others before it's too late—! As for tonight," he smiled cruelly, "there's a name for women like you, honey. Women who lead a man on, get 'em all hot and bothered, then run out on 'em—but it sure as hell ain't 'lady!'"

She flinched. "Go to the devil, Durango, you bastard!" she hissed, quivering all over with outrage. So saying, she drew back her hand and slapped him hard across the face, as she'd itched to from the first.

The silence that reigned in the carriage following her slap was suddenly charged, crackling, electric. Though she was trembling uncontrollably, Nick moved not so much as a nerve or a muscle.

When she'd finally composed herself, she risked a glance at his face in the light spilling from the doorway of the St. Pierre, and saw that her anger was nothing compared to the dark rage smoldering in his features. His face was frightening, an unreadable mask, the face of a dangerous stranger, with the marks of her fingers striping his left cheek.

"As far as I'm concerned, nothing happened between us tonight," she gritted softly at length, trying to control her trembling. "We enjoyed a pleasant supper—but that is all we enjoyed. Attempt to force yourself on me again—to do anything other than the job you were hired for—and you will bitterly regret it, I assure you. Goodnight, Mr. Durango. And my thanks for a most—unusual—evening!"

With that farewell, she rose, smoothed down her skirts, flung open the *fiacre's* door, and plunged through it, running inside the hotel's vestibule before Nick could do or say anything to stop her, had he wanted to—which he didn't, by God!

"Where to, m'sieu?"

"Rue des Courtesanes, Henri. And step on it!" he barked.

"Certainly, m'sieu! I know just the very place!" the cabbie agreed. There was a knowing chuckle in his tone.

That damned, teasing little bitch! Nick thought as he threw himself back down across the leather seat. Drawing a cheroot and matches from an inner pocket, he lit the end and inhaled deeply.

The cabbie flicked his whip over the chestnut's rump, and the *fiacre* rumbled on.

Chapter Thirteen

"Room service!"

"Door's open, *amigo*. Come on in."

Grinning, Juarez entered as bidden, carrying a bottle of cognac by the neck in one hand and two glasses hooked over the fingers of the other. "Ah, what a pity! I have come to your rescue too late, *no?*" he observed, nodding at the half-emptied bottle of Scottish whisky on the nightstand beside Nick.

"Better late than never, pardner," Nick drawled, smiling a tight smile that never reached his eyes. "Have a seat and choose your poison. I stole this little sweetheart from Martine's private stores. Tastes smooth as silk going down," he added, gesturing at the Scotch, "but then she kicks like a *burro!*"

"Thanks, but no thanks." Juarez poured himself a glass of cognac and carried it with him to the opened French doors. Drawing aside the lace curtain to peer into the street below, he observed a tall, slim man standing in the shadows opposite the hotel as he sipped. He wondered absently what he was doing there, apparently watching the St. Pierre's entrance, but continued, "I will not ask how your evening with señorita Angel went. You would not be back so early nor drinking alone—or so heavily!—if things had gone well!"

"Don't even ask, *amigo*." Nick sighed, thinking of the pretty little mamzelle he'd turned his back on at the high-class cat-house on Rue des Courtesanes he'd visited. He still wasn't sure why he'd left, exactly, other than that the girl's eyes had been the same smoky gray as Angel's. . . . "I'm not rightly sure if she's a woman or a she-devil!"

"Because her eyes say one thing, but her lips another?"

"Partly."

"Do not lie to me, *hombre*. I know you too well! It is because she reminds you of Savannah."

Nick's head snapped sideways. His silver-pale eyes were veiled now, his jaw hard. "Hell, no!" he growled, tossing off the dregs of his Scotch.

"Hell, yes," Juarez argued mildly. "I saw it, too, *hombre,* from the first. That is why you are so hard on her, *no?*"

"Hard on her?" Nick echoed incredulously. "You're talkin' *loco!*"

"Am I?" Juarez shrugged. "Suit yourself. Believe what you will. But I see what I see, Cousin, and I know what I know. You see Angelica, remember why it is her father hired you, and you think of your own father, and of Savannah's deceit and betrayal. These memories, they make you very angry, and so you cannot be yourself. You wear your bitterness like a mask—to hide the man you are inside."

"Aw, hell, Juarez, enough! I'm in no mood for you t' start quotin' Tía Magdalena at me, *hombre!* Fact is, I'm a sorry son of a gun all around tonight. Not fit company for anyone. Get out of here!" he growled without malice. "Go on back to that wild redhead's bed."

Juarez grinned and fanned himself. *"Aiee, madre!* If my little red flower would but permit me to share her bed, I would not be here with you!" he said ruefully.

Nick allowed himself a grin. "Well, I'll be damned! You've got it bad, eh, *amigo?*"

"Sí! Like an arrow through the heart!" he agreed dolefully. "That *bruja!* She bewitches a man! It is as if she were not one woman, but many—and all of them fascinate me! What is a man to do if he would keep such a woman for himself, tell me that, Nick?"

Nick grinned wryly. "Ever thought of marriage, pardner?" he suggested, expecting Juarez to roar with laughter at such a notion.

"I think perhaps you are right . . ." he said thoughtfully instead. "Perhaps . . . perhaps it is the only way to keep her, eh, Nick?"

And on that pensive note, Juarez left, looking thoughtful and broody as an old hen—and taking his cognac with him.

After he'd gone, Nick lay back on his bed with his arms folded behind his head. He stared up at the ceiling, lost in thought. Juarez had been right, damn him, he considered. Angel did remind him of Savannah, more than he cared to admit.

Savannah. Beautiful, faithless Savannah! First his sweetheart—and then his stepmother, for Pete's sake! He laughed mirthlessly, remembering the expression on her lovely face when he'd told her the truth; when she discovered she'd married the wrong man!

New Mexico, back in '84, it'd been. He'd returned from a trip to Albuquerque—a trip he'd taken solely to buy her the fanciest diamond wedding ring money could buy—earlier than planned, and had surprised them together.

He could still recall the blanching shock of flinging open that door; he could even recall the damn-fool whoop of welcome and the words he'd uttered.

"Savannah, honey! It's Nick! Where are you? I'm back—and I have a present for you!" he'd called, a lovesick fool, searching through the cool adobe *corredores* of his *hacienda* for the woman he'd loved and sworn to wed. But there had been no answer, no Savannah running to greet him . . . and moments later, sick to his belly, he had discovered why. The box with the ring and the sheaf of white roses had fallen unnoticed from his hands.

"Easy now, son. I can explain. This ain't what you think," his father had begun, holding up a hand as he slid nervously from the bed, reaching for his pants with a flickering glance toward Nick's gun hand. "Savannah and me, we were married yesterday, in Santa Fe. We love each other, son! We wanted to tell you, but—"

"—but we didn't know how to do it without hurting you, Nicky," Savannah had supplied for his old man in a

154

tone as smooth and sweet as honey.

Damn her, she'd sounded as if she was explaining a broken fingernail, not why his life had been torn up, turned inside out, his heart trampled on—!

As she drew the lace-edged sheets up about her breasts, her golden hair had been a wild tangle of silken skeins spilling down her back, spiraling down over her shoulders; her eyes had been languid, dewy; her lips reddened and swollen. She'd looked just as she'd looked after he'd spent the night making love to her, goddamn her! Seeing her that way had been a knife twisted in his gut, a blade that deepened the gaping wound already there. And there was nothing he could do about it. They were married, for Christ's sake. Behind his back, the woman he loved had been betraying him with his own father!

"Get out!" he'd breathed hoarsely, knowing he was walking a thin line between sanity, and a blinding white rage that could lead only to murder if they stayed. "Get out of my house. Get out of my life. Get out—and stay out!"

"I'm sorry, son," his father had tried to calm him.

"Sorry?" A smile of contempt had curled Nick's lips. "Sorry is what you claimed to be when you deserted me and Mama, remember, *Father?* She started dying the night you left—of a broken heart! And 'sorry' is what you were when you came crawling back here, eh, and heard that she was dead? Crawling back, whining that you'd made a mistake—that you'd loved us and should never have left? Ha. Like a fool, I believed you—goddamn it, I *wanted* to believe you—more than anything I've ever wanted in my life! Oh, sure, I was a grown man on the outside, but on the inside—! On the inside, you son of a bitch, you bastard, there was a little boy who still wanted his papa to come home to stay."

"Nick, I—"

"Shut up, old man!" he hissed. "Just . . . just shut up and go!"

"Please, son, hear me out! I've never been a strong man like I shoulda been, you know that, and so do I. You— well, I reckon you were born strong, like your mama's

155

people. Mighty proud folks, the Spanish. Tough. Smart. They know how to make the land work for them. But me, well, I'd never amounted to much. I left Texas when I was fourteen and never went back. I just drifted from place to place, doing enough work to put food in my belly and get by on 'til the money ran out and I had to start all over again. Guess you could say I was a cowboy, 'cos I did a little of everything. Riding herd. Some wrangling. Branding. Roping. And then one day, I hired on here at Rancho Diablo, to work for your grandaddy, Don Carlos. Helping out with the spring roundup, I recollect."

"Where's this going, old man? Hurry it up!" he'd gritted, knotting his fists.

"It was soon after that, I saw your mama for the first time. Doña Serena, they called her. Lord, she was the prettiest little thing I'd ever seen, and I had me an eye for beautiful women even then. Didn't take long, I knew I loved her something fierce—and I couldn't hardly believe it when your mother said she felt the same about me. 'Course, her pa wasn't none too happy about his high-born little gal marrying a drifter, one of his *vaqueros*, but when he saw he'd have to give in, or she'd run off with me first chance she got, he gave his permission and we were married. What I'm tryin' t' say is, I—I *meant* to do right by her, son, I swear it! I loved Serena! But . . . after you were born and your grandaddy Carlos passed on, the running of the ranch fell to me. I—I couldn't handle it, son."

"And so you ran."

"Yes!"

"You old fool! You don't have to explain anything to him—not a damned thing!" Savannah had flared triumphantly, reaching for the ruffled white robe at the foot of the bed and slipping into it. "His mother—Don Carlos—that's all in the past. Finished! You're back, Gil, honey, and you're in charge here now. You don't have to answer to him!"

"That's where you're wrong, Savannah," Nick'd said softly, a bitter smile curving his lips.

"What!"

"Did you tell your bride everything, Father? Or only

156

what she wanted to hear?"

Savannah turned to her new husband. Seeing his expression, his fear, her exquisite face had grown hard as nails, showing a side of her nature she'd kept well-hidden from Nick during their whirlwind courtship of three months, a romance that had begun with a waltz at the Governor's Ball in Santa Fe. "What's he talking about, Gil? Tell me!"

"I'll tell you. The *hacienda's* mine, Savannah, honey," Nick had drawled, relishing the horror that had crept into her eyes. "This house, and every damned thing in it. The land, the herd, the horses, the money—all of it's *mine*. My father doesn't have a dime to his name that doesn't come from me! You've hitched yourself to an old man, *muchacha*—to a brokendown, penniless old fool!"

"You're lying!" Savannah had screamed as she sprang toward him, her nails curved into talons to rake his face.

He'd caught her wrists easily and forced them down to her sides, hating and loving her at the same time as he held her back.

"No, Savannah! The only one who's been lying around here is you—and your husband. My mother learned what her husband really was—discovered that he was weak. She knew that if he came back here someday, tried to take over the land, he'd lose everything her family had worked for over the years. Don Carlos, my grandfather, had willed the land to her, as his eldest daughter. And she, upon her death, left it to me. Rancho Diablo is *my* inheritance from her—and he can't touch so much as a clod of Diablo earth or a nickel of her wealth without my say-so."

"Noooo!"

"Yes! You married the wrong man, Savannah, honey—but right or wrong, he's the one you'll be leavin' with . . ."

"You married the wrong man, Savannah, honey . . ."

Nick pressed his fingers to his temple where a knot of pain lodged, throbbing mercilessly, a result, he knew, of reliving that day. Over two, almost three, years had gone by since then, but remembering Savannah's betrayal still had the same effect on him. Maybe it was because he'd trusted her so completely, been betrayed so badly—and yet

157

had still loved her so desperately—he'd had to leave New Mexico to put her out of his heart. . . .

"Cor! Look at your lips! They aren't half swelled up!" Mabel exclaimed the following morning, gaping at Angel. She grinned slyly. "I don't need ter ask what you was up to last night, do I, you dark 'orse, you! 'Hateful' man indeed! Good kisser, was he, luv?" she asked innocently.

"I really don't know what you're talking about, Blunt," Angel, seated at the writing desk in her suite, denied aloofly, though color immediately filled her cheeks. Studiously ignoring Mabel's curious expression, she added a final flourish to her signature and carefully blotted the note she'd written with blotting paper, before rereading it with a critical eye. "There! That should do the trick." Standing, she folded the sheet of paper and handed it to the other woman. "Off you go, then, Mabel."

Mabel scowled. "This is bloomin' stupid, it is! Why should I go traipsin' down the bloody hall to 'is room, when the connecting door's right there? You could slide the note underneath it, easy as winkin', you could . . . ?"

"No! That won't do it. Durango has to see you *before* we switch places and clothes, for my plan to work," Angel explained with an exasperated expression. "Now, run along, do, and stop complaining. I feel a sick headache coming on."

"Sick headache?" She snorted. "La-di-da! What you've got, mi'lady, is a whoppin' great 'angover," Mabel corrected her. With a grin, she skipped from the room before Angel could argue the point—or throw something.

The corridor was deserted, Mabel saw. At this hour, most of the St. Pierre's guests were out on the terrace, enjoying a leisurely breakfast. She caught a glimpse of a maid's gray skirts and feather duster as she whisked inside a room farther down, and waited a moment before scampering down the hall herself.

She stopped before Nick's door. It was closed, but by pressing her ear to the jamb, Mabel could hear him moving around inside. Good. He was awake. Looking furtively up, then down the long, carpeted hallway, she unfolded the note and read it.

Mr. Durango, it began briskly,
I'm sure you'll understand that I find myself a little under the weather this morning. Accordingly, I shall forego my customary ride in the Bois in favor of a less strenuous excursion. To this end, I've ordered breakfast in my room, and requested that a landau be sent around for me at nine. I plan a quiet morning spent in prayer and meditation at Notre Dame Cathedral, should you question my whereabouts.

"Question my whereabouts!" Cor, she was as crafty as a bleedin' fox, Angel was, Mabel thought, almost choking with laughter. She knew bloody well Durango stuck to her like glue! She shook her hennaed head, making the long, curling feather in the big-brimmed green hat she was wearing jiggle. How much longer would it take the pair of 'em to realize which way the wind was blowing, and just why they always rubbed each other the wrong way . . . ? Poor old Nick! Angel knew bloody well he'd follow her, note or no note—or rather, *think* he was following her! The poor sod took his promise to Sid Higgins far too seriously not to—among other reasons for wanting to keep his eye on her! Still, what business was it of hers? With a shrug, Mabel rapped smartly on Nick's door.

"It's Mabel Blunt, luv," she called out. "Are yer decent?"

"Nope. But come on in anyway, Red."

She bounced inside, grinning as she saw Nick standing before the mirror. He was lathering his stubbled jaw, a shaving brush in one hand and a steaming water mug in the other. A cutthroat razor had been set neatly in readiness on a folded towel to his right.

"Mornin', ducks!" she sang out. "Post's here!"

"Post?" He frowned.

"Mail. See, I've a letter! A billy-doo for you from Her Majesty, no less." Mabel rolled her eyes, fanning herself

159

with the note as she admired Nick's bronzed bare chest, his lean flanks encased in fitted tan breeches. She made no attempt to hide her admiration. He was a loverly looking bloke, an' no mistake.

"Thanks, Red." Nick winked at her reflection in the mirror and grinned as he took up the razor. "You can leave it on the dresser."

"Right you are, luv. See yer later."

With that, Mabel left and returned to Angel's room.

"Well? How did it go?" her young mistress asked, rising from her chair before the dressing table with a look halfway between dread and breathless expectancy.

"Like clockwork, you twit. I in't stupid, you know. I am capable o' delivering one bleedin' letter!"

"I know, I know. Now, out of that gown and into this white one—and *do* hurry! It's half-past eight already! We don't have much time . . ."

At nine on the dot, a rented open landau with matched gray horses pulled smartly away from the pavement fronting the Hotel St. Pierre. The vehicle had a single occupant: a young lady, clearly of some refinement, lounged against the leather seats. She was wearing a pristine white morning gown, adorned with flounces of white lace and pink-silk rosettes. A huge white chapeau with a veil hid her face. A ruffled white parasol angled elegantly over her left shoulder completed her stylish spring ensemble. It was a gown the charming Mademoiselle Angelica Higgins favored, the *commissionaire* noted, doffing her a smart salute. She wore it often.

Before the open carriage had turned the corner and vanished from view amidst wagons and milk carts, horse-drawn trolleys, and similar vehicles that rumbled or clattered over the cobbles, a dark-haired man riding a frisky black stallion with a silver-trimmed American saddle exited the mews alongside the St. Pierre. He set off down Rue Cologne after the landau, to the delight of the pair of sparkling gray eyes peeking through lace curtains three stories above the boulevard.

Hugging herself with glee at the success of her diversion, Angel let the lace curtain drop. Nick had taken the bait, confound the man! For the moment, she was free of him!

She crammed Mabel's green velvet hat down on her upswept hair and thrust a hat pin in place to keep it securely atop her head, almost braining herself in her triumph. Turning this way and that, she inspected her reflection in the mirror. Satisfied that her "disguise"— Mabel's best green velvet jacket and matching skirt—was adequate, she left her suite for the St. Pierre's stables and the mount she'd reserved in Mabel's name.

Glancing at the fob watch pinned to the front of the velvet jacket as she trotted her chestnut gelding down Rue Cologne, she saw that the time was nine-fifteen. Perfect! A half-hour's ride to the Bois, fifteen minutes to the toy-sailboat pond, and she would meet her dearest Reggie. And, after last night's alarming faux pas with that awful Durango—a direct result, she'd convinced herself, of the large quantity of champagne she'd guzzled—she could hardly wait to see him again.

Renewing her affection for Reggie would force that awful Nick and the memory of his loathsome, brutal kisses and near violation firmly out of her mind! Why, just thinking about what had almost happened in the darkened coach made her heart thump uncontrollably with what must surely be fear? Her gloved hand left the reins. Her fingertip strayed to her swollen lips, touched them experimentally. That Durango was an animal—a crude, lusting brute who preyed on innocent young women he'd sworn to protect! Why, her mouth still tingled this morning, hours after the incident. Butterflies danced in the pit of her stomach just thinking about what he'd done to her, how boldly he'd caressed her, how brazenly, while breathing into her ear in a way that had made gooseflesh crawl the length of her arms.

Reginald, on the other hand, had never taken such liberties with her person, bless him. As she'd so hotly told Durango, he'd always been a perfect gentleman. A chaste, respectful kiss once in a while . . . a clandestine embrace in the darkened corner of some gaming hall they'd frequented with their "fast" crowd . . . a lingering look across the supper table from soulful blue eyes . . . all perfectly dull stuff. *Dull?* Good Lord! What was she thinking! She caught herself in midthought and gave a shaky little laugh. She'd meant "proper," not dull, of course she had! Or "correct"? Or "considerate," even? Yes, she amended firmly, something along those lines. Reggie was titled, a peer of the realm. Consequently, he could never be dull!

The usual plague of little boys in brown knickerbockers and jackets were hanging over the sailboat pond, urging their tiny craft across the glassy water with sticks. Beneath shady trees sat their uniformed nannies, gossiping, and benevolently nodding and smiling at their antics, perhaps with a younger brother or sister in lacy gown and frilly bonnet cooing in a perambulator at their sides. Lovers walked hand in hand along the little pathways circling the pond, starry-eyed shop girls and accounting clerks escaping their dreary jobs for a few blissful minutes in the spring sunshine. A *gendarme* swinging a night stick tipped his billed cap to her as she rode past and wished her a very good morning, which she coolly returned as she looked about her for some sign of Reggie. He was nowhere to be seen.

No matter. There was a wrought-iron post for tethering mounts close by the pond, a mounting block set conveniently before it. Angel dismounted and looped her horse's reins through the post, smoothing down her skirts as she crossed the grass toward a wooden bench beneath a tree. She would sit there, watch the passersby and wait for him. Punctuality, she recalled, was not one of Reggie's sterling qualities, though perversely he deplored anyone being late for *his* appointments. She supposed this annoying little character quirk had something to do with being raised with servants to attend one's every whim. . . .

"Angel, dearest!"

She rose and turned as Reggie plunged from the woods

at her back.

"Reggie!" she cried. She would have thrown herself into his arms had he not forestalled her by reaching out and taking her hand, decorously drawing it to his lips instead. "How—how wonderful it is to see you!"

"And you, poppet! I say, I hardly recognized you in that awful get-up. Hardly the latest in Paris fashion, what, old girl?"

"My maid and I switched clothes. It was the only way I could think of to meet you without Durango following me here."

"Durango. Oh. Yes. Durango's the man your father hired, the American fellow?"

"One of them, yes. And a simply awful brute he is, too. Oh, Reggie, he watches me like a hawk—won't let me out of his sight for a moment!"

"But you *did* manage to evade him this morning?" Reggie asked. He looked nervously about, as if expecting someone to leap out from between the dense trees at their backs and assault him.

"I did—tho' not without some difficulty."

"Thank God! Well, dear heart, shall we take a little promenade through the woods, away from all these noisy little brats? We can talk privately there." He offered her his arm, and with a smile, Angel took it.

Side by side, they wandered between the towering trees. The leafy boughs dappled their faces with sunlight and shadow as they strolled, arm in arm, amongst the Bois, Reggie going on and on about his doings since they'd seen each other last, Angel silent and thoughtful and—though she'd never admit it—more than a trifle bored, if truth were known.

Reggie seemed not to notice. He rabbitted on about how Neville, his tailor, was threatening legal action to recover the money Reggie owed him, and had already engaged a solicitor for that purpose. About how Bill Bligh had gotten wind that his creditors were closing in on him, and had called in his gambling markers, demanding immediate payment and threatening violence if he was unable to come up with the money.

163

"So you see, my darling, we have no choice, not anymore. My situation is terribly desperate!" he cried, suddenly grasping her by the upper arms and turning her to face him. "Angelica. We *must* be married!"

"What?" To be honest, she hadn't heard a thing Reggie'd said after the first few words. She thought she must have misheard his sudden declaration.

He scowled. "I said, we must be married."

To her amazement, he gathered her roughly into his arms and crushed his lips down upon hers, kissing her so roughly and so clumsily that Mabel's atrocious hat fell off and rolled away. Angel was breathless when he finally released her to demand, "So, poppet? When shall it be? Name the happy day!"

"When . . . ?" she echoed stupidly.

"Our wedding!" Reggie exclaimed, his eyes shining. Irritated, he shoved a blond cowlick from his brow. "Come on, old girl, don't be coy, there's a love. You knew very well that our wedding was the 'matter of importance' I referred to in my letter, didn't you?"

"Well, ye-es," she admitted truthfully. She'd suspected as much. "But—"

"But what? There are no 'buts,' Angelica. It's the obvious thing to do! The perfect solution to both of our financial—er—quandaries. Once we're man and wife, your father will have to accept me. And then—"

"And then the large settlement Da has promised to make me upon my marriage will get you cosily out of debt and see you comfortably off for the remainder of your life—oh!"

She broke off, astounded by what she'd said. Good God! Had she really been thinking that of him, let alone found the courage to say it, she wondered, shocked? The words had literally popped out of her mouth—and so coldly, too.

Reggie's adoring smile dimmed. For a fleeting second, his expression of bored indolence slipped, replaced by a twisted mask of fury and desperation that revealed a side of Reggie's character she'd never seen before or, for that matter, ever dreamed existed. A side that was, in all honesty, rather frightening. . . .

164

But then, just as swiftly as he'd changed, he resumed his good-natured smile, and she fancied the ugly expression she'd glimpsed must have been a trick of the light playing through the leaves.

"Oh, come on, old girl," he coaxed silkily, tracing the lovely contours of her face with a long tapered finger, "you know that's not the only reason. Not by half! I love you, Angelica. Truly, I do. More than anything in this world, I want you to be my bride. My own adorable Lady Angelica Smythe-Moreton."

Angel smiled. But . . . where was the carillon of bells, the covey of white doves, the bursting sky rockets she'd always imagined filling the air in the happy moment when Reggie confessed he loved her? She felt nothing, neither joy nor elation. Rather, his admission seemed forced to her ears, tainted by his earlier recounting of his debts. Every word he said seemed suddenly false, calculated, spoken to achieve a purpose. Suddenly fearful, she bit her lip. How could she tell if he truly loved her? How could she be certain that he was not simply a fortune hunter after her father's wealth, as her shrewd da had claimed after meeting him only a time or two? She'd been so eager to see him. So anxious to hear him say the words he'd just said. But now, after not seeing him for almost a month, her feelings toward him had changed beyond all recognition. His confessions of love made her feel peculiarly hollow inside, letdown. Used.

For an instant, her treacherous thoughts turned inexplicably to Nick. She found herself comparing him with Reggie for the teeniest instant—and in a way that made Reggie come off a sorry second-best. Not in a million years could she ever imagine Nick Durango swearing love to a woman in order to gain access to her fortune. Never! He was simply not the kind of man who would let a woman support him. When Nick found the woman he loved, Angel knew there'd be no shilly-shallying, no pleading or argument. He'd simply throw her over his shoulder—or rather, his horse—and carry her off, making her his in that no-nonsense, masterful way he had. . . .

"What's wrong, poppet? Overwhelmed you with my

165

admission, have I?" Reggie grinned nervously. What the devil was wrong with her? She wore a dreamy smile and had a faraway look in her eyes that was in keeping with his proposal . . . and yet, he couldn't shrug off the feeling that she'd hardly heard him. Taking her icy hand in his, he kissed it, darting an anxious look at her impassive face. What was going on behind those pensive gray eyes? Had the chit's father written to her, he wondered suddenly? Was that it? Did she already know somehow about the scandal that had driven him from England, cast an everlasting blot of suspicion upon his family's good name? Did that explain the changes he sensed in her feelings toward him?

"I can't marry you, Reginald," he heard her say as if from a long way off, and it was like a nail being hammered into his coffin. "Not now. Perhaps—perhaps never."

"What? See here, don't be hasty, old girl! At least think it over a day or two. You've been hinting that you'd like nothing better than to be my wife for the past three years, dash it all. Don't throw it all away in a moment of recklessness!" He was a drowning man, clutching at passing spars.

"That's true," she admitted slowly and then added in a firmer voice, "And I thought . . . I really believed that I loved you. But now, I'm not so sure anymore, Reggie. I think perhaps I was in love with the idea of being Lady Smythe-Moreton and not—and not . . ."

"And not me?" he ground out harshly, his fingers biting into her upper arms as he fought the urge to shake some sense into her.

Biting her lip, she shook her head. "No, I'm afraid not. You know, I do believe I've grown up a little this past month, Reggie. I suppose it's understandable—a result of being independent for the very first time in my life. Of having to make my own decisions. Perhaps there'll come a time—after I've tried my wings for a little longer—when I'll realize that I do love you, after all. But for now—!" she shrugged. "I'm very sorry. I can't accept your proposal."

"For now, you feel incapable of becoming my wife, is that what you're saying?" he rasped. "For now, you don't give a halfpenny for what happens to me! You don't care if my creditors are after my blood. Or if I live or die! Go ahead, say it, you common little upstart—you jumped-up little working-class nobody, always trying so very hard to be the lady of quality you never could be!—say what you really mean. Be 'Lancashire blunt,'" he sneered. "Admit that you don't give a tinker's damn about me!"

"Reggie!" she cried from the heart, wounded to the quick by his contempt, his jeering words.

"Don't 'Reggie' me, common Annie Higgins!" Reggie jeered. "In the future, you may address me as Lord Smythe-Moreton—*if* I should ever permit you to address me at all! So you think you're too good for the likes of me, hey? Ha! You and your father—you're the laughingstock of London, did you know that, Annie, dear? Sidney the Millionaire with his braces and his flat cap! Oh, crazy old Harry Brixton may well have left your father his fortune, but there are some things money can't buy. Breeding, dear heart. Class. Blue blood. You may have a thin veneer of culture over your country-bumpkin origins but that's all you have—a veneer! You'll die an old maid, Annie, luv!" he mocked, his expression contorted. "A filthy-rich, lonely old maid!"

The blood had drained from her face. Her eyes were huge gray pools of agony. A great weight lodged in her breast, one so enormous, it seemed to choke her throat. Scalding tears filled her eyes. "You bastard!" she whispered. "Is this how you've thought of me all along? You and the others were only using me, weren't you? You never accepted me, did you? All this time, you've been pretending—lying—!"

With a choked sob, she whirled and ran, fleeing blindly through the dense trees toward the pond.

Uttering a foul curse, Reggie started after her. He'd bungled everything and there'd be hell to pay now! He couldn't let her go, not like this. He had to smooth things over, somehow. . . .

"Angel, wait! Please, old girl, come back! I was upset. You turned me down, don't you see? I was hurt—I didn't mean a bloody word of it, I swear it! Angelica!"

He burst from the woods just as Angel viciously swung her horse's head about and kicked the poor animal into a swift canter, heading back down the path the way she'd come.

"Damnation!" Reggie ground out, his fists balled at his sides as he watched her ride away.

Unnoticed by Reggie, a tall dark-haired man wearing fringed buckskins was smoking a cheroot and watching him from the shade of a towering chestnut tree across the pond. A showy liver-and-white pony grazed the lush grass at his side.

After a few moments, the strangely attired man swung into the saddle and rode off in the same direction Angel had taken. Although the primly uniformed nannies, the *gendarme*, and the little boys by the pond stared after him with open curiosity, he gave no sign that he'd noticed any of them. He remained unsmiling and silent. His dark features were hard, his ice blue eyes glacial as they rested fleetingly on Smythe-Moreton's flushed, furious face.

And, as he rode past the Englishman, his gaze flickered away with an expression of contempt.

Chapter Fourteen

"That's enough fer now, gov'na."

"I'll decide when enough's enough, damn you. Gimme me that bo—hic!—bottle."

"Sorry, gov'na. Orders is orders. We've tried things your way. Now it's time t' try ours . . ." The man's fleshy lips parted in a wolfish smile over crooked, ivory teeth.

Reggie nodded nervously, glancing around the seedy room he'd rented above *Le Chat Mal*, a dingy little back-street restaurant on the Left Bank, as if searching for some avenue of escape. There was none, either from the dangerous situation he found himself in, or from the nauseating smell of boiled cabbage and garlic rising from the kitchen below to fill the windowless attic cell. Alas, the absinthe he'd gulped down after leaving the Bois had failed to dull his senses completely.

"It won't be easy," he said slowly. "There's the maid, Mabel Blunt? A tough little chit, I'd say. And there's that American lout her father hired to guard her, the one I told you about . . . ? Angelica says he watches her like a hawk."

"Durango?" The man chuckled, cracking his hairy knuckles. "Oh, I know all about bloody Nosy-Parker Durango and his sniffin' about! You let me and me brother worry about 'im, all right, gov'na?" His tone was almost kind, almost conciliatory. Almost.

Reggie nodded unhappily.

"Meanwhile," the man continued, an odd, anticipatory light in his eyes now, "The Boss told us t' be sure and send

169

you his fondest rgards . . ."

"Regards? From him?" Reggie echoed faintly. He half rose from the sagging *fauteil* as sudden understanding—and apprehension—squeezed his innards. "Good God! Surely you can't mean—!"

His answer was a set of brass knuckles that came out of nowhere and slammed into his face, blackening both eyes and smearing his broken nose across his face in crimson strings.

Angel's hands were still shaking when she wrenched open the door of her suite at the St. Pierre. Slamming it behind her, she leaned against the wood to catch her breath until she'd regained her composure somewhat.

Hands steadier now, she tore off Mabel's vulgar feathered hat and hurled it to the floor. With equal force and distaste, she yanked off her maid-companion's hateful green velvet jacket and skirt. She did so with such force, the buttons popped off and rolled under the bed. The buttonholes ripped. Wearing only her undergarments, she tottered to the bed and flung herself facedown across it. Her shoulders shook, then all at once she was sobbing uncontrollably, the scalding tears she'd held in check soaking the bedspread.

How could he? How could they? she asked herself, over and over. Anger had replaced much of her hurt on the return ride, yet she was still stunned, still unable to accept what Reggie'd scornfully flung at her. And yet, if true, it meant that he and Diana Forsythe, Corky Madison, Trudi Beauchamps, Algernon Fernsworth—all the members of the "fast" set she'd believed herself a part of—had been using her, laughing at her behind her back!

Hurt tears welled anew as she recalled how desperately lonely she'd been before Diana had befriended her, first at boarding school and in the years following, when her working-class origins had denied her a debutante's launching into society, and the coterie of female friends and eligible male suitors, the endless invitations, that went with a successful London season.

She bit her lower lip and blinked rapidly, her eyes

smarting. She'd tried so very hard to put the Lancashire cotton mills behind her and become one of them, so hungry for acceptance she'd not cared who she hurt in the process, from her dear father to the lowliest maid at Brixton Towers. In fact now, just thinking about the countless times she'd bullied poor Mabel into covering for her midnight excursions, filled her with shame and remorse.

Oh, yes, lies had piled up upon lies in her attempts to conceal her escapades from her father! In her efforts to be accepted, she'd risked everything that was important to her; her self-respect, her honor, her principles and values, and most precious of all, her father's trust. Conceivably she might lose his love, too, if he ever found out what she'd been up to, how she'd deceived him, lied to him, attempted to extort money from him. And for what? She swallowed another hiccupping sob. To impress a group of snobbish rakes and "fast" hussies who weren't fit for her da to wipe his mucky boots on, that was what!

Her joy when Reggie, Diana, and the others had finally seemed to accept her seemed pathetic now, the desperate, wishful thinking of a trusting child. Oh, how they must have laughed behind her back at her gullibility! How they must have chortled when they'd confided to each other how "dearest Angel" had eagerly loaned them a guinea or two without question on learning that they were "strapped" for funds. But, hungry for their approval— "You're a brick, Angelica! I shan't forget this!" or "Jolly good show, old girl! Thanks awfully!"—she'd never once refused them. Rather, she'd been *grateful* for the chance to help her "friends." Oh, how they must have snickered at her naiveté. . . .

"Damn it, woman, whatever that sidewinder said, it sure as hell ain't worth bawlin' over!"

On hearing Durango's deep voice, Angel shot bolt upright, as if she'd been stabbed with a pin. Twisting over onto her side, she saw him sitting in the wing chair beside the French windows that led out onto the balcony. He was twirling his Stetson about on one finger, while his right leg, booted to the knee in fancily tooled leather, was hooked over an elegant brocade arm. He was dressed, she

171

realized curiously, in the tan fringed buckskins that Juarez favored.

"Your room is next door, Durango, if you recall," she snapped frostily, ignoring his comment. "Please leave!"

His cool, assessing glance swept over her. Hooded ice blue eyes took in the sheen of tears on her damp, flushed cheeks, the mass of shiny cornsilk hair spilling about her shoulders in wanton disarray, all pins and combs lost. The tempting swell of her breasts, which rose like peaches from her lace-ruffled muslin chemise, promising soft-skinned delights he could remember only too well. . . .

Despite the promises he'd made himself last night in anger, after she'd fled the rented *fiacre*, damned if she still didn't make a mighty fetchin' sight, red-eyed an' bawling aside! But in answer to her imperious command, he only shook his head ruefully. "I'd like to, Angel. But—I can't!"

"Can't?" She sprang from the bed and stalked across the room, before whirling to face him, lips pursed, her fists planted on her hips. "And why not, pray?"

"Because you see, Miz Angel," he admitted with apparent reluctance, "this *is* my room."

"Your . . . ? Oh, don't be so ridiculous—!" she began, but couldn't help a furtive glance about her, all the same, just to make absolutely certain he wasn't telling the truth.

What she saw made her heart sink. There was not a single item of her clothing nor any of her personal belongings in the room, except for those she'd tossed carelessly aside earlier. However, masculine toilette articles were neatly arrayed on the bureau, and Nick's holster and six-guns were dangling from the back of an upright chair.

Seeing her dismay, he chuckled. "Aw, don't try to tell me you didn't know, sweet thing? That you didn't plan it this way—just the two of us, all on our little lonesomes?"

"I certainly did not!" she sputtered indignantly. "How dare you insinuate otherwise."

Nick grinned, his eyes dancing under lazy, sleepy lids. That was better, more like the Angel he'd come to know! She was so indignant now, she'd quit crying altogether— and he much preferred to see her outraged and spiritedly arguing than hurt and bawling. "How *dare* I? But you

172

know damned well there's not much Durango wouldn't 'dare'! Sashay on over here to me an' sit on my lap, angel lips. We can start where we left off last night, hmmm—?"

The challenging way he was looking at her, the tilt of his ebony head, that wicked sensual gleam in his devilish eyes, the lazy, teasing half-smile he was wearing, left her in no doubt what he meant.

A treacherous thrill of excitement skittered through her. Reluctantly, she remembered the swaying *fiacre's* darkened interior, the sharp turn that had spilled her into his hard lap, the hot, hungry kisses they'd—that *he'd*—enjoyed—let alone what he'd done next—the shocking intimacy he'd forced upon her. Closing her eyes, she swayed slightly, feeling suddenly dizzy, suddenly afire and icy-cold all at once. She was acutely aware that they were quite alone in his boudoir, that she was at his mercy, wearing only her undergarments—a scandalous combination of circumstances fraught with all manner of dire possibilities!

Durango was dangerous, a totally unprincipled rogue and libertine, a lecherous brute who might attempt any liberty upon a defenseless woman. He'd start with bold kisses, she suspected, as he had last night, kisses perhaps showered over throat and brow or even—shudder the thought!—forced upon her lips! Moist, masterful kisses that demanded some response! Intimate caresses would follow, those darkly tanned, callused male hands with sprinklings of black hair across the knuckles would stroke, would fondle, would roam everywhere over her helpless, trembling bare flesh. Next would come little nibbles at her fingertips—possibly even her toes. And then—she gulped, almost swooning—and then would come the coup de grace, when Nick tossed her, naked, to the bed and forced his hard body upon hers—! His hairy, tanned chest would crush her soft breasts as he pinned her beneath him . . . as he mastered her, possessed her utterly. . . .

Angel shuddered, rocked on her heels by her own fantasies. Dear Lord! The mere thought of Nick seducing her made her faint, weak at the knees—and far too excited for either decency or coherent thought. . . .

"I'm questioning neither your audacity nor your—" she

173

swallowed, tapered fingers straying to her ivory throat"—
your boldness, Mr. Durango. That dubious quality you
have proven beyond a doubt! I'm simply imploring you—
as a gentleman—to leave this room, so that I may dress and
return to my own."

"Sorry to disappoint you, honey, but I'm not leaving
you alone anymore—not even for a minute—because I
can't trust you, can I? You tried to give me the slip once
already today. And chances are better than even that you'll
try it again, sooner or later. So, I've decided t' go wherever I
have t' go t' keep an eye on you. Day or night."

"You mean, you intend to—to sleep in the same room as
I do from now on?" Her voice had grown shrill now.

"Yes, ma'am, I do! I figure if we're bunkmates, I can
make good and sure you don't go galloping off t' meet
that greenhorn pantywaist again."

"Reggie?" she blurted out without thinking, startled
that he knew about her rendezvous. She colored and
averted her face, furious at herself for her slip and
desperate to cover her mistake. "I'm afraid you're
mistaken, Durango. I went riding, that much is true. But I
certainly didn't 'gallop off' to meet anyone! I spent a
quiet morning in the cathedral of Notre Dame, praying
and thinking, so you see, I really don't know what you're
talking about. Now, if you'll be so g—"

"The hell you don't know! Shall I jog your memory,
Angel?" Nick suggested in a biting tone. He held up his
hand, counting off the points one by one as he covered
them. "First, you traded duds with Red and sashayed on
down to the Bois. Two, you left your horse by the sailboat
pond an' waited a spell. Three, Reggie showed up and the
two o' you took a real cozy little stroll beneath the trees.
You were arm in arm," he added, wondering at the sudden
sting of jealousy that bit him as he remembered. "Weren't
you, now?"

"You spied on me!" she cried. "You cad! You Peeping
Tom! You had no right, sir, none whatsoever!"

"Wrong, honey. I had every damned right," he argued
evenly and with no trace of remorse. "Your pa gave it to me
the day he hired me."

As he sprang to his feet and strode across the polished

wood floor toward her, he reminded her of a sleek, graceful panther, coiled to spring. She was suddenly afraid he intended to take her by the neck and choke her, so darkly furious was his expression, so cruelly thinned his lips. But to her relief, he halted a scant arm's length away and towered before her, his huge fists knotted at his thighs. "That's what I'm getting paid for, remember? To protect you and keep you out of trouble, right? Your pa's no fool. He had a hunch Smythe-Moreton might come sailin' across the Channel after you—or should I say, your fortune?" His dark brows rose. He smiled mockingly.

Tight-lipped, she said nothing. Besides, what *could* she say? It seemed everyone had guessed Reggie's true character but she, she thought miserably. Oh, what a silly goose she'd been!

That she made no attempt to defend Reggie, despite his insults, surprised Nick. Interesting. Whatever the pair had quarreled about, Angel'd obviously been hurt bad by it, he reckoned—perhaps the blinkers had finally been torn from her eyes, where Smythe-Moreton was concerned? Or was he way off the track? Maybe that sidewindin' Limey had tried to talk her into doin' something she didn't want to do—like stage another phony kidnapping? He wouldn't put it past him.

"Tell me, how did you guess—?" she demanded, wondering if Mabel had turned coat and told him everything.

"You mean, about you an' Red tradin' places?" Nick chuckled. "Honey, when a selfish brat like you bothers t' send a 'hired hand' like me a note t' let me know where she's going, it sets off alarm bells in my head! The minute I read it, I knew in my guts you were up to no good. 'Sides, Red's got more . . . jiggle . . . t' the way she walks than you do, if you know what I mean?" He winked lecherously. "The second she left the hotel, I knew my hunch was right. So, me and my pardner switched duds, too. I had Juarez follow her t' Notre Dame—and I followed you."

"I see. Then that explains it." The ease with which he'd seen through her "foolproof" ruse made her feel deflated like a pricked balloon.

Nick saw her crestfallen expression and grinned. "Aw,

don't look so down in the mouth, Angel. You gave it a damned good try. Trouble was, your pa wanted to hire the best—and that's just what he got when I took the job!"

"Oh, rubbish. The best, indeed. I've never met such an arrogant lout as you!"

"Why, thank you kindly, ma'am. Coming from you, I count that a real compliment."

"Compliment!" she retorted, frowning. "And just what do you mean by that?"

"Think about it some. It'll come to you, sooner or later."

"Then it will have to be later. Right now, I have neither the time nor the inclination for childish guessing games, Durango," she snapped, snatching Mabel's discarded skirt from the floor. She stepped into it with a wriggle that was a joy to behold, to Nick's thinking. Her breasts thrust forward as she reached behind her to fasten hooks and eyes with brutal finesse. She did the same with the jacket, almost wrenching the sleeves from the armholes in her haste to put it on. "Nor do I care to play those games with you!" she added. "Really, Durango, this ludicrous situation has gone on quite long enough. I refuse to answer to you for everything I do. To have you dictate to me whom I shall or shall not see one moment longer. And as for the two of us sharing a room—!" Her chin came up defiantly. Her gray eyes flashed. "I know I swore I'd never mention last night again, but since then, I've been thinking things over. First thing tomorrow morning, I intend to telegraph my father and demand that he terminate your employment immediately—! Good day, sir."

The infuriating man made no reply. Nor did he seem in the least perturbed by her threat. He merely inclined his head and grinned in that unsettling way he had.

Flinging about, she stalked toward the adjoining door, but remembered that it was stuck. Her dramatic exit ruined, she spun angrily about on her heels, headed for the door leading into the corridor—the door that Nick sprang to open for her with a mocking flourish and an overly courteous bow, damn his insolence.

"*Adios*, for now. I'll be joinin' you next door after I

change these duds, Duchess!" he promised with a wicked grin.

"Pray, don't hurry on my account!" she snapped. With a snort and a toss of her honey blond mane, Angel sailed past Nick into the carpeted hallway, flinching when the door behind her slammed shut so violently in her wake, it dealt her a hefty thwack across the bottom that jolted her forward. That weasel! He'd done that on purpose, confound him!

Holding the fronts of Mabel's ruined jacket together, she stalked down the hallway, alternately cursing Durango and thanking her lucky stars that there were no other guests about to witness her disheveled condition. But of course, there wouldn't be anyone, she reminded herself bitterly. *Normal* people were enjoying a genteel luncheon at this hour. Normal people who led normal lives unfettered by swarthy cowboys who kept closer to them than their own blasted shadows . . . How long would he give her to change for luncheon, before barging into her boudoir?

Muttering a descriptive, colorful curse that would have plunged her former headmistress into an immediate attack of the vapors, Angel flung open her door. With a sigh of relief, she stepped into the sanctuary of her sun-drenched room.

They jumped her the moment she entered!

Coarsely dressed men sprang from behind both door and dressing screen. They were on her so swiftly and suddenly, that for an instant, she froze. That instant proved her undoing, for when she opened her mouth to scream, someone stuffed a filthy rag between her teeth. Another someone threw a sack or something over her head.

Terror streaked through her. The intruders meant to suffocate her! To murder her! Blindfolded and gagged, she could hardly breathe! Her lungs were afire, bursting! Panicked, she blundered about, trying frantically to tear the sack from her head, spit the gag from her mouth, but rough hands grasped her wrists and wrenched her arms up, behind her back.

As bone ground against bone, she uttered a muffled

whimper of agony and struggled to escape, kicking out with her feet. Her riding boot struck one man solidly in the shin, but that small triumph was short-lived, for she was dealt a hefty punch to the side of her head that exploded stars in her skull and made her ears ring. Oh, God, she wanted to be sick—but if she was, she'd drown in her own vomit!

"That's quite enough o' that!" rasped a guttural voice. "Kick me again, Miss Toffee-Nose, an' you'll be bleedin' sorry you was born—!"

As she screamed impotently behind her gag, Angel's assailants wrapped her in something voluminous and stifling. It felt like her bedspread. Wound mummy-fashion about her, the folds pinned her arms to her sides and clamped her legs uselessly together. The blood pounded in her ears as the terrible truth struck home. There was to be no escape for her! She was their prisoner.

"I'll 'andle 'er Ladyship, Tiny. You check the 'all," growled a coarse voice.

A moment later, she was jerked off her feet and hoisted roughly over one of the louts' shoulders, much like a dusty carpet being readied for beating.

"All clear, then?"

"All clear it is. Get a move on!"

Her abductor lumbered forward, turning right so abruptly, her head thudded into the doorjamb.

"Careful, you bloody twit!"

She saw a shower of stars again but, careless of her discomfort, the oaf lurched on, wheezing loudly, with Angel flopping over his shoulder. They were taking her from her suite—probably leaving the St. Pierre altogether! She sensed that they were headed down the hotel corridor now—to the rear staircase? In another moment, it would be too late! Oh, please, let a maid or a bellboy—someone—see them! she prayed.

Off to her right, she heard the muffled click of a door opening, the squeal of hinges as it swung inward. *Thank God!* Her prayers had been answered. Someone was leaving their room. Surely they'd raise an alarm at the suspicious sight of two rough men carrying a body wrapped in a counterpane?

The man carrying her halted abruptly, his burly frame tensed for either flight or fight, she sensed. She wriggled and tried to cry out, but only gurgling grunts and piglike squeals escaped the gag and her binding.

"Well, well! 'S that you in there, Angel?"

She heard Nick's amused drawl and her spirits soared. The door had been his! Oh, thank God! Thank God! But her glee vanished as he continued in the same bantering tone, "High-tailin' it again, without tellin' me, huh? Shame, shame, you naughty girl! You didn't tell me you and your ugly friends were leaving so soon," he taunted with silky sarcasm.

"Shut yer trap, Yank!" growled the other man. "Just step back inside your door, nice an' easy—and don't try no funny business, mind! I'm good with this 'ere knife, see— and I in't afraid t' use it, neither! Make a move, an' the chit 'ere gets it good!"

"Hey, far be it for me t' keep you boys and lil' Miz Iron Drawers from your business. Fact is, I could use a spell away from wet-nursin' that little hellcat. *Adíos*, Angel, boys. Y'all have a fine old time, now!"

With that parting sally, Angel heard the door close and her hope of rescue died. Nick had gone! That—that bastard had left her to the tender mercies of these—these kidnapping *thugs*, sold her out without lifting so much as a finger to save her!

Anger surfaced as the two men bore her swiftly down the servants' rear staircase to the Paris back streets, pure, unadulterated fury that mercifully obliterated her fear. The man her father had trusted, admired, looked up to, and hired to protect her, had aided and abetted her abductors. And for that, he would pay! Ooooh, yes. Somehow, and in some way, she'd escape these uncouth ruffians—if only to come back and make absolutely certain that he did—!

Chapter Fifteen

"For Gawd's sake, get a move on, you chump! A toffee-nosed slut like her—lor, she's not going anywhere, are yer, darlin'—not 'alf dressed like that—so leave off with them bleedin' ropes and come *on!* We'll catch 'ell from the Boss if we're late, you know that."

"We'll catch more'n hell if she gets loose, you stupid twit!"

"I'm tellin' yer, Tiny, she won't get loose! She ain't that Houdini kid, now, is she?"

"Aw, all right. That's it, then, in'it? Them knots should hold 'er. Let's get goin'."

"What've I been telling yer, lad? It's past bloody time—!"

"I don't feel right about this, reely I don't," Mabel muttered as she and the two Americans strolled beneath the hissing gaslights that lined Rue Cologne.

Below the stone embankment on one side of the street, the Seine flowed silently, a dark ribbon shot through with braided ropes of moonlight. Above yawned a starry sky, the graceful spires of Paris's many churches pricking its spangled folds. A lamplighter was moving down the street with his cart, lighting each lamp in turn. The cool night wind carried the scents of coffee beans and carnations as it playfully tossed the horse-chestnut boughs and stirred wisps of hennaed hair about Mabel's face. It would have been a perfect spring evening, she thought, heaving a sigh, if not for her misgivings about Angel. . . .

"Trust me. There is nothing for you to worry about, my flower," Juarez crooned. He fondly squeezed the gloved hand Mabel had tucked through his arm, his expression adoring as he looked down at her.

Tonight, the Mexican roughrider wore his shoulder-length, straight black hair neatly fastened at his nape by a leather cord. His slim, dark good looks were striking in what Nick had once laughingly termed his "courtin'" duds—evening attire tailored in the style of the Spanish *hidalgo*. He wore a short bolero jacket over a snowy ruffled shirt with a black satin cummerbund spanning his narrow waist. His trousers hugged his lean hips and thighs but flared out below the knees to conceal all but the toes of his stilt-heeled boots. He looked, Mabel thought dreamily, "proper smashin'." On such a hunk's arm, she'd be the envy of every woman in Paris tonight, she didn't wonder. Well, let 'em look—!

"As Señor Nick told us, the señorita has not really been kidnapped," Juarez reminded her in the same coaxing tone. "It is just a hoax—like the last time, eh, Nick? A little trick to persuade Señor Higgins to part with his money."

"Hmm. I'd like t' think that, reelly I would," Mabel returned with a worried frown. "But, if that's the case, 'ow come Her Highness didn't let me in on the secret? She always has before!"

The possibility that Angel hadn't trusted her upset Mabel more than she cared to admit. True, she and Angel argued like bleedin' troopers most of the time, but despite that, she'd always felt they were friends, in a funny sort of way—or if not exactly friends, then surely partners in mischief? And friends and partners trusted each other. They shared their plans. So—why not this time?

Angel could be a right sod at times; no one knew that better than Mabel did. But she'd learned over the past three years that Angel's bark was invariably far worse than her bite. In fact, she tended to be highest-handed when she was afraid or out of her depth in some way. She was one of them what got riled up and attacked when they were most afraid or threatened. Not surprising, really. The poor little blighter had been left without her mum at a tender age, hadn't she? It couldn't have bin a bed o' roses having her life turned arse about face by Lord Bloody Harry Brixton's dying whim! Just fancy being sent away to a posh school, and having to learn how to fit in with them snooty bitches like that mi'lady Mucky-Muck Diana Forsythe—cor blimey, it hardly bore thinking about! Yes, as mistresses went, Angel treated her fairer than most, she had to admit, especially since her skills as a lady's maid were sketchy, t' say the least. Consequently, knowing Angel as well as she did, Nick's description of her quarrel with Smythe-Moreton and subsequent "abduction" bothered Mabel something fierce. When he'd told her about the two men he'd seen, a queer, heavy feeling had churned her innards. Angel'd said nothing about havin' another go at a ransom! Was everything all right? Or had that sod, Bill Bligh sent some of his lads across the bleein' Channel to collect what was due him?

"Juarez is right, Red. Come on, now, just relax and enjoy yourself tonight," Nick insisted, seeing her perturbed expression. "Let Angel play her spoiled-little-rich-brat games, while we have ourselves a hard-earned night on the town. This is Paris, Red! Paree! Right now, while you're fretting yourself sick, I'd bet Miz Iron Drawers is sippin' champagne from her slipper with that greenhorn Smythe-Moreton, laughin' her pretty head off thinkin' she's suckered us!"

"Weell, I *was* lookin' forward t' seein' the cancan," Mabel admitted at length, her foreboding lifting somewhat. "And likely you're right." Her eyes sparkled with anticipation. Her rouged gamin face dimpled naughtily as she added, "Sounds proper wicked, it do, what wiv all them French mademoyzelles doin' high kicks and showin' their knickers an' whatever!"

"Then swear that for tonight, you will forget Señorita Higgins?" Juarez pressed, his dark eyes tender as he looked down at Mabel. "Promise that tonight, there will be just two of us, *querida*, and you shall see all the cancan your heart desires, *sí*?"

Mabel sighed. How could she refuse those beseeching spaniel eyes anything? That mushy look of his reached clear down inside her and played merry-hell with her heartstrings. "Oh, all right, luv. You've twisted me arm!

No more Angel t'night, I promise. Cross me 'eart an' hope t' die!"

"If you turtledoves are done cooing, here comes a cab now!" Nick cut in with a grin. He stepped into the cobbled street to flag down the passing *fiacre*.

The coach rumbled to a halt beneath a wrought-iron streetlamp, a scrawny bay in the traces.

"Where to, m'sieu?" the bored cabbie asked, stifling a yawn.

"Montmartre, cabbie. The Moulin Rouge!"

Laughing gaily, the three clambered aboard the vehicle, Angel forgotten.

Angel bit back a whimper of pain. The coarse bonds had chafed her wrists, raising rope burns that smarted dreadfully. But, despite what felt like hours of struggling and straining, she'd succeeded only in slackening them a little. Oh, damn it all to hell! The ropes were nowhere near loose enough for her to wriggle free, though time was fast running out. At any moment, those dreadful men might return!

Earlier, she'd overheard her kidnappers talking when they'd believed themselves out of earshot. She'd pieced together from their coarse conversation that they intended leaving her alone for a short while, in order to meet someone arriving at the Gare du Nord train station. This man—whom they obviously feared and referred to simply as "The Gov'na" or "The Boss"—would tell them what to do with the "chit"—the "chit" being herself. From their tone, she'd had the distinctly unwelcome impression she might be tied in a weighted sack and thrown into the Seine, there to drown like an unwanted kitten. Her terror and her determination to escape had mounted accordingly. . . .

The ruffians had left soon after, taking with them Mabel's green velvet skirt and jacket despite her violent objections. They'd underestimated her, tho', in thinking she wouldn't try to escape in her undergarments. Ha! Wrong! Wrong! Wrong! She had no intention of becoming a sitting duck for those ruffians, thank you very much!

Gritting her teeth, she rocked from side to side on the ladder-back chair to which she'd been tied, violently throwing her weight from left to right again and again. At last, she succeeded in jolting the heavy chair off balance. She yelped with pain as she crashed to the floor, landing heavily on her shoulder, but to her delight, her ploy had worked. The woodwormed chair back had shattered with the fall, as had two of the legs. Thank God, she was now free, the ropes coiled loosely about her arms!

Panting, she hastily untangled herself, tore off the stifling pillow case blindfold, spat out the revolting gag, and gulped musty air. So great was her relief at being able to breathe freely again, tears filled her eyes. Her hands and legs trembled so, she wasted several precious moments before she was able to take stock of her surroundings.

Hmm. The sharp slope to the ceiling above her implied that she was in an attic somewhere, one with walls mapped with green islands of damp. Rotting, dusty sea trunks and several huge wicker hampers in better condition were stacked against one wall. Just above the topmost hamper was a small grimy windowpane, set high under the eaves. Could she escape through it? Perhaps climb out over the rooftops to freedom, she wondered, her heart beating very fast now . . . ?

Scrambling up the stacked hampers as if they were stairs, Angel eagerly peered through the murky pane, but could see nothing but darkness pricked with bleary light here and there beyond. Peering, alas, was all she *could* do, since only a cat could hope to escape by such a tiny opening!

Chafing smarting wrists and stamping numbed feet, she scrambled back down. And, as she did so, she noticed the low door set beneath the sharply angled ceiling. Crossing her fingers, she scampered across the attic to try the knob. Thank God for bungling fools! In their haste to leave, it had been left unlocked, she discovered!

Cautiously opening the door a crack, she saw a short landing and a steep, shabby staircase beyond, with bare wooden treads and a sagging bannister. Sounds of merrymaking carried from the ground floor below; deafening music, bawdy female laughter, male whoops and guffaws and the crash and tinkle of metal trays and glasses. The odor of stale perfume and sweat, old cigar smoke and liquor tickled her nose. A restaurant, perhaps? No, too noisy by far, and besides, she could smell no food. A dance hall, then? Far more likely!

Biting her lip, Angel looked about her. She could hardly hope to slip out of the building unnoticed by the dance hall patrons clad in her undergarments! For all she knew, those horrid men could well be carousing belowstairs and might see her and give chase. Could the hampers contain something that might serve as a disguise?

It seemed Lady Luck was smiling on her, for as she flung up the lid of the third hamper, she saw it was filled with several frilly costumes, all of the same color and style. Stepping into layer upon layer of ruffled scarlet satin petticoats, she pulled them up and tied the drawstrings about her waist. A flounced overdress of black satin followed. The neckline was immodestly low, the skirts indecently short, and while hardly an exquisite creation of Mr. Worth in style, beggars, she thought ruefully, could not be choosers!

Moments later, dressed as gaudily as many of the dreadful "unfortunates" to be seen strolling the seedier streets of London and Paris after dark, she slipped from the attic and made her way down the steep staircase to the ground floor below.

A long hallway ran at right angles to the stairs, numerous rooms leading off it. As she hesitated, trying to determine which way led outside to the street, one of the doors flew open. A blond woman dressed exactly as she was exploded through it.

"*Mon dieu, Babette!* Where 'ave you been? *Merde!* You new girls, you are all ze same—slow as snails! Come on—and quickly! Already zey are playing our music!"

"Our music?" Angel stammered in French.

"Of course, little idiot! Ze cancan!"

With this, the woman grasped Angel's hand and dragged her after her, back through the same swinging door she'd just exited. Just then, more squealing, garishly costumed girls burst from a dressing room down the hall, like a bouquet of gaudy satin flowers appearing suddenly from a magician's sleeve. They surged after Angel, filling the hallway, cutting off her retreat, sweeping her along on their cheaply perfumed, chattering tide!

Oh Lord, she had no choice but to follow them! And yet, if her kidnappers were out there, among the dance hall patrons, they couldn't fail to see her, dressed like this, unless she blended in. . . .

The blond woman, followed by Angel and the others, ran lightly across the sawdusted dance hall floor to the dais erected in the center. The rowdy patrons cheered loudly and surged forward with their entrance. They catcalled, stamped, and whistled as they greeted the dancers by name, saluting them with raised glasses.

"Vive La Mignon. Vive Mimi, la belle fille!"

"Vive la jolie Yvette!"

Borne aloft on a tidal wave of raucous noise, bright lights, heady scents, and brilliant colors, Angel found herself swept up onto the stage. Once there, she was chivvied into line by the other girls, whether she liked it or not.

"New, huh?" the pert brunette to her right asked, looking her over with a sniff.

"I—yes! I mean, no! Oh, please—I don't belong here! Some men are after me—I have to get away. You don't understand, I—!"

"I understand, *chérie*. Of course you're nervous, but you'll catch on. Just follow me—Gabrielle!—and kick— kick as 'igh as you can! Flirt your skirts and show the men lots of leg! These old goats are all half drunk already, *non*? They'll be more than happy, right, boys?" the girl asked in a louder voice, with a saucy smile and a wink for the mostly male audience. "If it's fancy steps and culture they want, then let them go to the ballet!"

To Angel's horror, the musicians picked up the tempo then. The bouncy music grew wilder, more strident, more bold, as if buildling to some bawdy orgiastic finale. And then, as one, the line of girls grasped the hems of their frilly skirts, raised them high above their knees, and let out a naughty squeal that drew whoops of approval from the grinning crowd. In time to the music, they began kicking high with their right legs and flaunting their white ruffled

186

drawers and scarlet garters.

And Angel, her cheeks aflame with mortification, had no choice but to kick right along with them! If she simply stood there, she'd draw attention to herself—the very last thing she wanted!

Following the other girls' lead, she shook her skirts furiously, squealed, kicked, then waggled her lower leg from the knee in time to the bawdy music, while balanced precariously on the other foot—all this in time to the thumping, blood-stirring rhythm and trombone slides of the wicked cancan!

When it happened exactly, she wasn't quite sure, but—somewhere between that first liberating kick and the next exciting few minutes of bawdy abandon—she completely forgot why she was there. Cast aside all inhibitions! Rather, she flung herself wholeheartedly into the dance, kicking and squealing with a wanton gusto that the girl beside her approved with a saucy wink and, "That's the way, *chérie!*"

At a small, stained table in one corner of Montmartre's Moulin Rouge, an untouched drink before her, sat Mabel. Her cheeks were flushed with enjoyment as she gazed at the chorus of dancers, both transfixed—and thrilled—by their shocking antics. Nick and Juarez, seated on either side of her, were little less entranced by the cancan's lively sensuality. Both men wore broad, appreciative grins from ear to ear.

"Now those are what *I* call women!" Nick approved out of the corner of his mouth, raising his glass to the stage in salute. "No airs and graces. No pretending."

Juarez nodded agreement.

"You're right there! This 'ere's really somethink t' see, in't it?" Mabel exclaimed, forced to shout to make herself heard over the raucous blare of the music and the patrons' whoops of laughter. "These Frenchies know 'ow to have good old 'knees-up,' don't they?" Her face had a flush of excitement to it now that owed nothing to either rouge or gin. Her eyes were bright as new pennies as she looked avidly about her.

Smoke wreathed around the gas chandeliers suspended above the dance hall. Thick clouds of blue smoke also drifted between the tables, giving the scene a surrealistic quality. Like hell might look, she wouldn't wonder! Fancily dressed toffs in evening attire lounged at some tables, enjoying an evening of working-class diversion. In one gloomy corner, a dwarfish artist wearing a derby sketched rapidly on his drawing pad with a stub of charcoal, the high-kicking ladies of the Moulin Rouge coming to life beneath his clever fingers. Working class female patrons, not to be outdone by the naughty cancan girls, entered into a high-kicking contest of their own, off to one side. Egged on by their male escorts, each woman was lifting her skirts to shamelessly expose her drawers, stockings, and legs, while vying to successfully kick her male companion's hat off his head with her foot. It was a scene of vitality, of spontaneity, laughter, irrepressible movement, and color, with a flavor that was uniquely French.

"That dancer, third from the left—she looks a bit like Angel, she do," Mabel decided, pursing her lips and frowning.

"Mabella *mía*, you promised. No mention of the señorita, not tonight, hmmm?" Juarez scolded.

"Ooops! Sorry, luv. I forgot meself."

Just then, the cancan dancers finished their number with a cartwheel, then leaped high into the air in turn. They landed in a full split, one after the other, uttered a final ear-splitting squeal, before flinging their skirts over their heads in triumph. The bourgeois audience went wild, whooping and stamping for more, good-naturedly cursing the two rough Englishmen who tried to elbow their way between them to reach the stage.

"Eh, boys, not so rough, eh? The girls will wait for you!" they grumbled.

Nick turned back to his drink just as the pair squeezed by his table. He had his back to them and was still chuckling over Mabel's outrageous comment when the third cancan girl from the left suddenly spotted the men's rapid advance. She blanched, scrambled to her feet and fled from the stage.

"Red, honey, if you can get Miz High-and-Mighty Iron

Drawers t' dance the can-can, hell, I'll eat my hat!" Nick drawled.

Her head down, her elbows tucked into her sides, Angel exploded from the side door of the Moulin Rouge like a bull charging a matador's cape. She dashed through the littered alley that ran alongside the dance hall and erupted onto the boulevard fronting the Moulin Rouge.

Many private coaches, wagonettes, and *fiacres* lined the curb, disgorging their passengers. Angel ran from coach to coach, desperately looking for a friendly face, wondering how on earth she could hope to hire a cab without a penny to her name. Suddenly, she heard the thud of racing footsteps on the pavement and a coarse shout of, "Hey! You! Come back 'ere!" The bellow came from one of her kidnappers—and he was not far behind her, either!

Scrambling over a dog-collared vicar who'd bent over to tie his green cross-gaiters, Angel muttered, "I do beg your pardon. So frightfully sorry, Reverend!" and vaulted into the *fiacre* the vicar'd commandeered for himself. Without further ado, she hammered on the coach roof and yelled at the cabbie to lay on at once, just as two nightmarish faces appeared through the coach window.

The pair glowered at her, shaking their fists and screaming obscenities as they tugged at the coach door, determined to wrest it open. Somehow, Angel managed to hold it shut with one hand and pull down the rolled blind with the other. In the next instant, thank God, the coach jolted forward, throwing her across the interior. Its wheels clattered over the cobblestones, forcing the men to back off or be crushed beneath them.

Weak with relief, Angel slumped back against the black-leather seats to recover her composure as their shouts grew mercifully fainter.

Thank God, she'd escaped! Time enough later to bother about paying for the bloody cab. Right now, all she cared about was returning to the Hotel St. Pierre—alive. And settling accounts with that bastard Durango, of course—!

Chapter Sixteen

The foyer of the Hotel St. Pierre was ablaze with light despite the late hour when the three merrymakers spilled from their cab.

"That was the best bloomin' grub I ever tasted!" Mabel declared with a smack of her lips and a contented sigh. "What was it we 'ad again, Nick? Boolibase? Yescargo?"

"Somethin' like that, Red," Nick confirmed with an amused grin. He was pleased by the little woman's unabashed enjoyment of the evening they'd spent together, first at the dance hall and after, at a modest out-of-the-way restaurant. The food had been sensational, the bill pleasingly low, and Red had enjoyed everything with unabashed relish. "Evenin', Henri!" he greeted the *commissaire.*

"Good evening, M'sieu Durango." The stout little man beamed. "I trust you and your companions had a pleasant ti—*mon Dieu!*"

Henri's cordial greeting was abruptly cut short as the double doors he was standing before flew outward, slamming him behind the knees and almost knocking him to the cobbles in the process. As the concierge Paul Martine made an explosive exit, Henri bit back a curse and stepped aside.

"M'sieu Nick! Thank God you are back! I was watching through ze glass, praying you would soon return!" Martine exclaimed excitedly, wringing his hands.

"Martine, ole buddy, what's wrong?" Nick demanded.

"It is your Mademoiselle Higgins, m'sieu! She is dressed

very strangely, and I fear—oui!—I fear she 'as gone mad, sir! She 'as your guns, and she is threatening to shoot you when you return. You 'ave had a—a lovers' quarrel, per'aps?"

"Little Annie an' me quarrel? Hell, no! We're jest a pair o' turtledoves, *mon ami*, always billing and cooing. Sounds more like my little gal's rehearsin' our act for the new show—it's one we've been talkin' about some. Er, where did you say she was?" Nick soothed the man casually, casting a long, meaningful look at Juarez and Mabel.

"She is in the lobby, m'sieu! No one has been able to persuade her to put down her weapons. I thought—I thought it best to keep the area clear. Our guests 'ave been asked to use the rear staircase until further notice. Oh, forgive me, M'sieu Nick, but I had no idea the young lady was rehearsing! She seems so—so convincing!" He shuddered delicately.

"Aw, that Annie, she's a real trouper, ain't she? Puts all she's got into her work, body, heart, and soul! Now, you jest settle down, pardner an' I'll take care of Annie, *pronto.*"

"What's going on, Nick?" Juarez asked softly, drawing Nick aside.

"Damned if I know," Nick admitted out of the side of his mouth with a shrug. Lighting a cheroot with a match struck against his boot heel, he drew deeply, then exhaled. "But my pal Martine says Angel's holed up in the lobby with my guns—and threatenin' to use 'em on me, if I show my face."

"Wot!" Mabel exclaimed, round-eyed. "Shoot *you*, Nick? But why?"

"Beats me, Red. My best guess is that Miz Iron Drawers didn't take kindly t' havin' her playactin' ignored this afternoon. Maybe she's sore we went out on the town, 'stead of hangin' around here, waiting for her phony ransom note to be delivered? Aw, who knows! Right now, I have t' take those guns away from that damned little fool before she kills somebody. Juarez, count to a hundred, then go in the front door. Keep her talkin' as long as you can, *amigo*. I'll take the back stairs and try t' get the

191

jump on her . . ."

Juarez nodded solemnly, his dark eyes concerned. "Very well, *amigo. Vaya con Diós.*"

"You too, *hombre.*"

"And wot about me? What do I do?"

"You stay right here, Red, honey, and wait."

"Stay here? Wait? But I—"

"No 'buts'! Henri, keep an eye on Mam'zelle Blunt, y' hear? She tries t' give you the slip, jest sit on her."

Mabel glowered and crossed her arms over her chest, tapping her foot.

The *commissaire* grinned. "It would be my pleasure, m'sieu!"

With a nod, Nick tossed his butt to the gutter and left, circling the hotel and entering by the service entrance at the rear.

". . . surely? Come," Juarez's lilting voice coaxed, "beautiful lady, give Juarez your guns, eh? You don't want to hurt anyone—I know this. You are all that is kind and good. Truly, you could never do such a terrible thing."

"You're quite correct, Señor Juarez," Angel agreed in a low, clipped tone. But though her face was pale, her gray eyes were fairly smoking with fury. "I really don't want to hurt anyone except *him!* And, after I've killed Durango, I fully intend to throw myself on the mercy of the law. You have my word."

The apprehensive onlookers, trapped in the lobby for the past hour by Angel's dramatic appearance, coupled with the chilling announcement that she intended to shoot that cad Nick Durango stone-cold dead when he showed his ugly face, were now pressed flat against the walls, as if trying to melt into them. The brace of wicked-looking, heavy revolvers she'd brandished so coolly at the outset were trembling in her dainty fists now. Time had taken its toll. She was wearying, and fatigue bred carelessness. Just one slip of those delicate fingers curled about the trigger and—boom!

Nick's pale eyes narrowed as, bootless, he eased his way silently down the thickly carpeted corridor to the polished

192

oak balustrade overhanging the lobby below. Flattened against the wall, he craned his neck to peer over it.

Juarez stood some fifteen feet inside the main doors. Martine and a few other hotel employees were huddled close to it, half-hidden behind a potted palm. All appeared shaken and bug-eyed. Two waiters, a bellhop, and a maid were plastered against the frescoed walls, held rigidly in place by their fear of the young woman who stood at the foot of the stairs.

Her back to him, her black-stockinged legs braced apart, her honey blond hair a wild mane that spilled about her bare shoulders, toting a Colt .45 in each hand, Angel stood. To his astonishment, she was all gussied up in a dance hall doxie's gaudy duds, and had never looked more beautiful—nor more deadly!

Seeing her, Nick remembered his rash vow at the Moulin Rouge and groaned. Mabel had been right. It *had* been Angel kicking up her heels at the Moulin Rouge. Aw, Jeez! Red'd never let him live this one down, no sir. . . .

Silent as a panther stalking its prey, Nick edged toward the bannister just as the little maid happened to look up. He knew she'd spotted him when her eyes widened! She opened her mouth to scream just as he pressed his finger across his lips to silence her. To his relief, she caught the signal in the nick of time and hurriedly looked away.

Juarez was still doing a damned fine job keeping Angel distracted by talking nonstop as Nick gingerly slung a leg over the polished bannister as if mounting a wild bronco.

". . . cannot understand why you would wish to kill him? Trust me. Tell Juarez what is wrong? Nick is a good man, señorita. I know this. Many times he has saved my life. He is the best! A man of his word. A man of courage and honor—"

"Honor and courage be damned!" Angel spat. "And as for his word—! Fiddlesticks and horsefeathers! Durango's word is worthless—less than worthless! He accepted payment from my father on the understanding that he would guard my life with his own. And what does your 'honorable' Mr. Durango do?" she scoffed, tossing her hair. "He stands by and allows those awful thugs to—to abduct me—bound, gagged, and utterly helpless—without lifting a finger to stop them! Why, I barely escaped with my life, no thanks to *him!*" She shook her head so that the frilly white ornament in it jiggled madly. "Had I been less resourceful, I would be lying in a watery grave at this very minute! No, Señor Juarez. I'm sorry, I cannot be dissuaded. Enough is—*enoooooouaaagh!*"

Her words ended in a shriek as Nick—who'd whooshed soundlessly down the entire length of the highly polished bannister to the ground floor—caught her around the waist and propelled her with him across the green marble floor!

He'd been banking on her threat being an empty bluff, convinced she wouldn't have known how to reload his empty Colts, but he'd been dangerously wrong on that score. As he and Angel crashed to the floor in an untidy tangle of arms, black-stockinged legs, and scarlet petticoats, both guns discharged.

The deafening shots elicited screams from both maid and waiters, as well as Martine and the others. The first wild bullet went skywards, severing the chain to one of the teardrop chandeliers. The huge fixture crashed to the ground. Fortunately, there was no one standing below it, but crystal shards sprayed everywhere. The second stray bullet creased Juarez's shoulder, ripping through coat and shirt with a spurt of crimson before ploughing into the frescoed walls beyond with a puff of plaster powder.

One knee jammed against the small of Angel's back, Nick's expression was murderous as he leaned over the girl. He twisted a gun from her clenched right hand, wrenched a second from her clamped left, then skidded both Colts across the marble floor, out of her reach. Juarez bent quickly to retrieve them.

"Damn fool woman!" Nick gritted as he jerked Angel roughly to her feet. "You could have killed someone!"

"Yes! *You*, you bastard," she gritted, so much venom in her tone that Nick was startled, despite himself. Why the hell did she hate him so much?

"Well, I'm real sorry t' disappoint you, Miz Iron Drawers," he drawled mockingly, "but when I'm ready t' meet my Maker, I don't reckon on a spoiled little brat bein' the one to send me there. Now, *move!*"

194

Still keeping a firm grip on her wrists, which he twisted painfully up and behind her back, he gave her a nudge to get her going up the staircase. Under his prodding, Angel was forced to climb them.

At the second floor landing, he jerked her to a halt and hissed in her ear "Turn around and take a bow."

"A *what?*"

"I said, take a bow, goddamnit, or so help me God, I'm gonna strangle you, woman."

To his relief, she did as he'd ordered. He took a bow himself before chivvying her on up the next flight of stairs to the third floor. Over his shoulder, he added in a loud, ringing voice, "The show's over for tonight, folks! If you've a hankerin' for more, tickets t' Buffalo Bill Cody's Wild West Show go on sale next month! For now— *Adiós—!*"

Apparently, his cocksure showman's tone and his broad grin convinced at least some of those below that what they'd seen had been only an act. A chorus of disappointed "ohs"! and a halfhearted spattering of applause and nervous laughter broke out behind his back as he marched Angel up the stairs to their suite.

Once inside, however, his good humor abruptly vanished. He shoved her forcefully away from him and kicked the door shut behind them.

"All right. You've got one minute to start talking—and honey, make it good." He smiled nastily. "See, I'm still in two minds about strangling you!"

"I don't have to explain my behavior to you, you cad. You deserve to be shot! You took money from my father under false pretenses!"

Her tone was icily controlled, her haughty composure remarkable considering she was still smoldering with anger as she stalked as far away from him as she could get. It seemed prudent to put distance between them, for she'd never seen Nick's handsome face so hard and dark with anger, nor his pale blue eyes so silvery, glacial with contempt. He showed every appearance of becoming violent in the very near future. . . .

"False pretenses? And what in the *hell* do you mean by that?" he snarled.

"Correct me if I'm wrong, Durango, but—weren't you hired to protect me from kidnapping?"

"I was," he gritted.

Two spots of vivid scarlet flared in her cheeks as she whirled to face him, hands planted on her hips like a fishwife. "Then what the bloody hell were you doing this afternoon, when those two louts dragged me out of this suite, right under your nose?"

"Aw, come on, honey! Quit playin' me for a fool! We both know those two sidewinders were pals of your friend, Reggie. You were never in any real danger—so drop the act. This is Nick you're talkin' to, remember? The same *hombre* you tried t' get t' help you with your dirty little charade. After I turned you down flat, you sweet-talked ole money-grubbin' Smythe-Moreton into bein' your sidekick—"

"That's a lie!" she protested, unable to meet his blazing eyes. "I never had the chance to put my plan into action in London because—because I really *was* kidnapped!"

"The hell you were, Angel—and don't think you can make me believe otherwise. See, I *know* what you two did in London! Before I ever agreed to work for your pa, I did some nosin' around. And in one evening, I knew everything there was to know about you and Reggie and the fast crowd you ran with."

"Everything?" she echoed, dry-mouthed.

"Everything, sweetheart," he scoffed, relishing the suddenly fearful light in her eyes. "All your little secrets that weren't so secret after all! About your gambling losses. All about your so-called 'kidnapping.' And all about the disgraceful way Angel Higgins would do *anything* to hitch up with a title. You have a real bad name in London, Angel—but then, I reckon you know that, right, sugar pie?"

She laughed in an effort to conceal the sudden gallop of her heart. "Why, I've never heard such—such rubbish! I have no secrets, Durango, so stop trying to trick me into confessing something I never did."

"Rubbish? Is that what you call it? He smiled a thin, disquieting smile that turned her insides to jelly. "Oh, I don't think it was 'rubbish,' Angel. See, money has a way

196

of switching folks' loyalties. Of greasin' their tongues. Reggie's faithful valet, ole William, hadn't been paid a farthing in wages in over a year. He told me an earful about your middle-of-the-night visits to ole Reggie's town house—!"

"I don't believe you!"

"—then there was Diana Forsythe's maid, Winnie. Now, that little gold digger would have sold her own grandmother for half a crown! For an extra guinea, she hinted I should try Bligh's gaming hall if I was curious about you." He shrugged. "I did—and I met a passel of desperate people at that high-class snakepit. Every damned one of 'em would have traded their soul t' the devil, if the price was right. Fortunately, mine was." He smiled mockingly as her defiant stance wilted just a fraction. "You believe me now, sweet thing?"

"Oh, go ahead! Gloat all you want! If you knew so bloody much, why didn't you tell my father what you'd learned?" she suggested bitterly.

"And break that poor devil's heart?" Nick shook his head. "No, lady. I liked Sid from the first. Higgins is a straight-shooter with a heart of gold—and you don't deserve a father like him! His only fault is thinking the sun sets on your scrawny tail! I reckon he'll find out soon enough that his precious daughter's nothin' but a deceitful, selfish little snob who uses those who love her. But—not from me, he won't."

"Why did you take the job, then?"

"Damned if I know, honey bunch." He paused. "Let's just say I'd had a gutful of playin' cowboy every night, and your pa's offer seemed . . . interestin'."

"Oh, come now. You're not seriously expecting me to believe that the money had nothing to do with it?"

"Believe what you want, but a price never even entered into it." A derisive half-smile twisted his darkly handsome features. "I'm no fortune hunter like Smythe-Moreton, hangin' on a woman's skirts, lookin' for a free ride or a handout. Nope. I already have more than enough for my . . . needs."

The blasted man had an answer for everything, Angel thought, choking back the retort she would dearly have loved to make, but didn't dare. Though he seemed less volatile now, less like a loaded bomb with its fuse lit and about to go off, anger still crackled around him. She drew a deep breath. "Very well. I won't waste any further time in pleading my innocence about what happened in London. Just answer me this. Do you have any explanation for today's kidnapping?"

His insolent, knowing smile was back, curling his upper lip. "Why, heck, Miz Higgins, I thought I'd let *you* explain it to me this time," he drawled insolently.

"Me?" She snorted. "Sorry, Durango, but I can't oblige you. You see, I'm telling the truth. *I* haven't a clue who those men were, nor why they abducted me."

His raven brows rose mockingly. "You really expect me to swallow that?"

"Yes!"

"Give me one good reason why in hell I should?"

"Because it's the truth, damn you!"

"The truth?" He snorted. "Pardon me for saying so, honey, but I doubt you'd recognize the truth if it up and bit you in the eye! Was it that greenhorn's idea?" he asked suddenly. "Is that why you took off and left him in the Bois?"

She shook her head. "That was another matter entirely. I told him my feelings for him had changed, and Reggie was hurt, I suppose. In his anger, he said some hateful things and we—we quarreled. That's why I ran off. The *only* reason." She bit her lower lip and blinked rapidly to dispel the disgusting urge to cry. "I swear to you, Durango, on my mother's grave, that I had nothing to do with it. Today, I was their—their innocent victim!"

"Let's suppose I believe you. If *you* didn't have a hand in it, and Reggie didn't arrange it, then who did?"

"Bill Bligh, perhaps? Oh, I don't know, I tell you! I only wish I did," she insisted heatedly, adding, "And stop looking at me like that, damn you, Durango! I know what you're thinking, and I know it's asking a lot, expecting you to believe me, considering my—um—past record, but I'm telling you the truth this time—so help me God!"

He crossed his arms over his chest, looking as impassive and stony as the Matterhorn. "All right. Prove it to me."

"How?" she wailed.

He shrugged. "Beats me. That's your problem, Angel."

She thought for a moment, her lovely face creased in concentration, then brightened. "All right. What about these." Taking a step toward him, she held out her wrists for his inspection. "Proof enough?"

Angry, raised welts, livid against her fair skin, encircled her slender wrists. His brows rose as he grimaced. "Rope burns?"

"Yes! And they smart like the devil! Be serious, Durango—would I inflict these on myself?"

"I reckon you just might—! Hell, Angel, you're about as sneaky as a ring-tailed polecat! I wouldn't put anythin' past you, honey!"

She ignored that. "Well, what about this bruise, right here? And this one, here?" She touched her cheek, then turned her bared shoulder toward him.

He shook his head. "I don't see a blamed thing."

"You might, you brute—if you'd turn up the gaslight!" she flared.

"All right." With a curt nod, Nick strode across the carpet to the milk-globed gaslights that branched out from the wall. He turned up the wick.

Angel followed him, hovering at his elbow. As he turned to face her, she swept back her honey gold hair, baring her cheek so that he could see the shadow of the huge bruise forming along the curve of her jaw.

Cupping her chin in his huge tanned hand with surprising gentleness, Nick turned her face from side to side beneath the light. His mouth thinned, then pursed. His eyes narrowed. Truth was, his thoughts were only marginally on inspecting the obvious bruise there, for unbidden, a wave of lust swamped over him, heady lust bred of tawny gaslight gleaming on her exquisite features and caught in the shiny mass of her glorious hair. He swallowed and flicked his head, trying to escape the sweet musky scent of her that filled his nostrils. Yet the memory of her lips, the remembrance of her soft curves pressing sweetly against his in the shadowed *fiacre*, the very taste of her, returned to torment him.

"Well?" she demanded when he made no comment.

"Could be a bruise," he admitted grudgingly in a husky voice, suddenly dry-mouthed.

"*Could* be? It is, I swear it!" she protested. "One of those ruffians struck me in this very room. I suppose he was angry that I kicked him in the shins . . . Surely you believe me now?" Her tone, though still demanding, was the tiniest bit hopeful now.

"Nope."

"Oh, you obstinate brute! What more must I do to convince you?" she cried. "What about this bruise, then, here on my shoulder? It happened when I overturned the chair they'd tied me to—you know, to escape? I landed on my shoulder."

This time, even Nick couldn't deny that the mottled, darkened area on her creamy upper arm appeared to be a bruise. His angry expression betrayed as much.

"There, you see! Are you convinced now?"

"Nope," he insisted obstinately.

"No? But why not, for heaven's sake?" she wailed. "What possible reason would I have for inflicting these bruises on myself?"

"Maybe you didn't." He smiled nastily. "Maybe ole Reggie lost his temper—? Some women enjoy being roughed up." Even as he uttered the words, Nick realized that the thought of Reggie hurting her filled him with jealous rage and anger—anger at himself, that he cared; anger at her, because despite everything, she'd somehow made him care so much. Damn it, he didn't want to feel this way about her, didn't want to get involved—! He hadn't asked for this—!

"So I've heard—but I'm not one of them!" she protested.

"Aren't you?" His softly spoken question was murmured insinuatingly in her ear and his warm breath sent goosebumps prickling down her arms, her spine.

With a curse, she angrily flung about, fully intending to stalk away from him, to tell him exactly what she thought of him in no uncertain terms. As the coup de grace, she'd add that he might consider his employ terminated as her parting shot. But instead of letting her go, his fingers knotted in her hair. She found herself jerked roughly back against the front of his body, held immobile against the breadth of his chest.

His body heat branded her back. His warmth was everywhere, all around her, enveloping her. She could feel his very breath in her hair, stirring against her nape, her spine, and the fiery pressure of his fingers encircling her waist.

"Let me go!" She drew a shaky breath, wanting to break free, determined to do so—but she was held immobile by a force more potent than any magnet.

His hand left her waist to sweep her tangled mane aside and bare her throat, caressing the fluid column with his fingertips. She stiffened, for she knew what was coming even before his lips touched hers.

"Durango, don't you da—!"

"Shut up, Angel . . ." he growled.

A heartbeat later, she was shivering as Nick's lips nuzzled the sensitive flesh of her throat, his tongue tracing a path ever so slowly up and around her delicate little ear in a way that made her squirm with pleasure.

Heat streaked through her—sizzling, scorching heat! She gasped and arched back against him, raising her arm to encircle his neck. Her breathing sounded shallow and rapid on the gaslit hush, like the panting of a small wild animal run to ground. The hand he'd curled about her waist traveled slowly up the front of her body, grazing the curves of her hips, her abdomen, with heat and sensation, before he cupped the fullness of her breasts in both palms.

She sucked in a shaky breath, close to swooning as Nick teased both breasts to aching fullness by rubbing the balls of his thumbs over the hardening peaks again and again.

No! No! a voice screamed in her head. But, with a will of their own, her breasts tautened, swelled. They threatened to spill from the cancan gown's low neckline into his waiting hands if she drew too deep a breath. Her nipples had become tight berries, centers of exquisite sensation.

"Nick, please, stop this! I swear I . . ." she began in a desperate, last-ditch effort to return matters to their former plane.

In answer, he turned her to face him. Her toes left the floor as he slid her up the length of his hard, lean body.

"Damn me for a fool . . ." he muttered, then his dark

201

head dipped. She had a glimpse of his swarthy, handsome face, of silvery-blue eyes grown dark, heavy-lidded and sensual, in the instant before his mouth claimed hers, then his mouth silenced her protests. He held her against him while he ravished her mouth with a brutal thoroughness of lips and tongue that left her limp, weak with rising desire, all thoughts of escape forgotten and abandoned.

With a low moan of surrender, she curled her hands about his tan throat to caress the crisp waves of inky hair that clung to his nape like commas of raw silk. *At last!* she thought dreamily as she began to kiss him back, opening her mouth to his, yielding him all.

Their open mouths met. Their tongues entwined, pressing. They shared greedy kisses, deep, hungry kisses that sizzled like oil on a hot griddle. As he kissed her, his hand slid feverishly down her body to cup her bottom, to lift and press her hips to his arousal. His manhood rubbed against the pit of her belly, hard and hot even through their layers of clothing. That he wanted her—and badly!—was undeniable, and the knowledge thrilled and terrified her at the same time.

She should demand that he stop, before he ruined her. But . . . oh, damn propriety! Damn morals! Damn outrage and ruination! She'd already gone beyond the point of no return. There'd be no turning back. Not now. Not with a dangerous, determined man like Nick—not with that *look* in his eyes . . . thank God!

Her anxiety evaporated like morning mist beneath the scorching sun, consumed by the conflagration of her own rising desire.

Still kissing her, Nick jerked the straps of the gaudy gown from her shoulders, hungrily branding the faint lines they'd left on her subtly perfumed flesh with his lips. Made for a more voluptuous woman than she, the garment needed no further unfastening. It slithered to the carpet with a whisper of satin folds. He kicked it aside, still kissing her hungrily, slanting his mouth savagely across hers as his hands sought hooks and fastenings. Seconds later, her scarlet petticoats slipped over her hips. Angel was unaware of it—unaware of anything but Nick. Of the feel of Nick's arms, holding her close, keeping her safe. Of the taste and scent of him. Of the glorious new sensations he sent exploding through her body like fireworks on Guy Fawkes' Day, skyrockets and spinning Catherine wheels ignited by his lips, his hand.

Their mouths still hungrily moving against each other, he swept her up into his arms and carried her through the suite.

"Where are you taking me?" she asked breathlessly, tearing her mouth from his to speak. She half feared his answer, while knowing it—craving it!—in her heart of hearts.

"Where I should have taken you days ago, you damned little witch!" he growled, his voice ragged with desire as he halted before the connecting door.

"And where's that?" she whispered.

"To bed—!"

Chapter Seventeen

Nick's room lay in heavy shadow. The draperies were drawn, the gaslights extinguished. Lowering Angel to the sheets, he followed her down and kissed her tenderly.

"Don't run away," he murmured teasingly, grinning as he looked down at her, "I'll be right back."

She nodded, feeling faint as, her cheeks still flaming from his caresses in the suite's parlor, her lips still tingling from his feverish kisses, she watched with widening eyes as, his back turned to her, Nick stripped.

Hauling off his boots, he tugged the tails of his shirt free of his pants and unbuckled his belt, his hands clumsy in his impatience. Jumpin' Geronimo, he was like a green kid takin' his first woman! Damned if that shy, reluctant act Angel was putting on wasn't driving him wild, now that he'd finally admitted she was under his skin and that bedding her was the only way he could get her out of his blood.

"Miss me, darlin'?" he asked huskily, stretching out beside her on one elbow as he rubbed a long, silky strand of her hair between his fingers.

Stunned, Angel couldn't answer, she was trembling so violently. His magnificent bare torso was only inches from her, the . . . magnificent *rest* . . . of him not much farther way—and a completely naked Nick Durango was a far more threatening proposition than a clothed one had proven!

Oh, Lord, what was she doing here? This close, she

could *smell* the pleasant, musky male scent of his naked body, mixed with the soapy tang of his last shave, feel the heat of him rising against her, like the warmth given off by a fire. His chest hair had brushed her arm when he'd sprawled alongside her. It was prickly, coarse, and had raised gooseflesh down her spine. She swallowed. Dear God, his hairy animal maleness and his nudity made her want to swoon.

"Cat got your tongue, sweetness?"

Hooking a finger under the lace-trimmed ribbon of her bodice, he slid it down from her shoulder, just as he had the straps of the cancan gown earlier. She stiffened and placed her hand over his to stop him.

"Easy, there, sweetheart. I'm not fixin' to hurt you. I just want to look at you, my pretty Angel," he murmured caressingly.

With a start, she realized that he'd bared her breast as he spoke. She felt a draft on her skin in the instant before he ducked his head. Then Nick's burning lips claimed her puckered nipple, drew the soft pink nubbin deep into his mouth to be suckled.

"Stop!" She gasped, almost jumping out of her skin. The drawing sensation of his mouth was unlike anything she'd ever felt before. The contact threw her emotions into turmoil, made her feel as if she'd been skinned alive, and the nerve ends left exposed, screaming with sensation. Her hands moved quickly to frame his dark head, hovered there on either side of it as if uncertain where to go, what to do. She was torn between wanting to tear his mouth from her body and in holding him fast; so fast that he could never, *ever* stop the incredible things he was doing. In the end, she made no attempt to draw him away. Instead, her fingers laced through his jet black curls, feverishly caressing his hair as little whimpers of pleasure broke from her lips.

Drawing back a little, Nick relinquished her nipples. Instead, he shifted his attention to the exquisitely sensitive deeper pink areolas that surrounded them, swirling his tongue around them and from time to time, teasing the flushed, tightly furled buds that rose from their center with an occasional flick of his tongue. She whimpered his name. Oh, the drawing sensation of his mouth, the rasp of his stubbled cheeks against her soft skin, the feel of his work-roughened hands cupping and fondling her breasts—it was all so unbelieveably new to her—and so incredibly erotic! Everything he did seemed to detonate a chain of reactions, miniature explosions that raced from her breasts to her belly and that secret place between her thighs, then back again to her mouth. Her fingers tightened in his hair, doing so so painfully, Nick winced, though Angel didn't notice.

Never—oh, never had she imagined this sweet torment! What he was doing sent firefly thrills skittering through every part of her, made her very toes curl. A throbbing pulse began in the pit of her belly. It became the questing, roaring hunger for release she recognized from the *fiacre.* Oh, how that pulse quivered, made her squirm with longing. And his mouth—! She didn't want him to stop—!

"Angel?" he murmured lazily, coming up for air.

"Mmmmm hmm?" she murmured, knowing she sounded like an idiot incapable of speech.

"These here are the prettiest breasts I've ever seen," Nick whispered, nuzzling her creamy flesh.

"Uhh . . . really? Well, umm, thank you," she managed to stammer inanely in response to his compliment, as if he'd commented on her hat or gloves.

Nick threw back his jet black head and whooped with laughter. Straightening up, he caught her by the chin and planted a smacking wet kiss full on her lips that was more teasing than passionate.

"'Thank you'? Damn it, woman, if you don't beat all, then I don't know what does!" he declared, before scooping her into his arms and rolling her over with him, so that she was above him now.

He'd moved before she could so much as gasp in surprise. She was still breathless when his hands slid down to fondle her bottom. She jumped as he splayed his long fingers across the springy globes and squeezed, silvery blue eyes lidded under brooding dark brows as he watched her face. The emotions that flitted across it were unfathomable as he lustily kneaded her bottom through her clothes.

"Don't know about you, but I can't wait much longer," he whispered huskily, his handsome face dark with desire. "This sinner's a-ready and a-rarin' to go, just as soon as you say the word!"

She smiled uncertainly. "Word? And what word, precisely, is that?"

Nick's sensual grin wavered. Was she joshing him? He frowned. Apparently not! Her lovely face was the picture of consternation as she awaited his answer. "Well," he began hesitantly, feeling stupid now. "There's no *real* word, as such, I don't reckon. I guess you could say 'Go'? Or maybe 'Yeeehaaah'? Had a gal once in Laredo was fond of that one. Her name was Dusty, I recall." He grinned and winked up at her while caressing her breasts, rolling the hardened nipples between his thumb and finger. "She wore spurs and a Stetson every time we hit the sheets. Damn me if bedding that little filly wasn't like tumbling a Fourth of July bronc when she lit out of the rodeo chute!"

"Bronc?" She frowned down at him. "Chute?"

"Never mind, darlin', I was just teasin'," he explained with a heavy sigh. As he'd once thought, Angel—for all her beauty—had about as much humor in her bones as an undertaker!

"Oh! I see," she exclaimed. "A joke!"

But it was obvious she didn't understand, and his bodily needs were raging now.

"Come on, sweet thing. Undress for me, hmm?" he urged.

Her stomach turned over. "Very well. Um, what should I take off?"

Nick's jaw dropped. Was she really that innocent—or teasing him? "I figured you'd want to take off everything, right—?" he whispered, and when her gray eyes widened in pretended shock, his patience splintered. "Aw, come on, Angel. Enough's enough! I want you so damned bad, I can't stand it! Quit playin' little miz innocent and strip, 'fore I strip you myself!"

"*Strip!*" Her cheeks flamed. "Oh, I couldn't. It's quite out of the question! A true lady never bares herself completely, not even to her husband in their marriage bed. And may I remind you, sir, that *we* are not married."

Perplexed now, Nick sat up, Angel still curled in his lap—a circumstance that was uncomfortable in the extreme, considering his advanced state of arousal and her lamentably partial state of undress.

"Where in the hell'd you learn that bullsh—er—hogwash?" he wondered aloud, incredulous.

"At the Ellen Clarke Boarding School for Young Ladies," she confessed with an edge of pride to her voice. Leaning back, she curled one slender arm around his neck, smoothing the commas of inky hair back from his temple with her other hand. "It was a rather progressive establishment . . ."

Progressive, hell! Nick shook his head. Now he'd heard everything! "You mean, all the other times, you left your—er—drawers—on?" The mechanics of such a feat fascinated him. Sure, he'd figured the reserved British for a breed apart, but damned if this didn't beat all!

She blushed and looked away, drawing a circle around and around one of his flat dark rose nipples, curiously watching it stiffen amidst a sprinkling of curly black hairs. She appeared completely unaware that her little experiment made Nick feel as if he was being tortured. Looking down, she shyly confessed, "I'm afraid there—um—were no—er—other times."

"You don't mean—? Oh Jeez, don't tell me you're a *virgin?*" From his incredulous tone, he might have said "headhunter" or "cannibal." Or even "leper."

"I'm afraid so, yes."

"Damn it all to hell!" Nick cursed, the urge to strangle her returning full-force now. Here he was, rattlin' down the rails like a locomotive with a full head of steam, and she was a blamed virgin, for Pete's sake!

"Does it—does it make a difference, Nick?" she inquired in a small, worried voice.

"Some," he ground out curtly, shifting her smartly to the bed beside him—an action that gained him only minimal relief from the arousing pressure of her bottom squirming against his tender parts.

"Oh dear! I'd so hoped it wouldn't." Biting her lower lip, she laughed nervously. "Diana and the others girls bragged that they'd—well, you know!—heaps of times. So, I let them think I had, too."

"You did, huh?" he gritted, the ache in his groin unbearable now. "Well, sweet thing, you sure had me fooled!"

"I knew it! You're angry!"

"Me? Angry?" Nick bellowed, then recovered himself. She looked close to tears, and that made him feel even more of a sidewinding polecat than he did already. "Hell, no, sweet thing. I'm—I'm just as happy as all get-up t' hear it. Real happy," he reassured her in a more level tone, kissing the tip of her nose. And he had to admit that, on one level, it was no lie. "Any man would be real proud you chose him t' be the first."

"But are you?"

"I am. It just means we'll—er—have t' slow down some, that's all." He hesitated before adding firmly, "But either way, honey, fast or slow, those clothes have to come off."

Again, she gnawed her lower lip. "You're quite certain?"

"I am."

"Oh, well, then . . . If you'd close your eyes—?"

As Nick obediently did so, Angel squirmed from her chemise and drawers and hastily pulled the rumpled counterpane over her nakedness.

Nick leaned up, swept both counterpane and her protests aside and planted his lower body across her naked hips.

The contact of his middle with her skin made him shudder with lust, almost undid his remaining self-control. *Slow down hombre!* he cautioned himself. Gathering her up into his arms, he kissed her lingeringly while he gently explored the curves she'd bared so hesitantly to his touch, aware as he did so that he was the first to touch her as he was touching her, and pleased by that knowledge. A tender smile curved his lips. He was a pioneer exploring virgin territory—and how sweet that territory was! He'd never felt skin as soft, as smooth, as hers. Everywhere he touched, she was just as warm and silky as a kitten, as fresh as prairie wildflowers you just wanted to bury your face in and breathe deep of their fragrance. . . .

He groaned as she took his lower lip between her teeth and gently tugged on it, for virgin or no, she seemed to know instinctively just how much pressure to use to drive him wild. If anything, the brief delay had only served to heighten her arousal, to sharpen her responses to his lovemaking. She clung to him, kissing him back as he'd kissed her, doing so with an openmouthed, innocent sensuality that stampeded his already galloping senses.

"Angel, my pretty angel," he murmured raggedly. Slipping his tongue inside her mouth, he kissed her deeply, while his hand traveled down over her abdomen and flat, velvety belly to caress the trembling thighs she pressed so tightly together. After a moment's resistance, she parted her legs and let him caress her between them. As his fingers drifted higher, circling the silky inner flesh, rising to explore the downy golden curls of her mons, her breathing quickened. Each gasp became a panting litany beneath his hungry mouth as he parted the soft petals of her sex and slipped a finger inside her, readying the tightness of her virginal body for his entry with slow, rhytmic thrusts.

To her shame, she felt herself grow moist with his intimate caress, a wildly exciting caress that was both far too much and far too little, in some mysterious way she had no words to define. She was afraid—and yet perversely, she wanted more—!

"Oh-oh!" she gasped, pressing her lower body shamelessly against him, clinging to his shoulders as if she were drowning. "Oh, Nick, Nick . . . ! What's happening to me? What's wrong with me?" she whimpered.

"Nothing's wrong, sweetheart. Trust me. Everything's just how it should be, when a woman starts to want a man." He stroked her hair. "Your body's getting ready, same way mine is. We'll take it slow and easy," he promised, kissing her cheeks, her closed eyelids, as he reassured her. "One step at a time. There's a long night still ahead of us, darlin' . . ."

But how could she take things slow and easy, when what he was doing made her feel so excited, so impatient? Not even Miss Clarke's avante-garde education had prepared her for this delicious madness, this wanton delight! What made it all even more incredible was that she'd never dreamed she'd *enjoy* the Unmentionable Act. She'd anticipated a distasteful few minutes spent in utter darkness, wherein The Man lifted her nightgown a few inches, fumbled beneath it and had his disgusting male way with her. Meanwhile, she would lie still and submissive and entertain noble, patriotic thoughts while pretending she was elsewhere until It was over! Was it like this for all women? Did all women experience this euphoric sensation when a man made love to them? Did they crave such shamelessly intimate caresses—or was she in some way a freak, her responses a result of her humble working-class origins?

Through the golden haze of pleasure that surrounded her, filled her, she sensed Nick moving to kneel between her thighs. He took her hand and guided it to his manhood, firmly insistent that she caress him, too, when she would have pulled away in fear.

Curiosity overwhelmed her. Tentatively, she took him in her palm, slowly curled her fingers about his length.

"Oh, God . . . !" he muttered, gritting his teeth.

To her surprise, he didn't feel in the least disgusting or snakelike down there. He was all throbbing heat and a lovely velvety hardness, though she had to admit, he did seem abnormally large for The Act, as she understood it. Apprehension filled her. Surely she would be split in two if he attempted to—to—!

Heart pounding, she drew quick, gasping breaths that were every bit as shaky and rasping as his had become. Perhaps there was still time to reconsider? To change her mind? To plead a sick headache . . . ? To leap up and run for her very life—!

Yet even as the panicky thought took form, he was looming over her.

"Please, Nick, don't. Stop! I've changed my mind. I

don't think I—I can! That we—we should!"

Nick made no answer. Instead, the breadth of his muscular shoulders blotted out the silvery bluish moonlight spilling through the windows as he leaned forward. Bracing his weight on his palms, which he planted on either side of her, he murmured, "You don't have to be afraid, Angel, trust me. Sure, the first time a man has her can be a mite hard on a woman—"

"I know!" she cried, her face paling.

"—but it doesn't *have* to be. Not if that man knows what he's doin'." He smiled and grazed his lips over her swollen mouth.

"And you—you know?" she ventured timidly.

He chuckled softly. "Believe me, darlin', I know. C'mon. Relax. Give me those sweet lips. Kiss me, sweetheart, and I'll show you . . ."

Slowly, oh, so slowly, he lowered his ebony head to hers, claiming her mouth with infinite tenderness. And this time, his kisses were slow and arousing, like the trickle of warmed honey drizzled lazily from a spoon.

Sensation unraveled through her in golden ribbons of pleasure. The gently insistent pressure of his mouth, his lips, steadily fanned the lambent passions that panic had doused, kiss by honeyed, langorous kiss. After a few heady moments, she forgot her fears, forgot what lay ahead. Her limbs grew loose and boneless. Her entire body seemed to float, drifting weightlessly as a silver balloon. Her world narrowed to the cradle of Nick's arms, Nick's lips, to Nick's kisses and caresses, and the dreamy spell of delight they wove about her.

When it happened, it was over in an instant. Still kissing her, he thrust forward. There was a momentary feeling of enormous, unbearable pressure, an instant of burning pain that made her stiffen and struggle, made tears well. Her nails bit deep into his upper arms as, in a blind panic, she tried to squirm from beneath his hurtful, prodding body and thwart his entry. But by then, it was over, done with.

"That's my girl," he murmured as if she were a child, gently stroking her hair until the tension had left her body and her breathing had returned to normal. He kissed her eyelids, the corner of her mouth, the tip of her nose. "That's my lovely Angel . . ."

Only when her resistance had ebbed did he attempt to deepen his entry, to lodge himself fully in the untried sweetness of her virgin flesh that, dear Lord, sheathed him so perfectly in its tightness. And, when he did so at long last, moving his hips slowly, carefully, to fill her, he saw her gray eyes widen with the dawning knowledge of a pleasure so great, wars had been fought over it; lives had been given for it; civilizations lost on account of it.

"Nick! Oh, Nick it feels so—so—good! Oh, don't stop—don't stop don't—ever!"

Slowly, he began to move in her, flexing his muscled hips, whispering silly, wonderful endearments in her hair as he loved her. To his delight, she soon began to move with him, slowly at first, first arching her body to accept his thrusts, then to match them, clinging to him as they moved together. She caressed his back, his hard buttocks, feeling the muscles there tighten and relax, again and again. Each plunge of his flanks, each powerful thrust, carried them closer to the golden rapture that lay but a trembling heartbeat away!

To Angel, it was as if she moved in some glorious dream from which she never wanted to wake, a sensual, erotic dream in which pleasure was the air she breathed, the wine she drank, the song she sang, the music to which they danced.

Holding her fast, Nick rolled over, onto his back, taking her with him. "Now. You love me, sweet thing," he commanded huskily.

Angel, lost in the sweet madness of first desire, needed no second invitation.

Lifting her hair above her head so that it spilled in wanton abandon between her fingers and down her back in glorious tangled skeins, she straddled him, undulating her hips experimentally.

"Like this?" she whispered, her eyes dark with her passion.

Unable to speak, Nick could only clench his jaw, nod,

and grunt. Sweat beaded on his brow, bled from him. Didn't she know? Couldn't she tell? Virgin or no, was it possible she was really so innocent, she had no idea what she was doing to him—had been doing to him for what seemed an eternity?

Groaning, he caressed her thighs, her high, full breasts, the almost concave sweep of her velvety belly, before finally devoting his attentions to the tiny bud of her passion. Suddenly, she arched backwards and grew still. Her moist lips parted in a throaty cry. Her eyes slid closed in silent wonder as the shower of blossoms that had swirled in her mind's eye suddenly exploded in a scarlet storm of petals.

She panted, gasped, and as her body pulsed around him, Nick offered up a fervent prayer of relief and fiercely gripped her hips to hold her down upon his aching length, groaning through clenched jaws as he reached his own long-awaited release with a muted roar of triumph.

They rocked together until, with a final sob of pleasure, Angel fell limply forward across his chest, her long, honey gold hair wrapped about his throat.

For endless moments, they lay still and sated in the aftermath of their loving, waiting until the pounding of their hearts had ebbed to a more measured tempo. It was Nick who broke the silence at long last.

"Don't run away, sweet thing. I'll be right back," he whispered at length.

"Where are you going?" Angel queried softly, sitting up. Her hair and body were a pale blur against the darkness.

"To open the windows so I can sleep. I get t' feelin' like I've been roped and hog-tied when I'm closed in. Guess I'm used to sleeping outdoors, under the stars."

Under the stars? He was used to sleeping outdoors, in the open air? Oh, her poor, proud Durango, she thought tenderly. Despite his devil-may-care attitude, he must not have so much as a roof over his head back in his primitive New Mexico! No wonder he'd joined the Wild West Show and jumped at her father's proposition. He'd needed the money, but been too proud to admit it . . . She bit her lip, remembering the countless times she'd privately called him uncouth or gauche, the spiteful way she'd criticized his outlandish attire or deplored his lack of manners. Now, knowing what she did, she was thoroughly ashamed of herself for her condescending manner. There, but for the grace of God and crazy Lord Harry Brixton, go Papa and I, she thought contritely, her heart going out to him.

"There's no need to explain, Nick," she scolded drowsily. "This is your room. And a cool breeze would be rather welcome right now . . ." her voice trailed away.

Before he returned to bed, she was fast asleep.

Chuckling, Nick curled his arms around her and kissed her brow, before pulling the coverlet up over them both and joining her in sleep. By his figuring, he'd earned it.

Chapter Eighteen

As a nearby church clock chimed three, Nick glanced one last time over his shoulder before slipping from the room.

Angel was still deeply asleep, a contented smile curving her lips. Her long, unbound hair spilled across the pillows in a river of captured light that gleamed like gold veins in a miner's pan. The coverlet was twisted around her body as she lay on her side, one hand cradling her flushed cheek, the other arm loosely hugging the pillow she'd accepted in his place. Her slender, ivory thighs and the high, rounded swell of her bottom were delightfully bared, patterned by tiger stripes from the alternating shadow and blue-white moonlight that spilled through the French doors he'd just locked.

"Sweet dreams, lil' Miz Iron Drawers," he murmured under his breath.

An unaccustomed tenderness filled him as, chuckling softly, he slipped through the door and out into the corridor. Taking no chances, he also carefully locked the second door behind him.

Two hours later found him walking his horse back toward the Hotel St. Pierre, deep in thought as he smoked a cheroot.

Dawn was showing a rosy pink blush above the rooftops of Paris. The birds were beginning to stir and warble matins in the chestnut trees that lined the boulevards.

Farmers driving wagons piled high with produce were entering the city, headed for the morning markets. Street vendors with their barrows of wares passed him, yet Nick saw none of them.

His visit to the Moulin Rouge's attic in the wee hours had confirmed the story Angel had told him. He'd found the overturned chair she'd described, the ropes still coiled about its spindles, the tiny murky window beneath the eaves, the wicker hampers filled with gaudy cancan costumes, stacked against the mildewed walls. What he had not found were any traces of the two men.

"D'you recollect seeing two Englishmen and a young woman here this afternoon, mam'zelle?" he'd asked one of the bleary-eyed dancers.

The girls were sitting about the deserted dance hall, which at this hour smelled strongly of stale cigar smoke and sour wine. Night people by nature, they were enjoying an early breakfast before they headed home to sleep away the daylight hours. However, they were not so exhausted they hadn't visibly brightened with the handsome *Americain's* entrance.

"Two rough English fellows, *chèri? Oui*, they were here," a blond woman volunteered in answer to his questions. "They offered Jacques—he's the manager— money to rent the attic for a few hours. Jacques, he is a greedy peeg. Of course, he accepted. But the girl . . . ?" Mignon shrugged, stifling a yawn. "No. I did not see 'er until this evening, m'sieu, when she somehow slipped in among us. Then, during our first number, she jumped from the stage and ran out of that side door, over there." She nodded in that direction. "I followed and saw her running away from the men down the delivery alley, yes? She jumped into a cab and—poof! She was gone." Mignon smiled ruefully. "Those British idiots were very angry that they lost her, believe me."

"Are they still around here?"

"*Non*, m'sieu. Jacques, he told them to get out. Their bad manners upset the customers, you see? Jacques wouldn't stand for that. It is bad for business."

He nodded. "Could you describe the men for me?" Angel had been blindfolded and able to add very little to

217

his own brief impression of her abductors, but fortunately, Mignon was shrewd and observant and able to give him a vivid description of both men.

When she'd finished, Nick nodded and tipped his hat, sliding a thousand franc note across the table. "*Merci*, mam'zelle."

"My pleasure, m'sieu," Mignon purred, fluttering her lashes at him coyly as she tucked the bill down her jiggling bosom. "Per'aps, if you are alone in Paris, Mignon could show you ze sights, hmm . . . ? I am free during the day . . . ?"

"Maybe I'll take you up on that offer, *chèrie*," he'd said with a wink, and left the Moulin Rouge.

One block from the Hotel St. Pierre Nick heard the nasal drawn-out bleats of police whistles. Moments later, caped gendarmes on horseback appeared from several different directions, hastening their clopping mounts toward the source of the sound. Kneeing his black stallion into a trot, Nick did likewise.

As he rounded a corner, he saw a crowd had gathered. People were leaning over a small stone bridge that crossed the Seine, gesturing excitedly at something floating in the river below.

Nick peered over the embankment. He saw one of the colorful flyboats, bobbing about on the current below the picturesque bridge. Her captain hung over the boat's railing, grappling at something dark in the water with a boat hook. As Nick watched, one of the *gendarme's* removed his cape, jacket, and boots. The crowd cheered its approval as the young officer dived off the bridge, surfacing alongside the boat. Nick could see no more as the onlookers surged forward, obstructing his view.

Clicking to Diablo, Nick cantered his horse closer, mounting the bridge just as the crowd parted. The *gendarmes* were helping their fellow officer and the boat's captain heave a dripping object up onto the bridge.

It was a body, he realized, his curiosity piqued. A suicide? Probably. The Seine's watery depths attracted its fair share of despondent lovers. Dismounting, he hitched his horse to a lamp post and approached the crowd on foot, elbowing his way through the crush of flower

218

vendors, bakers, fishmongers, clerks, and farmers to see.

The body was that of a young man who seemed vaguely familiar to Nick at first glance, somehow, though it was hard to be certain. His blond hair was now dark with river water and his narrow-featured, pale face mottled with purple bruises and the lividity of death. The vacant eyes that stared up at the dawn breaking over the city of Paris were blue and bulging with terror, as if he'd expected to die.

"Mon Dieu! C'est l'Anglais!" cried an excited voice.

The man next to Nick dropped a half-dozen smelly blue-and-silver fish to the pavement. He brandished the sheet of crumpled newspaper they'd been wrapped in in Nick's face, shaking it to add emphasis to his words. "Look, m'sieu, his picture is right here!"

A daguerreotype of the dead man stared up at Nick from beneath a glaring headline, smiling indolently and fully recognizable in what had obviously been a far happier time for him. The headlines screamed in French:

BRITISH GAMING-HALL OWNER SLAIN! FUGI-TIVE PEER PRIME MURDER SUSPECT!

With a low whistle, Nick grabbed the newspaper from the man and quickly scanned the column printed beneath it. Three European tours with Bill Cody's troupe had left Nick with just enough knowledge of French to be able to translate the report:

Inspector Jamieson of Scotland Yard announced this morning that Lord Reginald Smythe-Moreton, son of the late Lord Cavendish Smythe-Moreton, has been implicated in the shooting death of William Bligh, proprietor of Bligh's West End gaming establishment. Smythe-Moreton is urgently being sought for questioning both in Britain and at all Continental ports.

Bligh's body was discovered in his mews apartment three days ago, shortly after midnight. He had been shot between the eyes. Inspector Jamieson further stated that a warrant has been issued for the arrest of Smythe-Moreton, whom Pansy Loveness, a female companion of the deceased, witnessed fleeing the mews shortly after hearing the loud report of a firearm.

Any person having information regarding this crime, or knowledge of the whereabouts of said fugitive, should contact Inspector Jamieson at Scotland Yard, Whitehall, London, without delay.

Nick's eyes flickered to the date in the top corner. The newspaper was almost a week old! And, that being the case, Bill Bligh had clearly taken no active part in masterminding the kidnapping of Angel that afternoon. Hardly—he'd already been dead over a week! What was more, judging by the bloated condition of Smythe-Moreton's sodden corpse, it seemed unlikely he'd had a hand in it, either. . . .

With a nod of thanks, Nick returned the crumpled newspaper to the man and crouched down beside the body. His gaze traveled over the sorry sight, taking in the injuries done to the face before finally coming to rest on the mottled and puffy blue-white hands. One was open, the other tightly clenched. Acting on gut instinct, Nick reached for that closed fist. It was cold and stiff as marble in his hands. There was no way he could pry open the fingers without breaking bones, he realized.

He was about to leave when he noticed something shiny protruding between the rigid knuckles. A prickle of excitement raised the hackles on his neck. A button torn from his murderer's clothing as Reggie struggled for his life? Curious, Nick worked it loose with his fingertips. But to his disgust, the "button" was only a tiny scrap of sodden paper that disintegrated in his grip. Disappointed, he extricated himself from the ghoulish crowd, retrieved his horse, and continued on to the St. Pierre at a brisk canter that made Diablo's hooves clatter loudly over the cobbles.

Hell if he didn't feel uneasy about having left Angel alone, all of a sudden. Sure, Reggie and Bligh were dead and were of no further threat to her, but the same couldn't be said of the two ornery sidewinders Mignon had described. Or whoever *they* were working for.

* * *

The morning breeze promised summer was on its way as the four sat at breakfast on the stone-flagged terrace of the St. Pierre the following morning.

Their wrought-iron table, shaded by a gay red-and-white striped umbrella, overlooked the Seine and the colorful pleasure boats riding its current. The silver serving trays set before them held an assortment of warm croissants, hot rolls, butter, and preserves. There was also a platter of sliced fresh fruits, a steaming pot of café au lait, and dainty demitasse cups.

Hungrily devouring his fourth croissant, Nick found himself longing for the kind of breakfasts he'd been used to back home: platters of perhaps a half-dozen eggs fried over-easy with chili-pepper salsa spooned over them, a mess of country-fried potatoes or Spanish rice and refried beans, along with a sizzling beefsteak cooked rare over a mesquite fire, the whole washed down with scalding black coffee, bitter and strong enough to burn the roof off his mouth. . . . Hell if these papery-light rolls didn't tickle his belly, 'stead of filling it!

Glancing up, he saw that Angel was watching him wolf the croissant like a scared jackrabbit fascinated by a snake. Grinning, he slowly licked a flake of pastry and a golden droplet of butter from his lower lip and let his gaze roam lazily over her. Meeting her eyes again, he winked and murmured, "Good mornin', Miz Angel," amused when she blushed deeply and smartly returned her attention to her plate. She was obviously thoroughly unsettled by his gaze and the memories it brought back of the night they'd shared.

Damn, but she looked lovely this morning—like a bride the morning after her wedding! Just looking at her across the table made his groin grow tight with the longing to make love to her all over again in a thousand different ways, to teach her everything he knew about making love. Instead of confining her hair in a severe knot with pins and combs, she'd used only a wide band of deep-pink velvet ribbon to draw it back and up, off her cheeks and brow. Beneath a summery white straw boater trimmed with a flirty matching ribbon, loose ringlets of honey-gold spiraled down her back. He remembered how those silken

221

skeins had felt in the night, wound around his throat, pooling across his chest, and his mouth grew dry as a desert. Her gown was also deep rose in color, with a square sailor collar and long sleeves that had wide buttoned cuffs. Both cuffs and collar were of crisp white linen. Yes sir, all pink and white and gold, she looked good enough to eat this morning, vulnerable and innocent and wide-eyed as a schoolgirl who'd been up to mischief, and was now fearful of being caught by the grownups and punished for her misdeeds.

"Did you sleep well, Miz Higgins?" he drawled, aware of Red and Juarez's covert glances at them both over their coffee cups.

"Like a top, Mr. Durango," she replied demurely, with just a hint of a sexy, conspiratorial gleam in her long-lashed gray eyes and the faintest of smiles curving her tempting pink lips. "And I have such an appetite this morning, too! I suspect the spring weather must have had an invigorating effect on my . . . ummm . . . appetite. Don't you?" She raised her lashes to him once again and shot him a sultry side-look that could have singed paper.

"Spring weather, my arse!" Mabel muttered into her napkin.

"Mabel? I'm sorry, dear, I didn't quite catch your last remark. What did you say?" Angel inquired, darting Mabel a sharp look.

Dear? "Oh, nuffink. Just silly ole me, thinkin' out loud!" Mabel covered with a nudge and a wink for Juarez, who was also smiling broadly across the table, first at Nick, then back at the redhead. Stiffly, he reached out, took Mabel's hand from the tablecloth and pressed his lips to her knuckles.

"Oh, Señor Juarez, do forgive me!" Angel exclaimed as she noticed the difficulty with which he moved. She blinked as if aroused from a trance. "Your poor, poor arm! How is it this morning? I quite forgot—I injured you with my unpardonable behavior last evening, did I not?"

"Truly, it was but a scratch, señorita. Do not concern yourself."

Filled with shame and remorse, Angel pressed her hand to her bosom. "Just a scratch, indeed! I shall never forgive

222

myself! I could have killed you—or—or—Nick—with my foolish, irresponsible behavior."

"Sí—but the important thing to remember is that you did not. The bullet only winged me. Mabe—the lovely señorita Mabella here cleaned and bandaged my small wound, and now, Juarez is as good as new."

"Really and truly? You swear it? Oh, I do hope you're not just saying that to make me feel better." She grimaced and bowed her head, toying with her napkin. "I feel so ashamed this morning, so awfully guilty about what I did. I suppose—I suppose I really owe M'sieu Martine an apology for frightening the hotel guests, too . . ."

"Martine thinks you were rehearsin' an act for the Wild West Show, Angel. Let it go at that, hmm?" Nick suggested.

"Very well. If—if you say so, Nick."

"I do."

Their eyes met over the table centerpiece of carnations again, uncertain gray melting into bold, hungry ice blue and locking there as if transfixed. Both Juarez and Mabel noticed the sudden acceleration of the bluish pulse at the base of Angel's throat, the way her fingers tightened convulsively over the folds of her napkin as a lazy smile curved Nick's lips.

"I do," he murmured again.

Mabel coughed loudly and cleared her throat, forcing the pair to guiltily turn their heads to look at her. "Talking of acts, Angel luv, that *was* you we saw, kicking up your heels at the Moolon Rooge last night, weren't it?" she asked with archly raised brows.

"Why, yes, Mabel, I'm afraid it was." Angel admitted ruefully, embarrassed that they'd seen her scandalous charade. "As I told Nick last night, I was desperate to escape those dreadful men. In the process, I somehow ended up on the stage with the cancan dancers!"

"Hmm," Mabel said serenely, giving Nick a pointed, smug glance that screamed "I told-you-so." "I said as much to these two. 'That's our Angel up there,' I said, 'showin' off her drawers—'! But Nick said if it were, he'd—"

"That will be quite enough of that, Mabel," Angel cut

223

in sharply, red-cheeked with mortification. "As far as I'm concerned, what happened yesterday was a frightful nightmare, but is now over and done with. Finished! I'd just as soon forget it, pretend none of it happened, if it's all the same to . . . all the same to . . ."

Her voice suddenly trailed away.

Looking up curiously from his jelly-laden croissant, Nick saw that she was staring across the terrace. Her face had paled. Her eyes widened with alarm. Her mouth rounded with shock.

"Angel? What's wrong? What is it?" Nick rasped, following her frightened gaze.

"That man on the steps—the fellow paying M'sieu Martine?" she whispered. "I only caught a glimpse before they jumped me, but—I'm almost certain he's one of them!"

"Your kidnappers?"

"Yes!"

"Stay with the women, *amigo!*" Nick growled.

He sprang to his feet, toppling the wrought-iron chair beneath him as he quickly wove his way between the busy tables, crossing the stone-flagged terrace at a run.

Both Martine and the man saw him coming before he was halfway there. He knew it by the fear that leaped into their eyes. But, just as he was about to close in on them and head off their escape, a party of white-wimpled Breton nuns suddenly exited the hotel conservatory, blocking his way!

At what seemed like snail's pace, the sisters walked past him in a close-knit, unbroken cavalcade, two by two, each one with her head piously bowed in prayer, clasped hands fingering a rosary. Fuming with impotent fury, Nick was forced to stand there and wait 'til they'd gone past.

By the time he could continue the chase, the pair had split up, the man taking the flight of lichened, crumbing steps down to the stone quay below the hotel terrace, while Martine vanished elsewhere. As Nick leaped after the first man, he scrambled aboard a small boat. A second man waiting inside it hurriedly cast off. The boat had already moved out into the middle of the Seine when Nick skidded to a halt on the mossy quay.

"Damn!"

Still cursing, he retook the steps two at a time, but despite his haste, there was no sign of Martine on the crowded terrace. Looking about, he saw Juarez point to the hotel. "Inside, Nick! He went that way!"

Needing no second telling, Nick ran through the hotel kitchen and storage rooms in search of Martine, asking startled chefs, maids, and waiters if they'd seen the manager. Luck was with him. Some had, and they pointed the way. At length, he found the man cowering in the hotel pantry, clearly terrified. He threw up his pale hands in surrender as Nick strode toward him with a face like thunder.

"Don't 'urt me! I beg you, M'sieu Nick, do not shoot me!"

Gripping him by the coat lapels so forcefully, his patent-leather shoes quit the ground, Nick slammed Martine up against the pantry door.

"All right, *mon ami*," he ground out, his silvery eyes crackling. "If you don't want to get hurt, talk! Then I'll decide whether t' shoot you or not."

"Talk about what, m'sieu?" Martine babbled, almost incoherent.

"That man! I want his name, damn you!"

"But I do not know it . . ."

"Yeah? Then why was he paying you?"

"For—for information, m'sieu. He—he said he was a newspaper reporter—and that he was doing a story about you and—and Mademoiselle Oakley—er—Higgins, and the Wild West Show. He wanted me to watch you and the young lady. To let him know when you went out and she was alone in her suite. He said—he said he only wanted to interview her, and I believe 'im! Oh, forgive me, Nick, I beg you! A hotel manager's salary, it is very small, *non?* And the—the money he offered, it was so very tempting, m'sieu—!"

"Never mind that!" Nick growled. "How were you to contact him?"

"I was to send a messenger to a room above the Le Chat Mal—it is a small restaurant a few streets from here. The food, it is not very—"

"And today was the first time he approached you?" Nick cut in.

"The very first. I swear it on my mother's grave!"

"Dirty liar—!"

"*Non! Non!*"

Nick tightened his grip on Martine's throat. "You're sure?"

"I'm sure, *oui*, very sure!"

Nick released Martine, who slithered to the cold tile of the pantry floor in a heap. Sobbing, he sat there with his face buried in his hands. With a look of contempt, Nick turned on his heels and returned to the terrace.

"Our pal got away," he announced in response to the three expectant faces lifted to his. "Seems he was trying to pay our friend Martine to keep him notified about our whereabouts."

"Blimey! Then those bastards ain't given up on our Angel?" Mabel exclaimed indignantly.

"I'm afraid not," Nick admitted, taking his seat once again and squeezing Angel's clammy little hand to reassure her. "Now. Since I scared the sidewinder off, you ladies may as well finish your breakfasts, before you go on up to your rooms to pack."

"Pack?" Angel echoed, brows raised.

"That's what I said, sweet thing. I reckon it's high time we were movin' on down the trail, don't you?"

Soberly, his three companions nodded agreement.

They halfheartedly returned to their meal and their cooled coffee, trying to restore their former lighthearted mood with breezy chatter that fell horribly flat. Nick was scowling and preoccupied and it was obvious that Angel had completely lost her appetite. The atmosphere resembled a wake rather than a holiday breakfast.

Just then, a waiter halted at their table. He was smiling indulgently. "M'sieu Durango?"

"Yes?" Nick said, glancing up suspiciously.

"Go away!" Mabel hissed, flapping her hand and signaling frantically at the waiter to make himself scarce with her rolling eyes. "*Allez!* Shoo!"

"Shoo? *Shoo*, madame? But I have a special order for M'sieu Durango," the young man insisted.

226

"Just get lorst, lad. Scarper, I said! The monsewer's full, he is. He don't want no more grub, believe me, he don't! So, shove orf—!"

"But I have my orders, madame," the young man protested, sniffing in distaste. With a flourish, he set a silver platter covered with a large dome before Nick. "With the compliments of Mademoiselle Blunt, m'sieu," he declared pompously, and bowed before leaving them.

"From you, Red? But it's not my birthday! What in the world is it—?" Nick began, casting her a curious glance.

Mabel laughed nervously. "It's nothing, reelly it ain't. Er—in fact, all things considered, per'aps it'd be better if you didn't look inside, eh, love?" Mabel suggested in a wheedling tone, pushing back her chair and hurrying to Nick's side. "Just pass it over here t' me, lad. I'll take care o' it for you."

"Heck, no, Red," Nick intervened, wrestling the platter from her hands when she reached for it. "If you ordered a surprise treat for me, then I intend to eat it," Nick vowed with a wink and a smile for the redhead. "Finish your coffee and rolls, honey. We've plenty of time."

Mabel sighed heavily and returned to her seat with sagging shoulders and an expression of doom. "All right. 'Ave it your way. But remember—keep your sense of humor, Nick, there's a good lad," she pleaded. "And *don't* say I didn't warn you, ducks!"

Frowning, Nick lifted the silver dome. There, basking in solitary splendor upon the ornate silver platter, complete with parsley garnish, knife and fork, was his Stetson hat!

Chapter Nineteen

"Well, ladies, next stop, Italy!" Nick declared. He clambered over one of Angel's hatboxes and her bulky drawstring purse to take his seat upon the bench facing Mabel and Juarez.

Angel gave him a rueful smile. "If we survive the journey, that is!" She was uncomfortably squeezed into the corner by the window. It was only with some difficulty that Nick managed to fit his tall frame between her and a buxom farmer's wife. The woman had a basket of eggs on her plump knees and two fidgety little girls tucked under her arm, like chicks nestled under a hen's wing.

"You'll survive," Nick promised in a tone that brooked no possible alternative, and was enormously conforting to her. "I'll see to that."

"Then you believe I had nothing to do with yesterday's kidnapping attempt?" she whispered, wondering if the night they'd shared had brought about his new proprietary tone, or if he'd learned something new.

"While you were sleeping, I paid a little visit to the Moulin Rouge."

"You did? And your visit proved I was telling the truth?"

"My visit, and a few other things," he hedged, deciding to postpone telling her about Reggie and Bligh's deaths until a more suitable time. The farm wife was peering at them curiously.

She bit her lip. "Thank God! I thought I'd never be able to convince you, and it was all my fault that I couldn't—

like the little boy who cried 'wolf' so many times, when the real wolf came along, no one believed him." She sighed. "You have no idea how I regret the dreadful hoax I tried to pull off! Despite how it seems, I do love my father very deeply, Mr. Durango."

"Surely you can call me 'Nick' by now, can't you?"

"Very well. Nick. Truly, I would never have done anything to hurt my father in the usual way of things. It was just that . . . I was so terribly ashamed of losing all that money at the gaming tables, I could see no other way out of my dilemma. Da would have been so shocked if he'd learned the truth. And that hateful Bligh was threatening to tell him everything! Oh, Nick, Da's such a dear, dear man, and he trusts me completely. I suppose—I suppose you could say I acted badly out of desperation, but did so with the best possible motives . . ."

"Figuring with all his millions, your pa'd take the loss of three thousand pounds easier than learning you'd lied to him?"

She looked up at him with surprise and no little admiration. "Why, yes. That's exactly how I felt!"

"Well, I guess I can understand that," he admitted reluctantly.

"This morning, when I realized I'd wounded poor Juarez, I knew things had gone far enough. I've made a decision, Nick. When I go home, I'm going to tell Papa everything, make a clean slate of it. He'll be hurt and angry, no doubt, but I must do what I should have done from the very first. Face up to the consequences and take my punishment."

"Good girl. Sid loves you, Angel. He'll be riled as a wet hen at first—but he'll come around."

"Thank you. I do hope so."

"Say, was anyone else in on your plan, other than Red and Reggie?"

"Just Simmons, the groom. He drove the carriage."

"No one else who might stand to profit from your kidnapping?"

She shook her head. "Not that I can think of. That's why I've come to the conclusion those dreadful men must work for Bill Bligh. Who else could possibly have any reason to harm me! You didn't discover something at the Moulin Rouge?" she asked hopefully. "Something you're not telling me?"

"Not exactly, no. But as for a motive—! Angel, your pa has millions of 'em!"

"His money, you mean?"

"That, coupled with his love for you. Add greed, and you have a deadly combination, by any man's reckoning."

On that sobering note, they both fell silent, Nick pondering the identity of Angel's kidnappers, Angel determinedly casting such unpleasant thoughts aside. Instead, she dreamily reflected on their blissful love-making the night before.

She was a little tender in certain areas today, but except for those minor discomforts, she felt wonderful, blooming, alive as she'd never felt before, no longer a naive young girl, but an experienced woman of the world who had dared the Ultimate, she considered, and tasted the heady wine of illicit passion. And, since she'd burned her boats, so to speak, by turning down Reggie's proposal, that single night with Nick might be all the passion she ever knew. After all, she thought practically, she'd received only one other offer of marriage since she'd turned sixteen, and that one made by Uncle Teddy, bless him, out of pity; an offer her da had thanked him for making, but gently refused. No, she might as well face up to it; it was unlikely she'd marry. She was too wealthy for the young lads that her working-class birth would have suited her for, yet too "common," too lacking in blue blood, to marry into society. She imagined she and Da'd retire to their country estate in Suffolk when her age and the fact that she was still unwed became an embarrassment. There, her days would no doubt be spent in caring for her father and doing good works about the nearest village.

The steam train that would carry them down into the south of France then on across the Alps into Italy was so crowded, the stuffy, warm compartment made Angel yawn. The monotonous chuffa-chuffa song and the lulling, swaying motion as the train rattled through winding green valleys, vineyard terraces, past ancient, rambling chateaux or quaint country inns only added to her sleepiness. Her eyelids began to droop so heavily, it was an effort to keep them open!

"Didn't you tell me you slept like a top?" Nick murmured as he noted her fatigue.

"But I did," she argued, stifling yet another yawn that popped out of nowhere. "I don't know what's wrong with me this afternoon!" She straightened her spine, trying very hard to sit up and be more alert, as befitted a young lady traveling the Continent. But, it was a battle she was destined to lose.

"Must have been that cancan dancing got you tuckered out, then I guess," he suggested as she stifled yet another yawn. He was rewarded by a bright pink blush. They both knew it wasn't the dancing that had drained her so completely, but the glorious interlude that had come much later.

"Cad!" she hissed under her breath, smiling nonetheless. "A true gentleman would refrain from reminding me of what transpired last night!"

"If I was a true gentleman, there wouldn't have been anything to remind you of, sweetness," he whispered back, quick as a flash. "Any regrets?"

She looked up shyly, then smiled a dazzling smile of such sweetness, such open honesty and sincerity, it was like the sun coming out after a shower. "Actually, no. None at all," she admitted candidly. "And you?"

"You need to ask?" he murmured, seeking her hand, which was hidden by the folds of her skirts.

The combinaton of his husky admission and the intimate way he linked his fingers through hers and squeezed pleased her to the point of confusion. They exchanged quick, embarrassed smiles and, still holding hands, looked as quickly away, both pretending to be suddenly fascinated with the countryside.

Only moments later Angel fell asleep with her head lolling snugly against Nick's chest, while he drifted off with his chin propped on the top of her head and his Stetson angled over his eyes.

Mabel and Juarez exchanged knowing grins before

following suit in similar cosy fashion. Sleep was by far the simplest way to make a long, uncomfortable journey pass quickly.

It was late afternoon when Juarez woke them, urgently shaking Nick's shoulder.

"*Amigo!* Wake up! We have company—!"

Nick came fully awake instantly, an old habit acquired riding herd he'd never lost. Shoving back his hat, he sat up. "Where?"

"Back there, the carriage behind this one—and coming up fast! I saw them when I went back to the smoking car. They're dressed as ticket collectors, but I recognized one from this morning. Nick, they look like they mean business!" Juarez rolled his eyes.

"Guns?"

"*Sí.* Both are armed. The left-hander wears his gun in his belt, about here. Crooked Nose has a knife. In his boot."

"You did real good, *hombre.*"

Juarez's eyes darkened. "These are dangerous *hombres.* Something about them . . . aiee, I can tell. They will not rest until they have Señorita Angel—or until the one they call *jefe* calls them off. I think you should take Angelica and go. Leave the train, if you have to."

"My reckoning, too!" Nick agreed hurriedly, with a grim smile. "If things go wrong and we get split up, I'll see you in Rome, pardner. You know where. Wait for us there, eh?"

"I will. Be careful."

Their eyes met. Nick nodded. "We will. Angel, honey, let's you and me take a walk, hmmm?"

Sleepily, she opened her eyes. "A walk?" She yawned. "Where?"

"You'll see, honey. Grab your bag, now." When she'd done so, he gripped her elbow and all but lifted her from her seat. "Excuse me, folks! Make way! Sick woman comin' through! Give the little lady some air!"

Chivvying Angel ahead of him, they wove their way between the strap-hanging passengers to the door at the far end of the carriage. Nick frowned. If they were in luck, the rear of another carriage would be joined to this one by an

232

accordion link-up, and they'd be able to pass on through into the next compartment. If not—*Dios!* There'd be nowhere to run and nowhere to hide—and they'd be in real trouble—!

Nick risked a glance behind him. He saw two now-familiar, ugly faces appear through the far door, heads bobbing as the pair craned to see over the crush of passengers in the public car. It'd be only a matter of minutes before they'd checked all the passengers and realized he and Angel were not there!

"Hey, you thievin' blighter!" he heard Red screech at the top of her lungs of a sudden. "You took my bleedin' seat, didn't you? I was sittin' here!"

"But you are mistaken! I was here first, señora!" he heard Juarez protest in a wounded tone.

As the pair intended, with their little diversion the passengers began jostling forward, trying to find out just who and what were causing all the ruckus.

Thanking God for loyal friends, Nick plunged forward, battled the carriage door against the wind, then stepped through it, dragging Angel after him.

The wind slammed the door shut behind them. It whipped their faces and stole their breath away. Sooty smuts stung their cheeks where they stood on a narrow ledge, bordered by a low railing. Beyond this, the locomotive's iron wheels, the endless rails and the French countryside peeled away in a blurred frieze of green-and-brown, seeming perilously close and threatening. Alongside the narrow door they'd exited, an engineer's spindly iron-runged maintenance ladder led up onto the roof of the railway carriage. Grinding coupling separated their car from the one behind. They were trapped!

The sudden breathtaking rush of cold air, the dizzying speed at which they were traveling, brought Angel around. Gripping the railing, she blinked and looked around her, exclaiming, "Nick? What are we doing out here?"

"Those men are on the train. Juarez spotted them. They're searching the car for us now."

"No!" Wildly, she looked around, holding down her wind-whipped hair with one hand and gripping the

233

flimsy railing with the other. "But—where can we go?"

"Up there!" He pointed to the ladder that led above. "Are you game?"

With only a moment's hesitation, she nodded, to his enormous relief, and released the railing long enough to tuck her skirts into the sash of her dress, out of the way.

"There! All set!" she declared gamely, despite the fear that had sprung into her eyes.

In that moment, Nick fancied he might be falling in love.

"Good girl! You go first. I'll be right behind you."

One after the other, they scrambled up the ladder onto the carriage roof.

To Angel's relief, it proved far broader than she had anticipated, broad enough to walk along with relative ease, once one's equilibrium had adjusted to the repeated rocking motion. Everywhere was sooty and grimy.

"Oh, my word!" she exclaimed as she looked about. The scenery was breathtaking from up here, little green valleys and terraced vineyards on either side of the tracks, farms and deeply wooded forests spreading out in all directions. Further away, just before a steep hillside, a wooden train trestle crossed a sparkling lake, before the tracks arrowed straight into the dark belly of the hillside. "It's lovely!"

"Keep your voice down and don't move around, Angel. I think our friends are down below," Nick hissed.

She held her breath, watching as Nick stepped gingerly to the top of the ladder and peered over the edge. Moments later, he returned to her.

"Well?"

"I think we've given them the slip for a while. They thought they'd missed us somehow and went back inside for another look." He grinned. "How's that for luck?"

"Thank heavens for small mercies! Are we anywhere near a station, do you know?"

"Judging by all this countryside, I don't reckon so."

"Then we'll have to stay here indefinitely, and pray those men don't put two and two together and guess we must be up here, hmm? Nick? Is that what you're saying?"

He was staring straight ahead, as if he hadn't heard her. "Nick? Will we have to stay up here indefinitely?"

The look in his eyes when he turned was one she was certain she didn't want explained.

"Not indefinitely, no," he said tightly, a muscle ticking in his jaw. "In fact, I reckon we should be moving on real soon—say, in about five minutes?"

"Five minutes! But why? And where can we go?" she demanded, her voice growing shrill with panic now. Wasn't it enough that she'd climbed up onto the roof of a moving railway carriage? What more did the confounded man expect of her?

"The 'why' of it's easy, honey. See, there's a little old tunnel up ahead. The train tracks run clear through that hill."

"And?"

"Well, sweet thing . . . while there's room for the train to go on through, I'm not sure there's room for us." He grinned. "If you get my meanin'?"

She did, and paled. "We could—we could lie flat on our stomachs, couldn't we?"

"We could, you're right. But . . . if we've misjudged the clearance, it'll be too damned late to change our minds at the last minute. We'll hit the tunnel and—splut!"

She swallowed nervously. "All right. Forget that. We could climb back down and take our chances?" she suggested, suddenly very certain that this option was not one Nick would even consider.

"We could—but we won't."

"But the only alternative is—"

"—rushing up on us right now! Here, take my hand and stand up, honey. That's the way!"

"Balderdash! This is utter madness—and you're utterly mad! It's insane. I won't do it—I shan't! We'll be killed!"

The train was hurtling toward the wooden trestle and the dark mouth of the tunnel at its far end. She could feel it picking up speed beneath her feet as it mounted the incline, and panic filled her.

"Do you trust me, Angel?" Nick shouted, just as the steam engine let out a triumphant whistle.

"Never! Not in a million years!" she screamed back. "You're a maniac! A stark, raving lunatic!"

"Maybe I am!" Nick yelled, unabashed. "Either way,

you c'n badmouth me later. For now—*juuummmp!*"

Never—even should she live to be a hundred!—would Angel forget Nick grabbing her hand and pulling her after him; she would never forget the jolting terror as the train slipped from beneath her feet and she plunged suddenly down, down in midair.

During that seemingly endless drop through space, the momentous details of her life flashed before her eyes.

Her da's smile of pride and love—

—and Nick, kissing her in the rented *fiacre*.

Her da's comforting hugs—

and Nick as he'd looked last night, when he'd loomed above her and shown her what it meant to be a woman.

Her da's loving concern—

and Nick's expression when he'd taken her hand in the railway carriage.

Please God, she had to survive—had to!—if only to tell that madman if he ever dared to touch her again, she'd take back her apology and kill him—!

The sudden shock of plunging into the ice cold waters of the lake at its spring flood drove all thoughts of vengeance from her mind—temporarily.

She sank, her sodden clothes dragging her down, tangling and weighting her limbs. Her poor lungs were screaming for air when at last, she managed to fight her way back to the surface, inch by painful inch. She saw Nick treading water only a few feet away but he seemed far more concerned about recovering his stupid hat than her welfare!

Ignoring him, she kicked madly for shore, her arms windmilling to keep afloat. Her teeth were chattering uncontrollably when she staggered out onto the shale banks just moments ahead of Nick. Her jaw set, her gray eyes smoking with fury, she lifted her drawstring purse over her head.

"Well?" he demanded between panting breaths as he lurched up the banks toward her. "We made it! Do you trust me now?"

She answered by swinging her purse around on its long, narrow strap and lambasting him across the head with it. The wet, hefty thwack sent him reeling off-balance,

236

sprawling to the shingle.

"Does that answer your question, you great dolt? No, Durango, I bloody well don't trust you! And I'll never, ever—so long as I live and breathe—trust you again, you foolhardy, reckless, stupid, crazy, impossible *American!* You could have gotten us both killed, you sorry lout! Ye daft bastard! Eeeh, by gum, you—you—ohhh!—you bloody *cowboy,* you!"

"Careful, honey-pie! That nobby accent's slipping!" he taunted, ice blue eyes dancing wickedly against his wet tanned face.

"Ooooh! I hate you, Durango! You could try the patience of a saint!" With that, she lunged and swung her sodden bag again, this time in the opposite direction.

But Nick ducked this time and threw up his hands in self-defense, weaving backward like a prizefighter as she came after him with fire in her eyes. "Hey, lady, what's got you so riled up?" he demanded. "You're not hurt, are you?"

"No thanks to you, I'm not!" she retorted, her breasts heaving against the now almost-transparent sodden layers of her clothing, he noted appreciatively. "But we could easily have been, and you know it! What about these great big guns you're so proud of? Why didn't you use those to—to intimidate those men, make them leave us alone, instead of risking this—this harebrained escape?"

"Because those 'great big guns,' as you call 'em," he explained levelly, "were stowed in the baggage car in my carpetbag, Miz Angel. Where I, against my better judgment, loaded them this mornin', so I wouldn't embarrass Miz High-and-Mighty Higgins by drawin' attention to myself."

"Oh, that's right, go ahead! Try to blame everything on me!"

"What's more, I couldn't have used 'em anyway, not on that crowded train. Too risky! Too easy for a ricochet plug t' hurt someone innocent."

"More excuses!" she retorted with a snort, but she had the grace to look guilty, remembering her own lack of caution had resulted in Juarez's flesh wound. And, guilt being the uncomfortable emotion that it is, she hastily changed the subject. "That's all well and good, but what are we to do now, pray? It'll be getting dark soon and we seem to be miles from anywhere. We have no food, precious little money and are soaked to the skin, besides. Spring nights tend to be rather chilly here in Europe, Mr. Durango, even in the South of France! Perhaps you, being the hardy individual that circumstances have made you, find nothing amiss with the idea of sleeping out in the open, under the stars. I do, however! I intend to find the nearest inn with quilts and a hot bath. You may follow or not, as you choose."

With that, she raised her bedraggled skirts and, mustering as much dignity as her ruined appearance would permit, she began striding off across the grass, toward a fringe of trees.

"Hey! Wait up, you darned fool of a woman!" Nick yelled after her, cramming on the dripping Stetson he'd recovered from the lake. "You don't know what might be over that rise—!"

But even as he spoke, he saw his warning had come too late. Angel screamed, threw up her arms and vanished from sight.

Cursing obscenely, Nick tore across the grass. He skidded to a halt at the tree line, finding himself on the edge of a grassy slope that swept down to a shallow-bottomed valley below in two steep stages. His concern that she'd plummeted to certain death from a steep cliff rapidly became amusement, for she was rolling sideways down the incline at considerable speed, looking for all the world like a blurred pink log! She'd be dizzy as all get-up at the bottom, but he doubted anything but her dignity would be wounded! Heck, it might even have taken some of the starch out of her drawers!

About halfway down, the steep slope leveled out some. Here, Angel came to a sudden halt. But, rather than quickly scrambling to her feet, she remained immobile, he saw. Too dizzy to stand unaided, huh? Shaking his head, Nick started down after her at an easy lope that allowed him to keep his balance.

"Could I help you up, ma'am?" he drawled, offering her his hand.

"If you'd be so kind," she gritted, looking greenish about the gills as she extended her hand to him. Yet as he took it, the vixen suddenly yanked back on his wrist with all her strength. The surprise action jerked him off his feet, flung him past her into a dramatic, head-over-heels somersault that cartwheeled him down the remaining slope!

When he came to a shuddering halt at the bottom, he was too winded to do more than lie in the tall grass, breathing heavily, as Angel's shadow fell across him. Looking up, he found her grinning down at him, hands on hips.

"Sidewindin' little witch!" he growled, scowling.

"Pompous ass!" she hissed back. But there was a naughty twitch to her lips and a mischievous sparkle to her gray eyes that belied true anger and ignited the laughter in his. A deep rumble convulsed him as Angel, also laughing helplessly, fell to her knees alongside him.

"Oh Nick, I must have looked a sight," Angel declared at length, wiping her tears on her fist. "I know you did!"

"'Sight' hardly begins t' describe you right now," Nick agreed with a teasing grin. "Honey, I've seen drowned cats look more fetchin' than you do!"

"That's quite enough of your insults, thank you! You didn't have to agree with me, you bounder!" she chided wiht mock severity. "But, all joking aside, we really should be making plans for tonight."

"T' hell with t' night, sweet thing," Nick said huskily, drawing her into his arms. "I have plans for right now . . ."

"Oh? But—surely they don't include 'drowned cats'?" she challenged breathlessly. Dear Lord, her knees felt weak! Her heart was hammering so loudly, surely he could hear it?

"Oh, baby," Nick crooned as he pressed her down onto her back in the tall grasses, "you wouldn't believe what they include—!"

And with that, he followed her down and showed her.

Chapter Twenty

Where was the sense in denying it any longer? Angel wondered moodily several nights later, watching Nick's dark, handsome face in the ruddy shadows of their campfire.

All those weeks of pretended loathing in Paris, the confusing mood swings that had flung her either to the heights of elation, or into the deepest sloughs of despair, had been her silly heart's feeble attempts to deny the truth: *She'd fallen in love with Nick Durango!* Fallen for a man who'd made no bones to hide the fact that he disliked her intensely until the first time they'd made love—and who'd made it clear once or twice since that night that he'd like to see his job finished and be well rid of her!

How could you be so blind, Angelica? How could you have allowed this to happen—and with such an unsuitable fellow, besides? she asked herself bitterly, but there was no denying it, not any longer. And, when she looked back, she could see all the telltale signs with the crystal clarity of hindsight! The pounding of her heart whenever he'd been nearby . . . The trembling weakness in her knees his smoldering glance could evoke . . . Her aching hunger for the tiniest crumbs of his approval . . . The irrational fury that man could arouse her to . . . Ye gods, her every waking moment—and most of her sleeping ones, too—had been consumed by thoughts of Nick Durango on one level or another, since the very first time they'd met!

True, she'd fussed about his outlandish dress, his casual manners, his arrogance. She'd convinced herself the

American brute figured so largely in her thoughts because he irritated her so, but—she'd only been lying to herself! She'd reacted that way because secretly, she found Nick a devilishly handsome man, and because—rough-and-ready cowboy or no—she'd been attracted to him from the very first. Denial had been her only defense against admitting the dangerous alternative! She sighed. What was worse, although they'd been forced to spend every moment together over the past week of "roughing it" since they'd jumped from the train, familiarity had served only to intensify her feelings, rather than diminish them, blast him, she thought with treacherous fondness. . . .

They'd passed the days trudging down endless dirt roads that meandered past fairy-tale castles, through beautiful avenues of trees or terraced vineyards, and alongside green fields dotted with sheep and lambs. They kept away from the villages and towns, since Nick figured the less people who saw them pass and could tell which direction they'd taken, the safer they'd be. Instead, they traveled winding country roads that led them steadily southward toward the French Riviera. Italy lay beyond the Alps, and from there they'd travel down the coast to Rome.

Nights they'd slept camped out in the open, like the caravans of Gypsies they'd seen, making their beds wherever the fancy took them, be it a dry ditch, some leafy hedgerow, an abandoned shed, or—one rainy night—beneath an overturned hay wagon, from which they'd stolen a ragged, probably verminous, horseblanket! The only constant features to their nightly "lodgings" had been the starry sky and the smiling spring moon that had twinkled down upon them—and the passionate love-making they'd shared, which had tumbled them both into deep, blissful sleep when it was over.

Night after dew-scented night, Nick'd taught her new ways for a man and a woman to make love, and each time he'd fanned and built the innocent fires within her until they'd blazed out of control and engulfed her in ecstasy. For her part, she'd proven an eager pupil. She knew now how to caress his hard body in the ways he loved; where the brush of her lips pleased him most, or the graze of her fingertips would enflame him most strongly, until he'd

241

trembled with desire, taken her in his arms, and returned her passion tenfold!

Oh, yes, for seven idyllic days and seven glorious nights, she'd been drunk on the wines of pleasure, able at last to satisfy her longing to run her fingers through his glossy black curls, to trace at will the rugged angles of his cheek, jaw, and chin, the margin of his sensual lips. Night after night she'd leaned over him as he slept and pressed her mouth to his closed eyelids, just so she could feel the flutter of his thick black lashes, quivering like sooty moths beneath her lips. She'd thrilled to the rasp of his beard shadow against her own burning softness, the exciting, coarse texture of his chest hair beneath her fingers, and to so many other new delights, exploring each one like a child on Christmas morning, presented with a heap of gaily wrapped presents. . . .

Dear God! Though she wore Nick's fringed buckskin jacket over her gown tonight, Angel shivered as if it were midwinter, though she felt almost feverish at the same time. That was nothing new! She'd come to accept that she was obsessed with the man, that just thinking about Nick, or watching him perform the simplest tasks, from building them a cooking fire to washing his face and bare, sun-browned torso in some sparkling stream, had the same peculiar effect of making her shiver, although her body flamed in the sultry warmth of the night. Just watching him pile kindling on their fire moments ago had stirred her! Her nipples had risen against the confining cloth of her chemise in a shameless, wanton fashion that was so exquisitely pleasurable, it bordered on pain.

"Cold?" he asked, noting the shudder that ran through her. "Come on over here. I'll warm you, sweetness," he invited. There was a heavy-lidded, sleepy look to his eyes she'd come to know only too well.

"Really, I'm perfectly fine over here," she reassured him in a sharper tone than she'd intended, though a part of her yearned to accept his invitation.

His gaze narrowed. "Are you under the weather?"

"Uh uh. Certainly not."

"Still hungry, then?"

"No, not a bit, thank you. The roasted rabbit you

cooked was delicious."

"Are you mad at me, then?" His eyes caught the light of the fire and gleamed roguishly. Damned if he didn't enjoy their fights almost as much as making love to her!

"Not right now, no," she insisted, but it was a lie. She *was* angry at him, angry that he didn't seem to notice her feelings had changed in the past week—and angry that he didn't return them. Angry that he held their relationship so casually, when to her, it had quickly become so very much more than a brief, meaningless *affaire de coeur*, despite her sternest efforts to keep things in proper perspective. Perhaps their lovemaking meant very little to a man of the world like him—was just another harmless diversion with yet another giddy woman in a long stream of willing, giddy women—but she'd never given herself to anyone before him, had never felt for any man what she was beginning to feel for him. Maybe—maybe she was a naive little goose for caring so very deeply, but she did!

Oh, Nick! Damn you, Nick, can't you see? Are you blind, that you haven't guessed? I'm in love with you, you infuriating, wretched man! And God help me, each day and night, I want you more!

The thought of her Grand Tour ending and the heartbreak that parting from him would cause hurt so very much, she wept silent tears in the shadows. How she longed to look him straight in the eye and say, "Nick! Oh, Nick, I love you so!" And yet, perversely, her greatest fear was that Nick *would* guess her secret. That he'd return to his old, scornful ways and throw her declaration of love back in her face. Or worse, use it as a weapon against her.

"Well, well, Miz Angel!" she imagined him saying in his insolent drawl. *"Guess you've finally found somethin' your pa's money can't buy, huh? Nick Durango!*

The scenario she imagined was far too real! She could almost hear his laughter, husky with mockery, on the shadows, and her tears flowed faster. The painful, choking lump in her throat swelled unbearably. Oh, she could bear anything but that! Endure anything but Nick's laughter, his scorn, his rejection. They could destroy her.

She was reminded suddenly of the miserable first weeks she'd spent at boarding school, alone and desperately

243

unhappy and ridiculed by everyone. She had survived by
adapting, by becoming a mirror image of her snobbish
tormentors, and had thus defused their scorn. If she
intended to survive this, she must be equally strong, she
told herself. She must play the game as Nick played it;
must laugh and tease—but never, *ever* let him suspect that
she loved him. Perhaps, if she played the game hard
enough, she would come to believe it herself. . . .

Her mind made up, she fell asleep at long last with her
tears still damp on her cheeks, not waking even when Nick
pulled the ragged horse blanket over them both.

Brushing his lips against her cheek, he stretched out
beside her and drew her into his arms.

Provence in late spring. How beautiful it was! How
wonderful the colors, the smells! The peculiar trick of
atmosphere and light which forecast a spring thunder-
storm bathed everything in surrealistic wine gold hues two
afternoons later, and turned the sky an unearthly,
glowering shade of faded blue. The strawberry fields that
bordered the dusty lane they traveled were covered with
low green vines. Most of their dainty white blossoms had
been replaced by ripe red fruit, still glistening like rubies
with dew, Angel noticed, leaning over a wall.

"Strawberries! Look, Nick! There must be thousands of
them!" Angel exclaimed, her mouth watering. The rabbit
population had refused their invitation to join them for
breakfast that morning; the fish in the streams had proven
equally reticent about a luncheon appointment. Consequently, she was so hungry that her belly was growling
horribly. "Oh, I love strawberries more than anything!
What about you?"

"Never tried 'em," Nick admitted with a grin. "But I'm
starving. Let's pick some, 'fore the storm breaks."

They clambered over the gray stone walls that bordered
the strawberry fields and were soon crouched among the
low, tidy rows of plants, filling their mouths with luscious
red fruits. Angel filled her skirts, too, teasingly batting
Nick away when he tried to poach from her.

"These little treasures are mine, all mine, sir! Go pick

your own, you thieving rascal!" she challenged, her gray eyes sparkling, her enchanting lips parted in a merry smile as she skipped away down the rows.

Nick adopted a moody Latin pout as he chased after her. "Aiee, Doña Angelica—my lovely, heartless Angelica! Why do you always deny your poor Durango the treasures within your skirts, eh?" He rolled his eyes wickedly.

Angel giggled at his bawdy double entendre. "Heavens! You sound exactly like that horrid Prince Antonio di Soriso! But—since I know very well it's not my strawberries you're after, you rogue—be gone with you!"

"I, Don Nicholas de Montoya y Durango, a rogue? Aiee, madonna, how you wound me with the daggers of your tongue! I am but a poor cowboy, accustomed to sleeping under the stars. The only riches I possess are my horse, my saddle—my pride and my good name. I insist you take back your harsh words, señorita—or I shall be forced to demand satisfaction—!" He twirled the ends of an imaginary mustache.

"Satisfaction? A duel, you mean? Well, come on, then, 'Don' Nicholas. I accept your challenge. Choose your weapons—then do your damnedest, sir!" she declared saucily.

"Very well, wench! I choose loaded strawberries at thirty paces. Run, mi'lady—or accept the consequences!"

"Loaded *strawberries!*" she exclaimed, then with a shriek of laughter, she fled.

With a whoop, Nick lunged for her, hurling strawberries after her retreating back. But in this, Angel proved faster and lighter on her feet! She fled for the trees at the edge of the strawberry field, with her skirts still bunched up before her, scattering "ammunition" as she ran.

"I have you now, my proud beauty!" Nick threatened, racing after her. "You cannot escape me!"

"Oh, can't I? We'll see about that, sir!" Angel laughed as she whirled about to face him, lobbing berry after berry at his head as if they were indeed dangerous missiles. Her hair was a wild honey gold tangle about her grubby face, giving her a look more hoyden than haughty. Her lips were stained deep red with glistening strawberry juice. More dribbled down her chin. When Nick made a wild grab for her, she'd succumbed to her hunger and was trying to pop a glistening berry into her mouth, instead of flinging it at him, and wearing a delightfully guilty, greedy expression as she did so.

"Truce! Give quarter, sir!" she begged huskily, another berry en route to her mouth. "I'm famished!"

Nick's hand froze in midair. *Oh, Lord!* Just watching the way her reddened lips nuzzled the plump strawberry made his groin tighten. And, as her moist lips closed around the luscious fruit, he moved his lips and swallowed as if he'd eaten it, by God, rather than her. . . .

Their eyes met. Their gazes locked for moments that were an eternity to Angel. And then—was it just wishful thinking on her part? Imagination? Or did something flare up in the depths of his? Something that was desire, surely, but—please God!—mingled now with the fragile stirring of another, deeper emotion . . . ?

Perhaps. Oh, yes, perhaps . . . !

The very air, strawberry-and-rich-earth-scented, tanged sharply with the coming rain. It seemed suddenly charged, brooding and expectant, as if the world were holding its breath, waiting for him to say—to say—to say—

"It looks like rain," he murmured huskily.

She almost sobbed with disappointment. "Yes. It does."

"We'll get soaked again."

"I suppose we shall, yes."

"I saw a barn, back there a-ways."

"Me, too. By—by the little stone bridge?" she recalled, her poor crumpled heart beating, beating frantically against her rib cage, like a snared bird.

"That's it. In the field across from the mission fish pond."

"You mean the convent fish pond?" she corrected by rote.

"Yep. That's it. That's the barn, all right."

"Yes, the very one," she agreed shakily.

"No sense wasting it, right . . . ? I mean, what with this rain an' all . . . ?"

"Oh, none at all. How very sensible of you to think of it . . ."

He grinned. "I'm a practical *hombre*."

"As I'm f-fast discovering. Stolen blankets. Snared rabbits. Fish hooked on my hat pin. Indeed, you've proven a remarkably practical fellow this past week!" She dared to glance up at him, then looked quickly back down at her feet, brought close to swooning by the look in his eyes. Disappointed or not, she couldn't deny her desire for him. "Sh-shall we, then?"

"Hell, why don't we just? Like I said, I'd surely hate t' get soaked again . . ." he repeated softly, so softly.

With her nod, he took her by the hand and led the way.

They ran through the fields like children, hopping over the low rows of strawberry vines or the furrows between them, laughing gaily at nothing and at everything: the way the strawberries they trod on squelched juicily beneath their feet, the way a big old toad hopped frantically out of their path, the thwarted expression of the black bull they came upon, staring belligerently from a field they'd almost tried to cross—but luckily hadn't!

As Nick had foretold, the storm broke. Thunder rumbled ominously in the near-distance. Lightning flickered like white sprites in the now-greenish sky. Rain pelted down in fat drops long before they'd reached the cover of the barn. Squealing, Angel halted. Flinging back her head so that her battered straw boater rolled away, she raised her face to the downpour, opened her mouth and stuck out her tongue, letting the raindrops fall on it.

She looked so carefree, so breathtakingly lovely with the rain spiking her lashes and glistening like dewdrops on her flushed cheeks, the breath caught in Nick's throat. Oh, Jesus! It was happening again! The thin fabric of her dress was damp and clinging. It outlined the curves of her breasts, plastered to her hips like a second skin. Startled, he realized his heart was thundering, that the breath was squeezing up from his lungs as if forced through bellows, making his chest heave in and out as if he were drowning. . . .

"Angel? Damn it, you're getting soaked—!"

"Oh, I know, I know!"

"And you don't care?"

247

"Nope!" she sang out, playing the game, suddenly determined to play it better and harder than he. "Not a bit!"

"*Nope?*" he echoed, grinning. Angel, teasing him again? That was somethin' new! Before this past week, he'd figured her for about as much fun as getting a tooth pulled—maybe less. But then, he'd been proven wrong about her in so many ways since they'd jumped the train. 'Til then, he'd underestimated the core of steel that ran beneath her wilting violet, nobby exterior; her amazing ability to adapt to even the worst situation, and even to thrive on it, both qualities he admired in a man or a woman.

"Nope," she repeated. "Heck, I don't give a dern 'bout this here rain, cowpoke!"

"Is that how I sound to you?" he asked, forgetting for the moment his own pose as the "crude colonial."

"You shorely do, pardner."

"I say you're plumb *loco*, Miz Higgins!" he declared, remembering.

"Oh, I must be, I reckon. After all, I'm here with you, ain't I, cowboy?"

Laughing and shaking his head, he raised the wooden bar and flung open the barn door. They both tumbled inside, heading by mutual consent for the huge mound of clean, fragrant hay heaped in one corner.

Once again, it happened as it always happened between them, just exactly how, neither of them would remember afterwards. Somehow, between the barn door and the hay, Angel felt Nick's hands encircle her waist, his warm breath in her ear, and her heart skipped a beat.

"Angel!" he murmured. With that solitary word, he gathered her up into his arms and carried her across the flagstoned floor. Looking up at him, she saw how his eyes smoldered in the scented shadows, like the pale blue flicker of flames that devoured the pine logs on a cold winter's night. Their silvery pallor was striking against the swarthy darkness of his complexion!

As if in a dream, his dark head dipped toward hers even as he lowered her to the hay. He covered her mouth with his, taking full possession of her lips with a mastery that

248

stunned and thrilled her—and broke her poor heart all over again. He offered her the placebo of passion, the amnesia of lust, when what she craved from him was true love and the tumultous ecstasy of mutual desire that was its crown!

"*Love me! Say that you love me!*" she begged silently.

But, "I want you, darlin'!" was all he breathed on the hush, his fingers lacing through her hair to draw her head back down to his.

Despite her unspoken yearnings, his very first kiss unlocked the lambent fires within her; freed them to flame anew. Too soon, his lips left her mouth to brand her sensitive throat, her ears. His tongue delicately followed each intricate little shell-whorl of pink flesh until she squirmed in his arms, for his moist breath made shivery tingles sweep down her spine and arms. Damn him, damn him—! His every caress built the delicious tension that was gathering deep inside her, like storm clouds heavy with rain.

His heavy-lidded gaze intent upon her face, Nick watched Angel's changing expressions as his hand swept down the length of her throat to cup her breasts. Gently, he caressed each one, rubbing the ball of his thumb over the stiffened peaks before unfastening the row of pearl buttons that impeded his hands. Parting the fronts of her damp bodice, he drew an uneven breath as he pushed aside her filmy chemise to bare her bosom. Dipping his ebony head, he brushed his lips over the exquisite mounds of her petal-soft skin. Her tiny nipples engorged beneath his mouth, grew as full and ripe as the berries they'd gathered in the fields. Her skin was salty and scalding hot to his lips, as if a fever raged through her, her fragrance as fresh and sweet as the icy, thaw-swollen stream in which she'd splashed with him that morning—and he could never get enough of the taste of her!

She glanced down. His head, his hands, were both dark, sun-browned as a tinker's nestled against her creamy fairness. His knuckles were sprinkled with coarse black hairs that were oh, so exciting, so deliciously male and virile, so very different from her own body! Framing his head between her hands, she pressed him to her bosom, overwhelmed by the fierce emotions teeming through her veins.

Her quivering arousal and her ardent responses set Nick afire. Pulling down her skirt, her petticoats, he undressed her with hands made unsteady by impatience and rough with urgency. In moments, she curled before him on the hay with only the flimsy scrap of her chemise twisted about her waist. She was the most beautiful woman he'd ever seen, he thought, dry-mouthed—and she was giving herself to him!

Leaning down, he nuzzled then kissed her sleek, flat belly, drawing his tongue across the velvet plateau with little dancing flickers that made her gasp uncontrollably, as if he'd flayed her with a silken whip. The fragile strokings were a heady contrast to his beard. His cheeks felt deliciously rough against her skin as he nuzzled the jut of her hipbones. And then, still kissing her stomach, he moved to kneel between her thighs, circling her navel with his tongue bathing her in fiery sensation.

"No! Oh, Nick, you mustn't do that! Please, stop it!" she whispered, moaning helplessly as his lips trailed lower still, to kiss the fleecy golden curls of her mound. Shocked but wildly excited at the same time, and terribly ashamed that she should feel so, she tried to draw his head away, desperate to prevent a more intimate kiss, but he would not be denied. He held her wrists fast at her sides and continued his maddening torment, until she ceased to resist.

Dear Lord, his lips, his tongue were delicately ravishing her, possessing her in shocking ways she'd never dreamt existed! A whirlwind swept her up, whipped the fires within her into a crackling bonfire of passion that made her writhe like one tormented. Unable to help herself, she cried out and arched beneath his mouth, pressed herself shamelessly against him.

The scented gloom exploded into a million star shards! Rapture splintered through her, filling her loins and belly, her aching breasts, with a throbbing, nectared sweetness so sharp, so intense, so incredibly pleasurable, it was almost unbearable. In the midnight-velvet of the stillness that followed the whirlwind's passing, she lay in silent wonder, uncertain if she still lived, or had died and flown to paradise itself. . . .

The breath rasping from between his parted lips, Nick tore the shirt from his back, shucked off his pants and boots like a man possessed, falling upon her as hot and ready as a stallion.

"Love me, sweet thing! Love me!" he growled deep in his throat as he covered her with his hard, tanned body. The fingers of one hand linked through hers, with the other, he guided his manhood home.

His thrusts were deep and swift, each powerful flexing of his hips driving his passion higher, rekindling the embers of hers. The virile power of his possession swept her up into the maelstrom of his passion. Soon, she cried out in dazed wonder a second time. When he heard her love song, the sound trilling on the gloom like the fluting call of some lovely bird, Nick could delay no longer. His roar of fulfillment met hers as they clung together, gasping, sobbing; fiercely reaching, fiercely meeting, fiercely blending into one, glorious being, as Nick felt himself erupt deep within her body.

Drained for the moment, he rolled beside her, wanting nothing more than to hold her close, to sleep for a spell with her head pillowed on his chest. But—it seemed his contrary Angel had other ideas. . . .

"Come on!" she urged, scrambling to her feet and brushing wisps of hay from her body. "I have the most wonderful idea!"

He opened one eye. "Your perkiness is none too flattering to my ego, Miz Angel," Nick grumbled, scowling at her.

"How so?" she asked, frowning.

"Well, you see, I'd have bet hard money you'd sleep an hour or two, after . . ." he let the sentence go unfinished and cocked his dark brows.

"Oh, that," she acknowledged airily, her eyes sparkling. "To be honest, the first time made me want to sleep—but somehow, the second time I—er—um—well, you know!— it was so very lovely it quite woke me up again! Now, come on, do, before we're too late and the rain stops!"

Resigned that he'd have no peace—or rest—until he

complied, Nick reached for his breeches.

"Eee, lad, we'll have none o' them there trousers!" she teased in a broad Lancashire dialect, tugging them from his hands. Naked as a jaybird, she ran outside into the roaring rain, pulling Nick after her.

There were mud puddles everywhere in the barnyard. White ducks with red bills were taking a joyous bath in them, quacking and beating their wings so that the water fanned about them in glorious arcs.

"You see? Now, isn't this wonderful? Isn't a rain shower far more refreshing than, say, a swim in some murky pond or other?" she demanded. Her gray eyes were shining, her face glowing as she rubbed the rain all over her rosy, nude body, then twirled about so that her long wet hair sprayed water over him in fans, like the ducks.

"Wonderful!" he agreed wryly, wanting to tell her to grow up, to quit acting like child, but—he couldn't. Couldn't hold on to his exasperation at her crazy, wonderful delight in such a simple pleasure as playing in the rain. And, what was even stranger, he knew deep down in his heart that he didn't want to change her, that he liked her fine just the way she was. Heck, her quicksilver change of moods fascinated him, kept him on his toes! She could be prim and snooty as hell one minute, then all-woman, all-passion, as sexy as all-get-up, in the next. She could be serious and thoughtful one minute, and in the blink of an eye, a little girl playing games! Shoot! For the first time since Savannah's betrayal with his spineless father, he was having *fun*, for crying out loud—and damned if little Miz Iron Drawers wasn't the reason why!

Dark hair plastered seal-like against his head by the rain, rivulets streaking down his handsome face, he swung her up into his arms and spun her around and around, until they were both dizzy, laughing helplessly, and hardly able to stand.

"Hey! You over there! What are you doing naked in my barnyard, eh, you immoral rogues! Up to no good, stealing my strawberries, I'd bet!" bellowed an angry voice in thick country French.

Startled, Nick abruptly set Angel down and whirled around. "Damn! It's the farmer—! The old coot's armed

252

and headin' this way!"

"He wants to know what we're doing here, and says he wagers we've stolen his—"

"Darlin', what he's saying doesn't need translatin'—not with that big ole shotgun he's totin'. Make tracks—!"

They fled, both quite naked, down the muddy lane, the angry farmer brandishing his shotgun and hobbling after them on gouty legs.

"Well, well! Do you see what I see, *Sister* Angelica?" Nick asked soberly, peering between some bushes an hour later.

"Indeed I do, *Father* Nicholas!" Angel agreed with a muffled giggle.

In the forest clearing before them, a band of Gypsies were encamped. Smoke rose into the air from between their colorfully painted and gilded *vardos*, which were drawn up in a circle on the grass. Gypsy menfolk were tending to the string of shaggy ponies and horses they'd staked out some yards away, while the younger women of their band prepared supper and the older crones smoked their clay pipes and gossiped as they minded the children. Above their shrieks and laughter, Nick and Angel could hear someone playing a guitar and singing a melancholy love song. The rippling chords of the Spanish melody, the singer's plaintive voice, seemed perfectly appropriate here in the shadowy forest, somehow—an echo of her own heart's hopeless longing, Angel thought, darting a quick, hopeful glance at Nick. The savory smell of the stew simmering in the Gypsies' black kettle made her mouth water. The few strawberries she'd gobbled down had done little to ease the growling of her stomach.

"Well? What do you think? Shall we beg for our supper?"

"I don't think we have much choice, not now. We had to leave everything we owned in that barn, including your knife! And no knife, no rabbits, right?"

"Right."

"I'm sorry. It was all my fault!"

"The hell it was—you didn't have to break my arm, did

253

you? Besides, it was worth it . . ." He winked. "Come on, now! Maintain a stiff upper lip and put your best foot forward, old girl! We may as well get it over with. All they can say is 'no,' right?"

"They won't do that. Who'd be so callous as to turn away a 'priest' and a 'nun' . . . ?"

"No decent folks that I know of," Nick came back solemnly yet his eyes twinkled as he eyed her in her stolen nun's habit, complete with wimple, which he'd snatched from the convent's laundry line, along with his own vestments.

"Nor I!" Angel agreed firmly, smiling encouragement. Personally, she thought Nick made a rather dashing priest. That snowy clerical collar was a pleasing contrast to his devilish, wind-tanned face. "And by the way, Father Nicholas, you do look simply marvelous in that cassock! If I were a Catholic girl, the thoughts I've been having would keep me in confession for a month, at least!" she observed impudently, fluttering her lashes. "I wonder, did you ever consider taking orders and becoming a priest?"

He scowled. "Honey, the day I wear skirts and swear off women is the day you can bury me in a pine box!"

She giggled, looking decidedly impish rather than angelic in the severe dark habit. "Somehow, I thought you might feel that way—! But, no matter. Just forget I asked and—lead on, Father MacDuff!"

Irreverently making a gesture that was certainly *not* the Blessing, Nick led on.

Chapter Twenty-One

"Did you ever see so many stars? There must be billions of them!"

Nick smiled in the shadows. "Pretty near that many. On clear nights like this, they seem close enough to pick like daisies."

Angel rolled over and propped herself on her elbows in the grass, grinning up at him in delight. In the flickering light of their campfire, auburn highlights gleamed in her golden mane. Her gray eyes shone with an incandescence he'd come to look forward to in the quiet, intimate moments like these that followed their lovemaking; moments when they'd talk and share their thoughts and feelings on countless different things, before falling asleep in each others' arms. Nick had come to treasure those times, much to his surprise, for he'd found in them an intimacy that went beyond the physical intimacy of their passion. It was, he fancied, almost a sharing of souls.

"Why, Mr. Durango, that was so poetic!" Angel murmured in response to his observation.

"You sound surprised. How come?" he asked. "Do you think a cowboy can't be a poet, too?" Teasingly, he tugged her hair. "Seems to me, Miz Angel, that the best poets would be those who live closest to nature—like cowboys do."

"The best poets? Then you enjoy poetry?"

"Some."

"But that's wonderful! So do I! Come on, tell me, who's your favorite?" she demanded eagerly, sitting up with her chin resting on her bent knees now.

"My favorite? Oh, a man named Willie Kerr, I guess I'd say. He was a Rocky Mountain fur trapper in the days when the American West was still young. He wrote about simple things in a no-nonsense, down t' earth sort of way. Cut right through to the heart of matters, I reckon."

"Really? Can you remember any of his poems?" she pressed, both surprised and curious that Nick should be interested in poetry at all, let alone have a favorite poet.

"Well, there's one that goes something like this." He cleared his throat and in his deep drawl began, "'A woman's like a treasure chest. Her secrets she keeps hid. A woman's hard to shut up nights—but a chest comes with a lid!'"

"With a li—why, you rogue! You made that up!" she accused, swatting his nearest leg.

"Guilty as charged, ma'am!" Nick admitted with a wink and a grin. He made her a mocking bow from the waist without leaving his seat against a handy tree trunk.

"Oh, you! Can't you be serious for once? Tell me another of your favorites—and this time, make it a real poem, please, Durango?"

"All right, teacher. Let me think for a spell." Nick thought, and then he recited softly:

> Love 'n marriage are only for gamblers,
> Who'll wager their hearts on a whim.
> At the turn of a card,
> They'll give up the free life—
> They'll hang up their saddles,
> Hitch up with a housewife—
> Lassoed by some gal's shapely limb!
>
> O, Love is for lonesome young cowboys,
> Who melt with a female's false smiles.
> But it ain't 'til she's got you
> Corralled with a ring—
> 'Til you've wedded and bedded
> That purty young thing!—
> You discover her four-flusher's wiles.

Smart is the bachelor fellow
Who won't bet against Lady Luck's whim!
All the days of his life
He'll hoard money and heart—
Should his stake reach the rafters
From neither he'll part!—
Love makes no gamblin' fool outta him!

"Well! A somewhat cynical choice, I'd say, sir—but quite revealing in regards to your attitude toward women!" she observed dryly, only half teasing.

He shrugged. "You asked me for my favorite," he reminded her, casting a piercing glance her way. "Like it or not, that was it."

"I'm sorry, Nick. I didn't mean to criticize, honestly I didn't. It—it's really a very interesting piece. More of your—er—Mr. Kerr's ponderings?"

"No."

"Then may I ask the—er—poet's name?"

"Durango. *Gil* Durango. My father," he added in a bitter, knifelike tone, before she could jump to the conclusion he'd composed it. Abruptly, he stood. "You should turn in, get some sleep. We've a long day's walk ahead of us tomorrow."

She flinched as if he'd struck her, for his voice had grown so hard and clipped, it was that of a stranger, despite his innocuous words! She swallowed, desperate to recapture their easy mood of moments before. Something she'd said or done must have angered him terribly. Or—had something about the poem brought back painful memories . . . ? Whatever the reason, she'd never heard him sound so cold, nor so bitter! In a small voice, she murmured, "Ye-es, I suppose I should. G-goodnight, Nick. Sweet dreams."

"Angel?"

"Yes?"

"I won't be long," he added gruffly, sensing the need to say something to soften his curt words of moments before. "I—well, I thought I'd ask Manolito if I can borrow a smoke before I turn in."

She nodded, knowing it was an excuse and that he wanted to be alone. She watched as his dark frame moved with surefooted grace away from their fire, into the deeper shadows beyond the circle of Gypsy caravans. There, she knew, the Gypsy youth, Manolito stood sentry over the horses and ponies. He played his Spanish guitar each night to calm the animals when a fox was on the prowl and they grew restless, filling the camp with the brooding melancholy and bittersweet pathos of his music. . . .

"Caray! I think El Diablo wou' never leaf you alone, eh!" exclaimed a husky voice in fractured English.

A slim dark whirlwind emerged from the bushes before Angel and scampered across the grass toward her, long black curls flying. Without so much as a by-your-leave, the young Gypsy girl flopped down upon Angel's borrowed quilt. Countless gold chains, earrings, bracelets, and coin ornaments made a noisy jingle as she sat, squirming about to get comfortable. The tiny fragments of mirror appliquéd to the hems of her skirts and her velvet bolero caught the firelight and reflected it in a hundred winking prisms—yet none were as bright as Lucia's mischievous shining eyes! "Here, English! You ask, and Lucia, she is your goo' frien'. She find, yes? I think this meck you mush more *bonita*—preety—than those holy rags, no? Here! You take!" So saying she thrust a bundle of clothing into Angel's lap.

"But—I have no way to repay you for these!" Angel exclaimed, touched by the girl's generosity. "Or for the many kindnesses you and your family have done for us this past week. You've fed us, let us ride with you, shared your fire—"

Lucia dismissed her gratitude with any airy grimace. "So? Is small thing, while you—! Aiee, you have teach Lucia how for cheat at cards! And Lucia, she has learn all her many, many fren's. So! Wash out, all you stupid *gorgios!* Lucia and her friends, they are comin' t' town. We goin' take all you *dinero!* Ha! Ha!" She grinned wickedly, her strong white teeth flashing in the firelight against her dusky complexion as she greedily rubbed the balls of her thumb and index finger together and translated, *"Di-*

258

nero—money! Truly, English, is trade enough."

Angel's eyes widened. "You mean . . . ? Oh, no, Lucia, you mustn't even *think* it, let alone try it! Promise me! Swear you won't? I showed you those silly card tricks for fun—something to do to pass the time!—not so you could steal from people. What if you're caught? You'd be sent to prison! Did you think about that?"

"If I am lock in a cage like poor lit' bird, Lucia, she die," Lucia agreed with a mournful sigh. But then her brown eyes sparkled anew as she added, "And so, Lucia not be caught. She run fast like wind! Like—so!"

With that dramatic farewell, Lucia sped off back to her parents' *vardo*, both arms spread like a soaring bird's, leaving behind a very perturbed Angel, who was now far too upset to sleep a wink.

Did the sixteen-year-old minx seriously believe the hotel managers would let her enter the glittering casinos of Monte Carlo, clad in her motley gypsy finery—let alone stay there long enough to cheat them out of their money? Faint hope!

In fact, if Angel hadn't felt so terribly guilty, so responsible for encouraging the girl, the picture her imagination painted would have been a funny one! But alas, the idea of naughty, engaging Lucia being marched off to prison by some cruel *gendarme* for what could prove a very long time . . . of the carefree, enchanting Lucia confined in some airless dank cell for years on end . . . was far too dismal to permit even a solitary smile.

What on *earth* had possessed her to teach that impressionable child Reggie's silly parlor tricks? For herself, she'd never so much as practiced the sleight of hand or the card-palming he'd taught her that rainy winter's afternoon. Nor had she even once considered using her skills to cheat at Bligh's, not even in her darkest hour. Certainly not! The very proper British sense of honor and fair play she'd acquired at boarding school had firmly ruled out such chicanery.

Lucia, however, was governed by no such constraints. The Gypsy philosophy her band lived by seemed to be one in which all nonGypsies, or *gorgios*, were fair game. If a *gorgio* were taken for every penny he possessed by a Gypsy ruse, then more power to the Gypsy—it was the *gorgio's* own stupid fault for being so gullible! Angel sighed heavily. She'd have to keep a sharp eye out for Lucia until they reached the mountains of Monaco some time tomorrow morning. After that, there was little she could do to keep her out of trouble, for she and Nick and the Gypsy band would go their separate ways. . . .

Speaking of Nick, why hadn't he returned as promised, she wondered belatedly, fidgeting to get comfortable beneath the satin quilt Lucia's mother Anna had loaned her. And when he did, would he be his old self again, or the hard, embittered man she'd glimpsed? The man who'd dared to love in the past, perhaps, but been made a "gamblin' fool" of—?

"*Adiós*, señorita! I woan see you again, so—*vaya con Diós!*"

"Lucia, wait! Where are you going?" Angel demanded, running down the mountain path after the girl.

Below, on the high bluffs overlooking the sparkling sapphire of the Mediterranean, lay the charming town of Monte Carlo. Even from up here, the sails of the yachts and other luxury vessels anchored in the marina could be seen, along with the Catholic cathedral and the numerous casinos lining La Condomine.

Lucia halted and turned to face her. "Me? Mama, she send Lucia into town—you know, to sell lucky heather? The rich *gorgios* at the casinos, they buy plenty, so much plenty! They belief it bring *buena suerte*—good luck!"

Pouting, Lucia held up a basket filled with white sprigs to prove her claim, but Angel wasn't convinced. Her eyes, her expression, were too wide and innocent by far!

"Don't lie to me, Lucia," she threatened sternly.

"Lucia, she doan lie to you! Never!"

"Oh, yes, she does. But, mark my words, young lady: if you try to leave this camp, I'll tell your father. And Ramon will send El Diablo after you!" For some reason—probably because he was not easily hoodwinked and because his shrewd pale blue eyes missed little—Lucia had feared and disliked Nick from the first night. She also called him El Diablo—the Devil!—behind his back, the silly little goose!

Her threat paid off. Lucia's shoulders sagged. "Oh, all right. I come back. But Lucia, she *hate* you now, English!" she added in a burst of anger, then fled back to the circle of caravans on the edge of the woods.

Hate me all you want if it keeps you safe, silly child! Angel thought as she retraced her own path, certain she'd been far more mature at sixteen.

Nick was with Lucia's father, Ramon, over by the horses. The two men had their dark heads together and were in heavy conversation. Angel wasn't surprise to see them talking. Rather, she crossed her fingers and hoped with all her heart that he'd be successful, for when he'd returned to their fire last night, Nick had told her he meant to try and talk Ramon into letting them take two of the horses when they went their separate ways. The only problem was that, without money or possessions, Nick had nothing to trade for the animals, except his strong back and his cowboy talents. He and Manolito'd come up with the idea of persuading Ramon to let him stage a one-man show on the outskirts of town: a demonstration of his skills with the lariat, whip, and knife. The Gypsy women could tell fortunes and sell their clothes pegs, lace, and lucky white heather to the crowd, while the "take" Nick's performance brought in would hopefully pay for the horses. This was what they were discussing now, she guessed.

Sure enough, moments later, Ramon whistled for his young son, Gino, and sent him off in search of a rope. He returned in moments, and as Nick knotted the rope to form a running noose, Gypsies gathered from all sides of the camp, sitting either on the grass or on fallen logs or else standing in groups to watch.

Angel forgot about Lucia as she watched Nick go through his act. She was mesmerized by the whirring rope that either zipped through the air with ease, like a child's bowling hoop twirled on a string, or whizzed about his

261

body in dazzling figures-of-eight, drawing cries of *"Olé"* and admiring gasps from the Gypsies. Showmen themselves, they could appreciate Nick's skill more than the average audience, for he handled the lariat with grace and breathless expertise they knew had been earned by years of hard work and practice. The way he moved—hopping smartly to one side or the other, or turning his upper body from the waist in a wide curve that made the spinning rope dance around him, reminded Angel of pictures she'd seen of *matadores*, bullfighters swirling a cape about their bodies, their consummate skill making a difficult task seem deceptively easy. He ended his act by lassoing Ramon, pinning the grinning Gypsy leader's arms to his sides.

A roar went up as Nick took his bow. Ramon came forward to clasp his arms and slap him across the back in approval. They conferred for a few moments, and then Ramon reached into his belt and, with a grin, handed Nick a knife.

"You, Gino!" Ramon snapped his fingers before his son's face. "Give Papa your smoke!"

The young Gypsy boy sulkily handed his father his cigarette. Ramon clamped it between his own teeth and strolled several paces away, across the grass. "Far enough, *amigo?*" he called to Nick.

"Back a few feet—good! That's fine, right there. Easy now, *amigo*. Don't move!"

Angel's heart was in her mouth as Ramon turned sideways, standing with his hands on his hips and the half-smoked cigarette jutting from between his lips, for she'd realized what Nick meant to do.

Clothed in a borrowed full-sleeved white shirt and black breeches, and looking like a Gypsy himself, his tanned face set in concentration, Nick sighted on the smoldering tip of Ramon's cigarette. Slowly, he raised the knife above his head, holding it by the blade as he prepared to throw.

The Gypsies fell silent to a man, watching. The morning air grew tense, thick, and heavy with anticipation. Angel held her breath and crossed the fingers of both hands, praying fervently that Nick's arm would be steady, his aim true. If not, Ramon could be badly injured—

perhaps even killed . . . !

A tugging at her skirts broke her concentration.

"Señorita! Did you see my worthless sister?"

"Lucia? She was here a moment ago . . ." Angel looked around but couldn't see the girl either in the crowd or in the camp. Alarm swept through her. Surely that little idiot hadn't gone into Monte Carlo after all—? "Where did you look for her, Gino?" she demanded, taking the boy by the shoulders.

"Everywhere! Papa, he took my last smoke—and Lucia, she has tobacco to roll more."

"I'll find her. And when I do, I'll tell her you're looking for her, all right?"

"Sí," Gino agreed sullenly, wandering off with his fists dug deep into his sagging pockets.

Without bothering to waste precious time in searching the camp, Angel ran through the woods to the Monte Carlo road. She knew only too well where to find Lucia. . . .

"My good man, did you see a young girl pass this way— dark-haired, about sixteen years old?"

"Your 'good man'? What nerve! Be off with you, you shameless hussy. I'm a married man—with grown children, too! Go away!"

"Sir, how about you? Did you see her?" Angel pleaded, plucking at the man's companion's coat sleeves.

"Filthy Gypsy! Take your dirty hands off me, or I'll call a *gendarme!"*

A third man was walking briskly down the opposite side of the street. An elderly woman clung to his arm for assistance. She ran across the road toward him, imploring, "Sir, please, won't you help me? Did you by any chance see a young Gypsy girl—about my height—wearing a red dress?

"I saw nothing and no one. Here! Take this and leave decent people alone! Better yet, leave Monte Carlo altogether, and do your begging elsewhere, girl!"

The man flung a creased thousand franc note at her and

on reflex, Angel caught it, clutching it to her bosom as her mouth dropped open in shock at his rudeness.

"You see, *maman?*" the man exclaimed smugly, as he hastened the woman past her. "Give the rascals what they want, and they soon leave you alone! It's much easier than bickering with the rogues."

"*Oui,* Julian—but did you have to give 'er quite so much?" the old woman snapped, rapping her walking cane across his shins.

Still clutching the forgotten thousand-franc note in her fist, Angel ran down the street toward the center of the little town, where she was certain she would find the famous gambling house of Monte Carlo, which had been made popular worldwide by the patronage of Europe's wealthy since 1856.

In her haste to find Lucia before she got into trouble, she was oblivious to the curious stares she was drawing, the heads she was turning as she went. It was not often, even in Monte Carlo, where outrageous things happened all the time, that you saw a beautiful young woman with flowing blond hair—dressed in a swirling gypsy skirt and embroidered peasant blouse—running barefoot through the town's main throughfare!

But as Angel made to dive through the casino's impressive entrance, a uniformed doorman stepped in front of her, blocking her way.

"Now, now! Stop right there. We'll have none of your riffraff in here! Be off with you!"

Angel stopped dead in her tracks, her mind racing as she glowered up at the man. Smoothing down her windswept hair to stall for time, she wondered what Reggie would say—do—in such a situation?

"'Riffraff,' my deah, misguided fellow?" she said crisply in her haughtiest tone, "Pray tell, do you know to whom you are speaking?"

Her plummy uppercrust accent floored him momentarily. It was so at odds with her appearance! "Well, I—"

"No? Then permit me to enlighten you, my good man. You see before you the world-acclaimed diva, Princess Angelica di Soriso, bride of the Italian *prince,* His Royal

Highness, Antonio di Soriso."

"The prince has married?" the doorman whispered, brows raising almost to his retreating hairline.

"Why, most assuredly so," Angel confirmed icily. She stared down her nose at him. "I have been his bride for thirty idyllic days and thirty heavenly, glorious nights!" She made a sweeping theatrical gesture and clasped her hands to her bosom, to hide the absence of a wedding ring.

"But—forgive me!—you do not—er—look like a—a princess, er, madame?"

"Indeed I do not, at this moment, you bumbling imbecile! Darling Poopsi—my dear husband, the prince, bless him—insisted I should continue to enthrall my adoring public, following our marriage. One does so hate to disappoint all the little people, doesn't one? Consequently, the Royal Italian Opera Company and myself are en route to Venice. We shall give *Il Trovatore* at La Scala next week, and so I was rehearsing for my role as Leonora—hence this gaudy Spanish costume you see me in!" She gave a delicate shudder and gestured at her colorful skirts with a grimace, as if they were verminous— "We were halfway through the first act when I was simply overcome by the urge to—how shall I express it? *Indulge* myself in a teeny little game of—chance!"

She made a little *moué* with her lips, and the doorman's frown dissolved into a conspiratorial chuckle. This sudden urge to "indulge in games of chance" was nothing new, not to him, and not in this town! The doorman had seen far more rich, titled women fall victim to the gambling fever than he had men in his five years of employment—and wealthy female gamblers, riding high on a winning streak, tended to be generous with their tips!

Accordingly, he simpered, "Come, come, Madame la Princesse, you have absolutely no need to explain yourself to one such as I! Please, allow me to escort you to the manager. He will, of course, see you personally to our very best table . . ."

"But of course," Angel agreed languidly, feigning a bored yawn to cover her urge to smile.

Taking her elbow and bowing and scraping, the

doorman led her inside the casino. Angel permitted him to do so, thinking as she summoned her most aloof expression that Reggie would have been bloody proud of her!

She successfully evaded the fawning casino manager within minutes of him escorting her to the casino's best table, and went in search of Lucia.

One hand on her hip, she glided a regally as any queen over the deeply piled white carpet, her head held as high as if she'd been gowned by Worth himself. She rebuffed any curious looks sent her way with a genteel nod of her head and a dismissing sniff. Both implied she was fabulously rich and eccentric—and had neither the time nor the inclination to exchange pleasantries with those she considered beneath her. Despite her attire, snobbery had convinced everyone in the gambling house that Angel was of the blood royal, when she was done with them. She simply *had* to be richer than rich, and with impeccable background and connections, to boot! After all, no one of lesser standing would have deliberately committed social suicide by snubbing the blue-blooded aristocrats of Europe—!

The gambling house was fabulous—Bligh's quite paled beside its grandeur! Crimson figured-velvet wallpaper graced the walls, and despite the early hour, enormous crystal chandeliers blazed with candlelight. Beneath them, crowded around by elegantly dressed patrons, were the gaming tables—baccarat, roulette, rouge-et-noir—and Lucia! Angel caught a glimpse of her red skirts as she dove between two satin-gowned dowagers watching the roulette players!

Weaving swiftly between the crush of gambling men and women, Angel forced her way to the front of the crowd and saw Lucia across from her, on the opposite side of the table now, her brown eyes shining with greed as she avidly watched a lucky winner rake in his winnings.

"Place your bets, mesdames et monsieurs, *s'il vous plait!*" the *croupier* announced by rote in a bored monotone. Bejeweled hands slid sheafs of notes onto one or other of the diamond-shaped areas marked off on the tablecloth.

"You must place a bet or leave the table, mademoiselle," the croupier cautioned her.

"I must what?" Looking up, Angel saw that everyone was looking at her, and with cross, impatient expressions, too. She was delaying the game! "But I have no . . ."

It was then she remembered the thousand-franc note that odious man had flung at her, wadded now into a damp little ball in her fist. Hastily unfolding it and smoothing it out, she slapped it down onto the nearest marked section. "There!" she told the croupier, who nodded.

"Thank you, mademoiselle." He spun the red-and-black colored wheel, then tossed a marble ball onto its spinning compartments. Over the loud clicking of the wheel, Angel hissed at Lucia, "Don't be such a little fool! Come back to the camp with me, before it's too late!"

"But I never try nothin' yet, English," Lucia pouted. "I doan want to go back!"

"Red seven wins," the croupier declared and a chorus of groans followed.

"But you have to go back! Your mother will be frantic, worrying about you! Your father will be furious!"

"Congratulations! You won, mademoiselle!" a man seated at Angel's left declared, tapping her elbow to get her attention.

"Please, don't bother me, m'sieu. This is very important!" Angel muttered, waving him away.

"Mademoiselle, you must either permit your winnings to ride a second time, 'else leave the table. House rules," the croupier informed her.

Irritated by so many interruptions, Angel gritted her teeth. "Oh, very well. Let the blasted money ride until I tell you otherwise!" she snapped. "Now, Lucia, don't try to run away from me again, please. Just come here to me this very instant. I shall take you back to the others."

"You say you wou' send El Diablo after Lucia," Lucia challenged her cheekily with a flash of her dark eyes. "You lie!"

"Oh, but I shall—if you don't agree to leave here with

267

me immediately."

"But I cannot. Lucia, she have more heather to sell . . ."
Lucia said sweetly, turning away. *"Adiós*, English!" And
withthat, she squirmed her way between the gamblers and
those standing three-deep behind them, and vanished from
view again.

"Oh, botheration!" Angel exclaimed crossly. She rose
from her chair, intending to go around the table and cut
her off.

"Miss? Your winnings!" a young Englishman declared.
"Miss! Surely you don't mean to leave without them,
what?"

"My winnings?"

"Red seven? You lucky girl! It came up three times in a
row! Here. Careful you don't lose any—after all, it's not
exactly lettuce, is it?" So saying he thrust an enormous
heap of money into her arms. "I say, you don't mind if a
fellow countryman takes your place, do you, miss?
Perhaps your good fortune will rub off on me, don't ye
know!"

"By all means, be my guest, sir," Angel dismissed the
man, and plunged back into the champagne-guzzling
crowds.

To her surprise, it was Lucia who approached her, this
time, rather than the other way around. The Gypsy minx
cornered her.

"Look! Look, English! You win plenty much *dinero*,
eh?" Her bright dark eyes were as greedy as any jackdaw's
as she stared at the money Angel was cradling. *"Caray!* I
never seen so much!"

"If I promise to give you some, will you leave here with
me?" Angel suggested, inspired. Unwittingly, she now
possessed the perfect carrot to persuade this particular
donkey to do what she wanted.

"English, I follow you to end of world," Lucia vowed.
"Because—because I love you *so* plenty much!"

"Bloody little liar!" Angel ground out under her breath.

"What you say to me, eh?" Lucia demanded suspiciously.

"Never mind what I said. Just . . . come on."

*   *   *

Once outside again, Angel took the first normal breath she'd taken in the hour she'd spent inside the casino.

"Why he call you 'Princess'?" Lucia demanded, rudely sticking her tongue out at the doorman over her shoulder as Angel chivvied her briskly away.

"Never you mind."

"I doan like it when you angry," Lucia said sulkily.

"I doan like it when you misbehave, either, miss!"

"Pah!" Lucia dismissed her mild reprimand with a shrug. "I wan' bonbons . . . and fresh winkles . . . and silk stockings! Come on! There are place down by the harbor—they have everythin'! You'll see!"

When they struggled back up the winding mountain road to the woods and Ramon's camp three hours later, both young women were almost buried beneath numerous parcels.

Face to face with a dazzling array of items in the exclusive little shops Lucia dragged her into, it had finally dawned on Angel that she'd won a considerable amount, and that—failing clothes, food, and some means of transportation for herself and Nick—the money was actually a godsend!

Accordingly, she had embarked on a shopping spree that had left even Lucia breathless, purchasing blouses, skirts, underthings, sturdy shoes, and one darling little straw hat she hadn't been able to resist, for herself; shirts, breeches, and riding boots for Nick. She also had two bottles of excellent champagne, some paté and crackers, fresh fruits, expensive Cuban cheroots for Nick, and newspapers, some British and others French, so that they could catch up on what had been happening in the world since they'd left the train. The results of her efforts were tucked under her arms and dangling from strings looped through her hands.

Oh, she couldn't wait to see Nick's face when he saw the presents she'd bought him with her unexpected windfall! How he would laugh when she told him all about her foray into the casino for Lucia, and her pose as an opera

269

diva—! They could drink champagne and nibble on crackers spread with goose-liver paté while she recounted the droll little tale. . . .

"We've been combing these mountains for you two for three hours! Where in the *hell* have you been, woman?" Nick roared when she made her reappearance in the Gypsy camp. "And how in the name of all that's holy did you buy all that!"

Biting her lip, she haltingly explained, the funny way she'd planned to do so falling by the wayside in the face of his murderous tone and lethal expression.

A crackling silence followed her explanation. Angel risked a glance at Nick's face. If he was amused, he was hiding it awfully well. . . .

Chapter Twenty-Two

"Where the devil do you think you're taking me—?" she cried indignantly.

"Somewhere we can talk, missie—without half the Gypsies of Europe listening to us!" Nick growled. His fingers tightened about her wrist like a vise as he dragged her after him through the woods, far away from Manolito's camp.

"Did you consider that I might not want to accompany you?" Angel demanded hotly through gritted teeth, trying to squirm free.

"Nope. But then, I didn't consider givin' you a choice, either," he snapped, halting and releasing her hand at last.

"Humph!" she snorted, rubbing her sore wrist. "On reflection, that's hardly surprising, coming from you. You've manhandled me, threatened me, browbeaten me— you've never given me a choice in anything, not since the hour my father hired you, you—you bullying—arrogant— wretch!" she flung at him, tears of self-pity welling behind her eyes. An achy knot tied a double-hitch in her throat. Why, oh, why did he have to be this way? She'd wanted so very badly to please him, to impress him, to make him proud of her ingenuity and resourcefulness just this once, and this was how he rewarded her: with that—that *look* of his, like Satan himself, and with his domineering, hateful words! Knowing he was right didn't help, either. . . .

"Sit!" he snapped, his voice like the crack of a whip.

Like an obedient lapdog, she actually sat for one insane second, but then—realizing what she'd done—she immediately sprang to her feet again, popping up right under his nose like a jack-in-a-box. "No, *master*. I will *not* sit on command. What's more, I refuse to stay here and listen to yet another of your pompous lectures. Damn your arrogance, Durango! I'm a grown woman—not a little child to be scolded and dismissed to her room!"

Color flamed in her cheeks. Her gray eyes smoldered as he'd not seen them smolder since the evening she'd come gunning for him at the Hotel St. Pierre.

"All right. If you don't want to be treated like a child, then for Pete's sake, quit acting like one and show some savvy! This mornin', you went running off into the nearest town with that sixteen-year-old Jezebel without telling anyone where you were going—or that you were leaving the camp at all! Neither me nor Manolito nor all the men combined could find hide nor tail of you for over *three hours*. Now, maybe you didn't stop to think, but three hours of searching for someone you care about who's lost—who could be hurt, or in trouble, or danger—is one hell of a long time. It's an eternity, Angel!"

There was, for an instant, such raw agony in his eyes, it filled her with shame—and an uncomfortable twinge of guilt that her pride demanded she dispense with immediately.

He continued, "Sweet Christ! What went through my head in that time hardly bears thinking about—!"

"Oh, pooh! I was never in any danger. You're overreacting—again," she disclaimed airily.

She turned as if to rejoin Manolito, Lucia, and the others, but Nick's hand snaked out. He gripped her elbow, spinning her back to face him, his swarthy complexion dark with fury, his eyes hooded silver-blue points of fire.

"No danger? No *danger*, damn it? Tell me, just how do you know that, Angel? How can you be so sure of where those two sidewinders are? For all you know, you hotheaded, fool' woman, they could be in these here woods right now, just waiting t' ambush you!"

She tossed her head and laughed. She tried to sound scornful and deprecating as she did so, too, but—she couldn't quite resist an uneasy peek over her shoulder, just to be certain there was no one there. Nick had sounded so

272

bloody sure of the possibility.

"Oh, balderdash! You sound like an old woman who thinks there's a robber hiding under her bed each night, Durango! You're the one who should grow up. The one who should stop playing cowboys and Indians. Not me!"

"Maybe. Either way, one of us has to take this seriously, wouldn't you say, Angel, unless . . . you really were lyin' to me back in Paris?" His eyes narrowed. His jaw tightened—and so did his painful grip on her arm. "Have you known who's been after you all along, and why? Is that why you're so damned sure you're not in any real danger? Answer me!" he barked.

Her composure crumpled. "No! I swear it isn't that! Everything I told you is true! It's—" she sighed, blinking rapidly, "it's just that—that—I can't believe anyone would really want to hurt me so badly, they'd scour the countryside for me! I know those men dragged me off to that awful attic, but still—it doesn't seem *real*. And besides, if—if the kidnappers were well-informed enough about our plans to know we'd be on the train for Rome that day, they'd know our entire itinerary, surely? Wouldn't they simply continue on to Rome? Follow Mabel and Juarez to our hotel, and wait until we join them?"

He nodded curtly. "That's just what I'm betting they did, after we jumped the train. But—there's no way t' be sure! So, until we know where they are, we have to act as if they were holed up behind every tree. And that means, if you plan on harin' off someplace, sweet thing, you have to tell me first," he finished in a far gentler tone.

To her surprise, he suddenly drew her into his arms, turning her to face him. And, after tensing momentarily, she softened and let him hold her, curling her arms around his lean waist and resting her cheek against his chest.

Oh, he felt so strong, so very powerful. The throb of his heart in her ear was like the beat of a drum, its tempo sure and measured. His arms were a fortress, a citadel against all danger. She suddenly felt certain that as long as she remained within them, nothing on earth could harm her. . . .

"Oh, baby, I was so damned worried about you!" he murmured, his chin resting in her hair, his free hand

273

stroking her tangled curls.

"Were you? Were you really?" she whispered, her voice catching, she was so happy that he cared.

Nick nodded. "Worried? I was closer to going 'loco'!"

"And all because I didn't stop to think!" she bit her lower lip and looked up at him tremulously. "You're right, Nick. I'm such a silly goose sometimes! It was stupid of me to run off without telling you, but—but all I could think about was keeping that minx Lucia from being thrown in gaol because of the card tricks *I'd* taught her. My—er—gambling windfall really was an accident, you know," she added earnestly. "I meant it when I promised never to gamble again. It happened just as I told you."

"Honest Injun?" he challenged, tilting her chin between his thumb and finger so that she was looking up at him. A smile tugged at the corners of his mouth and twinkled in his eyes. "The next time you take it into your pretty head to make tracks, you'll tell me? Cross your heart 'n hope t' die?"

She smiled with relief at his silliness and nodded, solemnly raising her palm. "Honest Injun."

He dipped his head and pressed a lingering kiss full upon her lips; a kiss that melted her bones and made her giddy with its sinful sweetness.

"All forgotten and forgiven, then," he murmured huskily. "Now. Let's go take a look-see at what you bought with your ill-gotten gains, woman—before I forget it's only high noon . . ."

"Later," she said huskily.

The gleam in his eyes was a lusty, wicked one as, laughing, she tugged him toward a rough bridle track between the trees.

"Where the devil do you think you're taking me, missie?" he growled, parroting her earlier words.

"Somewhere I can really drive you *loco*, Durango!" she declared impudently, a look in her smoky gray eyes that almost brought him to his knees. "Somewhere we can . . . make love . . . without half the Gypsies of Europe looking on!"

* * *

By noon the following day, after a total of almost sixteen hours spent astride one of Manolito's swaybacked nags, Angel was bitterly regretting having bought clothing and luxuries with her windfall. Now, she wished with all her heart—and throbbing body!—that she'd invested her funds in two first-class railway tickets to Rome, and some decent food, instead of frivolous treats like paté, crackers, champagne, and week-old British newspapers. As Nick had pointed out when she'd bewailed her numb derrière earlier that morning, if she'd bought the train tickets instead of underdrawers and shirts, they'd have been reunited with Mabel and Juarez by now, her belongings at her disposal, looking forward to a tasty supper of scampi and pasta and spumoni served on some starlit Roman terrace, no doubt. . . .

As it was, although they'd crossed through the mountain passes leading from Monaco into Turin, then ridden on into the Lombardy region of Italy the day before, they'd somehow lost their way and wandered far from the coast road they'd planned to travel, not discovering their mistake for many miles. Now, they were traveling through grassy hills dotted with Alpine wildflowers above sparkling lakes, heading instead for the nearest Italian city of Milan, where Nick hoped he could find work for a day or two and earn enough to buy them train tickets to Rome.

The extravagant foodstuffs she'd purchased had been quickly consumed the evening before, worst luck. . . . They'd had nothing to eat upon rising, and for their midday meal, only a half-loaf of coarse bread and a little sausage and cheese. These Nick had earned by drawing water for an old woman in an isolated mountain chalet they'd passed. Obviously believing from their shaggy mounts and casual attire that they were either thieving Gypsies or tinkers, who'd return after dark to steal from her, she'd flung the food at Nick, then set her watchdogs to worrying their horses' heels, in order to speed them on their way.

"That old crone was near as tough as her bread!" Nick said ruefully when they halted to rest and eat their sorry luncheon that noon. His exaggerated chewing was not so much an act as a necessity!

"Hmm," Angel agreed absently, glancing up briefly from one of the newspapers she'd bought in Monte Carlo. She'd been reading avidly ever since they'd dismounted, for it had been too dark to read by firelight the evening before, and she'd been too exhausted then to try. "Here. Why don't you read one of these while you're eating? This ghastly cheese is almost palatable if you can take your mind off the waxy texture!"

"Thanks. Say, that must be Lake Como down there," he observed as he resumed his cross-legged position. He nodded toward the sparkling lake far below their picnic spot as he shook open the newspaper.

Angel looked up. "Did you say Lake Como?"

"That's what the signpost over there says. Why?"

She frowned. "You know, I believe Da inherited a small villa from Lord Brixton that was on the shores of Lake Como. Villa—villa something—Oh, what was it? Alejandro? No, no, it wasn't a name. The word was Italian, though. It meant house of happiness or joy, Mr. Hamilton said. Villa Allegra? Yes, that was it!" The sudden, breathless excitement in her voice was marked. "Oh, Nick, do you think we could go there? It can't be very far, and I'd give anything to soak in a real bathtub with soap, instead of in a muddy stream. And I'd give my little finger to sleep in a real bed tonight, too, instead of on the ground!" Her gray eyes shone.

Nick chuckled. "Heck, if you're sure your pa owns a villa near here, I don't see why we couldn't look for it. There's a village down in the valley—Santa Marianna. Maybe the folks there have heard of the place. But don't be disappointed if it's in poor shape. Lord Harry's been dead for a spell, after all . . ."

"I believe Mr. Hamilton mentioned that there was a caretaker who saw to its upkeep, but I might be wrong," Angel said thoughtfully, trying to remember. "Either way, I'd really like to see the villa, now that it's Da's—and any roof over our heads for the night would be better than nothing, right?"

"Sure, some folks swear by 'em!" Nick admitted with a grin. "But as for me—heck, I'd just as soon have the stars and the sky and a big old moon shinin' down on me . . ."

"Some folks swear that eating daffodils on St. David's Day improves your health, too," she countered pointedly, "But that doesn't mean they're right—or even sane!" She stuck out her tongue at him, then returned to her newspaper reading.

Grinning, Nick opened his own copy. For several minutes, there was silence.

"Well, look at this! There's an accounting of Diana Forsythe's wedding here," she exclaimed with a wistful edge to her voice. "It sounds as if it was quite the talk of the town, don't you know!"

"Diana?"

"Yes. One of my—er—old schoolchums," Angel explained, reluctant to mention Reggie and risk making Nick angry. Or—were his reactions to Reggie's name jealous ones? Hmm. It was an encouraging possibility she hadn't considered before. "Diana and I met at boarding school years ago. I'd always thought she was my friend, but now—? Well, I rather doubt she was anything of the sort, on reflection. Diana was always looking for something outrageous and daring to do, you see. She often used to say how very amusing it was to pretend to befriend those of the lower classes and rub shoulders with the 'common folk.' She claimed she found their manners and speech quaint, and that the way they dressed and acted was quite uproariously funny."

"Your Diana sounds like a real peach of a gal!" Nick said dryly.

"She does, doesn't she? I realize now that I was probably just another of her little lower-class diversions. Perhaps the biggest laughingstock of them all! Quaint, stupid little Annie Higgins from the mills of Lancashire. The cloddish daughter of a multimillionaire, a guttersnipe who wore clogs and did her hair in pigtails. A stupid little idiot who wanted everyone to like her and said 'nowt' and 'by gum' and who didn't even kn-know which s-spoon or f-fork to use at d-dinner—"

"—and who was worth two Dianas any damn day of the week, but was too darned blind—and scared—t' see it," Nick finished softly, without a trace of teasing.

"Thank you," she murmured gratefully, drawing a

deep, shaky breath. "But I'm afraid Annie was something of a rough diamond. One who, right or wrong, felt herself lacking and sadly in need of polish. I suppose, in my desperation to fit in, I became even more of a snob than the others were!"

"Aw, at least. Much, *much* more, I'd say," Nick agreed solemnly. "Why, the first time I met you, I reckoned you were lookin' down your nose so darned hard, you could see your upper lip through your nostrils!"

She giggled, blinking back her tears. "Oh, you dear, sweet idiot! Did I—was I really *that* horrid?"

"Honey, if I close my eyes, I can still see the expression on your face after I dropped you on that chaise the first night! Your pa was so darned relieved we'd agreed to hire on with him, he took us off for a drink to celebrate. He told Red to put you to bed with a glass of warmed milk, remember? As we walked off down the hall, I glanced back. And sweetness, you looked jealous enough t' spit nails!"

"Oh, but I was!" she confessed, remembering that night. "You see, Mabel and I had heard noises. I was convinced Bill Bligh's boys had broken in downstairs and meant to kill me! That's why—when I saw you and Juarez in the doorway—I fainted. But my da didn't even seem to care, he was so taken with you both! I was furious. It had been just the two of us for so very long, I was green with jealousy. I hated it that Da liked you so much. Poor Nick. I'm afraid I didn't try very hard to be pleasant, did I?"

"Not by a long chalk! But—I reckon you got your come-uppance for it."

She frowned. "I did? When?"

"When you upchucked over the sides of the *Pelican!* Y' know, I don't reckon I ever saw a sorrier sight than you tryin' to act the lady in that oversized sou'wester, with your face all green and pukey . . . *That* was well worth watching!"

"You horrid man! Go back to reading your newspaper and let me continue with mine, do!" Angel said with a sniff. Though she sounded cross, she was smiling none-theless.

An article about the Wild West Show caught Nick's eye, and he was soon immersed in reading himself, a slow grin tugging at his lips as he did so.

According to the column, the female sharpshooter Annie Oakley's manager-husband, Frank—Frank Butler—had taken over the role of "King of the Cowboys" for Nick when—according to the reporter's story, "former 'King' Nick Durango was forced to leave the Wild West Show due to pressing family matters that required his return to his native New Mexico!" It also stated that Edward, Prince of Wales, had gifted Cody with a gold pocket watch that boasted a huge oval amethyst, set in gold, on the fob, following a recent performance. Her Majesty, Queen Victoria—equally enthralled by the show's exciting performances in her honor—had presented Buffalo Bill with a gold brooch that featured a crown and the royal insignia. "Good t' see you're doing well without me, Cody," Nick murmured to himself, surprised and pleased that he still felt no regret for having quit the show.

Just then, he happened to glance across at Angel and was felled by what he saw.

She was sitting upright on the grass as still as any statue, her legs curled to one side. But the newspaper she'd been reading was now crushed to her breast, held in clenched fists that trembled uncontrollably. Her face was streaked with rivers of silent tears, drained of all color. Her mouth was working soundlessly.

He looked. He saw. And—he knew without needing to ask what newsworthy item she'd read, and damned himself for a fool. What in the hell was he thinking of? He knew she'd bought papers in Monte Carlo and that she might find out from their pages about Smythe-Moreton and Bligh's deaths, but for some reason, it hadn't registered. Christ! He should have told her long since—'else seen those damned newspapers hidden away from her until he had!

"Nick . . ." she choked out. "Oooh, Nick. It's—Reggie—he's—Reggie's dead!" A tremendous shudder ran through her. "It—says—here—that he—that he committed suicide in Paris, after m-murdering Bill B-Bligh in L-London!" The anguished eyes she turned beseechingly to him were dilated with shock. "How can that be? I talked to him just last month. We quarrelled and now—he's gone.

Just like that," she whispered. "I—I can't believe it."

Seeing her shock, her grief, Nick felt as if someone had slammed him in the gut with a hefty boulder. She hadn't deserved to find out like this, but it was too late now. The damage was done. Christ! What could he say to comfort her? What words could he use that wouldn't sound hypocritical or callous to her, knowing how he'd felt about both men?

Instead, he took the coward's way out. He went to her, held her, stroked her hair, and offered his broad chest to the tears and the weeping that finally spilled forth, figuring on saying as little as possible.

As his arms enfolded her, the dam broke. He felt the hot flood of her tears dampen his shirt and chest, and the sobs that wracked her slender body.

"Oh, Nick," she managed at length, her voice thick and muffled with weeping, "now that it's too late, I realize how very desperate he must have been, how very badly he needed my help! Even if I refused to marry him, I had Da's letters of credit. I could have loaned him the money he needed—but I didn't! I called myself his friend, but when he needed me the most, I let him down. Oh, poor, poor Reggie!"

That damned, sidewindin' Limey just wouldn't stay dead! Nick thought, exasperated, pushed to break his judicial silence by her words.

"Sure, Angel," he ground out, "you were his friend, all right—his own little Bank of England, there whenever that lily-livered, spineless leech needed you for a stake or a loan! Come on, Angel! Open your eyes! Don't let his death turn him into a saint—see him for what he was! He used you. For years he'd been using you—dangling his title before you like a carrot, knowing how badly you wanted the acceptance that being his wife would bring. He told you himself he considered you beneath him, that he'd only wanted your pa's money, remember?"

"But he was desperate! I know he didn't mean it—he couldn't have!"

"He meant it, honey—and don't you ever forget it. I don't hold with talkin' ill of the dead, but I'd bet hard money that cuss got no more than he deserved, if the truth were known. Suicide, my a—er—my stars! He's the first damned suicide I saw that gave himself a pistol-whippin' 'fore he threw himself in the Seine—!"

The silence thundered in the wake of his outburst. Crackled. Breathed. Nick's faint hope that Angel had been too upset to realize what he'd said died as she stiffened in his arms. Slowly leaning back and removing his hands from her waist, she stared at him as if he were a stranger.

"What did you say?" she whispered.

"That he got no more than he deserved?" Nick gritted.

"Not that—the rest of it. You said—you said you *saw* him!"

"You heard me wrong." Christ! His eyes couldn't meet hers.

"Perhaps. But it doesn't say in this article how Reggie died. Yet, you knew! You said he threw himself in the Seine. Just how—how do you explain that, Nick?"

"All right. Just calm down, quit shaking, and I'll tell you."

"Go right ahead."

"Well, the night I went back to the Moulin Rouge—you know, while you were sleeping?—I saw the *gendarmes* fishing his body out of the water," he admitted, resigned. In as few words as possible, he told her everything.

"Then you've known all these weeks that Reggie was dead?" Her tone was shrill with incredulity and accusation now. "That he fled England because he was accused of murdering Bligh?"

Reluctantly, he nodded.

"And yet you said nothing?"

"I . . . thought about it, some," he admitted. "But we'd jumped off the train by then and you seemed like you were—aw, enjoying yourself, I guess—and I couldn't see the sense in upsetting you."

"Upsetting me? And finding out like—like this is supposed to be easier on me?"

"I should have told you long since, I know. I was wrong, honey, and I'm sorry, and I'd have done anything t' spare you findin' out this way, but—whatever I say can't bring him back. Can't we go on from there?"

"Did you kill him?"

"What!"

"Reggie. Did you kill him?"

"Hell, no!" he rasped. "Is that what you think I am—a cold-blooded killer?"

"Right now, I don't know exactly *what* you are, Mr. Durango." She shot him a look that was pure poison. "I only know that you have one rule for yourself, and another for others. If you want people to be honest with you, sir, then I would strongly suggest that from here on, you be honest with them." She bit her lip. "Now. I suggest we leave here and try to find the villa before it gets dark. Do you agree with that plan?"

"Yes, ma'am," he ground out, a muscle ticking at his temple, his fists knotted at his sides.

"Good. Then let's waste no more time. Mount up."

Those crisp orders were the last words she spoke to him for the remainder of that day. She retreated into her haughty facade of the proper British lady and try as he might to bring her out, to trick her into answering or make her smile, she stonily ignored him, acting as if she'd either not heard his attempts to smooth things over, or by following his suggestions without question or comment.

In the end, he decided she'd have to work things through for herself, and quit trying. A flesh-and-blood man he could compete with on his own terms—but there was no way in hell he could compete with her distorted memories of a dead man.

In the final hour of their journey that day, the brilliant cornflower sky and the hazy lavender-blue Alps changed color, the sky darkening to a smudgy bluish violet beyond the charcoal mountain ridges.

They followed the villagers of Santa Marianna's directions and at last their weary horses ambled to a halt before a sweeping wrought-iron gateway, framed by tall white walls. Sure enough, in one of the gateposts, below a tarnished plaque with the legend "Villa Allegra" engraved in curling letters, a rusty bellpull had been set. Through the gates, they could see ranks of lofty cypress sentinels, guarding either side of a white-pebbled driveway that clambered up to where the villa stood, upon terraced slopes overlooking Lake Como. Nick dismounted his horse. He tried the gate, found it locked, and pulled the bell chain instead.

"I don't reckon there'll be an answer so late in the day, but it's worth a try," he observed.

Angel nodded coolly, unsmiling. Despite a long and difficult ride over hilly terrain that had left her with an aching back, chafed thighs, and a numb derrière, she was still angry, still stunned by the news of Reggie's violent death. How dare that—that rat speak and act as if he'd done absolutely nothing wrong—as if *she* was the one who should feel guilty, rather than him? He'd *deliberately* concealed the knowledge of Reggie and Bligh's deaths from her, despite knowing how close she'd once been to Reggie and how terrified she'd been of Bligh. That sly fox, that—that unscrupulous weasel! If he could hide that from her, what more secrets might he have up his sleeve?

It was a seed of doubt that, once planted in the fertile ground of her anger, quickly took root in a dark, mistrustful corner of her soul. . . .

Just when they'd both given up on anyone answering their ring, an old woman suddenly appeared from a pathway that followed the villa's walls for some yards, then disappeared between some bushes.

Though dressed all in widow's black like most of the older peasant women of Italy, wearing the ubiquitous black lace shawl over her hair, she carried her tall, thin frame erectly, and her dark eyes snapped under winging black brows with no traces of gray.

"*Sì?*"

"*Buona sera, signora,*" Nick began, exhausting the extent of his knowledge of Italian with his greeting.

"And to you, sir," she answered in perfect English, spoken in a suprisingly rich contralto voice for one her age. "How may I help you? Have you lost your way?"

"No, ma'am. See, this young lady here is Signorina Angelica Higgins—the daughter of Signore Sidney Higgins, ma'am—the new owner of Villa Allegra since Lord Brixton passed on? She—er—that is, we . . ."

"Please, signore, forgive my interruption, but there's no

need to explain. I know very well who Signore Higgins is," the woman confirmed, her tone defensive. "The new heir to Villa Allegra—a very kind gentleman who graciously permitted my brother and myself to stay on here as . . . caretakers . . . following Harry's death. Signore Higgins's secretary is most efficient. He sees that we are paid promptly each month for our services. If you and the signorina have come to inspect the villa, I can assure you, you will find everything in order."

"Ma'am, I know we will. But that's not why we're here," Nick reassured her. "See, Miz Higgins has been traveling across-country for several weeks. She's worn out and she'd like to spend a few days here at the villa, resting up, before we go on to Rome."

"Stay here? But the villa is hers! The young lady is always welcome. If you'll ride on up to the villa, I will meet you there in a short while. Giorgio—my brother— will see to your horses. You have left your baggage in the village, perhaps . . . ?"

"No. We have none, signora—?"

A ghost of a smile curved the old woman's tightly clamped lips. "You may call me 'Maria,' sir."

With that, she reached into a pocket in her black dress and withdrew an ornate key. After she'd opened the gates, they rode their horses through and she locked them behind her, gravely handing the key over to Angel saying, "Until you leave, Signorina Higgins . . ." when she was done. Then she vanished down the path as mysteriously as she'd made her appearance.

"There must be a cottage back there somewhere," Nick observed. But to his regret, Angel didn't deign to answer even this casual comment. Scowling himself, he caught the flicker of irritation that crossed her lovely features and wondered—not for the first time over the past few hours— what the infuriating woman'd do if he quit pussyfooting around her? Maybe he should quit patiently waiting for her to regain her common sense, and instead just toss her over his knee and paddle the livin' daylights out of her backside! He grinned evilly, for the image was one he found immensely satisfying. "Why, yes sir, Nick. I agree one-hundred-and-fifty percent. There surely must be a cottage through there," he answered himself, and clicked to his horse before riding on.

At a slower pace, Angel followed him, feeling a tiny twinge of guilt at her pettiness in refusing to talk to him—but maintaining her stony silence nonetheless. He deserved being made to squirm for little longer, confound him.

Despite her mood, she couldn't help a gasp of delight as they reached the house proper. The villa was enchanting! A tiny replica of a Florentine palazzo, set in a miniature formal garden that meandered over steeply sloping terrain, it boasted three levels, roofed with terra cotta tiles and walled with dark beige stucco that looked almost pink in the fading light. Dark blue shutters framed the windows, and the arched double entry doors had a lighted carriage lamp of wrought iron on either side. A terrace of weathered gray crazy-paving stones encircled the villa, with earthenware vases of deep red bougainvillea set at intervals along it. Beyond a shallow flight of grassy steps that wound between azalea hedges off to the right of the house, Angel glimpsed Lake Como. A balustraded terrace that fronted another wing of the villa overlooked what promised to be a magnificent vista of mountains and water.

"Welcome to Villa Allegra. Please, come inside, signorina."

Angel smiled her thanks and entered the door Maria held open for her, looking about the arched portico with interest as she did so.

Inside, the stucco walls had been painted a pale yet sunny yellow. Fat yellow candles flickered in the wrought-iron sconces that branched out from the walls, drenching everywhere in golden light. It gleamed on highly polished tables, danced over heavy chairs with exquisite tapestry or satin seats, winked gaily off tall candlesticks of brass or silver and made them shine with a spanking, new-cast luster.

Some of the doors that opened onto large, airy rooms boasted hand-painted panels, while many of the tall windows had been paned with glass etchings of birds, fruits, or flowers. Elegant French Provincial furniture contrasted sharply with heavy Tuscan antiques in many of the rooms they passed through, yet the overall effect was one of casual luxury and perfect harmony, of good taste combined with an eye for comfort and a flair for color.

"You're doing a splendid job of upkeeping the place. The villa looks beautiful, Maria," Angel complimented the woman, trying to keep up without actually breaking into a run as Maria swept down a long corridor. As she hurried along, she wondered guiltily if her dusty boots were scuffing Maria's gleaming red-tiled floor and hoped if they were, the imperious old woman would forgive her. "I—um—I don't believe you could take better care of the place were it your own. My father will be very pleased with what you're doing here. I shall be certain to recommend an increase in your wages when I see him next."

"Thank you, signorina," Maria murmured, a slight edge to her tone now that made Angel wonder if perhaps her praise had seemed patronizing to the woman, though she'd meant it sincerely. "I thought perhaps you and the young gentleman might be hungry after your journey," Maria continued without slowing her pace, "and so I brought some supper up with me from the gatehouse. Tomorrow, I shall go into the village to buy food. I will also have the dustsheets removed from the dining room. But for this evening, with your permission, I shall serve you in the kitchen. There is a fire lit, and it is more . . . cozy . . . yes?"

"It sounds perfect! Really, you shouldn't have gone to so much trouble. I do hope we're not depriving you and— Giorgio, was it?—of your own suppers?"

"No, signorina. We have more than enough."

The kitchen Maria led her into was clearly the heart of the villa. It was dominated by the huge old farm table in the center of the cotto-tiled floor. Two places had been set upon its scarred scrubbed surface, blue bowls of Sardinian design alongside blue-and-white checkered *serviettes*, spoons, a bread board with a long golden loaf, a dish of sliced tomatoes sprinkled with curls of pale *parmegiana*, a platter of sliced sausage, a basket of white grapes and oranges, and a bottle of wine. Between them sat a black soup kettle with a lid and a handle.

The lower walls were tiled with square ceramic tiles in a Tuscan-blue floral motif. Wrought-iron utensil racks hung with pots, spoons, pestles, and ladles vied for space on the upper half of white stucco, along with narrow shelves that held pretty blue pottery, baskets of geraniums, or copper butter molds. Strings of garlic and onions hung from the rough rafters above. And, as Maria had said, a welcoming fire had already been lit in the rustic arched fireplace, which looked as if it had once been an outdoor oven, used for baking bread.

A charming iron-grilled window along the farthest wall overlooked a tiny courtyard where grapevines rambled over a wooden trellis. Angel glimpsed a pump and a weathered dovecote there. Fan-tailed doves were fluttering home to roost, their cooing loud on the hush of dusk. Inhaling, she caught the spicy scent of an herb garden on the cool evening breeze that drifted into the kitchens, basil, sweet rosemary, oregano—and flowers.

"If you would like to refresh yourself, there is a pump outside, but I'll have Giorgio fill the bathtub with hot water while you're eating. Enjoy your supper, signorina, while I prepare your rooms for the night."

"I'm sure I'll enjoy it. Everything looks delicious! Thank you so much, Maria."

After Maria had gone, Angel forgot all about washing her hands and instead sat down at the table. Lifting the lid of the soup kettle, she peeked inside, sniffing eagerly. The savory soup within smelled deliciously of shrimp, tomatoes, onions, white beans, celery, squash, and other tasty vegetables, all simmered with spices, herbs, and wine. Her mouth watering, she ladled herself a generous helping, filling the bowl to its very rim, breaking off a generous heel of the crusty bread, then digging into the meal with unladylike gusto. Lord, she was so famished and the food smelled so mouthwatering . . . !

Nick joined her when she was already halfway through her second bowl of soup, ducking his tall frame through the low kitchen door that led outside to the tiny courtyard.

She glanced up and saw that his hair was wet. Droplets of water still clung to his ebony curls. His face and hands appeared freshly washed, too, and his white shirt clung to his damp chest as he took his seat at the table opposite her. She felt a tug at her heartstrings as she stole a covert glance at him, a yearning to mend the rift between them so that she could sleep the night away in the fortress of his arms, safe and secure from all harm. But—that would require calling a truce on her part, would require the offering of the olive branch of peace. She, apologize, when he was in the wrong? When he'd intentionally concealed the truth from her? Never! Not even for the joys of sharing a real bed with him would she lower herself to eat humble pie for the second time in two days.

She stole another look at him. Blast the man! He looked so impossibly handsome, so bloody cool, refreshed, and relaxed, as if he hadn't spent the past two days being jounced around like a sack of potatoes, carried up hill and down dale on the bony back of a gypsy nag. By contrast, she—with her clothes travel-stained and wrinkled, her hair snarled and badly in need of a thorough washing and brushing, and her hands reeking of horse sweat and leather—felt suddenly grubby and decidedly uncomfortable beneath his pale blue gaze. Angel grimaced. She probably looked like something the cat had dragged in, she thought irritably!

"Hungry?" he asked casually, nodding at her drained bowl. It was a statement rather than a question. She'd used the last morsel of her bread to sop up every last trace of soup!

Muttering something, she flung aside her *serviette* and sprang to her feet, leaving Nick staring after her as she stalked from the kitchen.

Let Durango enjoy his supper all alone! she told herself as she climbed the staircase to the second floor of the villa. Maria had promised a bath would be waiting for her when she'd finished her supper, and she intended to take it at her leisure before she tumbled into bed—alone.

Chapter Twenty-Three

She awoke the following morning to the melodic tinkle of campanile bells from the church in Santa Marianna, and the nearer, plaintive bleating of a goat in need of milking.

Maria's? she wondered, yawning and stretching blissfully on the lace-edged sheets, then discounted the idea. Somehow, despite her position as caretaker of the villa, and the fact that Maria dressed humbly in black, there was something almost . . . sophisticated . . . something that bordered on elegant about the woman. It was in the imperious tilt of her head, in her confident carriage. Self-possessed Maria didn't strike one as a woman who kept goats! Even the way she spoke, in that throaty contralto without a hint of an accent of any kind, suggested an educated woman; someone who'd done more in her life than see to the upkeep of a small Italian villa for an absentee landlord.

Still contemplating the enigmatic Maria, Angel luxuriated in the dreamy limbo that lies between waking and dozing, dreamily aware of the lazy slap of the lake as it lapped at the grassy shores below her terrace, idly watching the rippling reflections of water and sunshine shimmering on the ceiling and walls above and around her.

How marvelous! The filtered light that fell through both wooden louvers and French doors transformed her bedchamber into an underwater grotto! In it, the enormous poster bed on which she'd slept became a mahogany sailing ship. Its tapered posts were the masts, its hangings of white silk with *broderie anglaise* borders the vessel's billowing sails. The matching white curtains at the windows, dancing in the breeze, added to the illusion of bellying sails, she thought fancifully, stroking the cool white satin sheets beneath her.

Birds were singing their little hearts out to the dawn, and the dangling crystal teardrops that decorated the shade of the bedside lamp tinkled like windchimes. Such civilized sights, such nonthreatening, everyday sounds. Oh! What bliss! she thought, yawning hugely and stretching again. After so many nights of sleeping outdoors on the hard ground, plagued by insects and damp, the luxury of sleeping in a real bed upon a real feather mattress, between satin sheets that smelled of sunshine and rose-petal sachets was sheer heaven—or very close to it. . . .

She must have drifted off again, for when she awoke the second time, dawn had long since fled. She frowned. Golden sunlight now flooded the room, but there was something else that had altered, besides the light. Ah, yes. The background of sounds to which her hearing had grown accustomed while asleep had changed. The birds were no longer warbling, frightened away by a repeated low, grinding sound that was somehow familiar. She thought for a moment, then placed the sound and smiled with satisfaction. Someone was clipping a hedge with a pair of gardening shears!

Flinging her newly washed hair over her shoulders, she threw aside the sheet and headed toward the terrace to enjoy the view. Last night it had been too dark to see much from her balcony, and besides, she'd been too worn out to care much.

But halfway across the room, she froze. Her hand flew to her mouth. Involuntarily, she cried out, for the sunlight streaming through the filmy white curtains on the French doors had cast a shadow upon their surface—the blunt-featured profile of a man she recognized!

Unable to believe her eyes, she shook her head from side to side. No. It couldn't be Bill Bligh! He was dead—it was impossible!

The door to her bedchamber suddenly flew open. It

slammed back against the plastered walls as, barechested, Nick exploded into the room. He took one look at her ashen face, saw the direction in which she was staring and strode quickly out onto the balcony. He looked around, but saw nothing that would have frightened her.

"I heard you scream. What was it? An intruder—?" he demanded.

She nodded, chilly and trembling with shock. Hugging herself about the arms, she whispered, "I think they're gone now."

"They?"

"He. I saw—I saw a shadow on the curtains. Right there." She pointed. "A man's profile. Nick, I know this sounds foolish—and I know it couldn't really be him—because—because he's dead—but I'd swear it was—Bill Bligh!"

Frowning, Nick returned to the balcony. This time, he peered over it, and the tension drained from his broad shoulders. "Come out here. Let me introduce you to your mysterious 'shadow.'"

Hesitantly, she joined him and leaned over the stone railing of the terrace. Several feet below, standing upon a wooden ladder with shears in his hands as he pruned the camelias that rambled about her terrace, was an elderly man dressed for gardening.

"Giorgio, Signorina Angelica would like to meet you," Nick called down. "Angel, this is Giorgio—Maria's brother."

The man looked up. He drew the stub of a cheroot from between his fleshy lips, saluted and smiled, showing crooked teeth. Masses of sunbrowned wrinkles crinkled about his faded blue eyes. "Good mornin', miss. Loverly day, in'it? I do 'ope you slept well?"

Angel stared at him. His nose appeared to have been broken at some time in the past, and his other features were coarse, as Bligh's had been, but there the striking resemblance she'd glimpsed in his shadow ended—or had been no more than her imagination all along. Whereas the gaming-hall proprietor had been in his forties, swarthy, burly, and tall, this man was old enough to be Bligh's father. He was also gray-haired and fair-complected, his

291

stooped frame of average height and build! Embarrassed, she realized she'd been mistaken.

"I slept very well, thank you, Giorgio," she managed to say. "The gardens are beautiful."

"Thank you, miss. I do me best, though Gawd knows, I in't gettin' any younger! The roses are bloomin' a proper treat this summer, though. If yer like, miss, I could cut some for yer room?"

"Thank you. That would be lovely." Angel went back inside, feeling silly for making such a fuss over nothing.

"Well, he *did* look like Bligh in silhouette," she insisted defensively, catching Nick's expression as he followed her inside.

Tight-lipped, he shrugged. "I'll have to take your word for it, won't I? I never saw Bligh." He started to leave.

"Wait!" she called after him, wanting to kick herself the moment she'd spoken, because there was no reason to call him back.

"Yes?"

"Um, did you, er, notice that Maria doesn't seem the caretaker sort?" she asked. It was the first thought that popped into her head.

"Really?" he drawled, his expression derisive as he looked down at her. "Silly old me! See, I didn't know people had 'sorts.'"

She flushed. "Oh, stop it! I didn't mean it how it sounded. It's just that—Maria speaks beautiful English, without any accent whatsoever. And Giorgio sounds like a Londoner, rather than an Italian! There's something about both of them that isn't quite right . . ."

"For gardeners and caretakers, you mean?" he added with heavy sarcasm.

"I mean exactly that!" she agreed with a defiant, irritated toss of her head. "Maria is so . . . she's so *poised.*"

"Well, I'm damned if I noticed anything odd about the poor woman. She seems fine to me. Charming to talk to— and the best cook I've come across in quite a spell. Giorgio's harmless, too, from what little I've seen of him. Wrapped up in his battles with greenfly and Japanese beetles. Did it occur to you that Lord Harry—being English himself—might simply have preferred to hire

292

himself a couple of English caretakers? That that's all there is to it?"

Of course. It was the obvious solution to the mystery she'd dreamed up, but she hadn't thought of it, and it showed in her deflated expression.

"By the way," Nick continued, "Maria said to tell you that breakfast's ready, if you're hungry. Do you want a tray brought up?"

She shook her head. "No. Tell her I'll come down."

"Then if there's nothing else you want, I'll be off."

"No, nothing else. Oh, there is one thing! I forgot to thank you for coming to my 'rescue'!" she added in a shamefaced tone.

"All in a day's work, ma'am," he said curtly, turning on his heel.

Angel scowled at his retreating back and rudely stuck out her tongue. So he'd decided to become his old arrogant, mocking self, to remain impersonal and aloof and let her make the first move toward any reconciliation between them, had he? Well, he was in for a long, long wait, if that was his plan. It'd be a cold day in Hades before she went crawling to him! she thought.

After Nick'd gone, she looked for something to wear, but could find nothing in any of the dressers or the carved armoire but mothballs and yellowed newspaper liners. Maria had taken her dirty clothing away to be laundered—or perhaps burned!—last night. At the time, she'd been too exhausted, too upset about Reggie's death and Nick's deception to care which, only too grateful to accept the fresh cotton nightgown Maria had offered her after a heavenly bubble bath, before she fell into bed.

She called to Maria from her doorway but, receiving no answer after several minutes, went down the hall to the next room and looked inside. The dark Spanish furnishings and claret-colored hangings in the room suggested it had once belonged to the master of the house. No female clothing in this masculine domain!

The next room down the hall looked more promising. Decorated in delicate yellows and creams, with accents of ivy green in the charming French provincial furnishings and pillows, the spacious sunlit chamber could only have

293

belonged to a woman. The etched windows behind the cream-brocade draperies framed a view of sparkling Lake Como and the hazy lavender mountains, as did her own.

From the very first, her search was rewarded. Kneeling, she pulled open a dresser drawer and found frothy underthings scented with rose sachets inside it. Holding them up against her, she was certain they would fit. Now, something to wear over them . . .

She flung open the door to the hand-painted wardrobe and was about to examine the crush of gowns that hung within it when she noticed the corner of a picture frame tucked behind the last gown, as if someone had wanted the picture hidden. Curious, she withdrew it and carried it over to the windows and the light.

It was a framed theater poster, she realized, printed in somewhat lurid colors that had retained much of their brilliance over the years. "Shakespeare's *Macbeth* As You Have Never Seen It!" the title promised. Beneath it, a beautiful dark-haired woman in period costume stood in a dramatic, tragic pose. The back of her hand was pressed to her brow, while in the other, she held a dripping dagger. Beneath the Thespian beauty's feet were the words, "With Mary Appleby starring in the role of Lady Macbeth. Performances nightly, June 7—Aug. 8, 1834."

Angel held the poster up to the light and peered at the woman's face. She was very beautiful, with jet black hair, haunting dark eyes, fine bone structure and an ivory complexion.

"So. Have I changed so much that you don't recognize me?" asked Maria from the door.

Angel jumped guiltily at being caught snooping. She turned to the woman. "You're Mary Appleby?"

"I am. Or should I say, I was."

"Then that explains it. Nick was right—you are British! How stupid of me. You see, I was puzzled that you spoke English without a trace of an Italian accent! You have such a lovely speaking voice, Maria. Now I know why." To her relief, the woman didn't look or act in the least annoyed.

As if to prove it, she laughed. "Thank you, my dear.

Dramatic training helps. You're quite right, I'm British by birth—and proud of it, too, though it's been many, many years since I was last in England. Unfortunately, it's not often I have the chance to speak my own language these days, except with my brother, or on those rare occasions when my son comes to visit me. Alas, no one calls me Mary Appleby any more, either. I've been simply 'Maria' for . . . what is it? Forty . . . ? No, almost fifty, years. How time flies! I expect most of the people who saw me perform are either very old, or dead by now, but I was a celebrated Shakespearian actress in my youth. The toast of London's theatres in the thirties.''

"Really? How exciting!"

"Oh, yes, it was. My loyal audiences adored me! And the handsome young gentlemen who used to flock to my dressing room door after each performance—! I was so very happy, my dear. It almost broke my heart to leave it all behind, turn my back on success and the stage I loved. But, I survived, somehow!" She gazed through the window at the mountains in the distance with a faraway, wistful look in her eyes. "So many years ago, that was, but to me, it seems like only yesterday."

"But if acting made you so happy, why on earth did you give it up?" Angel asked.

Maria sighed and her happy expression faded as she went to perch on the edge of the bed. "Because when I was at the very height of my career, I made the foolish mistake of falling in love, and everything changed. If you will take a sentimental old woman's advice, Signorina Angelica, you'll be very careful to whom you lose your heart. Or— have you already lost it to that handsome Signore Nick?"

Angel blushed and seemed at a loss for words as Maria's brows rose in inquiry.

The woman clicked her teeth. "There, now, look what I've done. I've embarrassed you with my silly advice and my impertinent questions! Pay no mind to me, my dear, or my ramblings. When one becomes old, one forgets what it was like to be young, when Love counts for everything in life! Now. What was it you were looking for? Something to wear, I expect?''

"Please. Our—er—my—baggage was left on the train. I expect it's in Rome by now." She grimaced. "Or Timbuktu!"

"Ah. Then let's see what we can find for you in here." She stood, walked gracefully across to the wardrobe and ran her hand caressingly over the beautiful gowns within it. "These were mine, and I wore them all, once upon a time," she murmured. "Pretty dresses. Outrageous hats! Jeweled ball gowns—ah, clothes were my one passion! Even as a little girl, I used to love to dress up and pretend I was a grand lady or a princess. Didn't you?" Angel smiled and nodded. "I suppose my ambition to become an actress began with those childish games."

"I'm sure it did. When I was little, my passion was hats. I'd watch the ladies in church on Sunday mornings, and think that wearing a stylish, flamboyant hat must be the grandest thing to do! I decided I wanted to become a milliner and own dozens of them someday, all different, all stunning, all of my own design." She laughed and waited a little while before asking, "Maria, forgive me if I'm being nosy, but . . . what brought you here, to Italy?"

"Harry," Maria confessed with an arch smile.

"Harry? Lord Brixton?" Angel appeared puzzled. Then, when she realized what Maria was implying, she blushed bright pink. "Oh! I see."

"Yes, my dear. I know it's shocking and perhaps hard to believe now, but many years ago, I was Lord Brixton's mistress. I was beautiful then, and he was young and handsome and so very dashing. His wife, Cecilia, had been thrown from her horse while hunting quite soon after she and Harry were married. Sadly, the accident left her paralyzed. She'd been an invalid for many years when Harry and I first met. He was a young man with a man's needs, and he was lonely. I was there, and . . . well, I'm sure you can imagine how it was? One thing led to another and since we could never be married, we became lovers.

"Harry would come to Villa Allegra each year and stay all summer long with me and the child, you know, but in the autumn, it was to Cecilia he returned, and I missed him so. In his fashion, I believe he really loved his wife—perhaps more than he loved us—but that didn't matter to me. You see, I knew I had enough love for both of us!" She laughed, a little sadly, Angel thought. . . . "My brother George, who used to be my manager, said I was a little fool. He told me I should force Harry to divorce his wife, marry me, and give our child a name. George said he owed me that much for sacrificing my stage career for him, but . . . I was proud. I didn't want to win him that way. I was content to accept whatever part of himself Harry was willing to share—even if that part was only summers spent by the lake here. Harry loved Italy so! The warmth of the climate, the dazzling sunshine, the blue of the sea, the gaiety—oh, all of it! On weekends, we'd leave the villa and stay at the finest hotel in Milan. We'd go to wonderful balls and masquerades, drink champagne, and dance the night away . . . ! But—how I do go on. I'm sure I'm boring you, aren't I, you poor child?" Maria apologized. "I forget sometimes that those days are over, finished. I'm an old woman now—and Harry is gone!"

"Oh, Maria, you could never be old," Angel insisted, touched by the woman's willingness to confide in her at such length and in such detail.

"Old enough, child. Old enough! I have no use for these pretty gowns anymore. Since Harry's death, I dress only in black, and my brother Giorgio and I live very quietly. Your coming here is such a treat for us, you have no idea! We rarely have visitors, you see, and since we leave the villa only to go into the village to buy food, we make few friends."

"But you mentioned a child? Surely he visits you?"

"Children grow up, signorina. They grow up, they have their own minds, their own lives, and they forget their mothers. Their visits become few and far between. But— perhaps it is for the best, yes? For many years now, young Harry and I have not seen eye to eye. He comes, we fight, he leaves in anger." She sighed. "He blames me, you see, for the way his life turned out, and at my age, I find quarreling about things that cannot be changed so very upsetting! To be honest, I think it's far better that he stay away . . . Now, come, help me to take down these gowns. I'm sure we'll find something suitable in here that will fit you, yes?"

Wearing one of Maria's white blouses and a blue striped skirt of a charming if outmoded style, Angel passed a pleasant day alone.

She spent the morning exploring the flagstoned paths that sectioned off the villa's gardens, admiring the yew hedges clipped into animal or bird shapes, the fronded palm trees, the masses of lavender-blue hydrangeas or rhododendrons that Giorgio tended with such pride and care. There were formal water lily ponds in some shady arbors, where lichened stone cherubs frolicked and fountains played. Everywhere, the scent of roses and camellias drifted on the balmy breeze. The Alps, Maria had explained as she served breakfast, provided a buffer against the harsh winds and violent storms swooping down from the north, resulting in a delightfully mild climate for these parts; one so warm that tropical plants and vegetation flourished.

In the afternoon, after a light luncheon of cheese, sausage, bread, and fruit, she wandered down the terraced slopes to the trellised white gazebo she'd spotted, perched on the shores of Lake Como like a pretty bird cage. She stepped inside and looked around.

A deeply padded wooden window seat with pillows and a hinged lid for storage ran the length of the wall overlooking the lake. Curious, she raised the lid and looked inside, finding the memorabilia of a lifetime of lazy summer afternoons stored within. It held a torn and mildewed parasol, a broken toy sailboat, several frayed tennis and badminton rackets, shuttlecocks, and a tangle of nets, as well as a few grass-greened balls, croquet mallets and hoops, wickets, bails, and cricket bats. In the handle of one of the bats, the initials H.E. had been crudely carved by some earnest young hand, she noticed idly, running her fingers over the ragged lettering. A third initial—perhaps an "O" originally, or even a "D," but more probably a "B"—for Brixton—had been gouged out, so that it was no longer identifiable. Had Harry and Maria's young son eradicated it in a fit of pique? she wondered as she carefully replaced the lid.

She settled herself comfortably upon the window seat with a heap of pillows tucked beneath her head. There, she lounged in delicious idleness, watching the sparkling deep blue lake and the banks of high-scudding clouds drifting above the mountains.

From time to time, tiny rowboats or spritely pleasure boats with crisp triangular white sails would skim by. Their crew members—well-to-do Italian families who were staying at their own lakeshore villas for the summer—would wave to her and call out in greeting. Languidly, Angel waved back, smiling ruefully at her laziness. She simply felt too idle and limp for anything more strenuous today! Perhaps it was a combination of the fresh air off the lake and mountains, or the dazzling sunshine, but even the most perfunctory wave exhausted her. *Too many nights spent sleeping out of doors in the damp air, Angelica,* she told herself, dabbing at her perspiring brow and upper lip with a lace hanky.

When she returned to the villa shortly before dusk, following an unplanned and lengthy nap curled up on the gazebo window seat, she found Maria in the kitchen, slicing a loaf of freshly baked bread. She looked up and smiled in greeting as if the two of them were old friends.

"There you are! I thought perhaps you were lost, and was about to come and look for you. So. Are you enjoying your little holiday with us, signorina?"

"Very much. This place—it's heavenly! So—so tranquil. I can't wait to tell Da—my father—all about it. I'm sure he'll want to come here and see it for himself."

"We would be honored to meet the new master of Villa Allegra," Maria acknowledged with a smile. "Here, won't you have some grapes while you're waiting? Supper will be a little while yet, I'm afraid."

"Thank you," Angel murmured, plucking the juicy white grapes one after the other and greedily devouring them. "Hmm. Delicious! I didn't realize my throat was so dry. Are these from the villa's vines?"

"They are, yes."

"Mmm. They're awfully good—sweet, too. Did—er—did Signor Durango try them?" She wanted to ask Maria where Nick was, but was embarrassed to admit that she was in any way curious about the horrid man or that she didn't know his whereabouts for herself.

Maria seemed surprised. "Didn't he tell you? Signore Nick has gone to Milano. He left this morning, soon after breakfast, and said we should not expect him to return until tomorrow, or the day after. I believe he said something about wanting to send a telegraph to Rome . . . ?"

"Oh. I see." Crushed that she'd been told nothing of Nick's intentions or his departure for Milan, she could think of nothing more to say.

"I removed all the dustsheets from the dining room this morning. It has been airing all day, with the windows open to the breeze. If you will follow me, Signorina Higgins, I will serve you your supper there, when it is ready."

Angel wrinkled up her nose. "Do I really have to?"

"Signorina—?"

"Oh, I know you've gone to a lot of bother on my account, but to be honest, I'd much rather eat in the kitchen, Maria, if it's all the same to you?"

Maria laughed. "You would?"

She nodded eagerly.

"Very well, then—if you won't mind me preparing everything in front of you?"

"Not at all. To be honest . . . what I'd *really* like to do is help," Angel confessed. "It's been years since I've done anything really useful—not since before Da inherited crazy Lord Brix—I mean, Lord Brixton's estate—and I do so love to cook. Could I? Help you, I mean? I won't make a mess of your kitchen, I promise. I used to be quite good at chopping and dicing, though Mam always said I wasted too much when I peeled the potatoes."

Maria laughed, impulsively hugging the young woman. "This is your villa, signorina. You may do anything you wish! Here." She handed Angel a wooden meat mallet, a slab of beef, a dish of mixed spices and a wooden chopping block, with the instructions, "Pound this for me, if you would, my dear? It looks as tough as old shoe leather, doesn't it? Ha! I intend to give Signore Tagliari—our old butcher in the village—a piece of my mind next time I see him!" she added grimly.

Angel set to work, smiling as she sprinkled the thick slab of beef with the spices and started tenderizing it by pounding it with the mallet. Maria couldn't have chosen a better task to delegate to her in her present mood, she decided as she hammered the unwieldy meat again and again. Each satisfying, fleshy thwack made the dishes on the shelves jiggle about, but better than that, if she closed her eyes, she could pretend the leathery beef was that impossible man. . . .

"Signorina! There is no need for such violence!" Maria scolded gently, trying hard not to smile. "Believe me, it is already dead!"

"Well, if it wasn't, it most certainly is now," Angel declared, grinning.

Chapter Twenty-Four

The sun was reflecting off the waters of the lake, making the whitewashed walls of her bedchamber waver and ripple. No, she told herself uncertainly, that wasn't it; the walls *were* water—she was in a watery grotto, adrift on a sailboat with four tall wooden masts and billowing white sails.

On, she drifted, on . . . and on . . . and on . . . until she came to that magical dream place where the gossamer light is liquid gold, and time has ceased to exist. It was that place where the endless blue of the lake met the endless lavender horizon and became sky and infinity. . . .

Surely her sailing boat must come about soon, tack on some other course, she thought idly as they neared the far banks of the lake. One of her hands trailed languidly in the waters off the starboard side as they sped over the waves, the thrilling swiftness of their passage misting her burning face with spray.

But at the farthest shore, the boat neither came about nor dropped anchor. It simply went on and up, spreading its sails like glorious wings as it left the water and took flight, soaring up into the sky as effortlessly as a white-winged swan to swoop and tumble amongst the fluffy eiderdown clouds.

The sun! Oh, the glorious Italian sun! It was directly above her now, smiling a dimple-lipped smile. That smile . . . oh that sunny, funny smile! But then, she shivered, suddenly chilled. She'd been wrong, terribly wrong, about the benevolent sun. It wore no dimple-lipped smile but an orange *tiger's* grin, one that hid twin rows of fiery, gnashing teeth. . . .

Too late, she'd seen behind the smile—seen the tiger's yawning maw, the cavernous jaw, and the empty, roaring furnace-belly beyond! The craft on which she was bobbing so sweetly amongst the fluffy clouds was doomed if it did not alter its course; it was heading straight for hell—sailing directly into that yawning, golden mouth of fire! They were being drawn into it, sucked into it, swallowed alive by some demonic force she could not vanquish or evade.

So hot! So hot! Her throat was parched, her lips cracked, her tongue swollen to twice its former size. . . . Panic flew up like a great, dark moth to clog her throat with its furry wings and stifle her cries for help.

As the flying boat was drawn closer, she scrambled aft, crouching on her pillow and babbling like a frightened child as she felt the intense heat licking at her hair now, singeing her eyebrows, scorching her cheeks and nightgown with flaming kisses. The edges of her clipper bed began to smolder, smoke, and curl. The masts exploded—became pillars—then flaming torches—of fire in turn! The sheets and the hangings turned gray, then pink, then orange, then burst into flame. A wall of orange tongues was racing toward her, licking and leaping toward her, forcing her farther and farther back until she had no place to run—no corner in which to hide from the fire, the heat, the sun.

"Nooo!" she screamed, and screaming, flung herself over the edge of the bed, hurled herself overboard. She began falling . . . down . . . falling head over heels, tumbling and somersaulting, oh so very slowly, among the clouds. . . .

Falling, drifting, sinking down down down, until the lake took her fevered body in its watery embrace and dragged her beneath the surface.

The noisy pigeons he'd noticed everywhere upon his arrival in the city of Milan that morning were gone as Nick crossed the Piazza del Duomo. Although the sun had set only moments ago, the square was already dark, for it lay in the shadow of the huge, many-spired cathedral with its thousands of statues that towered above it like a protective hen over a cherished chick. Nick shrugged his shoulders and hurried across the piazza, anxious to be out of the depressing gloom, to find the lights and warmth, laughter and song his brooding spirit seemed to crave tonight.

Choosing one of the many streets that led away from the square like spokes from the hub of a wheel, he started down it, deep in thought, oblivious to the passersby— old women dressed in black, for the most part, on their way to evening mass—or the ancient churches and the royal palace that rose in the distance or soared magnificently skyward to either side of him.

Angel, he thought, and scowled. The fierce expression on his darkly handsome face was enough to cause the tomcat that had slunk from a nearby alley to wind itself about his legs, to hiss and arch its back, instead. Its eyes turning emerald in the gloom, it scampered away.

It was hardly surprising. Jesus, just thinking about her, just murmuring her name aloud, filled him with such powerful, conflicting emotions that anger quickly took their place, drove out his softer feelings, rendering cool logic and decision-making impossible. So it was that each time he'd tried to think about her—what she meant to him, what he might mean to her, and what sort of life they could have together, if by some miracle they chose to stay together—he came no closer to discovering what his true feelings for her might be. He only knew that he'd needed an excuse to get away from her for a while; needed space to think, without the pressures upon him that being near her brought to bear.

He sighed heavily. That damned, contrary woman! Why couldn't she simply have accepted his reasons for keeping the knowledge of Reggie and Bligh's deaths from her, so they could have gone on as they had before, enjoying passionate nights and endless, carefree days? Why did she assume his excuses that he'd "forgotten" to tell her and later, that he'd said nothing for her own good, must be lies?

Because she knows you, hombre, a small voice nagged

in his head. *Because she knows you, and she suspects there's far more to it than that. And she's right, isn't she? You, Nick Durango, forget something like that? Never! Be honest, man. You don't want to admit the real reason you didn't tell her, because the real reason is petty and childish and unworthy of you—and by its very pettiness and unworthiness, it says more about your true feelings than you want her to know or suspect . . . !*

"You isa Americano, eh, signore?" a smoky voice challenged him from a darkened doorway.

Abruptly, he halted his brisk pace. Scowling, he glanced up to find his path blocked now by three young prostitutes, all dressed in the garish finery of their profession, all possessing luxuriant curly raven manes, full-lipped smiles, flashing dark eyes, and smooth golden skin, much of which was exposed by their low-cut gowns, all three representing the promise of total oblivion, of a brief but pleasurable respite from the knotty entanglement of his emotions. Well, well! Lady Luck had answered his secret prayers! Here was the promise of lust quenched without guilt or commitment, self-recrimination or even thought!

Fists on hips, he grinned in delight, his pale blue eyes kindling lecherously as he cocked his dark head to one side and looked them over, one by one. His slow, wicked grin deepened as he murmured, "Evenin', pretty ladies. And yes, I'm an American."

"You isa lookin' lonely, signore," the one who'd spoken accused, trailing a painted fingernail down his shirt front. "Me and my cousins, we makea you very happy tonight, *sí*? Soon, you is no morea lonely, eh?"

"No morea lonely? Hell, it sounds good to me, ladies!" Nick agreed as he gallantly offered the two girls nearest him his arms, and apologized with his eyes and a rueful grimace for having none to escort the third. She, with a careless shrug, fell in step beside the linked trio as they moved gaily on down the narrow street. "So, what'll it be, ladies? Your place—or mine?"

He'd rented a small room in a respectable lodging house upon his arrival in Milan, using the money he'd received from the sale of the Gypsy Ramon's two horses to a farmer on the outskirts of the city. He'd done so because he

305

needed an address to receive any replies to the two telegraphs he'd sent soon afterwards. The first he'd sent to Juarez at the hotel in Rome, to let his cousin know that he and Angel would be joining them there soon, along with instructions regarding some business transactions he needed handled. The second telegraph had gone to Sidney Higgins in London, reassuring the man that his daughter was unharmed, but that there had been other attempts to kidnap her. He'd also included a brief description of the suspects and what little he'd learned of them. After leaving the telegraph office, he'd also made arrangements with the Bank of Milan to have funds transferred there from a bank in Rome. To his relief, the bank manager had assured him he would have no difficulty in receiving funds in a day or two, provided Juarez had carried out his instructions and could verify Nick's identity, using the letters of introduction that had gone on to Rome with his luggage when he'd jumped from the train. All in all, he was pleased with the way things were coming together. Within the week, they would be in Rome, spend a month there, and then on to their last destination, Egypt.

"Our place, signore," the prostitute said firmly. "But first, we eat, eh?"

Her suggestion amused him. So. The girls were hungry, huh . . . ? Well, so was he, by God! he realized. It'd been hours since he'd eaten, and then only some fruit and rolls. "Some chow sounds real good to me right now, *muchachas*. Lead the way!"

The girls, delighted by their handsome benefactor's easy capitulation, led the way to a shabby tavern that was obviously a favorite of theirs. The atmosphere was boisterous rather than elegant, the patrons loud rather than refined, the wine potent and plentiful rather than expensive—and the pasta lip-smacking good. In all, it was exactly the sort of place he'd have chosen for himself tonight, with this broody mood full upon him.

He ate his fill, devouring hot bread, a crisp salad of lettuce, tomatoes, and onions with a robust dressing of olive oil, vinegar, garlic, oregano, and other spices, delicate pasta, cooked al dente, swimming in a savory cheese, meat, and tomato sauce. As he did so, he enjoyed the sight of the three pretty gals—Sophia, Gina, and Claudia, their names were—relishing their own heaped platters as if they hadn't eaten in days. Throughout the meal, they chattered gaily and argued and waved their hands about between mouthfuls like a trio of noisy parrots. Watching them and their unabashed enjoyment of the good food and companionship was a sensual experience in itself, he thought, raising a glass brimming with blood-red wine in a silent toast to their beauty.

As that merry, bawdy evening wore on, Nick—who drank only whisky, as a rule, drank far too much of the cheap but potent red wine, first from the glass, then straight from the bottle, until at last, the time came for him to stand and escort his ladies of the evening to their room.

But after several unsuccessful attempts to rise, he discovered that standing was a feat he could no longer accomplish unaided! With giggles and shrugs, the three girls slung his dangling arms over their shoulders and half dragged, half carried him from the tavern between them. They were laughing raucously as they huffed and puffed to get him up the steep, dark stairs to their room, because for every three steps they managed to drag him up the flight, he stumbled another two back down!

"Naughty girls! Hic! Bad . . . naughty lil' girls!" Finally deposited upon the wide brass bed in their spartan attic room with its sharply sloping ceiling, Nick was frowning groggily and hiccupping as he waggled an admonishing finger at them. They ignored him as they stripped him down to his breeches and eagerly examined the contents of his pockets. With no words but several sly smiles and winks exchanged, they relieved him of the few thousand lira he had left after paying for their feast, then undressed themselves, all three naked women joining him in bouncing about on the now overcrowded bed like children.

Through bloodshot eyes, Nick reflected that he'd never seen so many well-rounded, jiggling breasts at any one time before, nor so much golden flesh so delightfully exposed as it was now, in a dizzying tangle of sturdy olive legs and firm thighs, dirty broad feet, plump buttocks, and smooth, flat bellies. Only dimly was he aware that thirty seductive fingers rumpled his dark hair, that six hands stroked his bare chest, his back, his arms, while three pairs of pouting red lips nuzzled his throat, trailed hot little kisses all over his body, and whispered sweet nothings while nibbling on his earlobes!

"He isa beautiful, thisa man I find you, eh, Cousins?" Sophia declared throatily, a gleam in her sultry dark eyes as, tossing back her black mane of glossy curls, she knelt beside him. Licking her red lips, she pouted and cupped her full breasts, then arched forward and offered them to his lips.

Grinning broadly, Nick pulled back his head. He blinked several times, until he was able at last to focus his attention on the nude girl and what she was doing. Damned if she wasn't golden-skinned and curvy in all the right places—a real armful, just the way he liked 'em!

"Oh ho!" he murmured lecherously. "C'mon over here t' ole Nick, beautiful little filly!" he slurred. Breathing heavily, he reached out to fondle the ample treasures she offered, for he was quite unable to capture the dark, engorged nipples that swayed so tantalizingly before him with his lips, in his drunken state. He snorted and laughed, slapping his thigh in self-disgust, thinking that after so much red wine, it was like bobbing for apples on a string! Cupping the firm ripe flesh in his hand, instead, he hauled Sophia down across his lap for a kiss. Shrieking with delight, Sophia readily obliged.

"Aah, you isa very much a man, eh, Nicky?" she purred huskily, her dark catlike eyes half-closed now as she tugged free of his arms. "Come, my darling. We take offa you trousers, yes?"

Six eager hands deftly tackled the task and in mere seconds, Nick was stripped, bareback-naked, sprawled across the rumpled white sheets like a Turkish sultan, surrounded by a harem of three golden Italian beauties whose only desire was to arouse him to the fullest degree, and then to satisfy his smallest whim.

There was no need for trust between them, not with these little darlins', he thought smugly. Hell, no man in his right mind would trust working gals like these *muchachas* an inch—! And nor was there any need for him to inspire trust in them, he considered, or to swear his undying love in order to sample their charms, either. No, sir! You just paid your money and got the lusty tumble you paid for. Nor was there anyone looking up at him from beneath a veiling of dark gold lashes, her pleading, wistful gray eyes framed by silky honey-gold hair, no one wearing their heart on their sleeve for him to see and feel guilty about, no one silently imploring him with the very timbre of her voice and every subtle nuance and response of her body for him to love her, please, love her, too! Nope. There were no hidden currents here, no unspoken wishes, no veiled pleas. All the cards were on the table, where he could see 'em. What he had here was the simple promise of a night's pure pleasure just for pleasure's sake, nothing more and nothing less—and by God, that's what he wanted! he told himself. Night after night. Day after day. Week after week, year in and year out, that was *all* he wanted. Pleasure with a capital "P"! No hurtful, pride-destroying mistakes, like Savannah. No messy involvement. No commitment. And certainly no love! He was done with love, had had all of it he cared to, in this life, thank you kindly, ma'am.

By God, he vowed, when he returned to Villa Allegra, he'd tell Angel straight out that whatever had been between them was over. Ended. That their relationship from now on would be strictly business, as he'd intended from the first—until that disastrous moment of weakness in the darkened *fiacre* had destroyed his noble intentions. He'd tell her firmly that it was for the best. That—as she'd said herself, many times before—they were quite wrong for each other, strangers from two different worlds.

She needed a stuff-shirted Limey, he'd say, a British greenhorn who dressed in correct duds and had the right breeding, the best social connections, a man who could give her the nobby uppercrust life she craved, not a cowboy from New Mexico who dressed in chaps and spurs, and who was more at home in the saddle than in a fancy drawing room, sipping dainty cups of tea!

Angel would find happiness as the wife of such a man, as the mistress of an ancient graystone mansion, surrounded by rolling green estates. He sure as hell couldn't picture her in his *casa grande*, nor as the mistress of Rancho Diablo, with its red-tiled roofs, its cool adobe walls, its dark wooden beams, and its shady *corredores* beneath the blazing skies of New Mexico. And as for estates—! He snorted. His "estates" were thousands of acres of grama grass and coarse rabbit brush, grazing lands bordered by desert, by the beauty of the rugged Sangre de Cristo mountains, by deep canyons and arroyos that scarred the red earth like gaping wounds, by soaring buttes and milling cattle, that he found beautiful beyond compare—an alien world he knew she could never love. . . .

"Go to it, gals!" he whooped suddenly, feeling strong and unshakeable in his convictions that he must sever all ties with Angel. "Yeehaah! Nick Durango's back in business and he's all yours, you little darlins."

With delighted squeals, the trio fell upon him like a bevy of feasters at a Roman orgy. He went down laughing under a rain of kisses and embraces and naughty, sensual caresses that any other man would have yielded up his all and died for—and yet, for Nick, it was somehow still not enough. His mind responded, hell, yes! And his will surrendered, easy as winking. But his damned body—or at least that ornery part of him that was vital to the task at hand!—refused to rise to the occasion, so to speak. He started cursing under his breath, uttering a stream of cowboy invectives that were colorful enough and graphic enough to make even these three hardened hussies blush, despite their meager command of his language!

"Doana you worry, eh?" Gina reassured him with huge tears of pity in her lovely Madonna eyes. "It's a-gonna be all right. We're a-gonna make-a you a very happy tonight. One way or another . . ."

"*Sí*, you poor, poor man. You 'ave come to the right girls, yes? Tonight, with the 'elp of me and my cousins here, you will becomea a man again. On the chastity of Our Blessed Virgin, I swear it!" Claudia vowed, pouting her wide, moist mouth.

Nick blinked. "Hey, what's that you're sayin'? Real man? Aw, gals, you've got it all wrong! This here's just a temp-or-ary delay, see? Hell, I'm more'n man enough for the three o' you little fillies," Nick bragged, planting a kiss on Claudia's inviting lips and another on the swell of Gina's cute little rump as she leaned over him.

"No, signore," Sophia corrected him sadly moments later, rocking back on her heels. "Tonight, I think not Sophia, nor even the Blessed One Himself could raise your poor little man from the dead—no, not even if he was called Lazarus! Believe me, I 'ave tried *everything*," she added darkly, rolling her eyes expressively.

Her cousins gasped.

"Everything?" Claudia and Gina echoed simultaneously in disbelief, for they knew Sophia's amorous repertoire was enormous.

"*Every* thing, I say," Sophia confirmed, making a face and looking cross that they'd doubt a seasoned professional like her.

"Aiee!" The other two girls groaned in commiseration.

"Then it is quite 'opeless, yes? Aiee, *Diós*, poor, poor Nicholas! What a tragedy! He is such a handsome man, too! Aiee, Madonna, how cruel life is, eh, for a young man to have so much to offer a woman, but to be stricken with impotence!"

"Impotence, my backside!" Nick growled. "Honey, I'm as about as impotent as the stud bull I have on my ranch back in New Mexico. Sired me three hundred calves since I bought him, he did!"

"But what has happened to *you*, Nicky, darling?" Gina demanded. "Perhaps—*sí*, perhaps it is us, yes? We are at fault! You doana like me and my cousins, maybe?"

"Hell, that ain't it! I like you gals just fine. It's—" he paused and scowled.

"Yes?" they eagerly chorused together, breathless for his answer.

"It's because of—?"

"Yes? Tell us! We only want to help you, Nicky, darling? To lift this terrible curse from you!"

"It's that damned woman!" he exploded suddenly. "That contrary Limey filly! She did this! She's ruined me for other women—ruined me!"

"A 'Limey' filly? What is this? And who is she, this woman? Your wife?"

"Naw. They call her Angel, see . . ." he began through gritted teeth, "but if you ask me, she's more like a she-devil, the way I see it . . ."

The three prostitutes cupped their chins in their fists and listened intently as Nick told his story. They sighed when he was done.

"Poor thing," Gina sighed.

"Doggone it, I knew you'd see it my way!" Nick crowed triumphantly.

"Not you, you heartless rogue—my pity is all for Signorina Angelica!" Gina corrected him sternly.

"Angelica?!"

"And mine!" Sophia admitted.

"And mine!" Claudia confirmed. "Men! All they want is a good time! They climb on top of you, grunt a few times, yelp like dogs, and they are happy 'til the next time! What do they care for us, eh? About how we feel? Nothing—less than nothing. We are dirt. They treat us like animals!"

"The poor little thing was a virgin, you say, and yet you stole her innocence, you rogue—! A good girl, and you used her like a whore for your pleasure, all the while knowing that you did not love her—that you could *never* love her, because of what that little bitch Savannah had done to harden your heart. I say you are a dirty cockroach for using her, Durango. A filthy peeg for breaking her heart! You do not deserve the love of such a fine girl!" Gina exploded, her dark eyes flinging daggers at him now.

"*Sí!*" Sophia agreed with a glare of contempt cast his way. "It is one thing to treat us that way—we know the score, eh? We whores are paid for what we do. It is our choice to sell our bodies or not. But that poor little Angel—! Think how very frightened she must have been—a young, innocent girl like that, deeply in debt to that monster, Bill Bligh. Forced to deceive the father she loved so very much, in order to protect him from the knowledge that she had failed him! And then you, Durango—the big, brave man who was supposed to protect her, you came along and stripped her of her innocence—you seduced her, turned her first innocent passions against her!"

312

"I agree with my cousins," Claudia stated, murdering him with her half-closed eyes. "You are a rat. Vermin! A louse!"

Despite his wine-induced stupor, Nick realized that the tide of their good will had somehow been turned against him, and it infuriated him. Damn! The three women he'd fed just a short while ago with what precious little remained of his meager resources were now close to biting the very hand that had fed them—perhaps *literally* so, if their outraged expressions were anything to go by!

"Now, you gals just see here—!" he began indignantly, struggling to sit up, fully intending to argue his case and convince them of his worth.

"No, signore, you see here!" Claudia snapped, thrusting him back down with a well-placed palm planted in the very center of his chest. "We want to have a leetle talk with you, right, girls?"

"Right! And then we throwa the bastard downa the stairs, eh—?"

"*Si!*" the others agreed with far more enthusiasm than Nick thought the situation warranted.

Bad enough he was in the doghouse with Angel, but now he'd gotten on the wrong side of these three pretty *putas*, too—and he was too blamed drunk to do a damned thing about it but listen to what they had to say. With a sour expression, he sank back onto the bed.

There were water weeds everywhere, Angel realized with delight as she gave herself up to the lake's embrace. Rich, green vegetation hidden here beneath the water that was as thick and luxuriant as any earthbound garden. The tall water weeds danced bonelessly with the lake's restless tide, swaying green-fronded hips gently . . . gently . . . to and fro, to and fro, like Polynesian dancers, even as her hair swirled and eddied to and fro behind her. She swam, then. Swam deeper and deeper without needing to surface to breathe; swam like a mermaid amongst the watery garden until, looking down, she spied a huge creamy pearl—someone's treasured keepsake—forgotten among the weeds.

313

She dived down, her arms outstretched to scoop up the giant bauble from its watery nest and claim it for herself. She smiled in delight at her find, her hands embracing the enormous jewel lovingly, gently, as she held it aloft, turning it this way and that way to admire its pearly beauty in the sunlight that illumined even the lake's deepest reaches. But—as she turned it to face her, she saw that it was not a giant pearl, as she'd thought. No! It was a horrid skull—a grinning skull with blackened sockets for eyes, for nose, for mouth!

She tried to cast it away, to hurl it from her in horror, yet—it would not leave her hands! It was bound there, stuck to her palms. Her flesh had now merged with its lipless jaws, its sucking mouth. For the love of God, it was *feeding* upon her—it was a parasite, sucking the life from her veins to restore life to its own!

Sure enough, as she watched, the engorged skull began to change, to grow. Fat with her blood, replete as a maggot with the life it drew from her, the flesh returned to it, layer upon layer, grayed rotting inch by rotting inch, until she knew whose skull it was—what name it had borne in life:

"Reggie!" she shrieked, for his drowned eyes stared at her accusingly, his mouth was open in a scream of condemnation. "No, get away—uggh! Get it away from me—please oh please I can't bear iiiit—!"

"Hush, now, hush. You're safe, darlin'. I'm here—I've got you. And I won't let anythin' hurt you, I swear it . . .''

Nick's deep voice reached down into the water. Like a hand, it plucked the skull from her grasp—crushed it to chalky powder that scattered on the tide. Then his strong hands were holding her, lifting her up, bearing her away to that other place, leaving the lake far behind, carrying her to that place where she could feel again, to that place where there was pain behind her eyes and in her throat, her joints, but which was far, far better than that fearful *other* place, because pain was *real* and she could withstand it and Nick's voice promised that it would soon be gone, anyway, and that she'd be well again. She believed that voice implicitly.

Drifting in and out, she'd open aching, gritty eyes to see white curtains billowing on the breeze. A sun-browned face frowning down at her. A dazzling smile of welcome rising between stubbled cheeks, laughter twinkling in ice blue eyes that were red-rimmed from lack of sleep.

Another time, she drifted up to shadows, to the scented, velvet darkness of night, to find his warm hand enfolding her own. To see silvery blue eyes reflecting myriad candle flames, and always, always there was his warm voice enfolding her spirit. He was always there, always talking in that easy, musical drawl she loved, speaking nonsense, telling her of little doggies and of scorching deserts, of cactus and roundups, golden-skinned girls, fiestas, and brandings; telling her of heartbreak and unfaithful sweethearts and so many other strange and wonderful things, while she would smile tho' she didn't understand, not wanting it to end or for him to leave. She felt safe, aahh, she felt so very, very safe, kmowing he was there, watching over her. . . .

"How . . . she . . . today?"

". . . feeling better . . . ?"

"Alas . . . fever rises . . . but perhaps tomorrow . . ."

"Drink, signorina . . ."

". . . strong and well, honey . . ."

"Fight, Angel . . . don't . . . give up!"

Those tiny scraps of reality, those remembered tidbits of conversation, were anchors for her reason in those frightening days of her illness, crutches for her crippled spirit and exhausted will. Oh, those soothing words, those endless questions she couldn't find the strength to answer, but which forced her to think—! They drifted through her consciousness like autumn leaves plucked from a tree and tossed on a whirlwind, and although sometimes she managed to grab one, just for a second, it always slipped through her fingers and blew away. . . .

Then, quite distinctly she heard someone say, "Sí . . . lung fever, signore . . . yes, I am, quite certain . . . Sad to say, she . . . follows the disease . . . many times . . . worse than the measles itself . . . be back to see her in the morning . . ."

More drifting.

Chapter Twenty-Five

"Welcome back!"

She smiled drowsily as she opened her eyes to find Nick seated at her bedside, looking down at her. She was aware as she stirred that the burning behind her eyes had gone, disappeared. The deep aching beneath her ribs and the hacking cough were gone, too.

"I've been ill." It was a statement of fact, rather than a question.

"Very, I'm afraid."

"What—?"

"Measles, then lung fever. At one point, we didn't know if you'd make it. You were so bad, I was just about to telegraph your pa when you started to get better."

"Then he doesn't know?"

"Uh uh."

"Thank God! The poor dear would have worried himself sick. How long have I been in bed?"

"Ten days."

"That long? Good Lord!" She ventured a wan smile. "What a lazybones!"

"You had a high fever. You were delirious most of the time."

"I'm not surprised to hear it. I remember scraps of the most awful nightmares. Giant pearls that became skulls with Reggie's face—delightfully gruesome stuff!" She shuddered, hesitating for a moment before shyly admitting, "I also remember that when the nightmares were at their worst, you would be there. I'd hear your voice and the—monsters—would slink away. Was that part real? About you being there, I mean?" She posed the question almost hopefully.

Nick shrugged. He looked embarrassed, maybe even ready to bolt. "Aw, I guess I was around someplace. You know, off and on." He frowned. "Hey, don't go thanking me, Angel, making more of it than there was. I had my reasons. Selfish ones, too." He winked.

"Oh? And what were they?"

He grinned. "I figured your pa'd take a bullwhip t' my back if he found out I'd saved you from being kidnapped, but lost you to the measles!"

The idea of her father wielding a bullwhip—or any whip at all, for that matter—coupled with the image of Nick, cowering in fear of her father's anger, wrung a deeper smile from her.

"You silly man!" she chided fondly.

Nick grinned in satisfaction. Damned if she wasn't looking more like her old self with every passing minute, to his relief! The image of her lovely face splattered with the frightening, angry red rash of the disease was still fresh and sharp in his mind, as were the seemingly endless nights when he'd sat by her bedside, spelling Maria until morning, working hard to bring down the fever with cold-water compresses, or to spoon a trickle of liquid between her cracked lips, or to help her to sit up when the harsh coughing fits of the lung fever wracked her and seemed bent on stealing her very breath away. Between times, she'd lain so very still he'd found himself checking frequently to see if she was still breathing, his heart thundering with dread until he'd reassured himself that she was, however shallowly. In those moments, she'd seemed smaller and far more vulnerable than he'd ever seen her, her face a small, delicate oval against the mane of honey gold hair that fanned across the pillow, the face of a little lost flower strewn amidst the snowy whiteness of the vast Spanish four-poster.

"Mr. Durango's far too modest," Maria disagreed from the doorway. She came into the room bearing a basin and cloths. "Since he came back from Milan and heard that you were ill, he's hardly left your side for a minute! Why,

I've had to bully him to make him leave you long enough for me to bathe you, and make sure he ate his own meals." Maria clicked her teeth. "It's no thanks to him I didn't have two of you sick," she scolded, smiling nonetheless.

"Aw, be honest! You weren't afraid I'd get sick—you just like bullying folks, Maria, honey!" Nick disclaimed teasingly. But taking a good hard look at him, Angel decided Maria wasn't exaggerating. Nick looked rough—rougher than she'd ever seen him! Several days' growth of bristly black beard gave him the unkempt look of a bandit or an escaped convict, but even those fierce whiskers couldn't hide the lines of exhaustion that bracketed his eyes and mouth.

"Thank you, both of you," she murmured, tears sparkling in her eyes. "You've both been so good to me. I don't know how I'll ever be able to repay you."

"Oh, but I do, my dear! You'll repay us by doing as you're told. And by eating well and resting and getting a little better every day," Maria declared firmly. "The physician warned us that you could have a relapse if you try to resume your normal activities too soon. He's recommended a light, nourishing diet, lots of rest and *no* excitement—or traveling—for at least two more weeks."

"Two more weeks—? But we have friends waiting for us in Rome. They'll be frantic!"

"No, they won't," Nick reassured her. "I wired 'em, told 'em you were ill. Juarez wired back that he and *his bride* would pray for your recovery. They said for you to get well real soon, an' that they'd wait for us in Rome." Brows arched, he waited for the reaction he knew would be forthcoming.

"Did you say Juarez and his *bride?*" she echoed, uncertain if she'd heard him properly. She struggled to sit up, but was too weak. She sank back down to the pillows, trembling from the effort. "You mean, Juarez and Mabel are *married?*"

"Yep. Sure seems so."

"My stars! Who'd have thought it!" For all Mabel's outlandish behavior, she realized suddenly that she'd somehow grown very fond of her over the years, and that despite her happiness for her, she would genuinely miss having her around to battle wits with. "If she and Juarez are married, I suppose she'll be going to America once my Grand Tour is over?"

"Reckon so," Nick agreed heavily, not at all sure if he liked all this talk of marriage, nor the wistful glint it had put in her eyes. "A woman's place is with her husband, after all, right?"

"Of course," Angel agreed, jealously imagining the three of them off on jolly adventures in America without her, while she returned to her da and the myriad humdrum tasks that running Brixton Towers entailed. It was not a prospect she found exciting in the least. "And what will you do? Will you live with them in New Mexico, after you've returned me to my father?"

"Me? Muscle in on a pair of newlyweds, billin' an' cooing like turtledoves? No, thanks! I have my own place t' get on back to. It's small and none too fancy, but I call it home."

"You have a house? Really? I'm surprised. I had the impression you slept outdoors?"

"And so I do, most nights. But ole 'Villa Durango' comes in real handy in winter, when the blizzards start whistling down across the Plains into New Mexico. Man needs a roof over his head then—any damn roof he can get!" If she'd glanced up at him just then, she would have seen the laughter in his eyes, known—or at least suspected—that he was teasing her. But, she closed her eyes instead, quite exhausted by the effort it'd taken to talk, and so she missed the merry twinkle in his eyes. "Well, you're looking sort of wearisome, Angel, so I guess I'll let Maria take over for now." He hesitated, the teasing smile gone, replaced by another expression. "I'm real glad you're feeling better, Angel."

She smiled and caught his hand, brought it to her lips to kiss. "Me too, Nick. Thank you again. For everything."

With a curt nod, he drew his hand away and left the room.

"At last!" Maria exclaimed, bustling over to the bed. "I thought he'd never go! Now. If you're not too tired, signorina, I thought I'd sponge you down and change your nightgown? Then we'll see if you feel up to trying a

319

little of my soup. It's very nourishing—minestrone, with pasta and herbs and beef broth."

"It sounds marvelous. Maria, have I—have I been a terrible nuisance to you? Oh, what a goose I am, asking such a silly question! Of course I must have. I'm truly very sorry to have made so much work for you."

Maria bent down and kissed her cheek, smoothing a soft blond curl from Angel's brow. "Stop it, before I *do* get cross with you. You couldn't help being ill, could you? And besides, I did very little, other than spoon some broth into you, and sponge you to lower the fever. No, my dear. As I said, it is Signore Nick who deserves all the credit for your recovery. What a fine young man he is! He sat up with you each and every night. When the coughing attacks were at their worst, he helped you to sit up and pounded your back so you could cough, time after time. When the lung fever was at its worst, he never left your side. You are a very fortunate young woman."

"To have survived my illness, you mean? Yes, I suppose I am, when so many die of it."

"For that, yes, but also for having a man like Nick. I've watched him these past two weeks. I've seen the gentleness in his hands when he touched you, the fear of losing you in his eyes. I'm not certain he even knows it himself, but he loves you very deeply, signorina."

"I'm sure you're wrong. He's never told me he loves me," she murmured doubtfully.

"No? Then perhaps he's afraid. Some men are like that. They shy away from committing themselves, but the feeling is there nonetheless. Perhaps you will have to . . . encourage . . . your young man to find his tongue? Help him to find the words to tell you, yes?"

Angel frowned as she looked up at the old woman. "How would I do that?"

"There are ways, signorina!" Maria confided with a naughty wink that made her face young and beautiful again. "Remember? I was once a scarlet woman—an actress, no less!—the wicked hussy who was Lord Harry Brixton's mistress and the scandal of London! If anyone knows how, it should be me!"

"But we quarreled, Maria. Nick was very impatient with

me before I fell sick . . . and I was angry with him," she recalled ruefully. "I doubt things could ever be the same between us again."

"Perhaps, perhaps not. Take the time to recover your strength and we will see what we can do. You have nothing to lose by trying, hmm, my dear?"

The fragrance of the camellias filled his nostrils with their heady perfume as Nick stepped out onto the terrace where Angel was waiting for him. He felt almost intoxicated by their scent, drunk on the warm velvet of the Italian evening. Fireflies twinkled in the bushes, and the trill of the crickets in the grass set up a reedy melody. The sky was a dreamy canopy of midnight blue, scattered with tiny, pulsing stars. As he saw her, leaning over the balustrade with her hair stirring like a cloud of gold on the night wind, the image she created caught the breath in his throat. Her loveliness seemed fragile, otherwordly since her illness, but no less intoxicating than the magical night. Clothed only in a shimmering gray silk dressing robe and matching nightdress, her hair flowing loose over her shoulders, she turned as she heard his footsteps and slowly crossed the terrace to meet him.

"Maria said you needed me?" he told her gruffly. For the past two weeks, he'd been consciously avoiding her, mindful of the sound advice given him by Sophia, Claudia, and Gina in Milan. The girls had told him that, unless he loved her, he should leave her alone. That he had no right to expect a girl who'd been raised as Angel had been raised to settle for an affair, with no hope of marriage in the future. He'd recognized the wisdom in their words and once he'd reassured himself she was recovering, he had tried to cut her loose by making himself scarce. It had been hard at first—harder than he'd dreamed—but now he reckoned he'd gotten over the worst of it and could be detached, could be the protector her pa had hired, and nothing more.

"I've missed you, Nick," she admitted in a low, musical voice.

"What was it you wanted?" he demanded curtly, disliking the flood of emotion that suddenly filled him, the longing to take her in his arms and to hell with what was right!

"Oh, just to talk, I suppose. To be with you. You've been avoiding me these past two weeks while I've been recuperating."

"I've been busy."

"Doing what?"

"Aw, things."

"Nick, please don't be this way! We have to talk. We quarreled, remember, and it's high time we sorted things out."

"Okay. What do you want t' talk about?"

"About us. About you and me." She raised lashes like fans to look him full in the face, and the pain he saw there was like a knife twisted in his vitals. "We can't go on like this, Nick! *I* can't go on like this. It's breaking my heart."

He hardened his jaw, not wanting to, but doing it anyway. It hurt suddenly to breathe. "What is it you want?"

"I want—I want us to be like before—you know, when we were traveling down through France? I want to be able to talk to you and share my thoughts, and for you to share yours with me. I want the—the coldness that was between us before my illness gone. I want to be able to reach out in the darkness, and know that you'll be there, that I can hold you when I'm afraid and that you'll make the nightmares go away. And I—I want you to make love to me," she whispered, so softly he wondered for a moment if she'd really spoken, or if he'd only conjured her words from the soughing of the night wind in the cypresses, the lazy wash of the lake against the shore—and his own heart's desire.

"It's been too long, Nick. Far too long! Don't you feel it? Don't you feel the hurt, the emptiness? It's time we put our silly misunderstanding behind us. I suppose I—I overreacted—you know, about Reggie and Bligh's deaths?—and I'm sorry. I'm willing to forgive and forget and I think—I hope!—you are, too. Come back to me, Nick. Forget the things I said. They don't matter. What we had is what matters . . ."

He watched, dry-mouthed, as she let the silk robe slide down from her arms. It fell about her feet and she stepped

322

away from the gleaming puddle, came toward him clad only in the sheer nightgown. Lifting it over her head, her bewitching eyes held his transfixed as she held out her hand and carelessly let this last wisp fall in a shimmering swathe from her fingers. She wore nothing beneath it. Veiled only by her gossamer cloud of hair, she padded barefoot toward him, moving across the flagstoned terrace in a graceful ballet of silver and gold.

Her alabaster flesh was bathed in moonlight. Her rose-tipped breasts were half-hidden behind skeins of shining hair. She cupped them in her hands, as if offering her loveliness to him. Her slender waist flowed into rounded hips, ivory thighs and long, shapely legs. Watching her turned Nick's blood to fire, made his pulse a roaring thunder in his ears. He cursed silently. She was right—God help him, he'd failed! He still wanted her. Wanted her so badly, it took all his willpower to stand there, to keep from reaching out, from taking her in his arms. He'd thought about this moment—imagined it—a thousand times since his return from Milan, telling himself he would overcome his desire for her sake. But now that the moment was here, he was afraid; afraid if he moved, he'd be lost. Afraid if he moved, the magical moment would shatter into a thousand maybes. . . .

Casting him a sultry invitation from smoky gray eyes, she took both his hands in hers and placed them upon her breasts, curling his tanned fingers over the creamy mounds with her own.

"Angel, honey, don't!" he whispered hoarsely.

"You don't have to be afraid of hurting me, Nick. I'm better. I won't shatter if you make love to me—Honest Injun!" Her smile sweet with promise, she gently pressed him back against the stone balustrade, then leaned over him to brush her lips across his. The warmth of her mouth, the feathery, tantalizing texture of her lips, enflamed him beyond reason. "There? You see, darling?" she whispered. "All better . . ."

His senses leaped as their breaths commingled, their bodies touched. Leaning over him as she was, her hair was pooled across his chest; her breasts were crushed against his, each tiny, hard peak as fiery as the head of a lighted match, so fiery, he could feel their heat scorching through his clothing.

"Enough, *mi pequena bruja!*" he groaned. "Stop, before you drive me crazy, my lovely witch—! I don't want to hurt you." He drew his hands from her to grasp the balustrade at his back instead. In the moonlight, his tan fingers were bleached white where they gripped the railing.

"Nick, don't push me away! I love you," she whispered aloud for the very first time, caressing his clean-shaven cheek with her fingertips. "I think—I think I've loved you from the moment I first saw you! Nicky, I'm well again—and I need you so! Touch me. Kiss me. Have me! I want an end to this coldness between us, now and forever. Tonight, I want to sleep with your arms around me. I want to wake up tomorrow morning with my head beside yours on the pillow. But most of all, I want you to make love to me. To—to hear you say you love me, too!"

Her impassioned plea destroyed the resolve he'd made in Milan, turned to ashes the solemn promises he'd made to Sophia, Claudia, and Gina. He'd sworn he'd turn over a new leaf. That he'd fight his desire for her. That he would show her the respect he'd denied her when they first met, when he'd believed her a good-time gal, a gambler, and a hussy who knew the score. But . . . when he was close to her, his good intentions flew out the window, his resolve turned to mush; his promises became so much dust on the wind, he wanted her so—!

With a growl, he caught her to him. Weaving his fingers through her hair, he drew her head down to his, trapping her lower lip between his teeth. He nipped gently, then deepened the glorious kiss, parting her lips beneath his to plunder the hidden sweetness of her mouth with his tongue.

A shudder ran through him. Christ! It had been so long. She tasted so sweet. Smelled so pretty. Felt so damned soft. He drank from her lips like a man dying of thirst. Yet, far too soon for his liking, she drew away.

Gray eyes heavy-lidded and smoky-sensual, her reddened lips parted in a seductive smile, she slowly unfastened his shirt buttons, one by one. Inch by inch, she

324

branded the sun-browned chest she'd bared with her mouth, until at last, the final button gave beneath her fingers. Barechested, his lean legs braced apart, he stood before her in the moonlight like a gladiator of old. His ebony hair clung to his fine head in inky commas, framing the swarthy symmetry of his handsome face. His shoulders were broad, his torso magnificently muscled, his belly flat and firm as a slab of oak, his waist very lean and narrow. He was so overtly male, so very masculinely beautiful, he made the breath catch in her throat. Made the bones melt within her.

She leaned forward and pressed her lips to his breastbone; heard the wild thunder of his heart as she did so. With a groan, he whispered her name, tried to embrace her in return, but she laughed throatily and pushed his hands away.

"Soon, my darling. Very soon!" she whispered as she tugged his shirttails free of his belt, and eased his garment down, off his arms.

Muscles bunched across his shoulders and over his upper body, hard curves that shimmied under sun-bronzed flesh. She shivered with pleasure, aching, postponing the pleasure of caressing him in a single shivery moment of glorious anticipation. Oh, Lord, that tanned skin—that inky hair—those ebony brows—such striking contrasts to the gorgeous ice-and-fire, silvery blue of his eyes! She would never grow tired of looking at him, or weary of being with him, she thought as she ran her fingernails lightly down his trousered thigh, laughing softly as Nick shuddered and sucked in his hard belly in response.

Dipping her head to his bared chest, she reflected that here was a man worth fighting to keep, a man worth risking everything for, even her pride. A man she knew she could love forever—and would, if only she won the game! Her confession that she loved him, Maria's help with her plan to seduce him, were the last cards in her hand, all the aces she had left to play. But now, more than ever, she was gambling to win! Immoral wanton, beguiling seductress, teasing temptress—tonight, she would become them all, if that was what it took to make Nick hers forever. . . .

She flicked the tip of her tongue across his hardened

325

nipples, swirled it around and around the areolas of rose-and-tan goosebumps that now encircled each one, then ran it lightly through the shadow of dark hair that surrounded them.

To Nick, her tongue felt like wildfire racing over his skin, leaping from nerve to nerve in a blaze that only one thing could douse! With a heated curse, he caught her roughly to him, slamming her up against his body with a passionate urgency that bordered on violence.

She gasped, for the rough contact of their bodies was electric, sizzling—unbelievably exciting! Grasping her waist to steady her, Nick dropped to his knees at her feet. He kissed and stroked her everywhere, suckling her breasts, teasing her navel, nibbling on her fingertips and toes, gently biting her shoulders and buttocks, trailing his tongue over the delicate bumps of her spine. He engulfed her in an orgy of sensation that left no soft curve unexplored, no tiny hollow unloved. To Angel, standing before him on legs grown weak and trembly with desire, it seemed an eternity had passed before his calloused palm stroked her belly and, traveling still lower, his fingertips gently grazed the curls that crowned her mons.

She cried out, and he stood, capturing her mouth beneath his, kissing her hungrily again while he stroked her inner thighs. Wild with need, she whimpered. Begged! Shamelessly, she pressed her hips against his hand, his thighs, silently pleading for more, more. He slipped his tongue into her mouth, while at the same time he slid his fingertip deep into the flaming heat of her loins. He groaned with sensual pleasure against her lips. *Madre!* She was already moist with longing for him, silken fire and sweet, wild nectar to his touch. Damn it, what was it about her? She was no different from the other women he'd made love to, surely? But then—why was it that just holding her, caressing her, triggered such violent responses in him? Aroused a lust in his loins that was like a herd of wild horses, stampeding out of control? Could it be . . . was there a chance? . . . that he loved her, too—?

No. Damn it, no!

"Angel?"

"Yes . . . ?" she whispered shakily.

326

"I can't go on like this, not without telling you something."

Her heart skipped a beat. "Yes? I'm listening."

"Angel, sweetness, I can't lie to you," he began as gently as he could. "I have to tell you straight where we stand, before this goes any further." He paused as he looked down, searching her face, then drew a deep breath, before saying, "Darlin', if I ever love again, the woman I love will be you," he breathed. "But I was—burned—real bad by someone in the past, and honey, I can't seem to forget what she did to me. Angel, I can't say the words you want—need—to hear. I want to be with you—not just this way, but in every way. And I'd die before I'd let anything or anyone harm a hair on your pretty head. But—honey, I don't rightly know if you'd call that love? If what I'm feeling is *enough* to be called love?" His shoulders slumped. "There. I've said it. I owed you the truth, and the truth's what I've told you. If you want to stop right now, just say the word. I'll understand and I'll leave."

The crushing disappointment that filled her was like nothing she'd ever felt before. It was the morning Reggie had shown his true self all over again—only a billion times more painful, because she'd never really loved Reggie! Oh, God, her gamble had failed. She'd lost the game. She's lost Nick. There would never be skyrockets exploding overhead, nor coveys of white-winged doves soaring up, up into the sky; no joyous carillons ringing out from a thousand steeples when Nick said he loved her, because Nick *didn't* love her—and, what was worse, he'd said he didn't know if he ever would.

The knot in her throat grew huge. She didn't trust herself to speak, hardly dared to breathe, for fear she would shatter into a thousand brittle pieces that no one could put back together again. And yet—the yearning for him was still there, still as fierce, as aching and bittersweet as ever. She shook her head and buried her face against his shoulder, her very silence implying that he should continue.

"You're sure this is what you want?"

She nodded, tears of sorrow trickling from beneath her lashes as he pressed his lips to hers and tried to regain the

327

passion they had shared but moments before.

You bastard! his conscience accused. *You say your pride yourself on honesty? Then quit actin' like a yeller-bellied coward and tell her the truth! Don't do this to her—she loves you!*

I can't say it. It'd be a lie.

Lie, hell! You were half crazy when you thought she'd die of lung fever. You love her, Durango, you goddamned fool! Say it!

As the truth he'd denied for so long slammed through him like a bolt of lightning, sweat sprang out upon his brow. The throbbing hardness at his groin bucked like a wild bronc. Aroused to explosion point by her loveliness, Nick could stand it no longer. No, it wasn't love he felt for her, he argued with himself. It couldn't be. Hadn't he established that much in Milan? What he felt for Angel was only *lust*, pure and simple. And lust was an emotion he could understand, could deal with and accept, whereas love—! Hell, love hurt. Love destroyed a man. Love trampled on pride, on honor, on trust. It gouged and clawed and left wounds too deep to heal. Hell, Love was something he'd vowed never to feel again!

"Take me!" she whispered shakily. "Oh, Nick, please—now!"

Reaching between them, he freed his throbbing manhood and lifted her astride his flanks.

"Nick!" she sobbed, curling her arms about his throat, wrapping her legs about his waist as he lowered her onto his throbbing length.

Their bodies united, he carried her across the terrace and into the candlelit chamber beyond, where a hundred dancing candle flames held back the night.

Lowering her to the bed, he crushed her beneath him on the cool satin sheets. His eyes, reflecting the candle flames, blazed into hers with a silvery intensity that made the breath come hard and fast in her throat as he began to move, filling her again and again with his deep, swift thrusts.

They were both breathing so very hard, so very fast, that when he broke away in that heart-stopping instant before rapture could claim them, they were both panting, both hoarse. Their chests heaved as if they'd run a mile flat out.

His gaze swept over her like a hot desert wind, scorching her body, before returning to her lovely face. Their gazes, naked with desire in the candles' light, locked for one breathless, painful instant.

Guilt flooded through him. "Angel," he began, "I— I—!" But damn it, he couldn't go on, couldn't bring himself to say it, or to lie, and he was filled with remorse and guilt even as his treacherous body found its release.

"I'm sorry, Angel," he murmured a short while later, when it was over and he'd rolled to her side. He stared up at the ceiling. "I should have left well enough alone tonight—and back in Paris. Damn it, you were a virgin! An innocent little girl! I had no right—not from the very first. Damn me for a son of a bitch, but you deserve better than this—a damn sight more than I have t' offer you."

"It's all right, Nick," she whispered tremulously, feeling the tears begin as she stroked his cheek. "Truly it is. What you've given me is more than enough."

But it was a lie. Angel knew it, even as she spoke, and so did Nick. She loved him—blindly, deeply, utterly—no matter how poorly matched they might be, how different, or how unsuitable her heart's choice had proven. And the passion they shared was empty, meaningless, if he didn't love her in return. . . .

Chapter Twenty-Six

"No, signore, we have no tickets left for the train to Roma, not a single one for today. Everyone goes to Roma for the festival tomorrow, you understand? I am so sorry, signore!" The railway official in the ticket window at the Milan train station was apologetic but adamant.

Frowning, Nick turned back to Angel. "Well, I guess we'll either have t' find another way to Rome, or check into a hotel for a night or two. Either way, we won't be leaving Milan by train today!"

Angel was only half listening to Nick. Rather, she was staring at a bill posted on the wall of the train station behind his head, one that showed an artist's rendition of the city of Venice in earth tones that resembled faded oils, a cityscape painted in dark rusts, browns, and ochres of picturesque buildings overlooking a canal. Sunlight slanted off grotesque little gargoyles and statues, bouncing a sunburst off the still green water, while in the foreground of the bill rode a graceful black gondola in which reclined two genteel ladies, their parasols unfurled. They were smiling as they were poled along by a moustachioed gondolier.

"Ask the ticket seller if he has any tickets to Venice instead," she murmured wistfully. "I've always wanted to go to Venice!"

"Venice? Hmm. I don't know about that. Venice wasn't on the itinerary Mr. Hamilton worked out with your pa," Nick reminded her doubtfully.

"Oh, fiddlesticks, I know that—and it's precisely what

makes going there an even better idea! Those awful men will be sitting back, waiting for us to meekly show up in Rome like good little sitting ducks—but we won't be there. We'll be in Venice!"

Her face, so pale these past few days, was flushed and pink, animated with excitement. Her gray eyes sparkled for the first time since the night on the verandah.

"Oh, come on, Nick, let's go! Don't let's tell anyone— don't let's send any telegraphs or postcards—let's just *go* there, the two of us, and have *fun!* I'm sick and tired of having my Grand Tour ruined. Of having this once-in-a-lifetime visit to Europe destroyed by having to look over my shoulder and watch myself every minute. Oh, Nick, we could float down the canals on a gondola . . . visit the museums and the churches . . . dance to the music of the bands in the Piazza San Marco—! It'll be wonderful, you'll see!"

He smiled, warming to the idea himself now. The way she described it, it sure sounded more appealing than Rome, where those two sidewinding thugs were no doubt holed up, just biding their time, watching Red and Juarez's comings and goings while they waited for Angel and him to show up. Heck, the jaunt she'd suggested would be just the thing right now, a much-needed breathing space for the two of them; one their time at Villa Allegra would have supplied, had Angel not fallen ill through no fault of her own. His own mind made up, he asked, "You're sure that's what you want to do?"

"Positively," she declared, her stubborn little chin taking on that obstinate cast he'd come to know so very well.

"All right then. You're the boss-lady on this here trail drive, ma'am. Venice it is!"

"Wonderful! You won't regret it, Nick. We'll have a marvelous time, you'll see!"

Venezia!
Venice, or the "Queen of the Adriatic," as she was fondly known, was everything Angel had imagined! Her streets were not streets at all but serpentine waterways,

green canals that snaked between a dozen mud piles on which ancient buildings with facades of colonnades, loggias, and colorful mosaics had stood for centuries. The one hundred and twenty small islands of Venice were linked by four hundred picturesque bridges with names as romantic-sounding as their history—the Rialto Bridge, the Bridge of Sighs, to name but two. Her carriages and hackney cabs were not horse-drawn vehicles but flat-bottomed black gondolas, narrow boats with high, graceful prows poled by gondoliers—bold, handsome fellows in striped jerseys who, for a small fee, would also strum the mandolin, and make the hearts of their female passengers flutter as they flirted their liquid, dark eyes and sang of moonlit bridges, stolen kisses, of Venice and love. . . .

Nick and Angel arrived in the city on August fifteenth, the day on which the Roman Catholic Church celebrated the Feast of the Assumption, commemorating the union of the Blessed Virgin's earthly body with her soul in Heaven, the "Falling Asleep of the All Holy Mother of God." Since the eighth century, devout Catholics had observed this holy occasion with three days spent in fasting, prayer, and vigils, followed by processions, feasts, masquerade balls, dancing, and merrymaking. Catholic Venice was no exception. As had Rome, the city had attracted hundreds of visitors like themselves, Nick and Angel discovered upon their arrival, all of them eager to join in with the festivities!

The hotels were crowded, the best of them booked solidly for the entire week. It was only by the greatest of good fortune that they were able to find two Spartan rooms in an unpretentious yet clean hotel. Overlooking the Piazza San Giovanni, a tiny square far from the city's heart, their lodgings were nevertheless close enough so that they could hear the glorious bells of the Campanile when they awoke the next morning.

After breakfast, they left the hotel and wandered the narrow streets and alleys of Venice hand in hand, exploring her museums and marveling at the priceless collections of paintings to be found there, before finding their way at last to the largest square of all, the Piazza San Marco.

332

Here, in the heart of Venice, stood Saint Mark's Cathedral and the Doges' Palace, famous for its wonderful, colorful mosaics and its statues of winged lions. These two ancient buildings loomed in Gothic splendor over the eastern side of the square, while on the southern and northern sides were the New and the Old Procuraties, the official residences of Venice's government officials—called *procurators*—since the sixteenth century. There was also a fifteenth century clock tower with bronze figures, and a bell tower—the Campanile—that had awakened them so thrillingly that morning. Newer shops and cafés were clustered between the Procuraties.

As they strolled the ancient flagstoned square, hundreds of pigeons took flight, their feathers white as meringues against the brilliant blue of the Italian sky. At Angel's urging, Nick bought a loaf of bread from a baker's shop on the square to feed to them. Side by side, they sat on the steps of the cathedral and scattered crumbs for the pigeons. Many were bold enough to perch on their fingers or shoulders to feed. They gobbled pieces torn from the warm, fragrant loaf themselves, too, for with the carefree holiday mood upon them now, everything tasted doubly delicious and their appetites were voracious, their other senses heightened.

Why, here in this wonderful city, alone with Nick, Angel reflected happily, the very colors of the world around them seemed brighter, richer, the music more stirring and poignant, her cares and doubts less weighty—perhaps even her heart a little less broken? Here, in this magical city of history and romance, anything seemed possible. One's dearest wishes might even come true! Yes, oh yes! Perhaps here, Nick would realize—as Maria suspected—that he'd been wrong, and that he was in love with her after all. . . .

Tossing a coin into a lichened fountain where water splashed from the mouths of playful stone dolphins, she closed her eyes. Crossing her fingers, she prayed with all her heart that her wish would come true.

"Well? What did you wish for?" Nick asked, amused. She looked like a little girl, standing there with her eyes tightly shut and her fingers crossed. Her somewhat old-

333

fashioned gown, given to her by Maria, added to the effect.

"Oh, I'll never tell! They say if you do, it won't come true!" she came back gaily. "Come on, Durango! Never mind my silly old wishes. Let's see what everyone's doing over there. Look at the crowd! Something must be happening."

Taking his hand, she tugged him across the square to where a crowd had gathered to watch a religious procession crossing the piazza. Far above their heads, borne reverently on the backs of six strapping Italians, bobbed a life-sized statue of the Virgin Mary, dressed in a white gown and mantle trimmed with gold. Behind her came priests swinging smoking censers before them, sweetly chanting nuns with bowed heads, and angelic white-robed choirboys. As the respectful crowd parted to let them pass, the procession crossed the square and filed down the steps leading to the Grand Canal, where several gondolas waited.

Along with countless others, Nick and Angel hung over the Rialto Bridge and watched as the gondolas, each one decked with red, white, and pink carnations and crimson and yellow roses—glided in stately procession down the Grand Canal. In the first gondola, the beautiful statue of the Virgin had been erected amidst a bank of still more flowers. She rose from the blossoms' fragrant midst with her carved and painted face smiling and serene. Her right hand was lifted, as if she were bestowing her blessings on one and all. After carrying the Virgin in ritual procession through all the canals of the city, the gondolas would return to the Piazza San Marco and the Virgin would be ceremoniously replaced in her niche in the cathedral there.

When the gondolas had vanished, they left the bridge and returned to the square to explore the shops, marveling over fabled Venetian glassware and exquisite Burano lace, jewelry and wood carvings. Another shop featured wonderful masks and exotic costumes of velvet and silk, many of them dripping glass jewels and sparkly sequins, or festooned with yards of lace and gold braid. Depending upon one's whim, one could masquerade as a Venetian *doge* of old, a French courtesan, a shepherdess, perhaps a humble friar, or even a Valkyrie. Whichever choice one

334

made, there were glittering accessories to match! The *costumier* was doing brisk trade this morning, for a masked ball would follow the solemn religious services of the holy day in true Italian tradition, with masks, or the customary religious plays, followed by lively dancing to entertain the costumed revelers.

"Look at this!" Nick exclaimed while they explored the lacemaker's shop. Between his arms was draped a lovely white shawl, a cobweb of the finest handmade lace Angel'd seen. The center was worked in an intricate love-knot design, while about the border flew pairs of turtledoves. Each bird had a tiny ribbon clasped in its beak. Long fringes gave the exquisitely crafted shawl an exotic touch.

"It's lovely!" Angel exclaimed as Nick lifted it over her head, draping it carefully about her shoulders to admire the effect. In the muslin gown that Maria had altered for her, sprigged all over with tiny periwinkle-blue flowers and deep-green leaves, she lived up to her name. The gossamer shawl made an angel's halo about her head, aided by a trick of the light that streamed through the opened doorway into the gloomy shop.

"*Sí*, signore! You have the eye. Is *belissima!* Perfect for the signora!" the old lacemaker exclaimed, clapping her spotted brown hands together in delight. She'd obviously mistaken them for newlyweds.

"We'll take it," Nick decided without hesitation.

"Nick, don't. Really, you shouldn't," Angel protested, wanting to tell him it was far too expensive for their straightened means, but reluctant to embarrass him by doing so in front of the old woman.

"Wrap it up, signora," Nick told the shopkeeper, blithely ignoring her protests. Turning to Angel, he murmured, "And as for you, missie, not another word! When Nick Durango goes a-courtin', he doesn't go empty-handed, *comprende?*"

Startled by his choice of words, she looked up into his serious face. The expression in his eyes made a peculiar little flutter stir in the very pit of her stomach. ". . . *goes a-courtin' . . .*" he'd said, but what did he mean by that? What was he trying to tell her, if anything? That there was a chance he could change? That he wasn't yet sure of his

335

feelings? That he did care, in his own way, but was too uncertain as yet to commit himself? Whatever the reason, her heart soared on wings of hope! Instead of arguing and refusing his beautiful gift, she clasped it to her bosom and murmured, "Very well. I'll just say 'thank you,' with all my heart! It's beautiful, Nick! The most beautiful thing I've ever seen!" And it will be doubly treasured because you gave it to me, she added silently.

"Wrong," he murmured softly, taking her hand and kissing her fingertips before slipping it through his arm. "It's you that makes it beautiful. Now. Shall we move on, mi'lady?"

The shawl proved only the first item in what proved quite a shopping spree! After they left the lacemaker's, Nick tugged her after him into the *costumier's* next door.

After rummaging through baskets of fantastic costumes, he found something to his taste, swirling cloaks of shiny scarlet and royal blue sateen. He also chose two outrageous masks for them to wear at the lavish costume ball that was scheduled to begin at dusk in the Piazza San Marco.

"Everyone'll be wearing 'em, Angel," he explained, grinning like a little boy at the prospect of donning a costume. "Don't want to stick out like sore thumbs, now do we?"

Come evening, the *costumier* told them, costumed merrymakers would spill out into the narrow alleys, streets, and canals of Venice to dance as the wine flowed more and more freely and the night wore on to dawn.

Passing up the more commonplace domino masks, Nick selected one for Angel and another for himself, unaware that they were not the only customers in the gloomy, cluttered *costumier's*. Someone stood behind a rack of Medieval courtier costumes, listening intently as the couple selected their masks.

"This one's yours. Here you go."

Made of stiffened pasteboard, Angel's mask reached to the tip of her nose, covering only the upper part of her face. Long, silky white fur had been glued to the base to resemble an Angora cat with plump, furry cheeks and pert pricked ears lined with pink velvet. Sapphire blue sequins set off the slanted eyeholes, while gold wire whiskers and a heartshaped pink velvet nose finished off the "purrfect" mask, designed to be held up before the face on a stick, medieval fashion. Nick's mask, equally exotic, fitted over the head. It was of a crested hawk or a falcon, she wasn't sure which. It had glossy black feathers, layered one upon the other, and a cruel golden beak covered his nose. The round eyeholes were rimmed with glittering amber sequins.

"Careful, Miz Kitty, or I'll swoooop down from my aerie and carry you off!" Nick threatened. Holding the mask up before his face, he curled his fingers into talons.

"Try it, Sir Rooster, and Miz Kitty'll scratch your eyes out!" she meowed haughtily, doing likewise. She ended her challenge with a curtsey and a feline-sounding, "Hsss!"

"Rooster, hell!" Nick disagreed, pretending to be annoyed. He took a second, longer look at the mask. "It's a hawk. Or maybe an eagle. Either one. But it's sure as heck no barnyard rooster!"

Angel grinned and shrugged airily. "Oh, really, Durango, I don't know what you're making such a fuss about? I'd have thought a rooster mask would be perfect for you! You're always strutting about, arrogantly preening yourself, crowing, 'Cock a doodle doo'!"

"The devil I am, you little—!"

With a giggle, Angel cheekily stuck her tongue through the cat mask's open mouth and sidestepped around him. He made a grab for her, but she outran him and fled the cluttered *costumier's* for the sun-drenched piazza outside.

Hoisting her skirts a little, she sped quickly down the square, while Nick—who'd yet to pay for the masks and capes—lost precious minutes waiting for his change.

When he ducked out of the shop, his purchases tucked under his arm, he was momentarily blinded by the brilliant light outside. By the time he'd recovered, he managed to catch only a glimpse of Angel's blue-sprigged skirts as she ducked quickly into a nearby alley. Ah ha!

Hugging the shop fronts, unaware that he had been followed outside, Nick sidled toward the mouth of the alley, suddenly turning into it. There was Angel! She'd hidden halfway down the gloomy alley, her back pressed up against the wall to make herself as small as possible.

"Ah ha! Hiding from someone, Miz Kitty?" he taunted, grinning as he stalked slowly down the alley toward her. "The Terrible Tickling Rooster of Venice, mayhap? If so, dear damsel, you are *doomed!*"

Like a panther, he pounced, trapping her up against the wall. The hand he planted on either side of her head cut off escape. Mercilessly, he lightly scratched his fingers against the soft web of flesh between her neck and shoulder. Promptly squealing, she thrust her chin down, burying it against her collarbone to make him stop. Squirming and giggling helplessly, she tried to push his hands away, but he only redoubled his torture.

"Ohh, you beast! You rotter! You utter bounder, Durango! I loathe being tickled more than anything!" she wailed, tears of laughter rolling down her cheeks.

"More than anything?" he countered softly, tickling her in the ribs now, thinking how adorable she was, how beautiful, how funny, how unlike any other woman he'd ever met.

"Anything—*anything!*" she groaned, reckless in her torment.

"More than this?" he asked huskily. He ducked his dark head and gently pressed his lips over hers. Willpower—or lack of it—didn't even enter his thoughts in that moment. Truth was, he couldn't seem to help himself!

It was a sweet kiss, a long, lingering, gentle kiss, a kiss laden with tenderness. It was also the first time he'd kissed her since that night at Villa Allegra two weeks ago. The memories it brought back, the hunger it stirred in him, were stunning.

"Oh, much, *much* more than that," she confessed shakily when he broke the kiss to look down at her. "At least, I think so," she amended coyly. "To be absolutely certain, I suppose you'd have to—"

"—kiss you again?" he supplied, smiling.

"Hmm. Rather! At *least* once more, don't you think?" she murmured as his arms enfolded her.

He drew her against his chest and, tilting her lovely face up to his, kissed her again, moving his mouth against hers

338

slowly but oh, so very surely. His kisses sent a warm flood of sensation pouring through every fiber of her being, a sensation that deepened as he parted her lips to explore the inner sweetness of her mouth. He gently massaged the undercurve of her chin with the ball of his thumb, then lazily caressed the fluid column of her throat with trailing fingertips until she was gasping against his mouth, uttering little sighs and oohing and aahing sounds of contentment.

"Why, you sound as if you're purring, Miz Kitty," he teased, his voice deep and sensual against her ear, his warm breath sending delicious, tickly quivers down her spine.

"I am, I am," she admitted happily, nuzzling her cheek against his broad chest as she wrapped her arms around him. "Do you know, I think I could stay in this awful old alley forever!"

Nick wrinkled his nose in disgust. "Maybe you could, sweet thing—but I couldn't! What do you say we go on back to the hotel? We could rest up for a spell before dinner and tonight's masquerade ball? Who knows, it might be a long night, if it's half the fine old time these folks say it is . . . ?"

Their eyes met. Silent currents raced between them.

"That's a splendid idea," she agreed softly, with just a heartbeat's hesitation.

Chapter Twenty-Seven

Mellow afternoon sunlight fingered its way through the wooden louvers, striping the mosaic-tiled floors and stucco walls of the bedchamber where Angel and Nick lay entwined in the lazy afterglow of their lovemaking.

From the eaves beneath their wrought-iron balcony came the low, cooing refrain of doves, and from time to time, the quick flash of wings from the swallows who roosted there cast a darting shadow across the walls.

The melodious sound of the gondoliers' voices as they called to each other on the canal below was muted by distance from here. Only the bonging of the brass figures in the ancient clock tower of San Marco marked the passage of the hours, as did the gradually fading brilliance of the blue sky framed by the window.

The afternoon was slipping away; a beautiful sultry summer evening was taking its place. Soon, the city's nightwatchmen would begin their rounds, lighting the torches that would bring another Venice to life. The bands would play in Piazza San Marco that evening. Throngs of exotically masked and costumed revelers would flock to the square to dance; the plays would begin, as they'd been performed on this day for centuries, and after, the wine would flow like water and the merrymaking would commence in earnest.

"Any regrets?" Nick murmured, leaning up on one elbow to look down at Angel's lovely face. Her delicate features were a little blurred now, her gray eyes dreamy with the languor of spent passion.

"You asked me that once before, remember?" She smiled.

"And?"

"My answer's the same now as it was then. No. No regrets. Yes, I was upset before, at the villa. But I realize now I should be grateful for your honesty. I'm sure it wasn't easy for you. A more unscrupulous man would have said what I wanted to hear, and taken advantage of me for his own ends. No. It's far, far better to know the truth—even if what you said wasn't what I wanted to hear! I've learned the repercussions that dishonesty can have all too thoroughly," she added a little ruefully, remembering. If she and Reggie hadn't tried to dupe her father, Nick would have had no reason not to trust her in Paris. He would have taken swift action when those two horrid men abducted her from the St. Pierre, instead of standing by and letting them do so. And perhaps, in the process, he might have ended their attempts to kidnap her once and for all that afternoon. As it was, he'd believed it yet another ruse on her part, and had done nothing. Why, she could have been murdered, and it would have been no one's fault but her own. . . .

But Nick looked uncomfortable and far from reassured, despite her words. Truth was, her calm, reasonable acceptance of the circumstances only made him squirm with guilt, rather than serving as a balm to his conscience. He would have felt better if she'd gotten mad or had tried to argue with him or plead her case.

"Er . . . you do know that if there should be any . . . er . . . consequences of this afternoon, I won't run out on you?" he said gruffly.

"If I should find myself with child, you mean?" She caressed his cheek. "I'm sure you wouldn't. You're an extraordinarily honorable fellow beneath that brash American facade, aren't you, Nick—though I would have been the first to deny it a few weeks ago! But you need have no concern on that account. Should I find myself in such a position, I promise I'll make no claims or demands on you. I made love with you with my eyes wide open, knowing full well what could transpire. As I said, I did so with no regrets, and no illusions. If there should be some

341

consequence of our actions, I accept sole responsibility for it. I could never use an innocent babe to bind you to me."

He scowled. It wasn't what he'd wanted her to say, not at all! Nor had he intended for her to interpret his concerns as a reluctance to accept responsibility. Hell, the thought of her having his child alone was unimaginable! His mellow mood had evaporated now. It was fast becoming irritation, instead. That darned woman, it was all her doing. She was always so blamed noble and coolheaded, always so practical and unruffled. "Sole responsibility"—hell! What did she take him for, anyway? The kind of sidewindin' love-'em-an'-leave-'em lowlife who took his fun where he could find it, then rode off into the badlands and left the gal without a backward glance? Did she think him incapable of doing the decent thing, the noble thing, the *right* thing, if circumstances warranted it? His scowl deepened. More than likely that was exactly what she thought! But then, whose fault was that? What else could he *expect* her to think? He'd been all too eager to resume the intimate side of their affair today, despite making it daylight-plain the last time they'd made love that on no account should she expect her love returned. Damn it! What was eating at him? He'd never felt so confused before, nor so turned inside out.

"Oh, my! You look very stern, Mr. Durango," she observed, frowning as she idly trailed her fingernail through the mat of black hair on his chest. She circled his flat dark rose nipples. "A penny for your thoughts!"

"Right now, I don't reckon they're worth half that much," he said sourly.

"Really? Hmm, we'll have to do something to improve your mood. We're on holiday, remember, Mr. Durango? Frowns—" she poked him in the belly, "—and scowls—" she poked him again, "—and grumpy, stern expressions—" she poked him a third time, "—are expressly forbidden! That, sir, is the law!"

"Whose law?"

"*My* law!"

So saying, she planted her palms in the middle of his chest and shoved him onto his back. Her breasts swung forward like bells as she leaned over him to dip her honey blond head to his. A loving smile curved her lips as she pressed her mouth to his closed eyelids, feeling the flutter of his thick lashes against her lips, then to the tiny indentations at each corner of his mouth, before fitting her mouth to his.

Hmm, heaven. His lips tasted of the sweet red wine they'd drank from a single glass, before urgently shedding their clothes and tumbling to the bed, there to make love with a passion that had bordered on frenzy, earlier that afternoon.

He smelled of aromatic tobacco and of shaving soap, clean, manly scents combined with an exciting, masculine musk unique to him; a beloved, exciting scent that even were she blind, she would yet recognize as his alone.

Her cool hands explored the sinewy hardness of his body as she kissed him. How smooth he felt here, how hairy he was there, how coarse . . . how powerful . . . how male . . . how wonderful! Her eager hands traveled up his corded arms to his shoulders, then found the vulnerable spot between his throat and chest. She planted a kiss on the smooth skin there, where she could feel his pulse beating strongly beneath tan flesh.

"Mabel would say I'd gone 'proper barmy,' but I love you, Durango," she murmured. She expected no response and he gave none as, lapping diligently, like a kitten lapping up a bowl of cream, she flicked her tongue over the salty maleness of his chest, trailing it down his breastbone, across his rib cage to his flat belly. There, she sighed and rested her flaming cheek like a weary traveler, before continuing her caresses. Her fingers skimmed his powerful horseman's thighs, lingering at an old, knotty scar on one, before grazing the forest of coarse, dark hair that framed his quiescent sex. Boldly, she took his manhood in her hand. He grunted with pleasure as she stroked him.

His throbbing maleness, ensheathed by her palm, quickly stirred and grew proud and firm again. How strange, how magical it was, almost, to feel his sleeping manhood answer her touch, to know that it had been she who'd aroused him. There was a certain feeling of power in such a talent, she decided, smiling a wicked little smile. Leaning up, her hair spilling about her shoulders and making golden arabesques against the paler tan of his lower body, she saw that his eyes were no longer troubled and angry. They'd grown heavy-lidded and sensual now, their silvery blue all but hidden. His hard-lipped scowl had also vanished, replaced by an expression of intense pleasure that made her smile again—this time in female triumph.

"She-devil!" he drawled huskily, knowing she was watching his face, guessing the reason for that smug little grin. "What'll I do with you, huh? You'll wear me out, woman! Wear me out and plant me in a pine box up on old Boot Hill!"

"Perhaps I shall—but what a way to go, hmmm?" she challenged naughtily, her pewter eyes bright with mischief.

He burst out laughing and caught her to him, hauling her up the length of his body to be hugged tightly in his arms. "It's almost dusk, Miz Angel," he reminded her. He stroked her back, fondling the firm curves of her delectable bottom. His breathing grew steadily more shallow and thick with desire as he did so. "If we stay in this here bed much longer, you're gonna miss the dancing."

"The *dancing!* Oh, that's right! I'd quite forgotten! Then, enough of this nonsense! Let's go—!" she began, sounding eager to be free of him. She laughed helplessly as he jerked her back down—just as she'd known he would.

He held her fast and threatened, "Let's *go?* Just like that? Huh! Tease me, would you, you minx? The heck I'll let you go now, missie! Guess you'll have to stay here and finish what you started, hmm, darlin' . . ."

"But the dancing—!" She pouted, pretending disappointment.

"Damn the dancing!" he growled, sweeping her beneath him.

The band in the square played waltz after waltz as they danced around and around the torchlit piazza. They moved together so perfectly, Angel fancied their feet hardly touched the flagstones. Hers certainly weren't earthbound. She was dancing on air!

344

"You dance divinely, dahling!" Angel declared in a plummy British accent. She looked like a fairy tale character in her Angora kitten mask and swirling red cloak, Mistress Puss-in-Boots, in the flesh.

"I do at that, don't I?" Nick agreed immodestly.

She sensed his roguish grin as he gallantly turned her in time to the music, for she could not see his face beneath the concealing hawk mask.

"Durango, Dancer Divine. I kinda like that! It'd look just dandy up on a circus tent."

"'Dancer Divine,' really. You're crazy!"

"If I am, so are you."

"I know! *I* admit it."

"Do you also admit you've had too much wine, Miss Know-it-All?"

"I do indeed, sir—and I don't care. I just wish this night—this holiday!—would never end. I wish we could go on dancing and dancing forever!"

With a blissful sigh, she threw back her head and let Nick guide her as she gazed up at the midnight blue sky, enjoying the way the stars ran together in a sparkling blur way above her as they twirled. "So many stars—and so very bright—just like that night in the Gypsy camp! And do you smell that air? Hmm! Foreign herbs. Exotic spices. Wine and flowers and leftover sunshine—heavenly!"

All about them swirled costumed couples—most dressed far more elaborately than themselves. There was the devil, horned and cloaked in crimson satin, whirling in his arms a dainty wood nymph wearing a gauzy Grecian toga. To their left, a barbaric Viking escorted a striking French courtesan, her costume complete with black velvet pox-patches and orange pomander. A Dutch girl danced with a ferocious-looking corsair to their right, while a few feet away a bearded centaur, complete with horsetail, cavorted merrily with a buxom shepherdess, a Roman gladiator squired an ethereal sylph with powdered cheeks and hair, while another dressed in the traditional Italian *domino* costume of flowing black cloak with a small black half mask, twirled an exotic Arabian belly dancer in his arms, making her bells and coins tinkle madly.

Their faces safely hidden beneath the masks, the shy

became bold; the already-bold became buffoons or strutting braggarts as the masks served to loosen everyone's inhibitions.

On every side, the sounds, the smells, the sights—the sparkle, the glitter, the hectic gaiety in the air—intoxicated. It seemed to Angel as if the whole world had lost its senses, had gone mad and donned costumes and masks to join in the festival and dance—and still the enormous crowd was growing! More overladen gondolas were arriving every minute, coming alongside the broad, shallow steps that led up from the canal to the square itself. The gondoliers would pause below for a few moments to allow their passengers to disembark and accept their fares, before poling their crafts on down the moon-and-torchlit, glinting black water in search of new customers.

"Whoa!" Angel exclaimed, tottering off course. "I'm so dizzy! Down's up—and up's down!"

"If you stare up at the stars and dance at the same time, I'm not surprised. Come on, sit down over here for a spell."

Nick took her hand in his. He led her between the dancing couples to a low, crumbling wall that bordered the steps leading to the Grand Canal below.

"Better?"

"Much." So saying, she drew off the cat mask and fanned herself with it. Pretty as it was, the fur made it very hot to wear. Her cheeks were red as apples.

"I'd say an Italian ice would be real welcome right now."

Her mouth watered at the thought. "Rath-er. But . . . do we have enough money?" she wondered longingly.

"Let me worry about that. You sit here. I'll be right back."

"Lemon for me, if they have it!" she called after him, and he waved to show he'd heard as he plunged back into the crowd.

She passed the time waiting by tidying her hair, which she'd caught up in an elegant chignon. The tiny tendrils of short hair that framed her brow had escaped the pins. They were curly as vines from the night's warmth and her exertions.

"May I have the honor of this dance, beautiful one?" a voice asked, and looking up, she saw a handsome Italian youth standing before her, costumed in the suit of lights of a Spanish matador.

"Thank you, signore, but I'm with someone, you understand?" she refused.

"But of course, signorina. The loss is mine." Inclining his head, the young man bowed and moved on in search of another partner.

Angel looked idly about her. She enjoyed watching all the different costumes and the heady carnival atmosphere and couldn't help thinking how Mabel, with her fondness for loud music and boisterous fun, would have loved an evening like this. . . .

She flinched suddenly as a weighty hand clamped over her shoulder but glancing up, she saw it was only Nick and smiled her relief.

"Oh! You startled me! Didn't they have any ices?" He'd come back empty-handed she realized, disappointed.

He shook his head.

"Oh, well. Never mind."

Suddenly, he took her elbow and almost dragged her to her feet. His fingers bit cruelly into her arm.

"Nick? What on earth are you doing?"

"It's a real pretty night. Let's take a gondola ride," he rasped. His words sounded muffled.

"I'd enjoy that. What's wrong with your voice?" she asked.

"The mask," he muttered. "Come on. Here's one now."

With that, he chivvied her quickly down the steps. At the bottom, he helped her into the gondola bobbing alongside with far more force than was necessary.

"Where to, signore?" the gondolier asked, thrusting his pole against the stone jetty to get them on their way. Nick muttered something she couldn't quite make out.

"This is so romantic," she murmured as the high-prowed black gondola slipped beneath the arches of the Rialto Bridge. On either side of the canal, the ancient palazzos were ablaze with the light of crystal chandeliers, the candlelight reflected a thousandfold in the dark, oily waters of the canal. Music carried from many of them. "Where did you say we were going?"

Nick didn't answer.

For a moment, she was angry, furiously angry at his mercurial change of mood. His sudden sullenness was ruining their magical evening! But then, she happened to glance down at the hand still gripping her wrist, and her anger became fear.

The hand about her wrist was fair-skinned, not tan. The knuckles sprouted blond hairs!

Whoever was sitting beside her, cloaked in royal blue satin and wearing a black hawk's mask, she had no idea. Of one thing she was certain, though. That man was not Nick. . . .

Chapter Twenty-Eight

"Nicky—! *Amore!*"

"Cooeee! Over here, darling!"

The shrill feminine voices caught Nick's attention despite the laughter of the crowds and the noise of the band in the torchlit piazza. Looking about him, he saw Sophia, Claudia, and Gina bearing down on him across the square with big smiles and open arms. He groaned. For a moment, he was tempted to hightail it in the opposite direction and pretend he hadn't seen them. But, it was too late for that! They'd recognized him, and there'd be no avoiding them now, he thought, resigned. Damn it! Why'd he have to take off the hawk hood? But, it was a warm evening and the feathered hood had been hot and irritating. . . .

"Well, well! Good evenin', ladies," he sang out, forcing a smile of greeting as they surged around him like piranhas in a feeding frenzy. They clung to his arms, pulled his head down by the ears, planted smacking wet kisses on his lips, and gave him boisterous hugs. "What are you gals doing here?"

"We wanted to go to Rome for the Feast of the Assumption—we go there every year for a few days, you see? It is our—how you say?—our little holiday," Claudia explained.

"That's right," Gina agreed. "But this year, we heard there is a outbreak of typhoid in Roma, and so we come 'ere to Venice instead, to visit our Uncle Giacomo."

"And what about you? What are you a doin' here, in Venice, Nicky, darling?" Sophia demanded.

349

She was, he noticed, blinking, dressed in the costume of a Vestal virgin. Darn it, he realized belatedly, they *all* were!

"Me? Oh, I'm here for the festival, too. Doing a little sightseeing, an' such."

"All . . . alone?" Claudia asked in a purring tone, running her fingernail down his chest.

"Yes sir, all alone!" he lied, but Claudia archly eyed the two cardboard cones of Italian ice he was holding—they'd melted, dripping sugary liquid down his arms—and his shoulders sagged. "Well, maybe not all alone," he admitted guiltily. "Er, Angel's with me."

"Angelica? *The* Angelica? Shame, shame, Nicky!" Gina scolded, her tone stern as she waggled her finger at him.

"Yes. You isa naughty man! You promise us faithfully you let 'er go, eh? But now, you say you isa here with her?" Sophia said, pouting her lush red lips. "Bad boy!"

"Guilty, ladies," Nick admitted. "You caught me this time, fair and square! And I'd sure like to stay and visit awhile, but Angel's waitin' for me over there . . . and these ices are meltin' fast. I'd best be gettin' on back to her. It was real nice seein' you again. Adios!" He started to go.

"Nicky, *amore*, don't run away! Me and my cousins, we want to meeta you sweetheart," Sophia declared, pouting as she hurried after him. The other girls followed her.

"You want . . . to meet . . . Angel? Whoa, there. You gals hold your horses a minute! I don't know about that—!"

"*Sí!*" Claudia exclaimed. "Why not? You doan have to tell her what we do, eh? You can tell her we isa all you old, old friends. Friends from—from—"

"Catholic School?" Nick suggested with raised brows. "I've got it! You can say you were nuns there. How about that?"

"*Sí!* Is very good story! You will tell the signorina we were nuns. Holy sisters—very devout." Claudia sighed wistfully. "You know, from when I was a little girl, I 'ave always wanted to be a nun."

"Hey, I was kidding—Angel'll never swallow that!" But then Nick sighed and grinned, unable to help himself. The whole idea of these three pretending to be nuns was just too crazy for words! "Aw, all right, then. What harm can it do? Come on, *sisters*, I'll introduce you—but not a blamed word about what you gals really do for a livin', okay? Angel'll throw a fit if she ever finds out you're not . . ."

"Vestal virgins?" Sophia suggested coyly.

He snorted. "Something like that."

"Okay!" they chorused. "We take a vow of silence, eh? Our lips, they isa sealed." All three girls giggled and pressed fingers over their lush mouths.

"This way, then, ladies."

Like the Piper Piper of Hamlin, Nick led the bevy of Italian beauties in and out of the dancing couples.

At the crumbling steps across the square, he pulled up short. Angel had vanished! The wall where she'd been sitting was now empty. Frowning, he looked around, scanning the crowds for her red sateen cloak and sassy white kitten mask. If she wasn't here, she must be dancing with someone, he figured.

"Well? And where isa she, you Angel?" Gina asked, her hands planted on her hips as she looked around.

"Damned if I know," Nick said slowly, his frown deepening to a scowl. He thrust a cone of lemon ice into Claudia and Sophia's hands and strode across to the nearest couple. He tapped the young bullfighter on the shoulder, smiling his apologies to his partner, a sultry brunette dressed as Cleopatra. "'Scuse me, friend, but there was a young lady sittin' on the wall over there. You didn't happen t' see where she went, did you?"

"The blond goddess holding a cat mask?"

"That's her."

"*Sí!* I asked her to dance, but she said she was with someone. A few moments later, her escort returned and she left with him, signore."

Alarm leaped through him like wildfire. "Escort?"

"*Sí*, signore. He wore a blue cloak—like your own—and a mask. It was a bird. A hawk, I think. Or maybe an eagle?"

"A hood like this?" Nick held up the mask he'd removed.

"That's it!"

"You didn't happen t' see which way they went?"

"I did, my friend," the youth said with a conspirator's

351

grin, obviously mistaking Nick as a rival for Angel's affections. "They left by gondola. It was headed that way. Toward the Piazza Santa Maria." He pointed.

"And she left with this man willingly?"

"She—er—seemed willing, signore, yes."

Nick thanked him, ignoring his jovial cry of "Good luck!" as he hastened down the mossy steps to the canal.

The dark green water reflected torch and candlelight on its rippled surface, but as he'd expected, there was no gondola, no Angel, nor any stranger in a blue cloak there now.

Dread raised the hackles on his neck. Who could have taken her? Why? And where? Had her would-be kidnappers found them, somehow? Or was the man she'd gone with, thinking he was Nick, some sidewindin' lowlife who'd duped her for reasons of his own . . . ? He didn't know, couldn't begin to guess, and a wildfire was raging through him now, out of control, a wildfire of anxiety and apprehension that only holding Angel safe in his arms again could extinguish.

He imagined the man lifting the hood, and her terror on finding he was not Nick, as she'd believed. He imagined her frightened and helpless, at the mercy of a terrifying strangers's whims, and his gut tightened.

"Hold on, sweet thing. I'll be there. I'm coming, darlin'! Don't give up—just hold on!" he prayed silently.

"Nicky! What's wrong? Where are you going? Nicky! Wait for us—!"

At a ground-eating lope, Nick left the square in the direction the youth had pointed, and kept on going.

Wherever possible, he used the narrow pavements that flanked the Grand Canal. Soon, however, the pavements ended. From there on, the buildings fronted the water itself. Nick was forced to continue his search around them, using the lanes and alleys that ran between the merchants' homes, the museums, and palaces, in a serpentine, mazelike course that forced him to leave the waterways completely for several minutes at a time.

Each diversion took him down narrow, murky alleys that were either black as pitch, or lit eerily by flickering torches. Sometimes, he almost collided with drunken masked revelers who'd lost their way, or stumbled upon lusty lovers enjoying themselves in some dark, littered corner. The alleys reeked of mildew and rotting vegetables, of urine and decay. Rats scampered and squeaked there, in the shadows. Mating cats howled like newborn babies. Bats flapped leathery wings as they left the bell towers to hunt in squeaking flights. And each time Nick stumbled from some foul back street and back to the canal proper once again, he'd hope against hope that this time, please God, the gondola he sought would be there.

But there was nothing, damn it! Not a sign of her anywhere! But then, perhaps it had been madness to even try? The gondola she'd been in could have stopped anywhere, at any one of over a thousand places!

Chest heaving, Nick sank down onto the steps to catch his breath. He hung his head in his hands. How could he hope to find Angel at night, on foot, in this rabbit warren of a city? Damn it, *how?*

"Gondola, signore?"

He looked up, saw that one of the high-prowed black gondolas was bobbing on the canal just below him, and shook his head angrily. "No."

With a shrug, the gondolier braced his long oar against the stone embankment and began pushing off.

"Wait!" Nick called after him.

"Yes?"

"I'm trying to find someone. A man and a woman. The woman was blond and wearing a red cloak. His was blue, like mine. They left the Piazza San Marco in a gondola about twenty minutes ago, and were headed in the direction of the Piazza Santa Maria."

"I'm sorry, sir," the gondolier apologized. "There are so many new faces in the city these past few days. The festival attracts tourists by the thousand—you understand?"

"The woman might have been wearing a cat mask."

"Like I said, there are so many people here in Venice tonight, sir, and all of them costumed or masked! Forgive me, but I would be lying if I said I remembered one woman among so many."

Nick nodded. "Thanks anyway. It was a long shot, but I figured I'd ask."

"Why not let me take you to Piazza Santa Maria? Who knows, perhaps we can find the gondolier who took the fare? If so, there's a chance he could tell you where he let them off?"

Nick nodded. It was the only chance he had. "All right. You've got yourself a fare, *amigo*. If we find her, I'll make it worth your while. Let's go!"

"Hmmm. What about Uncle Giacomo? He has won the gondolier's regatta for seven years running. He'll know howa to find Nicky's sweetheart, eh, Sophia?" Claudia said hopefully.

The women had learned from the youth dressed in the bullfighter's costume why it was Nicky had left the square so hurriedly, and without so much a word of farewell, and they were determined to help him.

"If Uncle can't, no one in Venice can, Cousin. He knows these canals like the lines on his palm. After all, that's why they call him the Prince of the Waterways, no? But first, cousins, we 'ave to find *him!*" Sophia reminded them with a frown. "Gina, you will take a gondola to the Piazza San Giovanni. Claudia, you'll take another to the Palazzo di Gregorio. I will go that way, after Nick. We'll meet at the Piazza Santa Maria in one hour. And remember, if you should run into Uncle on the way, tell him everything that's happened. He will 'ave gondoliers all over the city watching for them. And if, by some stroke of luck, you should spot the girl and her abductor instead, follow them, see where he takes her—but don't take any chances. Remember, cousins, Signorina Angelica has golden hair. She's wearing a red cloak and, perhaps, the mask of a white cat. Got it?"

The other two nodded eagerly.

"Then, be off with you!"

"Let go of me, you animal!" Angel ground out. She struggled to escape her captor's fierce grip about her shoulders and arms, desperately trying to free her hands. Her frantic struggles rocked the gondola so violently,

354

the gondolier cried out in alarm and tried to peer beneath the pavilion that hid the couple from him in deep shadow.

"Please, signore, don't move about so! My gondola, she will overturn!"

The man laughed harshly and answered him in the fluent Italian of a native, "Forgive me, my friend. It's the woman. I gave her her asking price. Now the lovely little whore is playing hard to get, if you know what I mean? What's a hot-blooded man to do, eh?"

The gondolier chuckled. "With one so beautiful, you need to ask, signore? Lucky dog! That one, she'll be well worth your wait, I fancy. And the thrill of a little chase always sweetens the victory, no?"

"Quite so, my friend! Quite so."

The gondolier burst into rapturous song as he poled the gondola down the Grand Canal. They were headed for Marghera, the port that handled the city's trade. The light that spilled from the *loggias*, or galleries of the waterfront palaces, of Byzantine, Gothic, and Renaissance arthitecture, bathed the girl's face. It was pale as a shroud and stark with fear as she struggled with the man in the hawk's mask.

"I warned you once, didn't I?" he rasped under his breath in a frightening, muffled voice. "Keep still, blast you, or I'll slit this pretty throat from ear t' ear! Understand?"

She felt the cold prick of a knife point just below her jaw, and knew he'd made no idle threat. Swallowing a whimper of terror, she nodded, bracing her hands against the crosspiece upon which they sat, side by side like lovers, in an effort to recover her nerve. As she did so, her fingers brushed against something soft, something furry. It was the mask, the cat mask Nick'd bought her! Her heart skipped a beat. Darting a nervous side glance at the man—who was still wearing his own horrid hawk mask—she could tell by the dull glitter and hint of movement behind the eyeslits that he was looking straight ahead now, rather than at her, probably scanning the canal ahead for any sign of pursuit.

She bit her lower lip. Dare she? Could she . . . ? She had to try something—!

Moving her hand up, behind her back, just an inch at a time—hardly daring to breathe as she did so, for fear that he'd turn and see what she was doing—she edged the mask over the side of the gondola and let it fall. . . .

"Ahoy, there, Geraldo! How's business tonight, eh, my friend?"

"Brisk, Lucio! Indeed, better than brisk—thank the Blessed Virgin, eh?"

Nick drummed his fingers impatiently while his gondolier, Lucio, exchanged a few low words with the other fellow. While the two stationary crafts bobbed side by side on the torchlit waters of the Grand Canal, the couple beneath the other gondola's small pavilion were kissing and cuddling so ardently, they rocked the narrow flat-bottomed vessel. Nick grimaced, envying them their total preoccupation with each other. It was doubtful they'd even noticed the brief halt, while to him, every moment that passed seemed a lifetime!

He cursed under his breath as Lucio turned to him with a rueful frown and slowly shook his head. His tan hands were knotted into fists of impotent rage. They'd poled down what seemed like a hundred miles of inky water in the past hour, glided beneath dozens of picturesque stone bridges, had stopped every darned gondola they'd passed to ask the gondoliers if they'd seen the couple he sought. But none had. It was as if Angel and her abductor had vanished into thin air, though logic reasoned that that was impossible.

"Shall we go on?" Lucio queried doubtfully.

"What choice do we—I—have?" Nick growled, drawing a cheroot from beneath his cloak and cupping the match to light it. He drew deeply on the slim cigar.

"I'm sorry, signore."

"Forgive me. It's not your fault, my friend. Please, go on."

They were gliding past a brightly lit hotel not long after when Lucio gave a cry. "Signore, look! There, in the water!"

Immediately, Nick shifted to the side to look, while

356

Lucio deftly fished something furry and white from the water with his long oar.

At first, he thought the gondolier had found someone's prized pet that had fallen into the canal and drowned. But as the blue sequins bordering the eyeholes caught the light like sapphires, Nick saw what it was. His eyes narrowed. Had Angel lost the mask as she struggled with her abductor, or had she thrown it into the canal, leaving a desperate clue so that he could find her? Was it even the same mask? There must be a hundred others like it in Venice tonight! Perhaps it had fallen from Geraldo's gondola? Perhaps it had been lost in the ardor of the moment as his amorous passengers embraced? He smiled thinly. They'd sure seemed lively about their courting, the way that gondola had been bobbing about!

His head snapped up. A chill ran through him and his gut tightened. Had the couple been courting? Courting— or struggling? It was only a hunch—and a long shot, at that—but he'd be damned if it didn't feel *right.*

"Lucio, your pal Geraldo—did he say where he was headed?"

"He mentioned Marghera, signore. The harbor, it's back that way. Geraldo said his fat fare meant he could spend Saturday in bed!"

Nick looked back the way they'd come, but the other gondola had already disappeared around one of the serpentine bends of the Grand Canal. He could see only a broad swathe of glittering black water, framed by ancient buildings on either side.

"Geronimo!" Nick exclaimed, and snapped his fingers. "Bridges, Lucio! Are there any bridges?"

"In Venice you ask this?" Lucio grinned. "But of course!"

"Then take me ashore, pardner—then tell me the fastest way t' get to 'em, on foot."

Silent tears streamed down Angel's face. Beneath the gondola's pavilion, her head was turned sideways to the moonlight at an oddly stiff and unnatural angle, exposing her throat and the glint of the blade angled across it. Her

357

abductor—furious that she'd struggled and tried to break free when they'd stopped for the American's gondola—had cruelly knotted his fist in her hair, then brought the knife to her throat. In a low hiss that had made her blood run cold, he'd warned her that if she uttered so much as a squeak, he'd kill her first—then do the same to Nick. With that, he'd thrown his arms around her to make it appear they were embracing, kissing.

She swallowed, only too aware of the weapon at her windpipe as she did so. It felt like a splinter of ice against her skin.

"Promise t' be a good little girl?" the man rasped.

"Ye-es," she whispered shakily, and to her relief, he withdrew the blade, though he retained his painful grip on her wrist beneath the folds of their cloaks.

"Who are you? Tell me why you're doing this?"

"Shut up, Angel."

"But if it's money you're after, I know I could—"

"I said, shut *up!*" he snarled. Turning to the gondolier, he rattled off some questions or instructions, again in Italian.

"It won't be long now, signorina *belissima*," he murmured with a chuckle, and leaned back comfortably, as if certain he no longer had anything to fear.

A graceful bridge arched across the obsidian water ahead of them. Behind it, the velvety midnight blue of the night sky was spangled with a million golden stars, like a wizard's cape. A bell tower rose beyond it, silhouetted by the huge, round moon, floating high and free as a globe of Venetian crystal. It was a beautiful night, Angel thought miserably, her stomach feeling as if it were tied in knots of fear. She shivered as the gondola glided beneath the bridge into absolute darkness, wondering if he intended to rape then kill her. Tears choked her throat. *Please, help me, God!* she prayed. She didn't want to die! It was far, far too beautiful a night for whatever awful fate her captor had in mind for her—

The gondola lurched violently off-balance as a man dropped from beneath the bridge!

He landed on all fours behind the gondolier, like a cat, and at once managed to stagger upright in the flat-bottomed craft. As the gondola's reeling prow nosed out from under the bridge, Angel recognized his silhouette. She shouted, "Nick! Oh, thank God!"

With Nick's arrival, her fear fled and anger replaced it. Furious, she turned and shoved her abductor in the belly as hard as she could. But, instead of falling obligingly onto his back, he reached out and gripped her wrist before yanking her to her feet.

"Let me go, you pig!" she spat, tearing at his fingers.

With all the movement, the gondola rocked dangerously, threatening to spill them all into the water.

"Hey, have a care, you rogue!" Geraldo exclaimed. Deciding Nick was the guilty party, he swung at him with his oar. Nick ducked. He leaped across the gondola and made a grab for the other man, but he heard his muffled chuckle as he jerked Angel off her feet and stopped dead in his tracks.

"Let her go, *hombre*," he ordered with deadly softness.

"You want her? Here, take her! She's yours!" the man crowed, and before Nick could stop him, he'd turned and shoved Angel over the side, headfirst into the canal!

Under normal circumstances she was a strong swimmer, but her cloak, skirts, and petticoats were tangled about her limbs. The wet clothing dragged her down, making swimming impossible!

She hit the water and went under like a stone, without drawing so much as a single breath. There was nothing but blackness all about her; water filled her lungs. Choking, she tried to fight her way up to the surface, but failed. Oh, God! The wet folds of the cloak had wrapped about her, pinning her arms to her sides!

She tried to kick out, but even her strongest kicks were useless—less than useless!—with the weight of her petticoats and boots weighing them down. As she struggled, the watery blackness closed in around her, filling her mind as it filled her lungs, driving out thought, eroding all will. . . .

"Bastard!" Nick roared. He swung at the man, but in his haste, the roundhouse punch missed his jaw and slammed into his shoulder instead. He toppled backwards into the gondola—which had taken on water now—as Nick

hauled off his boots and dived into the canal.

Black water—water and darkness everywhere! Where the hell was she? Holding his breath, he dived beneath the surface, as close as he could remember where she'd fallen in, then swam back and forth, feeling with his hands for her, thanking God when at last, he encountered her limp body. He hooked his arm beneath her chin and brought her to the surface, hoping against hope that she was still alive, silently offering up every prayer that Mamacíta and Tía Magdalena had taught him that he was not too late, that she was not dead.

The gondolier had poled his craft to some nearby steps and moored her to one of the red-and-white striped mooring poles that jutted up from the water. When he saw Nick resurfacing with the girl, he dived in and helped him to carry Angel up the steps of the Piazza Santa Maria.

Nick knelt beside her, his tan face ashen as he unfastened her red cape and unwound the folds. Her glorious honey gold hair was streaming rattails now, her face bluish white in the flickering torchlight, her gray eyes closed. She was as still as death, a sleeping beauty! Pressing an ear to her chest, he could discern no signs of life.

"No, damn it!" he rasped. "No!"

Grimly, Nick rolled her over, onto her stomach, and turned her limp head to one side. Drawing both of her elbows up, he firmly pressed the middle of her back. Dirty canal water spewed from her mouth and nostrils. He repeated his actions once, twice, and on the third effort, she coughed and sputtered and drew a deep, shuddering breath. Color returned immediately to her cheeks and bloodless mouth. Closing his eyes momentarily, he offered up a heartfelt prayer of thanks.

"Nicky?"

He looked up and saw Sophia standing there.

"I'll take care of the signorina for you. Me and my cousins will see her safely back to your hotel, yes? You must go after that—bastard!"

Nick agreed. There was nothing he would have liked better than to get his hands on him!

But despite a good hour spent searching the square, the surrounding alleys, and even extending his efforts to the harbor of Marghera, where Geraldo, the gondolier, said he'd asked to be taken, and despite the help of Sophia's Uncle Giacomo and his friends, Nick recovered only the man's blue satin cape and hawk mask.

He returned to the hotel exhausted, but brightened considerably on finding Angel cozily tucked in her bed amidst a half dozen feather pillows and feather quilts. Sophia had been true to her word. Angel had been bathed, her hair had been dried and brushed out, a fresh nightgown had been slipped over her head, and then a doctor had been summoned to examine her and ensure that she was none the worse for her ordeal. She was obediently swallowing the hot broth Claudia was spooning into her when he entered the room. The smile that lit her face when she saw him was worth a million dollars in gold!

"Nick! Oh, Nick, thank you! You saved my life! But, that awful man—did you find him?"

He shook his head. "'Fraid not. Are you all right, sweet thing?" he asked gruffly.

"Better than I dared to hope a short while ago—thanks to these charming ladies. We've been getting acquainted. I understand they're friends of yours? That they used to be nuns at the Catholic School you attended?"

"Hmm, something like that," he agreed evasively, and cleared his throat.

"Isn't that wonderful—and what a coincidence that they should be here in Venice at just the right time to run into you!" Angel murmured.

Nick shot her a startled glance, but if she was suspicious or doubted the tall story the gals had told her in any part, she was doing a hell of a job of hiding it!

"So, Nicky, how long will you and Signorina Angel be staying in Venice?"

Angel shuddered. "I don't know about Nick, but I'm ready to leave for Rome first thing tomorrow morning, after what happened tonight."

"Rome isa no good. They 'ave typhoid there! Seven new cases since yesterday, according to the newspaper. Better

361

you not go, eh?"

"Surely the risk of catching it in such a big city would be slight?"

"I agree with Sophia," Nick said with a frown. "It's safer not to take any chances."

"Well, now that you isa back, we musta be going! Uncle Giacomo, he has invited us all to his home for supper, you see? *Ciao*, Nicky, Angelica. You two, take care of each other, eh?" Sophia instructed.

"*Si*. And Nicky, if you should ever be in Milan . . . ? Claudia reminded him, following Sophia.

"I promise, I'll be sure to look you ga—sisters—up."

"Good night, little lovebirds!" Gina murmured. She blew Nick a kiss as she followed her cousins through the door.

"What wonderful young women," Angel declared, leaning back on her pillows after they'd left. "Former nuns, but still so very devout. Did you know that Claudia has taken a vow of chastity, although she left the sisterhood?"

"What a gal that Claudia is, huh?" Nick agreed wryly, shaking his head as he peeled off his still-damp clothing. Naked, he found a clean towel and briskly toweled his hair, then dried his body, before slipping beneath the covers with Angel.

At once, she snuggled up to him, winding her arms around his chest. "My poor Nick. You must be exhausted! The girls told me what you did. And the way you dropped down from that bridge—oh, it was wonderful!"

"Did you drop the mask in the canal on purpose, hoping I'd find it?"

"Yes! And did you?"

He nodded. "That was how I figured out you might be inside Geraldo's gondola. Just a hunch, true, but as it turned out, a damned good one."

"It was, indeed."

"Angel, you didn't get a look at that sidewinder's face did you?"

"I'm afraid not. He kept the mask on the whole time. You know, I've been thinking about that. I've come to the conclusion it means one of two things. Either he knew I would have recognized him without it—which means he's probably one of the kidnappers from Paris. Or else he simply wanted to keep his identity hidden. Hmm. Come to think of it, that observation's not much help to us, unless we have some way of knowing which!"

"Unfortunately not. . . . My bet is that he's got nothing to do with the other attempts. That he's *loco*—crazy. That he saw us this morning when we were sightseeing and decided he wanted you for himself. So, he bought himself a costume like mine, bided his time until he saw you alone—and the rest is old news."

"You could be right. He spoke Italian fluently and his English did sound peculiar. I'd agree with you—except for one thing."

"And what's that?" Nick asked, stroking her hair.

"He called me 'Angel.'"

Chapter Twenty-Nine

The news of the outbreak of typhoid in Rome was especially disturbing to Nick, who'd seen victims of the terrible disease firsthand in his travels through the West as a youth. He doggedly refused to take any unnecessary risks by visiting the city, despite Angel's observation that with so few cases confirmed, their chances of catching the disease were slight.

"Maybe so, but those are odds I won't gamble on. Rome's been around for a spell, Angel," he reminded her wryly. "I reckon it'll still be standing next year, Lord willin'! You can always come back. Meantime, we're making tracks for Cairo."

"But Mabel and Juarez are expecting us in Rome!"

"I'll send them a wire. We can meet them in Egypt, instead."

Though disappointed that she would have to postpone seeing the Vatican City, and Michelangelo's "Last Judgment" and glorious Old Testament paintings in the Sistine Chapel, Angel had to agree it was the most sensible, safest thing to do.

Accordingly, telegraphs were sent to Juarez and Mabel to advise them of the change in plans; their goodbyes were said to Sophia, Claudia, Gina, and the plump little widow, Mama Lydia, who'd run their hotel, and on a hot, sunny August morning, they sailed from Venice aboard the *Circe*.

The *Circe*, a trim white yacht, was captained by a wonderful Greek named Miklos, who regaled them with outrageous fishing stories by day, and sang them naughty Greek love songs at night. He also prepared them wonderful Greek meals, using olives and *feta* cheese, eggplant, grape leaves, and other exotic items. The *Circe* carried them swiftly across the calm, sparkling deep blue waters of the Mediterranean, and under such idyllic sailing conditions, Angel suffered none of the mal de mer she'd experienced aboard the fishy *Pelican* and enjoyed herself tremendously.

By day, Nick and Angel took to sunning themselves stretched out in deck chairs upon the *Circe's* decks, drinking long, cool glasses of fruit juice. Sometimes, they slipped over the *Circe's* side and swam in the warm turquoise water, while Miklos watched them, nodding and smiling approval like a benevolent gnome.

Each starry night, they squeezed together in the single bunk in Angel's tiny cabin, laughing and giggling at the naughty edge the inconvenience added to their lovemaking, which lasted until the rosy circle of sky through the porthole promised dawn was imminent.

Soon, they saw the magical island of Crete off their port bow, while to starboard lay the coast of Africa. They followed the coastline until at last, the *Circe* dropped anchor in the fine harbor of Port Said, where the Nile Delta spread its green and fertile fingers. Here they bade farewell to the *Circe* and Miklos, and boarded another, smaller vessel that would carry them up the fabled waters of the Nile to the ancient city of Cairo.

Angel shaded her eyes and looked about her in delight as they disembarked, for Cairo was everything she'd imagined, a beautiful city of blinding white buildings, fairy-tale towers, mosques, and minarets, that seemed exotic beyond her wildest dreams!

Lofty palms tossed fronded heads high above the wharves, where handsome, dark-eyed natives called to each other in singsong Arabic as they toiled to load the waiting vessels with cargoes of cotton, silk, brassware, spices, and dates. Camels and donkeys were everywhere, too, swaying sedately or gamely plodding along, bearing their native masters or a bulging load of some sort with stoic indifference. Canopied carriages were much in evidence, as were two-wheeled ox carts, wagons, and even a handful of bamboo rickshaws, borrowed from another land.

Nick good-naturedly waved aside the beggars and fruit-sellers that clamored about them and, taking Angel by the elbow, led her to where a number of canopied carriages waited beneath a shady awning.

They rode up from the wharves to the hotel in one of the mule-drawn gharrys, or open carriages, that were for hire. Their vehicle—which boasted a smart red fringe about its canopy and matching red wheels—was driven by a talkative native driver named Hanif, who fancied himself a tour guide. He gave them a running commentary in fractured English as he guided his mule through the crush of the Cairo wharves.

"Cairo is a marvelous place, don't you know? Very fine hotels. Very fine shops for the missie. You will enjoy very much your holidays here—this I promise. You are liking to go some place, Hanif will take you in his very fine gharry. Ah, look, young American master! Finest Egyptian cotton! It is bound for the most splendid cotton mills of that fairest of queens, Victoria of England, May Allah bless her!" he observed.

He yanked sharply on the reins to steer his mule around an enormous mountain of cotton bales awaiting lading, and almost flattened one of the barechested, brown-skinned *fellahin* toiling beneath the blistering sun in the process. Seemingly unconcerned by the near accident, he bellowed, "Out of my way, thou slow-footed oaf! Make room for Hanif and his honored passengers!" He flashed them a gold-filled smile and whipped his poor mule into a trot.

In no time, they'd been whisked through Cairo's wide boulevards, lined with lofty Royal palms, past the white-walled consulates and offices of the European quarter, to the section of Cairo where the fine hotels that catered to European visitors were to be found.

The Grand Sphinx Hotel was no exception. Bowered by still more palms, her walls white and opulent, her facade embellished with enormous white columns that looked

366

like medieval drum towers, mysterious with arched entryways and grilled windows, the hotel had the sumptuous appearance of a sultan's castle, rather than a place of lodging!

The hotel proved little less exotic on the inside. The lobby floors were of pale green marble. Fronded palms potted in brass containers were much in evidence, as were beaded curtains that cleverly divided some areas from others. The overstuffed chairs scattered about seemed incongruous in such a setting, which was more fitted to lounging upon brocade divans heaped with plump, tasseled pillows, in Angel's opinion.

Nick led the way to the front desk and exchanged a few words with the desk clerk before signing the register.

"Mabel and Juarez beat us to it," he told Angel.

Her brows rose. "They're here already?"

"According to the register, they are."

"I can't wait to see Mabel again!" Angel exclaimed. Realizing what she'd said, she smiled ruefully. "My, how I've changed! I never thought the day would come when I'd say that about Mabel!"

Nick chuckled, staring at something—or someone— over her shoulder. "Well, you'd better think of some more nice things to say about her—'cos here she comes now!"

"Well, blow me down wiv a feather, if it ain't Her Royal Majesty, in the flesh!" Mabel exclaimed, swooping across the lobby in Angel's direction. "About bloody time, too, I say. Wot kept yer, ducks?"

Angel giggled and ran to meet her. "Oh, Mabel, bless you, you never change, do you?"

"Me? Change?" Mabel grinned. "Nah, luv. In't no sense in *me* changing, now is there? See, yer can't improve on perfection!"

"You look wonderful—positively radiant!" Angel told her later, in her hotel room, where she'd gone to freshen up and change, so that she and Nick might join the Juarezes for luncheon. Taking Mabel's hands in her own, she kissed her cheek. "Congratulations! I'm truly very, very happy for you both."

"Ow, you!" Mabel sniffed, but she beamed with

367

pleasure, nonetheless. "Ta ever so, ducks. But I can't take no credit for 'ow I look. It's all due t' love, in'it? I 'spose what's inside a body shows up on the outside, sooner or later."

As she spoke, Mabel glanced over Angel's shoulder at her reflection in the dresser mirror and patted her hair. Its virulent red-dyed coloring had grown out over the weeks since Angel had last seen her, but for a few hennaed inches at the ends. These she'd artfully woven into a knot of curls that spilled charmingly about her nape. The softer reddish brown of her natural hair coloring was very flattering, as was the modest yet attractive lavender morning gown with pristine white collar and cuffs that she sported—a new addition to her somewhat frowsy wardrobe since she'd seen her last, Angel noted. Why, Mabel looked positively pretty now. Younger. More settled. Blooming!

"You know, I 'aven't touched a drop of 'Mother's ruin' since we left the Towers," Mabel confided, whispering although they were quite alone in Angel's room.

"I'm glad to hear it, Mabel. Clearly, love and marriage have succeeded where my efforts failed! You've never looked better," Angel admitted, a trifle enviously. "How did it happen?"

"Me gettin' wed, ye mean?"

"Yes. Do tell me!"

Angel finished dressing while Mabel perched on the bed to tell her story.

"Well, after we got t' Rome, Warez checked us inter the hotel, an' I realized right off that he planned on the two o' us sharin' a suite—you know, like in Paris? Well, that did it! 'Excuse me, sir!' I told him. 'We'll have none o' those naughty goings-on here. Me, share a suite with you? Alone? Not bleedin' likely! My name'll be dirt, it will,' I sez. 'Me poor dead mother'll be turnin' bloody cartwheels in 'er grave, she will!' I tells him. She raised me proper, warned me t' be a good girl, Ma did. 'Don't you give them lads wot they're after 'til ye've a ring on yer finger, Mabel, ducks,' she always used ter say. 'Keep yer legs t'gevver, 'cos them randy sods won't go buying the whole bloody cow when the bloomin' milk's free, now, will they?' Me ma was ever so clever, she was. An' despite what me big mouth might ha' led you to believe, I listened to 'er, I did. Went to me marriage bed a virgin, didn't I?" she added proudly. "Anyway, I told Warez, all prim an' proper, 'It's not like we was married, after all, is it?'" Here Mabel grinned, remembering. "Well, that got 'im thinking on the right track, didn't it?' 'Married?' sez he, them spaniel eyes o' his lookin' all sad and thoughtful. 'You mean, you would marry me?' 'That depends,' sez I. 'Are you askin', luv?' I sez, looking flustered. 'I am,' sez he. 'Well, then, me answer's yes,' sez I. And that were it!" She giggled. "We were wed by special license the very next day. Imagine that—me, Mabel Blunt, married to a Spanish nob! Who'd have thought it!"

"A Spanish nob?"

Mable nodded. "Warez's grandad was a Spanish don, see—that's sorta like an English 'sir' or a 'lord,' ye know—one o' them forrun titles? Don Carlos, 'is grandad was called. Like as not, I'm Lady Mabel or summat now, *Miss* Higgins! Happen you'll 'ave t' curtsey t' me, an' all—!" she added with a mischievous wink.

Angel grinned. "I'd be happy to. You've done very well for yourself, in more ways than one. Good for you!"

"I have, haven't I? But, wot about you and Nick? The two o'yer, all alone—all those weeks . . . ?"

Angel frowned and sighed. "Ah, yes, Nick. I rather fancy some of your wise mother's advice would have benefitted me," she said ruefully.

"Uh oh. Gave the milk away fer free, did ye, ducks?" Mabel commiserated.

"I love him so," Angel said simply and with such a woe-begone expression, it cut the other woman to the heart. "I love him—but he doesn't love me!"

"He told you that?"

Angel nodded. "More or less. He said—he said he'd been badly burned by a love affair in the past. That he doubted he could love anyone, let alone me."

"Oww, what a load of cod's wallop!! But it'll be that Savannah cow he's talkin' about, I suppose. Now, there's a right bad lot!"

"He told you about her?" Angel exclaimed, burning with curiosity. Nick's manner that night at Villa Allegra hadn't encouraged her to ask questions, though she'd been dying to hear the whole story.

"Warez did, though he wouldn't say much. Said it weren't his place t' talk about Nick's business. Anyway, the way I heard it, your Nick was fixin' to marry that Savannah chit. He went orf t' buy her a weddin' ring, but when he come back, unexpected, like, he caught that trollop red-handed. In bed with another man!"

"No!" Angel exclaimed, deeply shocked. "That's awful!"

"And that ain't the worst of it, neither," Mabel continued with a darkling look. "The man she were with was Nick's dad."

"His own *father?* Oh, dear Lord! That poor, poor man."

"Poor ain't the word fer it! Anyway, he found out later that while he was gone, she'd up an' married him, too! Oww, it were a terrible blow, to all accounts. Took poor ole Nick right in the bread basket, it did—knocked the bloody wind out o' his sails, good an' proper. That's why he and my Warez joined the Wild West Show. Your Nick wanted ter get away from New Mexico, you know, ter forget? He and Warez were close, so Warez decided to go with him."

There came a knock on the door. *"Querida? Senorita Angel?* Are you ready to go down to luncheon?"

"Oops! That's me old man, ducks. Sounds as if he's starvin', don't he, bless 'im? Are you ready yet? I am—ready an' rarin'! They serve up some smashin' grub here. Get a move on, do."

Angel nodded absently, still thinking about what Mabel had told her. If true—and she had no reason to think it wasn't—it helped to explain Nick's determination not to fall in love again as nothing else had. "Once bitten twice shy"—wasn't that how the saying went?

"I'll get my hat and we'll be on our way," she promised Mabel, who was clearly chafing to be off.

The kitchens of the Grand Sphinx Hotel were staffed with some of the finest chefs in the world, and the meal was as delicious as Mabel had promised. The large number of patrons luncheoning in the opulent dining room proved that she was not alone in her opinions of the "smashin' grub" served there!

For luncheon they enjoyed a delicate consommé, followed by tender slices of roasted lamb with a pearl-onion sauce; savory rice with tiny pieces of vegetables and morsels of meat accompanied it, along with salads. The dessert was equally delicious, a sort of flaky pastry layered with honey and nuts, accompanied by tiny cups of thick, sweet coffee.

"Good?" Nick asked, smiling as Angel pushed her plate away and sighed.

"I couldn't eat another bite!" she confessed.

"O' course you couldn't ducks. You've et everything already!" Mabel teased, giving her a nudge in the ribs.

They all laughed.

"Miss Higgins?"

"Why, yes. What is it?" Angel asked, smiling up at the native waiter, wearing white robes and red fez, who hovered at her elbow.

"There is a gentleman in the smoking room asking after you. He said he did not wish to intrude upon your luncheon, but asked me to tell you that he wishes to speak with you as soon as you have finished your meal. He awaits you in the saloon."

"Oh? Did he leave his name?"

"I'm afraid not, missie."

"Tell him Miss Higgins will be right there," Nick cut in. "I'll come with you, Angel."

"We'll all go," Juarez added, standing and pushing back his chair and helping his wife with hers.

The saloon, a cavernous room with high ceilings and arched doorways, was wreathed with cigar smoke. The divans and overstuffed chairs scattered in small, intimate groups about low rattan tables on the marble floor were occupied for the most part by elderly retired gentlemen, enjoying a drink and a good afterluncheon cigar. One portly, pompous old fellow with a heavily bandaged leg was arguing with one of the waiters, complaining that the poor fellow'd put too much soda water in his whisky. His loud voice carried like a fog horn. The smokers and drinkers ignored him, but looked up in frank curiosity and displeasure at the two young women who'd invaded the saloon's masculine domain. The rotund gentleman, however, ceased his grumbling for long enough to give Angel an appreciative, ogling glance better suited to a far younger man.

Angel looked about, but could see no familiar faces.

"Please to follow me this way, missie," the waiter murmured, bowing. He led them through the saloon to a distant, cozy corner, hidden by fronded potted palms.

"Angel, my dear! How very good it is to see you again!" cried the man seated in an armchair there. He rose to greet her, casting the newspaper he'd been reading aside.

"Uncle Teddy! How wonderful to see you!" she exclaimed, returning the hug he gave her. "But—what on earth are you doing here in Egypt?" Her smile wavered. "Nothing's wrong—? My da! He's all right, isn't he?"

"Come, my dear girl. Sit down, and I'll tell you why I'm here. First of all, there's no need for alarm. There has been an accident—but nothing too serious, thank God."

"An accident?" she whispered.

"Yes, I'm afraid so. Your father took a fall about a week ago—from that feisty chestnut hunter he acquired before you left?"

Dry-mouthed, she nodded.

"Well, my dear, I'm afraid he's laid up with a broken hip. And, since he's likely to be bedridden for quite some time to come, he's anxious to have his little Annie back home, to see to his care. He sent me to fetch you, post-haste. I arrived on the *Cleopatra* two days ago, expecting you'd be here, but to my surprise, I discovered otherwise. I telegraphed the hotel in Rome, and they wired back that you'd never arrived! Angelica, I've been dreadfully worried about you."

"We were somewhat delayed in Italy. I was ill myself . . . then we spent a week in Venice . . . and then, en route to Rome, we heard that several typhoid cases had been reported there, and so we decided to come straight here instead. It's a long story, but never mind all that for now. I'll tell you all about it later. Tell me about my poor da. Is he—is he in terrible pain?"

"I'm sure he must be, but you know dear old Sid, he never complains. What a brick the man is!" Teddy Hardcastle frowned. She looked so pale, suddenly. "I say, old girl, I do so hate to be the bearer of these bad tidings. I promised you I'd take care of him, didn't I? I've let you down dreadfully! Are you sure you're quite all right?" Tears had filled her eyes now. "Perhaps a stiff brandy—?"

"No, really. And it's not your fault—please don't think I'm blaming you. I—I just hate to think of Da suffering, of him being bedridden—he's always hated being helpless. Tell me, when are we to leave?"

"There's a liner, the *Empress of Egypt*, sailing for England in one week. I took the liberty of booking berths for us upon her. You do approve?"

"Oh, of course. But a week . . . There's nothing leaving sooner?"

"Alas, no. It was the best I could do."

"I'm sure it was. And I suppose we'll just have to be patient 'til then. What other choice do we have?"

"None, I'm afraid. But I'm certain Sidney wouldn't want you to worry. A week isn't such a long time. And besides, Sidney's in no danger. Merely uncomfortable. I suggest, since you've just arrived here, that you enjoy the sights of Cairo, stick to your plans as if nothing has happened. The time will pass more quickly that way, my dear girl."

"You're right as usual, Uncle Teddy," Angel murmured, flashing the dear, sweet man a grateful smile. Poor thing, he obviously felt terrible at being the bearer of bad news! "And what about you? Have you seen the fabled pyramids yet?"

"No, worse luck. I haven't left the hotel since my arrival, I was so anxious to speak with you the moment you got here. But, now that I've told you about your father, well, I certainly intend to see them while I'm here! Perhaps I could escort you? I'm sure Durango would welcome a brief respite from his duties?"

"That would be lovely!" Angel agreed, quite unaware that Nick was now bristling. "You don't mind, do you, Nick?" she asked airily over her shoulder.

"Oh, not at all, Miz Higgins," he gritted sarcastically,

tugging at an imaginary forelock in peasant fashion—a gesture that Angel was too preoccupied to notice. "A respite from my duties'd be just fine about now!"

"Good man!" Hardcastle murmured. "When would you care to go, my dear?"

"Why not right now? The pyramids aren't far from the city, I understand?"

"Ten miles into the desert. It'd be pitch dark by the time you headed back."

"I say, what a topping idea! Seeing the pyramids by moonlight would be a once-in-a-lifetime experience," Uncle Teddy exclaimed, ignoring Nick's comment.

"Indeed it would. But as Nick said, it'd be awfully late by the time we got back.... And besides, I've half promised Mabel we could visit the native bazaars this afternoon. Or perhaps do a little sightseeing in the city..." She shrugged expressively and gave Hardcastle an apologetic smile. "Tomorrow morning would be a much more sensible time for our excursion, don't you think?"

"Very well, as you wish. Tomorrow morning it is, then. I'll have a gharry waiting at say, tenish?"

"Perfect! Oh, it's so wonderful to see you again!"

"And you, my dear. I'll be looking forward to tomorrow's outing."

"As will I."

"What's this then? A council o' war?" Mabel inquired, for she'd returned to their suite later that afternoon to find Nick stretched out comfortably on their bed wearing his natty black Western get-up, complete with stilt-heeled, silver-trimmed boots. Her husband had pulled a straight-backed chair close to the bed. He straddled it backwards while they talked.

Nick jumped from the bed and guiltily smoothed down the rumpled coverlet. "Sorry, Red. I keep forgetting ole Juarez here ain't footloose and fancy-free anymore. Bad habits die hard."

"Never mind bad habits. Wot're you two up to?" she demanded suspiciously. The air'd been thick enough to

374

cut with a knife when she entered the room, and the all-too-innocent expressions the men wore was a dead giveaway that what they were up to was anything *but* innocent!

Juarez coughed. "Nick has decided it's high time he confronted those *diablos*—got them out in the open before they make their final move, *querida*. Cairo is the last city on the *señorita's* itinerary—and their last chance to abduct her before we return to England. After failing in Paris, Venice, and Rome, they must be desperate, *no?* They'll make their move here—and they'll do it soon."

"Sounds good—but we in't seen hide nor hair of them buggers since we left Rome. Couldn't we 'ave lorst 'em?"

"I don't reckon so—not for a minute," Nick disagreed. "Since Paris, they've stuck closer to us than a tick on a hound dog's tail. They're out there somewhere, waiting, watching, or I'll eat—" He grimaced and amended, "—or my name's not Nick Durango."

"You say you want ter bring 'em out in the open, right?" Mabel said thoughtfully, her index finger pressed to her chin.

"Right. We want the man behind those sidewinders—the one who's jerking their chains, calling all the shots."

"But how'll you do it?"

Nick shrugged. "We don't know how—yet. That's what your husband and I were discussing when you came in."

"Any good ideas?"

"None so far."

"Well, I've got one. An' it'll work, too—*if* it's done right," Mabel opined with the shrewd air of a seasoned strategist.

Nick and Juarez exchanged amused glances.

"Where's Angel?"

"Fast asleep in her room. This bloomin' heat an' all the sightseeing we did this afternoon wore her out, poor lamb," Mabel revealed with a grin. "I reckon as how she'll sleep 'til dinner time."

"Good. She's been like a cat on hot bricks since that incident in Venice. And now she's worried about her father, too . . . I'd as soon not tell her what we've got planned, unless we have to?"

"Mum's the word, ducks. Cross me 'eart and hope ter die! So. Wot now? Do you want ter hear me idea, or not?" Mabel asked impatiently.

"All right, Red. Fire away." Nick urged.

On her way downstairs the following morning, Angel paused to knock on Nick's door.

After dinner the evening before, he'd complained that he was feeling out of sorts, had left the table, and retired to his hotel room alone. Angel had been concerned, and she said as much to Juarez. In all the time she'd spent with Nick, she'd never known him to be unwell before. But when she said that she intended to look in on him before retiring for the night, Juarez had hastily suggested she should not.

In a somewhat shamefaced manner, Juarez had confessed that while she and Mabel were out sightseeing that afternoon, he and Nick had gone carousing in one of the dark little native taverns, and that Nick's attack of the "grippe" was more than likely the aftereffects of too much drinking!

Then, early that morning, Nick'd sent Mabel to her room with the message that although feeling much better, he was still a little under the weather and would see her after she returned from her jaunt with Uncle Teddy. It had sounded perfectly plausible, but for some reason, Angel had the strongest intuition they were all lying to her, though she could think of no reason why they should.

Receiving no answer to her knock, she shrugged and went downstairs, running into Juarez on the way down.

"Good morning!"

"And to you, señorita!"

"Thank you. Juarez, I knocked at Nick's door just now, but there was no answer. Is he in there?"

"He is—and fast asleep, señorita. Tell me, will you be going to the pyramids with your uncle as planned?"

"Of course—that is, unless you think I should stay here with Nick?"

"*No!*" Juarez coughed and smiled apologetically. "What I meant was, no, there is no need for you to stay.

Should he need me, I will take good care of him, never fear. And perhaps next time, he will remember this little lesson and know when enough is enough, eh? Look, there's your uncle, over there."

"So he is. Good morning, Uncle Teddy. Here I am!" Angel sang out gaily as they crossed the lobby to meet him. Nattily dressed in a Panama hat and sporting a beige suit, white gloves, and walking cane for the tropical clime, he cut a dashing figure, she thought fondly. "I'm all set to see the fabled pyramids in the company of my distinguished escort!"

"So I see, my dear. And how very charming you look, too," Uncle Teddy complimented her, smiling. "Just as fresh and lovely as a daisy!"

Angel smiled, basking in his praises. Today, she wore a pastel-flowered white muslin gown with puffy leg o'mutton sleeves and a high, ruffled neck. The cuffs and neckline were trimmed with tiny bands of broderie anglaise and porcelain buttons. Upon her upswept hair, she sported a broad-brimmed pink straw hat with a filmy pale pink scarf wrapped about the crown, the ends left trailing. The hat matched the long strand of pink glass beads wound about her throat—the ones she'd bought in Paris on one of her and Mabel's afternoon shopping sprees on Rue St. Honoré. She'd had no occasion to wear them, 'til now. White kid shoes, white gloves, and a lace-edged parasol completed her ensemble. She felt wonderful, more herself again than she had in ages, for this morning was the first time since she'd jumped from the train upon leaving Paris that she'd felt properly dressed in her own clothes!

"You're far too kind, good sir," she rejoined gaily, holding out her skirts and making Teddy Hardcastle a deep, graceful curtsy. "Shall we be on our way? I'm sure you have a carriage waiting, and I'm so looking forward to seeing the pyramids—!"

"Quite so, my dear. As am I! But first, I'm afraid we must make a short detour to the British Consulate. I ran into someone in the lobby here yesterday evening, after I spoke with you. Someone I believe it's very important that you talk to," he added mysteriously.

"Oh? Who is it?"

Teddy glanced across at Juarez and grimaced. He was still hovering at Angel's elbow and eavesdropping shamelessly on their conversation. He shot him a meaningful look, leaned toward Angel and murmured in a low, confidential voice, "I'd rather not say just yet, if it's all the same to you, my dear? I thought we'd get this—er—business over with, then ride on out to the pyramids. Perhaps we could have a late tea together at the Grand?"

"Splendid!"

"Shall I find you a gharry, Señor Hardcastle?" Juarez offered.

"Thank you, but I have one waiting. Shall we, Angelica?" He offered Angel his arm.

Juarez followed them outside to where a gharry waited in the cool, dark shadow cast by the enormous hotel. The driver was dozing under the canopy, his mule looking equally bored and moth-eaten as it whisked flies away with its tail.

Angel looked about appreciatively. Towering palms lined the broad boulevard, which basked in a shimmering midmorning heat haze. The dust thrown up by passing gharries, other wheeled vehicles, camels, ox-drawn carts, donkeys, and scores of pedestrians—some Europeans, dressed in tropical whites and kepis, other natives wearing flowing white robes—only added to the exotic, foreign atmosphere of heat and haze. On the opposite side of the street, squatting like a mushroom between two tall, white office buildings, flying French flags, and a mosque with a pretty minaret, was a dark little café with striped awnings. European tourists occupied most of the tables, enjoying cool glasses of sherbet or fruit juice or tiny cupfuls of thick, sweet coffee. It was no wonder such places seemed to do brisk trade! The heat made one thirsty all the time, she'd found yesterday, and drained one's energy in no time. . . .

"Angel? Angelica, dear!"

"Hmm? Oh, sorry, Uncle. I was daydreaming!"

"May I assist you?"

"Of course."

Uncle Teddy handed her up into the carriage, then

378

sprang up after her and took his seat.

"Señorita y señor, have a wonderful day!" Juarez urged, smiling. "And don't hurry back, señorita. I will take good care of Nick—this I promise you."

With a lurch, the gharry rumbled off, leaving Juarez standing there, waving and smiling more broadly than before.

Chapter Thirty

Nick slipped through the door of Angel's hotel room, using the key he'd pocketed earlier that day, to find Juarez already there and waiting for him, as they'd planned.

"About time!" Juarez murmured, scowling. "I'd begun to think you'd run off with my woman, *hombre!*"

"Can't say I didn't think about it," Nick shot back with a grin. "So? Where's Angel? Did you manage to get her away from the hotel?"

"As luck would have it, *sí!*—and I didn't have to do a thing!" Juarez' scowl dissolved into a smile. "She left with Señor Hardcastle—something about having an appointment at the British Consulate? She has not returned."

"Perfect." Nick nodded in satisfaction.

"And where is my little red flower, my beloved bride?"

"Safe and sound in your suite, pardner, taking a well-deserved rest. You know, I have to admit I was wrong. Your little lady's plan and her disguise worked like a charm. Our 'friends' were on our tails the moment we left the hotel."

"And you're certain they did not suspect the woman with you was not Señorita Angelica?" Juarez asked, his dark eyes anxious. Though Mabel had been determined to take part—even eager to play the decoy and pretend to be Angel—he'd been reluctant to expose his bride to danger.

"Not a chance! Hell, they stuck with me and Red through a tour of the pyramids, a stroll through the native quarter and the bazaar, and skulked in an alley while your missus bought three carpets, a shawl, and some other female fol-de-rols I didn't pay much mind to! They were still trailing us when we came back to the hotel, so I reckon it won't be long now. You can vamoose whenever you're good n' ready. From here on, it's my show, pardner," Nick murmured, clamping his hand over his cousin's shoulder in thanks. "Go ahead, go join your little lady. Take her out for the fanciest supper in town—my treat! God knows, she earned it! There were times she even had *me* convinced she was Angel!"

"Leave—and let you have all the fun with those two *hombres?*" Juarez snorted, rolling his eyes. "Think again, Don Nicholas!"

"Aw, don't be a fool, Juarez. You're a married man now. Don't take chances—you have a wife to think of," Nick reminded him soberly.

"*Sí.* And if I let you do this alone, *mi querida* Mabella would never let me forget it! *Aiiee, Diós,* I would spend the next ten years sleeping in the *ramada.* No, Nick. I'm staying!"

"Okay, you ornery cuss. But, don't say I didn't warn you—! So. What'll it be? The bed or the wardrobe?"

Juarez grinned evilly as he withdrew a hunting knife from his belt. He ran the ball of his thumb down the blade. A thread of blood welled instantly. "I'll take the bed. I like the idea of those *diablos* pulling back the covers, expecting the señorita, but instead finding me—with this!" He gestured with the wicked skinning knife and frowned thoughtfully. "I think I'll introduce them to my *amigo,* Panther-Who-Stalks, too."

It was Nick's turn to grin now. "You son of a gun! I'd bet hard money you won't be what those rattlers are expecting—but you'll sure as hell be what they deserve!"

Nick drew his gun, sighted down the barrel of the Colt, and spun the chamber. "If this setup works, *amigo,* there's no way in hell they're leavin' here without telling me everything I want to know, starting with who they're working for. And maybe—hell, who knows?—maybe not even then . . . ?"

The two men exchanged glances. Neither Angel nor Mabel would have liked what they saw in Nick and Juarez's faces in that moment.

"No, thank you. I would not care to take tea, or lemonade, or anything else! Rather, I would like to know exactly what it is you're trying to say, Inspector Jamieson?" Angel demanded impatiently. "Please come to the point, without mincing words!" She scowled. Nick, Mabel, and probably Juarez, too, were up to something, she just knew it. She was itching to get back to the hotel and find out why they'd wanted her out of the way for the afternoon! The hasty way Juarez had bundled her and Uncle Teddy into the gharry, and the broad grin he'd worn as he did so, had been highly suspicious. . . .

But, here she was, instead, and that dratted Scottish haggis of a detective was still dithering, as he'd been doing ever since Uncle Teddy had escorted her into the offices of the British Consulate almost an hour ago.

He'd been rabbiting on, slyly hinting that *Nick* had been involved in the attempts to kidnap her, of all the preposterous ideas, without once having the courage to come right out and say what he meant! Her initial shock at seeing the horrid inspector here, in Cairo, had rapidly dwindled, as had her patience, once it'd dawned on her that he'd come to Cairo on a wild goose chase!

"Verra well. I can be blunt, if you insist! I'm saying that ye mustna see the American again, Miss Higgins!" a redfaced Inspector Jamieson declared, slamming his fist down on the desk. "That I canna guarantee your safety, if ye do. There! That's it, in a nutshell."

Two crimson spots flared in Angel's cheeks. That detestable, officious little man! How dare he say she mustn't see Nick, or imply that he was a danger to her?

"I wasn't aware that I'd asked you for any such guarantees, Inspector," she snapped. "And as for Nick—Mr. Durango—being implicated in these attempts on my person—! What utter balderdash! I've never heard such nonsense! If this is what you came to Egypt to tell me, then I'm very much afraid you've had a wasted journey!"

"Now, now, my dear. Let's not lose our temper, shall we, hmm? I can well imagine how very upset and—er— confused you must be, under the circumstances. After all, you trusted Mr. Durango implicitly, did you not? But I'm afraid the inspector is right, my dear," Uncle Teddy murmured consolingly, placing his hand on her shoulder to steady and comfort her in her upset. "It would appear your Mr. Durango is a dangerous man—a charming confidence-trickster who's quite capable of convincing you that he was working for, rather than against, you. I admit, your father and myself were quite taken in by him."

"That's ridiculous! Nick is nothing of the sort! He's innocent—I know he is! He—he would never do anything to hurt me," she protested, stricken to the core. "Ever since my father hired him, he has been committed to protecting my life with his own. To ensuring that the two men who abducted me in Paris were unable to do so again."

"On the contrary, miss. From what me and Mr. Hardcastle here have been able to piece together, we're almost certain those two men are the Figg brothers, 'Tiny' and 'Knuckles'—petty criminals well known to the law. And, according to a reliable informant, they are currently in Nick Durango's employ!"

"What!"

"It's true, Angelica," Hardcastle confirmed in a regretful tone. "I discovered that after Sidney'd hired those rogues, the Americans did some investigating of their own."

"Aye," Jamieson cut in. "And as a result, the wee prank you and the late Lord Smythe-Moreton played on your father came to light. We have good reason t' believe it was probably then that their dastardly plan was conceived!"

"What *plan?*" Angel demanded scornfully.

"Their plan to kidnap you. To ransom you to your father themselves."

"Rot! Hypothetical rubbish!" she scoffed, tossing her head. "I don't believe a word of it! Not one."

Uncle Teddy continued gently, "We speculate that Bill Bligh promised to become something of a fly in the ointment, hounding you to settle your—er—gambling debts as he was . . ."

"Aye. And so—what with young laird Reggie desperate t' wed you and use your dowry t' pay off his own markers—Durango and Juarez decided they must be gotten rid of!

383

The Americans callously plotted Bligh's murder. They cleverly set it up so that Reggie would appear the guilty party. No doubt they expected the law t' take care of Reggie for them, but instead, he panicked, and fled the country for France, forcing them to change their plans. So, they murdered Smythe-Moreton. Cold-bloodedly killed him in such a way, his death would appear t' be a suicide!" Jamieson's piercing eyes gleamed ghoulishly, causing a shudder to run down Angel's spine.

"How very plausible you've made your little fairy tale sound!" Angel crowed, forcing a trill of derisive laughter. "Why, if I didn't know better, I could almost believe it. Alas for you, I do not."

Contempt in her tone and in her expression, she looked from the inspector's unsympathetic face, then back to Uncle Teddy's kindly, troubled one. Neither man would meet her eyes, and all of a sudden, her unshakable conviction wavered just a tiny bit. The inspector and Uncle Teddy both appeared so very certain they were right. Was there the smallest chance that they were?

She bit her lower lip, remembering the grassy hill above Lake Como where she and Nick had stopped to picnic, before going on to Villa Allegra.

"Did you kill him?" she'd asked, still reeling with the shock of learning about Reggie's death from the newspaper, and discovering that Nick had known about his death, but kept it from her.

"Is that what you think I am—a cold-blooded murderer?" he'd demanded.

Her stomach churned over with doubt. A tiny seed of mistrust had been planted in her that day—one Jamieson's accusations now seemed to encourage, and Uncle Teddy's very kindness seemed to underscore. *Could* Nick have killed Bill Bligh and Reggie, after all . . . ?

Never.

She remembered the tender way he'd cared for her when she'd been ill. Nick, a murderer? Nick, the devilish scamp who'd suggested they "duel" with loaded strawberries? Dashing Nick, who'd leaped from a moving train, rather than confront her abductors in a crowded railway carriage, and chance an innocent person being hit by a ricochet bullet? No, she couldn't believe it of him. Not Nick—not her darling, gentle Nick! Maybe he acted the rough 'n tough cowboy on the outside, but inside, he was a pussy-cat, a sweetheart, incapable of hurting anyone.

"H-have you charged him yet?" she whispered. "Is he in custody?" She hadn't seen Nick since dinner last night.

"Och, no. I regret not. Ye see, we have only our suspicions, as yet, Miss Higgins. We need proof—solid evidence—before we can make an arrest, right, Hardcastle?"

"Quite, Inspector. Innocent until proven guilty beyond a shadow of a doubt—that's what the law says, my dear. Until then, the hands of Justice are tied—and Durango walks the streets a free man."

"I see. Then I suppose I should thank you for warning me, Inspector Jamieson, and apologize for doubting you. Rest assured, I shall take the utmost care where Durango is concerned until I am safely aboard the *Empress of Egypt*, bound for home. Forewarned is forearmed, after all, is it not?" she said with every appearance of sincerity, forcing a brittle smile as she rose to leave.

"Aye. It most certainly is, my dear lassie. Now, remember what I said: *Stay away from Durango*. However, if ye should accidentally run into the mon, say nothing of our suspicions. Act as normally as possible, until ye can get yoursel' safely away from him. If he suspects that the Yard's on t' him—! Whist, it could be verra dangerous for ye!"

"I understand completely," she murmured demurely, drawing on her lace gloves and unfurling her parasol with a practiced flick of her wrist. "May I go now, Inspector?"

Jamieson nodded. "Aye, ye certainly may, miss. Please extend my verra best wishes t' your father for a complete recovery when ye see him next?"

"I shall. Thank you, Inspector."

They shook hands.

"My pleasure. Guid day t' ye, Miss Higgins."

"And to you, sir."

Teddy Hardcastle rose to follow her to the door. "I'll escort you back to the hotel, my dear, and see you safely into Miss Blunt's—er—capable care. You poor child.

385

What a day this has been for you! First the news about poor Sidney's accident and then right on its heels, this nasty business—!" He shook his graying head and clicked his teeth. "You really shouldn't be alone at a time like this," he sympathized, taking his Panama hat, white gloves and walking stick from the desk.

"Thank you, Uncle Teddy, but I'd really prefer to be alone for just a little while, if it's all the same to you . . . ?"

To her relief, he frowned, then nodded in understanding. "Of course. I quite understand."

"Thank you," she murmured gratefully, going on tiptoe to kiss his cheek. "I shall look forward to seeing you at dinner tonight—that is, if you're free?"

"You can count on it, Angelica. We'll meet at seven or thereabouts, in the hotel dining room. Meanwhile, do take care of yourself, won't you, my dear girl?"

"I shall, I promise!"

Once outside, she ignored the waiting gharry and its dozing driver, and walked briskly to the nearest corner. There she looked about her, then broke into a run, oblivious to the shocked stares of the *fellahin*, the native peasants, and Europeans who watched from within their shady colonial office buildings or from the doorways of dark cafés as she sped past them, all but running through Cairo's European quarter's wide, clean boulevards. Far above the fronded heads of the date palms, the sun was a white disc, pulsing down on the ancient city from a sky of such brilliant blue, it pained the eyes to look at it. No one but a mad dog or an Englishman would be out in this, the hottest hour of the day, those watching eyes said. But then, the missie was obviously British! That explained much. . . .

As Angel sped down the street, the cry of the *muezzin* rang out from the pink minaret of the nearest mosque, calling the Followers of Islam to noon prayer.

Please God, let Nick be in his room! she prayed as she ran up the staircase to the deserted hotel's second floor, deserted because every devout Moslem who worked there was at his prayers.

She was panting for breath, for she'd not stopped

running since she left the British Consulate offices. A stitch had painfully cramped her side long before she'd gone even half the way, and her hair, her clothing, were sodden with perspiration, too. She could feel it trickling down her reddened face to sting her eyes, feel it plastering her muslin gown to her spine like a second skin. She wanted nothing so badly as a cool, refreshing bath in that moment, but first—first she must warn Nick, must urge him to get out of Cairo before that well-intentioned idiot, Inspector Jamieson, could act on his and Uncle Teddy's ludicrous suspicions, fabricate the "solid evidence" they needed, and have Nick arrested!

Angel had no illusions about the British judicial system. While an effective and fair one, for the greater part, she believed, it was also convoluted in its workings and incredibly slow. A foreigner like Nick might languish in gaol at Her Majesty's Pleasure for months—perhaps years—before he was brought to trial and found innocent. And caging an outdoorsman like Nick in an airless cell would be tantamount to a death sentence. . . .

"I'm a real patient man," Nick drawled, slapping the blade of the knife against his palm as he circled the chair. "But pardner, my patience is fast wearin' out. Unless you start talkin'—and soon!—me and my friend are gonna get real rough."

"Tiny" Figg was a coarse Englishmen of enormous size. His bulk almost hid the chair to which Nick and Juarez had bound him after a tremendous tussle that had destroyed the room's furnishings. He'd been cocky when they'd first overpowered him, cussing up a blue streak, jeering and refusing to say a word. But once Nick had withdrawn the silver-bladed knife from his belt, the dawnings of fear had crept into Tiny's piggy, deep-set eyes. He'd gulped and wetted his fleshy lips—a dead give-away that he was starting to feel a mite skittish. Nick grinned. Despite Tiny's greater size, both Nick and Juarez had figured he'd be the easier of the two men to break. The nervous glances he kept darting at Juarez told Nick just how best to do it!

Glancing across the room at his cousin, Nick was forced to hide a smile. It was little wonder Tiny appeared ready to spill his guts!

Juarez towered before the window, his long, raven black hair falling loose about his chiseled face. The intense North African sunlight pouring through the lace curtains created a nimbus about his tall frame, made him seem larger, broader than life—and infinitely dangerous! His muscular arms were crossed over his chest. Eagle feathers and beads dangled from his scalp lock. A necklace of bear claws and a medicine pouch hung over his chest. Both it and his face had been war-painted with stripes of red and black. A fringed buckskin breechclout and thigh-length leggings hugged his lean lower body as he stared straight ahead, looking neither to left nor right, but simply standing there in menacing silence. Gone was the shy, gentle, *civilized* man of an hour ago, the man who'd fretted about his bride sending him to sleep in a shed! Juarez had become the bloodthirsty Apache, Panther-Who-Stalks, the character he'd created for old Bill's Wild West Show!

"Who hired you?" Nick barked, leaning over Tiny with his dark face inches from the sweating Englishman's.

"Get stuffed, Yank!" Tiny stammered in a show of bravado. "If yer want some fink that sings, get yerself a bleedin' canary!"

"I don't need a canary, pardner—I can make *you* sing. And you know how? By handin' you over to my pal here, so the two of you can finish this friendly little chat! Say— you did meet my blood-brother, Panther-Who-Stalks, right? No? Well, heck, let me tell you all about him. His mama was a full-blooded Apache. A killer! Legend says his daddy was half Injun, half cougar. He don't say much, but he's real handy with a skinning knife and awful good at getting folks t' sing." Nick shook his head ruefully. "Only trouble is—hell, I reckon you might be singin' *soprano* 'stead of tenor, when Panther gets through with you."

"He's bluffin', Tiny!" Knuckles cried out. "Don't listen to 'im!"

"Bluffing, am I?" Nick chuckled, and the sound was

388

enough to stir the hackles on Juarez's spine, and almost cost him his menacing pose. "Go ahead. Try me, *hombre*—! They're your balls, after all . . ."

"Wot—wot'll you do—you know, if I—if I talk?" Tiny whispered, sweat pouring down his pouchy face.

"If you don't make me good an' mad," Nick drawled, lighting a cheroot and exhaling a thin spiral of blue smoke in leisurely fashion before continuing, "I was figurin' on makin' a deal with your boss. I handle the woman, he can handle Higgins and taking delivery of the ransom money. We split the proceeds fifty-fifty. Sounds fair t' me."

"But the snooty chit's seen our faces! She can identify us t' the law!"

"I told you, I'll handle her. Once Higgins has handed over the loot, it's *adios* and godbye for lil' Miz Iron-Drawers," Nick swore grimly.

In the crackling silence that followed his ominous words, both Nick and Juarez heard the muffled gasp and sudden "thwunk" that came from behind the suite's connecting door. Neither man could afford to investigate its cause, however. Tiny was close to cracking, and they'd worked too hard to give it up and start over now.

Chapter Thirty-One

Angel reached the ground floor in record time after accidentally dropping her parasol.

She stood on the pavement fronting the Sphinx Hotel with the vacant look of the deeply shocked in her eyes. Her heart was thudding painfully, and she was trembling all over in reaction to what she'd overheard. Yet—it was as if on one level, she were also quite numb, unable to force her limbs to move properly or to form a coherent plan of escape. And yet, escape she must!

Where could she go? she wondered frantically. To whom could she run? And who dare she trust, now that Nick—oh, Nick!—had shown his true colors, proven to be the biggest liar, the grandest deceiver, of all times?

Home! a tiny voice cried out inside her. *Go home to Da and Brixton Towers, where it's safe, Annie, lass!* But she couldn't, not yet. The *Empress of Egypt* wasn't scheduled to sail for five more days.

Mabel must be in on it, as Juarez's wife. Asking her to hide her, help her, was out of the question. Uncle Teddy was the obvious choice, but she had no idea where to find him before their dinner engagement that evening at seven—almost five long hours from now! Where could she hide until then?

"Angel! Wait! We have t' talk!"

Nick's loud bellow from the balcony three floors above the boulevard made up her mind for her. Looking up, her heart skipped a beat in fright as she saw Nick swing a leg over the verandah railing and begin climbing down. Dear

God! He knew she'd eavesdropped on his conversation—and he was coming after her!

"Good afternoon, mam'selle? You are desiring of a carriage, yes?"

Angel blinked as if awakening from a dream, to find a carriage had halted before her. A grinning Turk with gold teeth, wearing a red fez and a striped robe, sat in the driver's perch. She leaped into the vehicle unaided with an impassioned cry of, "Desiring, yes! Lay on, do!"

"Mustapha possesses the swiftest mule in the city, missie!" the driver boasted, whipping his mule into a spanking trot that swiftly carried her down the boulevard and around the corner, before Nick—she was relieved to see—reached the ground floor.

"The swiftest bar none, thank God!" Angel agreed fervently.

"Where is it you would have Mustapha and this noble beast transport your most glorious self, missie?"

"To the harbor—no, no, that won't do! To the native quarter, then—yes! That's it! Mustapha, take me to the native quarter, at once!"

"Non! Non! That would be most unwise, I fear. It is said that some pretty European ladies such as yourself have visited the bazaars—and never been seen or heard of again. It is believed some powerful *jinn* spirited them away . . ."

"I'll take my chances on a genie any day," Angel crisply cut in, "rather than let that devil Durango catch me!"

The broad, shady boulevards of the European quarter with its elegant white buildings rapidly gave way to poorer, meaner streets, then to the narrow twisting alleys of the native quarter as the gharry rumbled along.

On either side of the alleys they were passing through now, tall, crumbling buildings soared four, perhaps five stories into the air, blocking out the fierce sunlight and replacing it with shadows, dirt, and mystery. The many windows of these buildings were arched, grilled with fanciful arabesques of iron, while others had balconies that almost met the balconies of the houses opposite them. From behind one of the grilles, the dark eyes of a merchant's *hareem* peered jealously down into the street below, noting the bright gold hair and pretty clothes, the milk-white skin, and dangling pink jewels of the shameless woman riding alone in the gharry—an unveiled Christian hussy with no male family member to protect her!

The carriage jounced along the narrow streets, its progress growing slower and slower by the minute as Mustapha was forced to halt while ambling donkeys and camels passed before his mule's nose, or to navigate the street stalls of the bazaar that littered the dusty ground with their wares. There were rugs, brass bowls, trays or jugs, sacks of tea, coffee beans, spices, finely crafted camel or horse trappings, cages of exotic birds, as well as street performers such as jugglers, fortune-tellers, astrologers, physicians, scribes, snake charmers, belly dancers, fire-eaters and more.

Merchants were everywhere, holding out samples of their goods for Angel's inspection, singing the praises of their merchandise and naming prices in strident voices. Beggars were everywhere, too, old and young alike. The small brown hands of the ragged children clung to her carriage wheels, while other, bolder urchins swarmed like naughty monkeys over the vehicle itself, each reed-thin ragamuffin imploring her for a coin or two, or something to eat. Moved despite her own plight, she flung them a handful of Italia *lira* and French *centimes* from her bag to get them out from beneath the gharry's dangerous moving wheels. To the last child, the last blind or crippled old man, they fell on the coins like starving wolves upon a lamb.

"Can't you go any faster? Please!" Angel called loudly, trying to make herself heard over the deafening noises of the bazaar, for the cacophony of sounds was second only to the overwhelming odors hanging in the still, sultry air, camel dung and perfume mingled with hot oil and clarified butter, coffee and almonds, and the smoke of Turkish cigarettes. There were the vendors' cries, braying donkeys, spitting camels, screaming children, chinking tambourines and wailing flutes, all crashing together with the plaintive haggling of those who would buy what was offered for sale.

"Faster? By Allah, Mustapha can go no faster—nor any

further, missie! The streets, they are too narrow, yes? The people are too many! Please. You must pay me and get down—or wiser yet, go back!"

Biting her lower lip in consternation, she turned on the shabby leather seat, intending to look about, consider her alternatives, and come to some decision. Could she while away three, four hours here?

But as she did so, she saw Nick's black Stetson bobbing above the sea of turbaned, red-fezzed and white-robed heads, as he steered his prancing stallion through the crush of the bazaar. She had no choice, not now! He'd be alongside her in seconds!

Jumping down from the side of the carriage furthest from Durango, she tossed her remaining change into the air, and dived headfirst into the sea of people.

As she'd hoped, her little diversion bought her precious minutes. As beggars and merchants' apprentices alike scrambled for the loot, they created a formidable human barrier—one that Nick could not penetrate without trampling some small body underhoof! While he cursed, fumed, and roared at the beggars to make way, Angel was off and running. . . .

The street she blindly chose for her escape route was named the Street of the Carpetmakers. Through opened doorways, she could see men in robes seated upon high stools, either weaving at huge, intricate looms, or embroidering beautiful carpets. Few looked up to mark the passing of the strange European woman. If they had, they would have seen a demented creature, one whose hair had escaped its pins and now tangled about her shoulders in a golden mop, whose straw hat flopped down her back, held precariously to her hair by but a single pin—and whose smoky eyes were as wild as any demon of the night!

She ran without stopping until she reached the corner. Here, the Street of the Carpetmakers ran at right angles to the Street of the Tentmakers. Another agonizing stitch in her side forced her stop and recover her breath. Her face crimson, she flopped forward, her arms dangling loose at her sides like a puppet. Her breasts were heaving against her dainty muslin morning gown—which was beginning to show every evidence of hard wear. She sucked in each breath in gulping, hiccupping sobs that hurt her ribs so much, the very act of drawing breath brought tears to her eyes.

It's no use! I can't go on! I simply can't! Oh, damn these bloody stays! And damn this stupid dress! And to hell with these blasted shoes! she ranted silently, kicking off the offending footwear one at a time.

And then, as if in the throes of a nightmare, she heard the merry jingle of harness, the quick, noisy clatter of metal-shod hooves on the cobblestoned street at her back. Turning, she saw *him* astride his demonic coal black beast, dressed as she'd first seen him, head to toe in black and silver.

Larger and larger, taller and taller in the saddle he grew as he rode toward her, but—like a rabbit entranced by a deadly cobra, she made no attempt to run. She simply stood there, fascinated, watching with glazed eyes and slack-jawed mouth as he came on.

"There is no god but Allah; Mohammed is the Messenger of Allah!"

The *muezzin's* first wailing call to afternoon prayer was the catalyst that jolted her into action once more.

With no time to waste, she hastily looked left, then right, then flung herself into the last carpet merchant's on the street. The Moslem weavers, all of them men, were in the act of spreading their prayer rugs upon the ground and facing east toward Mecca for their devotions. They let her pass through their midst unhampered, with only a shocked widening of their dark eyes to tell that they had seen her at all.

Angel's heart was in her mouth as she skidded to a halt. The game was well and truly up, now! She couldn't run straight out of the carpetmaker's back door, as she'd hoped, for the weaving room led onto a high-walled courtyard, surrounded by a covered walkway, onto which looked still other rooms. She glimpsed women and children in some, men at prayer in others—people who could *see* her, could tell Durango which way she'd run! She'd have to go back the way she'd come, unless—she could hide somewhere and wait?

She slipped into the first room she came to, one with a

massive, nail-studded door. It looked quite capable of repelling even Attila the Hun! She swung the door shut behind her and slid the giant bolt home.

Inside the storeroom were hundreds of beautiful carpets, embroidered with trees, flowers, and vines in glowing colors; rectangles, squares, ovals, circles, all rolled and neatly fastened with cord, ready to be unfurled in the bazaars to catch a buyer's discerning eye. There was a stack of unrolled rugs, too, piled one on top of the other. Her eyes lit up!

Running across to the stack, Angel gingerly lay down upon the very edge of the topmost rug. She firmly grasped the fringe, then rolled herself sideways, over and over, just as she'd rolled down the hill after she and Nick leapt from the train.

It was very hot and smelled of sheep's wool and vegetable dyes in her thick cocoon. But it would, she decided, serve. Beggars—and desperate fugitives—could not, after all, be choosers!

Trying to be very still, she waited . . . and waited . . . and waited . . . and . . .

She came to with a sickening, panicky jolt. Her palms and upper lip were slick with sweat. *Dear Lord!* Her poor heart was galloping so fast, it felt ready to explode from her breast!

As reality returned, scalding tears trickled from beneath her tightly closed eyelids, for in all honesty, reality was only a smidgeon more preferable to her dreadful nightmare!

She'd fallen asleep and dreamed that Nick had caught her, that he'd buried her alive in an underground tomb!

"Adiós and goodbye, lil' Miz Iron Drawers!" he'd jeered, twirling the ends of a villainous moustache. Then he'd pulled some monstrous lever that had made the walls cave in, to suffocate her.

She gagged suddenly as something nasty, something hairy, fell into her open mouth, then spat several times in a most unladylike fashion to empty it. Had her dream been real, after all? Had whatever it was been, perhaps, a trickle of dirt? A furry spider leg? *What?* She felt around very gingerly, but the hairy "something" proved only a strand of carpet fringe, thank God! Horrid, but harmless.

Still, it was but small relief to come to her senses and remember what had transpired, only to find herself still wrapped in the carpet like a particularly generous sausage roll.

How long had she been asleep? Minutes? Hours? And was it yet day, or night? Had Nick been there, searching for her? She had no way of knowing the answers to any of her questions, for within the rug's thick folds, it was always night. She frowned. Dare she unroll herself and attempt a return to the hotel and with it, Uncle Teddy's sane, familiar presence? Or—should she wait a little longer? She knew Nick must have seen her run inside the carpet-maker's but if so, had he already searched the place then left, convinced she was elsewhere? Or was he lying in wait somewhere nearby, ready to pounce on her when she crawled from her hiding place? It was a knotty dilemma, to say the least!

She stiffened suddenly, hearing voices nearby, muffled by the carpet's folds. Trying hard to breathe as shallowly as possible, she strained her ears. Was the voice Nick's? No. There were two voices, both male, both speaking in Arabic, but neither was his.

"You are in luck, my illustrious friend!" declared Akbar, the carpet merchant, though Angel could not understand him. "Your lord-master's carpets are finished and ready to grace his tents! Here they are—and what beautiful weaving! What glorious colors and workmanship, eh?"

"You've already been paid by my master, the sheik, you old rogue. There's no need to boast of your wares. Come. Make haste! The hour grows late. I would leave the city by moonrise."

The merchant clapped his hands. "And so you shall, sir. Abdul! Kahlil! By Allah, was ever a good man cursed with such lazy apprentices as this? Move your bones! Faster, you idle sons of a constipated camel! Load the rugs for our lord Rashid!"

Angel muffled a squeal of protest as she felt herself—or

rather, the rolled carpet—hefted up between two strong pairs of hands that carried her from the room in which she'd hidden!

Surely, oh surely, they would notice the extra weight, find her, and then—! Oh, what would they do to her? she wondered apprehensively. But it seemed they noticed nothing untoward.

Moments later, she was bent almost in two and slung across some peculiar conveyance she could not name, before being soundly whacked across the derrière a time or two with what felt like a stout stick.

It was only when the vehicle began to move with an unsettling, sideways swaying motion, combined with a jerky back-and-forward lope, that she knew what it was she was riding upon: her conveyance was none other than a ship of the desert, a hissing, spitting, ill-natured camel!

And—if the snarling quality to his thick Arabic was anything to go by—its master was in the foulest of moods. . . .

Chapter Thirty-Two

Nick knelt on the floor of the carpetmaker's storeroom and picked up the pink bead he'd spotted there, sparkling in the light of the dish lamps. Looking about him, he found another, and yet another.

"And you say you saw no sign of the woman after she ran through your weaving room at the time of prayer?"

"No, kind master, none at all," Akbar the merchant told him truthfully, excited by the return of the famous American "King of the Cowboys" to his city. He had enjoyed very much the show Pasha "Buffalo Bill" Cody had put on two years ago—especially the daring riding and roping of the man before him, for Akbar was Arab, and as such he respected one who was skilled in the saddle, and who had great knowledge of horses. "We searched for her everywhere, as I told your most gracious self earlier. But—it was as if the mademoiselle had vanished into thin air." He snapped his fingers. "Poof!"

"Or else climbed over the wall?" Nick observed, his pale blue eyes narrowing.

"Nay, I do not think so, master. the walls, they are very high, are they not? No man—forgive me, but not even a magnificent, tall man such as yourself!—could climb them unaided, let alone a helpless maiden."

"Helpless, hell!" Nick muttered under his breath, straightening up. Angel Higgins was about as helpless as a wagonload of monkeys! There wasn't much he'd put past her!

Whistling through his teeth, he pushed back his Stetson

and looked carefully around the storeroom. As it had when he'd searched earlier, it held nothing but carpets, carpets, and more carpets, either stacked in bulky rolls or layered like flapjacks. His eyes gleamed suddenly. "Say, have you sold any carpets from this storeroom today—since the woman vanished, I mean?"

"Ah, yes, indeed I have, sir! Rashid—he that is known as the Ungrateful?—came here shortly before dusk. He left with the carpets his master, Sheik Abdullah the Fruitful, ordered in the months of winter. But—surely you do not believe the maiden was hidden within a carpet, master?"

"I wouldn't put it past this little filly," Nick said grimly. "How was this Rashid fella travellin', and where?"

"How else but by camel, master? He was going into the desert to join his chieftain and their tribe at the oasis of Siwa!"

"Aw, Christ!" Nick growled with a sense of more bad news to come. "Show me where they loaded up the carpets, Akbar."

"Very well, Durango-Pasha. Please, follow me."

Outside in the darkening streets, almost hidden among the dust, camel droppings, and refuse, the pearly pink sheen of yet another glass bead gleamed in the moonlight. Nick groaned and his gut squeezed in apprehension, but his hunch was all but confirmed by this find. He'd bet hard money that that impossible, infuriatin' woman had rolled herself up in one of those carpets to hide from him; that she was even now slung over a camel, headed across the Arabian desert in the surly company of an Arab named Rashid. Hell, if he was wrong about this, he'd eat his . . . his . . . He caught himself in midthought and stopped dead, remembering all too clearly the last time he'd rashly vowed to eat his hat if he was wrong. Uh uh. Nope. No way! Damned if he'd tempt fate by saying that again . . .

"Master Akbar, I'd like to send a message to the Grand Sphinx Hotel in the European quarter. Could you help me out? I'd go myself, but a fresh trail's easier to follow than an old one."

399

"It would be an honor, Durango-Pasha. I will send my youngest son."

"Thanks, pardner."

As he watched the young messenger leave, Nick thought grimly, *I sure hate to leave you high and dry, Juarez, amigo, but there's no other way. If I don't go after Angel tonight—right now!—she might disappear with this Rashid fellow forever. The desert's a mighty big place t' hunt for one little gal. You're on your own for now, cousin. If Tiny and Knuckles set up a parlay with their boss, you'll just have to do the best you can . . . alone.*

It was almost dawn when Rashid halted his string of camels at the oasis of Barrakah. Commanding his own beast to couch, so that he might dismount, he stepped down from its neck and stumbled across the sand to relieve himself against a rock.

Meanwhile, his serving boy, Ali, hurriedly set about the hated female task of building them a camel-dung fire, erecting the tent of goatskins, and spreading rugs upon the sand within it for his master's bed.

Irritably, Ali unfastened the rope that held the rugs loaded onto one of the camel's backs. The bundle dropped to the sand with a weighty thud. To Ali's amazement, from the midst of the carpets came an angry female voice.

"You bloody idiot!" it shrieked. "You stupid nincompoop! You could have brained me!"

Young Ali fell to his knees, prostrating himself on the sand with his forehead touching the ground.

"What nonsense are you up to now?" Rashid growled sourly, his fists planted on his hips. "This is not the hour of prayer. Get up and raise the tent, oh worthless jackal, before the sun rises!"

"But m-m-master, the c-carpet spoke to me!" Ali babbled, his dark eyes round as moons. "It is s-surely p-p-possessed by a *j-j-j-j-j-inn!*"

"*Jinn?*" Rashid boomed. "Pah! I will thrash your plump buttocks for this foolishness! Out of my way! Let me pass! I would hear this 'Genie of the Carpets' for myself!"

So saying, Rashid shoved poor Ali roughly aside with the toe of his boot, and kicked out at the heap of carpets on the sand. To his amazement, a pained shriek rose from their folds.

"Owwwch! That was my knee, you damned baboon! Kick me again, and you'll be sorry!"

Prodding at each of the carpets in turn, Rashid found one that was plumper than all the rest.

"You, you lazy scorpion! Unroll this one," Rashid ordered with a sneer of contempt, jerking his thumb at Ali. "I would see this *'jinn'* of yours face to face!"

Ali obediently grasped the fringe of the carpet Rashid had selected, and pulled as hard as he could. It unrolled swiftly, catapulting a disheveled Angel out of its confines, and rolling her like as log onto the moonlit sands of the desert.

"By Allah and His Prophet, it is truly a *jinn*, master!" Ali breathed almost reverently. He was dazzled by the beautiful golden-haired, ivory-skinned woman sprawled before him. "She is as fair as any *houri* sent from paradise!"

In response to his worshipful gaze, the vision scrabbled to its feet in crablike fashion, tottered to and fro for a moment, as if to get its balance, then stalked toward him.

Wearing a furious scowl, Angel drew back her foot and kicked the youth square in the shins, using all the force she could muster without her shoes. "Kick me, would you, you barbaric little rotter? Well, take that!" she snapped. "I've had quite enough of your Arab hospitality!"

And with that, she tossed her head haughtily and stalked past poor, innocent Ali, clearly intending to strike out across the gray silk dunes and valleys of the desert on foot, without either water or food—and to do so quite alone.

Rashid's igneous eyes grew beady and bright with cunning as the woman stormed past him. Her hips twitched enticingly beneath her ridiculous skirts as she did so. Her glorious hair lifted on the night wind like a cloud of spun gold. Rashid's avaricious mind raced, performing lightning calculations with the speed of an abacus. The woman was European, a fair-skinned, golden-haired, pale-eyed beauty—and one who clearly possessed fire, spirit, and a reckless courage that was rare in a woman, too. In all, she was just the sort of rare woman sheik Abdullah would covet for his *hareem!*

Rashid rubbed his pudgy hands together greedily, and imagined the riches that would be his when his lord-master accepted his gift of the girl. It was well known that others who had presented his chieftain with less than beautiful concubines had seen their generosity richly rewarded! For such a beauty, surely his master would reward him tenfold . . . ?

"After her, boy!" Rashid bellowed. "Why are you standing there? Run! She must not escape!"

"But, master, she kicked me—!" Ali protested, his lower lip jutting mutinously, tears of pain still dampening his eyes.

"Kicked you? Pah! *I* shall see you put to the Torture of a Thousand Daggers, if you do not obey me!" his master thundered. "Now, run!"

"Unhand me, you scamp!" Angel protested when Ali caught up with her and attempted to force her back to the oasis. Reaching out, she soundly boxed his ears, first the left, then the right, hoisted up her skirts and struck out at a run—no easy feat to accomplish on the dragging sands.

Ali raced after her, pulling at her skirts, tearfully imploring her in Arabic to be kind and return with him to his master, Rashid, who would surely kill him if she escaped. His answer was another kick—this one landing solidly in the unfortunate lad's groin. Ali set up a whirling-dervish dance and an unearthly howling that could have awakened the sleeping pharaohs in their tombs—a performance that put Angel sharply in mind of Prince Antonio di Soriso's cunning little dance on a similar occasion several weeks ago.

"I warned you, did I not, boy?" she scolded as Ali clutched his middle and squealed. "And yet—like the majority of your cloth-eared sex—you thought yourself far superior to a lowly woman, and would not heed me! Well, let this serve as a lesson to you!"

With that farewell, Angel recommenced stalking across the sand, moving at a lively clip in her outrage. Men! It would be a happy circumstance if the lot of them were to die out, like some dwindling species of wildlife—perhaps in the fashion of the unfortunate dodo bird, now extinct? The world in general would be a far happier, better-balanced place without men to complicate matters. There would be fewer wars, if any, with a sensible, intelligent woman at the helm of the universe. The poor would be well-fed and adequately clothed, for a woman would no doubt administer the budget of the world as she would her own efficiently run, well-budgeted kitchen, pantry, and household. Better yet, without men, there would be no cause for heartbreak among young ladies such as herself, who had tasted the fruits of love, and now must swallow the bitter pill of deception that came after . . .

She flicked her head to clear it as she marched along, fighting tears as she traveled over sands bathed in cold moonlight, lit almost as brightly as by day. Ever since she'd overheard Nick's damning conversation with her abductors, she'd been trying to pretend it hadn't happened, that she hadn't really heard him trying to deal himself into the dirty game they'd played. Rather, she'd thrust her feelings aside and instead forced her mind to dwell on escaping Nick and trying to decide what she should do next.

But here, amidst the vast emptiness and silence of the desert night, with only the frosty sparkle of the stars to spy upon her, it was suddenly impossible to act as if her heart hadn't been broken clean in two. It had. It was.

She swallowed, and the lump in her throat was like a rock lodged there. Inspector Jamieson and Uncle Teddy had been right about Nick, ultimately, she thought, her breast aching with misery. Perhaps he hadn't been in on it from the first, as they'd believed, but he certainly was now—up to his horrid, deceitful neck in it! It was the money, of course, she reflected with a sigh as a huge tear rolled down her cheek and plopped onto the sand. The temptation had proved too great for a man like Nick to withstand. Perhaps he'd wearied of the penniless rough-and-ready outdoor life he'd claimed to love, and now sought a more comfortable existence, one that guaranteed a fine roof over his head, rather than sleeping outdoors beneath the sky and the stars, and a soft feather bed, instead of a saddle for a pillow, and a cowboy's bedroll . . . ?

Once she had succumbed to her misery, she was too steeped in it to care when she heard Rashid ride up behind her on his camel. She halted and looked up into his hooked-nosed, olive face with little curiosity or even fear, feeling suddenly bone-weary and utterly careless of her own future.

"Yes?"

"The day is dawning," Rashid said in adequate, decipherable French, spoken with deceptive kindness. "Soon, the fierce sun will rise to scorch the desert sands. One with your fair skin will not last long, I fear, mademoiselle. Forgive my servant's clumsy invitation to travel with us, and instead, accept mine, oh most gracious lady."

"Where is it you're going, m'sieu—?"

"Rashid. I journey to the oasis of Siwa, missie, and will there present carpets from the merchant, Akbar, to Sheik Abdullah, a most worthy chieftain who is grazing his flocks nearby. When I have accomplished this, we shall return to the city of Cairo."

"I see." It all sounded quite reasonable to Angel, though she promised herself to be wary of the man. There was something decidedly shifty about his coal black eyes and his silky tone that warned her not to take his kindness at face value. "And when do you expect to return?"

"Three days—four at most, missie, if it is the will of Allah that my journey be swift and without delay."

"Oh, but of course. All matters are in His hands, ultimately," she agreed. Four days, at most, he'd said. If this fellow was to be trusted, she could still be back in Cairo with enough time to board the *Empress of Egypt* five days hence! Besides, Rashid was perfectly correct about her fate if she chose to keep walking. What choice did she have, really, but to accept his invitation? "I would be delighted to accompany you, sir," she accepted primly.

Without further ado, Rashid commanded his camel to couch. The beast folded its front legs, then its back. Rashid sat there, waiting, his expression impatient.

Realizing belatedly that it was not the way of Arab men to extend a hand and assist a lowly woman in mounting, she clambered up onto the camel's neck unaided, scrambled over its front hump, and perched gingerly before Rashid upon the saddle. Hiding his triumphant smirk, Rashid whacked the animal with his camel stick to urge it up and into a lope.

Within what seemed only a few minutes, they were once again at the oasis. The greenish pool beneath the straggly date palms that she'd glimpsed before her hasty departure reflected the rising sun now, and the sky above was washed with lemon and lavender.

In the interim, Ali had returned to camp. Moving somewhat guardedly, he had erected the tent of black goatskins. Scowling, he cast his master a furtive look, before turning back to the skewers of meat he'd propped over the fire.

Rashid dismounted his camel and went to one of the other kneeling beasts. He withdrew a bundle from its heavy load.

"Here, woman. Go into the tent and change into these," Rashid rasped, flinging the bundle of clothing at Angel.

"Oh! But I really don't think I—"

Fast as a striking snake, Rashid's hand darted out and wound in her hair. He cruelly jerked her toward him. His spittle flecked her cheeks as he hissed, "I do not care what you *think*, oh garrulous one!" he snarled, withdrawing a pointed dagger from his sash. Smiling evilly, he touched its tip to the soft flesh just beneath her chin. She felt it prick the skin, and knew he'd drawn blood. "You will do as I say!"

She bit her lip and whispered. *"Oui!"*

With a grunt, he returned his dagger to its scabbard, gripped her shoulder, and shoved her headlong into the tent.

Her hands were trembling uncontrollably as she removed her garments and replaced them with the ones Rashid had given her. They were, to her mind, indecently brief, else almost transparent—or both! The thought of Rashid—or anyone, for that matter!—seeing her so scantily attired made her nauseous.

The heavily embroidered, short-sleeved amethyst jacket reached only to a point just below her breasts, and was

405

fastened at the front by a single frog of braided purple silk. The baggy gauzy pantaloons were of filmy lavender cloth, and far too skimpy for either modesty or decency. Even when she fastened the bejewled and embroidered waistband, her entire stomach remained exposed—including her navel!—like a common belly dancer's in the bazaar—while drawstrings about the ankles gathered the wide legs of the garment snugly above the feet. The flowing maidenly veil intended to cover her head was fashioned of sheer lavender cloth, shot through with silver threads, and had a narrow band of deeper amethyst woven about its borders. It seemed rather pointless to cover her hair, when she was so dreadfully exposed elsewhere. But, touching the dried bead of blood beneath her chin, she decided she'd not argue the matter with that plump toad, Rashid.

Dressed, she sat down upon the heaped rugs, uncertain what to do next. She had not long to wait. Only seconds later, Rashid ducked under the raised tent flap. His surly expression became a beaming smile when he saw her.

"Truly, Ali was right, for once! You are beautiful as any *houri* from paradise!" he crowed in Arabic. "My master, Sheik Abdullah the Fruitful, will give anything to possess you, my beauty! By the next rising of the sun, Rashid will be a wealthy man!"

Angel frowned, unable to understand his words, but his actions were easy enough to follow. Drawing a length of rough rope from his robe, he grabbed her hand and tied one end about her wrist, knotted the other about his own, then flopped down onto the rugs beside her. He promptly fell asleep.

Obviously, he intended to take no chances of her escaping! she thought, dismally thinking she'd been right about not trusting him. She sighed. She was now his captive, for whatever reason he had for making her so. But the alternative—a slow, agonizing death, broiled alive by the scorching desert sun—was even less palatable, she told herself. After all, captives at least had the option of attempting to escape, when opportunity presented itself, while corpses did not.

Chapter Thirty-Three

"Yuck! Rashid, couldn't you *please* find something more platable for me to drink instead of this dreadful spoiled goatsmilk? I am so terribly thirsty, I can hardly swallow!" Angel wailed from the back of her camel.

"Silence, woman!" Rashid bellowed, his oily face turning purplish beneath his brown complexion. "You have done nothing but complain for the past two days. Ewellah, I am heartily sick of your nagging voice! Another word—a mere squeak!—and I swear before Allah that I shall slice your noisy tongue from your mouth and feed it to the hawks of the desert!"

"Hmph. It's all very well for you natives," she muttered. "You're used to this loathsome stuff, while I'm accustomed to far better. Ugh! Look at this bread! It's moldy! No wonder you have such a spleenish disposition, Master Rashid. Anyone who chooses to exist on soured milk, yogurt, moldy flat bread, syrupy black coffee, and gamey goat meat as you do could hardly be otherwise. And there's really no need for it, you know. There are foodstuffs available in every bazaar that are both tasty, nourishing and very beneficial for—er—regulating the—er—workings of the body. Take dried fruits, for example. They're in plentiful supply in the native markets—I saw them there myself. A handful of raisins, a few figs or dates, a nice sweet, juicy orange or a prune or two, perhaps, would travel perfectly well in this desert heat, and yet take up very little—"

"Enough!" Rashid yelled in desperation, his arms

raised to the heavens in supplication. "Silence—before I slit your cursed throat from ear to ear! By Allah, is this the price I must pay to become a wealthy man?"

"I believe it is working, missie-Angel!" Ali whispered over his shoulder to her.

"I do believe you're right, Ali," Angel agreed with a conspiratorial grin, glad she'd made her peace with the lad and that they'd allied themselves against Rashid.

Just the evening before, she'd apologized for her mistake in kicking him rather than Rashid. In return, Ali had confided that his master had lied to her. He'd told her that Rashid had no intention of returning her to the city of Cairo in three or four days, as he'd implied, but instead meant to give her to Sheik Abdullah the Fruitful, his chieftain, as a gift to add to his *hareem*.

"You must escape Rashid before my lord-master, the sheik has seen you, for you are truly most beautiful, missie. Once he has set eyes upon you, Sheik Abdullah will never let you go!"

"Really? But how can I possibly leave Rashid without food or water or camels?"

"There are many caravans traveling the desert, missie. At least half of them are bound for Cairo, with honest men who lead them. Now, if you could convince my master to part with you—persuade him that for some reason, you would prove a most unsuitable gift for the sheik—it is my feeling Master Rashid would be only too willing to rid himself of you!"

And so, they had hit upon their little plan!

From dawn to dusk the following day, Angel had complained and grumbled about everything under the sun, using, as a role model for her performance, Katherine in Shakespeare's play *The Taming of the Shrew*. And shrewish she had been!

The milk was sour, she'd grumbled with a disgusted sniff and a wrinkling of her nose when they broke the night's fast the next morning. The bread was too tough, too hard to chew. The goat meat smelled rancid. The rope around her wrist chafed terribly. The black robe Rashid had forced her to wear over her scanty lavender ensemble was scratchy and very possibly lice-ridden, because she itched all over. The camel's back was too bony, its gait uncomfortable. The days were far too hot and the nights far too cold. The flies annoyed her. The sand got into her mouth and made her eyes smart with grit. Her bottom was numb. Her thighs were chafed. Her temples throbbed from squinting against the brilliant sun—her grievances were endless!

Before too long, Rashid had broken his clenched-jawed silence to bellow at her, threatening her with all manner of dire and agonizing consequences if she did not cease her nagging and whining. But—as Ali had so cleverly foreseen—she was quite safe from his master's violence. As angry as he might become, Rashid dare not make good on any of this threats, for fear of marring her beauty in some way. A woman with a black eye or bruises upon her creamy flesh—? Unthinkable! It would never do to insult Sheik Abdullah with damaged merchandise!

"I do believe Rashid's ripe for part two of our plan, Ali," Angel observed as they made camp the second evening. She'd been covertly watching Rashid talking to himself as he actually petted his camel. "He's a man ready to break, if ever I saw one!"

"It is so, missie," Ali agreed with a grin. "Go into the tent and rest, and leave everything to me."

That evening, as Rashid sat before the fire, staring moodily into its flames, Ali murmured slyly, "My poor, poor master! What shall Ali do when he is no more . . . !"

"What do you mutter, oh worthless dung beetle?"

"Me, master? I but asked what I should do without your gracious care and protection, oh thou kindest of masters," Ali said innocently.

"How so? Where should I go, that I'd not be your master, boy?" Rashid demanded.

"Why, to paradise, I fear, sir!" Ali blurted out, to all appearances terribly distraught at such a thought.

"Paradise! But I am yet young in years, and blessed with perfect health!"

"By the grace of Allah, ewellah, this is so. But—oh, my master, I fear you will not be long for this world, if—if you give that—that *Englishwoman* to Sheik Abdullah!"

"How so?" Rashid snapped, then his brows rose. "Ah.

Now I understand! Can it be that you, my little sugared almond, are—jealous of her?"

"No! Of course I'm not! It's just that—oh, no, I cannot—will not!—speak of it—!"

"Speak of what, maggot? Tell me—or be sorry."

"Very well. As you wish, master," Ali sighed reluctantly. "You see, the way I see it, at first, all will be well when we return to our tribe. Our lord chieftain will be enchanted by the woman's golden-haired loveliness, by her fair skin that is as white as the milk of his finest mare, and by her eyes, which are the gray of the smoke from his campfires. He will reward my gracious master accordingly, with generous gifts to show his gratitude and his delight in her beauty. But then—" Ali paused ominously.

"But then what? Go on, boy!"

"But then, as the days pass, Sheik Abdullah will discover the flaws in the priceless jewel you have given him, and he will become very angry!"

"Flaws? But the woman is without fault! She is a perfect pearl, a sweetmeat to be savored!"

"Sweet and toothsome, indeed, master—until she opens her mouth, that is. And then—! Alas, *then* she is as disagreeable as a flatulent she-camel, as soured as old wine, as tart as vinegar—! As bitter as aloes! You have heard her, master. You know I speak truly! When Sheik Abdullah hears her complaining and quarreling day in and day out, causing discord amongst the formerly happy, contented women of his *hareem*, he will remember the man who gave him the woman—and not with gratitude!"

A film of sweat suddenly dewed Rashid's upper lip as he absorbed Ali's words. His pudgy fingers strayed to his throat as if he already felt the kiss of Sheik Abdullah's mighty blade, feeling out the pulse that beat within those pouchy folds of flesh. "Ewellah—I believe you could be right, lad. Had my lord-master to endure what I have endured for the past two days, he would hack my head from my shoulders!"

"And so, it will be as I said. My beloved master will no longer be my master," Ali wailed, rocking back and forth as he wept his crocodile tears. "Woe is me, for when Rashid the All-Wise, the All-Bountiful goes to Paradise,

I shall belong to no one! Have no one to love me!"

"Calm yourself, boy," Rashid soothed thoughtfully, clumsily patting Ali's scrawny shoulder, then stroking his bony buttocks with a lascivious palm. "You shall share my rugs this night, and your master will prove the great affection he feels for you. But as for the woman . . ." he scowled, "you are right. She is flawed, alas. I must rid myself of her, and quickly, lest she prove my undoing! Wait here—!" he commanded, and drew his dagger as if he meant to put an end to his problem straightway.

"Wait! Not that way, sir! 'Twould be a waste to slay her. Now, if there was a passing caravan, perhaps . . ." Ali suggested craftily, stroking Rashid's leg, "my clever master might yet turn some small profit on her beauty, yes? He could sell the woman quickly to a stranger he will never see again—without care for the consequences!"

Rashid, to Ali's surprise, actually giggled. "Oh, but thou art a clever boy, Ali! A clever boy, indeed. I'll do it! At daybreak tomorrow, I will find that caravan! Meanwhile, come, my pretty lad. Sit here, close beside me. Truly, I have missed your company of late . . ." he cooed.

With a triumphant wink for Angel, who sat in the entrance to the tent and had been trying—without success—to understand their conversation, Ali crawled onto Rashid's lap. He was smiling smugly as he did so.

By Allah, he would sleep well this night, he told himself, secure in the knowledge that very soon, the English missie who looked like a *houri*—an angel—but who kicked like a long-eared ass, would soon be gone, and no longer a possible rival for his master's affections . . .

Nick knelt at the oasis, grimacing with distaste as he filled the hairy goatskin Akbar had loaned him. Behind him, his black stallion Diablo nibbled on a solitary blade of grass, the only vegetation that grew from the mortar of the low wall of mud bricks encircling the watering hole. The stallion nickered in disgust and tossed its ebony head, circling nervously.

"Yeah, old buddy, I know what you're saying," Nick muttered. "This here's about as bad as it gets, hmm?" He corked the goatskin and set it aside, before removing his Stetson. Dipping it in the green, scummy water, he filled it to the brim and carried it to Diablo, so that the horse could drink its fill without fouling the watering hole—though such precautions seemed kind of stupid, considering the unappetizing condition of the water to begin with!

His horse seen to, Nick wetted his bandanna in the water and swabbed his gritty face and throat, squinting up at the sky between the shredded date-palm fronds. By his reckoning, night would soon fall with the abruptness peculiar to the East. He may as well take a siesta before riding on through the cool hours of night.

He stretched out under a palm tree, drew one of the Colt .45s from his holster and placed it in readiness at his side, where it'd be handy in case of trouble, then tipped his damp Stetson over his face. But although he was exhausted, sleep wouldn't come. His churning thoughts and emotions wouldn't let it.

Damn it, where in the hell were they? he wondered. Had he passed them up somehow? He didn't think so. He'd followed the directions Akbar had given him to the letter, traveling the old caravan routes southwest, and had located the two oases the carpet merchant had described right on schedule; the first the oasis of Barrakah, the second this one, but he'd seen no sign of the Arab, Rashid, who'd unwittingly ridden off with Angel.

The depth of his anxiety for her safety and well-being amazed him. Not a minute had passed without him thinking about her since he left the Sphinx Hotel. He'd caught himself ghoulishly imagining finding her dead, and had been disgusted to find his eyes were wet with tears, his heart aching, even at the thought. He'd also tried to imagine going on with his life without her in it, and failed miserably.

Fact was, that damned, contrary, highfallutin iron-drawered Limey had gotten so deeply under his skin, she'd just about become a part of him. He'd gotten used to the way she woke up in the morning, stretching like a kitten and snuggling up against him. He even like the way she acted schoolmarmish, uppity, and bossy when she felt he was taking advantage of her. He couldn't stand seeing her

412

cry because, innocent or guilty, her tears made him feel so blamed useless and responsible. But he loved to see her smile with delight or hear her laughter just about more than anything on the face of this good earth—next to making sweet, wild love with her.

Back in Italy, on that unforgettable, sultry night when she'd seduced him on the terrace of Villa Allegra, and they'd made love in a room filled with the light of a hundred flickering candles and the perfume of camellias and roses, she'd said she loved him. But—if that was true, wouldn't she trust him? he asked himself. Trust was a part of love, after all. And, that being the case, why had she run when she overheard him setting up the Figg brothers in order to learn the name of their boss? Why hadn't she waited—at least given him a chance to tell her what he was up to—before she lit out of the hotel like a cat with a firecracker tied to its tail?

He sighed, thinking, *Durango, you son of a bitch, be honest! What did you expect? Did you ever once tell Angel that you loved her, too? That you couldn't imagine a day without her in your life? That you reckoned you might as well get hitched, because—as stormy as it was living with a contrary female like her—it'd be pure, lonely hell-on-earth without her?*

Hell, no! You said a heap of things, all right—but you never once mentioned love or marriage. And as for trust—? Admit it, old son! There's still a wary, watchful part of you that can't forget what Savannah did, nor that it was the hacienda and the money she was really in love with all along, 'stead of yours truly. A part that's still raw and bleeding with hurt deep inside, just waitin' for Angel to let you down, so that you can turn around and say, "See? I told you so!" A crippled part that, if you're honest with yourself, might never heal well enough to let you trust another woman completely. . . .

He must have drifted off to sleep with his uneasy thoughts, because Diablo's whicker of greeting awoke him just after dusk. He came instantly awake, as was his custom, the handle of the Colt snug in his hand even before his eyes had fully opened.

Scrambling to his feet and taking what cover there was

413

behind the slender date palm trunks, he saw a string of five heavily-laden camels, plodding down the dunes toward the oasis in the fading light. Three of the beasts had riders, though their flowing native robes made it hard to tell if they were men or women.

"Greetings!" called the youth riding the first camel, speaking in French as they approached the watering hole. "May we join you, master, and rest ourselves and our beasts for the night?"

Eyes narrowed, Nick's gaze flickered over the trio, noting that while the second rider was a porky Arab fellow who appeared to be the head honcho of the little outfit, the third rider was female. His heart thudded. Was it Angel? Damn! It was impossible to judge the woman's age or anything else about her, for she was dressed in the enveloping black robes of a native woman, and only her eyes were visible. What color they were, he couldn't tell in this light.

"Help yourselves, son," he offered. "I'd offer you some chow and coffee, but truth is, I left home sorta low on supplies!"

"You are American, yes?" the boy asked eagerly, springing down from his kneeling camel's back. When Nick nodded, he turned and said something in excited Arabic to the second man. Unknown to Nick, his words translated, "There! Did you hear that, beloved master? He's an American! Truly, Allah has smiled upon us this night! Instead of some lowly caravan, upon which we might have squandered the woman's true worth, He has send us a wealthy, stupid foreigner! Is it not known that all Americans possess great riches?"

Rashid answered sourly, "He does not appear wealthy to me, boy. Where are his camels, his possessions, his women?"

"Ah, the ways of foreigners are not our ways, master. Look at his fine beast, instead! Is it not beautiful? Sheik Abdullah would give many pieces of gold and many sheep and camels for such a fine stallion to breed with his mares!"

Rashid pursed his fleshy lips. "Once again, you are right. And besides, what choice do we have? Time flies

414

past! We must rejoin our people on the morrow, and we have met not a single caravan this day! Go, then. Ask the infidel if he would share the warmth of our fire, and our humble supper. And, when his belly is full and he is content, we will offer him the woman."

"The American is a fine figure of a man, is he not, master? One so tall and well-muscled, so very pleasing of face, would no doubt prove virile indeed, and very fond of women! What a pity, yes . . . ?"

"Careful, maggot," Rashid hissed in warning, wearing an ugly expression, "lest I sell you to the American you find so very handsome and virile—and keep the girl for myself!"

"I hear and obey, most kind and indulgent of all masters!" Ali amended hurriedly, wiping the sly grin from his face. Turning to face Nick, he said, "M'sieu, I have spoken with my master. He insists that you partake of our humble meal. He also bade me explain to you that the hospitality of our Bedouin poeple is well-known to all men, and that he will be offended if you should refuse."

Nick grinned. "Son, in that case, I accept! Tell your master—?"

"Rashid," Ali supplied.

"Ah," Nick murmured, and his pale blue eyes kindled. "Tell your master Rashid it's real neighborly of him."

His glance flickered to the woman, though his expression was unreadable. Was it his imagination, or did the eyes within those dark robes slide quickly away, reluctant to meet his . . . ?

A milky moon was hanging in the sky above the silvery sands like a huge pearl when Rashid finally handed his water pipes to Ali. His fleshy features took on a deceptively benevolent expression that the boy knew meant he would soon broach the subject of the woman.

"My master begins, ewellah!" he whispered gleefully to Angel, who was huddled in the opening of the tent. "Soon, you will be gone—! I—er—I mean, free! Soon you will be free."

"And I told *you* I'm not going anywhere with the

American!" Angel hissed, her eyes flaring behind the narrow slit of the ridiculous robe. "You can tell Rashid not to bother with extolling my virtues—I'll take my chances with Sheik Abdullah any day, thank you very much!"

"But, missie, we have—as it is termed in your country, I believe—burned our bridges behind us, yes?" Ali reasoned. "For the past two suns, we have done everything in our power to make my master realize how unsuitable a gift you would be for the sheik, by reason of your complaining nature. Alas, we have done such a bloody fine good job, it will be quite impossible to persuade him otherwise now! I believe that if he cannot sell you to the American, he will cut your throat and have me bury you in the sand!"

Angel's face paled behind her robe. "Please, Ali, you must let me go—! Don't you see? It's the only chance I have left. Let me escape with one of the camels, I beg you! The American is the reason I hid in the carpets in the first place. He's come here, hunting me down! I was running away from him when I saw the carpetmaker's and decided to hide there. Please Ali, you have to do something—he means to kill me! Can't you untie my hands, at least—?"

"Should I untie you, my master would know who to blame—and like you Englishwoman, I have no eagerness to cut short the span of years Allah has granted me! Here. Take this. It is the best I can do. So. Ask no more of me." So saying, he slipped a small knife into her bound hands.

"Thank you," she murmured, close to tears in her fear.

Ali nodded, then, his young face hardened. "Be warned, missie. Should you attempt to use the dagger on my master, I shall know of it—and will slay thee myself!" he added before scuffling away.

After what seemed an eternity of fumbling beneath her heavy outer robe, Angel managed to jiggle the weapon into the waistband of her Turkish pantaloons, no easy task, since Rashid had bound both of her wrists tightly together.

There was nothing left to do now but wait, she thought miserably, uncertain whether to pray that Rashid would succeed in selling her to Nick, or to hope he'd fail and be forced to deal with her himself. She sniffled, and a tear rolled down her nose and dripped off the end. It was a classic example of being between the devil and the deep blue sea . . .

"Do you have many wives in your native America, sir?" Rashid asked congenially, offering his guest a thimble-sized cup of the sweet black coffee the Bedouin people favored.

"In my country, a man's allowed only one wife at a time, Master Rashid," Nick answered, accepting the coffee. "For most men, that already's one too many!" Was it his imagination, or did he catch a snort of outrage from the tent opening where the female huddled like a great black buzzard?

Rashid chuckled. "But that is precisely why a man needs more than one wife, is it not? So that if one should displease him, he may spend the night on his rugs taking his pleasure with another!"

Nick chuckled and raised his cup. "I'll drink to that, pardner! Seems to me there's a lot the folks back home could learn from your customs."

"Ewellah, indeed so." Rashid beamed and inclined his head, showing gold teeth that winked in the firelight. "But, you did not answer my question! Have you a wife?"

"No, sir, I'll be honest with you, I haven't," Nick admitted slowly, convinced now that this was the Rashid he'd been looking for, and that the wily coyote was steadily leading up to a propositon of some kind. "Truth is," he continued in a drawl, watching Rashid's face with a deceptively lazy, heavy-lidded, silvery blue gaze, "I've never much felt the need for one. See, in my country, women t' see to a man's . . . needs . . . are a dime a dozen."

"How fortunate for you, gracious master! However, it is rare that women of great beauty can be persuaded to squander their favors so easily, yes?"

"Hmmm. You got that right on the money, pardner," Nick chortled. "Ugly? Geronimo! Let me tell you, I've woken up beside a few *muchachas* that'd make my horse look mighty fetchin'! But—aw, heck! When you blow out the lamp, there ain't much to choose between 'em, if you know what I mean?" He winked and tapped the side of his nose.

Rashid scowled. The strangely attired, loutish American was proving more difficult than he'd anticipated.

"Say, is that your wife?" the man asked suddenly, tipping his head toward the tent and raising his hat gallantly. "Or should I say, one of 'em?"

Rashid almost wept with relief. Here was the opening he'd been waiting for! "Alas, she is not—though any man would give a sultan's ransom for such a beauty as she! Her name is Desert Nightingale. She is called this because no *houri*, no angel from paradise, sings nigh as sweetly—nor as often—as does she," Rashid enthused. "She was promised to Sheik Abdullah the Fruitful, a peerless virgin jewel intended to grace his *harem* of lovely gems! A budding flower brought from her native climes to join his garden of dusky desert blossoms. But—alas!" Rashid shrugged expressively, "It was not to be. My master soon discovered that his Nightingale was a delicate bud from the north, one that quickly wilted beneath the harsh desert sun. He was forced to accept that she would never flourish or give him strong sons, if she were forced into the hard life of our wandering people. My lord-master has a soft and tender heart where women are concerned, and so, he took pity on the girl and made an enormous sacrifice. With tears in his eyes, he bade his humble servant Rashid take his beloved Desert Nightingale away. He commanded me to find her a rich, honorable husband—one from the city, such as yourself, perhaps?—who could afford to possess such a goddess?" he ended, his brows raised in inquiry.

"Now, whoa, there! Slow down, pardner! You're way ahead of me! I told you, the last thing I need—or want—is a woman!"

"But she is beautiful, I say! To see her is to want her. And to have her but once is to desire her forever—or, so my lord-master says," he added hurriedly, catching a certain look in Nick's eye.

"That doesn't make no never-mind t' me, Rashid, my friend. I like the bachelor life myself . . . most times." He seemed to hesitate. "And besides, I started down this trail with my pockets empty, and they're still empty."

"Empty pockets—pah, what of it? You are a man of honor, as am I. Such trifling details can be discussed at leisure. I implore you, but take a single glance at the woman—to please me, if for no other reason, most gracious master?" Rashid cajoled in silky tones. "After all, it will cost you nothing to look upon her, eh? And besides, have I once mentioned money to you? Never! I would not insult you by speaking of such matters! You and I, we have shared the warmth of a fire. We have shared a meal. We have taken coffee together. You have accepted the hospitality of my camp—ewellah, we are friends, are we not?"

"Weell, I reckon we are, at that . . ."

"And friends do not haggle over money like merchants and beggers in the bazaar, eh? Ali, bring the woman here!" Rashid commanded, clapping his hands. To Nick, he added in a lower voice, "I swear by Allah, if her beauty does not make your man-staff grow harder than ever before, I will return her to her bed with the camels, and speak of her no more!"

"Get up, foolish one! It is time!" Ali hissed in Angel's ear, yanking hard on her elbow.

"No!" Angel refused, digging in her heels. "I won't be paraded before that—that bastard! I won't! 'Dime a dozen' indeed!"

"Would you rather my master slit your throat then, obstinate daughter of a cross-eyed camel? Do as I say, or I shall wash my hands of you and let your Christian God see to your fate!"

He half dragged, half carried Angel across the sand and deposited her in the firelight before the two reclining men. As if made of stone, she sat there, cross-legged, arms folded over her breasts, exactly as she'd been when he pried her from the ground. She was muttering curses beneath the enveloping cloak and looked and sounded, in all honesty, like a black volcano bubbling to an eruption.

"Off with her robe, boy!" Rashid ordered, gesturing to Ali.

With a grin, the boy grasped the headpiece of the robe and pulled, jerking Angel to standing by her hair along with it.

419

"You grinning baboon! You—you spiteful little imp!"

Fuming, she stood in the moonlight with her honey golden hair spilling in glorious streamers over her shoulders, where it had escaped the sheer veils that crowned her lovely head. Her flawless skin was the color of palest pink Italian marble. Its silken smoothness matched the sheen of pearls beneath the stars. The exquisite beauty of her figure was set off to perfection by the sparkly amethyst bolero that skimmed only the upper curves of her breasts, and left their lower fullness bared, with only a single fastening to preserve her modesty. From her rib cage and down over her flat belly, which had the shadow of her dimpling navel at its center, she was all supple, satin flesh, below which the lissome curves of her hips and bottom vanished beneath clouds of gauzy lavender pantaloons that fastened with a belt of the same glittery purple cloth as the skimpy blouse. She was beautiful, magnificent, sensual, exquisitely feminine—and utterly and completely furious.

"Gerrr—onimo!" Nick breathed, letting out the breath he'd been holding. Staring, he whistled under his breath, stunned speechless despite himself. Oh, he'd expected to see Angel, all right—but not looking anything like this—!

"Ah," Rashid murmured softly, rubbing pudgy hands together as he saw the transported expression on Nick's face. "You see? Did I not tell thee she was lovely beyond compare . . . ?"

"Lovely ain't the half of it, pardner," Nick managed to gasp hoarsely, his eyes meeting Angel's smoking gray ones. Damn if she didn't look about ready to eat him alive, then spit out the pieces! "She's Eve," he stammered, "straight from the Garden of Eden! She's Venus risin' from the foam. She's Betsy Ross and Martha Washington, Queen Victoria an' lil' Annie Oakley all rolled into one! Damn it, ordinary words just ain't fancy enough t' describe this little filly, Rashid!"

Rashid smiled slyly. He had been correct in his earlier assessment of the fellow. The American was nothing more than a foolish peasant, an infidel dog who was ruled by his man-staff. The woman was as good as sold! Only her price remained to be settled . . .

"Ewellah, my friend, you do like her very much, I can tell," Rashid murmured silkily. "Enough, perhaps, to exchange her for your . . . stallion?"

Nick's head jerked up. "My horse in trade for the woman? Hell, no! Nothin' doin', Rashid. That horse an' me, hell, we've come a long ways together, we have. There's nothing on the face of this earth I'd trade for ole Diablo, no siree!"

"Come, come, my friend. Relax and have just another little cupful of coffee. We are in no hurry, after all. There is more than time enough to discuss this little matter at our leisure, yes?"

Nick pointed his finger at Rashid. "We'll discuss it all you like, pardner, but hear this. Diablo ain't a part of this trade, understand?"

"Of course. I understand very well. A man's horses, his racing camels, his hawks, and his dogs—they are dear to his heart, yes? If you say there will be no horse in our discussions, then there will be no horse, my fine friend . . ."

Chapter Thirty-Four

"This came about five minutes ago. That Knuckles Figg bloke slipped it under Nick's door. I stuck me head out in the 'all an' saw 'im meself."

Juarez nodded and eagerly unfolded the sheet of hotel notepaper Mabel handed him. He quickly scanned the message—block capitals scrawled in smudgy pencil. "It's on for tonight at eight, *querida*. They want us to meet with them at the Brixton cotton warehouse, down by the harbor."

"But Nick's not back yet! We don't even know where the bloody hell he an' Angel are! How'll you . . . ?" Mabel caught the expression on her husband's face and paled. "Oww, Gawd, luv, no! Tell me you in't thinkin' of meetin' them alone?"

Her husband shrugged, refusing to meet her frightened eyes. "If it's the only way to get these *hombres*, little one, I have no choice."

Panic filled Mabel's eyes. "Of course you've got a choice, ducks! You can wait 'til Nick gets back, can't you? This ain't your fight, it's Durango's and Angel's."

"*Sí*. But they are our friends—and friends look out for each other, yes? That makes their fight my fight, too. Nick would do no less for me, were things reversed and your life in danger, and you know it."

"I do," she admitted, "but—but you've already done more than enough, luv," she wheedled, slipping her arms around his waist and pressing her head against his chest. "Please, Antonio, I'm afraid! An' I'm beggin' yer, don't do

422

it luv! Don't go!"

The softly spoken, pleading way she said his given name, the caress of her fingers as they trailed over his chest, almost swayed him. "Mabella, *querida mía*, please . . . don't make it any harder for me, eh? This is something I have to do. I could not live with myself if I did nothing."

She sighed heavily. "Oww, all right, then. If you won't be sensible, you won't. Go an' meet those bleedin' thugs, if yer must—but I'm comin' wiv yer!"

"You—? Never!"

"Oh ho, 'never,' is it? Ooo, we'll see about that!" Mabel promised defiantly, sticking out her tongue and smiling a cheeky grin as she whirled away from him.

"Disobey me, woman, and you will be sorry," Juarez warned sternly, waggling a finger at her.

"I will, will I? Wotcha gonna do, then, you big old bully? Beat me bum 'til it turns black and blue?" She rolled her eyes naughtily. "Who knows, I just might like it!"

Despite his anger, Juarez couldn't help laughing. "You! My darling, you are incorrigible!"

"In-co—? In-ca—? Wot's that mean, then?" she demanded suspiciously, not at all certain he wasn't insulting her.

"It means that you are quite impossible—but that I love you more than my life, little kitten," Juarez said simply, catching her around the waist and planting a kiss on her pert nose. "And, because of this great love I have for you, you will do exactly as I say, yes? You'll be a good girl and wait here for me to return."

"Oh, all right, then. I give up. You're the boss, I s'pose," she acquiesced with a rueful smile. "I'll wait right here."

Her sudden turnabout should have warned him, but he was so preoccupied with thoughts of the confrontation that evening, her promise brought him feelings of relief, rather than suspicion, and he smiled and nodded absently. All going well, this evening he would at last learn the name of the animal who wanted to kidnap *pobrecita* Angelica so very badly, he would murder anyone who got in his way. Excitement and the thrill of danger pumped through his veins. He would go alone, and he would play the game as Nick had planned, pretending he wanted to be dealt in on the señorita's kidnapping and share a hefty cut of the ransom. And, when his cousin returned with the girl, he, Antonio de Montoya y Juarez would have the name of the man who had eluded them for so long . . .

"Now. Movin' right along, ducks, do you want t' feed that bleedin' monkey its breakfast this mornin', or shall I?" Mabel asked, cutting into his thoughts. She selected a ripe banana from the fruit bowl on the table and deftly peeled it.

Juarez grinned at his wife's description of Tiny Figg. Before leaving, Nick'd suggested they hold Tiny in Angel's suite as insurance, after releasing his brother Knuckles to act as a go-between. His dark eyes were soft with tenderness and passion as he gazed at her. "Don't worry, I'll take care of him. And when I return . . . aiee, *then* I shall take care of my little red flower, no?"

Mabel blushed and giggled. "And we know *how* you'll take care o' me, too, don't we, you randy young devil, you!" She was suddenly breathless, her eyes as soft and yearning with passion as his. "Just—just get a move on, Warez!" she urged in a shaky whisper, trailing a fingertip down his chest and flat belly to the fringes that hemmed his buckskin shirt. "I'm a *very* impatient girl, I am. I don't like t' be kept waitin . . ."

"*Sí*. I know." Juarez grinned and blew her a kiss as he left her to tend to their hostage, peeled banana in hand.

"Damn it, keep walking or I'll drag you along!" Nick growled.

"Why don't you just kill me and be done with it, you bastard?" Angel panted, pulling back on the lariat he'd looped about her wrist on leaving Rashid's camp. "Why prolong the agony? I'm not a little mouse you can play with like a . . . like a cruel tomcat!"

Nick halted and spun about on his heels to face her. "Kill you? If I've told you once, you infernal woman, I've told you a hundred times since we left the oasis: *I never intended to kill you!*" he thundered. "Maybe now . . . it doesn't seem such a bad idea! . . . but back then, it was all part of an act. A plan that Red came up with, so's Juarez and me could flush the Figg brothers' employer out into the open. Why can't you believe that?"

She grimaced. "Hmmpph! With your past record, you can't seriously expect me to believe *anything* you'd tell me?"

"Frankly, honey, right now I don't give a hot-damn on a larded griddle *what* you believe! I'm done tryin' to convince you, see? Ever since I met up with you, I've lost more of my clothes, my guns, my gear, and my dignity than I lost in a whole lifetime before! Fact is, I'm getting pretty damn tired of walking all over this damn world barefoot and half-naked with you hangin' on my tail, complaining!"

"Oh, I'm sure you are. And speaking of walking, don't forget about your precious horse! I'm sure you'll want to include losing Diablo among your list of losses when you present my father with the bill!"

"Losing my horse is the smallest part of my problem. Right now, I'd like a hat and a shirt to wear—any hat, any shirt!—before the sun comes up and fries me alive. I'd like my guns, too—so's I can shoot anyone that gets me t' feelin' any more ornery than I am right now!" he added, casting her a darkling look. "But more than anything, right know I'd like my bandanna back . . ." he ended with grim feeling.

"Why that?" she demanded, curious. "So you could use it to strangle me?"

"No! So I could tie it around your blamed mouth and shut you up for a spell!" he bellowed, halting and whirling on her again with such abruptness, she actually flinched and took a step backward. "Damn it, woman, for someone who's been rescued from rape, torture, and death at the hands of that sidewinder Rashid, you ain't exactly brimmin' over with gratitude, are you?"

"No, I'm not! In fact, you were the very last person on earth I wanted to be rescued by, Durango! You see, I overheard you and Juarez and those awful men cooking up your sneaky little double cross in my hotel suite, so there's no way you can convince me to trust you, ever again! I don't believe your claims of innocence and I sincerely doubt I ever will. What's more, Uncle Teddy

425

took me to see Inspector Jamieson at the British Consulate the other day. Jamieson told me that the Yard has been on to you for quite some time!" she flung at him triumphantly. "So you may well kill me, Durango—but you'll *never* get away with it!" Somehow, the latter idea wasn't half the comfort to her it should have been.

"Jamieson? Who the hell's Jamieson?"

"He's an Inspector of Detectives from Scotland Yard in London—the biggest, most efficient, and advanced police agency in all of England, as I'm sure you're perfectly well aware. Jamieson's been investigating the murders of Bligh and Reggie. He was also called in to investigate my—er—false kidnapping."

"You mean, he's here, in Egypt?"

"He is indeed—and following hot on the scent of a trail that leads directly to you, Mr. King of the Cowboys! Pray tell, how does it feel to know the net's closing in around you?" she asked with relish. "To feel the noose tightening about your neck? How does it feel knowing the coppers are just waiting to batter down your door?" She laughed and tossed her head in a grand show of bravado she was far from feeling. "Show your ugly face in Cairo again, Durango, and Jamieson'll have you arrested before you can say 'Geronimo'!"

"Lady, that's the biggest load of bullshit I ever heard!, even from you," Durango growled. Scowling, he proceeded to ignore her, striding along wrapped in thought. Damn, but there was something about this whole mess that just got fishier and fishier! He had a sneaking hunch he already had the answer to the puzzle somewhere, if he could just fit all the pieces together the right way. But for now, he had to concentrate on getting them back to the city in one piece—and hopefully do so before Knuckles set up the meeting with his boss. There was slim hope of that, though, once the blazing African sun came up in an hour or two. Once day broke, without camels or horses, no shade, and only a half goatskin of foul-tasting water, Angel wouldn't last long, not with her fair skin and delicate female constitution. He'd be cooked alive himself, soon after, half-dressed as he was, before they'd gone more than a mile or two.

His eyes narrowed. His ferocious scowl deepened. How could he have let this happen, he asked himself furious at no one but himself now? He'd always fancied himself for a pretty slick trader, but that sidewinder Rashid took the biscuit! The oily Arab had weaseled him out of everything in trade for Angel, that ungrateful, carping little witch. He'd been forced to surrender his Stetson, his red silk bandanna, his pearl-handled Colts, his second-best black silk shirt, his vest with the silver conchas, his stilt-heeled Spanish leather *vaquero* boots—hell, that slime-suckin' leech had even taken his socks, for Pete's sake! And of course, Rashid had Diablo—though Diablo had been the one part of the deal he'd figured on losing all along, knowing how the Arabs coveted fine horses, he considered with a thin, humorless smile. Which reminded him . . .

"Sit down and take a breather," he rasped, thrusting the goatskin into Angel's hands and planting his palms on her shoulders and shoving her to make certain she sat. "Have a swig of water or something. We'll rest here for a few minutes before going on."

Without comment, she tilted the hairy waterskin's spout to her lips and drank, her gray eyes following him warily as he climbed, slipping and slithering in the sand, to the very top of the dune at their backs. Raising his fingers to his mouth, he gave three piercing whistles, waited, then repeated the signal a second time, before sliding back down the hill on the seat of his pants.

"An old cowboy custom—or are you expecting company?" she inquired sourly, flinging the waterskin back at him so forcefully, it drove the wind from his belly.

"In a manner of speaking, yes," he admitted, taking a swig himself.

"Ah. Your trusty cohorts, the faithful Figg brothers, perchance?"

"Aw, grow up. And quit being bitchy. I've had enough!"

"*You've* had enough? What about me?" she shrieked at him, her nerves shredded. "I certainly didn't ask to be stranded out here in this godforsaken desert, nor ask to be left at the mercy of someone whose sole aim in life is to—is to wish me 'adiós and goodbye'—*permanently!*"

"People who eavesdrop never hear good about themselves, Angel—didn't your mama ever tell you that?"

"How could she! Mam died when I was eight."

"Sorry. I forgot."

"Don't mention it," Angel muttered, trying to sniff back her tears of self-pity. But, trying didn't help much, and crying within the full robe's musty confines made her feel hot and overwhelmingly claustrophobic. With a curse, she lifted the hated tentlike garment over her head and flung it aside, grateful for the cool kiss of the nightwind against her skin, which was inflamed and reddened in several places from the wool robe's scratchy fibers. Blinking back tears, she rubbed her hurts.

Nick, sitting next to her, involuntarily swallowed as he looked her up and down. Her bared skin was the color of alabaster; her hair, tumbling loose about her shoulders, a river of gold shot through with copper threads. It was a blamed mystery, but somehow, she seemed more naked than naked in the moonlight, wearing only those sparkly folderols—and far too damned lovely for comfort! He felt his groin tighten in response to her charms and wetted his lips, trying to quell his lustier inclinations. His manhood clearly had other ideas, however, damn it, despite the seriousness of the situation. Right now, his peter was straining against his trouser buttons, standing straight up like a goddamned totem pole!

"Damn it, you're asking for trouble, dressed like that," he rasped huskily. "Put that tent thing back on!"

"I will not. It's too hot and besides, it itches like mad. And as for my choice of clothing—! As I recall, I didn't have much say in selecting this delightful ensemble," she hiccupped. "It was 'Wear this, woman, or d-d-d-ie'!"

"Damn it, don't cry," he barked. "Do any damned thing but start blubbering!" He reached out, meaning to brush a tear from her damp cheek with his knuckle, but quick as a flash, she rolled away from him, drawing a small dagger from her belt that winked silvery fire in the fading moonlight as she righted herself.

"I am *not* blubbering. It's—it's p-p-p-perspiration, that's all!"

Snorting with disbelief, he made another motion

428

toward her, but quick as a wink, she brought her knife hand up and brandished the hidden blade defensively. "Oh, no, you don't! Just keep your bloody distance, Durango! You tricked me once into thinking you cared for me, with your sweet talk and your kisses and your sympathetic, protective act, but it won't work a second time. Lay a finger on me and I'll—I'll slice you from—from stem to stern!" It was an expression she'd picked up from a pirate novelette ages ago, one that sounded appropriately bloodthirsty.

"Goddamnit! What does a man have to do to convince you?" Nick exploded, running his hands through his black hair. "Everything I've done since the night your father hired me, I've done to protect you. And the kisses and sweet talk, they were *real*, God-help-me, lady. Angel, honey—darlin', sweet thing!—be sensible, huh? If I wanted to kill you, baby, I could have strangled you a hundred times with my bare hands since we left Rashid's camp!"

"No, you wouldn't have, not *yet*. Do you think I'm that stupid? You can't finish me off, because my father might demand some proof that I'm still alive before he'll pay your bloody ransom! Once you have the money, though, it'll be quite another story, eh, Durango?"

"That does it. Think what the devil you want! You're too blamed mule-headed to believe me, so if you'd rather take the word of this Inspector Jamieson, you go right ahead! I've been wastin' my breath all along, haven't I? There's nothing I can do to convince you or change your mind, is there?"

"You lied about Reggie and Bligh's deaths! How could I ever trust you completely after that? If you lied about that, then perhaps you lied about everything?"

"But I didn't lie," he gritted.

"All right, all right, you didn't actually lie. You just—neglected—to tell me about them. But why, Durango? Why haven't you explained? Why did you let me go on thinking Bligh was alive—that it was his boys following us?"

"Because if I told you about Bligh, then I figured I'd have to tell you about Reggie being fished out of the Seine," he admitted grudgingly.

"I see. And exactly why didn't you want me to know about Reggie's death?"

"Not because I killed him, that's for sure!" he shot back.

"But what other reason could there be?"

Silence yawned between them for several moments before Nick sighed heavily and spoke again.

"I didn't tell you because—aw hell, because I was *jealous*, goddamnit. Satisfied? If you must know—I was jealous as hell! I knew you were still hoppin' mad at Reggie for the way he'd treated you, and truth was, I liked things just fine the way they were—with you sore at him. But I knew once you found out Reggie was dead, you'd get all mushy and sorry about the way things had finished between you—and I was right, remember? So I just plain . . . forgot . . . about it."

"Jealous? You were jealous of Reggie? But—why?" she exclaimed, stunned, her knife hand falling slack at her side.

"Never mind why," he snarled, his handsome, dark face swarthy in the starlight, his pale eyes silvery slits beneath hooded brows. "It's old news—history."

"No, it's not. *I* don't know. Tell me!"

"Why bother? You wouldn't believe me if I tried."

"Try me. I might."

"Uh huh. That moon up there don't look blue to me— and a blue moon's about what it'd take to convince you of anything, woman!"

"Well, at least give me the option," she cajoled, her heart racing.

He sighed heavily. "All right." He paused, then looked her straight in the eye. "I was jealous . . ."

The world grew very still in that instant, not even the cry of the nighthawk rupturing the desert hush.

". . . because . . ."

The stars ceased to pulse. The night wind stilled. The full, nonblue moon held her breath—and so did Angel.

". . . I was falling in love with you!"

"Falling in love? With me, you mean? Oh, what utter nonsense! You've disappointed me, Durango. I could believe almost anything but that!" she accused bitterly.

"You asked me why I didn't tell you about Bligh and

Reggie, and I've told you the truth—the whole truth," he ground out in a dangerously soft tone.

"You certainly did—but let's face it, words really mean very little," Angel said stiffly, certain he hadn't meant it, afraid to dream for even one joyous moment that he had, and risk the hurt that discovering he was lying would bring. "When you get right down to it, it's a man's *actions* that count. I'm afraid there's been very little in your past behavior to support your claims."

"Support my—aw, Geronimo! I just knew it!" Nick bellowed, the last shred of his patience scattered to the winds.

Barechested, bareheaded, barefoot, his holsters slapping empty leather along his thighs, he flung the lariat aside and began striding off across the sands alone, headed for still more undulating sandhills at furious speed. "Goddamned woman! Y' just can't win with her, no matter which way you play it. Tell the truth, she says you're lying. Lie, and she reckons it's the gospel truth! Tell her you love her, an' she says you don't. Say you *don't* love her—and she cries because she wants you t' say you do! Fact is, tell her anything at all and it don't count because actions speak louder than words. Hell and damnation, I give up. Stay out here, woman. Roast! Die of thirst! Get bit by scorpions an' snakes! Eaten alive by ants and sandflies! I don't *care* anymore, 'cos I'm goin' home—home t' good old Santa Fe. Now, there's a place where folks say what they mean, and mean what they say—and there ain't a blasted Limey in spittin' distance for a thousand miles . . . !"

Chapter Thirty-Five

The wharves were deserted and cloaked in heavy shadow when Juarez, costumed as Panther-Who-Stalks, rode between the warehouses to the meeting place that night.

Halting his paint mustang in the moonlight, he double-checked the address on the note, comparing it to the tall black letters stenciled on the warehouse doors before him. "Brixton Cotton Mills, Brixton, Lancs, England," they read. This was the place.

He dismounted and hauled Tiny Figg down after him by the scruff of his lardy neck, leaving the little mare ground-tied with a quick, fond pat before padding up to the building on moccasined feet.

The huge lading gates were barred and padlocked for the night, but there was a small door off to one side that stood ajar. Drawing his knife, Juarez shoved Tiny's massive bulk through it, ahead of him.

Silence awaited them within; cottony silence and shadows. Juarez, sweat trickling down his face in the stifling heat, stood very still, listening, waiting, until his eyes adjusted to the gloom.

He could hear the scratch and scurry of rats; the slap of Nile water lapping at the piers, as well as his own heart beating, and Tiny's labored breathing. He could smell the cotton and the odors of old sweat, dirt, stagnant water, and, very faintly, the tangy, alien fragrance of fruit. Lemons?

He looked about him. Bale after white bale of the finest Egyptian cotton rose in stacks to the rafters on every side of him, while a solitary narrow pathway led between the textile towers, like the paths in a great white boxwood maze. There was no sign of anyone else there.

"Move, *hombre!*" Juarez growled softly, shoving Tiny in the small of the back. Oxlike, the bigger man grunted and lumbered forward through the opening. When Juarez judged that they were in the center of the warehouse, he halted. "That's far enough. Now. Sing out, Señor canary! Let your friends hear your pretty voice, eh?"

Tiny bellowed, "Knuckles! It's me, Tiny. You in 'ere?"

Tiny's voice was the last sound Juarez heard before a plank clipped him across the back of the skull. With a startled grunt, he folded unconscious to the dirt.

"Damn!"

Angel's head jerked up as Nick, stomping along a few feet ahead of her, suddenly lurched backwards. He writhed in the sand, clutching his bare foot.

"What is it?" she cried, dropping to her knees alongside him. She cast him a wary look, anticipating some subterfuge or other on his part.

"My foot! I stepped on somethin'."

"Really?" she echoed suspiciously. "Here. Let me see."

"Uh uh. Thanks, I'll pass," he refused her offer, looking pointedly at the knife in her hand.

"Oh, you," she grumbled, tossing it aside. "Satisfied? Now, turn over, give me your foot, and let me have a look at it."

Gingerly, he did as she told him, taking the knife she'd dropped into his own keeping when she wasn't looking. As she probed gently, he could feel the warm flow of blood pouring down the sole of his foot and gritted his teeth at the stabbing pain even her gentle touch caused him. "What the hell is it?"

"It's hard to tell in this light, it's so bloody, but . . . I think it's a gigantic thorn. I'm afraid it'll have to come out as soon as possible. You're bleeding like a pig, you see. And besides, the wound'll fester very quickly in this climate, if it stays in there."

Nick groaned. This was all he needed! "Can you grab a

433

hold of it, maybe pull it out?"

She pursed her lips. "I'll certainly try. Hold still."

He gritted his teeth again while she did her best, but though her nails were long enough, the thorn—a huge one with a base almost a half-inch across—was firmly embedded in his tough sole. Even the slightest effort to dislodge it made fresh blood gush from the wound, and it was so painful, the sweat stood out on Nick's face, though he staunchly refused to cry out.

"I'm sorry, it's no use. My fingers just aren't strong enough. I think I might be able to hook it out with the knife blade, though." Her expression said that she knew very well he'd palmed the weapon.

"You don't say! But the real question is, ma'am, could I trust you not to stick it between my ribs instead?" he asked in a mocking tone, eyeing her speculatively.

A wry smile curved her lips. "I think you might safely do so, yes," she assured him sweetly. "You see, British decency—the code by which I live—absolutely forbids taking advantage of one's enemy when he's wounded and helpless."

"Well, ain't that mighty reassuring t' hear," Nick muttered insincerely, wincing as she callously dropped his foot.

"Isn't it, though?" she agreed, rocking back on her heels to consider him. Despite his flippant tone and her own response, she knew having such a huge thorn embedded in his foot must be dreadfully painful, not to mention potentially dangerous. And—though she loathed the horrid man, mistrusted him, detested him, God help her, she still cared enough to empathize with his suffering and want to ease it.

"What now? You sitting there, waiting for me t' die, like a blamed buzzard?" he asked, cocking a brow up at her when she'd sat there for some time without speaking.

"Patience is a virtue—but alas, I doubt I'd ever be that lucky. Nor that you—infuriating man that you are— would prove so obliging. So, I was waiting for you to hand me the knife."

"Is that what would make you happy, Angel?" he asked huskily, his gaze flickering over the exotic picture she

434

made, kneeling beside him in her sparkly harem attire. "Watching me die?"

For a fleeting instant, her horror at such a thought was mirrored in her eyes, but then her jaw hardened—a feat her heart just couldn't seem to accomplish, where he was concerned, dash it all, no matter how hard she tried.

Ignoring his question, she insisted, "Your foot, Durango. The knife, man! Give it here! Do you want me to remove that thorn for you, or not?"

"Wh-what thorn?" he murmured weakly. His eyes crossed, then suddenly fluttered shut. A great shudder moved through his body, one so violent, she thought she heard his teeth chatter. Or—had it been the death rattle?

Panic leaped through her. If he was to die, she'd be all alone out here! She grasped his shoulder and shook him. "Durango! Don't you dare pass out on me! Wake up!"

"Ye-es? I hear you. What was it you said, *mama?*" he babbled, and then with a terrible groan, his eyes closed completely once again. His head lurched to one side and he lay very, very still—so still, her heart skipped a beat. Had the thorn been from some virulently poisonous tree? Had it, perhaps, contained a poison that had raced through his veins to still his heart forever—? Was he even now dying, while she looked on, helpless to save him . . . ? Anything was possible in this loathsome country! She stared at his bare, tanned chest without blinking, her gray eyes enormous with dread as she searched for signs of movement.

Nothing.

Oh, Lord, no! It was true. In the cold gray moonlight, she could discern no rise and fall of his chest whatsoever. Nick had stopped breathing—

She pressed her ear to his chest, frantically praying, *Please, oh, please, let him be alive! I love him, even if he's a rogue and a thief! Don't let him die!*

To her relief, her prayers were answered. She heard a strong thump, followed by a second stout heartbeat. Then—in the same moment she realized he'd been faking—Nick's arms snaked around her waist, holding her fast.

"Come here t' me, sweet thing," he murmured thickly in

435

her ear as he rolled her to the sand beside him.

"What are you doing? Don't you dare touch me! Let me go, you brute!" she protested, flailing her clenched fists at his head and shoulders.

"No way, sweetness." He grinned down into her lovely furious face, a swarthy handsome devil with a determined gleam in his ice-and-fire eyes now that boded ill. "See, you claimed back down the trail a ways that a man's words don't count. You claimed it was his actions that really counted—that actions spoke louder than words, remember? Well, honey, I've decided you're right! I've decided to give up talkin' right now, and let my little old actions speak for themselves. Come sun-up, if you have any doubts left in your pretty little head that I love you, and that I'd sooner die than harm a single golden hair on it, damn it, I'll become a—a monk! Now. Pucker up, angel lips!"

Juarez groaned. He tried to sit up, but failed. The pain in his skull was excruciating! It sent waves of nausea and agony pounding through him, pain so violent, it made him tremble with weakness.

"*Jesús y María!*" he moaned, clutching his head, trying to remember what had hit him as he reached out into the darkness, seeking handholds by which to haul himself to standing.

His fingers encountered a stout length of two-by-four planking at his side, then brushed against something else—something warm and bulky just beyond it.

He stiffened, for he'd touched a burly arm, a fleshy face with something coppery-smelling trickling down over a misshapen nose to pool in the folds of a paunchy neck. He groaned as memory flooded back. He was in the Brixton cotton warehouse. Someone had laid him out cold with that length of wood—and it was Tiny sprawled there, probably dead! Fumbling in the gloom for the man's wrist, he found it, and felt for a pulse. There was none. Tiny was dead, all right—killed by the same bastard who'd knocked him out. . . .

Hooking his fingers through the baling wire of the

cotton bales that towered on either side of him, he hauled himself to standing and began staggering back the way he'd come, if memory served, headed for the small side door by which he'd entered the warehouse. With the stink of Tiny's blood full in his nostrils, and the pounding torture in his skull, he needed fresh air, and badly!

Sure enough, he found the door with ease—but it was now closed and, he discovered, securely bolted from the outside. His efforts to open it made sweat pour off his brow, made his limbs tremble uncontrollably, but failed. *Por Diós!* The blow had left him weak as a kitten! Mumbling a curse, he reeled groggily away, trying to remember if he'd seen any other exits to the warehouse, other than the massive, heavily barred lading doors.

The towers of cotton bales on either side of him were all alike. Their similarity robbed him of his sense of direction, made him feel as if he were a tiny mouse running through a gigantic maze—a maze which, in his sorry state, seemed to have no way out! Left, then right, then straight, then left again, he stumbled in and out as if caught in the coils of a nightmare. But then, suddenly, his moccasined toe caught on something huddled across his path. He pitched forward and was sent sprawling on his belly, the wind knocked from him.

When he'd recovered a little, he thought at first he'd been walking in circles, for his hands had encountered yet another body, firmly wedged across the pathway between the bales. But it was not Tiny Figg who lay there. Narrow shafts of moonlight streaming down from a small slit of a window way above revealed the ferrety face of Tiny's brother, Knuckles. He was, Juarez quickly ascertained, also quite dead. The rear of his skull had been shattered like an eggshell.

Juarez sat very still. His throbbing head cocked to one side, he listened intently. Whoever had killed the Figg brothers had surely intended to kill him, too—or had they? He frowned. They'd dispatched the other pair so efficiently, it seemed unlikely they'd bungle his death! They'd either mistakenly left him for dead, like the others, or for some reason had wanted him kept alive . . . ? Moving gingerly, he stood up and waited for the knives of pain slicing through his skull to dull a little, realizing suddenly that if his first suspicion was correct, whoever had done this terrible thing might still be here, in the warehouse. They might find only two bodies, instead of three, and try to remedy their mistake! He must try very quietly to find a way out, before they came looking for him.

His back pressed to the cotton bales, his arms outstretched on either side of him, Juarez resumed his search for an exit. He'd gone only a few yards when the acrid smell of burning cotton seared his nostrils. . . .

Angel was fuming with impotent rage as Nick dipped his head to kiss her.

It seemed unimportant to him that he had to hold her wrists above her head in the loose sand to prevent her escape, or that his leg thrown across her hips was needed to keep her from squirming free, or even that she was screaming to the very stars for him to stop, to let her go *at once!* Oh, no! Holding her immobile, the villainous, double-crossing rogue kissed her thoroughly, expertly, stirring her senses with the light brush of his lips moving over hers—a touch here, a caress there, a teasing little nibble everywhere—never lingering in any one spot long enough to truly satisfy, curse him!

Tossing her head from side to side, she told herself she was trying to escape his kisses, that her sudden desire to move against him had nothing at all to do with the way his maddening lips were making her feel, any more than did the warmth and hardness of his body pressed against hers. "Nick Durango," she warned, breathless, "if you don't stop right now, I'll—"

"Hush, darlin'," he murmured, nuzzling the hollows of her throat, trailing his mouth upwards to tug very gently on her succulent little pink earlobe with his teeth. "No talkin', remember? Actions, darlin'! Actions speak louder than those empty, meaningless little ole words!" As if to add emphasis to his taunting words, he transferred both of her wrists to his left hand and with the right, worked the silk frog fastening of her bodice free. She gasped as the too-short bolero fell away, exposing the creamy mounds of her bosom to his scorching gaze beneath the light of the stars and the moon. "Damned if you weren't right all along, Angel!" he murmured huskily. "That action said 'I want you, desire you,' clear as day, didn't it?"

"You know bloody well that's not what I meant!"

But he gave no reply, and as his lecherous gaze devoured her bosom, she moaned silently, for both breasts had surged, both tiny, rose pink nipples had also grown hard as rubies beneath his eyes, inviting him to taste, to adore.

Sure enough, like a pagan supplicant, Nick knelt at her shrine and bowed his head in worship, delicately drawing first one ripened morsel then the other into the flaming heat of his mouth, swirling the very tips of her breasts with the tip of his tongue.

A sizzling jolt of sensation traveled a hot wire through her that reached from her breasts to the very pit of her belly, one so arousing, she could not help but utter a strangled moan.

"Damn you, damn you . . . !" she sobbed, her gray eyes veiled and heavy-lidded with mounting passion. She caught her moist lower lip between her teeth to staunch any further such shameless outbursts, but if Nick heard her or was aware of the torment raging through her, he gave no sign.

Moments later, he covered her nipple with his mouth and began to suckle her so deeply, so pleasurably, she arched up, rising clear off the sand in her frenzy. Nick tut-tutted his disapproval and pressed her back down, only to continue his maddening assault on her second breast. Cupping it in the warmth of his big, tanned hand, he expertly plied her with his lips, his tongue, and gentle teeth, to drive her to the brink of madness—a madness she vowed to withstand, come hell or high water! No, he wouldn't have his way with her so easily, not this time, she swore. She'd never again surrender to this—this lying scoundrel, no matter how much—how very, very much!—she loved him, or how very much he made her burn for him. His "actions" could do all the talking he wanted them to! She'd be damned if she'd encourage them, or welcome so much as a single caress. . . .

Nick trailed his mouth down over her rib cage, hiding a

grin against her creamy body as she sucked in her belly in a desperate effort to evade his lips. Undaunted, he lapped at the tiny indentation of her navel, kissed it noisily and wetly, then growled and ran his tongue beneath the sparkly waistband of her gauzy pantaloons, tugged at it with his teeth like a naughty pup.

His warm breath, the sensation of his lips against her belly, were incredible! She wanted to shriek, to squeal like a wild animal as a jolt ran through her body—one Nick felt against his mouth. Grinning and glancing up, he saw that in the moonlight, a tiny solitary bead of sweat stood out on her lovely brow like a jewel. Her lower lip was caught between her teeth. Her eyes were closed in rapture. He chuckled softly. She was doing a mighty fine job of pretending to be immune to what he was doing—but surer than water was wet, she was losing the fight!

Leaning up, he shifted his "attack" to her feet, tugging off the curly-toed Turkish slippers one by one to massage her arches. She squirmed with his tickling touch, clamping down even harder on her lower lip than before. With a lazy smile, Nick picked up her bare, pink little foot and began kissing her toes, one by one, raking his teeth over all ten of them and playfully biting the plump little pink pads underneath each upper joint. He did the same with her other foot, then stroked her calves and knees above her pantaloons with sweeping caresses that ended just short of the joining of her thighs. She was, he noted with a surge of triumph, holding her breath now as his hand hovered over her lower belly—and not, he was certain, holding it with anything approaching apprehension. Hell, no! Unless he missed his mark, it was anticipation that made the breath catch in lil' Miz Iron Drawers' throat!

Moving at a lazy pace that made her want to scream, Nick's warm fingers slipped beneath the waistband of her pantaloons, fondling her lower belly with the flat of his palm. Her wrists, still locked in the vise of his fingers, were rigid now, her fingers knotted so tightly into fists, the knuckles were white in the moonlight. She didn't even react as he released them! And, on the desert hush, he could hear the fluttery rasp of her breathing, see the quickened rise and fall of her bared breasts and the slight but rapid undulation of her hips. Grasping the waistband, he unfastened the cord ties and slowly began to slide the garment down, off her hips, enjoying the vision of flat ivory belly, the tuft of gold fluff and slender, milk white thighs that were bared as he did so.

"Now . . ." he murmured wickedly as he cast the garment aside, eyeing her like a lecherous wolf as he knelt between her thighs, ". . . you're gonna get all the 'action' you ever *dreamed* of, sweet thing!"

Chapter Thirty-Six

Juarez flinched as a bale of cotton suddenly exploded behind him, but he didn't dare look back. His skull still throbbing, his breathing now wheezing pants, he scrabbled on hands and knees between the towering walls of cotton bales like a crab, keeping low to avoid the dense, choking smoke that was quickly filling the warehouse, singeing his nostrils and throat with its acrid stench.

Could he hope to outrun the fire and escape? Casting a hurried glance over his shoulder now, he was, for the first time, afraid. A roaring wall of fire reached clear to the warehouse rafters behind him, devouring the spot where he'd tripped over Knuckles' body only seconds ago! If he didn't find a way out—and soon!—he'd be cut off, surrounded by it, consumed! The greedy, crackling fire was feasting on the dry bales. It had already spread with lightning speed, leaping from stacked bales to stacked bales like a predatory orange monster, engulfing fresh fuel in its crimson jaws, before moving rapidly on to its next meal. The white maze of cotton bales had become a maze of fire—a deathtrap!

Coughing now, his eyes streaming, the searing pain in his lungs more excruciating with every shallow breath, Juarez wriggled on his belly and elbows the last few yards to the side door, almost weeping with relief when his outstretched hands confirmed that he'd found it once again, *Gracias a Diós!* With the darkness and with smoke everywhere, he'd known of no other way out, and dared not waste precious time in searching for other exits. The fire was rapidly gaining on him from behind, while far above his head, the rafters were succumbing to its jealous, snapping jaws, tongues of flame licking along the beams. Before too long, the roof would cave in. This time, he *had to* break the door down with his fists—before the fire caught up with him or the smoke overpowered him—or he would die.

Dragging himself upright, he began battering at the door with his bare fists, unaware that it was blistering his hands.

"Help!" he croaked, throwing his body full-weight against the door. It shuddered but remained solid. "For the love of God, someone—! Help me!" he rasped as the warehouse swam in his vision. . . .

"*Warez?*" Mabel screamed from the other side of the door. "Aw, Gaawd, luv, push! Push!"

He heard her beloved voice and almost wept with relief that she was there; that he had heard the voice of his little red flower once more. "Querida, get away from the door!" he roared. "It might collapse!"

"I'm not leavin' here without you! Push!" she screamed back.

With his remaining strength, Juarez threw his shoulder against the door again, while she desperately tugged at the padlock. The metal was already too hot to touch, but in her panic to save him, her burns also went unnoticed. She had to get him out. She loved him so—! She had to!

To think, just moments earlier, she'd been tippytoeing around the warehouse, congratulating herself on pulling the wool over her husband's eyes.

She'd followed him on foot to his assignation with the Figgs and their mystery boss, thinking that whether he liked it or not, he wouldn't meet with those bleedin' bastards alone, not if she could help it. She'd seen him vanish through this door and had circled around the building, looking for another way in so she could eavesdrop on the meeting. But, to her dismay, she'd discovered there was no other way into the warehouse, except through the barred lading gates and the side door he'd entered. And so, she'd returned to it, only to discover that, during her brief absence, someone had padlocked it!

Stymied, Mabel'd been forced to resign herself to waiting for Juarez to reappear. He hadn't, but then—about ten minutes later—she'd heard a crack and a popping sound, and looking up, had seen the narrow air slits at the top of the warehouse fill with orange light, and realized the place was ablaze.

Now here she was, fighting desperately to free Juarez before he was burned alive, but she was no bleedin' use to 'im—no bleedin' use at all! She was too weak, and if—if he died, it'd be all her fault, she thought bitterly, sobbing as she pulled and pulled, splinters splitting her fingers, her nails tearing so that they bled. But, the door was far too solid, the hefty bar held firmly in place by a padlock. Try as she might, Mabel couldn't break the bloody thing off, for all that she was strong as a horse—!

The horse! The bloomin' horse!

Reeling away from the door, she staggered across the docks to where Juarez's little paint mare yet awaited her master, still ground-tied by only her dangling reins. She could have galloped off ages ago, but was too terrified by the smell of smoke and the fearful poppings and cracklings of the fire to move.

As Mabel approached her, she shied and snorted, her sides heaving. Her panicked eyes rolled back, white and enormous as she screamed in terror. Grimly Mabel snatched for her reins, caught them and wound them about her fist, in the very instant the mare seemed about to panic and run.

"Give over, you stupid nag! You in't runnin' away from Mabel, you 'ear me, horse? Your master's in there, he is, an' you an' me are gonna get 'im out, or I'll have your bleedin' guts fer garters! An' *then* I'll see you sent to the glue factory—!" she threatened luridly. "Now, *move!*"

The paint mare obediently trotted after her.

Juarez's lariat was still looped to the saddle, thank Gawd. Hastily grabbing one end, she tied it about the cantle of the mare's saddle, then tugged on the reins to bring the animal closer to the door, so she could slip the other end around the bar and knot the two tightly together. Sweat streamed down her face by the time she'd succeeded—time that had seemed like hours passing, but

444

was in fact only seconds.

"Yeeeaaah!" she screamed the instant the knot was secure, and at the same time, slammed the horse across the backside with her fist as hard as she could.

The mare bolted, tearing the door free of its hinges in a single lunge. Mabel whooped and jumped back as, still trailing it, the terrified animal thundered off across the Cairo wharves.

The heat was intense—hotter than an oven against her cheeks—but she could think only of her husband as she plunged inside the doorway.

Aw, Christ, no!

Through streaming eyes and a billowing cloud of choking black smoke, she saw Juarez, sprawled motionless just beyond the threshold, where he'd fallen behind the door, overwhelmed by smoke. The fire was only a yard from his feet now, almost licking at his heels, the fringes of his moccasins already smoldering! There was a sudden loud "whoosh" as the flames fed on the fresh air and doubled their size, roaring like a demon as they reached out for Mabel. Heat singed her hennaed curls, shriveled her eyebrows and lashes as she bent to pick up her husband's legs. She began dragging him, inch by painful inch, through the ruined doorway and out of the warehouse, away from the inferno, to safety.

She'd not gone far—tugging and panting with the effort to move her unwieldy but precious burden—when she felt a strong hand clamp over her shoulder. Startled, she looked up into a familiar face.

"Well, I'll be buggered!" she exclaimed. "You're that Jamieson bloke. The detective!"

"Och, aye, I am. Step aside. I'll carry him now, lassie. You make a run for it! Unless I miss my mark, this place'll go up like a wee bomb before verra long!"

Too exhausted and fearful for her husband's safety to argue with the man, Mabel nodded and stepped aside, tears of reaction rolling down her scorched, sooty cheeks. Jamieson bent and hefted Juarez easily over his shoulder in a fireman's lift. Seeing her standing there, watching him, the Scot snapped, "Damn it, I said 'run,' lassie!"

With Jamieson loping at her heels, and Juarez dangling

over his shoulder, Mabel sped across the wharves. They'd not gone far when, as Jamieson had anticipated, the Brixton cotton warehouse exploded with a deafening report! Flames, sparks, and shattered timbers showered against the midnight blue of the Egyptian sky, lighting the dark waters of the ancient Nile in an unearthly fireworks exhibition.

"Bloody hell!" Mabel exclaimed, cradling Juarez's head in her lap and kissing his poor blistered hands while Jamieson soaked a cloth in water from a nearby horse trough. "We was almost goners, we was!" He was coming to, now, much to her relief, coughing so painfully it tore at her heart. The whites of his eyes were stark against his smoke-darkened complexion as he opened them. With an exhausted, painful grin, he croaked, "Mabella, my little flower, you—you disobeyed me, eh?"

"Bloody lucky for you that I did, too!" she retorted, scowling crossly at him. But she couldn't hold the stern expression for long, her poor love looked so bleedin' battle-worn. She kissed his cheeks gently and her lower lip quivered. Her eyes filled with tears. "I thought I'd lorst you, I did, luv!" she sobbed. "I really thought I'd lorst you . . . !"

"Here, wrap ma hanky aboot his hands, lassie. It'll ease the pain a wee bit, 'til we can fetch a physician t' tend him," Jamieson instructed, squatting down at her side. "I've a gharry close by, if ye dinna think he'll need an ambulance?"

Mabel took the handkerchief he'd soaked in water and moistened Juarez's cracked lips before wrapping his hands. To her relief, the burns on his palms didn't look too severe, thank God, though she was beginning to feel the sting in her own. And, now that the panic was over and she was beginning to feel more like her old self again, her natural wariness reasserted itself. Someone had locked her poor luv in that bleedin' warehouse before they fired it, after all—and until she knew who, she wasn't about to trust anyone, not even the bloomin' Pope hisself, far less a bleedin' Scottish copper! In a polite but chilly voice, she thanked him, saying, "The carriage'll be luverly, Inspector. Thank you."

446

"Not at all. I'm happy t' have been of service t' ye, Señora Juarez. Another few seconds and—!" he grimaced. "Well, who knows? Your story might ha' had a far unhappier ending to it, hmm?" The detective's creepy, piercing blue eyes made Mabel's skin crawl in the eerie light of the flames from the fire as it finished its work of gutting the warehouse. Now that it was all over, they could hear the distant clanging of mule-drawn fire wagons, the sound growing louder as they neared the wharves. "If ye're feeling up to it, there's a wee question I'd like t' ask ye, before I fetch the carriage around?"

"Right you are. Fire away, ducks," Mabel agreed airily, thinking she'd tell him only what she felt he should bloody well know, and not one bleedin' thing more.

"May I ask what you and your husband are doing here t'night?"

Mabel's lips pursed. She fluttered her lashes and smiled. "Us? Well, Mr. Inspector, wot a co-in-ci-dence! See, I was about to ask *you* the very same question . . . ?"

Nick's strong hands lifted her hips, opening her. Dipping his ebony head, he traced circles on the silky flesh of her inner thighs with his lips. As his mouth moved higher, she arched her body, offering herself like a wanton as she moaned in ecstasy, writhed with delight. Little grasping cries escaped her, cries she couldn't have silenced, not had her very life depended on it!

Dear God, dear God, how could she bear this wonderful torment—? She couldn't wait, not a moment longer—!

Despite the chill of the Arabian night, a film of moisture dewed her body. She caught her lower lip between her teeth. Her hands clawed at the sand beneath her in her passion, tightened into fists, then let it slip away between her fingers like grains through an hourglass. His hands and mouth seemed everywhere, every kiss, each caress, firing her need, bringing new nerve endings to life with tingling, aching awareness and sensation. Shamelessly, she begged him to have her, to take her, to possess her—here!—now!—all pride and fear vanquished as she tossed in the throes of her raging desire. Yet madden-

447

ingly, he delayed, murmuring huskily, "Soon, sweet thing. Soon . . ."

When at last, he raised her up and entered her, the swift deep glory of his first plunge made her cry out to the very stars with the blinding pleasure of his possession. Her nails scored his back as she returned his savage kisses with a savagery that matched his own, twining slender legs about his hips.

"Nick, oh, Nick," she moaned against his cheek, her breath mingling with his. "I love you so!"

"And I love you, Angel," he whispered back, his eyes tender as he took her, filled her to the depths, then withdrew, only to thrust deeply, powerfully into the fiery sweetness of her body again and again.

"Really?" she sobbed, twining her fingers through his inky curls, framing his devilishly handsome face with her palms.

"More than anything. More than my life! Damn it, I love you, Angel—never doubt it! Never—again—doubt—*me!*"

"Oh, Nick, I won't. I swear it. Hold me, my darling. Don't let me go! Hold me forever!"

"I will, baby. I will. I'll hold you, and I'll keep you safe, always. From now on, there'll be you and me, forever, sweet thing!"

Joy filled her utterly, making her want to laugh and cry and dance, all at once. *He loved her! He said he loved her!* It was a glorious moment carved from time, one that she'd never, ever forget. There were no white doves filling the sky. No carillons of bells. No fireworks with rockets exploding. There was only the vast beauty of the midnight sky yawning above them, sprinkled with stars that glittered like tiny silver spurs: the sweeping gray majesty of the moon-washed sands, and the yawning silence of the desert—but it was enough. *More* than enough! She—little Annie Higgins—a jumped-up nobody without title or blue blood—a common Lancashire working-class lass who'd sprung from the shadows of a cotton mill, was richer than Midas, if Nick loved her. And she had the only title she'd ever want or need, if he would call her "Beloved." It was everything—it was all that mattered!

With a glad cry, she arched her soft curves to the strength and power of his hard male body, surrendering herself completely as they loved, holding nothing back, driving him crazy with the sensual abandon of her surrender.

In that glorious moment nothing existed but the two of them, and the giving, the taking, the rapturous joining, they shared. Her honey gold tresses spilled about them as they moved together as one. His unshaven cheeks were rough against the creamy smoothness of her own, his hairy chest, a delicious counterpoint to the mounds of her breasts, which he crushed beneath it. The slight coarseness rubbed her nipples, inflaming her to even greater heights of passion. Oh, he was magnificent, her fiery, plunging stallion, in one moment, virile and hot, and her tender, sensual lover in another, a lover whose possessive thrusts spun her like a top, whose caresses flung her headlong into a dizzying maelstrom of delight, a lover whose loving fulfilled her deepest desires, her every need—and far exceeded her wildest dreams!

They found violent release together, wrapped tightly in each others' arms. His roar of triumph mingled with the softer, joyous sobs of her release as, whispering his name again and again, tears flowed down her cheeks.

Taking her in his arms, Nick smiled as he cradled her to his chest. He kissed her tenderly, told her again and again how very much he loved her, that he would always, always love her.

A curious contentment filled him as he did so—one that went deeper than the sating of his physical needs. And, when she curled into his arms and pillowed her head upon his chest, he knew that nothing—*nothing!*— had ever felt so right before. . . .

He was still kissing her, still saying he loved her, when they drifted into exhausted sleep.

"Hmm, stop it, you beastly man," she scolded drowsily, smiling nonetheless as she squirmed to evade the wet rasp of a tongue raking the sole of her foot. Her eyes were closed as she snuggled against Nick's chest, grumbling, "It tickles so!"

"Darlin' you wore me out! I'm not doing anythin'," Nick drawled in protest, smothering a huge yawn as he drew her closer. "You must have been dreamin', hmm? Go on back to sleep, darlin'."

But the tickling continued, first one foot, then the other, and try as she might, she couldn't evade it. "You darling rogue! Are you insatiable, hmm? Is that what it is?" she demanded sleepily, but there was fond amusement in her voice. The tickling grew harder, more exquisitely tormenting. "Ohh, Nick, don't!" she cried, playfully punching his chest. "I simply can't stand being tickled. Please leave my feet alone!"

"Darn it, how can I be tickling you when I've got both arms around you?" Nick demanded.

"Well, something keeps licking my feet! If it's not you, then who is it?"

"A scorpion? Holy Geronimo!"

They both sat bolt upright then, their alarmed expressions turning to smiles and laughter as they realized the "tickler's" identity: Nick's black stallion.

"Diablo, you old son of a gun! You sure took your sweet time getting back t' me!" Nick exclaimed. "What have you got to say for yourself, huh?"

In answer to his question, the stallion—to Angel's delight—shook its beautiful head.

"Nothin', huh?" Nick asked, pretending to be angry. "Then I suppose you'd rather have stayed with that Rashid fella, right?"

This time the horse nodded, its silky black mane rippling.

Angel laughed aloud. "Oh, but he's wonderful! Is he who you were whistling for last night?"

Nick nodded and grinned. "Yep." Standing, he stratched the flat area between Diablo's eyes. The stallion nickered in appreciation and tossed its head. "He is. I had him from a colt—trained him myself to come back to me when I whistled the signal, right, boy?" With the key word "right," the stallion again nodded, looking uncannily as if he understood every word Nick said. "He knows no end of tricks. Say "howdy" t' my lady, Diablo."

Obediently, the stallion bent a foreleg and gave a fair

imitation of a bow, receiving another pat for his cleverness.

"With Diablo, we can cover several miles—maybe find an oasis or a native village or something—before it gets too hot. Damn it, look! Dawn's already breakin'! I reckon we'd best make tracks, pronto, 'fore it's too late. Get dressed, honey."

While Nick pulled on his pants and quickly checked the stallion to make sure it hadn't been injured, Angel dressed once again in the harem outfit, though she balked at pulling the hated black robe over it. She was humming as she did so. As Nick had said, dawn was breaking. The sky was awash with pastel saffrons and lavenders, the charcoal clouds of night only shredded streamers now that would soon be banished. It was a heavenly dawn—and a heavenly, glorious morning! Unable to keep from smiling, she was so very happy, she breathed deeply of the cool, sweet air and turned to look about her at the dunes encircling their camp. Why, this morning, knowing herself loved, even the endless desert sands seemed halfway pret—

"*Nick!*"

The strangled urgency in her low voice snapped Nick's head about in her direction. "Angel? What's wrong?"

"Up there. Look! All around us!" she whispered hoarsely.

Nick looked where she'd indicated. And, as he did so, he saw still other Arab tribesmen cresting the dunes all about them to join the handful of riders she had spotted. Mounted on their fine Arabian horses or upon white racing camels, with ammunition belts and rifles slung over their shoulders or brandished in their fists, their robes stirring gently in the breeze, this was no friendly native caravan. And, even as he watched them through hooded eyes, his mind churning for a plan of some kind, he heard the tribesmen's bloodchilling cries began:

"*Ul-ul-ul-ul-ul!*"

First one man took it up, then another and another, until the cries were all around them, a wall of ululating sounds that were calculated to strike terror in an enemy's heart.

"What is it they're saying? Why are they doing that? Dear God, Nick, what do they want with us?" Angel cried, running to him and lifting her ashen face to his.

"I'd say they're plannin' to attack," Nick revealed grimly, refusing to meet her wide, frightened gray eyes.

"Attack *us,* you mean?" she echoed in a squeaky voice.

He gave her a thin-lipped smile that turned her blood to iced water. "I don't see anyone else out here, do you, darlin'?"

"Jamieson! Thank God, man! I've been asking after you everywhere! Do you have any news about Angelica's whereabouts?"

The sandy-haired Scot shook his head ruefully, his piercing eyes muddied for once with thought as the Englishman sprang to his feet, drawing the notice of the few early-afternoon drinkers in the Sphinx's palatial saloon. "Och, nay, I'm afraid not, Mr. Hardcastle," he murmured as he took a seat in an overstuffed chair opposite Hardcastle's. "Miss Higgins and Durango have vanished from Cairo—or so it would appear!"

Hardcastle sat down abruptly, apparently felled by the inspector's news. "Damn it all!" he exclaimed irritably. "To be honest, when I couldn't find you either here or at the consulate, I'd hoped you'd uncovered a lead and gone haring off to find the poor child. Four days she's been missing, with no word. What, in God's name, am I to tell her father, Jamieson? I'll have to tell him something! The *Empress of Egypt* sails from Cairo tomorrow, and I promised Sid that Angelica would be aboard her—that I'd bring her home to him with all possible haste!"

"Och, dinna give up, laddie," Jamieson soothed, gesturing to the waiter and ordering himself a whiskey. "There's still time."

"Time? Then—you know where they are? Thank God! Tell me where that rogue has taken her and by God, I'll rescue the poor love myself!"

"Now, now, I didna say I knew where she is."

"No? Then what *are* you saying?"

Jamieson frowned. "The Figg brothers, the Mexican,

Antonio Juarez, and his wife, Mabel—they were killed last night, Hardcastle. All four o' them were burned alive, it would seem." His eyes narrowed under bushy, sandy brows. "It was nae accident, either. I believe Durango was responsible!"

"Good God, man! But—why? Why would he do such a thing to his own men?"

"I believe the scoundrel decided to rid himself of his cronies, who'd outlived their usefulness t' him and would ha' wanted their share of his ill-gotten gains. After all, he has the girl, and by now, nae doubt, he knows the Yard's onto him, and that the game's up—that it's way too late to hide his identity. Aye, he's decided t' work alone. Accordingly, I expect to receive some word from him verra soon."

"Word?"

"Aye. Ye see, I'd bet my last siller shilling Durango's had a change of plans. He feels the net tightening around him, an' he's grown desperate enough t' try to demand a ransom wi'out returning t' England. I have a wee hunch he'll try t' make the payoff through you, Mr. Hardcastle, sir."

"Me! Oh. I see," Hardcastle came back, visibly unsettled at such a thought. He took a hurried swig of his own drink from the brandy snifter on the table before asking, "And what would you have me do, should Durango present his demands?"

"Why, appear to go along with them, if ye would, sir? We've no other recourse, not now. It's Miss Higgins's safety—her very life!—I'm concerned aboot now. Stall for time, mon. Tell Durango ye must wire Sidney Higgins, to arrange for the ransom funds. And, while ye're at it, ask him for some proof that the lassie's still alive, puir bairn. When ye have it—and only then!—set up a time and a place for the exchange."

"All right, Inspector. Will do! There's no possible chance Angelica was in the warehouse when it burned, is there?" Hardcastle asked in a tone filled with dread.

Jamieson smiled and shook his head. "Nay, none at all. Dinna fret on that score, mon." He drained his glass with a satisfied grunt.

"Thank God for small mercies!"

"Aye," Jamieson agreed with feeling. "And now, I'd best be running along. I caution ye t' stay visible, Hardcastle. That way, Durango'll be able t' contact ye easily, all going well."

"I shan't leave the hotel until he does, or you tell me otherwise, Inspector. You have my word on it."

As he walked past Hardcastle, Jamieson clamped his hand over the other man's shoulder. "Good mon! I'll be in touch, but if ye should need me, urgent, ye know where t' find me?"

"I do. Good afternoon, Inspector."

"And t' ye, Hardcastle."

Sunk in thought, Teddy Hardcastle leaned back in his chair, swirling the brandy in the snifter he held up to the light, as if contemplating its color.

"I say, do you mind if I sit here, sir?" asked a voice in a clipped British accent.

Wearily, Ted looked up into a florid masculine face that boasted a white moustache and white muttonchop whiskers. The old gentleman was peering down at him through a monocle, while leaning heavily upon a brass-knobbed cane for support. "Not at all, sir. Please, be my guest," he murmured.

"Dashed gout! Takes all the bloody fun out of life, don't y' know. Can't eat this or that, can't do this or that—hrrumph!" he grumbled, waving his cane at the waiter. "Boy! Bring me a Scotch and soda—chop! chop!—and make it a double." As the waiter nodded and hurried off to do his bidding, the old man scowled and propped his gouty, heavily-bandaged leg upon the low brass table between them. "Blasted ragheads. Most of them can't even mix a simple drink, I've found. Much the same out in Inja, don't y' know? I say, don't I know you from out there, old chap? Weren't you in my regiment?"

"I think not, sir," Ted denied with a smile, "since I've never had the pleasure of seeing that country." He extended his hand, thinking the old goat probably suffered from senility as well as gout. "The Honorable Edward Hardcastle, Esquire, at your service, sir."

"Willers. Colonel Percival Willers, Her Majesty's Fourteenth Cavalry, retired."

"A pleasure, sir," Hardcastle returned warmly, shaking the colonel's hand.

Willers stared at him intently before finally releasing his hand. "Dash it all, are you quite *sure* I don't know you? I never forget a face, you know—like that pretty little gel you had hanging on your arm the other morning. Your wife, sir?"

"Alas, no."

"Daughter?"

"Niece would be more accurate, sir."

"Niece, eh, you young rogue?" Willers chortled and winked, patently disbelieving Teddy's claims. "Well, sir, in my opinion, your little 'niece' is a real English beauty. A corker! I envy you, old chap! I was quite popular with the pretty young gels meself in my time, believe it or not. By Jove, if I were only a year or two younger, I'd give you a good run for your money there, Hardgraves. I still might, at that. They say it's better to be an old man's darling than a young man's slave, what!"

"Quite so, Colonel," Teddy agreed amiably, thinking the gouty old goat would be hard put to give anyone a run for their money, anywhere. "And it's 'Hardcastle', sir, not 'Hardgraves.'"

"Close enough, old chap. Ah, here's my drink! Not too much soda in there, eh, boy?"

"I hope and pray not, sir," the native boy said smoothly, bowing as he left the two men.

"By George, look at the time! It's almost one o'clock and I'm starved! Forgive me, but I do believe I'll be off to the dining room for a spot of luncheon," Teddy murmured, springing to his feet. He nodded to the old man. "It was frightfully good meeting you, Colonel."

"And you, Hardacres."

Hiding a smile, Ted quickly made good his escape, leaving Colonel Willers frowning thoughtfully after him, his monocle raised to one eye.

Her heart in her mouth, her lips still tingling from the hard kiss he'd pressed to them, Angel watched as Nick rode Diablo into the center of the little valley in which they'd

455

passed the night. He had a plan, he'd said, one that might buy them a little time, if nothing else, but she'd known from the set of his mouth, the tightness to his jaw, that he held little hope of that.

"Trust me?" he'd asked her, and with tears in her eyes, she'd fiercely whispered "Yes!"

"Stay right here, then. Don't move!" Then he'd mounted Diablo and ridden off.

The howls of the native tribesmen dwindled, faded away on the cool dawn hush as Nick stood tall in the stirrups. Shoulders squared, his back ramrod straight, he raised his hand above his head in obvious salute. Then, with a flourish, he gave Diablo a heel signal to rear up. The wonderful stallion did so, powerful ebony forelegs pawing air, its mane and tail streaming in the light current of breeze.

"And now, for your entertainment, I present Myself— King of the Cowboys, Sultan of the Sands, Duke of the Dunes, ewellah!" Nick roared with a showman's flourish.

She knew then what Nick intended and her stomach turned over as she watched him, so proud, so very handsome, so magnificent and brave—and so utterly doomed to failure! It would never work, not in a million years . . . !

A ripple ran through the watchers on the dunes as, uttering a warlike whoop, Nick brought Diablo back down and kicked him into a ground-eating gallop. He circled once, twice, three times, at ever-increasing speeds.

When the stallion was moving at suicidal pace, he slipped his feet free of the stirrups and dropped, hanging along Diablo's side while the horse thundered across the sands. He nimbly regained his seat, then hung along the other side, Comanche Indian fashion, in what was a breathtaking display of trick riding. He ended by swinging himself up into a standing position on Diablo's broad black rump and balancing there, arms outstretched, while Diablo cantered in easy circles.

A ripple ran through the watchers once again. Displeasure? Anger? Boredom? Whatever its cause, Angel heard it plainly, and from where she sat—her knees buckled under her—it sounded like the muffled droning of a thousand discontented bees! Crossing her fingers, she offered up a silent prayer for their safety as Nick sprang down from the stallion, to the ground. He gave the animal a sign, pointed, and it galloped off without him, heading up the dunes toward the startled tribesmen before, at the very last minute, his piercing, single whistle turned its magnificent head, brought it racing back down the dune and across the sands. Diablo was galloping straight for him!

Risking death, with split-second timing he sprang up onto Diablo's back, in the instant he would have galloped past him. Diablo came on without breaking his stride, now heading straight for Angel! The hard purpose in Nick's eyes as Diablo thundered toward her brought her up on her feet, raised her to standing. *"Trust me!"* he'd asked, she remembered. And in that instant, she knew what he intended to do and was prepared for it.

As Nick drew abreast of her, she raised her arm and felt a shoulder-wrenching jolt as he leaned down and swept her safely up onto the saddle before him!

Diablo raced on at breakneck speed. The stallion was heading for a small gap in the wall of the riders ringing the dunes—a gap that, to her horror, was abruptly closed as a tall Arab, dressed in flowing white robes and mounted upon a prancing white horse, rode into it.

Nick reined Diablo in and they skidded to a halt less than thirty feet from where the man—obviously a sheik or chieftain of some import, judging by the ornate tasseled trappings adorning his magnificent Arabian steed—aloofly sat his mount.

"Well? Ain't you gonna say 'howdy' to the man, Diablo?" Nick growled in his horse's ear, and to his relief, the stallion bent a front leg and "bowed" respectfully to the chieftain.

Terror sliced through Angel as she heard the tribesmen suddenly began their high-pitched cries once again. The murmurs grew louder, more insistent. Men brandished their rifles over their heads, making what could only be threatening gestures, and her hopes died. She reached behind her, found Nick's hand, and squeezed it.

"Well, I suppose this is it, Nick, darling," she

whispered, tears filling her eyes—ones she bravely dashed away. "I know you did your very best. It—it just wasn't enough, not this time."

"The hell it wasn't! That was the best damn ridin' I ever did!" he protested gruffly in her ear, sounding wounded and indignant.

"Yes, my love, I know. But—listen! They've started that awful yodeling again. You said yourself it meant they were planning to attack!"

"They sure have started up, haven't they!" He grinned. "But . . . it's different! Can't you make out what it is they're sayin' now, darlin'?"

Frowning, she cocked her head to one side and listened intently. And, after a few seconds, she realized he was right. The tribesmen were no longer merely ululating. They were chanting a name, the same name, over and over again:

"*Nick Du-rango! Nick Dur-ango! Nick Du-rango! Nick Du-rango!*"

"They're calling *you!*" she exclaimed.

"They sure are," Nick acknowledged proudly, curling his free arm around her waist and dropping a kiss on her shoulder as he kneed Diablo forward to meet the Arab astride the white horse. The Arab also left the ranks of his followers. He rode to meet Nick halfway, grinning beneath his fierce black beard as he came.

"Angelica, honey, I'd like you to meet Sheik Fadil al-Alim. He's an old friend of mine! Sheik Fadil, this here's my woman."

"By the Grace of Allah, I offer you greetings, little missie. It is truly an honor to meet the chosen woman of my old friend, Nick Durango!"

"How do you do, sir," Angel murmured politely, muttering out of the side of her mouth to Nick, "First Martine in Paris, now Sheik What's-His-name! Tell me, Durango, is there *anyone* in this world you *don't* know? Anyone who hasn't seen your blasted Wild West Show?"

He grinned. "Might be one or two folks over in Portugal, but somehow—I kinda doubt it!"

"Come, Nick Durango. Ride with me to my camp!" Sheik Fadil insisted. "I have ordered my best lambs and my

458

finest kids butchered in honor of your return, my friend. We will feast and drink coffee, and afterwards, when you have known the full measure of my hospitality, you will tell me how you came to be here, in the desert, ewellah . . . ?"

"We're as good as home, honey," Nick murmured to Angel as he smilingly inclined his head and agreed. "Yes sir, we're as good as back in Cairo!"

Chapter Thirty-Seven

True to his word, Sheik Fadil feasted them royally that night, extending to Nick and Angel the hospitality for which his Bedouin people were known.

To Angel's relief, the Sheik laughingly declared that the native custom which decreed that men and women should eat separately would be set aside for that night, in her honor, and she was permitted to take her seat beside Nick. Seated cross-legged on soft woven rugs before Sheik Fadil's huge goatskin tent, part of the circle of men surrounding a huge fire of camel dung that burned with a fragrant grass-and-herb smoke, she shared in the feast. There were delicious chunks of lamb and vegetables speared on sticks and roasted, tender goat meat, savory rice dishes, yogurt, flat wheels of bread to sop up tasty sauces, delectable fried sweetmeats drenched with honey. When she had eaten her fill of the meats, she helped herself to fresh fruits—apricots, pomegranates, and plums, and to figs, dates, almonds, and dried fruits. After four days of unpalatable and inadequate food, everything tasted heavenly!

When Nick had dismounted upon reaching Fadil's encampment, it had become apparent that he was having considerable difficulty in walking due to the enormous swelling of his foot. The sheik had called upon one of his older tribesmen—a handsome man with a flowing white beard who, it transpired, tended to Fadil's own hurts. In no time he'd seen to the removal of the huge acacia thorn and to the poulticing of the infected wound.

The following morning, Nick was relieved and surprised to find his foot as good as new. There was nothing to prevent them from returing to Cairo immediately—if Fadil would provide them with a guide to lead them across the desert. True to his word, Fadil selected four of his men—all trustworthy fellows, he assured them with laughter in his magnificent, shining black eyes—to escort them safely to the outskirts of the ancient city of Cairo.

"May Allah watch over you and your woman until we meet again, my friend Nick!" he told them before they left his camp. "May you breed many strong sons and fertile daughters upon the lady Angelica, and may the seed of Nick Durango live forever!"

Nick chuckled, a little embarrassed by the Bedouin's flowery good wishes. "And may the foals and colts of Nick's stallion, Diablo, that he breeds upon the mares of Sheik Fadil, be as countless as the sands of the desert!" Nick returned in kind with a grin and a wink. He'd noted that his horse—which had perked up miraculously upon scenting the pretty fillies in season that the nomad camp had to offer—seemed a mite tuckered out this morning!

"Ewellah, indeed!" Fadil returned with a smile as broad as Nick's own.

Angel waved to Fadil's giggling bevy of black-robed, coin-adorned wives until they'd disappeared behind the last dune, then sighed as she was forced to direct all her attention to handling her fractious camel instead.

"Disappointed that we're leaving, sweetness?" Nick murmured, his eyes fondly meeting her sparkling gray ones.

"Disappointed about leaving these endless oceans of sand . . . of tasting grit in my throat . . . of swatting away the flies . . . of haggling for my life? Hrrumph!" she snorted, sounding uncannily like her camel, and demanded wryly, "What do you think, Durango?"

Heads turned in the lobby of the Grand Sphinx Hotel when they made their entrance. Curious eyes watched as Nick, in his borrowed Bedouin robes, led Angel to the front desk and asked the startled native desk clerk for the key to her suite.

"Ah, it is Durango Pasha! Forgive me, I did not recognize you, sir! Nor you, Missie Higgins. A thousand pardons!"

The curious continued to watch their progress as they crossed the marble floor and mounted the staircase to her suite. Irrepressible as ever, Nick couldn't resist turning and treating those who were staring to an expansive bow. Giggling, Angel grabbed his elbow and yanked him after her up the stairs.

"You're an impossible man!" she scolded, smiling nonetheless.

"But you love me anyway?"

"God help me, but yes, I do," she acknowledged as they made their way down the corridor.

They halted before her door. Nick unlocked it and gave her the key.

"Well, here we are. I guess I'll have to leave you alone for a while. I'm going next door to wash up and change into some real clothes, then I reckon I need t' have a word or two with your friend Jamieson, don't you?" She grimaced but nodded agreement. "And what will you do?" he asked.

"Me? Hmm, I'll take a long, lazy bubble bath, I think. Fill the tub to overflowing and just soak and soak in truly decadent fashion!"

"Sounds exciting. Maybe if I get through soon enough, I'll join you," Nick promised huskily, a wicked sparkle in his eyes.

"Join me indeed, you naughty man," she murmured, but then added, "What a heavenly idea!" She closed her eyes as Nick ducked his dark head to kiss her lingeringly, but then, with a few parting words, he had gone.

Angel let herself into the room. She leaned against the suite door after she'd closed it behind her, hugged herself about the arms, and sighed blissfully. The giddy sensation of happiness and well-being that filled her were like the heady bubbles in a glass of champagne, fizzily tickling her nose! She knew that her cheeks were flushed a rosy pink. Her lips still tingled deliciously from the pressure of Nick's ardent farewell kiss, the one he'd given her on the other side of this very door. Her heart still sang with the

462

joy of his parting words: "My love," he'd called her, and she echoed the precious words aloud now, smiling a dreamy smile. "My sweet—my only!—love."

A discreet cough jolted her from her romantic reverie. Blinking, she realized belatedly that she was not alone in the shadowed suite.

"Mabel?"

But no, it wasn't Mabel. Uncle Teddy was there, tucked in one of the overstuffed horsehair armchairs by the French windows that led out onto the verandah. He appeared to have been sitting there for quite some time, for on the small rattan table at his elbow was a half-empty whisky decanter and a solitary glass.

"Why, Uncle Teddy, hello there! I didn't see you in this dreadful, gloomy old room. You really should have opened the louvers to let in the light, you know. The half-dark is terribly damaging to one's eyesight."

Teddy shrugged, dismissing the matter as unimportant. He turned a weary eye up to hers as she leaned down to kiss his cheek.

"Frankly, my dear, I've been far too concerned about your disappearance these past few days to bother very much about failing eyesight or anything else, as I expect you can imagine. I came in here to think, to try to get some inkling of where the devil you could have gone . . . but, now you're back, just as suddenly as you vanished, smiling and apparently none the worse for wear, and quite oblivious to the heartache we've been going through."

"Uncle Teddy, I'm very so—"

"No. Don't bother to apologize, Angel. I suppose I should be bloody angry, after all the worry you've put me through. By rights, I should demand to know where you've been for the past four days, as any doting uncle would. But frankly, I'm going to do neither. You see, I fancy I already know the answer to my questions—and it isn't that you were kidnapped, but that you were with your lover!" He smiled in a sad sort of way that tweaked her conscience and her face flamed with guilt—not because she'd been with Nick, but because of the upset her disappearance had caused this dear man. "Ah. Then I was right! You really should learn to mask your emotions and bluff, my dear, as befits a real lady—or a gambler. Your lovely face quite gives you away!"

She laughed softly. "If you're tactfully asking have I been with Nick Durango all this time, then I'd have to admit you're right, Uncle Teddy. You see, I love him," she explained gently, "and Nick loves me."

Snorting in disgust, he tossed off the dregs of his Scotch and set the glass down upon the rattan table with a loud clunk. "Love be damned! On the contrary, you poor, gullible child, it's your father's *money* Durango loves, not you," Hardcastle said bluntly, standing and stalking across the room toward her.

Irritation bubbled up inside her. How could he say such a thing, with such hurtful disregard for her feelings? Clearly, he was far more annoyed than he wanted her to believe! She shrugged aside the hand he intended to place upon her shoulder and flounced across the suite, away from him, trembling with emotion. "You've disappointed me terribly, Uncle Teddy. I had anticipated just this sort of cavalier reaction from that horrid Inspector Jamieson upon my return to Cairo. But to be quite honest, I'd expected—hoped!—for better from you."

"Better? I'm afraid I don't understand . . . ?"

She whirled to face him, the flowing native robes swirling about her as she did so. With the voluminous hood shoved back and her honey gold hair spilling down about her shoulders, she could have been the noble, spirited heroine of some seventeenth century novel. "Yes, *better*. You cast aside my feelings, Nick's feelings, as if they were quite unworthy of any consideration whatsoever! Why is it that even you, Uncle, who profess to be fond of me, feel that no man could possibly love me for myself?" she demanded in a low, controlled voice. "Am I so very unworthy? So unlovable? Is it so very unlikely that any man could love me for the woman I am, rather than my father's fortune?"

Surprise and pain etched Hardcastle's face. "My dearest girl, forgive me! Truly, I never intended to imply any such thing. Surely you know how very much I admire you? And that I would do anything rather than hurt you, if there was an alternative? Alas, in this situation, there is none. What I have said is unpleasant but true, though you must never think that the fault lies in you, dear girl. Rather, the flaw lies in your innocent, trusting heart—and in its unfortunate ability to choose the most unsuitable of—er—suitors! As Reggie proved unworthy of you, so is Durango not the man he pretends to be. You *must* face up to that fact and accept it. You heard what Inspector Jamieson told us at the consulate the other day? Dear child, I'm afraid everything he suspected was true. The evidence against Nick is overwhelming! Furthermore, I have some bad news to tell you, I'm afraid—shocking news. Angel, while you were gone, there was a disaster—a fire—at your father's cotton warehouse. Durango's partner—the Mexican, Juarez, his wife, and those two scoundrels, the Figg brothers, Tiny and Knuckles . . . Angelica, they're all dead! Jamieson believes your cowboy was responsible for starting the blaze. That he killed them—just like Bill Bligh and Reggie."

"What!"

"Yes! Apparently he arranged a meeting with his cohorts at your father's warehouse, three days after you disappeared. Fire mysteriously broke out, and they were all killed . . . burned to death—"

"No!" she whispered, paling. Shock rendered her knees weak, unable to bear her weight. She staggered, reaching blindly for an armchair for support, knowing she would swoon if she didn't sit down immediately. "Not Mabel . . . no, not Juarez! For the love of God, Uncle, tell me you could be wrong? That it isn't so—!" she beseeched him.

"I wish with all my heart that I could, my dear, but I can't change the truth, horrible as it may be. Moreover, Jamieson has evidence that Durango was responsible for their deaths. There was a witness, I believe. Someone who saw the American at the warehouse that night, moments before and following the fire."

"Three days *after* I disappeared, you say? Then this witness must be mistaken, because that's impossible!" she protested weakly, sinking deep into the chair and gripping its plump arms for support. "Nick had nothing to do with any fire. He couldn't have. You see, he was miles from Cairo. Out in the desert, with me!"

"Angelica, Angelica, your attempts to defend the man are admirable—but your loyalty is just further proof of the diabolical cleverness of that . . . fiend . . . Who knows! Perhaps I have it wrong? Perhaps Jamieson meant that Durango had hired a thug to do his dirty work that night? But, whether he started the fire with his own hand, or hired someone to start it for him, he's guilty, all right—guilty as hell! A murderer and, I wouldn't doubt, your kidnapper—unless he's stopped before he can bring his final plan to fruition."

Hardcastle smiled consolingly. Drawing a large white handkerchief from his breast pocket and a small phial of liquid from another, he shook a few drops onto the cloth. "Angel, my dear child! You're completely overwrought, you poor, poor girl," he murmured, stroking her hair, squeezing her limp hand, noting as he did so the ashen pallor of her face, the clammy chill to her skin. "Fortunately, I happen to have some smelling salts here. Just the ticket to revive you in no time!"

"But I don't *need* smelling salts, Uncle Teddy," Angel denied, her voice husky with grief, breaking with sorrow in places. Springing from the armchair, away from him, she continued, "What I *need* is to talk to the inspector, before he makes a terrible mistake. I have to convince Jamieson that he's wrong about Nick—completely wrong. Would you have the front desk see that a gharry's sent around for me, please, Uncle? I simply must go to the consulate immediately, once I've changed!"

Teddy frowned. "Angel, dear girl, I'm afraid I can't let you do that. You see, the *Empress of Egypt* sails this very afternoon at three o'clock. Your father is expecting you to be aboard her when she docks in Southampton, and I have given him my sworn word that you'll be there. Besides, you'd only be wasting your time, going to the consulate. By now, I'm certain Durango has already been taken into custody."

"Well, I'll see about that!"

"There's nothing you can do, child. Durango's fate is up to the law to decide now, not you. Angel, won't you be the sensible, reasonable young woman that I know you for? Come along with your old Uncle Teddy, there's a

466

good girl. Pack your bags, forget your well-intentioned but foolish notions about defending that American rogue, and let's go home to jolly old England. Durango isn't worthy of your affections, you know."

Her eyes turned to smoke. Her obstinate little chin came up defiantly. Her jaw hardened. She tossed back her hair and stepped around Hardcastle as if he were a leper as she headed for the suite's door. Knowing herself loved by Nick and being *in* love had added a radiance to her beauty that no jewel, however costly, could impart—and given her an inner strength that was palpable and formidable.

"With all due respect, sir," she said in a tight, controlled voice, her fingers curled around the brass doorknob, "I'm no longer a child. I think I should be the judge of Nick's worthiness, don't you? If you won't help me to find Jamieson, so be it. That is your choice. I'll find him myself—!"

At the sidewalk café across the street from the Sphinx Hotel, seated at a table beneath a striped awning where they could observe the hotel guests' comings-and-goings without drawing undue attention to themselves, sat Nick and the detective.

Nick was scowling at Inspector Jamieson as native porters loaded luggage onto several gharrys drawn up before the vestibule of the Sphinx. There were weighty sea chests, trunks, and hampers, suitcases and hatboxes, as well as wicker cages containing chattering monkeys or squawking parrots.

"I think we're wastin' our time, sittin' here twiddlin' our thumbs, Inspector," Nick snapped, his ice blue eyes crackling with impatience as he sprang to his feet. "If what you suspect is true, Angel's in danger. Damn your hunches! I won't take any unnecessary chances with her life, man—not even to please you!"

"Och, ye young hothead, sit down! And be warned, laddie—if ye take a step oot o' this café, I'll have a pair o' cuffs slapped on ye before ye can say 'Macbeth.' It's been but an hour since ye bid the lassie farewell. Can ye no be patient a wee while longer, mon—and allow the pot t' simmer a bit before it comes to a boil?"

"All right," Nick gritted. "I'll give you another half an hour. No longer. But if nothing's happened by then, I'm doing things *my* way and getting Angel the hell outa that hotel room, onto the *Empress*, and home. Agreed?"

"Agreed, agreed. Now relax, laddie. Finish your drink. Like I told ye, my men are watching all the exits. That rogue'll no get away wi' the lassie—but if he tries, och, then we'll ha'e the proof of guilt we need!" Glee lit his brilliant blue eyes.

"You could be wrong about this, Jamieson. *Dead* wrong."

"I could, aye. But I'd wager every siller shilling I have that I amna."

Thirty minutes passed on feet of lead. At the end of them, even Jamieson's firm convictions were beginning to waver. He cast side-glances at Nick and drummed his hairy-knuckled fingers on the tabletop in a way that made the younger man want to hook him.

"That's it!" Nick rasped. "You had your chance. Now it's my turn," he gritted, obviously intending to carry out his threat and take matters into his own hands.

Quick as a flash, Jamieson's hand darted out. There was a metallic click as he fastened the bracelet of a pair of handcuffs about Nick's left wrist.

"What the hell are you doing?"

"Just a precaution, laddie," the inspector reassured him smoothly as he fastened the other cuff about his own wrist. "If we run into our suspect, we dinna want him t' guess we're onto him until he's shown his hand and we have the proof we need, do we now? This way, he'll believe that you're my man, and that he's home free!"

Nick shot him a darkling look that spoke volumes as to his opinion of Jamieson's methods. With a ground-eating stride, he started across the dusty Cairo street that basked beneath the afternoon sun. Jamieson had no choice but to follow him. Far above them, the fronded heads of the towering Royal palms that flanked the street like soldiers wafted gracefully to and fro.

Nick elbowed his way between the throng of native porters and British travelers outside the Sphinx, silently cursing the detective. The cocky Scot was so damned sure of himself, and of his pet theories! If he was wrong—and if Angel was hurt—or worse!—because of his shilly-shallying around, he'd kill the bastard, he swore.

"Leaving too, eh, Inspector?" bellowed a voice. "Returning home to jolly old Blighty on the *Empress*, are you, what?"

"No, Colonel Willers," Jamieson responded absently, craning his neck to see over the hats of the women instructing the porters in the stowing of their precious luggage aboard the open vehicles. The noise all about him was deafening for, like most British—and American—travelers in a foreign land when confronted by a foreign-speaking native population, the Grand Sphinx's guests had resorted to shouting their wishes and commands, in the belief that volume must succeed where translation failed! Jamieson had to yell to make himself heard. "I'm here on official business, ye might say, Colonel. I'm looking for a guest staying here, a man named Hardcastle. D' ye know the mon, sir?"

"Hardcastle, Hardcastle . . ." Willers frowned for a moment, then brightened up and smiled broadly. "By Jove, I couldn't place the name for a moment, old chap, but I never forget a face. You've missed him, Inspector. Saw the bounder meself about fifteen minutes ago, don't ye know?"

"Where?" Nick cut in sharply, almost yanking Jamieson off his feet as he shoved himself between the colonel and the detective.

"Right there, where you're standing, sir!" Willers chortled in high glee. "But if you're here to see him off, then you'll have to go down to the harbor, old chap. He left, you see. One of these bloody rag-headed fellows loaded his trunks and orf he went."

"Alone?" Nick demanded.

"What's that?" The colonel cupped his ear with his hand.

"I said, was he alone? Was there a young woman with him?"

"Pretty little gel, blond hair, absolutely stunning figure?"

469

"That's her!"

"'Fraid not, old chap. I'd have remembered if he had that little beauty with him, arf arf!" With a lecherous smirk, he nudged Nick hard in the ribs with his elbow, forcing the air from him in a started "oof." "No, Hardcourt was quite alone. The gel's his niece, or so he claims, but I fancy there's more to it than that, don't ye know!" He winked. "Something odd about that chappie—can't quite put the old finger on it . . . but it'll come, all in good time. I say, you're an American, aren't you? Haven't we met before . . . ? I never forget a face!"

Ignoring Willers' bumbling, Nick turned on his heels and dove between the crowd, hauling a red-faced and furiously muttering Jamieson after him across the lobby by the handcuff's short—and extremely painful—chain.

"Jamieson Pasha, wait! Missie Higgins asked me to give you this if I saw you!"

Nick halted abruptly as one of the hotel desk clerks bowed and solemnly handed Jamieson a letter.

Cocking his sandy brows at Durango, Jamieson tore open the envelope and scanned the contents, frowning as he did so. He read it aloud to Nick.

'My Dear Inspector,

Despite my Uncle Teddy's protests to the contrary, I regret I remain quite unconvinced of Mr. Durango's guilt. Indeed, I have conclusive evidence in my possession that he is not the scoundrel you believe him to be, but innocent of all wrongdoing. Since I would very much like to meet with you and discuss this grave matter in person as soon as possible, I am leaving the hotel immediately for the British Consulate, in the hope that I will find you at your offices there. However, in the event that our paths cross and you are out, would it be convenient for you to meet with me in the Sphinx's lounge at six o'clock this evening, instead?

Uncle Teddy has also asked me to convey his apologies to you for leaving Cairo without saying goodbye. However, the *Empress of Egypt's* imminent departure left him no alternative. I'm afraid

470

that, as of this writing, he is quite out of patience with my obstinacy and has determined to return to England alone.'

"It's signed 'Annie Higgins.'"
"Annie? Not Angelica?"
Jamieson shook his head. "Annie."
"Did the missie give you this note herself?" Nick barked, turning to the beaming clerk.

"Why, indeed, yes, sir—and very pretty she looked, as always!" the Turk confirmed with a grin. "She was wearing one of those very large hats she favors, with all the pretty flowers and veils. They are so very becoming to young British ladies, don't you think, sir? Sir—?"

But Nick had bolted across the lobby. He took the elegant curving marble staircase two steps at a time, forcing the inspector to do likewise for the entire three flights.

"What's the hurry, Durango. Och, the lassie's fine—ye read the note, mon! She's gone t' the consulate, looking for me!"

Nick smiled thinly. "That's what he wants you to think. No, Jamieson, she wrote that note under duress—because somebody *made* her write it. My Angel—call *you* her 'dear inspector'? Not a chance! I sure hate t' hurt your feelings, pardner, but I know for a fact she's none too fond of you! What's more, she signed herself 'Annie.' Now, the only note she ever wrote me, back in Paris, she signed *'Angelica'* Higgins. I could be wrong, but gut instinct says she was trying to tell us—you—something!"

Before the door to Angel's suite, he halted and tried the knob.

"Angel! It's me, Nick. Open up!"

The door was locked and, as he'd half expected, there was no answer from beyond it. Nick cursed foully under his breath. With hardly a pause, he turned sideways and threw his full weight against the paneled wood. Nothing. Without comment, Jamieson added his weight. Together, the two men slammed themselves against the door. After three attempts, the wood gave, the door tore free of its hinges and lock under their combined weight, and crashed into the suite beyond.

A hurried search confirmed Nick's fears. Angel was gone. The suite, its wooden louvers drawn against both light and air, was quite empty, and gloomy and stifling in the afternoon heat. The paddles of the ceiling fan were still, and the air smelled fusty and stale. He sniffed and frowned. There was another smell, too. One he couldn't place. The faint but unmistakable fragrance of something else, something other than dust and lack of use. Perfume? No. Not that. It was a tangy scent, more like citrus fruit . . . Lemons? That was it.

Lemons. With lemons you could make lemonade, or lemon meringue pie, his favorite. Tía Magdalena floated slices of lemons in iced water, used them to whiten and soften her complexion. Lemons . . . lemons . . . something to do with lemons . . . A buried memory had resurfaced, and was nagging at him to identify it. Damn it, it wouldn't come! What the *hell* was it?

Tugging Jamieson after him, he circled the room, searching, prowling like a dark panther on the hunt, his temper only a fraction from exploding in violence, so deep was his anxiety for the woman he loved and his conviction that he was missing something vitally important. And then, he saw it, and the truth slammed home, the pieces of the puzzle finally dropped into place!

Upon the desk, where Angel had no doubt been forced to sit to pen the note Jamieson had received, was a small, round but very fancy tin—the sort of tin the best British sweet and biscuit shops used as containers for their wares. Measuring some six inches or so across and perhaps two inches in depth, it was painted gold and further embellished with a painting of flowers and the name of the sweetshop. The lid, he observed, was merely resting upon the base. Sucking in a breath, he lifted it aside. Upon the lacy white paper doilie inside were a number of sweets, the kind he recognized as sherbet lemon bonbons—Angel's favorites—each one nestled in a pretty wrapper of gold foil.

"How about suckin' on one of these? It'll take the trail dust out o'yore throat?" he heard himself ask a bilious Angel upon the heaving decks of the Pelican.

And then memory flashed to the small stone bridge crossing the Seine, and to Reggie's waterlogged corpse, a corpse that had had something gold clenched in its rigid fist. A button, he'd hoped. Reggie's murderer's button, to be exact, but to his disgust, the gleaming something had proven only a scrap of soggy paper foil . . . the same gold foil wrapped around these lemon bonbons. Lemon bonbons, he saw now, that someone had carefully positioned in the bottom of the tin to form the letter "E"!

His heart was pounding unbearably now as he turned to Jamieson. "Y'see that? He's taken her all right—but she left us a clue t' find her by!"

Jamieson peered inside the tin. "Great Scott! It's an 'E'? The *Empress of Egypt?*"

"That's my bet."

"But how—? And what about the clerk who saw her—and the lassie's letter to me? And Colonel Willers, remember, laddie? He said Hardcastle left the Sphinx *alone.* Surely ye dinna think—?"

Nick's lips thinned. His jaw tightened. "I don't give a hot damn about how or about why, you hear me?" he growled, his ice-and-fire eyes blazing, his swarthy, stubbled, handsome face almost black with rage. With his free hand, he gripped the detective's lapels and, despite the Scot's considerable height, almost lifted him clear off the ground with only one hand. "I only know he's got her and she's in danger. By God, Jamieson, give me the key! Or unlock. These. Goddamned. Irons. Either. Way. Get—'em—off—me. *Now!*" he ground out, unable to formulate complete sentences in his fury.

"But—!" Jamieson spluttered in protest.

"So help me, one more 'but' outta you, pardner, and I'll tear your goddamned arm off, if that's what it takes t' leave you eatin' my dust!" Nick said so softly, chillingly, the blood ran cold in the detective's veins. "Now, my little gal's told us where she's headed, and that she didn't go along with that sidewinder willingly. I think we owe it to her to do the rest—don't you?"

"Aye, I do that," Jamieson agreed hastily, his hands shaking as he found the key and unlocked the handcuffs. His piercing blue eyes slid away from Nick's relentless gaze when he was done. "But—look here!" He withdrew a gold pocket watch from his coat that jiggled madly about in his trembling fingers. "We're too late t' stop the *Empress*, mon! It's a quarter past three! She's already sailed!"

Belatedly, he realized he was talking to himself. Nick was gone.

Chapter Thirty-Eight

More than one luxury ocean liner was moored alongside the Cairo docks, each proudly flying the nautical flag of its country of origin, but none could compare to the *Empress*'s sleek and slender modern beauty.

The *Empress*, which had been built by the Cunard line only five years earlier, was painted sparkling seagull-white-and-black. One of the first liners to be built entirely of steel, she had a straight up-and-down bow quite unlike the curved bows of her larger predecessors, and measured a little over four hundred feet from stem to stern. Although she boasted both paddle wheels and a screw propeller, she'd also been rigged as a four-masted bark, in the event her still-unreliable steam engines should fail. But even without taking on sail, the sleek *Empress* could reach a speed of fourteen knots and cross the Atlantic in only eight short days. The voyage from Cairo, Egypt, to Southampton, England, was even shorter.

"Careful with that, you clumsy oaf!" bellowed Colonel Willers as he heaved himself down from the gharry that had transported him from the hotel to the harbor. He was late, and his florid features were lobster-red beneath his white hair and whiskers. He angrily shook his cane at a native porter. The youth was struggling to hoist one of the colonel's heavy wooden boxes over his shoulder and carry it aboard the *Empress*. "No, no, you blundering nincompoop, keep it upright—*upright*, I said, dash it all! By Jove, what the devil's wrong with you ragheads? Can't understand the Queen's English when y' hear it, what?"

Willers' booming voice—due in part to his insipient deafness—carried the length and breadth of the bustling Cairo wharves. Cargoes of cotton, spices, and other exotic goods were stacked on every side, awaiting stowing in the holds of the ships anchored there.

The porters, laboring under the fierce afternoon sun, found their patience quickly evaporating in the heat of the old man's insults. The *fellahin* were beginning to look either mutinous or murderous, noted Captain Jonah McGuire from his vantage point on the bridge of the *Empress*. He motioned his first mate to take his place and, immaculate in spotless white uniform, trimmed with a quantity of gold braid, he strode down the gang plank to the wharf. "Captain McGuire of the *Empress of Egypt*, at your service, sir. What seems to be the problem here?"

As he spoke, the *Empress*'s steam engines roared to life, sending a shudder through the vessel.

Willers peered at McGuire through his monocle. "The problem, Captain, is these dundering idiots! If left to their own devices, they'll reduce Lady Willers' priceless Egyptian vases to potshards, don't ye know!" the colonel complained, loudly and sourly.

McGuire turned to the glowering porters. He murmured a few consoling words to them in their native Arabic, averting his face so that the blustering old thunderguts missed the wink he also cast their way. When he had finished, the porters—all smiling broadly now—nodded and bowed. They meekly began loading the colonel's baggage as if it were made of eggshells.

"There you go, sir. I believe that should take care of the problem, Mr.—?"

"It's Willers, Captain. Colonel Willers, Her Majesty's Cavalry. Fourteenth Regiment, retired."

"Colonel Willers, yes, of course! It's a pleasure to meet you, sir. Welcome aboard! Now, if you'd be so kind as to accompany my purser, Mr. Teasley, he'll be happy to personally escort you to your stateroom."

"McGuire? McGuire . . . By Jove, that name rings a bell! Would you be one of the Scottish McGuires? Or related to the Irish branch of the family—?"

476

"The Scottish. Now, if you please, Colonel, I really must ask you to hurry along. The *Empress* was scheduled to sail at six bells and it's long past that. We'll be getting underway in just a few minutes. Ah, Mr. Teasley, there you are! Be so kind as to escort the colonel to his stateroom on the first-class deck, there's a good fellow. Colonel, no doubt I'll have the pleasure of you and your wife's company at my dinner table during the voyage . . ."

With a bow, the captain marched smartly away, muttering in an aside to the purser, "Get the pompous old goat aboard immediately—even if you have to gag and bind him hand and foot to do it, Teasley! With or without him, we sail in five minutes, understand?"

"Very good, Captain!" Teasley promised with a cheeky grin. The passenger list tucked under his arm, he started down the gangplank. Taking the old man by the elbow, he murmured, "Good afternoon, sir. I'm Roger Teasley, the ship's purser, at your service, sir. If you'll come along with me, Colonel, I'll be—*Good Lord!* What the devil's going on there?"

Porters and passengers alike were scattering to left and right as a coal-black stallion thundered down the wharves. At first, Teasley thought the beast had thrown its rider and bolted, but as it drew nearer, he saw the grim-faced rider on its back, urging it on to still greater speed.

Dressed in fringed buckskins, the man was crouched forward over the racing stallion's arched neck, like a jockey. Even from a distance, he appeared steely-eyed with purpose. Indeed, so determined was he, that when a cargo of dates packed in wooden boxes blocked his path, he took the stallion up and over the obstacle as effortlessly as a steeplechaser jumping a hedge at Epsom Downs! Female screams and angry shouts followed in the wake of the horse's flying hooves, but neither horse nor rider paid them any mind. Relentlessly, the beast bore down on the *Empress of Egypt*'s lowered gangplank. And, in the last moment, Teasley realized the rider's intent and took action. He smartly pulled the colonel aside, out of harm's way. Leaving Willers, he ran back to the foot of the gangplank, waving his clipboard above his head in an effort to turn the horse's head. He only just missed being trampled for his efforts.

"Whoa, mister! Are you crazy? You can't take that brute on board!"

"No? Step aside, son, and watch me!" Nick snapped. He glared down at the fresh-faced youth as Diablo danced impatiently, tossing his ebony head. "We're comin' aboard, like it or not—*over*, if not around, you!"

The look in the rider's blazing eyes left no doubt that he'd do exactly as he threatened!

Gulping, Teasley fell back and let them pass. He gaped in amazement as the black stallion clattered past him, its wicked hooves thudding hollowly on the gangplank that led up onto the *Empress's* main deck, where passengers waving goodbye to family and friends crowded the rail.

"Eureka! I knew it'd come to me, sooner or later! That chappie's from Buffalo Bill's Wild West Show!" exclaimed Colonel Willers under his breath. He limped to Teasley's side.

Together, they watched the stallion's broad black rump and flowing ebony tail disappear onto the liner; seconds later they heard Captain McGuire's furious bellow from the bridge, threatening that "heads will roll"!

"Jolly good seat, that American fellow, what? Hardly surprising, though. 'King of the Cowboys'—that's what they call him, don't you know, Beezley? Real name's Mick, Mick d' Angelo! Descendent of the Milan d' Angelos, no doubt. Arf! Arf! You young whippersnappers can't fool me, not bloody likely. Granted, I might forget a name or two—but never a face . . . !"

So saying, he limped heavily up the gangplank, leaning on his cane and cursing his gouty leg. After a second, Teasley shrugged and followed, gloomily wondering if the captain had meant *his* head, or if he'd been indulging in hyperbole.

Angel came to with a groan. She tried to move, but discovered she could not. There was no room for movement. Her legs were bent up against her body, so that

478

her knees were almost touching her chin! Where on earth could she be? Inside a coffin? Swallowing a whimper of panic, she explored the walls of her cage with her fingertips. *Wicker.* That devil had locked her in a wicker hamper. She was trapped!

The effects of the chloroform Teddy had sprinkled on the handkerchief he'd held to her face—after he'd forced her to scribble the letter—had worn off. Fortunately, the drug seemed to have left few if any aftereffects, thank God! Her wits and her strength were unimpaired—as was her burning determination to escape, to see Hardcastle punished, emotions which quite overrode her fear!

She'd *trusted* Uncle Teddy, she thought, a lump in her throat that owed more to anger, disillusionment, and betrayal, than terror. She had loved him and had been touched by his kindliness and his affectionate little gifts. Her father had trusted him, too. He'd considered Teddy family, more like a favorite brother than a friend. He'd even paid him the supreme compliment of calling him a "reet champion lad"! but all the time, she and her da had been nursing a viper to their breasts.

Grunting, she rocked back and forth, throwing her weight violently to the left, then to the right, as she'd once done to free herself from the Figg brothers in the attic of the Moulin Rouge. At length, she succeeded in toppling the hamper over, right way up. Gritting her teeth, she began kicking out at the wicker walls as hard as she could in so cramped a space, hoping against hope that she could create a hole big enough to squirm through.

"So you're awake, are you, my dear?" came Teddy's voice. It had a hard edge to it she'd never noticed before. "What a pity. I'd really hoped it would be dark before the chloroform wore off, so that I could dispose of you before you came to. It would have been so much . . . easier . . . for me, and far, far less frightening for you."

"Why are you doing this? Tell me, what did I ever do to you?" she demanded hoarsely.

"Nothing, dear girl. Nothing but inherit the fortune that should by rights have been mine. I never wanted to hurt you, Angel. Can you believe that? In fact, I've grown rather too fond of you, over the years. And besides, you're very beautiful. I've coveted beautiful things ever since I was a little boy. Stately homes—fine wines—blooded horses—beautiful women—I love them all! But to own beautiful things, one must first acquire the money to buy them. That's why I asked dear old Sid for your hand that time, remember? It could all have been so very simple, so *right*, if only you'd said yes. Instead, you clung to your girlish dreams of marrying a man for love, and by so doing, selfishly assured that I would never get my hands on the Brixton millions that way. Who knows, my dear? You might even have grown to love me, then none of this unpleasantness would have been necessary!"

"Uncle Te—Mr. Hardcastle, there's something I must know. Did you—did you really fire the warehouse? Are Mabel and Juarez truly dead? And what about Reggie? And Bill Bligh? Did you—did you kill them?"

Hardcastle snorted. "Guilty as charged, luv—on all counts." He laughed mirthlessly.

She heard him moving around the hamper, and she could glimpse his patent leather shoes through the gaps in the wicker as he bent down, fumbling with something above her head. She sucked in a breath and stiffened in sudden expectation. She was almost certain he'd slipped the peg free of the hamper's latch . . . Did he mean to let her out? And if he did, what then . . . ? More chloroform?

"Poor, greedy old Cousin Bill," Teddy continued, as if talking to himself. "He had the lucrative proceeds from his gambling den, the loot from his shady little black-mailing schemes, but it still wasn't enough for him, was it? Oh, dear me, no! Billy-boy said he wanted half of whatever I got from kidnapping you, too—so, of course, he had t' be done away with. And Reggie, too. Spineless, that one was. Spineless as a bloody jellyfish! He would have murdered his own granny with an ax to pay off his debts and keep the old family name unsullied. Unfortunately, he made the mistake of visiting Bligh's unexpectedly one night when I was there with Bill. He'd come to beg for more time to pay off his gambling markers—but he overheard us quarreling about you, instead. He also saw me shoot dear Cousin Bill right between the eyes. *Bang!*"

She jumped as his voice rose.

"Well, what choice did I have? He *knew*, see! And I couldn't run the risk that he'd tell your father and ruin everything I'd worked for, now could I? So, I let the toffee-nosed fool believe I was willing to cut him in on the deal, and packed him off to France to keep an eye on you. Off he went, like a lamb, all the while thinking he was working for me." Teddy chuckled. "It kept him out of harm's way, until I had the time to deal with him properly. Knuckles said the stupid git tried one last time t' get you to run away and marry 'im. Is that right, luv?"

"What now?" she asked dully, ignoring his question. "I suppose the next step is to ransom me to my da?"

"Oh, certainly, my dear—and for a very large sum of money, too. One million pounds! A reasonable figure, don't you think? After all, a million is small change for me old friend, Sidney."

"A million pounds—? You're mad! He'll never pay it!"

"Oh, he'll pay it, all right. As day after day passes and his little Annie's still missin', he'll be falling over his bloody self to pay whatever I ask. Not that it'll do him any good. See, I don't intend to become a millionaire without having the freedom to enjoy my ill-gotten gains. The world'll be my oyster! Monte Carlo. Venice. Paris—maybe even America! But in order to remain free to enjoy the good life, my identity must remain a secret. Which leaves me with just one unpleasant job t' do, before I'm out o' the woods. If it's any consolation, Angel, luv, this'll hurt me almost as much as it'll hurt you . . ."

He didn't need to tell her how he would maintain his anonymity or what that "unpleasant job" might be.

The sharp, sweet odor of chloroform stung her nostrils through the coarsely woven slats as Teddy leaned over the hamper, kerchief in hand. She could see the white linen, smell the drug, even through the wicker. She turned her head aside, drew a deep breath and held it. Adrenaline streaked through her veins, sending new strength and energy zinging through her. She readied herself. She might have only one slim chance to escape with her life! *Please God, don't let me waste it!* she prayed.

She was coiled like a spring in the hamper, every muscle tensed for action, as Teddy flung back the lid. As he did so, Angel sprang upright like a jack-in-a-box.

Her head clipped Teddy solidly beneath the jaw. She shoved hard at his chest, toppling him onto his back with a startled grunt, before hopping from the hamper. *A cabin.* They were aboard the ship! Straightway, she flew to the cabin door, flung it open and hurled herself through it, before Hardcastle regained his feet. The chase was on, the prize, her very life!

Her heart was hammering as she fled down the passageway between the rows of third-class cabins, screaming for help at the top of her lungs as she went. But the cabin doors remained closed. Desperately, she wasted precious time trying first one, then another, but all were locked; the passageway was empty of stewards, pursers, or other crew members. The third-class deck was deserted! There was no one to hear her cries way down here, in the bowels of the ocean liner! The passengers must still be above deck, leaning over the rail, laughing and tossing streamers to those standing on the quay below as they waved farewell and received bon voyage wishes from their friends and family—quite unaware of the drama unfolding beneath them!

She risked a hasty glance over her shoulder as she hitched the flowing native robe up, about her thighs, to free her legs. The gangway steps leading up to C deck lay directly ahead, but Hardcastle had already turned the corner—was gaining on her! Her heart pounding, she grabbed hold of the rail and began scrambling up the stairs for all she was worth. . . .

A frantic Nick had almost convinced himself he'd been wrong about Angel's cryptic candy clue.

At their captain's command, McGuire's crew had searched the lower decks of the *Empress*, including the single berth cabin in third class that the purser's list showed Hardcastle had purchased for the voyage. But although they'd discovered an empty hamper in which she might have been slipped aboard, there'd been no sign of either Angel or the man she'd called Uncle Teddy. Had Hardcastle suspected that fool Jamieson was on to him? Had he left a false trail for them to follow?

Nick paced the bridge back and forth like a man possessed. He'd almost determined to find some way off the damned ship, when one of McGuire's crew sang out from his lookout point in the tiny crow's nest, far above the decks of the *Empress* and the sparkling Nile green waters surrounding the liner.

"Portside main deck, sir! A man and a woman! They're struggling—headed astern!"

Struggling! "McGuire? Where did he say they were?" Nick barked, beside himself with fear for Angel's safety.

"Back there," McGuire supplied rapidly, pointing. "Headed toward the stern—the rear of the *Empress!*"

"Captain, the man's desperate. I need a gun."

The two men's eyes met, green to striking ice blue. Without question, the captain nodded in understanding. For that, Nick would be forever grateful. The captain gestured to the first mate, who ducked inside the wheelhouse and returned with a loaded revolver in a leather case.

"Need I remind you that we've left the harbor, that the safety of these passengers is in my hands, Durango?" McGuire quietly reminded Nick as he handed him the gun.

"I won't forget it, sir," Nick acknowledged soberly. He took the weapon from its case and inspected it with a sharpshooter's practiced eye.

"Good luck, sir," murmured the first mate.

With a curt nod, Nick took the companionway down to the main deck.

Angel was choking. Hardcastle had his left arm anchored around her throat, his elbow hooked beneath her chin. He was dragging her backwards after him, heading

483

slowly but surely to the stern rail. Though she'd struggled and fought him ever since he'd jumped her at the head of the companionway, she couldn't break free of him! His forearm was pressed against her windpipe, cutting off her breath! Her blood was roaring in her ears. A terrible crimson blackness threatened. If he squeezed any tighter, she'd be out cold—and then it would all be over!

"Give it up, there's a luv. You're not going anywhere but over the side, darlin', and you know it!" Hardcastle menaced, his breath hot in her ear. "Make it easy on yerself. Give it up!"

In answer, she sank her nails deeper into his arm, frantically trying to tear it from her. She kicked backwards, too, rapping his shins with her heels.

"That's not very nice, now, is it, luv? Not a very nice way t' treat yer dear old Uncle Teddy at all!"

"You bastard! Let goooo!" she screamed. She clawed out, reaching above her, over her shoulder, in a desperate effort to stab her fingers into his eyes—to score his cheeks—tear out his hair—do *anything* to force him to break his grip.

"Not bloody likely, darlin'. You're goin' for a little swim, duckie—and you're not comin' back! Ta ra, our Annie! Cheerio, lass!"

Suddenly, he hefted her up, sweeping her off her feet by the arm he'd hooked around her waist. With a grunt, he swung her up and around, so that she was dangling half over the ship's rail.

Air yawned below her. Air! Angel screamed as she saw the blue-green water far beneath her flailing legs. It was rimmed with white foam thrown up by the vessel's churning screw. The propellers were directly below! Oh, sweet God—oh, dear Lord, if he let her go, she'd be cut to ribbons—!

"Hardcastle!"

Nick's voice rang out across the deck like the crack of a whip, slicing through the shu-shushing of the paddle wheels and the grinding thrum of the *Empress*'s screws. Angel felt a jolt run through Teddy's body like an electric shock as he recognized the voice and responded to it. It was

Venice all over again!

Releasing the breath he'd sucked in as a hiss, he slowly turned, dragging her back, onto the decks. He held her as a shield before him.

Nick stood only thirty feet away, a revolver gripped in his fist. Unsmiling, he towered like a dark, avenging angel against the seagull white of the superstructure at his back. His narrowed, glacial eyes were riveted to Teddy's face under raven black brows. Not a flicker gave any indication that he saw Angel there.

"Guess you've played out your hand, pardner," Nick drawled softly. "By my reckonin', you lose. A smart man'd know when he's licked, an' fold."

Teddy grinned. "Reckon so, cowboy?" he mimicked with uncanny accuracy. "Hell, Durango, I'm in no hurry for a gallows' necktie! And besides, you're wrong about my 'hand.' I still have an ace up my sleeve—and you're lookin' at her! Shoot me—and the little darlin' gets it. Now, wouldn't that be a cryin' shame?"

Nick said nothing. He simply stood there, coolly waiting, letting his very silence unnerve the man.

"What's wrong, cowboy?" Teddy jeered. "Cat got your tongue?"

Still Nick said nothing.

"All bloody right!" Teddy roared finally, obviously rattled by Nick's unnerving lack of response. "If you won't talk, then *I* will. I want a boat lowered—one of the lifeboats. Have the captain see to it. Me and Angel here are jumpin' ship, right, luv?" He tightened his grip around her throat, forced a gargling whimper from her. "See?" Teddy chuckled. "I knew she'd agree."

"No."

"No? *No?*" Teddy laughed brittlely in disbelief. "Do you know what you're saying, Durango? You're saying you don't care what happens to her, but I know better!" His jaw hardened. "See here, mate. I'm leavin' this bloody ship, one way or another. We can do it nice and civilized, in a lifeboat, with Angel all comfy-cozy—or I can jump over the bloody rail and take 'er with me—in which case, we aren't goin' to be a very pretty sight, not after the

485

propellers have had a go at us. Either way, my friend, you and that nosy detective won't take me back to England to stand trial! See, they'd hang me—and I'll take my own bloody life before I'd let 'em do that!" He paused and nervously wetted his lips. The dawnings of fear, of doubt, were in his eyes now. "Well?" he asked after a lengthy pause, during which Angel thought she'd swoon from sheer terror.

"No boat. No deals."

A sound came from between Teddy's lips. It was the strangled cry of a cornered animal run to ground, with no place left to run. The cry of an animal that knows its death is imminent. Teddy's "ace" in the hole had become the ace of spades, the hand he'd held, the Deadman's Hand.

"Don't say I didn't warn you, you son of a bitch!" he yelled, and edged backwards, leaning over the trail, dragging Angel backwards with him.

Nick raised the revolver chest high. He took aim, steadying it with both hands as Teddy hooked one leg, then the other, over the rail. There was a split second when he had a clear shot—a single, fleeting moment when Angel jerked her head aside. He took it and fired!

The thunder of Nick's shot—Angel's cry as Teddy released her and toppled backwards—his screams as he hit water and was churned under by the liner's screws—all were drowned out as the *Empress of Egypt* blasted her deafening whistle. The cheers of over two hundred blissfully unaware passengers echoed in its wake. To them, the whistle blast signaled only the beginning of a pleasurable voyage. They had no inkling it was one man's requiem.

Nick smiled grimly as he strode across the deck and lifted a sobbing Angel into his arms. McGuire's diversion had come just a moment too late, he thought as she wrapped her arms around him. She buried her face against his chest and hung on, clinging to him like she was planning on never letting go—which was just fine and dandy, by his reckoning.

486

"You okay, sweetness?" he asked tenderly, smoothing her tangled hair back from her face.

She nodded, blinking back her tears. "I've never been better, pardner," she managed to murmur with a brave little smile, though her voice sounded hoarse and her poor throat was mottled with bruises.

"Honest Injun?" he pressed, caressing her hurts with a gentle hand.

"Honest Injun!" she murmured, and lifted her face for his kiss.

Chapter Thirty-Nine

"Pitiful bloody speciment, what?" Colonel Willers observed to no one in particular, using his walking cane to draw back the tarpaulin which someone had thrown over Hardcastle's body. Stiffly, he bent down, peering through his monocle at the bruised but otherwise unaltered face, indifferent to the pools of pink-tinged water in which he stood. "Came to a bad end, didn't you, eh, my lad? Arf! Arf! Doesn't surprise me one bit! You made as big a bloody mess of dying as you did of living, if you ask me."

"You knew him, Colonel Willers?" Angel asked, surprised. Exchanging glances with Nick, she drew away from him and went to the colonel, carefully avoiding the tarpaulin.

"I most certainly did, my dear—though I'll be demmed if I could put the name he used with that face, 'til now! Hardgraves, indeed! Or was it Hardacres, he called himself . . . ? Well, no matter! *I* knew him as Bligh, Harry Bligh."

"Did you say *'Bligh,'* Colonel Willers?" Angel asked breathlessly. Taking his elbow, she drew the rotund old gentleman after her down a short companionway to a table in the saloon below, where they could talk without being overheard.

Nick, his clothes leaving trails of water behind him on the stairs—for despite Angel's protests, he had helped in the recovery of Hardcastle's body—followed them, gratefully accepting the stiff brandy and Turkish towel the waiter offered him, compliments of Captain McGuire, as he followed them down.

"Are you quite sure that was his last name?" Angel asked the colonel, for he had struck her as the dithery sort, prone to forgetfulness.

"Oh, rather, mi' dear! Once I'd remembered the name, it all came back t' me, plain as day. Bligh was a second-rate actor—actor turned confidence-trickster, rumor had it, though I wouldn't know about that. Saw him perform once, in Blackpool—or was it Brighton? Disgraceful performance, anyway! He couldn't hold a candle to his lovely mother in her hey day, let me tell you! Beautiful woman, Mary—demmed fine little actress, too. To my mind, no one's been able to match her Lady Macbeth since the 30's. The only thing that can be said to young Bligh's credit, is that he knew he hadn't the talent, and chose to confine his pitiful efforts to the Italian stage—thus sparing all of us loyal British theater-lovers a great deal of unnecessary suffering, what!"

Willers brayed with laughter, playing to the circle of ghoulish spectators who'd gathered at the head of the companionway to gape at the body. His loud voice had drawn their attention.

"Y' see, mi' dear, Appleby was just his mother's *stage* name," Willers continued, encouraged in his tale by the expression of incredulity in the stunning young woman's face. "She was born plain Mary Bligh of Camden Town, London, but she changed her name when her dramatic talents began to be recognized. In my youth—before I met my dear Lady Willers, of course—yours truly was a regular stage-door Johnnie!" He chuckled. "Meself and the other chappies used to bring bouquets of roses and champagne to pretty Mary Appleby's dressing room door after a performance. Oh, we'd wait for simply hours in the hopes of a wave or a smile. But—Mary had eyes for only one of us young blades. His name was—"

"Harry, Lord Brixton," Angel supplied, glancing across at Nick.

"Quite right, m' dear. Of course, young Harry already had a wife, Cecilia. The poor gel was an invalid, don't you know? Left crippled by a fall while riding to the hounds. It happened within months of their marriage. But naughty

489

Mary didn't seem to care that Harry was a married man."
Willers chuckled wheezily again. "Lucky bounder—the
gel was absolutely potty over the chap! Anyway, to cut a
long story short, within a matter of months we heard
rumors that Mary'd—um—become his mistress and was to
bear him a child. She left the London stage soon after and
never returned. Terrible loss."

Willers' rheumy eyes grew mistier still. His hand shook
upon his cane before he recovered himself sufficiently to
continue. "There was some nasty talk bruited about that
her brother and manager, George Bligh, had tried to
blackmail Harry into divorcing his wife and marrying
Mary, so he could give the child his name. I suppose it's
possible. Poor old brother George must have resented the
affair, since it had cost him his family's livelihood as
Mary's manager, but—Harry wouldn't even consider
divorce. He had his own way about him, did Harry.
Something of an eccentric, I always thought. Anyway, he
set Mary up in a nice little villa in northern Italy, and
spent summers with her and the child there. Otherwise, he
seemed quite content to leave matters as they were. When
Cecilia passed away, there was speculation that Harry
might marry Mary and recognize Harry Edward Junior—
who was a young man himself, by then—as his son. But
they were only rumors. He never did."

"And Harry Junior resented being his father's il-
legitimate son?"

"Oh, most assuredly so. Bitterly and violently resented
it, in fact! For years, he plagued Harry to name him as his
heir, but Harry was a stubborn fellow and flatly refused. I
often thought he questioned whether the boy was really
his, you know. Mary was such a lovely young gel, and so
very popular—and I'm sure you're aware that actresses
haven't the best—er—reputations? I believe Harry Brixton
felt that if Mary could dally with him, she might well have
dallied with others, what?"

"Poor, poor Maria," Angel murmured with a faraway
look to her own gray eyes. "She loved him all those years—
faithfully, loyally—and yet that cad couldn't accept that
the child was his."

"There's more, you pretty little thing," Willers said,

winking broadly at Angel over his bristly white moustaches. "Harry Brixton went quite mad shortly before his death—completely off his rocker, what! He left every blasted ha'penny he owned to some illiterate millworker he fancied had saved his life shortly before. Can you credit that? The Brixton millions—squandered on a working-class nobody and his snotty-nosed offspring! It was the talk of the town at the time, but I'll be dashed if I can remember the Lancashire bumpkin's name . . ."

"Don't bother yourself, sir," Angel supplied frostily, suddenly bristling. "You see, I already know it. It was Higgins. H-I-G-G-I-N-S. *Sidney* Arthur Higgins, to be exact. His snotty-nosed daughter was named Annie. And as for him being a working class nobody—! You've got your bloody nerve, looking down your nose at the likes o' him! I'll thank you to consider, Colonel Willers, that without such hard-working, decent people as Mr. Working-Class Sidney Higgins, there'd be no fine Egyptian cotton shirt to clothe your idle back. No soft woolen cravats to tuck beneath your sagging jaw. No sturdy polished leather boots upon your gouty old feet—and no over-rich foods in your enormous belly! What's more, milord Willers, Sidney Higgins is a reet champion lad—one you and others like you aren't even fit to wipe their mucky boots on! I know, because *I'm* that Lancashire bumpkin's daughter. Annie Higgins—and bloody proud of it, too!"

She was breathing heavily in the wake of her impassioned speech, but as her last word died away, a sailor somewhere to the rear of the crowd which had gathered yelled, "Bravo! That's the ticket, little lady! You put old thunderguts in his place good an' proper!"

"Toffee-nosed snobs! Who the 'ell do they think they are, anyways?"

"Now, listen here, you ruffians—! I hardly think you're in any position to . . ."

Pandemonium broke out as first-class passengers turned to argue heatedly with those from third class, each spokesman extolling the various merits of their own position or class in life. The resulting ruckus was deafening.

Ignoring them, Nick took Angel's hand. He squeezed it comfortingly, then slipped it through his elbow. "Well done, darlin'! That was quite a speech—!"

"And I meant every word of it, too!" Angel said with a prim and righteous little sniff.

"If it's not too soon t' ask, will you take a stroll on the decks with me? The moon's up an' it's a real pretty night."

"I'd like that—just as long as it's not along this deck," she accepted with a tiny shudder, glancing over her shoulder. Several sailors had wrapped Uncle Teddy/ Harry Bligh's body in the tarpaulin, and were carrying it away. Another was swabbing the deck. She looked quickly back to Nick. "It's foolish, I know, but in a way, I feel quite sorry for him—and for his mother, Mary, or Maria, or whatever you want to call her. They could have made the best of what they had and had a happy life at Villa Allegra. Maria loved Brixton, Nick! She was prepared to accept whatever part of himself Lord Harry was prepared to give—but that wasn't enough for their son. No. He wanted the inheritance he felt was due him by blood, and not a penny less—even if he had to kill to get it . . ."

"Don't feel too sorry for him, darlin'. He would have had to kill you, too—just like he killed Reggie, Bill Bligh, and the Figg brothers—if he meant to ransom you to your pa. With even one of you left alive to talk, he could never have kept his identity a secret long enough to enjoy the ransom money."

"I suppose you're right." She sighed. "Poor Da. He thought they were such good friends. It'll be awfully hard on him when he finds out the truth."

"Not near as hard as losing you would have been!"

"And then there's Mabel, and p-poor Juarez. She has— had—a sister in Whitechapel who'll have to be told."

"Told wot?" chirruped a voice. "I in't dead ducks— though happen you might wish I was! The inspector here, he's had us in hidin', he has!"

"*Mabel?*"

"Mabel Warez, in the flesh! Who'd you think it was, then? Bleedin' Queen Victoria 'erself? Come 'ere, you silly twit. Come 'ere an' give us a hug!"

With a most unladylike whoop of delight, Angel flew

across the deck and flung her arms about Mabel. The two women—both with tears in their eyes—hugged each other fiercely, while Juarez, quite recovered from his burns, smiled, and Inspector Jamieson looked on, smugly grinning.

"Och, Nick, laddie, ye see? All's well that end's well, eh?" the detective murmured, his piercing eyes twinkling. "My suspicions were right, were they no'? It was Hardcastle! Tell me, what d' ye think o' my investigative methods now?"

Nick's jaw hardened as he recalled how very close to death Angel had come, on account of the detective's mule-headed determination to see his theories proved correct. He took two long-legged strides across the deck to stand before the detective and asked him softly, "You sure you really want t' know, Jamieson?"

"Aye, laddie. I do!" Jamieson insisted.

In answer, Nick drew back his right fist and threw a smacking punch at the Scot's jaw. The blow clipped him beneath the chin with such force, the detective flew backwards. He landed on his backside in an astonished heap.

Turning his back on the man, Nick flexed his bruised fingers. "There! That just about sums up my opinion! Now, ladies. And you, *amigo*. How's about us rustlin' up some chow? I don't know about you, but I'm hungry enough t' eat a horse!"

Later that evening, Nick and Angel stood by the rail on the promenade deck and looked out over the midnight blue Mediterranean Sea. It was crested with sparkling whitecaps in the bright moonlight, as if the stars had fallen into the water. Angel's hair was blowing about in the warm gusts of breeze, while behind her, the fringes edging Nick's tan buckskins flapped furiously. Slipping his arms around her, he drew her back against his chest. And, when she looked up at him, he kissed her lightly on the curve of her cheek.

"Still believe I wanted to kill you?"

Shamefaced, she shook her head.

"Still want to marry one of your nobby blue bloods and be Lady Angelica Iron Drawers?"

She stuck out her tongue. "You beast! Will you never stop reminding me about just how awful I was? I've changed, really I have," she insisted, her gray eyes sweet and sincere.

"Enough to consider marrying an 'uncouth cowboy' . . . ?"

To her astonishment, Nick suddenly knelt on the deck at her feet. He removed his hat and took her hand between his. Her heart skipped a beat as she looked down into his darkly handsome, serious face, for the ice-and-fire pale blue of his eyes shone out against his sun-browned skin like twinkling stars.

"Are—are you proposing, Mr. Durango?" she stammered incredulously.

He grimaced. "Honey, I sure as hell ain't kneelin' here t' say my prayers! So. What's your answer? Will you do me the honor of marrying me, Miz Higgins?"

She stroked his cheek, gazed deeply into his eyes, and whispered, "I will!"

It could go on record, Nick fancied, as the shortest speech she'd ever made!

"Eeh, lass, I can't say as how I'm surprised. Fact is, I'm proper chuffed with your choice o' husband! I couldn't have chosen better myself. Ye've got a fine young lad 'ere, an' no mistake! And Nick, son, there's no grander lass than my little Annie! Be good t' each other, children. Be 'appy and love each other. And while yer at it, make me a dozen little babies t' dandle on me knees! Congratulations, love," Sid exclaimed, cupping Angel's face between his hands and planting a smacking kiss on her lips. Beaming, he turned to Nick, clasped his hand and clapped him warmly across the shoulder. "And t' you, Nick, my boy! Now, let's all have a drop of summat fancy t' toast the happy couple in style! Some o' that bubbly stuff'll do reet nicely, our Arthur," he suggested to the butler.

j Prickard smiled. "Very good, sir. I'll have some—er— bubbly stuff brought up from the cellars at once."

"Good lad! And now, I've been meaning t' give you two lovebirds summat all day. It's not a weddin' present, mind," he added in a lower voice for just the two of them to hear. "It's more on the lines of a—dowry—say. And there's the fee I'm owing you, Nick, for the champion job ye did of seeing t' my lass's safety," Sid added.

Angel gasped in surprise.

"Aye, lass. The lad's gotten nowt for his pains all this time. I just knew he was summat special when he wouldn't take the money I offered him up front. 'No, sir. You can pay me when I return your daughter to you safe and sound, Mr. Higgins, an' not a moment before,' he told me, just as proud as can be."

Sid reached into his waistcoat pocket and withdrew a bank draft. "Here you go, my loves. Take it with your old da's blessing—and all his love."

Tears sprang into Angel's eyes. Sniffling, she stepped forward and hugged her father tightly. "Thank you, Da," she whispered. "You shouldn't have, really."

"I agree with my fiancée, Mr. Higgins," Nick said gruffly. "It's very generous of you, sir, very generous indeed, and I thank you, but—I'm afraid I can't accept it."

"No? And why not, lad?" Sid asked softly.

"I asked Angel to be my wife, and she's done me the honor of accepting, sir. I wouldn't have offered her marriage at all, unless I was prepared to support her. Nor, I trust, would Angel have accepted my proposal, unless she was prepared to share whatever I have to give her, be it great or small. Isn't that right, Angel, darlin'?" Nick asked, smiling down at her fondly.

A deep frown had formed between her brows that she quickly banished—though not before Nick had noticed it. "Why, yes—yes, of course, darling," she murmured too hastily.

Grinning, Nick caught her against him. "You see, sir? We even think alike!"

"Aye," Sid approved. "And, son—there's nowt pleases me more than a lad with some old-fashioned pride!"

So saying, Sid tore the bank draft into little pieces and tossed it over the couple like confetti. If he noticed the moisture that welled suddenly in Angel's eyes as the pieces fluttered down around her shoulders, he no doubt thought it was tears of joy.

"So, it'll be a shipboard weddin' for the two o' ye, eh? Ta, lad," Sid observed, taking a glass of champagne from the silver tray Arthur offered him.

"I'm afraid so, sir. You see, I need to be home before the fall. The next vessel crossing the Atlantic leaves in just one week's time. If we can be aboard her, we can be back in New Mexico by the middle of September. There's way too little time t' have the banns called properly, or to prepare a fancy wedding breakfast, unfortunately. Right, sweetness?"

Angel nodded and forced a smile. She loved Nick with all her heart—truly, she did!—but she was still foolishly romantic enough to have dreamed of a glorious, fairy-tale wedding, one in which she wore a flowing white gown with a long train, the bodice sewn all over with diamonds and seed pearls, and a cunning white lace veil crowning her head—along with all the gorgeous rice and flowers, the dear, silly traditions, that went along with it.

"Angel, Mr. Higgins, excuse me for a moment. I must have a few words with Juarez. I'll be right back, Angel."

Angel nodded absently as Nick moved away.

"Angel? What's up? Ye look proper sorry, you do."

"What was that, Da?"

"I said, ye look a mite down in the dumps, lass?"

"Oh, perhaps I am, just a little. Everything's happened so quickly! I was just thinking how very much I'll miss you." She bit her lower lip. "You did mean what you said—about coming to live in America, I mean?"

"Aye, lass, I did. America's the very place for a man with 'brass' and ambition, Nick tells me. It's what a man makes of himself that counts fer summat there, rather than his pedigree. Aye, lass, I'll get my affairs settled an' in good hands, and still be there in plenty o' time time t' see your first babe born, never fear."

"Promise?"

"On your mam's grave, love," he vowed huskily. "Now, drink your bubbly and give your old da a smile!"

Nick returned to them then. As Sidney's brows rose in silent inquiry, he gave him a nod and mouthed, "All set!"

496

over Angel's head.

"All right, our Angel, look sharp. Me and Nick here, we cooked up a little summat t' surprise ye, lass. Come along."

"What on earth is it?" she asked.

"You'll see soon enough," Nick promised mysteriously.

Smiling now, she let herself be swept away, Nick on one arm, her father on the other.

Mabel was waiting for them by the front door. "No peekin', ducks!" she exclaimed as she slipped a scarf blindfold over her eyes.

With much giggling and laughter, they led her outside to the gardens of Brixton Towers, before removing it.

When they did, she blinked, unable to believe what she was seeing.

Every tree and bush, every immaculate hedge of the Towers' grounds, had been festooned with pink bunting, set off at strategic intervals with posies of deep pink roses and camellias anchored to fat pink satin bows. Little round tables had been set up on the lawns beneath a gaily striped tent, each spread with a snowy cloth and set with sparkling crystal, silverware, and dainty pink porcelain. On the lily pond, a pair of swans circled elegantly while a string orchestra in the arbor played a series of lilting waltzes. Closer to the house, under yet another tent, a groaning buffet table held a glittering white wedding cake of no-less-than four tiers, as well as tiny finger sandwiches, sponge cakes, vol-au-vents, sherry trifles, fresh strawberries and clotted cream. On a smaller table, a bubbling fountain spilled champagne into a crystal basin.

"Your wedding breakfast, our Angel!" Nick and Sid exclaimed together.

The incredulous delight on Angel's face was thanks enough for the two men in her life, who reached behind her back and shook hands to congratulate themselves on their cleverness and their ability to keep a secret.

"It's wonderful—simply wonderful! Oh, Nick—and Da—thank you, thank you both for everything!" Angel exclaimed, watching the guests mingling and moving about—and realizing only belatedly that she knew very few—if any of them!

"Um, forgive me for asking but . . . er . . . who *are* all these people?" Though the few ladies in attendance were dressed very properly in elegant afternoon gowns and hats, and the men correctly formal in their frock coats, there was something decidedly . . . peculiar . . . about the gathering.

"Eeh, they're nowt but the grandest folks ye could ever want ter meet, our Angel," Sidney began, beaming, "Come on and—"

His introductions were abruptly cut short as a prancing white stallion—ridden by a white-bearded man dressed head to toe in fringed buckskins—suddenly appeared from behind the boxwood maze.

As Angel's mouth dropped open, the magnificent stallion reared back on its hindquarters, its front hooves pawing air as its rider fired his Colt .45 into the sunny blue sky. There was a deafening report that scattered pigeons and starlings for miles around.

"The bride, the groom, my lords, ladies, and gentlemen!" the fellow roared with a showman's sweeping flourish. "We welcome you one and all this glorious afternoon to the fabulous—the one and only—the truly astounding and magnificent—"

"I know," Angel finished, leaning weakly back against Nick for support as she laughed helplessly. "Don't tell me—"

"—Buffalo Bill Cody's Wild West Show!"

Epilogue

"Still having doubts, Cousin? What does it take to convince you, eh?" Juarez asked Nick. "She loves you, *hombre*—any fool can tell that! It is in her eyes when she looks at you, in her smile—her voice! *Madonna*, she glows with love for you!"

"'E's right," Mabel agreed. "'Ead over 'eels, she is. And when she finds out who you really are an' everythink, she'll be over the bleedin' moon—!"

"Whoa, there, Red. She mustn't find out—not yet," Nick cut in sharply. "You've both got to promise me that you won't say a word. If she asks about me, about the family, change the subject."

"But, *amigo*—!"

"Swear it, 'Tonio. Swear it on our granddaddy's grave!"

"Why? Wot've you got up your sleeve?" Mabel demanded suspiciously, her eyes narrowed.

Nick frowned. "When I refused her pa's money back in England, there was a look in Angel's eyes that reminded me of—someone else?" He shrugged and frowned. "Oh, I don't know! Maybe I'm readin' too much into it. Anyway, it just . . . hell, it just seemed t' me like she was disappointed I turned him down, that's all. It's been eatin' at me ever since we left England!"

"Nick, *hombre*, you're talking *loco*. Just because she was disappointed you refused her father's money doesn't mean anything. She's not Savannah."

"I know that, damn it! But—knowin' it doesn't help! I don't know what the hell's wrong with me, but I can't seem t' shake the doubts. And the closer we get t' home, the worse it gets. But last night, I had an idea. Remember when Angel was talking about that Shakespeare fellow and his play?"

"*The Taming of the Shrew? Sí!* What of it?"

"Well, it was the story that gave me the idea. And if it works, it'll set my mind to rest once and for all. Will you help me?"

"Help you t' do wot?" Mabel asked, thoroughly confused.

"I have a plan—a test—in mind."

"A *test!* You're plannin' on *testin'* Angel's love for you? She married you, didn't she, you silly bloody twit? Ooo, you're a sneaky bugger, you are! All this time, I thought better of you. I'm reely disappointed in you, I am. Wot's more, I'm goin' t' tell our Angel just what sort o' bloke she's gorn and married 'erself to, I am—! 'Test' indeed! After she's followed you all these bleedin' miles across the ocean an' all—"

But before Mabel could storm off to carry out her threat, her husband caught hold of her elbow.

"No, *querida*, you must not interfere. This matter, it is between Nick and Angelica."

Nick grinned and slapped Juarez across the back. "There! I knew I could depend on you, pardner! Now. Here's what I want you to do—"

"Whoa, *amigo!* Slow down! I did not say we would help. Or that I would. Only that this matter is between you and your wife, no one else. We will keep quiet. We will say nothing about Savannah or your father or anything else, if that is your wish—but that is *all* we will do. Is that not so, my little red flower?"

"Bleedin' right it is, Warez," Mabel agreed indignantly. "And mark my words, Nick—if this plan o' yours falls through an' you end up losin' her—and I reckon as how it bloody well will!—don't come cryin' to us. Remember, ducks—we told yer so!"

"You two're makin' mountains out of molehills," Nick grumbled, a twinge of doubt pricking him, nonetheless. "Angel'll understand why I did it when she knows the whole story. We'll be laughing about it some day!"

"Don't bleedin' count on it, ducks!" Mabel said gloomily. "I wouldn't want to be in your boots when she finds out she's been 'tested.'"

"This is it. You can open your eyes now, darlin'. We're here at last!"

Angel lifted the hat veil off her face. A quiver of anticipation—of excitement!—ran through her as she opened her eyes expectantly.

But rather than delight, it was shock that slammed through her with all the force of a battering ram. The "Villa Durango" Nick'd described to her on the voyage across the Atlantic was a ramshackle hut. And "ramshackle" was a polite term for it!

Her gray eyes glazed over with crushing disappointment as she saw her new home for the very first time. This, then, was where she had traveled thousands of miles across land and ocean to live? Despite her sternest promises to herself that she would pretend she was delighted, whatever the condition of the home to which Nick brought her, she could not keep tears of dismay from welling behind her eyelids, nor from uttering a choked, "Oh!"

Nick dismounted and came to lift her down from her horse. There was a distinct swagger to his stride that she was very much afraid was due to masculine pride.

"See! Tears of joy! I just knew you'd be struck speechless with the place!" he chortled, beaming. "Thought I slept out in the open under the stars, didn't you, hon? You didn't reckon for a minute that old Nick had himself a place of his own, did you, *Mrs.* Durango? And half of everything I own is yours, too, now darlin'!"

"By my calculations, half of nothing is still nothing," she muttered under her breath, thinking, *The poor, poor man! He owns a crumbling hovel, and yet he's so terribly proud of it, it might as soon be his castle.* Or rather, *our* hovel, she amended silently, *our* castle, for she was now his bride, his wife—for better or for worse, for richer and—dear God!—for poorer, too.

Still, what did it matter if the roof above their heads was of rusted corrugated iron with flaking holes in it, when she loved him so? So what if the walls that surrounded them were of sagging logs, chinked with mud, that a stiff breeze—or a hearty sneeze!—might demolish, when she knew she'd always love him? They had each other. They had their love—and that alone was greater wealth than many people had in a lifetime!

"Sorry, honey, I didn't hear what you said?" Nick asked, taking her hand and kissing her fingertips in the tender way she loved. If he noticed that the wedding ring he'd slipped onto her finger aboard ship when Captain Van der Maark had declared them man and wife had turned green during the ten days of the voyage to America, he didn't remark on it.

"I said, my dear, that by my calculations, half of anything I share with you is worth everything!" she murmured, crossing the fingers of her free hand so the outrageous exaggeration wouldn't count as a sin.

"You little sweetheart, you!" he exclaimed, giving her a hug. "I sure picked a winner when I married you! Come on, wife. Let's go look at the inside. I know how you gals love to get your hands on a new place. I reckon you'll want to get started prettying it up, the minute you step inside. Up we go!"

Grinning, he swept her up into his arms and solemnly carried her across the dip in the sandy soil that could, theoretically, have been termed a threshold, *if* there'd been any door. Once inside, he planted a quick kiss upon her nose and put her down.

The instant Angel set foot inside "Villa Durango," her worse fears were confirmed! Her faint hope that external appearances might be deceptive and that the inside of the place could yet prove rustic but charming had been unfounded. One look, and she knew that "prettying up" this place would require a miracle of about the same magnitude as the raising of Lazarus from the dead!

The brilliant blue skies of New Mexico showed through the holes in the rusted roof. Patches of light slanted through the pine log walls where the mud chinking had crumbled away. A ragged patchwork quilt that had apparently divided the interior into two fair-sized rooms, one for cooking and eating and one for sleeping, draped in

502

rotted shreds from rusty nails. Every corner was heaped with piles of grit, dust, or tumbleweeds, and festooned with thick, sticky cobwebs—inhabited ones, she noted, with American-sized spiders.

The dirt floor was littered with the remnants of long-ago meals, old whisky bottles, bones, paper scraps and an assortment of broken and rusty tools or utensils. Still, the fireplace wasn't that bad, she noted with a tiny flare of optimism, built from attractively irregular gray stones, with only one or two missing about the mantle and chimney breast that could be readily replaced. If she squinted, she could imagine a fire crackling there in the hearth on a cold winter's eve, with perhaps a braided rag rug spread across the cleanly swept floor before it . . . ?

But as she stared at the fireplace and let her elastic imagination stretch to the far limits required by the hovel's present condition, something stirred in the shadows of the hearth! Some furry black-and-white creature that their intrusion had disturbed tumbled out from amidst the heaps of ashes and began scampering across the hut toward them. Angel let out a shriek and bolted outside, back to their horses, with Nick following at a speedy yet slower pace.

"Hey, hey, ain't no need t' get scared, Angel, honey," Nick reassured her. "That there's an old friend of mine, right, Stinky?" He turned to look back as the animal shot past him, obviously as frightened of them as Angel'd been of it.

"Stinky?" she echoed faintly.

"That's the little fella's name, all right."

"And what, exactly, *is* Stinky?" she inquired.

"Why, what else would he but a skunk?" Nick asked innocently. "Say, here comes Juarez with our provisions and stuff! I asked him to round us up a few things and to tote your trunks out here with him, too. I figured that way, we wouldn't have to go back to the hotel in Santa Fe again."

Looking up and shading her eyes, Angel saw that, as Nick had implied, a loaded wagon was coming over the nearest rise, a cloud of dust swirling in its wake as it rattled toward them, with Juarez handling the reins. Belatedly,

503

Nick's words registered like a deluge of ice water.

"You mean, we're staying here? Tonight?" she squeaked. "*All* night?"

"All night? How's about . . . forever?" He grinned and tweaked her nose. "Aw, honey, I know you! I knew you wouldn't be able to bring yourself to leave, once you'd seen our place. So, I checked us out of the hotel before we left. Go on, Angel—admit it! You can't wait t' get started on cleaning it up a mite, can you?"

Fortunately, her answer went unheard as Nick left her to go and meet Juarez.

"But I don't hate animals!" she insisted the following afternoon. "I *love* them—mice included. It's just that . . . I'd prefer they found somewhere other than our mattress to sleep in!"

"Aw, all right," Nick grumbled. "If you insist, I'll shake 'em out outside. But—the poor little critters are gonna be feelin' the cold awful bad tonight, come sundown."

"My heart bleeds for them, truly it does," Angel gritted as Nick brushed past her, hefting the straw-and-mice filled mattress after him. "But Nick . . . ?"

"Yes, hon?"

"Once the mice are out, burn that pallet!"

She leaned on her broom and critically inspected the results of her day's labor. Not a single cobweb remained, nor a scrap of litter. The hut had been vigorously swept clean of dust, grit, and tumbleweeds from top to bottom. The refuse, along with the rotted patchwork divider, had been carted outside and burned. The disgusting pallet would soon join it.

To her surprise, two narrow windows had appeared within the walls as a result of her efforts, one hidden behind a wood-wormed cupboard, the other boarded up completely. She'd pried off the boards, then—using the end of her broom—she'd seen the broken glass completely knocked out of both frames to permit air and light to enter the place and dispel the gloom and the musty odor of dirt and mouse droppings that had still lingered. Tomorrow morning, she'd ask Nick to ride into Santa Fe to purchase new glass panes and some putty to repair them, but for now, she had walls to wash!

The strong lye soap and disinfectant she'd insisted a peculiarly taciturn Juarez to return to town for that morning made her eyes smart and stung her hands as she wet her rag. Dipping the scrubbing brush in the bucket of water at her feet, she set to work, tackling one grimy section at a time. Reaching up, she briskly and methodically scrubbed and rinsed the lumpy, bumpy log walls from top to bottom, humming as she worked. In all honesty, she enjoyed cleaning. The work reminded her of her childhood, when she and Da had been alone after Mam's death. Once they'd recovered from their initial grief, she'd taken enormous pride in keeping their little cottage as neat as a pin, and in making it a warm, welcoming place her da had looked forward to coming home to each night, as he had when mam'd been alive. Being poor hadn't mattered to them then, for they'd been happy. Having very little wouldn't matter to her now. She had all she could ever ask for in Nick. . . .

Her perky blond ponytail bounced with her movements. Her breasts strained against the cloth of her crisp white shirtwaist. Her rounded hips twitched energetically from side to side as she labored. Nick—watching her from the doorway—found the whole business of housecleaning a perfectly delightful one.

"If you have nothing better to do than watch me, Mr. Durango," she said crisply without turning around, "I would suggest you fetch the river mud I asked for earlier. These walls are sadly in need of repair."

"Mud's right here, honey. Ready an' waitin' when you are."

"Good! I'll get started on the chinking the minute I finish scrubbing these walls. They're looking much better, aren't they?"

"Pretty as a picture and clean as a whistle!" he approved, ogling her trim ankles as she reached up, and the sway of her bottom beneath her skirts. "When's supper?"

"Supper? You mean, you're hungry *again?*"

"Starved, more like it. That's the funny thing about me.

505

I seem t' get that way about three times a day, regular as clockwork!"

"Oh, well," she said resignedly. "Perhaps I can do the other walls and start the chinking tomorrow. What did you bag for our supper pot?"

"Weeell, truth was, I didn't run across much in the way of game this morning, so I had t' settle on these ugly varmints instead. You ever cleaned one of these?"

She tossed the rag and scrubbing brush into the bucket, wiped her hands on her apron and turned around. Her perspiring face paled. "But . . . those are snakes!" she cried, eyeing the rattlers that dangled from his fists with slack-mouthed horror.

"Sure are. But skinned and fixed up right, then roasted over a hot fire, they taste just like fried chicken. Say, darlin', you feeling poorly—?" he asked as she rushed past him, almost knocking him flying in her haste to get outside.

To his astonishment, however, once she'd recovered from her initial, violent reaction, she not only cooked the repulsive snakes—she ate them, too, and with every sign of enjoyment!

"Hmm. One really must learn to adapt to one's surrounding when in a foreign country, mustn't one?" she observed, flashing him a sunny, sweet smile. "Go on, darling, do have some more. You were right. It's really quite tasty. Eat up, before it gets cold, and I'll serve you some more."

Gritting his teeth, Nick—who hated snake meat—had little choice but to oblige.

An entire month of cleaning and repairs, hammering and sawing, scrubbing and fixing passed before Angel would agree that the hut was finally ready for them to sleep in. Until then, they camped under the stars and reminisced about the nights they'd spent in similar fashion in France.

"Well, that's it! Tomorrow, we'll move the furniture in, and I'll cook us a wonderful supper to celebrate!" she declared, then frowned. "Umm, do try to find something a little more festive than snakes, won't you, darling?"

"I'll do my best!" Nick promised with a grin, ruefully remembering that supper and how his little trick had backfired on him.

Bright and early the next morning, he carried the small pine table he'd nailed together into the cabin. He had to move it to several different places before Angel finally settled on the perfect spot—one next to the newly glazed window that looked out onto the mountains. Curtains she'd sewn with her own hands framed the windows now, and the dirt floor had been swept as smooth as a baby's bottom, then sprinkled with clean sand, before she hid it beneath rugs she'd braided from rags, torn from her oldest clothing.

In the second room, behind the divider she'd rigged up using the old cupboard, which she'd given a fresh coat of blue paint, was their bed. Its wide frame was of rough wooden posts held together with pegs, then cross-strung with rawhide strips, in the old Western style. A tick mattress and beddings that a horrified Mabel had forced upon them when she and Juarez came to visit, covered it. Another rag rug had been set on the floor beside it, and upon one of Angel's sea trunks, placed beneath the window, sat a jelly jar crammed with the wildflowers the Spanish had named "cups of gold," orange-red poppies she'd gathered in an attempt to give their clean but humble home a tiny touch of grace, the coziness of color. On the second sea chest, beneath the window in the other room, she'd placed a chimney lamp that she lit each evening, although they'd not yet taken up residence in the hut. Curious, he'd asked her why.

"So that when you're riding home after a long day spent providing for me and the—the babies we'll have together, you'll see that light shining out in the darkness like a beacon," she'd told him with a shy smile. "When you do, you'll know that you're almost home, and that we love you and we're waiting for you."

Hearing that, seeing her efforts, had filled Nick with shame, and just about undone his flagging resolve to "test" her!

"Well? How do you like it?" she asked breathlessly,

nervously twining her hands together. Her expression was a mixture of dread and hope. In that moment, all of her fears were reflected in her gray eyes for him to see. She'd done her best with the little he'd offered her, asking for nothing but the barest essentials in their new life together. She'd changed, and she wanted so desperately for him to approve of her efforts. To approve of *her*, and believe at last that she wasn't the empty-headed, snobbish little nitwit he'd first taken her for, to whom climbing the rungs of society's ladder had meant everything.

Emotion choked his throat as he said huskily, "Like it? Honey, it's the best damn house I ever saw! It's a palace! Come on over here t' me, Mrs. Durango—!"

A month flew by, then two, the weeks slipping like fine sand through their fingers, with days spent in hard work and nights spent in passion, but both spent together—but still Nick couldn't bring himself to confess. Indeed the more time that passed, the harder it got!

After supper, they'd sit on the bench Nick had built and placed before the door. There they'd watch the fiery sun going down behind the Sangre de Cristo range, enjoying the gaudy sunsets until moonrise. Nick'd listen to Angel's animated plans to make their humble home more attractive and to the list of repairs she felt were still needed before winter came. He would nod in agreement from time to time as he watched her lovely face through hooded eyes, marveling that he never grew tired of being with her, whether it was in the quiet times, like these, or in the crazy, fun times they spent splashing naked in the creek, or fishing for cutthroat trout in the streams beneath the *manzanitas* in the hills.

She means it! She's real, he told himself, not for the first time, and a deep joy and a sense of peace filled him. There was no longer any doubt in his mind, no longer any question. The past weeks and her hard work, her sweetly determined commitment to making them a real home out of the line-camp hovel he'd brought her to—one filled with all the love and warmth she could provide—had convinced him. All first impressions and appearances

508

aside, his Angel was no Savannah. Heck, she was nothing like the cheating, fortune-hunting little bitch who'd trampled all over his heart! Angel loved him for himself. She'd meant her wedding vows with all her heart, including the part that had said "for richer or poorer, for better or worse." It was time to tell her the truth. . . .

"Nick?"

"Uh huh?"

"I know we don't have much money, but I—um—I'll be needing some things soon."

"More putty?" he teased. "No, no, don't tell me—! More lye soap? And a new broom?"

"Actually, no," she said evasively, reluctant to meet his eyes. "I'll be needing cloth to sew some clothes."

"You can only wear one dress at a time, sweetness," he pointed out. "Ain't two sea trunks of 'em enough?"

She shook her head. "I'm afraid not. Haven't you noticed? All of my clothes are getting too tight. Soon, I won't have a thing that fits."

"I guess there's nothing like snake meat for fleshing out a gal—" he began, but then the import of what she'd said slammed home with the impact of a rifle stock dashed against his thick skull. Damn! He could have kicked himself for not figuring it out sooner. "Wait a minute, now, woman" he began slowly. "Do you mean what I think you mean . . . ?"

She threw back her head and laughed merrily. Her gray eyes were sparkling in the firelight of their hearth. Her cheeks were flushed, and he noticed suddenly how very radiant she was, and how her lovely face seemed to glow from within. "If you mean, are you going to be a father, Durango, then the answer is yes!"

"Jumpin' Geronimo!"

In a single stride, he had her held tightly in his arms and was kissing her soundly, ignoring her laughing protests and attempts to squirm free as he whirled her around and around.

"Come on!" he said suddenly, taking her hand.

"Where are we going, you crazy idiot?" she demanded. "It'll be dark out soon!"

"I'm taking you where I should have taken you a long

time ago."

"I seem to recall you saying that once before, sir," she teased in a prim, disapproving tone, "and we ended up in your bed."

He grinned wickedly. "We will—later. For now, I want to show you something."

"And what if I don't want to see it?"

"Then I'll throw you up onto Diablo's back and carry you off, woman! What's it to be?"

"Do I really have a choice, you horrid, arrogant American?"

"Nope!"

Diablo carried them both to the crest of a high hill. Below them swept a huge valley with arroyos and canyons painted blood red and rust in the setting sun. Several thousand head of beef cattle grazed the enchanted valley below, while at its heart, she could see the red tile rooftops of a sprawling *hacienda,* the adobe walls of the *casa grande* stained rosy pink by the sunset.

"Well?" he asked.

"Well what?"

"What do you think?"

"Of the ranch?"

"The *hacienda.* The beeves. The ranch—all of it?"

"It's beautiful. The house reminds me of Villa Allegra."

"It's all mine."

"Oh, Nick, someday, perhaps," she corrected him gently, leaning back against his chest. She took his callused hand in hers and nuzzled her cheek against it. "We'll work hard, really hard. And one day, all our dreams will come true. You'll see. You'll have a ranch just like this, or one very like it. I believe in you, Nick. I just know you'll succeed, whatever you set your hand to!"

"You didn't hear me, Angel," he said gruffly, her words making him squirm with guilt. "*This* ranch is mine. This *land* is mine. All of it. Every last damned clod of earth and every blade of gramma, every bawlin' calf, belongs to me—Don Nicholas de Montoya y Durango!"

"Then you mean, you're not poor?"

"Hell, no! Aw, I'm not a millionaire like our pa, but Rancho Diablo is one of the biggest spreads around."

Her lips pursed. "I see. You just let me think you hadn't a penny to your name?"

He chuckled. "I did."

"And you didn't correct me, even when you knew I thought you slept out under the stars because you didn't have a roof over your head?"

"That's about it!"

"Ah. And would you mind very much telling me why?" she asked, two telltale spots of red beginning to flame in her cheeks.

He hesitated. "Because I needed to know if you really meant it when you said you loved me for richer or poorer—and honey, you passed every test I set you with flying colors!"

"*Test?*" she gritted, her gray eyes beginning to smoke. "You mean that hut was a—was a *test?* That crumbling—shack—I've come to love and think of as our home—it was all a part of some little *game* you were playing?"

"'Fraid so!" he admitted ruefully.

"Why, you arrogant clod! You—you blasted doubting Thomas—! You—loutish—insufferable—arrogant cowboy, you—!" she screeched. "You—you brash American! You odious colonial lout! How *dare* you presume to test me? How dare you ever doubt me—! I married you, didn't I, you skunk!"

She jerked back her arms, first the left, then the right, with as much force as she could muster, and jabbed him solidly in the ribs. The wind whooshed out of him in a startled "oof." He was still trying to recover his breath when she twisted on the saddle before him, braced both hands against his shoulder and shoved him sideways. Her efforts succeeded. To her delight, Nick slithered inelegantly from his horse's back. He landed hard on his backside.

"Angel, I—!"

"Don't 'Angel' me! Better yet, don't say another word, Durango," she spat, her gray eyes smoking. "Not a single one—or I'll encourage this clever beast to trample you underhoof—and laugh while it does so!" She gathered up

511

the reins and prepared to ride off.

"Hey! You can't do that! You can't just ride off and leave me here! Damn it, honey, it's a long walk back!"

"Quite so, Doubting Thomas. More than ample distance for you to reconsider your underhanded, deceitful actions of the past months, and to heartily repent your sins, I'd say. Come along, Diablo. Let's leave your master and go *home!*"

With that, she turned his horse's head and kicked the stallion into a canter, riding swiftly away in the direction of the line-camp hut. To add further insult to injury, Diablo's hooves enveloped Nick in a cloud of dirt as she rode off.

Cursing under his breath, Nick scrambled to his feet, retrieved his black Stetson and dusted it off by slapping it against his thigh. Darned Limeys! Who could figure any of 'em out! She'd seemed quite unimpressed with his beautiful home. Unmoved by the vast number of his beeves. Immune to the grandeur of his full name or his title. Numb to his considerable wealth.

"You damned, infuriatin' woman!" he roared at the moon. "I just can't win, can I? Is there no way to please you?"

But as he began eating her dust, a slow grin creased his sun-browned face. His pale blue eyes glinted with amusement. Hell, he might have been King of the Cowboys, once upon a time, but now Angel reigned, as Queen of his heart! And there was, he knew only too well, one surefire, guaranteed way to make her forget her anger. One certain way to please her . . .

"Light the lamp, little darlin'," he muttered wickedly under his breath as he strode along. "This cowboy's comin' home!"